Library of America, a nonprofit organization,
champions our nation's cultural heritage
by publishing America's greatest writing in
authoritative new editions and providing resources
for readers to explore this rich, living legacy.

O. HENRY

O. HENRY

101 STORIES

Ben Yagoda, *editor*

THE LIBRARY OF AMERICA

O. HENRY: 101 STORIES

Volume compilation, notes, and chronology copyright © 2021 by Literary
Classics of the United States, Inc., New York, N.Y. All rights reserved.

Published in the United States by Library of America.
Visit our website at www.loa.org.

This paper exceeds the requirements of
ANSI/NISO z39.48–1992 (Permanence of Paper).

Distributed to the trade in the United States
by Penguin Random House Inc.
and in Canada by Penguin Random House Canada Ltd.

Library of Congress Control Number: 2020950480
ISBN 978–1–59853–690–4

First Printing
The Library of America—345

Manufactured in the United States of America

Contents

EARLY SKETCHES,
STORIES, AND REPORTAGE

Bexar Scrip No. 2692

W HENEVER YOU visit Austin you should by all means go to see the General Land Office.

As you pass up the avenue you turn sharp round the corner of the court house, and on a steep hill before you you see a mediæval castle.

You think of the Rhine; the "castled crag of Drachenfels"; the Lorelei; and the vine-clad slopes of Germany. And German it is in every line of its architecture and design.

The plan was drawn by an old draftsman from the "Vaterland," whose heart still loved the scenes of his native land, and it is said he reproduced the design of a certain castle near his birthplace, with remarkable fidelity.

Under the present administration a new coat of paint has vulgarized its ancient and venerable walls. Modern tiles have replaced the limestone slabs of its floors, worn in hollows by the tread of thousands of feet, and smart and gaudy fixtures have usurped the place of the timeworn furniture that has been consecrated by the touch of hands that Texas will never cease to honor.

But even now, when you enter the building, you lower your voice, and time turns backward for you, for the atmosphere which you breathe is cold with the exudations of buried generations.

The building is stone with a coating of concrete; the walls are immensely thick; it is cool in the summer and warm in the winter; it is isolated and sombre; standing apart from the other state buildings, sullen and decaying, brooding on the past.

Twenty years ago it was much the same as now; twenty years from now the garish newness will be worn off and it will return to its appearance of gloomy decadence.

People living in other states can form no conception of the vastness and importance of the work performed and the significance of the millions of records and papers composing the archives of this office.

The title deeds, patents, transfers and legal documents

connected with every foot of land owned in the state of Texas are filed here.

Volumes could be filled with accounts of the knavery, the double-dealing, the cross purposes, the perjury, the lies, the bribery, the alteration and erasing, the suppressing and destroying of papers, the various schemes and plots that for the sake of the almighty dollar have left their stains upon the records of the General Land Office.

No reference is made to the employees. No more faithful, competent and efficient force of men exists in the clerical portions of any government, but there is—or was, for their day is now over—a class of land speculators commonly called land sharks, unscrupulous and greedy, who have left their trail in every department of this office, in the shape of titles destroyed, patents cancelled, homes demolished and torn away, forged transfers and lying affidavits.

Before the modern tiles were laid upon the floors, there were deep hollows in the limestone slabs, worn by the countless feet that daily trod uneasily through its echoing corridors, pressing from file room to business room, from commissioner's sanctum to record books and back again.

The honest but ignorant settler, bent on saving the little plot of land he called home, elbowed the wary land shark who was searching the records for evidence to oust him; the lordly cattle baron, relying on his influence and money, stood at the Commissioner's desk side by side with the preëmptor, whose little potato patch lay like a minute speck of island in the vast, billowy sea of his princely pastures, and, played the old game of "freeze-out," which is as old as Cain and Abel.

The trail of the serpent is through it all.

Honest, earnest men have wrought for generations striving to disentangle the shameful coil that certain years of fraud and infamy have wound. Look at the files and see the countless endorsements of those in authority:

"Transfer doubtful—locked up."

"Certificate a forgery—locked up."

"Signature a forgery."

"Patent refused—duplicate patented elsewhere."

"Field notes forged."

"Certificates stolen from office"—and soon ad infinitum.

The record books, spread upon long tables, in the big room upstairs, are open to the examination of all.

Open them, and you will find the dark and greasy finger prints of half a century's handling. The quick hand of the land grabber has fluttered the leaves a million times; the damp clutch of the perturbed tiller of the soil has left traces of his calling on the ragged leaves.

Interest centres in the file room.

This is a large room, built as a vault, fireproof, and entered by but a single door.

There is "No Admission" on the portal; and the precious files are handed out by a clerk in charge only on presentation of an order signed by the Commissioner or chief clerk.

In years past too much laxity prevailed in its management, and the files were handled by all comers, simply on their request, and returned at their will, or not at all.

In these days most of the mischief was done. In the file room, there are about —— files, each in a paper wrapper, and comprising the title papers of a particular tract of land.

You ask the clerk in charge for the papers relating to any survey in Texas. They are arranged simply in districts and numbers.

He disappears from the door, you hear the sliding of a tin box, the lid snaps, and the file is in your hand.

Go up there some day and call for Bexar Scrip No. 2692.

The file clerk stares at you for a second, says shortly:

"Out of file."

It has been missing twenty years.

The history of that file has never been written before.

Twenty years ago there was a shrewd land agent living in Austin who devoted his undoubted talents and vast knowledge of land titles, and the laws governing them, to the locating of surveys made by illegal certificates, or improperly made, and otherwise of no value through noncompliance with the statutes, or whatever flaws his ingenious and unscrupulous mind could unearth.

He found a fatal defect in the title of the land as on file in Bexar Scrip No. 2692 and placed a new certificate upon the survey in his own name.

The law was on his side.

Every sentiment of justice, of right, and humanity was against him.

The certificate by virtue of which the original survey had been made was missing.

It was not to be found in the file, and no memorandum or date on the wrapper to show that it had ever been filed.

Under the law the land was vacant, unappropriated public domain, and open to location.

The land was occupied by a widow and her only son, and she supposed her title good.

The railroad had surveyed a new line through the property, and it had doubled in value.

Sharp, the land agent, did not communicate with her in any way until he had filed his papers, rushed his claim through the departments and into the patent room for patenting.

Then he wrote her a letter, offering her the choice of buying from him or vacating at once.

He received no reply.

One day he was looking through some files and came across the missing certificate. Some one, probably an employee of the office, had by mistake, after making some examination, placed it in the wrong file, and curiously enough another inadvertence, in there being no record of its filing on the wrapper, had completed the appearance of its having never been filed.

Sharp called for the file in which it belonged and scrutinized it carefully, fearing he might have overlooked some endorsement regarding its return to the office.

On the back of the certificate was plainly endorsed the date of filing, according to law, and signed by the chief clerk.

If this certificate should be seen by the examining clerk, his own claim, when it came up for patenting, would not be worth the paper on which it was written.

Sharp glanced furtively around. A young man, or rather a boy about eighteen years of age, stood a few feet away regarding him closely with keen black eyes.

Sharp, a little confused, thrust the certificate into the file where it properly belonged and began gathering up the other papers.

The boy came up and leaned on the desk beside him.

"A right interesting office, sir!" he said. "I have never been in here before. All those papers, now, they are about lands, are they not? The titles and deeds, and such things?"

"Yes," said Sharp. "They are supposed to contain all the title papers."

"This one, now," said the boy, taking up Bexar Scrip No. 2692, "what land does this represent the title of? Ah, I see 'Six hundred and forty acres in B—— country? Absalom Harris, original grantee.' Please tell me, I am so ignorant of these things, how can you tell a good survey from a bad one. I am told that there are a great many illegal and fraudulent surveys in this office. I suppose this one is all right?"

"No," said Sharp. "The certificate is missing. It is invalid."

"That paper I just saw you place in that file, I suppose is something else—field notes, or a transfer probably?"

"Yes," said Sharp, hurriedly, "corrected field notes. Excuse me, I am a little pressed for time."

The boy was watching him with bright, alert eyes.

It would never do to leave the certificate in the file; but he could not take it out with that inquisitive boy watching him.

He turned to the file room, with a dozen or more files in his hands, and accidentally dropped part of them on the floor. As he stooped to pick them up he swiftly thrust Bexar Scrip No. 2692 in the inside breast pocket of his coat.

This happened at just half-past four o'clock, and when the file clerk took the files he threw them in a pile in his room, came out and locked the door.

The clerks were moving out of the doors in long, straggling lines.

It was closing time.

Sharp did not desire to take the file from the Land Office.

The boy might have seen him place the file in his pocket, and the penalty of the law for such an act was very severe.

Some distance back from the file room was the draftsman's room now entirely vacated by its occupants.

Sharp dropped behind the outgoing stream of men, and slipped slyly into this room.

The clerks trooped noisily down the iron stairway, singing, whistling, and talking.

Below, the night watchman awaited their exit, ready to close and bar the two great doors to the south and east.

It is his duty to take careful note each day that no one remains in the building after the hour of closing.

Sharp waited until all sounds had ceased.

It was his intention to linger until everything was quiet, and then to remove the certificate from the file, and throw the latter carelessly on some draftsman's desk, as if it had been left there during the business of the day.

He knew also that he must remove the certificate from the office or destroy it, as the chance finding of it by a clerk would lead to its immediately being restored to its proper place, and the consequent discovery that his location over the old survey was absolutely worthless.

As he moved cautiously along the stone floor the loud barking of the little black dog, kept by the watchmen, told that his sharp ears had heard the sounds of his steps.

The great, hollow rooms echoed loudly, move as lightly as he could.

Sharp sat down at a desk and laid the file before him.

In all his queer practices and cunning tricks he had not yet included any act that was downright criminal.

He had always kept on the safe side of the law, but in the deed he was about to commit there was no compromise to be made with what little conscience he had left.

There is no well-defined boundary line between honesty and dishonesty.

The frontiers of one blend with the outside limits of the other, and he who attempts to tread this dangerous ground may be sometimes in one domain and sometimes in the other; so the only safe road is the broad highway that leads straight through and has been well defined by line and compass.

Sharp was a man of what is called high standing in the community. That is, his word in a trade was as good as any man's; his check was as good as so much cash, and so regarded; he went to church regularly; went in good society and owed no man anything.

He was regarded as a sure winner in any land trade he chose to make, but that was his occupation.

The act he was about to commit now would place him forever in the ranks of those who choose evil for their portion—if it was found out.

More than that, it would rob a widow and her son of property soon to be of great value, which, if not legally theirs, was theirs certainly by every claim of justice.

But he had gone too far to hesitate.

His own survey was in the patent room for patenting. His own title was about to be perfected by the State's own hand.

The certificate must be destroyed.

He leaned his head on his hands for a moment, and as he did so a sound behind him caused his heart to leap with guilty fear, but before he could rise, a hand came over his shoulder and grasped the file.

He rose quickly, as white as paper, rattling his chair loudly on the stone floor.

The boy who had spoken to him earlier stood contemplating him with contemptuous and flashing eyes, and quietly placed the file in the left breast pocket of his coat.

"So, Mr. Sharp, by nature as well as by name," he said, "it seems that I was right in waiting behind the door in order to see you safely out. You will appreciate the pleasure I feel in having done so when I tell you my name is Harris. My mother owns the land on which you have filed, and if there is any justice in Texas she shall hold it. I am not certain, but I think I saw you place a paper in this file this afternoon, and it is barely possible that it may be of value to me. I was also impressed with the idea that you desired to remove it again, but had not the opportunity. Anyway, I shall keep it until to-morrow and let the Commissioner decide."

Far back among Mr. Sharp's ancestors there must have been some of the old berserker blood, for his caution, his presence of mind left him, and left him possessed of a blind, devilish, unreasoning rage that showed itself in a moment in the white glitter of his eye.

"Give me that file, boy," he said, thickly, holding out his hand.

"I am no such fool, Mr. Sharp," said the youth. "This file shall be laid before the Commissioner to-morrow for examination. If he finds —— Help! Help!"

Sharp was upon him like a tiger and bore him to the floor. The boy was strong and vigorous, but the suddenness of the attack gave him no chance to resist. He struggled up again to his feet, but it was an animal, with blazing eyes and cruel-looking teeth that fought him, instead of a man.

Mr. Sharp, a man of high standing and good report, was battling for his reputation.

Presently there was a dull sound, and another, and still one more, and a blade flashing white and then red, and Edward Harris dropped down like some stuffed effigy of a man, that boys make for sport, with his limbs all crumpled and lax, on the stone floor of the Land Office.

The old watchman was deaf, and heard nothing.

The little dog barked at the foot of the stairs until his master made him come into his room.

Sharp stood there for several minutes holding in his hand his bloody clasp knife, listening to the cooing of the pigeons on the roof, and the loud ticking of the clock above the receiver's desk.

A map rustled on the wall and his blood turned to ice; a rat ran across some strewn papers, and his scalp prickled, and he could scarcely moisten his dry lips with his tongue.

Between the file room and the draftsman's room there is a door that opens on a small dark spiral stairway that winds from the lower floor to the ceiling at the top of the house.

This stairway was not used then, nor is it now.

It is unnecessary, inconvenient, dusty, and dark as night, and was a blunder of the architect who designed the building.

This stairway ends above at the tent-shaped space between the roof and the joists.

That space is dark and forbidding, and being useless is rarely visited.

Sharp opened this door and gazed for a moment up this narrow, cobwebbed stairway.

After dark that night a man opened cautiously one of the lower windows of the Land Office, crept out with great circumspection and disappeared in the shadows.

One afternoon, a week after this time, Sharp lingered behind again after the clerks had left and the office closed.

The next morning the first comers noticed a broad mark in

the dust on the upstairs floor, and the same mark was observed below stairs near a window.

It appeared as if some heavy and rather bulky object had been dragged along through the limestone dust. A memorandum book with "E. Harris" written on the flyleaf was picked up on the stairs, but nothing particular was thought of any of these signs.

Circulars and advertisements appeared for a long time in the papers asking for information concerning Edward Harris, who left his mother's home on a certain date and had never been heard of since.

After a while these things were succeeded by affairs of more recent interest, and faded from the public mind.

Sharp died two years ago, respected and regretted. The last two years of his life were clouded with a settled melancholy for which his friends could assign no reason.

The bulk of his comfortable fortune was made from the land he obtained by fraud and crime.

The disappearance of the file was a mystery that created some commotion in the Land Office, but he got his patent.

It is a well-known tradition in Austin and vicinity that there is a buried treasure of great value somewhere on the banks of Shoal Creek, about a mile west of the city.

Three young men living in Austin recently became possessed of what they thought was a clue of the whereabouts of the treasure, and Thursday night they repaired to the place after dark and plied the pickaxe and shovel with great diligence for about three hours.

At the end of that time their efforts were rewarded by the finding of a box buried about four feet below the surface, which they hastened to open.

The light of a lantern disclosed to their view the fleshless bones of a human skeleton with clothing still wrapping its uncanny limbs.

They immediately left the scene and notified the proper authorities of their ghastly find.

On closer examination, in the left breast pocket of the

skeleton's coat, there was found a flat, oblong packet of papers, cut through and through in three places by a knife blade, and so completely soaked and clotted with blood that it had become an almost indistinguishable mass.

With the aid of a microscope and the exercise of a little imagination this much can be made out of the letters at the top of the papers:

B—xa—   ——rip N— 2—92.

Three Paragraphs

"COPY," YELLED the small boy at the door. The sick woman lying on the bed began to move her fingers aimlessly upon the worn counterpane. Her eyes were bright with fever; her face, once beautiful, was thin and pain drawn. She was dying, but neither she nor the man who held her hand and wrote on a paper tablet knew that the end was so near.

Three paragraphs were lacking to fill the column of humorous matter that the foreman had sent for. The small pay it brought them barely furnished shelter and food. Medicine was lacking but the need for that was nearly over.

The woman's mind was wandering; she spoke quickly and unceasingly, and the man bit his pencil and stared at the pad of paper, holding her slim, hot hand.

"Oh, Jack; Jack, papa says no, I cannot go with you. Not love you! Jack, do you want to break my heart? Oh, look, look! the fields are like heaven, so filled with flowers. Why have you no ice? I had ice when I was at home. Can't you give me just a little piece, my throat is burning?"

The humourist wrote: "When a man puts a piece of ice down a girl's back at a picnic, does he give her the cold shoulder?"

The woman feverishly put back the loose masses of brown hair from her burning face.

"Jack, Jack, I don't want to die! Who is that climbing in the window? Oh, it's only Jack, and here is Jack holding my hand, too. How funny! We are going to the river to-night. The quiet, broad, dark, whispering river. Hold my hand tight, Jack, I can feel the water coming in. It is so cold. How queer it seems to be dead, dead, and see the trees above you."

The humourist wrote: "On the dead square—a cemetery lot."

"Copy, sir," yelled the small boy again. "Forms locked in half an hour."

The man bit his pencil into splinters. The hand he held was growing cooler; surely her fever must be leaving. She was singing now, a little crooning song she might have learned at her mother's knee, and her fingers had ceased moving.

"They told me," she said weakly and sadly, "that hardships and suffering would come upon me for disobeying my parents and marrying Jack. Oh, dear, my head aches so I can't think. No, no, the white dress with the lace sleeves, not that black, dreadful thing! Sailing, sailing, sailing, where does this river go? You are not Jack, you are too cold and stern. What is that red mark on your brow? Come, sister, let's make some daisy chains and then hurry home, there is a great black cloud above us—I'll be better in the morning, Jack, if you'll hold my hand tight. Jack, I feel as light as a feather—I'm just floating, floating, right into the cloud and I can't feel your hand. Oh, I see her now, and there is the old love and tenderness in her face. I must go to her, Jack. Mother, mother!"

The man wrote quickly:

"A woman generally likes her husband's mother-in-law the best of all his relatives."

Then he sprang to the door, dashed the column of copy into the boy's hand, and moved swiftly to the bed.

He put his arm softly under the brown head that had suffered so much, but it turned heavily aside.

The fever was gone. The humourist was alone.

A Personal Insult

A YOUNG LADY in Houston became engaged last summer to one of the famous short stops of the Texas base ball league.

Last week he broke the engagement, and this is the reason why:

He had a birthday last Tuesday, and she sent him a beautiful bound and illustrated edition of Coleridge's famous poem, "The Ancient Mariner."

The hero of the diamond opened the book with a puzzled look.

"What's dis bloomin' stuff about anyways?" he said.

He read the first two lines:

> It is the Ancient Mariner,
> And he stoppeth one of three—

The famous short stop threw the book out the window, stuck out his chin, and said:

"No Texas sis can gimme de umpire face like dat. I swipes nine daisy cutters outer ten dat comes in my garden, I do."

When the Train Comes In

OUTLINE SKETCHES AT THE GRAND
CENTRAL DEPOT.

NEXT TO a poker game for a place to contemplate human nature in its most aggravated form, comes a great railway passenger station. Statistics show that nine-tenths of the human race lose their senses when traveling on the cars, and give free demonstrations of the fact at every station. Traveling by rail brings out all a man's latent characteristics and propensities. There is something in the rush of the train, the smell of the engine smoke, the yell of the butcher, the volapuk cries of the brakeman and the whizzing scenery visible from the windows that causes the average human being to shake off the trammels of convention and custom, and act accordingly.

When a train stops at the depot and unloads its passengers, they proceed at once to adopt for their style of procedure the idea expressed by the French phrase "sauve qui peut," or in polite language—"the devil take the hindmost."

An observer, unless he is of the "casual" variety, can find much entertainment in watching the throng of travelers and bystanders at any metropolitan depot. The scene presented belongs to the spectacular comedy. There are no stage waits; no changing of scenery; no forgetting of lines or casting about for applause. The mimes play their part and vanish; the hero with his valise is jostled by the heavy villain from the baggage room; leading ladies scramble, kiss, weep and sigh without boquets or applause; marionettes wriggle and dance through the crowd, putted by the strings of chance, and the comedian plays his part unabashed by the disapproving hiss of the engines, and the groans of the grinding wheels.

At the Houston Grand Central depot when the trains come in there are to be seen laughter and lanterns, smiles and sandwiches, palavering and popcorn, tears and tamales.

To the student of human nature is presented a feast; a conglomerate hash of the lighter passions and eccentricities of man; a small dish whereof, ye Post man will endeavor to set before you.

The waiting room is bright with electric lights. The line of omnibuses and hacks line the sidewalk on Washington street, and the drivers are crowding close to the dead line on the south side of the depot.

Scattered among the benches in the two waiting rooms are prospective travelers awaiting their trains. The drummers and old traveling men sit reading their papers or smoking, while new and unseasoned voyagers are pacing up and down, glancing uneasily at the clock, and firing questions at everybody that passes. The policeman at the door who has told the old man with the cotton umbrella at six different times that the Central arrives at 6:35, makes up his mind that if he inquires once more he will take the chances on getting a verdict of justifiable homicide.

The old lady with the yarn mittens who has been rapping with her spectacle case at the ticket agent's closed window for fifteen minutes says, "Drat the man," and begins to fumble in her traveling bag for licorice lozenges.

In the ladies' waiting room there is the usual contingent of peripatetic public. The bright-eyed, self-possessed young lady who is the traveling agent for a book, or, perhaps, a new silver ware polish, has learned the art of traveling. Haste and flurry are unknown to her. A neat traveling cloak and a light hand satchel comprise her accoutrements. She waits patiently, tapping lightly with a patent leather toe, and faintly humming the refrain of a song. Not so the large and copious family who are about to make the journey of their lives—at least fifty miles. Baskets, bags, valises, buckets, paper bundles, pot plants, babies and dogs cover the benches in their vicinity. The head of the family wears a look as deadly solemn as if he were on his way to execution. His face shows the strain of the terrible journey he is about to undertake. He holds his tickets in his moist hand with a vice like grip. Traveling is a serious matter with him. His good lady has taken off her bonnet. She drags out articles from boxes and bags and puts them back; she trots the baby and strews aprons, hairpins, knitted gloves and crackers far and wide. She tells John where she has hidden $13 under a loose board at home. She would never have mentioned it, but she is certain the train is going to run off the track and she may be killed. A few grimy looking men sit with their coat collars turned up, by the side of their weary spouses, who look as if they cared not for accidents, end of the world, or even fashions. A black-veiled woman with a prattling boy of five sits in a corner, disconsolate and lone; some aimless town stragglers enter and wander through the room and out again.

In the men's waiting room there is more life. Depot officials in uniform hurry through with lanterns. Travelers loll upon the benches, smoke, read and chat. From the buzz of voices fragments of connected words can be caught that read something like this:

"Got a $300 order from him, but it cost me $10 in drinks and theater tickets to get it—yes, I'm going to Galveston; doctor ordered perfect quiet and rest—a daisy, you bet; blonde hair, dark eyes and the prettiest—lost $20 on treys up; wired my house for expense money this morning—ain't seen Sam for fifteen year; goin' to stay till Christmas—loan me that paper if you're through with it—Red flannel scratches me, this is what I wear—wonder if the train's on time—No, sir, don't keep the North American Review, but here's Puck and Judge—came home earlier one night and found her sitting on the front steps with—gimme a light, please—Houston is the city of Texas—confound it, I told Maria not to put those cream puffs in my pocket—No, a cat didn't do it, it's a finger-nail mark; you see I put the letter in the wrong envelope, and—Toot—toot—toot—toot—toot."

The train is coming. An official opens the north doors. There is a scramble for valises, baskets and overcoats, a mad rush and a struggling, pushing, impolite jam in the doorway by a lot of people who know that the train will wait twenty minutes for them after it arrives.

The bell clangs; the single eye of the coming engine shines with what may be termed—in order not to disappoint the gentle reader—a baleful glare. A disciple of Mr. Howells' realistic school might describe the arrival of the train as follows: "Clang—clang—chookety chookety—chookety—clang—clackety clack—chook-ety—chook. Che—e—e—ew! Bumpety—bump—Houston!"

The baggage men, with yells of rage, throw themselves

upon the trunks and dash them furiously to the earth. A Swiss emigrant standing near clasps his hands in ecstasy. "Oh, Gott," he cries, "dess ees yoost my country like. I hear dot Avalanch come down like he from dot mountains in Neuchatel fall!"

The passengers are alighting; they scramble down the steps eagerly and leap from the last one into space. When they strike the ground most of them relapse into idiocy, and rush wildly off in the first direction that conveniently presents itself. A couple of brakemen head off a few who are trying to run back under the train and start them off in the right direction.

The conductor stands like a blue-coated tower of strength in the center of the crowd answering questions with an ease and coolness that would drive a hotel clerk wild with envy. Here are a few of the remarks that are fired at him: "Oh, conductor, I left one of my gloves in the car. How long does the train stop? Do you know where Mrs. Tompkins lives? Merciful heaven, I left my baby in the car! Where can I find a good restaurant? Say! Conductor, watch my valise till I get a cup of coffee! Is my hat on straight? Oh, have you seen my husband? He's a tall man with link cuff-buttons. Conductor, can you change a dollar? What's the best hotel in town? Which way is town? Oh, where's mamma gotten to? Oh, find my darling Fido; he has a blue ribbon round his neck," and so on, ad noisyam—as one might say. You can tell old travelers at a glance. They have umbrellas and novels strapped to their satchels and they strike a bee line for the open doors at the depot without creating any disturbance.

But the giggling school girls on their way home for the holidays, the old spectacled lady who punches your ribs with her umbrella, the country family covered with confusion and store clothes, the fat lady with the calla lily in a pot, the timid man following the lady with the iron-jaw and carrying two children, a bird cage and a guitar, and the loud breathing man who has been looking upon the buffet car when it was red, all these have tangled themselves into a struggling, inquiring, tangled Babel of bag, baggage, babies and bluster.

The young lady is there to meet her school girl friend. The escort stands at one side with his cane in his mouth; nervously fingering in his vest pocket to see if the car fare is ready at hand. The girls grapple each other, catch-as-catch-can, fire a broadside of the opera bouffe brand of kisses, and jabber out something like this: "Oh, you sweet thing, so glad you've come—toothache?—oh, no, it's a caramel—such a lovely cape, I want the pattern—dying to see you—that ring—my brother gave it to me—don't tell me a story—Charlie and Tom and Harry and Bob, and—oh, I forgot—Tom, this is Kitty—real sealskin of course—talk all night when we get home"—"Git out der way dere gents and ladies"—a truck piled with trunks four high goes crashing by; a policeman drags an old lady from under the wheels, and she plunges madly at the engine and is rescued by the fireman whom she abuses as a pickpocket and an oppressor of the defenseless.

A sour looking man with a big valise comes out of the crowd and is seized upon by a red-nosed man in a silk hat.

"Did you get it, old boy?" asks the man with the nose.

"Get your grandmother!" growls the sour man.

"That fellow Reed is the biggest liar in America. Feller from Maine got it. I'm a populist from this day on. Got the price of a toddy, Jimmy?"

The engine stands and puffs sullenly. The crowd disperses gradually, stringing by twos, threes and larger groups through the waiting room doors. Depot officials hustle along, pushing their way among the people.

A brakeman springs from his car and runs up to a dim female figure lurking in the shadow of the depot.

"How is the kid?" he asks sharply with an uneven breath.

"Bad," says the woman, in a dry, low voice. "Fever a hundred and four all day. Keeps a-calling of you all the time, Jim. Got to go out again tonight?"

"Orders," says Jim; and then: "No, cussed if I do. The company can go to the devil. Callin' of me, is he? Come on, Liz." He takes the woman's arm and they hurry away into the darkness.

A ragged man with a dreary whine to his voice fastens upon a big stranger in a long overcoat who is hurrying hotel-wards.

"Have you a dime, sir, a man could get something to eat with?" The big man pauses and says kindly, "Certainly. I have more than that. I have at least a dollar for supper, and I'm going up to the Hutchins House and get it. Good night."

On the other side of the depot the hack drivers are crowding to the dead line, filling the air with cries. A pompous man, who never allows himself to be imposed upon when traveling, steps up to a carriage and slings his valise inside. "Drive me to the Lawlor Hotel," he says, commandingly.

"But, sir," says the driver. "The Lawlor is—"

"I don't want any comments," says the pompous man. "If you don't want the job, say so."

"I was just going to say that—"

"I know where I want to go, and if you think you know any better—"

"Jump in," says the driver. "I'll take you."

The pompous man gets into the carriage; the driver mounts to his seat, whips up his horses, drives across the street, fully twenty-five yards away, opens the door and says: "Lawlor Hotel, sir; 50 cents, please."

He gets a dollar instead, and promises to say nothing about it.

The carriages and omnibuses rattle away with their loads; other travelers straggle in for the next train, and when it arrives the Grand Central will repeat its little farce comedy with new actors, and new specialties and various readings between the lines.

Why He Hesitated

A MAN with a worn, haggard countenance that showed traces of deep sorrow and suffering rushed excitedly up the stairs into the editorial rooms of the Post.

The literary editor was alone in his corner, and the man threw himself into a chair near by and said:

"Excuse me, sir, for inflicting my troubles upon you, but I must unbosom myself to some one. I am the unhappiest of men. Two months ago, in a quiet little town in Eastern Texas there was a family dwelling in the midst of peace and contentment. Hezekiah Skinner was the head of that family, and he almost idolized his wife, who appeared to completely return his affection. Alas, sir, she was deceiving him. Her protestations of love were but honeyed lies, intended to gull and blind him. She had become infatuated with William Wagstaff, a neighbor, who had insidiously planned to capture her affections. She listened to Wagstaff's pleadings and fled with him, leaving her husband with a wrecked home and a broken heart. Can you not feel for me, sir?"

"I do, indeed," said the literary editor. "I can conceive the agony, the sorrow and the deep suffering that you must have felt."

"For two months," continued the man, "the home of Hezekiah Skinner has been desolate, and this woman and Wagstaff have been flying from his wrath."

"What do you intend to do?" asked the literary editor.

"I scarcely know. I do not care for the woman any longer, but I cannot escape the tortures my mind is undergoing day after day."

At this point a shrill woman's voice was heard in the outer office, making some inquiry of the office boy.

"Great heavens, her voice!" said the man, rising to his feet greatly agitated. "I must get out of here. Quick! Is there no way for me to escape? A window—a side door—anywhere before she finds me."

The literary editor rose with indignation in his face.

"For shame, sir," he said, "do not act so unworthy a part.

Confront your faithless wife, Mr. Skinner, and denounce her for wrecking your life and home. Why do you hesitate to stand up for your honor and your rights?"

"You do not understand," said the man, his face white with fear and apprehension, as he climbed out the window upon a shed—"I am William Wagstaff."

Something for Baby

THIS IS nothing but a slight jar in the happy holiday music; a minor note struck by the finger of Fate, slipping upon the keys, as anthems of rejoicing and Christmas carols make the Yuletide merry.

A Post man stood yesterday in one of the largest fancy and dry goods stores on Main street, watching the throng of well dressed buyers, mostly ladies, who were turning over the exquisite stock of Christmas notions and holiday goods.

Presently a little slim, white faced girl crept timidly through the crowd to the counter. She was dressed in thin calico, and her shoes were patched and clumsy.

She looked about her with a manner half mournful, half scared.

A clerk saw her and came forward.

"Well, what is it?" he asked, rather shortly.

"Please sir," she answered in a weak voice, "mamma gave me this dime to get something for baby."

"Something for baby, for a dime? Want to buy baby a Christmas present, eh? Well now, don't you think you had better run around to a toy shop? We don't keep such things here. You want a tin horse, or a ball, or a jumping jack, now don't you?"

"Please sir, mamma said I was to come here. Baby isn't with us now. Mamma told me to get—ten—cents—worth of crape, sir, if you please."

Too Wise

THERE IS a man in Houston who keeps quite abreast of the times. He reads the papers, has traveled extensively and is an excellent judge of human nature. He has a natural gift for detecting humbugs and fakirs, and it would be a smooth artist indeed who could impose upon him in any way.

Last night as he was going home, a shady-looking man with his hat pulled over his eyes stepped out from a doorway and said:

"Say, gent, here's a fine diamond ring I found in de gutter. I don't want to get into no trouble wid it. Gimme a dollar and take it."

The Houston man smiled as he looked at the flashy ring the man held toward him.

"A very good game, my man," he said, "but the police are hot after you fellows. You had better select your rhinestone customers with better judgment. Good night."

When the man got home he found his wife in tears.

"Oh, John," she said. "I went shopping this afternoon and lost my solitaire diamond ring. Oh, what shall I——"

John turned without a word and rushed back down the street, but the shady-looking man was not to be found.

His wife often wonders why he never scolded her for losing the ring.

The Return of the Songster

H E WAS a busy man, and his ten years of married life had buried sentiment rather deep in his bosom, but it was not yet dead.

That morning at breakfast he and his wife had had some hard words, and when he had nearly reached his office an unusual feeling of tenderness for his faithful life partner, and regret for the things he had said came upon him. Without entering the office, he turned on his heel and went back home, resolving to acknowledge his fault, and spread the oil of love and forgiveness upon the troubled matrimonial waters. He returned by a slightly different route in order to post some letters he had forgotten.

After he had left home, his wife experienced the same feeling of remorse and affection, and putting on her hat, she started for the office, filled with the same laudable intent to make peace and restore the god of love to his old position in the household.

When she reached the office the boy informed her that her husband had not yet arrived. She took a chair and waited.

When he arrived at his home the servant girl told him that his wife had left the house soon after his own departure, volunteering the additional information that she seemed "powerful flustered and bothered like."

He sat down, thinking she had run over to a neighbor's, and would return presently.

After waiting an hour he began to grow alarmed. What was that she had said when they were wrangling that morning, about "putting an end to this kind of life"? Her nature was of the emotional kind that is apt to lose its balance when greatly affected. Had he driven her to desperation? A cold fear seized him, and he began to pace the floor nervously. He would have given all he was worth to have heard her step upon the stair. He strained his ears at every footfall upon the sidewalk. What course would her desperation take? He thought of her being dragged from the river, dripping and lifeless, and himself left in the world a prey of remorse, and morally responsible for her fate. And then, again, with a sharper stab, he thought of Sam

Sedberry, the man who was courting her when he won her. Only two days before, while walking on the street with her, Sam had come along, and she had stopped him and asked how the geranium was getting on that she had given his wife. Was it possible that—

He tore out his watch again and looked at it. She had been away two hours. She had not taken with her, the servant said, any satchel or bundle, or even a wrap. It could not have been flight; it must be—Oh, Laura, his love!—it must be suicide.

He seized his hat and hurried out, and down the street.

When the contrite wife had waited in her husband's office nearly an hour, and he did not come, her imagination began to suggest things that did not have a soothing effect. What could be keeping him? Had he—yes, Great heavens! she remembered now what he had said that morning. In the midst of their quarrel the words he had spoken: "I will not stand this another day" had seemed idle enough to her ears, but now they rang like funeral bells. He was a man of quick temper and high spirit: had he meant to take his own life? Or had he—her face paled. Only the day before he had leaned over the fence next door where that bold widow, Mrs. Fliply lived, and asked about her sick poodle. Had this designing creature persuaded him to run—No, no, no, that was too horrible to contemplate. He must be—Oh, John, dearest husband!—he must be dead!

She saw him, in her mind, already laid out in their parlor, and the men who had brought his body home standing around. She glanced at the clock over his desk. Two hours since she had come!

She hurried out, and homeward, with wildly beating heart.

About half way, they suddenly met each other as they turned a corner.

To do him proper credit, she recovered herself first.

"Nice business man you are," she said, "to leave your work to take care of itself while you go bumming around town half the day!"

"It's funny," he said, "that you cant resist your propensity to gallivant all over the streets long enough to even attend to the simplest of your household duties."

The moral will be found in the following verses:

Strange we do not prize the music
   Till the sweet voiced bird has flown:
But there is a fact that's stranger;
   And a fact we all must own.

That if that sweet voiced bird should fly
   Back once more, as he went,
We'd say, just as we said before:
   "You cant sing for a cent."

Book Reviews

UNABRIDGED DICTIONARY by Noah Webster, L. L. D. F. R. S. X. Y. Z. etc.

We find on our table quite an exhaustive treatise on various subjects, written in Mr. Webster's well known, lucid, and piquant style. There is not a dull line between the covers of the book. The range of subjects is wide, and the treatment light and easy without being flippant. A valuable feature of the work is the arranging of the articles in alphabetical order, thus facilitating the finding of any particular word desired. Mr. Webster's vocabulary is large, and he always uses the right word in the right place. Mr. Webster's work is thorough, and we predict that he will be heard from again.

Houston City Directory, by Morrison & Fourmy.

This new book has the decided merit of being non-sensational. In these days of erotic and ultra-imaginative literature of the modern morbid self-analytical school it is a relief to peruse a book with so little straining after effect, so well balanced, and so pure in sentiment. It is a book that a man can place in the hands of the most innocent member of his family with the utmost confidence. Its text is healthy, and its literary style excellent, as it adheres to the method used with such thrilling effect by Mr. Webster in his famous dictionary, viz: alphabetical arrangement.

We venture to assert that no one can carefully and conscientiously read this little volume without being a better man, or lady, as circumstances over which they have no control may indicate.

Guessed Everything Else

A MAN with a long, sharp nose and a big bundle which he carried by a strap went up the steps of the gloomy-looking brick house, set his bundle down, rang the bell, and took off his hat and wiped his brow.

A woman opened the door, and he said:

"Madam, I have a number of not only useful but necessary articles here that I would like to show you. First, I want you to look at these elegant illustrated books of travel and biography, written by the best authors. They are sold only by subscription. They are bound in—"

"I don't care to see them. We have sm—"

"Small children only, eh? Well, madam, here are some building blocks that are very instructive and amusing. No? Well, let me show you some beautiful lace window curtains for your sitting room, handmade and a great bargain. I can—"

"I don't want them. We have sm—"

"Smoking in the house? It won't injure them in the least. Just shake them out in the morning and I guarantee not a vestige of tobacco smoke will remain. Here also I have a very ingenious bell for awakening lazy servants in the morning. You simply touch a button and—"

"I tell you we have sm—"

"Have smart servants, have you? Well, that is a blessing. Now, here is a clothes line that is one of the wonders of the age. It needs no pins and can be fastened to anything—fence, side of the house or tree. It can be raised or lowered in an instant, and for a large washing is the most convenient and labor-saving invention that—"

"I say we have small—"

"Oh, you have a small family. Let's see, then I have here a—"

"I'm trying to tell you," said the woman, "that we have small-pox in the family, and—"

The long-nosed man made a convulsive grab at his goods and rolled down the steps in about two seconds, while the woman softly closed the door just as a man got out of a buggy and nailed a yellow flag on the house.

In Mezzotint

THE DOCTOR had long ago ceased his hospital practice, but whenever there was a case of special interest among the wards, his spirited team of bays was sure to be seen standing at the hospital gates. Young, handsome, at the head of his profession, possessing an ample income, and married but six months to a beautiful girl who adored him, his lot was certainly one to be envied.

It must have been 9 o'clock when he reached home. The stableman took the team, and he ran up the steps lightly. The door opened, and Doris' arms were flung tightly about his neck, and her wet cheek pressed to his.

"Oh, Ralph," she said, her voice quivering and plaintive; "you are so late. You can't think how I miss you when you don't come at the usual hour. I've kept supper warm for you. I'm so jealous of those patients of yours—they keep you from me so much."

"How fresh and sweet and wholesome you are, after the sights I have to see," he said, smiling down at her girlish face with the airy confidence of a man who knows himself well beloved. "Now, pour my coffee, little one, while I go up and change clothes."

After supper he sat in the library in his favorite arm chair, and she sat in her especial place upon one arm of the chair and held a match for him to light his cigar. She seemed so glad to have him with her; every touch was a caress, and every word she spake had that lingering, loving drawl that a woman uses to but one man—at a time.

"I lost my case of cerebro-spinal meningitis tonight," he said, gravely.

"I have you, and I don't have you," she said. "Your thoughts are always with your profession, even when I think you are most mine. Ah, well," with a sigh, "you help the suffering, and I would see all that suffer relieved or else like your cerebro—what is it? patient, at rest."

"A queer case, too," said the doctor, patting his wife's hand and gazing into the clouds of cigar smoke. "He should have

31

recovered. I had him cured, and he died on my hands without any warning. Ungrateful, too, for I treated that case beautifully. Confound the fellow, I believe he wanted to die. Some nonsensical romance worried him into a fever."

"A romance? Oh, Ralph, tell it to me. Just think! A romance in a hospital."

"He tried to tell it to me this morning in snatches between paroxysms of pain. He was bending backward till his head almost touched his heels, and his ribs were nearly cracking, yet he managed to convey something of his life story."

"Oh, how horrible," said the doctor's wife, slipping her arm between his neck and the chair.

"It seems," went on the doctor, "as well as I could gather, that some girl had discarded him to marry a more well-to-do man, and he lost hope and interest in life, and went to the dogs. No, he refused to tell her name. There was a great pride in that meningitis case. He lied like an angel about his own name, and he gave his watch to the nurse and spoke to her as he would to a queen. I don't believe I ever will forgive him for dying, for I worked the next thing to a miracle on him. Well, he died this morning, and—let me get a match—oh, yes, here's a little thing in my pocket he gave me to have buried with him. He told me about starting to a concert with this girl one night, and they decided not to go in, but take a moonlight walk instead. She tore the ticket in two pieces, and gave him one-half and kept the other. Here's his half, this little red piece of pasteboard, with the word 'Admit—' printed on it. Look out, little one—that old chair arm is so slippery. Hurt you?"

"No, Ralph. I'm not so easy hurt. What do you think love is, Ralph?"

"Love? Little one! Oh, love is undoubtedly a species of mild insanity. An over-balance of the brain that leads to an abnormal state. It is as much a disease as measles, but as yet, sentimentalists refuse to hand it over to us doctors of medicine for treatment."

His wife took the half of the little red ticket and held it up.

"Admit—" she said, with a little laugh. "I suppose by this time he's admitted somewhere, isn't he, Ralph?"

"Somewhere," said the doctor, lighting his cigar afresh.

"Finish your cigar, Ralph, and then come up," she said. "I'm a little tired, and I'll wait for you above."

"All right, little one," said the doctor. "Pleasant dreams!"

He smoked the cigar out, and then lit another.

It was nearly eleven when he went up stairs.

The light in his wife's room was turned low, and she lay upon her bed undressed. As he stepped to her side and raised her hand, some steel instrument fell and jingled upon the floor, and he saw upon the white countenance a creeping red horror that froze his blood.

He sprang to the lamp and turned up the blaze. As he parted his lips to send forth a shout, he paused for a moment, with his eyes upon his dead patient's half ticket that lay upon the table. The other half had been neatly fitted to it, and it now read:

ADMIT TWO

The Barber Talks

THE POST man slid into the chair with an apologetic manner, for the barber's gaze was superior and scornful. He was so devilish, cool and self-possessed, and held the public in such infinite contempt.

The Post man's hair had been cut close with the clippers on the day before.

"Haircut?" asked the barber in a quiet but thoroughly dangerous tone.

"Shave," said The Post man.

The barber raised his eyebrows, gave his victim a look of deep disdain, and hurled the chair with a loud rattle and crash back to a reclining position.

Then he seized a mug and brush and, after bestowing upon The Post man a look of undying contumely, turned with a sneer to the water faucet. Thence he returned, enveloped the passive victim in a voluminous cloth, and with a pitiless hand daubed a great brushful of sweetish tasting lather across his mouth.

Then he began to talk.

"Ever been in Seattle, Washington Territory?" he asked.

"Blub-a-lub-blub," said The Post man, struggling against the soap, and then he shook his head feebly.

"Neither have I," said the barber, "but I have a brother named Bill who runs an orange orchard nine miles from St. John, Fla. That's only a split hair on your neck; it's growing the wrong way. They are caused by shaving the neck in the wrong direction. Sometimes whiskey will make them do that way. Whiskey is a terrible thing. Do you drink it?"

The Post man only had one eye of all his features uncovered by lather and he tried to throw an appealing expression implying negation into this optic, but the barber was too quick for him and filled the eye with soap by a dextrous flap of his brush.

"My brother Bill used to drink," continued the barber. "He could drink more whiskey than any man in Houston, but he never got drunk. He had a chair in my shop, but I had to let him go. Bill had a wonderful constitution. When he got all he could hold he would quit drinking. The only way he showed it was in his eyes. They would get kind of glazed and fishy and wouldn't turn in his head. When Bill wanted to look to one side he used to take his fingers and turn his eyeballs a little the way he wanted to see. His eyes looked exactly like those little round windows you see in the dome of the postoffice. You could hear Bill breathe across the street when he was full. He could shave people when he was drunk as well as he could sober.—Razor hurt you?"

The Post man tried to wave one of his hands to disclaim any sense of pain, but the barber's quick eye caught the motion and he leaned his weight against the hand, crushing it against the chair.

"I kept noticing," went on the barber, "that Bill was getting about four customers to my one, even if he did drink so much. People would come in three or four at a time and sit down and wait their turns with Bill when my chair was vacant. I didn't know what to make of it. Bill had all he could do, and he was so crowded that he didn't have time to go out to a saloon, but he kept a big jug in the back room, and every few minutes he would slip in there and take a drink.

"One day I noticed a man that got out of Bill's chair acting queer and he staggered as he went out. A day or two afterwards the shop was full of customers from morning till night, and one man came back and had a shave three different times in the forenoon. In a couple of days more there was a crowd of men in the shop, and they had a line formed outside two or three doors down the sidewalk. Bill made $9.00 that day. That evening a policeman came in and jerked me up for running a saloon without a license. It seems that Bill's breath was so full of whiskey that every man he shaved went out feeling pretty hilarious and sent his friends there to be shaved. It cost me $300 to get out of it, and I shipped Bill to Florida pretty soon afterward."

"I was sent for once," went on the barber, as he seized his victim by the ear and slammed his head over on the other side, "to go out on Piney street and shave a dead man. Barbers don't much like a job of that kind, although they get from $5 to $10 for the work. It was 1908 Piney street. I started about 11 o'clock at night. I found the street all right and I counted from the corner until I found 1908. I had my razors, soap and mug in a little case I use for such purposes. I went in and knocked at the door. An old man opened it and his eye fell on my case.

"'You've come, have you?' he asked. 'Well, go up stairs; he's in the front room to your right. There's nobody with him. He hasn't any friends or relatives in town; he's only been boarding here about a week.'

"'How long since he—since it occurred?' I asked.

"'About an hour, I guess,' says the old man. I was glad of that because corpses always shave better before they get good and cold. I went in the room and turned up the lamp. The man was laid out on the bed. He was warm yet and he had about a week's growth of beard on. I got to work and in half an hour I had given him a nice clean shave that would have done his heart good if he had been alive. Then I went down stairs and saw the old man.

"'What success?' he asked.

"'Good,' says I. 'He's fixed up all right. Who's to pay?'

"'He gave me $30 to send his folks in Alabama yesterday,' says the old man. 'I guess your fee will have to come out of it.'

"'It'll be five,' I said.

"The old man handed me a five dollar bill and I went home very well satisfied."

Here the barber seized the chair, hurled it upright, snatched off the cloth, buried his hands in The Post man's hair and tore out a handful, bumped and thumped his head, shook it violently and hissed sarcastically:

"Bay rum?"

The Post man nodded stupidly, closed his eyes and tried unsuccessfully to recall a prayer.

"Next day," said the barber, "I heard some news. It seems that a man had died at 1908 Piney street and just a little while before a man in the next house had taken poison. The folks in one house sent for a doctor and the ones in the other sent for a barber. The funny part is the doctor and I both made a mistake and got into the wrong house. He went in to see the dead man and found the family doctor just getting ready to leave. The doctor didn't waste any time asking questions, but got out his stomach pump, stuck it into the dead man and went to work pumping the poison out. All this time I was busy shaving the man who had taken poison. And the funniest part of it all is that after the doctor had pumped all the other doctor's medicine out of the dead man, he opened his eyes, raised up in bed and asked for a steak and potatoes.

"This made the family doctor mad, and he and the doctor with a stomach pump got into a fight and fell down the stairs and broke the hat rack all to pieces."

"And how about your man who had taken poison?" asked The Post man timidly.

"Him?" said the barber, "why he died, of course, but he died with one of the beautifulest shaves that ever a man had.—Brush!"

An African of terrible aspect bore down upon The Post man, struck him violently with the stub of a whisk broom, seized his coat at the back and ripped it loose from its collar.

"Call again," growled the barber in a voice of the deepest menace, as the scribe made a rush for the door and escaped.

The Ghost That Came to Old Angles

DENNY TOOLE, who played the rôle of ghost is now leading man in a dramatic company of repute, "Raph," short for Raphael, who "made up" Denny for the scene is a rising marine painter, "The Angel," whose barbarous imagination conceived the infamous scheme, perforates our statesmen in Washington "specials," while I, aider and abettor in the affair, I—well, you should drop up into my den sometime and look over my splendid collection of "Editors' Regrets."

The long, two storied, moss grown brick college building in the lonely North Carolina woods, the cool, sandy roads flanked by sumac and blackberry bushes, through which ran, half hidden, the gray rail fences, the farm houses peering from shady groves across the fields of wheat and corn, the drone of the bees in the locust trees, the rattle of falling chestnuts upon the dry leaves at night, the dismal crying of the chicken hawks in the afternoons, the solemnity, the loneliness of the distant wooded hills, weltering in blue September haze and wooing us through the high, small windows;—all these things come back to me afresh as I recall the facts about the ghost that came to Old Angles.

We four boys, students at Oak Hill college, by reason of concordant tastes in the direction of the fine arts, a more discriminating and delicate choice in deviltry, and a fancied superiority to other people in general, were sworn and congenial associates. Our higher strung natures demanded loftier diversion than that afforded by the looting of watermelon and potato patches to set forth nocturnal feasts, and devising new forms of torture for the principal's cow. Wherefore, we sought out new, bizarre, and deeply pondered modes of rendering life a burden to our preceptors and the good folk unfortunate enough to dwell within the radius of the territory we covered.

By far the choicest butt of our waggery at Oak Hall was Professor Haliburton Chester Strayhorn, instructor in mathematics. At him we launched our masterpieces of wit and satire,—shafts that I now can see were but poor pinfeather darts of impudence and conceit.

Professor Strayhorn—or "Old Angles," as we called him privately,—a weak fancy evolved from his occupation and his bony figure—was a gloomy, solemn man with a sparse, reddish beard, and eyes totally devoid of humour. Mathematics he undoubtedly knew, but the rest of his soul he kept closed. It was rumored that he had once had a romance of some sort, but we four, who knew the world, laughed the idea to scorn. Old Angles, in his black dyed clothes, his frayed, with-collar-attached shirt, and his rusty brown string tie was too sorry a bird to have ever perched upon the bright pinnacles of romance. He always went through his lessons with painstaking care, and was sharp and intolerant with inattention or shirking. At all times he seemed a prey to some inward care that revealed itself in his restless, sometimes absent-minded, and always unhappy demeanour. After lessons he invariably retired to his room, a small log building upon the campus. To this room he seldom invited any one. Glimpses we caught of its interior in passing failed to reveal anything suggestive of romance or mystery. A table littered with books and papers, a frail bed in a corner, two or three chairs and a venerable hair trunk was about all it contained.

From some inexplicable, and, to us, tantalizing reason Old Angles had taken an uncommon fancy toward Denny. To him he explained equations with partial minuteness, and from him he bore with abnormal endurance utterly idiotic demonstrations of problems that from any other member of the class would have drawn swift and pointed reproof. Even in addressing Denny, Old Angles' voice would lose some of its harsh monotony, and I have seen him, during a lesson, watching the boy's face with a most peculiar soft and puzzling expression upon his own. He even went so far one day as to invite Denny to his room, and there regaled him with a glass of elderberry wine, and a lecture on the hypothenuse. Goaded by our ingenious and derisive speculations as to the reason of Old Angles' partiality, Denny received his favors with waxing hostility.

One day when Old Angles was feeling pretty sharp he kept in two of the duller boys after lessons in order to drum into them the whys and wherefores of a certain geometric design. We inevitable four companions left the recitation hall, and with ennui upon us, walked across the campus. As we came to Old Angles' cottage we observed that the door was open. Impelled by a common prompting to evil, we entered and looked about. The table in the center of the room alone offered matter worthy of inspection. It was piled high with books, mostly works on the higher mathematics, and scratch pads broken out all over with figures in pencil. There was his lamp with a spoonful of oil in it, and an old quill pen in an inkstand. Curiously enough, among the books lay an old volume of Tennyson's poems, which, when I picked it up opened easily at "Maud."

"Boys," I said, "Old Angles has deceived us. He reads poetry. Listen to this." A passage was marked with a pencil:—

> . . . "'Would die,
> For sullen seeming Death may give more
> life to Love than is, or ever was
> In our low world, where yet 'tis sweet to live'"

"Hullo! what next?" said The Angel, snatching up a square of cardboard that fell from a treatise on the differential calculus that he was contemptuously handling; "Shades of Cupid! Old Angles' Romance has turned up at last."

He held up a photograph of a woman, a young woman with a face such as an artist of real imagination pictures upon an angel; sweet, clear and tender, with eyes that accuse while they charm the beholder.

And—the secret of Old Angles' partiality to Denny was out—it was Denny's face feminimized; the same dreamy, holy expression that so belied Denny's interior, the same unimportant nose, the same curve to the mouth and same blonde curling hair. The Angel turned the card over. On the back was written in a sloping hand: "To Hal from Luella"; and underneath, in Old Angles' scrawl: "Died June 18th, 1868."

As I said before, it was The Angel who devised the infamous scheme. He stood balancing the photograph in his hand, looking first at it and then at Denny, meditatively chewing a black gum twig.

It was one of those marvelous resemblances that sometimes exist, not in families, but between people in no manner related.

"With the material on hand," said The Angel, as if he were arguing with some invisible antagonist, "it would be sinful not to do it. Denny in the rôle. Raph to rig him up, Mc. (that was I) to assist, and the glory mine;—boys, Luella is coming back to Old Angles tonight for positively her last reappearance."

We gathered close to The Angel while he began to set forth his plans, but at that moment a warning scurrying of feet from the direction of the recitation hall reminded us where we were, and we retreated hurriedly to a certain grape arbor which was held sacred to our councils of war, we having repeatedly proven by successful defence, our title to it against prying students.

I have no word of excuse to offer for what we did. Our youth might have accorded some, and the fact that The Angel swayed us by that masterful power of organization and leadership which has subsequently so distinguished his career, might add a little to it, but I shall plead nothing. I will only ask that the reader judge us by the end achieved, but as to his opinion of the affair, why, it matters little, since the question will never be settled either one way or another in this world.

That night, according to custom, Darius Hobbs, the janitor, blew a conch shell on the rear porch of the college building, signifying the arrival of nine o'clock, the hour for retiring. When the lights were out we four met in The Angel's room. He had everything ready,—sheet, vaseline, pearl powder, and a pair of curling tongs borrowed from a professor's wife. Raph, his artistic instincts well awakened, set to work on the "make up."

In forty minutes everything was done, and Denny stood before us in the classically draped folds of a linen sheet, his hair newly curled, and pearl powdered like a marshmallow. He was looking like a seraph, and swearing a little at the nippy fall air the September night had brought. In a properly dim light, we conceded, Luella's ghost itself could not have done better.

"Suppose he should shy something at me!" said Denny, with a not unreasonable qualm.

"Let it go clean through you," said The Angel, "like an orthodox conscientious ghost. Realism is what we want. But he wont do it. I wonder what he *will* do. A professor of mathematics ought to do something out of the ordinary *in re* a visit from a genuine ghost."

"Suppose," I said, "he should raise a row?"

"If the welkin rings," said The Angel, "it's cut and run, of course. Denny's clothes, or sufficient thereof, will be in the arbor, and he'll get them on and be elbowing among the alarmed bystanders in no time."

"I wonder who Luella was," said Denny;—"His girl?"

"Certainly," said The Angel; "And isosceles triangles parted them."

"But she died, you know," said Denny. "Isn't it—?"

"No, it isn't. It's not half as bad as the rapping tables and cabinet humbuggery. There's nothing to pay."

It was near eleven o'clock when we minced softly down stairs and out upon the campus. Denny's form was hidden by an overcoat, lest chance mortal eyes might gaze upon his spectral guise and be amazed. It was quite dark, for the autumn stars, sparkling frostily above, only drove the shadows into denser masses beneath the oaks. We heard nothing but a hound baying weirdly from the timber, and the muffled blows of a pillow fight somewhere in the smaller boys' dormitory. The principal's cow, grazing near, blew a deep breath of apprehension as we passed, fearing some fresh plot against her comfort.

Under his arm, The Angel—who thought of everything— carried a bundle of Denny's clothes, which, while we waited, he deposited in the grape arbor for the donning by the ghost in case of an alarm.

Old Angles' cottage was dark. His light always went out at ten. We halted under a cluster of trees thirty yards away, and The Angel went on a reconnaissance. He returned in ten minutes and said:

"He has'nt gone to bed. He's sitting by a handful of coals in the fireplace. He was smoking his pipe, but he dropped it and never picked it up. I think he's asleep, and the door and windows are open. Denny'll appear in the door. Raph, you take the bull's eye and stand about the corner of the house. Throw just enough light on Denny to make him a first class ghost. Denny, you—"

"Let up," said Denny, sweetly. "I dont need any coaching. I'm going to create a part. The light from the bull's eye is the only cue I want. Dont have it too strong."

"Spectators to the rear," said The Angel.

The Angel and I crept around to the back window under some thick fig trees that made an Erebus beneath them. All we could do now was to await the carrying out of the program by the leading actor and his assistant. Peering between the slats of the window blinds we made out the dim form of Old Angles sunk down in his chair beside the fireplace. The open doorway opposite us was black. The background was perfect. Old Angles stirred a little, and we heard him sigh deeply.

Suddenly, unaccompanied by any sound, a vision framed itself in the doorway; a vision so incorporeal, so faintly luminous and phantasmal, so beautiful that I gasped, and The Angel gripped my shoulder with abrupt violence. Was that unearthly, intangible thing really Denny, or was it—

"Hal!"

The word stole upon the silence, sweet and faint and far away, but the dim figure in the chair writhed at the sound, stumbled to its feet, and lurched down somewhere in the dark, crying a name in a voice that turned us cold where we stood.

"Lu-el-la!"

There was a whole life's history in that heart wringing cry, and we began to see what idiots we had been. Old Angles was crouching or kneeling somewhere on the floor. We saw the vague outlines of his arms upraised toward Denny, his fingers hooked and quivering like beech leaves. Then he began to speak, and it seemed that he was imploring forgiveness for something that had been done. The precise drift of the matter we could not follow with much understanding. He spoke indistinctly, and his words were upheaved by so violent an emotion that little continuity of idea attended them, but their import held us, ghost and all, in an indomitable spell. Thus he cried:

"Forgive, forgive! Luella—is it for that—you have come—or to judge? Have I not—lived in torture—these years—praying to Almighty God—that he might let you—but speak one word to me—from the grave—one word—to end this—all you had you gave—and I—ruined—ruined your life—Luella—my wife—forgive—"

Old Angles broke off with that harsh, wrenching, discordant sob that renders the grief of strong men unlovely. The ghost stood his ground manfully.

"Blind and unworthy—unfit to live—throwing away Heaven's gifts—I found too late—the angel you were—but one word of forgiveness—and I take up—my burden again—until I come—forgive!—"

I heard The Angel moisten his lips and whisper between his teeth:

"His chance! Now, oh, now; will the noodle take it!"

Then it was that Denny Toole rose to his opportunity and wrested *summum bonum* out of a very bad piece of business. His seraph's voice spake again, dulcet and clear, and seeming to come from the fixed stars:

"Hal, I forgive. I came to tell you. Be comforted. We shall meet again, and I wait for you above, where all is peace and love."

The ghost turned his head ever so slightly toward the corner of the house, where Raph stood, and vanished, leaving Stygian darkness in the doorway. We heard a hoarse, but exultant "Thank God!" from the darkness in the room, and a soft, crumpling fall as if something had relaxed.

The Angel and I rounded the house and overtook Raph and the ghost, who was hustling into his overcoat. Even in the faint light we could see the perspiration standing on his face. The ghost spake to The Angel.

"You damned fool!" he said.

"Right!" said The Angel.

When we filed into Old Angles' room the next day for our geometry lesson, we seemed to see another man in his chair. There was the same black dyed suit, the same rusty tie and straggling red whiskers, but out of the worn face shone a soul that had found peace. The old harassed, haunted look was gone, and in its stead was a calm exaltation that triumphed over its sadness.

And, considering all things, we agreed that it was well. Through a deception, it was true, had peace been brought to Old Angles, but judging from the face of Luella as shown upon the old photograph, and what is known of the all forgiving and all sacrificing deep tender heart of woman that passeth our understanding, I do not think that the words of forgiveness spoken by the ghost that came to Old Angles will be foresworn when he comes to face Luella's immortal spirit.

As we came out of the room one of the younger boys began—:

"Old Ang—"

The Angel's hand closed upon his windpipe.

"Professor Haliburton Chester Strayhorn," he said.—"Now, don't go and forget it."

Pursuing Ideals

THE MOMENT I met Curley I liked him. After we had talked an hour, in comparison with our relations those of Damon and Pythias would have appeared strained. Our tastes were identical, and we viewed life from a common standpoint of youth and disillusionment. When we spoke of Art we mentally spelled it with a big A, and referred to ideals as if they were as plentiful as blackberries.

Curley wrote, and he had been lucky enough to catch the return tide of Romance after it had been drawn away by the yellow spotted moon of Realism, and very nearly succeeded in being a Vogue. I was in the way of illustrating, and I had a "Girl" in black and white which (if I do say it) was referred to at least once where Charles Dana Gibson's was—say three times. Curley promised to drop into my studio, and I assured him I would fall up into his study—he was beyond calling it a "den"—as soon as possible.

But, to speak of my Girl.

Perhaps you have seen her. She is no stranger to the magazines, the backs of holiday numbers, or the galleries, where she has looked down more than once, in oils, unapproached in beauty by any of her living admirers. Her face was etched upon my heart. She was my Ideal, the pictorial incarnation of feminine charm. From my pencil or brush, whenever I had excellence in woman to portray, always grew this one Girl, and I loved to think she was mine alone.

I knew her as no one else ever could. I was familiar with her thoughts as well as her outward graces. I knew her little mannerisms of movement, her little tricks of turning her head quickly when she spoke, and her way of smiling suddenly out of a dreamy repose, like soft lightning from a gray cloud at twilight. To me alone she had opened the treasures of her heart. I cannot describe her as I knew her except to say that she was affectionate beyond the run of women, light hearted but unswervingly loyal, and with a flow of easy musical chat that revealed every sentiment she felt. She had a few distinguishing peculiarities that were characteristic of her and very dear to me. At home she always wore red; red house wrappers and pale red tea gowns, with a bunch of red geranium at her throat or waist. She loved to sit on hassocks instead of chairs, and in her gold brown hair she nearly always wore a silver pin. Her face was of no known standard of beauty. Rather heavy lidded her eyes were, with a look in them not to be described unless you understand what I mean when I say they were full of Fate. She was very fair, weighed 126, and her attitudes were impulsive, and so natural as to be sometimes unpicturesque. I loved her with my whole heart. She—

But, wait.

One day I had a note from a firm of publishers asking me to call. I did so. They handed me a manuscript novel to illustrate. Mr. Curley, the author, had requested that I be given the commission.

I was pleased at this evidence of friendship from Curley. He had not yet visited my studio, but I had met him repeatedly at other places, and we had become intimate friends.

A night or two afterward I opened the manuscript and began to glance over it. It was one of those romances that were quite popular then (and are still, today). Love was the motif, and the swift action of the plot carried the reader among scenes of royal splendor and knightly daring. The time was one long gone by, and the gallants and princesses played their parts at a court whose name you shall seek for in vain in the pages of history, but the living interest was there, and better still for the author, the kind of stuff was just what the people were asking for.

But it was neither Mr. Curley's style nor his plot that kept me chained to his manuscript until late that night. It was the startling fact that his heroine was my Girl. He had portrayed her with the utmost fidelity down to the red house gowns and her trick of smiling suddenly from deep reverie. He had described her person, her nature, her virtues, her every peculiarity so well that my admiration for Curley's delineative powers was swamped in an overwhelming flood of jealousy toward the writer. How had he come to know her? What right had he to drag into print for the perusal of a profaning public her sacred thoughts and attributes to which I alone had a prerogative? The picture must have been drawn from life, and by one who enjoyed an intimate association with the model. He must surely know her. The thought fired me with a sudden and stimulating resolve.

I would find out.

I finished my illustrations, and returned them with the manuscript to the publishers. I outdid all my previous efforts in the drawings of Curl— By Heavens! no—of my heroine. I selected for pictures only such scenes as her presence illumined, and I threw all my art and all my love into my work. My tribute to her charms should not be inferior to Curley's—he whom I now regarded as a base rival.

About three days after I had sent in my work, early one morning Curley walked into my studio. He greeted me pleasantly, in his charming way. Curley was a dreamer, and had the soul of an artist, but he made no cheap bid for fame by eccentricities of dress or manner. Neither did I. Curley might have been a stock broker, judging by his quiet, stylish dress and his close cut hair, instead of a rhapsodist and a sentimentalist. So might I.

My Girl was strongly in evidence about my studio. Sketches of her face and form were everywhere, in pastel, crayon, oil, water color, pen and ink—every vehicle by the use of which I could delight the eye with her beloved face.

After greeting Curley with assumed warmth I watched him closely. His eye wandered to my pictures, and he could not conceal a start of surprise when he saw Her face smiling at him from so many canvases.

I may as well state here that my Girl was a creature of my imagination. Her outward semblance was my ideal woman, whom I had not met but longed to meet, and her inward characteristics, as I have described them, were bestowed upon her by my own mind, and were such as my ideal woman might possess.

Curley had once told me that he always drew his characters from life. When I read his novel I knew that in the person of his heroine, when I met her, I should find my fate. I had resolved to find out who she was and win her, if possible. In what relation she stood to Curley I did not, of course, know. She was, unquestionably, something near, for his study of her was thorough, and portrait-like in its delineation. Curley was unmarried: she might have been a friend, a sister, or—painful reflection!—his fiancee. I would find out.

Curley walked over to where I was finishing a sketch, and mended the loose wrapper of a cigar with exaggerated carefulness.

"Joyce," he said, I thought a little constrainedly, "those illustrations were splendid; especially of Zenobia. I see that her face is a favorite study of yours. May I ask if the lady posed in person for the illustrations and sketches?"

I caught Curley's eye, and saw jealousy in it. Was it possible that my imaginary pictures of his heroine actually bore a resemblance to her, and he suspected me of being acquainted with her?

"Do you think the pictures do justice to Zenobia?" I asked, concealing my anxiety.

"They are admirable and faithful," he answered.

"The young lady," I said, "did not pose for the sketches. They were drawn from—memory."

"You are fortunate in knowing her," said Curley.

She was evidently not his sister, or he would have asked me point blank if I knew her. He was fencing with me. He looked upon me as a possible rival. I must dissemble.

"Anyone should be," I said.

"She is incomparable," said Curley, fastening his eyes on the sketches of Her face.

"The world has'nt her equal. I must compliment your portrayal of her character in your book."

"You think it very like her?" asked Curley, eagerly.

"A splendid characterization," I said.

"Joyce," said Curley, looking down at his cigar. "We have been pretty close friends; I am going to ask you a question. Do you love her?"

"Curley, old man," I answered, "I do. Do you?"

He looked at me, a little surprised, and said:

"I am sure of it."

I was playing a rather bold game, but the reward was worth it. I was determined to meet this woman whom Curley knew, and it was only through him that I could do so. She was the embodiment of my ideal, and she was reserved for me by fate.

Curley thought I already knew her. I conceived an impudent proposition and made it.

"Old man," I said, slowly, "Suppose we call on her together, and take a fair start. Then let the best man win."

Somewhat to my surprise, Curley did not demur. He sprang forward, grasped my hand, and exclaimed:

"Joyce, you're a noble fellow. Nothing could be fairer. Shall we call this evening?"

"The sooner, the better," I said. His prompt acquiescence puzzled me, but I was filled with delirious joy at the prospect of meeting her. Now that we were both at an understanding of each other's sentiments toward the woman we adored, and were taking no unfair advantage of our friendly relations, I felt my old amity for Curley return. He had acted with greater magnanimity than I would have shown, I told myself. We parted with effusive amiability.

I was two hours making my toilet that evening. I am not a bad looking man, and I was quite satisfied with my appearance in the mirror. Curley was to call for me at my rooms at eight, and take me to call upon her. Noble fellow! Would I have done the same by him? I tried to make myself believe so.

Curley was on hand promptly at the hour agreed upon. He was magnificently dressed, and I knew it was to be a battle to the death. We went down the stairs, and Curley turned slightly toward the left, with me close at his side. The evening was chilly, and we buttoned our Inverness overcoats up high.

We walked steadily down the street not conversing much, for I was full of happy anticipation of soon being in the presence of the woman I longed to meet.

We came to a quarter of the city built up with handsome residences, and I began to exercise my fancy by selecting this and that house for Her abode, but Curley went straight on, turning neither to the right or the left, and keeping pace with my stride.

Soon the houses began to grow further apart, and less pretentious in appearance, and still Curley kept straight ahead. After we had walked fully half an hour the street turned to a mere lane, the dwellings to mean and tumbledown cottages, and still Curley pressed forward upon a straight course.

I thought She must be in very humble circumstances, and thought how happily I would work for her if it should be my great fortune to win her favor.

Presently Curley tumbled into a ditch, and I helped him out, and began to scrape the mud off him. There were old fields on either side of us, a few squalid looking tenement houses, and the high black walls of factories and warehouses looming against the sky. A queer place for Zenobia to live, truly.

"Confound it," said Curley, "I've ruined my coat."

"Is it much further?" I asked.

"Dont you know where she lives?" said he.

"To tell you the truth," I said, "I've never been to her house. I've only seen her at other places."

"Then, how," he said, "How the devil did you expect to find it?"

"I—I was going with you," I said, rather weakly.

"What do you mean?" said Curley, "by asking me to call upon a young lady with you, and leading me into this villainous ditch, and then asking me where she lives?"

"I expected you to know," I said. "I was following you. Dont you know?"

"Of course not," he answered; "I never met her. You proposed—"

"Wait a moment," I said, "Whom did you think we were going to call upon?"

"Why, the young lady, the original of the illustrations you drew for my book. Did'nt you pro—"

"Wait another minute. Who was the original of Zenobia in your book?"

"Purely an imaginary character. And your pictures were drawn from—"

"Fancy."

We spoke very little of Ideals on the way back.

The Miracle of Lava Canyon

THE SHERIFF of Siskiwah county, Ari. had a secret. He never told it to his best friend, but it was never out of his own mind. He was a physical coward. A shot fired set his heart beating wildly, and he turned sick at strife and carnage. His pulse beats averaged 95 per minute and his heart turned cold every time a summons for arrest was placed in his hands. He experienced a sensation of nervous dread each time he swung himself upon the back of his high-spirited horse. Every sudden sound conveying presage of danger thrilled him with fright. His disposition was high-strung, sensitive and unalterably timid. And yet "Rad" Conrad was known as the coolest and most courageous sheriff in this territory. He had attained this reputation by a daily and hourly struggle with his whole moral force against his natural weakness. His fear of danger, great as it was, had been subordinated to a greater fear lest his failing be known. How to hide his cowardice from the world was his one aim. With a cold fear in his heart he sought danger with the eagerness of one who loved its every phase. Quiet, persistent, plodding in his way; without any of the western dash and audacity belonging to most men in his occupation, he continually sought the closest risks and hazards, driven by an abnormal desire to appear fearless. Men who had no conception of the meaning of the word "fear" sometimes stood apart, aghast at the man's daring, and admired him. Apparently without the slightest excitement, almost sullen of aspect, he trailed desperate criminals to their rendezvous, engaged in combat against mighty odds and waged such relentless war upon desperadoes and outlaws that his fame as an upholder of law and order was spread far and wide.

Radcliff Conrad kept his secret well. Not a man in Siskiwah county has ever seen him flinch from his duty, and tales were told in saloons and camps of his intrepidity and recklessness.

The sheriff's personal appearance aided him. He was strongly and finely formed. He possessed a blond head of classic mold, and a steel-blue eye under good control. His inward struggles kept him at a tension that gave him a reserved and somewhat preoccupied manner, and his every action seemed the result of deliberation instead of impulse. The giving away to impulse was the thing he was trying to avoid. He felt that some day his moral courage would fail him, and he would stand stripped to the gaze of his friends, the coward that he knew himself to be. No monkish ascetic ever scourged his fleshly sins as Radcliff Conrad did his one egregious failing. How well he succeeded in triumphing over it, his fame in Lava canyon and, indeed, in the mouths of men as far as the sage brush grew to east and west attested.

There came one cruel day when the sheriff was forced to apply the whip to his tortured spirit with double force. The town of Lava Canyon was built on a stretch of plain sloping down to a river from the exit of a mountain gulch. Within this gulch was a tangled wilderness. Two miles back from the town it converged to a fissure half a mile deep, like a sword-cut cleaving the hills. The sides, for its whole extent, were inaccessible, except to the rattlesnakes that made their dens among the boulders. Within the edge of the gulch, where the densely wooded sides began to straighten to steeper angles, stood the white painted cottage of Emmet Reed, the postmaster, and leading dealer in hardware, cutlery, arms and ammunition. Here, beside the mountain stream and among the moss-grown rocks, played the juvenile Reeds—little more than rushes in size—watched over more or less carefully by Boadicea, aged 20, eldest daughter of the house.

To these confines late one afternoon came Arizona Dan, worst man in the county, after breaking $500 worth of mirrors and glassware in the principal places of entertainment and introducing sundry slugs of lead into various citizens, to their great bodily anguish. Dan was not too drunk to entertain a wholesome fear of Rad Conrad, and it was his intention to conceal himself until darkness should lend him cover to escape.

On being apprised of these events the sheriff of the county, recognizing his duty, prepared to effect Dan's capture. A brave man in his place who properly estimated the value of a good citizen's life in comparison with the vital spark of a degenerate like Arizona Dan, as a furtherance of the survival of the fittest idea, would have summoned a posse and by moral force of numbers would have secured the surrender of the offender without risk of bloodshed. Radcliff Conrad was not the man to do this. He shunned all appearance of lack of courage, as he desired, in his heart, to shun the danger.

"What arms did he have?" asked the sheriff of some men who had seen Arizona Dan's retreat to the gulch.

"Nary a one," said a saloon keeper, who had suffered from the fugitive's iconoclasm. "He left both his guns in my place."

The sheriff unbuckled his revolver and shoved it across the counter.

"Keep that for me," he said. "I'll go and get Dan."

He passed slowly down the street, walking in the direction of the gulch, and the men gazed after him admiringly.

"Never knew what bein' afraid was. Rad never!" said the mail carrier.

"He 'uz born that a-way," said the county clerk. "A man as ain't got no skeer in him don't deserve no credit fur havin' sand. He wouldn't take his gun along, 'cause Dan had left his'n. With a creetur like Dan it 'pears to me that's a leetle reckless. Dan overweights Rad a matter of twenty-five pounds, the very least."

In the gulch things were as usual, to all appearances. The little mountain brook that dashed down the steep rocks purled in the deep shade and sent out diamond flashes where stray flecks of sunlight dived into it and the birds in the redwood trees whistled away as though there was no such unharmonious and degraded thing as Arizona Dan somewhere below, trying to conceal his desecrating presence. The little Reeds were at school and such noises as might have been heard by that legendary and overworked creature, the casual observer, were sylvan and well attuned. A critic in sight-harmony would also have found little to cavil at, unless his too fine-drawn perceptions had deemed the aspect of Miss Boadicea Reed, who sat negligently in a grapevine swing, too unsylph-like for perfect accord.

Miss Boadicea—called "Dicey" by her immediate family and friends, a diminutive evolved from their original and arbitrary pronunciation of her name—sounded a note which may have been a dissonance, but it had its true power of accentuating the soft melody of the wood. As she half reclined upon the giant vine, her freshly starched white muslin crackled about a form whose measurements faltered not an inch from the modern standard of perfection. Her glossy, black hair was arranged in the latest fashion shown in the most recently arrived ladies' magazine in Lava Canyon. Her features were clear cut and regular; she had the eyes of Melpomene and the heart of the ancient British queen whose name she bore.

Miss Boadicea Reed also had a secret. Being a woman, her dearest friends had often heard it divulged. But, as it was a secret, there needs must be those to whom it was not imparted. That portion of humanity was the one denominated by Miss Reed as "the gentlemen." This awful secret was that she had never, no never, felt the slightest sensation of fear or abashment at any person or thing since she could remember. Miss Boadicea despised and contemned all the little feminine weaknesses and terrors of her sex with all the prejudice of one who did not understand them. Had she been born with time and circumstances in her favor she would have led the overturning of a dynasty or two, captured by force the crown of some social queendom, or at least have gone up in a balloon as the special female representative of one of the several greatest newspapers on earth. Snakes, dogs, spiders, gossip, lightning, men—the partial list of the things regarded by Miss Reed with a serenity approaching contumely will afford a slight conception of her intrepidity of spirit. In the presence of man, the lord of creation, she felt no awe. Living in a frontier mining town and possessing the attractions she did, offers of marriage had come years before, but her suitors had never awakened in her a feeling softer than comradeship. She had laughed at most of them, pitched one out the window, and informed them all that they "made her tired." In fact, there was nothing in all creation, with or without life, that had ever caused her a qualm or a tremor. She regarded robbers as vulgar persons beneath notice, serpents, horned toads, mice and Gila monsters as uninteresting and unterrifying vermin too insignificant to dread. Her secret ambition, cherished in good faith until she was 18, had been to dress in man's clothes and travel round the world selling soap, or diamonds, or patent quartz crushers—anything would do. Since she was 20 her ideas had toned down to a firm resolve to be prima donna of an opera troupe, and the gulch had for many months echoed daily warblings that for clearness and volume, if not melodiousness, surpassed easily any vice in Lava canon. The form within the crinkling white muslin was a storage battery of impetuous life and force that needed continually some object upon which to exhaust its energy.

As Boadicea swung in the grape vine, some 300 yards up the gulch from the house, she turned her gaze idly toward a thick clump of bushes, and saw an eye with a good deal of red in the normally white portion of it looking at her between the leaves.

She sat bolt upright on the vine, and, as it appeared to be a man's eye, her hand, without any special volition of her brain, went to the knot of hair at the back of her head, smoothed it a little and thrust in the pins more securely.

"Come out of there," she said.

Red-faced and heavy-eyed from drink, Arizona Dan, hitching up his revolverless belt, shuffled his huge form through the flexible branches of the bushes into the path.

"Sh-sh-sh!" he said, his heavy face folding into a dull smile intended to be reassuring. "I ain't a-goin' to hurt you, miss."

"Hurt me," said Miss Reed, contemptuously. "I should think not. What are you doing here?"

"Just a-layin' low, miss, and waitin' for night. Yer see, I was on what you might call a sort of spree and broke a glass or two. Maybe somebody was hurt, too. The whisky done it. A good lookin' young lady like you, miss, wouldn't give the word on a man, now, I bet a hoss."

Arizona Dan's lumbering attempt at compliment produced no effect. Boadicea regarded him sternly with unswerving, disapproving eyes.

"You don't want to be loafing around these diggings," she said, substituting the local form of parlance for her ordinarily more elevated style of conversation, as being more worthy of her audience. "You are not afraid, are you?" with infinite disdain.

"I ain't afraid," said Arizona Dan, shifting his feet uneasily, "except of being took. I can't fight the whole town."

"Is any one after you?"

"If they ain't, they will be. Rad Conrad's in town and—"

Arizona Dan broke off with an oath and looked down the steep pathway. "Here he comes now," he muttered.

Boadicea rose to her feet and peered over the tops of the

intervening bushes. The sheriff, unarmed, in a light summer suit that set off to advantage his strong, graceful figure, was coming up the path with the sun striking golden lights from his head of curly blonde hair. Boadicea looked upon him and loved.

When in ten paces of his man the sheriff took off his hat and wiped his brow with a silk handkerchief.

"Dan," he said, in an even tone, "I want you."

Arizona Dan drew a nine-inch bowie knife from the leg of his boot. "Come and get me," he said, with a grin and a suggestive upward movement of his right hand.

The old, well known, nauseating, deathly, cowardly physical fear came upon the sheriff as he saw the shining blade held by the huge desperado he had come unarmed to capture. His pride and the wonderful moral puissance that ground out courageous deeds from heart-sinking apprehension urged him forward with another step. Arizona Dan laughed a low, half-sober, but chilling laugh. So quiet it was that the voice of the brook sounded in the sheriff's ears like the derisive mockery of men at his poltroonry.

For one instant Radcliff Conrad swung in the balance. An all-pervading panic seized him and the foot he lifted to take a forward step weighed 100 pounds. The rustling of a branch to his right above the path drew from him a swift glance and he looked for ten seconds into two dark eyes that seemed to flash some strange, exalting essence into his veins. A weight seemed loosened somewhere within him and he felt that he could hear it fall down, down to unsounded depths. He looked at Arizona Dan and laughed low and joyously, as a child does who has come upon a long-desired toy.

"Will you come?" said the sheriff in a tone a bridegroom might have used to his bride.

"I'll cut your heart out, Rad Conrad," said Arizona Dan, "if you come two steps nearer."

Boadicea, on the ledge above, rustled a little and the sheriff, without looking up, smiled again. Arizona Dan held his knife as one holds a foil, point outward, with his thumb against the guard. The sheriff crouched some three inches like a cat and seemed to gather himself together with his weight balanced evenly on each foot. Arizona Dan stood still with his knife ready. Was Rad Conrad fool enough to attack him with his bare hands?

The sheriff could have shouted for joy. Like a flash valor and audacious courage had come upon him. He felt that he would never know fear again. Something had passed into his blood that had made him a man instead of the spurious being he had been. He felt the two dark eyes above fixed upon him, but he kept his own upon Arizona Dan.

Heretofore the sheriff's exploits had been attended by a fortuitous chance that brought him safely out of them—a chance just as blind and incomprehensible as that which guards the ways of children and drunkards. Now he felt the caution, the indomitable intent to do coupled with the prudence of the successful general that gives bravery its value. Half a miracle had been accomplished. The other half was to follow.

It must have been that Arizona Dan's nerves were unstrung by his debauch, else when a small stone dislodged by Boadicea's foot rattled down to the path at his side he would not have bestowed the advantage of turning his head quickly to look. But he did so, and in the instant the sheriff had his knife arm by the wrist, and his other arm about his waist. Then Arizona Dan was filled with surprise to feel the arm that held his knife slowly twisting in spite of all his resistance—twisting outward, until the tendons and muscles were cracking. The sheriff's hand was like a steel clamp, and when the pain grew unbearable Arizona Dan dropped the knife. When the sheriff heard it ring on the rocks he released the wrist suddenly and laid his left forearm across Dan's throat. They were too close for blows, and there was little struggling or shifting of ground. The arm across Dan's throat pushed his head back, and the other iron band about his waist held him close. It was a silent, fierce, straining contention on one side for the displacement, and on the other to regain the center of gravity. The side for displacement won, and the gladiators went down with a crash. A small boulder in the way of Arizona Dan's head left him lying in a disgraceful heap oblivious to defeat. The sheriff knelt upon the vanquished distributor of leaden largess, drew cords from his pocket, and ignominiously bound him hand and foot. Then he sprang to his feet and turned his flushed face and yellow curls to the source of his new being, as a sunflower turns to the sun.

Boadicea slid down through the bushes like a young panther.

"You're a jim dandy," she said, "if there ever was one. I saw it. I—"

She stopped suddenly. The sheriff was looking straight into her eyes. She felt for the first time a strange heat in her cheeks, and thought she must have fever. Her eyes slowly dropped for the first time before another's. Her tongue for the first time tripped and faltered.

"It'll be dark soon," began the sheriff, and his voice sounded to her far away like the wind in the pines: "you'd better let me walk back to the house with you. I'll bring a horse back for this chap by the time he recovers. You are Miss Reed, I think. I know your father."

The evening breeze rustled airily through the redwoods. A squirrel frisked up a hickory, and the first owl hoot came from the shadows about the brook. The brook's babble no longer mocked: it sang a paean of praise. As they walked down the path together a scream of fright came from the namesake of the battle queen of the Britons.

"A horrid lizard!" she cried.

The sheriff's strong arm reassured her. The miracle was complete. The soul of each had passed into the other.

COUNTRY

Whistling Dick's Christmas Stocking

I T WAS with much caution that Whistling Dick slid back the door of the box-car, for Article 5716, City Ordinances, authorized (perhaps unconstitutionally) arrest on suspicion, and he was familiar of old with this ordinance. So, before climbing out, he surveyed the field with all the care of a good general.

He saw no change since his last visit to this big, alms-giving, long-suffering city of the South, the cold weather paradise of the tramps. The levee where his freight-car stood was pimpled with dark bulks of merchandise. The breeze reeked with the well-remembered, sickening smell of the old tarpaulins that covered bales and barrels. The dun river slipped along among the shipping with an oily gurgle. Far down toward Chalmette he could see the great bend in the stream outlined by the row of electric lights. Across the river Algiers lay, a long, irregular blot, made darker by the dawn which lightened the sky beyond. An industrious tug or two, coming for some early sailing ship, gave a few appalling toots, that seemed to be the signal for breaking day. The Italian luggers were creeping nearer their landing, laden with early vegetables and shellfish. A vague roar, subterranean in quality, from dray wheels and street cars, began to make itself heard and felt; and the ferryboats, the Mary Anns of water craft, stirred sullenly to their menial morning tasks.

Whistling Dick's red head popped suddenly back into the car. A sight too imposing and magnificent for his gaze had been added to the scene. A vast, incomparable policeman rounded a pile of rice sacks and stood within twenty yards of the car. The daily miracle of the dawn, now being performed above Algiers, received the flattering attention of this specimen of municipal official splendour. He gazed with unbiased dignity at the faintly glowing colours until, at last, he turned to them his broad back, as if convinced that legal interference was not needed, and the sunrise might proceed unchecked. So he turned his face to the rice bags, and, drawing a flat flask from an inside pocket, he placed it to his lips and regarded the firmament.

Whistling Dick, professional tramp, possessed a half-friendly acquaintance with this officer. They had met several times before on the levee at night, for the officer, himself a lover of music, had been attracted by the exquisite whistling of the shiftless vagabond. Still, he did not care, under the present circumstances, to renew the acquaintance. There is a difference between meeting a policeman upon a lonely wharf and whistling a few operatic airs with him, and being caught by him crawling out of a freight-car. So Dick waited, as even a New Orleans policeman must move on some time—perhaps it is a retributive law of nature—and before long "Big Fritz" majestically disappeared between the trains of cars.

Whistling Dick waited as long as his judgment advised, and then slid swiftly to the ground. Assuming as far as possible the air of an honest labourer who seeks his daily toil, he moved across the network of railway lines, with the intention of making his way by quiet Girod Street to a certain bench in Lafayette Square, where, according to appointment, he hoped to rejoin a pal known as "Slick," this adventurous pilgrim having preceded him by one day in a cattle-car into which a loose slat had enticed him.

As Whistling Dick picked his way where night still lingered among the big, reeking, musty warehouses, he gave way to the habit that had won for him his title. Subdued, yet clear, with each note as true and liquid as a bobolink's, his whistle tinkled about the dim, cold mountains of brick like drops of rain falling into a hidden pool. He followed an air, but it swam mistily into a swirling current of improvisation. You could cull out the trill of mountain brooks, the staccato of green rushes shivering above chilly lagoons, the pipe of sleepy birds.

Rounding a corner, the whistler collided with a mountain of blue and brass.

"So," observed the mountain calmly, "You are already pack. Und dere vill not pe frost before two veeks yet! Und you haf forgotten how to vistle. Dere was a valse note in dot last bar."

"Watcher know about it?" said Whistling Dick, with tentative familiarity; "you wit yer little Gherman-band nixcumrous chunes. Watcher know about music? Pick yer ears, and listen agin. Here 's de way I whistled it—see?"

He puckered his lips, but the big policeman held up his hand.

"Shtop," he said, "und learn der right way. Und learn also dot a rolling shtone can't vistle for a cent."

Big Fritz's heavy moustache rounded into a circle, and from its depths came a sound deep and mellow as that from a flute. He repeated a few bars of the air the tramp had been whistling. The rendition was cold, but correct, and he emphasized the note he had taken exception to.

"Dot p is p natural, und not p vlat. Py der vay, you petter pe glad I meet you. Von hour later, und I vould half to put you in a gage to vistle mit der chail pirds. Der orders are to bull all der pums after sunrise."

"To which?"

"To bull der pums—eferybody mitout fisible means. Dirty days is der price, or fifteen tollars."

"Is dat straight, or a game you givin' me?"

"It 's der pest tip you efer had. I gif it to you pecause I pelief you are not so bad as der rest. Und pecause you gan visl 'Der Freischütz' bezzer dan I myself gan. Don't run against any more bolicemans aroundt der corners, but go away vrom town a few tays. Goot-pye."

So Madame Orleans had at last grown weary of the strange and ruffled brood that came yearly to nestle beneath her charitable pinions.

After the big policeman had departed, Whistling Dick stood for an irresolute minute, feeling all the outraged indignation of a delinquent tenant who is ordered to vacate his premises. He had pictured to himself a day of dreamful ease when he should have joined his pal; a day of lounging on the wharf, munching the bananas and cocoanuts scattered in unloading the fruit steamers; and then a feast along the free-lunch counters from which the easy-going owners were too good-natured or too generous to drive him away, and afterward a pipe in one of the little flowery parks and a snooze in some shady corner of the wharf. But here was a stern order to exile, and one that he knew must be obeyed. So, with a wary eye open for the gleam of brass buttons, he began his retreat toward a rural refuge. A few days in the country need not necessarily prove disastrous. Beyond the possibility of a slight nip of frost, there was no formidable evil to be looked for.

However, it was with a depressed spirit that Whistling Dick passed the old French market on his chosen route down the river. For safety's sake he still presented to the world his

portrayal of the part of the worthy artisan on his way to labour.
A stall-keeper in the market, undeceived, hailed him by the generic name of his ilk, and "Jack" halted, taken by surprise. The
vender, melted by this proof of his own acuteness, bestowed
a foot of Frankfurter and half a loaf, and thus the problem of
breakfast was solved.

When the streets, from topographical reasons, began to shun
the river bank the exile mounted to the top of the levee, and
on its well-trodden path pursued his way. The suburban eye
regarded him with cold suspicion. Individuals reflected the
stern spirit of the city's heartless edict. He missed the seclusion
of the crowded town and the safety he could always find in the
multitude.

At Chalmette, six miles upon his desultory way, there suddenly menaced him a vast and bewildering industry. A new
port was being established; the dock was being built, com-
presses were going up; picks and shovels and barrows struck
at him like serpents from every side. An arrogant foreman
bore down upon him, estimating his muscles with the eye of a
recruiting-sergeant. Brown men and black men all about him
were toiling away. He fled in terror.

By noon he had reached the country of the plantations,
the great, sad, silent levels bordering the mighty river. He
overlooked fields of sugar-cane so vast that their farthest
limits melted into the sky. The sugar-making season was well
advanced, and the cutters were at work; the waggons creaked
drearily after them; the Negro teamsters inspired the mules
to greater speed with mellow and sonorous imprecations.
Dark-green groves, blurred by the blue of distance, showed
where the plantation-houses stood. The tall chimneys of the
sugar-mills caught the eye miles distant, like lighthouses at sea.

At a certain point Whistling Dick's unerring nose caught
the scent of frying fish. Like a pointer to a quail, he made his
way down the levee side straight to the camp of a credulous
and ancient fisherman, whom he charmed with song and story,
so that he dined like an admiral, and then like a philosopher
annihilated the worst three hours of the day by a nap under
the trees.

When he awoke and again continued his hegira, a frosty

sparkle in the air had succeeded the drowsy warmth of the day, and as this portent of a chilly night translated itself to the brain of Sir Peregrine, he lengthened his stride and bethought him of shelter. He travelled a road that faithfully followed the convolutions of the levee, running along its base, but whither he knew not. Bushes and rank grass crowded it to the wheel ruts, and out of this ambuscade the pests of the lowlands swarmed after him, humming a keen, vicious soprano. And as the night grew nearer, although colder, the whine of the mosquitoes became a greedy, petulant snarl that shut out all other sounds. To his right, against the heavens, he saw a green light moving, and, accompanying it, the masts and funnels of a big incoming steamer, moving as upon a screen at a magic-lantern show. And there were mysterious marshes at his left, out of which came queer gurgling cries and a choked croaking. The whistling vagrant struck up a merry warble to offset these melancholy influences, and it is likely that never before, since Pan himself jigged it on his reeds, had such sounds been heard in those depressing solitudes.

A distant clatter in the rear quickly developed into the swift beat of horses' hoofs, and Whistling Dick stepped aside into the dew-wet grass to clear the track. Turning his head, he saw approaching a fine team of stylish grays drawing a double surrey. A stout man with a white moustache occupied the front seat, giving all his attention to the rigid lines in his hands. Behind him sat a placid, middle-aged lady and a brilliant-looking girl hardly arrived at young ladyhood. The lap-robe had slipped partly from the knees of the gentleman driving, and Whistling Dick saw two stout canvas bags between his feet—bags such as, while loafing in cities, he had seen warily transferred between express waggons and bank doors. The remaining space in the vehicle was filled with parcels of various sizes and shapes.

As the surrey swept even with the sidetracked tramp, the bright-eyed girl, seized by some merry, madcap impulse, leaned out toward him with a sweet, dazzling smile, and cried, "Mer-ry Christ-mas!" in a shrill, plaintive treble.

Such a thing had not often happened to Whistling Dick, and he felt handicapped in devising the correct response. But lacking time for reflection, he let his instinct decide, and snatching off his battered derby, he rapidly extended it at arm's length, and drew it back with a continuous motion, and shouted a loud, but ceremonious, "Ah, there!" after the flying surrey.

The sudden movement of the girl had caused one of the parcels to become unwrapped, and something limp and black fell from it into the road. The tramp picked it up, and found it to be a new black silk stocking, long and fine and slender. It crunched crisply, and yet with a luxurious softness, between his fingers.

"Ther bloomin' little skeezicks!" said Whistling Dick, with a broad grin bisecting his freckled face. "W'ot d' yer think of dat, now! Mer-ry Chris-mus! Sounded like a cuckoo clock, dat 's what she did. Dem guys is swells, too, bet yer life, an' der old 'un stacks dem sacks of dough down under his trotters like dey was common as dried apples. Been shoppin' fer Chrismus, and de kid's lost one of her new socks w'ot she was goin' to hold up Santy wid. De bloomin' little skeezicks! Wit' her 'Mer-ry Chris-mus!' W'ot d' yer t'ink! Same as to say, 'Hello, Jack, how goes it?' and as swell as Fift' Av'noo, and as easy as a blowout in Cincinnat'."

Whistling Dick folded the stocking carefully, and stuffed it into his pocket.

It was nearly two hours later when he came upon signs of habitation. The buildings of an extensive plantation were brought into view by a turn in the road. He easily selected the planter's residence in a large square building with two wings, with numerous good-sized, well-lighted windows, and broad verandas running around its full extent. It was set upon a smooth lawn, which was faintly lit by the far-reaching rays of the lamps within. A noble grove surrounded it, and old-fashioned shrubbery grew thickly about the walks and fences. The quarters of the hands and the mill buildings were situated at a distance in the rear.

The road was now enclosed on each side by a fence, and presently, as Whistling Dick drew nearer the houses, he suddenly stopped and sniffed the air.

"If dere ain't a hobo stew cookin' somewhere in dis immediate precinct," he said to himself, "me nose has quit tellin' de trut'."

Without hesitation he climbed the fence to windward. He

found himself in an apparently disused lot, where piles of old bricks were stacked, and rejected, decaying lumber. In a corner he saw the faint glow of a fire that had become little more than a bed of living coals, and he thought he could see some dim human forms sitting or lying about it. He drew nearer, and by the light of a little blaze that suddenly flared up he saw plainly the fat figure of a ragged man in an old brown sweater and cap.

"Dat man," said Whistling Dick to himself softly, "is a dead ringer for Boston Harry. I'll try him wit de high sign."

He whistled one or two bars of a rag-time melody, and the air was immediately taken up, and then quickly ended with a peculiar run. The first whistler walked confidently up to the fire. The fat man looked up, and spake in a loud, asthmatic wheeze:

"Gents, the unexpected but welcome addition to our circle is Mr. Whistling Dick, an old friend of mine for whom I fully vouches. The waiter will lay another cover at once. Mr. W. D. will join us at supper, during which function he will enlighten us in regard to the circumstances that give us the pleasure of his company."

"Chewin' de stuffin' out 'n de dictionary, as usual, Boston," said Whistling Dick; "but t'anks all de same for de invitashun. I guess I finds meself here about de same way as yous guys. A cop gimme de tip dis mornin'. Yous workin' on dis farm?"

"A guest," said Boston sternly, "should n't never insult his entertainers until he 's filled up wid grub. 'T ain't good business sense. Workin'!—but I will restrain myself. We five—me, Deaf Pete, Blinky, Goggles, and Indiana Tom—got put on to this scheme of Noo Orleans to work visiting gentlemen upon her dirty streets, and we hit the road last evening just as the tender hues of twilight had flopped down upon the daisies and things. Blinky, pass the empty oyster-can at your left to the empty gentleman at your right."

For the next ten minutes the gang of roadsters paid their undivided attention to the supper. In an old five-gallon kerosene can they had cooked a stew of potatoes, meat, and onions, which they partook of from smaller cans they had found scattered about the vacant lot.

Whistling Dick had known Boston Harry of old, and knew him to be one of the shrewdest and most successful of his brotherhood. He looked like a prosperous stock-drover or a solid merchant from some country village. He was stout and hale, with a ruddy, always smoothly shaven face. His clothes were strong and neat, and he gave special attention to his decent-appearing shoes. During the past ten years he had acquired a reputation for working a larger number of successfully managed confidence games than any of his acquaintances, and he had not a day's work to be counted against him. It was rumoured among his associates that he had saved a considerable amount of money. The four other men were fair specimens of the slinking, ill-clad, noisome genus who carried their labels of "supicious" in plain view.

After the bottom of the large can had been scraped, and pipes lit at the coals, two of the men called Boston aside and spake with him lowly and mysteriously. He nodded decisively, and then said aloud to Whistling Dick:

"Listen, sonny, to some plain talky-talk. We five are on a lay. I 've guaranteed you to be square, and you 're to come in on the profits equal with the boys, and you 've got to help. Two hundred hands on this plantation are expecting to be paid a week's wages to-morrow morning. To-morrow 's Christmas, and they want to lay off. Says the boss: 'Work from five to nine in the morning to get a train load of sugar off, and I 'll pay every man cash down for the week and a day extra.' They say: 'Hooray for the boss! It goes.' He drives to Noo Orleans to-day, and fetches back the cold dollars. Two thousand and seventy-four fifty is the amount. I got the figures from a man who talks too much, who got 'em from the bookkeeper. The boss of this plantation thinks he 's going to pay this wealth to the hands. He 's got it down wrong; he 's going to pay it to us. It 's going to stay in the leisure class, where it belongs. Now, half of this haul goes to me, and the other half the rest of you may divide. Why the difference? I represent the brains. It 's my scheme. Here 's the way we 're going to get it. There 's some company at supper in the house, but they 'll leave about nine. They 've just happened in for an hour or so. If they don't go pretty soon, we 'll work the scheme anyhow. We want all night to get away good with the dollars. They 're heavy. About nine o'clock Deaf Pete and Blinky 'll go down the road about a quarter beyond the house, and set fire to a big cane-field there that the cutters have n't touched yet. The wind 's just right to have it roaring in two minutes. The alarm 'll be given, and every man Jack about the place will be down there in ten minutes, fighting fire. That 'll leave the money sacks and the women alone in the house for us to handle. You 've heard cane burn? Well, there 's mighty few women can screech loud enough to be heard above its crackling. The thing 's dead safe. The only danger is in being caught before we can get far enough away with the money. Now, if you——"

"Boston," interrupted Whistling Dick, rising to his feet, "T'anks for de grub yous fellers has given me, but I 'll be movin' on now."

"What do you mean?" asked Boston, also rising.

"W'y, you can count me outer dis deal. You oughter know that. I 'm on de bum all right enough, but dat other t'ing don't go wit' me. Burglary is no good. I 'll say good night and many t'anks fer——"

Whistling Dick had moved away a few steps as he spoke, but he stopped very suddenly. Boston had covered him with a short revolver of roomy calibre.

"Take your seat," said the tramp leader. "I 'd feel mighty proud of myself if I let you go and spoil the game. You 'll stick right in this camp until we finish the job. The end of that brick pile is your limit. You go two inches beyond that, and I 'll have to shoot. Better take it easy, now."

"It 's my way of doin'," said Whistling Dick. "Easy goes. You can depress de muzzle of dat twelve-incher, and run 'er back on de trucks. I remains, as de newspapers says, 'in yer midst.'"

"All right," said Boston, lowering his piece, as the other returned and took his seat again on a projecting plank in a pile of timber. "Don't try to leave; that 's all. I would n't miss this chance even if I had to shoot an old acquaintance to make it go. I don't want to hurt anybody specially, but this thousand dollars I 'm going to get will fix me for fair. I 'm going to drop the road, and start a saloon in a little town I know about. I 'm tired of being kicked around."

Boston Harry took from his pocket a cheap silver watch, and held it near the fire.

"It 's a quarter to nine," he said. "Pete, you and Blinky start. Go down the road past the house, and fire the cane in a dozen places. Then strike for the levee, and come back on it, instead of the road, so you won't meet anybody. By the time you get back the men will all be striking out for the fire, and we 'll break for the house and collar the dollars. Everybody cough up what matches he 's got."

The two surly tramps made a collection of all the matches in the party, Whistling Dick contributing his quota with propitiatory alacrity, and then they departed in the dim starlight in the direction of the road.

Of the three remaining vagrants, two, Goggles and Indiana Tom, reclined lazily upon convenient lumber and regarded Whistling Dick with undisguised disfavour. Boston, observing that the dissenting recruit was disposed to remain peaceably, relaxed a little of his vigilance. Whistling Dick arose presently and strolled leisurely up and down keeping carefully within the territory assigned him.

"Dis planter chap," he said, pausing before Boston Harry, "w'ot makes yer t'ink he 's got de tin in de house wit' 'im?"

"I 'm advised of the facts in the case," said Boston. "He drove to Noo Orleans and got it, I say, to-day. Want to change your mind now and come in?" ·

"Naw, I was just askin'. Wot kind o' team did de boss drive?"

"Pair of grays."

"Double surrey?"

"Yep."

"Women folks along?"

"Wife and kid. Say, what morning paper are you trying to pump news for?"

"I was just conversin' to pass de time away. I guess dat team passed me in de road dis evenin'. Dat 's all."

As Whistling Dick put his hands into his pockets and continued his curtailed beat up and down by the fire, he felt the silk stocking he had picked up in the road.

"Ther bloomin' little skeezicks," he muttered, with a grin.

As he walked up and down he could see, through a sort of natural opening or lane among the trees, the planter's residence some seventy-five yards distant. The side of the house toward him exhibited spacious, well-lighted windows through which a soft radiance streamed, illuminating the broad veranda and some extent of the lawn beneath.

"What 's that you said?" asked Boston, sharply.

"Oh, nuttin' 't all," said Whistling Dick, lounging carelessly, and kicking meditatively at a little stone on the ground.

"Just as easy," continued the warbling vagrant softly to himself, "an' sociable an' swell an' sassy, wit' her 'Mer-ry Chris-mus,' Wot d'yer t'ink, now!"

Dinner, two hours late, was being served in the Bellemeade plantation dining-room.

The dining-room and all its appurtenances spoke of an old regime that was here continued rather than suggested to the memory. The plate was rich to the extent that its age and quaintness alone saved it from being showy; there were interesting names signed in the corners of the pictures on the walls; the viands were of the kind that bring a shine into the eyes of gourmets. The service was swift, silent, lavish, as in the days when the waiters were assets like the plate. The names by which the planter's family and their visitors addressed one another were historic in the annals of two nations. Their manners and conversation had that most difficult kind of ease—the kind that still preserves punctilio. The planter himself seemed to be the dynamo that generated the larger portion of the gaiety and wit. The younger ones at the board found it more than difficult to turn back on him his guns of raillery and banter. It is true, the young men attempted to storm his works repeatedly, incited by the hope of gaining the approbation of their fair companions; but even when they sped a well-aimed shaft, the planter forced them to feel defeat by the tremendous discomfiting thunder of the laughter with which he accompanied his retorts. At the head of the table, serene, matronly, benevolent, reigned the mistress of the house, placing here and there the right smile, the right word, the encouraging glance.

The talk of the party was too desultory, too evanescent to follow, but at last they came to the subject of the tramp nuisance, one that had of late vexed the plantations for many miles around. The planter seized the occasion to direct his good-natured fire of raillery at the mistress, accusing her of encouraging the plague. "They swarm up and down the river every winter," he said. "They overrun New Orleans, and we catch the surplus, which is generally the worst part. And, a day or two ago, Madame New Orleans, suddenly discovering that she can't go shopping without brushing her skirts against great rows of the vagabonds sunning themselves on the banquettes, says to the police: 'Catch 'em all,' and the police catch a dozen or two, and the remaining three or four thousand overflow up and down the levees, and madame there"—pointing tragically with the carving-knife at her—"feeds them. They won't work; they defy my overseers, and they make friends with my dogs; and you, madame, feed them before my eyes, and intimidate me when I would interfere. Tell us, please, how many to-day did you thus incite to future laziness and depredation?"

"Six, I think," said madame, with a reflective smile; "but you know two of them offered to work, for you heard them yourself."

The planter's disconcerting laugh rang out again.

"Yes, at their own trades. And one was an artificial-flower maker, and the other a glass-blower. Oh, they were looking for work! Not a hand would they consent to lift to labour of any other kind."

"And another one," continued the soft-hearted mistress, "used quite good language. It was really extraordinary for one of his class. And he carried a watch. And had lived in Boston. I don't believe they are all bad. They have always seemed to me to rather lack development. I always look upon them as children with whom wisdom has remained at a standstill while whiskers have continued to grow. We passed one this evening as we were driving home who had a face as good as it was incompetent. He was whistling the intermezzo from 'Cavalleria' and blowing the spirit of Mascagni himself into it."

A bright-eyed young girl who sat at the left of the mistress leaned over, and said in a confidential undertone:

"I wonder, mamma, if that tramp we passed on the road found my stocking, and do you think he will hang it up to-night? Now I can hang up but one. Do you know why I wanted a new pair of silk stockings when I have plenty? Well, old Aunt Judy says, if you hang up two that have never been worn, Santa Claus will fill one with good things, and Monsieur Pambe will place in the other payment for all the words you

have spoken—good or bad—on the day before Christmas.
That's why I've been unusually nice and polite to everyone
to-day. Monsieur Pambe, you know, is a witch gentleman; he
——"

The words of the young girl were interrupted by a startling
thing.

Like the wraith of some burned-out shooting star, a black
streak came crashing through the window-pane and upon the
table, where it shivered into fragments a dozen pieces of crystal
and china ware, and then glanced between the heads of the
guests to the wall, imprinting therein a deep, round indenta-
tion, at which, to-day, the visitor to Bellemeade marvels as he
gazes upon it and listens to this tale as it is told.

The women screamed in many keys, and the men sprang to
their feet, and would have laid their hands upon their swords
had not the verities of chronology forbidden.

The planter was the first to act; he sprang to the intruding
missile, and held it up to view.

"By Jupiter!" he cried. "A meteoric shower of hosiery! Has
communication at last been established with Mars?"

"I should say—ahem!—Venus," ventured a young-gentleman
visitor, looking hopefully for approbation toward the unre-
sponsive young-lady visitors.

The planter held at arm's length the unceremonious visitor—a
long dangling black stocking. "It's loaded," he announced.

As he spoke he reversed the stocking, holding it by the toe,
and down from it dropped a roundish stone, wrapped about
by a piece of yellowish paper. "Now for the first interstellar
message of the century!" he cried; and nodding to the company, who had crowded about him, he adjusted his glasses
with provoking deliberation, and examined it closely. When he
finished, he had changed from the jolly host to the practical,
decisive man of business. He immediately struck a bell, and
said to the silent-footed mulatto man who responded: "Go and
tell Mr. Wesley to get Reeves and Maurice and about ten stout
hands they can rely upon, and come to the hall door at once.
Tell him to have the men arm themselves, and bring plenty of
ropes and plough lines. Tell him to hurry." And then he read
aloud from the paper these words:

To the Gent of de Hous:

    Dere is five tuff hoboes xcept meself in the vaken lot near de
road war de old brick piles is. Dey got me stuck up wid a gun
see and I taken dis means of comunikaten. 2 of der lads is gone
down to set fire to de cain field below de hous and when yous
fellers goes to turn de hoes on it de hole gang is goin to rob de
hous of de money yoo gotto pay off wit say git a move on ye say
de kid dropt dis sock in der rode tel her mery crismus de same
as she told me. Ketch de bums down de rode first and den sen a
relefe core to get me out of soke youres truly,

                                      WHISTLEN DICK.

There was some quiet, but rapid, manœuvring at Bellemeade
during the ensuing half hour, which ended in five disgusted
and sullen tramps being captured, and locked securely in an
outhouse pending the coming of the morning and retribution.
For another result, the visiting young gentlemen had secured
the unqualified worship of the visiting young ladies by their
distinguished and heroic conduct. For still another, behold
Whistling Dick, the hero, seated at the planter's table, feasting
upon viands his experience had never before included, and
waited upon by admiring femininity in shapes of such beauty
and "swellness" that even his ever-full mouth could scarcely
prevent him from whistling. He was made to disclose in detail
his adventure with the evil gang of Boston Harry, and how he
cunningly wrote the note and wrapped it around the stone and
placed it in the toe of the stocking, and, watching his chance,
sent it silently, with a wonderful centrifugal momentum, like a
comet, at one of the big lighted windows of the dining-room.

The planter vowed that the wanderer should wander no
more; that his was a goodness and an honesty that should be
rewarded, and that a debt of gratitude had been made that
must be paid; for had he not saved them from a doubtless
imminent loss, and maybe a greater calamity? He assured
Whistling Dick that he might consider himself a charge upon
the honour of Bellemeade; that a position suited to his powers
would be found for him at once, and hinted that the way would
be heartily smoothed for him to rise to as high places of emol-
ument and trust as the plantation afforded.

But now, they said, he must be weary, and the immediate
thing to consider was rest and sleep. So the mistress spoke to

a servant, and Whistling Dick was conducted to a room in the wing of the house occupied by the servants. To this room, in a few minutes, was brought a portable tin bathtub filled with water, which was placed on a piece of oiled cloth upon the floor. There the vagrant was left to pass the night.

By the light of a candle he examined the room. A bed, with the covers neatly turned back, revealed snowy pillows and sheets. A worn, but clean, red carpet covered the floor. There was a dresser with a beveled mirror, a washstand with a flowered bowl and pitcher; the two or three chairs were softly upholstered. A little table held books, papers, and a day-old cluster of roses in a jar. There were towels on a rack and soap in a white dish.

Whistling Dick set his candle on a chair and placed his hat carefully under the table. After satisfying what we must suppose to have been his curiosity by a sober scrutiny, he removed his coat, folded it, and laid it upon the floor, near the wall, as far as possible from the unused bathtub. Taking his coat for a pillow, he stretched himself luxuriously upon the carpet.

When, on Christmas morning, the first streaks of dawn broke above the marshes, Whistling Dick awoke, and reached instinctively for his hat. Then he remembered that the skirts of Fortune had swept him into their folds on the night previous, and he went to the window and raised it, to let the fresh breath of the morning cool his brow and fix the yet dream-like memory of his good luck within his brain.

As he stood there, certain dread and ominous sounds pierced the fearful hollow of his ear.

The force of plantation workers, eager to complete the shortened task allotted to them, were all astir. The mighty din of the ogre Labour shook the earth, and the poor tattered and forever disguised Prince in search of his fortune held tight to the window-sill even in the enchanted castle, and trembled.

Already from the bosom of the mill came the thunder of rolling barrels of sugar, and (prison-like sounds) there was a great rattling of chains as the mules were harried with stimulant imprecations to their places by the waggon-tongues. A little vicious "dummy" engine, with a train of flat cars in tow, stewed and fumed on the plantation tap of the narrow-gauge railroad, and a toiling, hurrying, hallooing stream of workers were dimly seen in the half darkness loading the train with the weekly out-put of sugar. Here was a poem; an epic—nay, a tragedy—with work, the curse of the world, for its theme.

The December air was frosty, but the sweat broke out upon Whistling Dick's face. He thrust his head out of the window, and looked down. Fifteen feet below him, against the wall of the house, he could make out that a border of flowers grew, and by that token he overhung a bed of soft earth.

Softly as a burglar goes, he clambered out upon the sill, lowered himself until he hung by his hands alone, and then dropped safely. No one seemed to be about upon this side of the house. He dodged low, and skimmed swiftly across the yard to the low fence. It was an easy matter to vault this, for a terror urged him such as lifts the gazelle over the thorn bush when the lion pursues. A crash through the dew-drenched weeds on the roadside, a clutching, slippery rush up the grassy side of the levee to the footpath at the summit, and—he was free!

The east was blushing and brightening. The wind, himself a vagrant rover, saluted his brother upon the cheek. Some wild geese, high above, gave cry. A rabbit skipped along the path before him, free to turn to the right or to the left as his mood should send him. The river slid past, and certainly no one could tell the ultimate abiding place of its waters.

A small, ruffled, brown-breasted bird, sitting upon a dog-wood sapling, began a soft, throaty, tender little piping in praise of the dew which entices foolish worms from their holes; but suddenly he stopped, and sat with his head turned sidewise, listening.

From the path along the levee there burst forth a jubilant, stirring, buoyant, thrilling whistle, loud and keen and clear as the cleanest notes of the piccolo. The soaring sound rippled and trilled and arpeggioed as the songs of wild birds do not; but it had a wild free grace that, in a way, reminded the small, brown bird of something familiar, but exactly what he could not tell. There was in it the bird call, or reveille, that all birds know; but a great waste of lavish, unmeaning things that art had added and arranged, besides, and that were quite puzzling and strange; and the little brown bird sat with his head on one side until the sound died away in the distance.

The little bird did not know that the part of that strange

warbling that he understood was just what kept the warbler without his breakfast; but he knew very well that the part he did not understand did not concern him, so he gave a little flutter of his wings and swooped down like a brown bullet upon a big fat worm that was wriggling along the levee path.

A Retrieved Reformation

A GUARD came to the prison shoe-shop, where Jimmy Valentine was assiduously stitching uppers, and escorted him to the front office. There the warden handed Jimmy his pardon, which had been signed that morning by the governor. Jimmy took it in a tired kind of way. He had served nearly ten months of a four-year sentence. He had expected to stay only about three months, at the longest. When a man with as many friends on the outside as Jimmy Valentine had is received in the "stir" it is hardly worth while to cut his hair.

"Now, Valentine," said the warden, "you 'll go out in the morning. Brace up, and make a man of yourself. You 're not a bad fellow at heart. Stop cracking safes, and live straight."

"Me?" said Jimmy, in surprise. "Why, I never cracked a safe in my life."

"Oh, no," laughed the warden. "Of course not. Let 's see, now. How was it you happened to get sent up on that Springfield job? Was it because you would n't prove an alibi for fear of compromising somebody in extremely high-toned society? Or was it simply a case of a mean old jury that had it in for you? It 's always one or the other with you innocent victims."

"Me?" said Jimmy, still blankly virtuous. "Why, warden, I never was in Springfield in my life!"

"Take him back, Cronin," smiled the warden, "and fix him up with outgoing clothes. Unlock him at seven in the morning, and let him come to the bull-pen. Better think over my advice, Valentine."

At a quarter past seven on the next morning Jimmy stood in the warden's outer office. He had on a suit of the villainously fitting, ready-made clothes and a pair of the stiff, squeaky shoes that the state furnishes to its discharged compulsory guests.

The clerk handed him a railroad ticket and the five-dollar bill with which the law expected him to rehabilitate himself into good citizenship and prosperity. The warden gave him a cigar, and shook hands. Valentine, 9762, was chronicled on the books "Pardoned by Governor," and Mr. James Valentine walked out into the sunshine.

Disregarding the song of the birds, the waving green trees, and the smell of the flowers, Jimmy headed straight for a restaurant. There he tasted the first sweet joys of liberty in the shape of a broiled chicken and a bottle of white wine—followed by a cigar a grade better than the one the warden had given him. From there he proceeded leisurely to the depot. He tossed a quarter into the hat of a blind man sitting by the door, and boarded his train. Three hours set him down in a little town near the state line. He went to the café of one Mike Dolan and shook hands with Mike, who was alone behind the bar.

"Sorry we could n't make it sooner, Jimmy, me boy," said Mike. "But we had that protest from Springfield to buck against, and the governor nearly balked. Feeling all right?"

"Fine," said Jimmy. "Got my key?"

He got his key and went up-stairs, unlocking the door of a room at the rear. Everything was just as he had left it. There on the floor was still Ben Price's collar-button that had been torn from that eminent detective's shirt-band when they had overpowered Jimmy to arrest him.

Pulling out from the wall a folding-bed, Jimmy slid back a panel in the wall and dragged out a dust-covered suit-case. He opened this and gazed fondly at the finest set of burglar's tools in the East. It was a complete set, made of specially tempered steel, the latest designs in drills, punches, braces and bits, jim-mies, clamps, and augers, with two or three novelties, invented by Jimmy himself, in which he took pride. Over nine hundred dollars they had cost him to have made at ——, a place where they make such things for the profession.

In half an hour Jimmy went down stairs and through the café. He was now dressed in tasteful and well-fitting clothes, and carried his dusted and cleaned suit-case in his hand.

"Got anything on?" asked Mike Dolan, genially.

"Me?" said Jimmy, in a puzzled tone. "I don't understand. I 'm representing the New York Amalgamated Short Snap Biscuit Cracker and Frazzled Wheat Company."

This statement delighted Mike to such an extent that Jimmy had to take a seltzer-and-milk on the spot. He never touched "hard" drinks.

A week after the release of Valentine, 9762, there was a neat job of safe-burglary done in Richmond, Indiana, with no clue to the author. A scant eight hundred dollars was all that was secured. Two weeks after that a patented, improved, burglar-proof safe in Logansport was opened like a cheese to the tune of fifteen hundred dollars, currency; securities and silver untouched. That began to interest the rogue-catchers. Then an old-fashioned bank-safe in Jefferson City became active and threw out of its crater an eruption of bank-notes amounting to five thousand dollars. The losses were now high enough to bring the matter up into Ben Price's class of work. By comparing notes, a remarkable similarity in the methods of the burglaries was noticed. Ben Price investigated the scenes of the robberies, and was heard to remark:

"That 's Dandy Jim Valentine's autograph. He 's resumed business. Look at that combination knob—jerked out as easy as pulling up a radish in wet weather. He 's got the only clamps that can do it. And look how clean those tumblers were punched out! Jimmy never has to drill but one hole. Yes, I guess I want Mr. Valentine. He 'll do his bit next time without any short-time or clemency foolishness."

Ben Price knew Jimmy's habits. He had learned them while working up the Springfield case. Long jumps, quick get-aways, no confederates, and a taste for good society—these ways had helped Mr. Valentine to become noted as a successful dodger of retribution. It was given out that Ben Price had taken up the trail of the elusive cracksman, and other people with burglar-proof safes felt more at ease.

One afternoon Jimmy Valentine and his suit-case climbed out of the mail-hack in Elmore, a little town five miles off the railroad down in the black-jack country of Arkansas. Jimmy, looking like an athletic young senior just home from college, went down the board sidewalk toward the hotel.

A young lady crossed the street, passed him at the corner and entered a door over which was the sign "The Elmore Bank." Jimmy Valentine looked into her eyes, forgot what he was, and became another man. She lowered her eyes and coloured slightly. Young men of Jimmy's style and looks were scarce in Elmore.

Jimmy collared a boy that was loafing on the steps of the bank as if he were one of the stockholders, and began to ask him questions about the town, feeding him dimes at intervals.

By and by the young lady came out, looking royally unconscious of the young man with the suit-case, and went her way.

"Is n't that young lady Miss Polly Simpson?" asked Jimmy, with specious guile.

"Naw," said the boy. "She 's Annabel Adams. Her pa owns this bank. What 'd you come to Elmore for? Is that a gold watch-chain? I 'm going to get a bulldog. Got any more dimes?"

Jimmy went to the Planters' Hotel, registered as Ralph D. Spencer, and engaged a room. He leaned on the desk and declared his platform to the clerk. He said he had come to Elmore to look for a location to go into business. How was the shoe business, now, in the town? He had thought of the shoe business. Was there an opening?

The clerk was impressed by the clothes and manner of Jimmy. He, himself, was something of a pattern of fashion to the thinly gilded youth of Elmore, but he now perceived his shortcomings. While trying to figure out Jimmy's manner of tying his four-in-hand he cordially gave information.

Yes, there ought to be a good opening in the shoe line. There was n't an exclusive shoe-store in the place. The dry-goods and general stores handled them. Business in all lines was fairly good. Hoped Mr. Spencer would decide to locate in Elmore. He would find it a pleasant town to live in, and the people very sociable.

Mr. Spencer thought he would stop over in the town a few days and look over the situation. No, the clerk need n't call the boy. He would carry up his suit-case, himself; it was rather heavy.

Mr. Ralph Spencer, the phœnix that arose from Jimmy Valentine's ashes—ashes left by the flame of a sudden and alterative attack of love—remained in Elmore, and prospered. He opened a shoe-store and secured a good run of trade.

Socially he was also a success, and made many friends. And he accomplished the wish of his heart. He met Miss Annabel Adams, and became more and more captivated by her charms.

At the end of a year the situation of Mr. Ralph Spencer was this: he had won the respect of the community, his shoe-store was flourishing, and he and Annabel were engaged to be married in two weeks. Mr. Adams, the typical, plodding, country banker, approved of Spencer. Annabel's pride in him almost equalled her affection. He was as much at home in the family of Mr. Adams and that of Annabel's married sister as if he were already a member.

One day Jimmy sat down in his room and wrote this letter, which he mailed to the safe address of one of his old friends in St. Louis:

DEAR OLD PAL:

I want you to be at Sullivan's place, in Little Rock, next Wednesday night, at nine o'clock. I want you to wind up some little matters for me. And, also, I want to make you a present of my kit of tools. I know you 'll be glad to get them—you could n't duplicate the lot for a thousand dollars. Say, Billy, I 've quit the old business—a year ago. I 've got a nice store. I 'm making an honest living, and I 'm going to marry the finest girl on earth two weeks from now. It 's the only life, Billy—the straight one. I would n't touch a dollar of another man's money now for a million. After I get married I 'm going to sell out and go West, where there won't be so much danger of having old scores brought up against me. I tell you, Billy, she's an angel. She believes in me; and I would n't do another crooked thing for the whole world. Be sure to be at Sully's, for I must see you. I 'll bring along the tools with me.

Your old friend,

JIMMY.

On the Monday night after Jimmy wrote this letter, Ben Price jogged unobtrusively into Elmore in a livery buggy. He lounged about town in his quiet way until he found out what he wanted to know. From the drugstore across the street from Spencer's shoe-store he got a good look at Ralph D. Spencer.

"Going to marry the banker's daughter are you, Jimmy?" said Ben to himself, softly. "Well, I don't know!"

The next morning Jimmy took breakfast at the Adamses. He was going to Little Rock that day to order his wedding-suit and buy something nice for Annabel. That would be the first time he had left town since he came to Elmore. It had been more than a year now since those last professional "jobs," and he thought he could safely venture out.

After breakfast quite a family party went downtown together—Mr. Adams, Annabel, Jimmy, and Annabel's married sister with her two little girls, aged five and nine. They came by the hotel where Jimmy still boarded, and he ran up to his room and brought along his suit-case. Then they went on to the bank. There stood Jimmy's horse and buggy and Dolph Gibson, who was going to drive him over to the railroad station.

All went inside the high, carved oak railings into the banking-room—Jimmy included, for Mr. Adams's future son-in-law was welcome anywhere. The clerks were pleased to be greeted by the good-looking, agreeable young man who was going to marry Miss Annabel. Jimmy set his suit-case down. Annabel, whose heart was bubbling with happiness and lively youth, put on Jimmy's hat, and picked up the suit-case. "Would n't I make a nice drummer?" said Annabel. "My! Ralph, how heavy it is? Feels like it was full of gold bricks."

"Lot of nickel-plated shoe-horns in there," said Jimmy, coolly, "that I 'm going to return. Thought I 'd save express charges by taking them up. I 'm getting awfully economical."

The Elmore Bank had just put in a new safe and vault. Mr. Adams was very proud of it, and insisted on an inspection by every one. The vault was a small one, but it had a new, patented door. It fastened with three solid steel bolts thrown simultaneously with a single handle, and had a time-lock. Mr. Adams beamingly explained its workings to Mr. Spencer, who showed a courteous but not too intelligent interest. The two children, May and Agatha, were delighted by the shining metal and funny clock and knobs.

While they were thus engaged Ben Price sauntered in and leaned on his elbow, looking casually inside between the railings. He told the teller that he did n't want anything; he was just waiting for a man he knew.

Suddenly there was a scream or two from the women, and a commotion. Unperceived by the elders, May, the nine-year-old girl, in a spirit of play, had shut Agatha in the vault. She had then shot the bolts and turned the knob of the combination as she had seen Mr. Adams do.

The old banker sprang to the handle and tugged at it for a moment. "The door can't be opened," he groaned. "The clock has n't been wound nor the combination set."

Agatha's mother screamed again, hysterically.

"Hush!" said Mr. Adams, raising his trembling hand. "All be quiet for a moment. Agatha!" he called as loudly as he could.

"Listen to me." During the following silence they could just hear the faint sound of the child wildly shrieking in the dark vault in a panic of terror.

"My precious darling!" wailed the mother. "She will die of fright! Open the door! Oh, break it open! Can't you men do something?"

"There is n't a man nearer than Little Rock who can open that door," said Mr. Adams, in a shaky voice. "My God! Spencer, what shall we do? That child—she can't stand it long in there. There is n't enough air, and, besides, she 'll go into convulsions from fright."

Agatha's mother, frantic now, beat the door of the vault with her hands. Somebody wildly suggested dynamite. Annabel turned to Jimmy, her large eyes full of anguish, but not yet despairing. To a woman nothing seems quite impossible to the powers of the man she worships.

"Can't you do something, Ralph—*try*, won't you?"

He looked at her with a queer, soft smile on his lips and in his keen eyes.

"Annabel," he said, "give me that rose you are wearing, will you?"

Hardly believing that she heard him aright, she unpinned the bud from the bosom of her dress, and placed it in his hand. Jimmy stuffed it into his vest-pocket, threw off his coat and pulled up his shirt-sleeves. With that act Ralph D. Spencer passed away and Jimmy Valentine took his place.

"Get away from the door, all of you," he commanded, shortly.

He set his suit-case on the table, and opened it out flat. From that time on he seemed to be unconscious of the presence of any one else. He laid out the shining, queer implements swiftly and orderly, whistling softly to himself as he always did when at work. In a deep silence and immovable, the others watched him as if under a spell.

In a minute Jimmy's pet drill was biting smoothly into the steel door. In ten minutes—breaking his own burglarious record—he threw back the bolts and opened the door.

Agatha, almost collapsed, but safe, was gathered into her mother's arms.

Jimmy Valentine put on his coat, and walked outside the

railings toward the front door. As he went he thought he heard a far-away voice that he once knew call "Ralph!" But he never hesitated.

At the door a big man stood somewhat in his way.

"Hello, Ben!" said Jimmy, still with his strange smile. "Got around at last, have you? Well, let 's go. I don't know that it makes much difference, now."

And then Ben Price acted rather strangely.

"Guess you 're mistaken, Mr. Spencer," he said. "Don't believe I recognize you. Your buggy 's waiting for you, ain't it?"

And Ben Price turned and strolled down the street.

Confessions of a Humorist

THERE WAS a painless stage of incubation that lasted twenty-five years, and then it broke out on me, and people said I was It.

But they called it humor instead of measles.

The employees in the store bought a silver inkstand for the senior partner on his fiftieth birthday. We crowded into his private office to present it.

I had been selected for spokesman, and I made a little speech that I had been preparing for a week.

It made a hit. It was full of puns and epigrams and funny twists that brought down the house (which was a very solid one in the wholesale hardware line). Old Marlowe himself actually grinned, and the employees took their cue and roared.

My reputation as a humorist dates from half-past nine o'clock on that morning.

For weeks afterward my fellow clerks fanned the flame of my self-esteem. One by one they came to me, saying what an awfully clever speech that was, old man, and carefully explained to me the point of each one of my jokes.

Gradually I found that I was expected to keep it up. Others might speak sanely on business matters and the day's topics, but from me something gamesome and airy was required.

I was expected to crack jokes about the crockery and lighten up the granite ware with *persiflage*. I was second bookkeeper, and if I failed to show up a balance-sheet without something comic about the footings or could find no cause for laughter in an invoice of plows, the other clerks were disappointed.

By degrees my fame spread, and I became a local "character." Our town was small enough to make this possible. The daily newspaper often quoted my sayings. At social gatherings I was indispensable.

I believe I did possess considerable wit and a facility for quick and spontaneous repartee. This gift I cultivated and improved by practice. And the nature of it was kindly and genial, not running to sarcasm or offending others. People began to smile when they saw me coming, and by the time we had met I generally had the word ready to broaden the smile into a laugh.

I had married early. We had a charming boy of three and a girl of five. Naturally, we lived in a vine-covered cottage, and were happy. My salary as bookkeeper in the hardware concern kept at a distance those ills attendant upon superfluous wealth.

At sundry times I had written out a few jokes and conceits that I considered peculiarly happy, and had sent them to certain periodicals that print such things. All of them had been instantly accepted. Several of the editors had written to request further contributions.

One day I received a letter from the editor of a famous weekly publication. He suggested that I submit to him a humorous composition to fill a column of space; hinting that he would make it a regular feature of each issue if the work proved satisfactory. I did so, and at the end of two weeks he offered to make a contract with me for a year at a figure that was considerably higher than the amount paid me by the hardware firm.

I was filled with delight. My wife already crowned me in her mind with the imperishable evergreens of literary success. We had lobster croquettes and a bottle of blackberry wine for supper that night. Here was the chance to liberate myself from drudgery. I talked over the matter very seriously with Louisa. We agreed that I must resign my place at the store and devote myself to humor.

I resigned. My fellow clerks gave me a farewell banquet. The speech I made there coruscated. It was printed in full by the *Gazette*. The next morning I awoke and looked at the clock.

"Late, by George!" I exclaimed, and grabbed for my clothes. Louisa reminded me that I was no longer a slave to hardware and contractors' supplies. I was now a professional humorist.

After breakfast she proudly led me to the little room off the kitchen. Dear girl! There was my table and chair, writing pad, ink and pipe tray. And all the author's trappings—the celery stand full of fresh roses and honeysuckle, last year's calendar on the wall, the dictionary, and a little bag of chocolates to nibble between inspirations. Dear girl!

I sat me to work. The wall paper is patterned with arabesques or odalisks or—perhaps—it is trapezoids. Upon one of the figures I fixed my eyes. I bethought me of humor.

A voice startled me—Louisa's voice.

"If you aren't too busy, dear," it said, "come to dinner."

I looked at my watch. Yes, five hours had been gathered in by the grim scytheman. I went to dinner.

"You mustn't work too hard at first," said Louisa. "Goethe— or was it Napoleon?—said five hours a day is enough for mental labor. Couldn't you take me and the children to the woods this afternoon?"

"I *am* a little tired," I admitted. So we went to the woods.

But I soon got the swing of it. Within a month I was turning out copy as regular as shipments of hardware.

And I had success. My column in the weekly made some stir, and I was referred to in a gossipy way by the critics as something fresh in the line of humorists. I augmented my income considerably by contributing to other publications.

I picked up the tricks of the trade. I could take a funny idea and make a two-line joke of it, earning a dollar. With false whiskers on, it would serve up cold as a quatrain, doubling its producing value. By turning the skirt and adding a ruffle of rhyme you would hardly recognize it as *vers de société* with neatly shod feet and a fashion plate illustration.

I began to save up money, and we had new carpets and a parlor organ. My townspeople began to look upon me as a citizen of some consequence instead of the merry trifler I had been when I clerked in the hardware store.

After five or six months the spontaneity seemed to depart from my humor. Quips and droll sayings no longer fell carelessly from my lips. I was sometimes hard run for material. I found myself listening to catch available ideas from the conversation of my friends. Sometimes I chewed my pencil and gazed at the wall paper for hours trying to build up some gay little bubble of unstudied fun.

And then I became a harpy, a Moloch, a Jonah, a vampire to my acquaintances. Anxious, haggard, greedy, I stood among them like a veritable killjoy. Let a bright saying, a witty comparison, a piquant phrase fall from their lips and I was after it like a hound springing upon a bone. I dared not trust my memory; but, turning aside guiltily and meanly I would make a note of it in my ever-present memorandum book or upon my cuff for my own future use.

My friends regarded me in sorrow and wonder. I was not the same man. Where once I had furnished them entertainment and jollity, I now preyed upon them. No jests from me ever bid for their smiles now. They were too precious. I could not afford to dispense gratuitously the means of my livelihood.

I was a lugubrious fox praising the singing of my friends, the crows, that they might drop from their beaks the morsels of wit that I coveted.

Nearly every one began to avoid me. I even forgot how to smile, not even paying that much for the sayings I appropriated.

No persons, places, times or subjects were exempt from my plundering in search of material. Even in church my demoralized fancy went hunting among the solemn aisles and pillars for spoil.

Did the minister give out the long-meter doxology, at once I began: "Doxology—sockdology—sockdolager—meter—meet her."

The sermon ran through my mental sieve, its precepts filtering unheeded, could I but glean a suggestion of a pun or a *bon mot*. The solemnest anthems of the choir were but an accompaniment to my thoughts as I conceived new changes to ring upon the ancient comicalities concerning the jealousies of soprano, tenor and basso.

My own home became a hunting ground. My wife is a singularly feminine creature, candid, sympathetic and impulsive. Once her conversation was my delight, and her ideas a source of unfailing pleasure. Now I worked her. She was a gold mine of those amusing but lovable inconsistencies that distinguish the female mind.

I began to market those pearls of unwisdom and humor that should have enriched only the sacred precincts of home. With devilish cunning I encouraged her to talk. Unsuspecting, she laid her heart bare. Upon the cold, conspicuous, common, printed page I offered it to the public gaze.

A literary Judas, I kissed her and betrayed her. For pieces of silver I dressed her sweet confidences in the pantalettes and frills of folly and made them dance in the market place.

Dear Louisa! Of nights I have bent over her, cruel as a wolf above a tender lamb, hearkening even to her soft words murmured in sleep, hoping to catch an idea for my next day's grind. There is worse to come.

God help me! Next my fangs were buried deep in the neck of the fugitive sayings of my little children.

Guy and Viola were two bright fountains of childish, quaint thoughts and speeches. I found a ready sale for this kind of humor, and was furnishing a regular department in a magazine with "Funny Fancies of Childhood." I began to stalk them as an Indian stalks the antelope. I would hide behind sofas and doors, or crawl on my hands and knees among the bushes in the yard to eavesdrop while they were at play. I had all the qualities of a Harpy except remorse.

Once, when I was barren of ideas, and my copy must leave in the next mail, I covered myself in a pile of autumn leaves in the yard, where I knew they intended to come to play. I cannot bring myself to believe that Guy was aware of my hiding place, but even if he was I would be loath to blame him for his setting fire to the leaves, causing the destruction of my new suit of clothes, and nearly cremating a parent.

Soon my own children began to shun me as a pest. Often, when I was creeping upon them like a melancholy ghoul, I would hear them say to each other: "Here comes papa," and they would gather their toys and scurry away to some safer hiding place. Miserable wretch that I was!

And yet I was doing well financially. Before the first year had passed I had saved a thousand dollars, and we had lived in comfort.

But at what a cost! I am not quite clear as to what a Pariah is, but I was everything that it sounds like. I had no friends, no amusements, no enjoyment of life. The happiness of my family had been sacrificed. I was a bee, sucking sordid honey from life's fairest flowers, dreaded and shunned on account of my sting.

One day a man spoke to me, with a pleasant and friendly smile. Not in months had the thing happened. I was passing the undertaking establishment of Peter Heffelbower. Peter stood in the door and saluted me. I stopped, strangely wrung in my heart by his greeting. He asked me inside.

The day was chill and rainy. We went into the back room,

where a fire burned in a little stove. A customer came, and Peter left me alone for a while. Presently I felt a new feeling stealing over me—a sense of beautiful calm and content. I looked around the place. There were rows of shining rosewood caskets, black palls, trestles, hearse plumes, mourning streamers and all the paraphernalia of the solemn trade. Here was peace, order, silence, the abode of grave and dignified reflections. Here, on the brink of life, was a little niche pervaded by the spirit of eternal rest.

When I entered it the follies of the world abandoned me at the door. I felt no inclination to wrest a humorous idea from those somber and stately trappings. My mind seemed to stretch itself to grateful repose upon a couch draped with gentle thoughts.

A quarter of an hour ago I was an abandoned humorist. Now I was a philosopher, full of serenity and ease. I had found a *refuge* from humor, from the hot chase of the shy quip, from the degrading pursuit of the panting joke, from the restless reach after the nimble repartee.

I had not known Heffelbower well. When he came back I let him talk, fearful that he might prove to be a jarring note in the sweet, dirge-like harmony of his establishment.

But, no. He chimed truly. I gave a long sigh of happiness. Never have I known a man's talk to be as magnificently dull as Peter's was. Compared with it the Dead Sea is a geyser. Never a sparkle or a glimmer of wit marred his words. Commonplaces as trite and as plentiful as blackberries flowed from his lips no more stirring in quality than a last week's tape running from a ticker. Quaking a little I tried upon him one of my best pointed jokes. It fell back ineffectual, with the point broken. I loved that man from then on.

Two or three evenings each week I would steal down to Heffelbower's and revel in his back room. That was my only joy. I began to rise early and hurry through my work, that I might spend more time in my haven. In no other place could I throw off my habit of extracting humorous ideas from my surroundings. Peter's talk left me no opening had I besieged it ever so hard.

Under this influence I began to improve in spirits. It was the recreation from one's labor which every man needs. I surprised one or two of my former friends by throwing them a smile and a cheery word as I passed them on the streets. Several times I dumfounded my family by relaxing long enough to make a jocose remark in their presence.

I had so long been ridden by the incubus of humor that I seized my hours of holiday with a schoolboy's zest.

My work began to suffer. It was not the pain and burden to me that it had been. I often whistled at my desk, and wrote with far more fluency than before. I accomplished my tasks impatiently, as anxious to be off to my helpful retreat as a drunkard is to get to his tavern.

My wife had some anxious hours in conjecturing where I spent my afternoons. I thought it best not to tell her; women do not understand these things. Poor girl!—she had one shock out of it.

One day I brought home a silver coffin handle for a paper weight and a fine, fluffy hearse plume to dust my papers with.

I loved to see them on my desk, and think of the beloved back room down at Heffelbower's. But Louisa found them, and she shrieked with horror. I had to console her with some lame excuse for having them, but I saw in her eyes that the prejudice was not removed. I had to remove the articles, though, at double-quick time.

One day Peter Heffelbower laid before me a temptation that swept me off my feet. In his sensible, uninspired way he showed me his books, and explained that his profits and his business were increasing rapidly. He had thought of taking in a partner with some cash. He would rather have me than any one he knew. When I left his place that afternoon Peter had my check for the thousand dollars I had in the bank, and I was a partner in his undertaking business.

I went home with feelings of delirious joy, mingled with a certain amount of doubt. I was dreading to tell my wife about it. But I walked on air. To give up the writing of humorous stuff, once more to enjoy the apples of life, instead of squeezing them to a pulp for a few drops of hard cider to make the public feel funny—what a boon that would be!

At the supper table Louisa handed me some letters that had come during my absence. Several of them contained rejected manuscript. Ever since I first began going to Heffelbower's my stuff had been coming back with alarming frequency. Lately I had been dashing off my jokes and articles with the greatest fluency. Previously I had labored like a bricklayer, slowly and with agony.

Presently I opened a letter from the editor of the weekly with which I had a regular contract. The checks for that weekly article were still our main dependence. The letter ran thus:

"DEAR SIR: As you are aware, our contract for the year expires with the present month. While regretting the necessity for so doing, we must say that we do not care to renew same for the coming year. We were quite pleased with your style of humor, which seems to have delighted quite a large proportion of our readers. But for the past two months we have noticed a decided falling off in its quality.

"Your earlier work showed a spontaneous, easy, natural flow of fun and wit. Of late it is labored, studied and unconvincing, giving painful evidence of hard toil and drudging mechanism.

"Again regretting that we do not consider your contributions available any longer, we are, yours sincerely,   THE EDITOR."

I handed this letter to my wife. After she had read it her face grew extremely long, and there were tears in her eyes.

"The mean old thing!" she exclaimed, indignantly. "I'm sure your pieces are just as good as they ever were. And it doesn't take you half as long to write them as it did." And then, I suppose, Louisa thought of the checks that would cease coming. "Oh, John," she wailed, "what will you do now?"

For an answer I got up and began to do a polka step around the supper table. I am sure Louisa thought the trouble had driven me mad; and I think the children hoped it had, for they tore after me, yelling with glee and emulating my steps. I was now something like their old playmate as of yore.

"The theatre for us to-night!" I shouted, "nothing less. And a late, wild, disreputable supper for all of us at the Palace Restaurant. Lumty-diddle-de-dee-de-dum!"

And then I explained my glee by declaring that I was now a partner in a prosperous undertaking establishment, and that written jokes might go hide their heads in sackcloth and ashes for all me.

With the editor's letter in her hand to justify the deed I had done, my wife could advance no objections save a few mild ones based on the feminine inability to appreciate a good thing such as the little back room of Peter Hef—no, of Heffelbower & Co.'s undertaking establishment.

In conclusion, I will say that to-day you will find no man in our town as well liked, as jovial and full of merry sayings as I. My jokes are again noised about and quoted; once more I take pleasure in my wife's confidential chatter without a mercenary thought, while Guy and Viola play at my feet distributing gems of childish humor without fear of the ghastly tormentor who used to dog their steps, notebook in hand.

Our business has prospered finely. I keep the books and look after the shop, while Peter attends to outside matters. He says that my levity and high spirits would simply turn any funeral into a regular Irish wake.

A Ramble in Aphasia

MY WIFE and I parted on that morning in precisely our usual manner. She left her second cup of tea to follow me to the front door. There she plucked from my lapel the invisible strand of lint (the universal act of woman to proclaim ownership) and bade me take care of my cold. I had no cold. Next came her kiss of parting—the level kiss of domesticity flavored with Young Hyson. There was no fear of the extemporaneous, of variety spicing her infinite custom. With the deft touch of long malpractice, she dabbed awry my well-set scarf pin; and then, as I closed the door, I heard her morning slippers pattering back to her cooling tea.

When I set out I had no thought or premonition of what was to occur. The attack came suddenly.

For many weeks I had been toiling, almost night and day, at a famous railroad law case that I won triumphantly but a few days previously. In fact, I had been digging away at the law almost without cessation for many years. Once or twice good Doctor Volney, my friend and physician, had warned me.

"If you don't slacken up, Bellford," he said, "you'll go suddenly to pieces. Either your nerves or your brain will give way. Tell me, does a week pass in which you do not read in the papers of a case of aphasia—of some man lost, wandering nameless, with his past and his identity blotted out—and all from that little brain clot made by overwork or worry?"

"I always thought," said I, "that the clot in those instances was really to be found on the brains of the newspaper reporters."

Doctor Volney shook his head.

"The disease exists," he said. "You need a change or a rest. Court-room, office and home—there is the only route you travel. For recreation you—read law books. Better take warning in time."

"On Thursday nights," I said, defensively, "my wife and I play cribbage. On Sundays she reads to me the weekly letter from her mother. That law books are not a recreation remains yet to be established."

That morning as I walked I was thinking of Doctor Volney's words. I was feeling as well as I usually did—possibly in better spirits than usual.

I awoke with stiff and cramped muscles from having slept long on the incommodious seat of a day coach. I leaned my head against the seat and tried to think. After a long time I said to myself: "I must have a name of some sort." I searched my pockets. Not a card; not a letter; not a paper or monogram could I find. But I found in my coat pocket nearly $3,000 in bills of large denomination. "I must be some one, of course," I repeated to myself, and began again to consider.

The car was well crowded with men, among whom, I told myself, there must have been some common interest, for they intermingled freely, and seemed in the best good humor and spirits. One of them—a stout, spectacled gentleman enveloped in a decided odor of cinnamon and aloes—took the vacant half of my seat with a friendly nod, and unfolded a newspaper. In the intervals between his periods of reading, we conversed, as travelers will, on current affairs. I found myself able to sustain the conversation on such subjects with credit, at least to my memory. By and by my companion said:

"You are one of us, of course. Fine lot of men the West sends in this time. I'm glad they held the convention in New York; I've never been East before. My name's R. P. Bolder—Bolder & Son, of Hickory Grove, Missouri."

Though unprepared, I rose to the emergency, as men will when put to it. Now must I hold a christening, and be at once babe, parson and parent. My senses came to the rescue of my slower brain. The insistent odor of drugs from my companion supplied one idea; a glance at his newspaper, where my eye met a conspicuous advertisement, assisted me further.

"My name," said I, glibly, "is Edward Pinkhammer. I am a druggist, and my home is in Cornopolis, Kansas."

"I knew you were a druggist," said my fellow traveler, affably. "I saw the callous spot on your right forefinger where the handle of the pestle rubs. Of course, you are a delegate to our National Convention."

"Are all these men druggists?" I asked, wonderingly.

"They are. This car came through from the West. And they're

your old-time druggists, too—none of your patent tablet-and-granule pharmashootists that use slot machines instead of a prescription desk. We percolate our own paregoric and roll our own pills, and we ain't above handling a few garden seeds in the spring, and carrying a side line of confectionery and shoes. I tell you Hampinker, I've got an idea to spring on this convention—new ideas is what they want. Now, you know the shelf bottles of tartar emetic and Rochelle salt Ant. et Pot. Tart. and Sod. et Pot. Tart.—one's poison, you know, and the other's harmless. It's easy to mistake one label for the other. Where do druggists mostly keep 'em? Why, as far apart as possible, on different shelves. That's wrong. I say keep 'em side by side, so when you want one you can always compare it with the other and avoid mistakes. Do you catch the idea?"

"It seems to me a very good one," I said.

"All right! When I spring it on the convention you back it up. We'll make some of these Eastern orange-phosphate-and-massage-cream professors that think they're the only lozenges in the market look like hypodermic tablets."

"If I can be of any aid," I said, warming, "the two bottles of—er——"

"Tartrate of antimony and potash, and tartrate of soda and potash."

"Shall henceforth sit side by side," I concluded, firmly.

"Now, there's another thing," said Mr. Bolder. "For an excipient in manipulating a pill mass which do you prefer—the magnesia carbonate or the pulverized glycerrhiza radix?"

"The—er—magnesia," I said. It was easier to say than the other word.

Mr. Bolder glanced at me distrustfully through his spectacles.

"Give me the glycerrhiza," said he. "Magnesia cakes."

"Here's another one of these fake aphasia cases," he said, presently, handing me his newspaper, and laying his finger upon an article. "I don't believe in 'em. I put nine out of ten of 'em down as frauds. A man gets sick of his business and his folks and wants to have a good time. He skips out somewhere, and when they find him he pretends to have lost his memory—don't know his own name, and won't even recognize the strawberry mark on his wife's left shoulder. Aphasia! Tut! Why can't they stay at home and forget?"

I took the paper and read, after the pungent head-lines, the following:

"DENVER, June 12.—Elwyn C. Bellford, a prominent lawyer, is mysteriously missing from his home since three days ago, and all efforts to locate him have been in vain. Mr. Bellford is a well-known citizen of the highest standing, and has enjoyed a large and lucrative law practice. He is married and owns a fine home and the most extensive private library in the State. On the day of his disappearance, he drew quite a large sum of money from his bank. No one can be found who saw him after he left the bank. Mr. Bellford was a man of singularly quiet and domestic tastes, and seemed to find his happiness in his home and profession. If any clue at all exists to his strange disappearance, it may be found in the fact that for some months he has been deeply absorbed in an important law case in connection with the Q. Y. and Z. Railroad Company. It is feared that overwork may have affected his mind. Every effort is being made to discover the whereabouts of the missing man."

"It seems to me you are not altogether uncynical, Mr. Bolder," I said, after I had read the despatch. "This has the sound, to me, of a genuine case. Why should this man, prosperous, happily married and respected, choose suddenly to abandon everything? I know that these lapses of memory do occur, and that men do find themselves adrift without a name, a history or a home."

"Oh, gammon and jalap!" said Mr. Bolder. "It's larks they're after. There's too much education nowadays. Men know about aphasia, and they use it for an excuse. The women are wise, too. When it's all over they look you in the eye, as scientific as you please, and say: 'He hypnotized me.'"

Thus Mr. Bolder diverted, but did not aid, me with his comments and philosophy.

We arrived in New York about ten at night. I rode in a cab to a hotel, and I wrote my name "Edward Pinkhammer" in the register. As I did so I felt pervade me a splendid, wild, intoxicating buoyancy—a sense of unlimited freedom, of newly attained possibilities. I was just born into the world. The old fetters—whatever they had been—were stricken from my hands and feet. The future lay before me a clear road such as an infant enters, and I could set out upon it equipped with a man's learning and experience.

I thought the hotel clerk looked at me five seconds too long. I had no baggage.

"The Druggists' Convention," I said. "My trunk has somehow failed to arrive." I drew out a roll of money.

"Ah!" said he, showing an auriferous tooth, "we have quite a number of the Western delegates stopping here." He struck a bell for the boy.

I endeavored to give color to my rôle.

"There is an important movement on foot among us Westerners," I said, "in regard to a recommendation to the convention that the bottles containing the tartrate of antimony and potash, and the tartrate of sodium and potash be kept in a contiguous position on the shelf."

"Gentleman to three-fourteen," said the clerk, hastily. I was whisked away to my room.

The next day I bought a trunk and clothing, and began to live the life of Edward Pinkhammer. I did not tax my brain with endeavors to solve problems of the past.

It was a piquant and sparkling cup that the great island city held up to my lips. I drank of it gratefully. The keys of Manhattan belong to him who is able to bear them. You must be either the city's guest or its victim.

The following few days were as gold and silver. Edward Pinkhammer, yet counting back to his birth by hours only, knew the rare joy of having come upon so diverting a world full-fledged and unrestrained. I sat entranced on the magic carpets provided in theatres and roof-gardens, that transported one into strange and delightful lands full of frolicsome music, pretty girls and grotesque, drolly extravagant parodies upon human kind. I went here and there at my own dear will, bound by no limits of space, time or comportment. I dined in weird cabarets, at weirder *tables d'hôte* to the sound of Hungarian music and the wild shouts of mercurial artists and sculptors. Or, again, where the night life quivers in the electric glare like a kinetoscopic picture, and the millinery of the world, and its jewels, and the ones whom they adorn, and the men who make all three possible are met for good cheer and the spectacular effect. And among all these scenes that I have mentioned I learned one thing that I never knew before. And that is that the key to liberty is not in the hands of License, but Convention holds it. Comity has a toll-gate at which you must pay, or you may not enter the land of Freedom. In all the glitter, the seeming disorder, the parade, the abandon, I saw this law, unobtrusive, yet like iron, prevail. Therefore, in Manhattan you must obey these unwritten laws, and then you will be freest of the free. If you decline to be bound by them, you put on shackles.

Sometimes, as my mood urged me, I would seek the stately, softly murmuring palm rooms, redolent with high-born life and delicate restraint, in which to dine. Again I would go down to the waterways in steamers packed with vociferous, bedecked, unchecked love-making clerks and shop-girls to their crude pleasures on the island shores. And there was always Broadway—glistening, opulent, wily, varying, desirable Broadway—growing upon one like an opium habit.

One afternoon as I entered my hotel a stout man with a big nose and a black mustache blocked my way in the corridor. When I would have passed around him, he greeted me with offensive familiarity.

"Hallo, Bellford!" he cried, loudly. "'What the deuce are you doing in New York? Didn't know anything could drag you away from that old book den of yours. Is Mrs. B. along or is this a little business run alone, eh?"

"You have made a mistake, sir," I said, coldly, releasing my hand from his grasp. "My name is Pinkhammer. You will excuse me."

The man dropped to one side, apparently astonished. As I walked to the clerk's desk I heard him call to a bell boy and say something about telegraph blanks.

"You will give me my bill," I said to the clerk, "and have my baggage brought down in half an hour. I do not care to remain where I am annoyed by confidence men."

I moved that afternoon to another hotel, a sedate, old-fashioned one on lower Fifth Avenue.

There was a restaurant a little way off Broadway where one could be served almost *al fresco* in a tropic array of screening flora. Quiet and luxury and a perfect service made it an ideal place in which to take luncheon or refreshment. One afternoon I was there picking my way to a table among the ferns when I felt my sleeve caught.

"Mr. Bellford!" exclaimed an amazingly sweet voice.

I turned quickly to see a lady seated alone—a lady of about thirty, with exceedingly handsome eyes, who looked at me as though I had been her very dear friend.

"You were about to pass me," she said, accusingly. "Don't tell me you did not know me. Why should we not shake hands—at least once in fifteen years?"

I shook hands with her at once. I took a chair opposite her at the table. I summoned with my eyebrows a hovering waiter. The lady was philandering with an orange ice. I ordered a *crème de menthe.* Her hair was reddish bronze. You could not look at it, because you could not look away from her eyes. But you were conscious of it as you are conscious of sunset while you look into the profundities of a wood at twilight.

"Are you sure you know me?" I asked.

"No," she said, smiling, "I was never sure of that."

"What would you think," I said, a little anxiously, "if I were to tell you that my name is Edward Pinkhammer, from Cornopolis, Kansas?"

"What would I think?" she repeated, with a merry glance. "Why, that you had not brought Mrs. Bellford to New York with you, of course. I do wish you had. I would have liked to see Marian." Her voice lowered slightly—"You haven't changed much, Elwyn."

I felt her wonderful eyes searching mine and my face more closely.

"Yes, you have," she amended, and there was a soft, exultant note in her latest tones; "I see it now. You haven't forgotten. You haven't forgotten for a year or a day or an hour. I told you you never could."

I poked my straw anxiously in the *crème de menthe.*

"I'm sure I beg your pardon," I said, a little uneasy at her gaze. "But that is just the trouble. I have forgotten. I've forgotten everything."

She flouted my denial. She laughed deliciously at something she seemed to see in my face.

"I've heard of you at times," she went on. "You're quite a big lawyer out West—Denver, isn't it, or Los Angeles? Marian must be very proud of you. You knew, I suppose, that I married six months after you did. You may have seen it in the papers. The flowers alone cost two thousand dollars."

She had mentioned fifteen years. Fifteen years is a long time.

"Would it be too late," I asked, somewhat timorously, "to offer you congratulations?"

"Not if you dare do it," she answered, with such fine intrepidity that I was silent, and began to crease patterns on the cloth with my thumb nail.

"Tell me one thing," she said, leaning toward me rather eagerly—"a thing I have wanted to know for many years—just from a woman's curiosity, of course—have you ever dared since that night to touch, smell or look at white roses—at white roses wet with rain and dew?"

I took a sip of *crème de menthe*.

"It would be useless, I suppose," I said, with a sigh, "for me to repeat that I have no recollection at all about these things. My memory is completely at fault. I need not say how much I regret it."

The lady rested her arms upon the table, and again her eyes disdained my words and went traveling by their own route direct to my soul. She laughed softly, with a strange quality in the sound—it was a laugh of happiness—yes, and of content—and of misery. I tried to look away from her.

"You lie, Elwyn Bellford," she breathed, blissfully. "Oh, I know you lie!"

I gazed dully into the ferns.

"My name is Edward Pinkhammer," I said. "I came with the delegates to the Druggists' National Convention. There is a movement on foot for arranging a new position for the bottles of tartrate of antimony and tartrate of potash, in which, very likely, you would take little interest."

A shining landau stopped before the entrance. The lady rose. I took her hand, and bowed.

"I am deeply sorry," I said to her, "that I cannot remember. I could explain, but fear you would not understand. You will not concede Pinkhammer; and I really cannot at all conceive of the—the roses and other things."

"Good-by, Mr. Bellford," she said, with her happy, sorrowful smile, as she stepped into her carriage.

I attended the theatre that night. When I returned to my hotel, a quiet man in dark clothes, who seemed interested in rubbing his finger nails with a silk handkerchief, appeared, magically, at my side.

"Mr. Pinkhammer," he said, casually, giving the bulk of his attention to his forefinger, "may I request you to step aside with me for a little conversation? There is a room here."

"Certainly," I answered.

He conducted me into a small, private parlor. A lady and a gentleman were there. The lady, I surmised, would have been unusually good-looking had her features not been clouded by an expression of keen worry and fatigue. She was of a style of figure and possessed coloring and features that were agreeable to my fancy. She was in a traveling dress; she fixed upon me an earnest look of extreme anxiety, and pressed an unsteady hand to her bosom. I think she would have started forward, but the gentleman arrested her movement with an authoritative motion of his hand. He then came, himself, to meet me. He was a man of forty, a little gray about the temples, and with a strong, thoughtful face.

"Bellford, old man," he said, cordially, "I'm glad to see you again. Of course we know everything is all right. I warned you, you know, that you were overdoing it. Now, you'll go back with us, and be yourself again in no time."

I smiled ironically.

"I have been 'Bellforded' so often," I said, "that it has lost its edge. Still, in the end, it may grow wearisome. Would you be willing at all to entertain the hypothesis that my name is Edward Pinkhammer, and that I never saw you before in my life?"

Before the man could reply a wailing cry came from the woman. She sprang past his detaining arm. "Elwyn!" she sobbed, and cast herself upon me, and clung tight. "Elwyn," she cried again, "don't break my heart. I am your wife—call my name once—just once! I could see you dead rather than this way."

I unwound her arms respectfully, but firmly.

"Madam," I said, severely, "pardon me if I suggest that you accept a resemblance too precipitately. It is a pity," I went on, with an amused laugh, as the thought occurred to me, "that this Bellford and I could not be kept side by side upon the same shelf like tartrates of sodium and antimony for purposes of identification. In order to understand the allusion," I concluded airily, "it may be necessary for you to keep an eye on the proceedings of the Druggists' National Convention."

The lady turned to her companion, and grasped his arm.

"What is it, Doctor Volney? Oh, what is it?" she moaned.

He led her to the door.

"Go to your room for a while," I heard him say. "I will remain and talk with him. His mind? No, I think not—only a portion of the brain. Yes, I am sure he will recover. Go to your room and leave me with him."

The lady disappeared. The man in dark clothes also went outside, still manicuring himself in a thoughtful way. I think he waited in the hall.

"I would like to talk with you a while, Mr. Pinkhammer, if I may," said the gentleman who remained.

"Very well, if you care to," I replied, "and will excuse me if I take it comfortably; I am rather tired." I stretched myself upon a couch by a window and lit a cigar. He drew a chair nearby.

"Let us speak to the point," he said, soothingly. "Your name is not Pinkhammer."

"I know that as well as you do," I said, coolly. "But a man must have a name of some sort. I can assure you that I do not extravagantly admire the name of Pinkhammer. But when one christens one's self suddenly, the fine names do not seem to suggest themselves. But, suppose it had been Scheringhausen or Scroggins! I think I did very well with Pinkhammer."

"Your name," said the other man, seriously, "is Elwyn C. Bellford. You are one of the first lawyers in Denver. You are suffering from an attack of aphasia, which has caused you to forget your identity. The cause of it was over-application to your profession, and, perhaps, a life too bare of natural recreation and pleasures. The lady who has just left the room is your wife."

"She is what I would call a fine-looking woman," I said, after a judicial pause. "I particularly admire the shade of brown in her hair."

"She is a wife to be proud of. Since your disappearance, nearly two weeks ago, she has scarcely closed her eyes. We learned that you were in New York through a telegram sent by Isidore Newman, a traveling man from Denver. He said that he had met you in a hotel here, and that you did not recognize him."

"I think I remember the occasion," I said. "The fellow called me 'Bellford,' if I am not mistaken. But don't you think it about time, now, for you to introduce yourself?"

"I am Robert Volney—Doctor Volney. I have been your close friend for twenty years, and your physician for fifteen. I came with Mrs. Bellford to trace you as soon as we got the telegram. Try, Elwyn, old man—try to remember!"

"What's the use to try?" I asked, with a little frown. "You say you are a physician. Is aphasia curable? When a man loses his memory does it return slowly, or suddenly?"

"Sometimes gradually and imperfectly; sometimes as suddenly as it went."

"Will you undertake the treatment of my case, Doctor Volney?" I asked.

"Old friend," said he, "I'll do everything in my power, and will have done everything that science can do to cure you."

"Very well," said I. "Then you will consider that I am your patient. Everything is in confidence now—professional confidence."

"Of course," said Doctor Volney.

I got up from the couch. Some one had set a vase of white roses on the centre table—a cluster of white roses, freshly sprinkled and fragrant. I threw them far out of the window, and then I laid myself upon the couch again.

"It will be best, Bobby," I said, "to have this cure happen suddenly. I'm rather tired of it all, anyway. You may go now and bring Marian in. But, oh, Doc," I said, with a sigh, as I kicked him on the shin—"good old Doc—it was glorious!"

Blind Man's Holiday

ALAS FOR the man and for the artist with the shifting point of perspective! Life shall be a confusion of ways to the one; the landscape shall rise up and confound the other. Take the case of Lorison. At one time he appeared to himself to be the feeblest of fools; at another he conceived that he followed ideals so fine that the world was not yet ready to accept them. During one mood he cursed his folly; possessed by the other, he bore himself with a serene grandeur akin to greatness: in neither did he attain the perspective.

Generations before, the name had been "Larsen." His race had bequeathed him its fine-strung, melancholy temperament, its saving balance of thrift and industry.

From his point of perspective he saw himself an outcast from society, forever to be a shady skulker along the ragged edge of respectability; a denizen *des trois-quartz de monde*, that pathetic spheroid lying between the *haut* and the *demi*, whose inhabitants envy each of their neighbours, and are scorned by both. He was self-condemned to this opinion, as he was self-exiled, through it, to this quaint Southern city a thousand miles from his former home. Here he had dwelt for longer than a year, knowing but few, keeping in a subjective world of shadows which was invaded at times by the perplexing bulks of jarring realities. Then he fell in love with a girl whom he met in a cheap restaurant, and his story begins.

The Rue Chartres, in New Orleans, is a street of ghosts. It lies in the quarter where the Frenchman, in his prime, set up his translated pride and glory; where, also, the arrogant don had swaggered, and dreamed of gold and grants and ladies' gloves. Every flagstone has its grooves worn by footsteps going royally to the wooing and the fighting. Every house has a princely heartbreak; each doorway its untold tale of gallant promise and slow decay.

By night the Rue Chartres is now but a murky fissure, from which the groping wayfarer sees, flung against the sky, the tangled filigree of Moorish iron balconies. The old houses of monsieur stand yet, indomitable against the century, but their essence is gone. The street is one of ghosts to whosoever can see them.

A faint heartbeat of the street's ancient glory still survives in a corner occupied by the Café Carabine d'Or. Once men gathered there to plot against kings, and to warn presidents. They do so yet, but they are not the same kind of men. A brass button will scatter these; those would have set their faces against an army. Above the door hangs the sign board, upon which has been depicted a vast animal of unfamiliar species. In the act of firing upon this monster is represented an unobtrusive human levelling an obtrusive gun, once the colour of bright gold. Now the legend above the picture is faded beyond conjecture; the gun's relation to the title is a matter of faith; the menaced animal, wearied of the long aim of the hunter, has resolved itself into a shapeless blot.

The place is known as "Antonio's," as the name, white upon the red-lit transparency, and gilt upon the windows, attests. There is a promise in "Antonio"; a justifiable expectancy of savoury things in oil and pepper and wine, and perhaps an angel's whisper of garlic. But the rest of the name is "O'Riley." Antonio O'Riley!

The Carabine d'Or is an ignominious ghost of the Rue Chartres. The café where Bienville and Conti dined, where a prince has broken bread, is become a "family ristaurant."

Its customers are working men and women, almost to a unit. Occasionally you will see chorus girls from the cheaper theatres, and men who follow avocations subject to quick vicissitudes; but at Antonio's—name rich in Bohemian promise, but tame in fulfilment—manners debonair and gay are toned down to the "family" standard. Should you light a cigarette, mine host will touch you on the "arrum" and remind you that the proprieties are menaced. "Antonio" entices and beguiles from fiery legend without, but "O'Riley" teaches decorum within.

It was at this restaurant that Lorison first saw the girl. A flashy fellow with a predatory eye had followed her in, and had advanced to take the other chair at the little table where she stopped, but Lorison slipped into the seat before him. Their acquaintance began, and grew, and now for two months they had sat at the same table each evening, not meeting by appointment, but as if by a series of fortuitous and happy accidents.

After dining, they would take a walk together in one of the little city parks, or among the panoramic markets where exhibits a continuous vaudeville of sights and sounds. Always at eight o'clock their steps led them to a certain street corner, where she prettily but firmly bade him good night and left him. "I do not live far from here," she frequently said, "and you must let me go the rest of the way alone."

But now Lorison had discovered that he wanted to go the rest of the way with her, or happiness would depart, leaving him on a very lonely corner of life. And at the same time that he made the discovery, the secret of his banishment from the society of the good laid its finger in his face and told him it must not be.

Man is too thoroughly an egoist not to be also an egotist; if he love, the object shall know it. During a lifetime he may conceal it through stress of expediency and honour, but it shall bubble from his dying lips, though it disrupt a neighbourhood. It is known, however, that most men do not wait so long to disclose their passion. In the case of Lorison, his particular ethics positively forbade him to declare his sentiments, but he must needs dally with the subject, and woo by innuendo at least.

On this night, after the usual meal at the Carabine d'Or, he strolled with his companion down the dim old street toward the river.

The Rue Chartres perishes in the old Place d'Armes. The ancient Cabildo, where Spanish justice fell like hail, faces it, and the Cathedral, another provincial ghost, overlooks it. Its centre is a little, iron-railed park of flowers and immaculate gravelled walks, where citizens take the air of evenings. Pedestalled high above it, the general sits his cavorting steed, with his face turned stonily down the river toward English Turn, whence come no more Britons to bombard his cotton bales.

Often the two sat in this square, but to-night Lorison guided her past the stone-stepped gate, and still riverward. As they walked, he smiled to himself to think that all he knew of her—except that he loved her—was her name, Norah Greenway, and that she lived with her brother. They had talked about everything except themselves. Perhaps her reticence had been caused by his.

They came, at length, upon the levee, and sat upon a great,

prostrate beam. The air was pungent with the dust of commerce. The great river slipped yellowly past. Across it Algiers lay, a longitudinous black bulk against a vibrant electric haze sprinkled with exact stars.

The girl was young and of the piquant order. A certain bright melancholy pervaded her; she possessed an untarnished, pale prettiness doomed to please. Her voice, when she spoke, dwarfed her theme. It was the voice capable of investing little subjects with a large interest. She sat at ease, bestowing her skirts with the little womanly touch, serene as if the begrimed pier were a summer garden. Lorison poked the rotting boards with his cane.

He began by telling her that he was in love with some one to whom he durst not speak of it. "And why not?" she asked, accepting swiftly his fatuous presentation of a third person of straw. "My place in the world," he answered, "is none to ask a woman to share. I am an outcast from honest people; I am wrongly accused of one crime, and am, I believe, guilty of another."

Thence he plunged into the story of his abdication from society. The story, pruned of his moral philosophy, deserves no more than the slightest touch. It is no new tale, that of the gambler's declension. During one night's sitting he lost, and then had imperilled a certain amount of his employer's money, which, by accident, he carried with him. He continued to lose, to the last wager, and then began to gain, leaving the game winner to a somewhat formidable sum. The same night his employer's safe was robbed. A search was had; the winnings of Lorison were found in his room, their total forming an accusative nearness to the sum purloined. He was taken, tried and, through incomplete evidence, released, smutched with the sinister *devoirs* of a disagreeing jury.

"It is not in the unjust accusation," he said to the girl, "that my burden lies, but in the knowledge that from the moment I staked the first dollar of the firm's money I was a criminal—no matter whether I lost or won. You see why it is impossible for me to speak of love to her."

"It is a sad thing," said Norah, after a little pause, "to think what very good people there are in the world."

"Good?" said Lorison.

"I was thinking of this superior person whom you say you love. She must be a very poor sort of creature."

"I do not understand."

"Nearly," she continued, "as poor a sort of creature as yourself."

"You do not understand," said Lorison, removing his hat and sweeping back his fine, light hair. "Suppose she loved me in return, and were willing to marry me. Think, if you can, what would follow. Never a day would pass but she would be reminded of her sacrifice. I would read a condescension in her smile, a pity even in her affection, that would madden me. No. The thing would stand between us forever. Only equals should mate. I could never ask her to come down upon my lower plane."

An arc light faintly shone upon Lorison's face. An illumination from within also pervaded it. The girl saw the rapt, ascetic look; it was the face either of Sir Galahad or Sir Fool.

"Quite starlike," she said, "is this unapproachable angel. Really too high to be grasped."

"By me, yes."

She faced him suddenly. "My dear friend, would you prefer your star fallen?" Lorison made a wide gesture.

"You push me to the bald fact," he declared; "you are not in sympathy with my argument. But I will answer you so. If I could reach my particular star, to drag it down, I would not do it; but if it were fallen, I would pick it up, and thank Heaven for the privilege."

They were silent for some minutes. Norah shivered, and thrust her hands deep into the pockets of her jacket. Lorison uttered a remorseful exclamation.

"I'm not cold," she said. "I was just thinking. I ought to tell you something. You have selected a strange confidante. But you cannot expect a chance acquaintance, picked up in a doubtful restaurant, to be an angel."

"Norah!" cried Lorison.

"Let me go on. You have told me about yourself. We have been such good friends. I must tell you now what I never wanted you to know. I am—worse than you are. I was on the stage . . . I sang in the chorus . . . I was pretty bad, I guess . . . I stole diamonds from the prima donna . . . they arrested me . . .

I gave most of them up, and they let me go . . . I drank wine every night . . . a great deal . . . I was very wicked, but——"

Lorison knelt quickly by her side and took her hands.

"Dear Norah!" he said, exultantly. "It is you, it is you I love! You never guessed it, did you? 'Tis you I meant all the time. Now I can speak. Let me make you forget the past. We have both suffered; let us shut out the world, and live for each other. Norah, do you hear me say I love you?"

"In spite of——"

"Rather say because of it. You have come out of your past noble and good. Your heart is an angel's. Give it to me."

"A little while ago you feared the future too much to even speak."

"But for you; not for myself. Can you love me?"

She cast herself, wildly sobbing, upon his breast.

"Better than life—than truth itself—than everything."

"And my own past," said Lorison, with a note of solicitude—"can you forgive and——"

"I answered you that," she whispered, "when I told you I loved you." She leaned away, and looked thoughtfully at him. "If I had not told you about myself, would you have—would you——"

"No," he interrupted; "I would never have let you know I loved you. I would never have asked you this—Norah, will you be my wife?"

She wept again.

"Oh, believe me; I am good now—I am no longer wicked! I will be the best wife in the world. Don't think I am—bad any more. If you do I shall die, I shall die!"

While he was consoling her, she brightened up, eager and impetuous. "Will you marry me to-night?" she said. "Will you prove it that way? I have a reason for wishing it to be to-night. Will you?"

Of one of two things was this exceeding frankness the outcome: either of importunate brazenness or of utter innocence. The lover's perspective contained only the one.

"The sooner," said Lorison, "the happier I shall be."

"What is there to do?" she asked. "What do you have to get? Come! You should know."

Her energy stirred the dreamer to action.

"A city directory first," he cried, gayly, "to find where the man lives who gives licenses to happiness. We will go together and rout him out. Cabs, cars, policemen, telephones and ministers shall aid us."

"Father Rogan shall marry us," said the girl, with ardour. "I will take you to him."

An hour later the two stood at the open doorway of an immense, gloomy brick building in a narrow and lonely street. The license was tight in Norah's hand.

"Wait here a moment," she said, "till I find Father Rogan."

She plunged into the black hallway, and the lover was left standing, as it were, on one leg, outside. His impatience was not greatly taxed. Gazing curiously into what seemed the hallway to Erebus, he was presently reassured by a stream of light that bisected the darkness, far down the passage. Then he heard her call, and fluttered lampward, like the moth. She beckoned him through a doorway into the room whence emanated the light. The room was bare of nearly everything except books, which had subjugated all its space. Here and there little spots of territory had been reconquered. An elderly, bald man, with a superlatively calm, remote eye, stood by a table with a book in his hand, his finger still marking a page. His dress was sombre and appertained to a religious order. His eye denoted an acquaintance with the perspective.

"Father Rogan," said Norah, "this is *he*."

"The two of ye," said Father Rogan, "want to get married?"

They did not deny it. He married them. The ceremony was quickly done. One who could have witnessed it, and felt its scope, might have trembled at the terrible inadequacy of it to rise to the dignity of its endless chain of results.

Afterward the priest spake briefly, as if by rote, of certain other civil and legal addenda that either might or should, at a later time, cap the ceremony. Lorison tendered a fee, which was declined, and before the door closed after the departing couple Father Rogan's book popped open again where his finger marked it.

In the dark hall Norah whirled and clung to her companion, tearful.

"Will you never, never be sorry?"

At last she was reassured.

At the first light they reached upon the street, she asked the time, just as she had each night. Lorison looked at his watch. Half-past eight.

Lorison thought it was from habit that she guided their steps toward the corner where they always parted. But, arrived there, she hesitated, and then released his arm. A drug store stood on the corner; its bright, soft light shone upon them.

"Please leave me here as usual to-night," said Norah, sweetly. "I must—I would rather you would. You will not object? At six to-morrow evening I will meet you at Antonio's. I want to sit with you there once more. And then—I will go where you say." She gave him a bewildering, bright smile, and walked swiftly away.

Surely it needed all the strength of her charm to carry off this astounding behaviour. It was no discredit to Lorison's strength of mind that his head began to whirl. Pocketing his hands, he rambled vacuously over to the druggist's windows, and began assiduously to spell over the names of the patent medicines therein displayed.

As soon as he had recovered his wits, he proceeded along the street in an aimless fashion. After drifting for two or three squares, he flowed into a somewhat more pretentious thoroughfare, a way much frequented by him in his solitary ramblings. For here was a row of shops devoted to traffic in goods of the widest range of choice—handiworks of art, skill and fancy, products of nature and labour from every zone.

Here, for a time, he loitered among the conspicuous windows, where was set, emphasized by congested floods of light, the cunningest spoil of the interiors. There were few passers, and of this Lorison was glad. He was not of the world. For a long time he had touched his fellow man only at the gear of a levelled cog-wheel—at right angles, and upon a different axis. He had dropped into a distinctly new orbit. The stroke of ill fortune had acted upon him, in effect, as a blow delivered upon the apex of a certain ingenious toy, the musical top, which, when thus buffeted while spinning, gives forth, with scarcely retarded motion, a complete change of key and chord.

Strolling along the pacific avenue, he experienced a singular, supernatural calm, accompanied by an unusual activity of brain. Reflecting upon recent affairs, he assured himself of his happiness in having won for a bride the one he had so greatly desired, yet he wondered mildly at his dearth of active emotion. Her strange behaviour in abandoning him without valid excuse on his bridal eve aroused in him only a vague and curious speculation. Again, he found himself contemplating, with complaisant serenity, the incidents of her somewhat lively career. His perspective seemed to have been queerly shifted.

As he stood before a window near a corner, his ears were assailed by a waxing clamour and commotion. He stood close to the window to allow passage to the cause of the hubbub—a procession of human beings, which rounded the corner and headed in his direction. He perceived a salient hue of blue and a glitter of brass about a central figure of dazzling white and silver, and a ragged wake of black, bobbing figures.

Two ponderous policemen were conducting between them a woman dressed as if for the stage, in a short, white, satiny skirt reaching to the knees, pink stockings, and a sort of sleeveless bodice bright with relucent, armour-like scales. Upon her curly, light hair was perched, at a rollicking angle, a shining tin helmet. The costume was to be instantly recognized as one of those amazing conceptions to which competition has harried the inventors of the spectacular ballet. One of the officers bore a long cloak upon his arm, which, doubtless, had been intended to veil the candid attractions of their effulgent prisoner, but, for some reason, it had not been called into use, to the vociferous delight of the tail of the procession.

Compelled by a sudden and vigorous movement of the woman, the parade halted before the window by which Lorison stood. He saw that she was young, and, at the first glance, was deceived by a sophistical prettiness of her face, which waned before a more judicious scrutiny. Her look was bold and reckless, and upon her countenance, where yet the contours of youth survived, were the fingermarks of old age's credentialed courier, Late Hours.

The young woman fixed her unshrinking gaze upon Lorison, and called to him in the voice of the wronged heroine in straits:

"Say! You look like a good fellow; come and put up the

bail, won't you? I've done nothing to get pinched for. It's all a mistake. See how they're treating me! You won't be sorry, if you'll help me out of this. Think of your sister or your girl being dragged along the streets this way! I say, come along now, like a good fellow."

It may be that Lorison, in spite of the unconvincing bathos of this appeal, showed a sympathetic face, for one of the officers left the woman's side, and went over to him.

"It's all right, sir," he said, in a husky, confidential tone; "she's the right party. We took her after the first act at the Green Light Theatre, on a wire from the chief of police of Chicago. It's only a square or two to the station. Her rig's pretty bad, but she refused to change clothes—or, rather," added the officer, with a smile, "to put on some. I thought I'd explain matters to you so you wouldn't think she was being imposed upon."

"What is the charge?" asked Lorison.

"Grand larceny. Diamonds. Her husband is a jeweller in Chicago. She cleaned his show case of the sparklers, and skipped with a comic-opera troupe."

The policeman, perceiving that the interest of the entire group of spectators was centred upon himself and Lorison—their conference being regarded as a possible new complication—was fain to prolong the situation—which reflected his own importance—by a little afterpiece of philosophical comment.

"A gentleman like you, sir," he went on affably, "would never notice it, but it comes in my line to observe what an immense amount of trouble is made by that combination—I mean the stage, diamonds and light-headed women who aren't satisfied with good homes. I tell you, sir, a man these days and nights wants to know what his women folks are up to."

The policeman smiled a good night, and returned to the side of his charge, who had been intently watching Lorison's face during the conversation, no doubt for some indication of his intention to render succour. Now, at the failure of the sign, and at the movement made to continue the ignominious progress, she abandoned hope, and addressed him thus, pointedly:

"You damn chalk-faced quitter! You was thinking of giving me a hand, but you let the cop talk you out of it the first word. You're a dandy to tie to. Say, if you ever get a girl, she'll have a picnic. Won't she work you to the queen's taste! Oh, my!" She concluded with a taunting, shrill laugh that rasped Lorison like a saw. The policemen urged her forward; the delighted train of gaping followers closed up the rear; and the captive Amazon, accepting her fate, extended the scope of her maledictions so that none in hearing might seem to be slighted.

Then there came upon Lorison an overwhelming revulsion of his perspective. It may be that he had been ripe for it, that the abnormal condition of mind in which he had for so long existed was already about to revert to its balance; however, it is certain that the events of the last few minutes had furnished the channel, if not the impetus, for the change.

The initial determining influence had been so small a thing as the fact and manner of his having been approached by the officer. That agent had, by the style of his accost, restored the loiterer to his former place in society. In an instant he had been transformed from a somewhat rancid prowler along the fishy side streets of gentility into an honest gentleman, with whom even so lordly a guardian of the peace might agreeably exchange the compliments.

This, then, first broke the spell, and set thrilling in him a resurrected longing for the fellowship of his kind, and the rewards of the virtuous. To what end, he vehemently asked himself, was this fanciful self-accusation, this empty renunciation, this moral squeamishness through which he had been led to abandon what was his heritage in life, and not beyond his deserts? Technically, he was uncondemned; his sole guilty spot was in thought rather than deed, and cognizance of it unshared by others. For what good, moral or sentimental, did he slink, retreating like the hedgehog from his own shadow, to and fro in this musty Bohemia that lacked even the picturesque?

But the thing that struck home and set him raging was the part played by the Amazonian prisoner. To the counterpart of that astounding belligerent—identical at least, in the way of experience—to one, by her own confession, thus far fallen, had he, not three hours since, been united in marriage. How desirable and natural it had seemed to him then, and how monstrous it seemed now! How the words of diamond thief number two yet burned in his ears: "If you ever get a girl, she'll have a picnic." What did that mean but that women instinctively knew him for one they could hoodwink? Still again, there reverberated the policeman's sapient contribution to his agony: "A man these days and nights wants to know what his women folks are up to." Oh, yes, he had been a fool; he had looked at things from the wrong standpoint.

But the wildest note in all the clamour was struck by pain's forefinger, jealousy. Now, at least, he felt that keenest sting—a mounting love unworthily bestowed. Whatever she might be, he loved her; he bore in his own breast his doom. A grating, comic flavour to his predicament struck him suddenly, and he laughed creakingly as he swung down the echoing pavement. An impetuous desire to act, to battle with his fate, seized him. He stopped upon his heel, and smote his palms together triumphantly. His wife was—where? But there was a tangible link; an outlet more or less navigable, through which his derelict ship of matrimony might yet be safely towed—the priest!

Like all imaginative men with pliable natures, Lorison was, when thoroughly stirred, apt to become tempestuous. With a high and stubborn indignation upon him, he retraced his steps to the intersecting street by which he had come. Down this he hurried to the corner where he had parted with—an astringent grimace tinctured the thought—his wife. Thence still back he harked, following through an unfamiliar district his stimulated recollections of the way they had come from that preposterous wedding. Many times he went abroad, and nosed his way back to the trail, furious.

At last, when he reached the dark, calamitous building in which his madness had culminated, and found the black hallway, he dashed down it, perceiving no light or sound. But he raised his voice, hailing loudly; reckless of everything but that he should find the old mischief-maker with the eyes that looked too far away to see the disaster he had wrought. The door opened, and in the stream of light Father Rogan stood, his book in hand, with his finger marking the place.

"Ah!" cried Lorison. "You are the man I want. I had a wife of you a few hours ago. I would not trouble you, but I neglected to note how it was done. Will you oblige me with the information whether the business is beyond remedy?"

"Come inside," said the priest; "there are other lodgers in the house, who might prefer sleep to even a gratified curiosity."

Lorison entered the room and took the chair offered him. The priest's eyes looked a courteous interrogation.

"I must apologize again," said the young man, "for so soon intruding upon you with my marital infelicities, but, as my wife has neglected to furnish me with her address, I am deprived of the legitimate recourse of a family row."

"I am quite a plain man," said Father Rogan, pleasantly; "but I do not see how I am to ask you questions."

"Pardon my indirectness," said Lorison; "I will ask one. In this room to-night you pronounced me to be a husband. You afterward spoke of additional rites or performances that either should or could be effected. I paid little attention to your words then, but I am hungry to hear them repeated now. As matters stand, am I married past all help?"

"You are as legally and as firmly bound," said the priest, "as though it had been done in a cathedral, in the presence of thousands. The additional observances I referred to are not necessary to the strictest legality of the act, but were advised as a precaution for the future—for convenience of proof in such contingencies as wills, inheritances and the like."

Lorison laughed harshly.

"Many thanks," he said. "Then there is no mistake, and I am the happy benedict. I suppose I should go stand upon the bridal corner, and when my wife gets through walking the streets she will look me up."

Father Rogan regarded him calmly.

"My son," he said, "when a man and woman come to me to be married I always marry them. I do this for the sake of other people whom they might go away and marry if they did not marry each other. As you see, I do not seek your confidence; but your case seems to me to be one not altogether devoid of interest. Very few marriages that have come to my notice have brought such well-expressed regret within so short a time. I will hazard one question: were you not under the impression that you loved the lady you married, at the time you did so?"

"Loved her!" cried Lorison, wildly. "Never so well as now, though she told me she deceived and sinned and stole. Never more than now, when, perhaps, she is laughing at the fool she cajoled and left, with scarcely a word, to return to God only knows what particular line of her former folly."

Father Rogan answered nothing. During the silence that succeeded, he sat with a quiet expectation beaming in his full, lambent eye.

"If you would listen——" began Lorison. The priest held up his hand.

"As I hoped," he said. "I thought you would trust me. Wait but a moment." He brought a long clay pipe, filled and lighted it.

"Now, my son," he said.

Lorison poured a twelvemonth's accumulated confidence into Father Rogan's ear. He told all; not sparing himself or omitting the facts of his past, the events of the night, or his disturbing conjectures and fears.

"The main point," said the priest, when he had concluded, "seems to me to be this—are you reasonably sure that you love this woman whom you have married?"

"Why," exclaimed Lorison, rising impulsively to his feet— "why should I deny it? But look at me—am I fish, flesh or fowl? That is the main point to me, I assure you."

"I understand you," said the priest, also rising, and laying down his pipe. "The situation is one that has taxed the endurance of much older men than you—in fact, especially much older men than you. I will try to relieve you from it, and this night. You shall see for yourself into exactly what predicament you have fallen, and how you shall, possibly, be extricated. There is no evidence so credible as that of the eyesight."

Father Rogan moved about the room, and donned a soft black hat. Buttoning his coat to his throat, he laid his hand on the doorknob. "Let us walk," he said.

The two went out upon the street. The priest turned his face down it, and Lorison walked with him through a squalid district, where the houses loomed, awry and desolate-looking, high above them. Presently they turned into a less dismal side street, where the houses were smaller, and, though hinting of the most meagre comfort, lacked the concentrated wretchedness of the more populous byways.

At a segregated, two-story house Father Rogan halted, and mounted the steps with the confidence of a familiar visitor.

He ushered Lorison into a narrow hallway, faintly lighted by a cobwebbed hanging lamp. Almost immediately a door to the right opened and a dingy Irishwoman protruded her head.

"Good evening to ye, Mistress Geehan," said the priest, unconsciously, it seemed, falling into a delicately flavoured brogue. "And is it yourself can tell me if Norah has gone out again, the night, maybe?"

"Oh, it's yer blissid riverence! Sure and I can tell ye the same. The purty darlin' wint out, as usual, but a bit later. And she says: 'Mother Geehan,' says she, 'it's me last noight out, praise the saints, this noight is!' And, oh, yer riverence, the swate, beautiful drame of a dress she had this toime! White satin and silk and ribbons, and lace about the neck and arrums—'twas a sin, yer riverence, the gold was spint upon it."

The priest heard Lorison catch his breath painfully, and a faint smile flickered across his own clean-cut mouth.

"Well, then, Mistress Geehan," said he, "I'll just step upstairs and see the bit boy for a minute, and I'll take this gentleman up with me."

"He's awake, thin," said the woman. "I've just come down from sitting wid him the last hour, tilling him fine shtories of ould County Tyrone. 'Tis a greedy gossoon, it is, yer riverence, for me shtories."

"Small the doubt," said Father Rogan. "There's no rocking would put him to slape the quicker, I'm thinking."

Amid the woman's shrill protest against the retort, the two men ascended the steep stairway. The priest pushed open the door of a room near its top.

"Is that you already, sister?" drawled a sweet, childish voice from the darkness.

"It's only ould Father Denny come to see ye, darlin'; and a foine gintleman I've brought to make ye a gr-r-and call. And ye resaves us fast aslape in bed! Shame on yez manners!"

"Oh, Father Denny, is that you? I'm glad. And will you light the lamp, please? It's on the table by the door. And quit talking like Mother Geehan, Father Denny."

The priest lit the lamp, and Lorison saw a tiny, towsled-haired boy, with a thin, delicate face, sitting up in a small bed in a corner. Quickly, also, his rapid glance considered the room and its contents. It was furnished with more than comfort, and its adornments plainly indicated a woman's discerning taste. An open door beyond revealed the blackness of an adjoining room's interior.

The boy clutched both of Father Rogan's hands. "I'm so glad you came," he said; "but why did you come in the night? Did sister send you?"

"Off wid ye! Am I to be sint about, at me age, as was Terence McShane, of Ballymahone? I come on me own r-r-responsibility."

Lorison had also advanced to the boy's bedside. He was fond of children; and the wee fellow, laying himself down to sleep alone in that dark room, stirred his heart.

"Aren't you afraid, little man?" he asked, stooping down beside him.

"Sometimes," answered the boy, with a shy smile, "when the rats make too much noise. But nearly every night, when sister goes out, Mother Geehan stays a while with me, and tells me funny stories. I'm not often afraid, sir."

"This brave little gentleman," said Father Rogan, "is a scholar of mine. Every day from half-past six to half-past eight—when sister comes for him—he stops in my study, and we find out what's in the inside of books. He knows multiplication, division and fractions; and he's throubling me to begin wid the chronicles of Ciaran of Clonmacnoise, Cormac McCullenan and Cuan O'Lochain, the gr-r-reat Irish histhorians." The boy was evidently accustomed to the priest's Celtic pleasantries. A little, appreciative grin was all the attention the insinuation of pedantry received.

Lorison, to have saved his life, could not have put to the child one of those vital questions that were wildly beating about, unanswered, in his own brain. The little fellow was very like Norah; he had the same shining hair and candid eyes.

"Oh, Father Denny," cried the boy, suddenly, "I forgot to tell you! Sister is not going away at night any more! She told me so when she kissed me good night as she was leaving. And she said she was so happy, and then she cried. Wasn't that queer? But I'm glad; aren't you?"

"Yes, lad. And now, ye omadhaun, go to sleep, and say good night; we must be going."

"Which shall I do first, Father Denny?"

"Faith, he's caught me again! Wait till I get the sassenach into the annals of Tageruach, the hagiographer; I'll give him enough of the Irish idiom to make him more respectful."

The light was out, and the small, brave voice bidding them good night from the dark room. They groped downstairs, and tore away from the garrulity of Mother Geehan.

Again the priest steered them through the dim ways, but this time in another direction. His conductor was serenely silent, and Lorison followed his example to the extent of seldom speaking. Serene he could not be. His heart beat suffocatingly in his breast. The following of this blind, menacing trail was pregnant with he knew not what humiliating revelation to be delivered at its end.

They came into a more pretentious street, where trade, it could be surmised, flourished by day. And again the priest paused; this time before a lofty building, whose great doors and windows in the lowest floor were carefully shuttered and barred. Its higher apertures were dark, save in the third story, the windows of which were brilliantly lighted. Lorison's ear caught a distant, regular, pleasing thrumming, as of music above. They stood at an angle of the building. Up, along the side nearest them, mounted an iron stairway. At its top was an upright, illuminated parallelogram. Father Rogan had stopped, and stood, musing.

"I will say this much," he remarked, thoughtfully: "I believe you to be a better man than you think yourself to be, and a better man than I thought some hours ago. But do not take this," he added, with a smile, "as much praise. I promised you a possible deliverance from an unhappy perplexity. I will have to modify that promise. I can only remove the mystery that enhanced that perplexity. Your deliverance depends upon yourself. Come."

He led his companion up the stairway. Halfway up, Lorison caught him by the sleeve. "Remember," he gasped, "I love that woman."

"You desired to know."

"I—— Go on."

The priest reached the landing at the top of the stairway. Lorison, behind him, saw that the illuminated space was the glass upper half of a door opening into the lighted room. The rhythmic music increased as they neared it; the stairs shook with the mellow vibrations.

Lorison stopped breathing when he set foot upon the highest step, for the priest stood aside, and motioned him to look through the glass of the door.

His eye, accustomed to the darkness, met first a blinding glare, and then he made out the faces and forms of many people, amid an extravagant display of splendid robings—billowy laces, brilliant-hued finery, ribbons, silks and misty drapery. And then he caught the meaning of that jarring hum, and he saw the tired, pale, happy face of his wife, bending, as were a score of others, over her sewing machine—toiling, toiling. Here was the folly she pursued, and the end of his quest.

But not his deliverance, though even then remorse struck him. His shamed soul fluttered once more before it retired to make room for the other and better one. For, to temper his thrill of joy, the shine of the satin and the glimmer of ornaments recalled the disturbing figure of the bespangled Amazon, and the base duplicate histories lit by the glare of footlights and stolen diamonds. It is past the wisdom of him who only sets the scenes, either to praise or blame the man. But this time his love overcame his scruples. He took a quick step, and reached out his hand for the doorknob. Father Rogan was quicker to arrest it and draw him back.

"You use my trust in you queerly," said the priest sternly. "What are you about to do?"

"I am going to my wife," said Lorison. "Let me pass."

"Listen," said the priest, holding him firmly by the arm. "I am about to put you in possession of a piece of knowledge of which, thus far, you have scarcely proved deserving. I do not think you ever will; but I will not dwell upon that. You see in that room the woman you married, working for a frugal living for herself, and a generous comfort for an idolized brother. This building belongs to the chief costumer of the city. For months the advance orders for the coming Mardi Gras festivals have kept the work going day and night. I myself secured employment here for Norah. She toils here each night from nine o'clock until daylight, and, besides, carries home with her some of the finer costumes, requiring more delicate needlework, and works there part of the day. Somehow, you two have remained strangely ignorant of each other's lives. Are you convinced now that your wife is not walking the streets?"

"Let me go to her," cried Lorison, again struggling, "and beg her forgiveness!"

"Sir," said the priest, "do you owe me nothing? Be quiet. It seems so often that Heaven lets fall its choicest gifts into hands that must be taught to hold them. Listen again. You forgot that repentant sin must not compromise, but look up, for redemption, to the purest and best. You went to her with the fine-spun sophistry that peace could be found in a mutual guilt; and she, fearful of losing what her heart so craved, thought it worth the price to buy it with a desperate, pure, beautiful lie. I have known her since the day she was born; she is as innocent and unsullied in life and deed as a holy saint. In that lowly street where she dwells she first saw the light, and she has lived there ever since, spending her days in generous self-sacrifice for others. Och, ye spalpeen!" continued Father Rogan, raising his finger in kindly anger at Lorison. "What for, I wonder, could she be afther making a fool of hersilf, and shamin' her swate soul with lies, for the like of you!"

"Sir," said Lorison, trembling, "say what you please of me. Doubt it as you must, I will yet prove my gratitude to you, and my devotion to her. But let me speak to her once now, let me kneel for just one moment at her feet, and——"

"Tut, tut!" said the priest. "How many acts of a love drama do you think an old bookworm like me capable of witnessing? Besides, what kind of figures do we cut, spying upon the mysteries of midnight millinery! Go to meet your wife to-morrow, as she ordered you, and obey her thereafter, and maybe some time I shall get forgiveness for the part I have played in this night's work. Off wid yez down the shtairs, now! 'Tis late, and an ould man like me should be takin' his rest."

The Ransom of Red Chief

IT LOOKED like a good thing: but wait till I tell you. We were down South, in Alabama—Bill Driscoll and myself—when this kidnapping idea struck us. It was, as Bill afterward expressed it, "during a moment of temporary mental apparition"; but we didn't find that out till later.

There was a town down there, as flat as a flannel-cake, and called Summit, of course. It contained inhabitants of as undeleterious and self-satisfied a class of peasantry as ever clustered around a Maypole.

Bill and me had a joint capital of about six hundred dollars, and we needed just two thousand dollars more to pull off a fraudulent town-lot scheme in Western Illinois with. We talked it over on the front steps of the hotel. Philoprogenitiveness, says we, is strong in semi-rural communities; therefore, and for other reasons, a kidnapping project ought to do better there than in the radius of newspapers that send reporters out in plain clothes to stir up talk about such things. We knew that Summit couldn't get after us with anything stronger than constables and, maybe, some lackadaisical bloodhounds and a diatribe or two in the *Weekly Farmers' Budget*. So, it looked good.

We selected for our victim the only child of a prominent citizen named Ebenezer Dorset. The father was respectable and tight, a mortgage fancier and a stern, upright collection-plate passer and forecloser. The kid was a boy of ten, with bas-relief freckles, and hair the colour of the cover of the magazine you buy at the news-stand when you want to catch a train. Bill and me figured that Ebenezer would melt down for a ransom of two thousand dollars to a cent. But wait till I tell you.

About two miles from Summit was a little mountain, covered with a dense cedar brake. On the rear elevation of this mountain was a cave. There we stored provisions.

One evening after sundown, we drove in a buggy past old Dorset's house. The kid was in the street, throwing rocks at a kitten on the opposite fence.

"Hey, little boy!" says Bill, "would you like to have a bag of candy and a nice ride?"

The boy catches Bill neatly in the eye with a piece of brick.

"That will cost the old man an extra five hundred dollars," says Bill, climbing over the wheel.

That boy put up a fight like a welter-weight cinnamon bear; but, at last, we got him down in the bottom of the buggy and drove away. We took him up to the cave, and I hitched the horse in the cedar brake. After dark I drove the buggy to the little village, three miles away, where we had hired it, and walked back to the mountain.

Bill was pasting court-plaster over the scratches and bruises on his features. There was a fire burning behind the big rock at the entrance of the cave, and the boy was watching a pot of boiling coffee, with two buzzard tail-feathers stuck in his red hair. He points a stick at me when I come up, and says:

"Ha! cursed paleface, do you dare to enter the camp of Red Chief, the terror of the plains?"

"He's all right now," says Bill, rolling up his trousers and examining some bruises on his shins. "We're playing Indian. We're making Buffalo Bill's show look like magic-lantern views of Palestine in the town hall. I'm Old Hank, the Trapper, Red Chief's captive, and I'm to be scalped at daybreak. By Geronimo! that kid can kick hard."

Yes, sir, that boy seemed to be having the time of his life. The fun of camping out in a cave had made him forget that he was a captive himself. He immediately christened me Snake-eye, the Spy, and announced that, when his braves returned from the warpath, I was to be broiled at the stake at the rising of the sun.

Then we had supper; and he filled his mouth full of bacon and bread and gravy, and began to talk. He made a during-dinner speech something like this:

"I like this fine. I never camped out before; but I had a pet 'possum once, and I was nine last birthday. I hate to go to school. Rats ate up sixteen of Jimmy Talbot's aunt's speckled hen's eggs. Are there any real Indians in these woods? I want some more gravy. Does the trees moving make the wind blow? We had five puppies. What makes your nose so red, Hank? My father has lots of money. Are the stars hot? I whipped Ed Walker twice, Saturday. I don't like girls. You dassent catch toads unless with a string. Do oxen make any noise? Why are oranges round? Have you got beds to sleep on in this cave?

Amos Murray has got six toes. A parrot can talk, but a monkey or a fish can't. How many does it take to make twelve?"

Every few minutes he would remember that he was a pesky redskin, and pick up his stick rifle and tiptoe to the mouth of the cave to rubber for the scouts of the hated paleface. Now and then he would let out a war-whoop that made Old Hank the Trapper, shiver. That boy had Bill terrorized from the start.

"Red Chief," says I to the kid, "would you like to go home?"

"Aw, what for?" says he. "I don't have any fun at home. I hate to go to school. I like to camp out. You won't take me back home again, Snake-eye, will you?"

"Not right away," says I. "We'll stay here in the cave a while."

"All right!" says he. "That'll be fine. I never had such fun in all my life."

We went to bed about eleven o'clock. We spread down some wide blankets and quilts and put Red Chief between us. We weren't afraid he'd run away. He kept us awake for three hours, jumping up and reaching for his rifle and screeching: "Hist! pard," in mine and Bill's ears, as the fancied crackle of a twig or the rustle of a leaf revealed to his young imagination the stealthy approach of the outlaw band. At last, I fell into a troubled sleep, and dreamed that I had been kidnapped and chained to a tree by a ferocious pirate with red hair.

Just at daybreak, I was awakened by a series of awful screams from Bill. They weren't yells, or howls, or shouts, or whoops, or yawps, such as you'd expect from a manly set of vocal organs— they were simply indecent, terrifying, humiliating screams, such as women emit when they see ghosts or caterpillars. It's an awful thing to hear a strong, desperate, fat man scream incontinently in a cave at daybreak.

I jumped up to see what the matter was. Red Chief was sitting on Bill's chest, with one hand twined in Bill's hair. In the other he had the sharp case-knife we used for slicing bacon; and he was industriously and realistically trying to take Bill's scalp, according to the sentence that had been pronounced upon him the evening before.

I got the knife away from the kid and made him lie down again. But, from that moment, Bill's spirit was broken. He laid down on his side of the bed, but he never closed an eye again in sleep as long as that boy was with us. I dozed off for a while, but along toward sun-up I remembered that Red Chief had said I was to be burned at the stake at the rising of the sun. I wasn't nervous or afraid; but I sat up and lit my pipe and leaned against a rock.

"What you getting up so soon for, Sam?" asked Bill.

"Me?" says I. "Oh, I got a kind of a pain in my shoulder. I thought sitting up would rest it."

"You're a liar!" says Bill. "You're afraid. You was to be burned at sunrise, and you was afraid he'd do it. And he would, too, if he could find a match. Ain't it awful, Sam? Do you think anybody will pay out money to get a little imp like that back home?"

"Sure," said I. "A rowdy kid like that is just the kind that parents dote on. Now, you and the Chief get up and cook breakfast, while I go up on the top of this mountain and reconnoitre."

I went up on the peak of the little mountain and ran my eye over the contiguous vicinity. Over toward Summit I expected to see the sturdy yeomanry of the village armed with scythes and pitchforks beating the countryside for the dastardly kidnappers. But what I saw was a peaceful landscape dotted with one man ploughing with a dun mule. Nobody was dragging the creek; no couriers dashed hither and yon, bringing tidings of no news to the distracted parents. There was a sylvan attitude of somnolent sleepiness pervading that section of the external outward surface of Alabama that lay exposed to my view. "Perhaps," says I to myself, "it has not yet been discovered that the wolves have borne away the tender lambkin from the fold. Heaven help the wolves!" says I, and I went down the mountain to breakfast.

When I got to the cave I found Bill backed up against the side of it, breathing hard, and the boy threatening to smash him with a rock half as big as a cocoanut.

"He put a red-hot boiled potato down my back," explained Bill, "and then mashed it with his foot; and I boxed his ears. Have you got a gun about you, Sam?"

I took the rock away from the boy and kind of patched up the argument. "I'll fix you," says the kid to Bill. "No man ever yet struck the Red Chief but what he got paid for it. You better beware!"

After breakfast the kid takes a piece of leather with strings wrapped around it out of his pocket and goes outside the cave unwinding it.

"What's he up to now?" says Bill, anxiously. "You don't think he'll run away, do you, Sam?"

"No fear of it," says I. "He don't seem to be much of a home body. But we've got to fix up some plan about the ransom. There don't seem to be much excitement around Summit on account of his disappearance; but maybe they haven't realized yet that he's gone. His folks may think he's spending the night with Aunt Jane or one of the neighbours. Anyhow, he'll be missed to-day. To-night we must get a message to his father demanding the two thousand dollars for his return."

Just then we heard a kind of war-whoop, such as David might have emitted when he knocked out the champion Goliath. It was a sling that Red Chief had pulled out of his pocket, and he was whirling it around his head.

I dodged, and heard a heavy thud and a kind of a sigh from Bill, like a horse gives out when you take his saddle off. A nigger-head rock the size of an egg had caught Bill just behind his left ear. He loosened himself all over and fell in the fire across the frying pan of hot water for washing the dishes. I dragged him out and poured cold water on his head for half an hour.

By and by, Bill sits up and feels behind his ear and says: "Sam, do you know who my favourite Biblical character is?"

"Take it easy," says I. "You'll come to your senses presently."

"King Herod," says he. "You won't go away and leave me here alone, will you, Sam?"

I went out and caught that boy and shook him until his freckles rattled.

"If you don't behave," says I, "I'll take you straight home. Now, are you going to be good, or not?"

"I was only funning," says he sullenly. "I didn't mean to hurt Old Hank. But what did he hit me for? I'll behave, Snake-eye, if you won't send me home, and if you'll let me play the Black Scout to-day."

"I don't know the game," says I. "That's for you and Mr. Bill to decide. He's your playmate for the day. I'm going away for a while, on business. Now, you come in and make friends with him and say you are sorry for hurting him, or home you go, at once."

I made him and Bill shake hands, and then I took Bill aside and told him I was going to Poplar Cove, a little village three miles from the cave, and find out what I could about how the kidnapping had been regarded in Summit. Also, I thought it best to send a peremptory letter to old man Dorset that day, demanding the ransom and dictating how it should be paid.

"You know, Sam," says Bill, "I've stood by you without batting an eye in earthquakes, fire and flood—in poker games, dynamite outrages, police raids, train robberies and cyclones. I never lost my nerve yet till we kidnapped that two-legged skyrocket of a kid. He's got me going. You won't leave me long with him, will you, Sam?"

"I'll be back some time this afternoon," says I. "You must keep the boy amused and quiet till I return. And now we'll write the letter to old Dorset."

Bill and I got paper and pencil and worked on the letter while Red Chief, with a blanket wrapped around him, strutted up and down, guarding the mouth of the cave. Bill begged me tearfully to make the ransom fifteen hundred dollars instead of two thousand. "I ain't attempting," says he, "to decry the celebrated moral aspect of parental affection, but we're dealing with humans, and it ain't human for anybody to give up two thousand dollars for that forty-pound chunk of freckled wildcat. I'm willing to take a chance at fifteen hundred dollars. You can charge the difference up to me."

So, to relieve Bill, I acceded, and we collaborated a letter that ran this way:

Ebenezer Dorset, Esq.:
   We have your boy concealed in a place far from Summit. It is useless for you or the most skilful detectives to attempt to find him. Absolutely, the only terms on which you can have him restored to you are these: We demand fifteen hundred dollars in large bills for his return; the money to be left at midnight to-night at the same spot and in the same box as your reply—as hereinafter described. If you agree to these terms, send your answer in writing by a solitary messenger to-night at half-past eight o'clock. After crossing Owl Creek, on the road to Poplar Cove, there are three large trees about a hundred yards apart, close to the fence of the wheat field on the right-hand side. At the bottom

of the fence-post, opposite the third tree, will be found a small pasteboard box.

The messenger will place the answer in this box and return immediately to Summit.

If you attempt any treachery or fail to comply with our demand as stated, you will never see your boy again.

If you pay the money as demanded, he will be returned to you safe and well within three hours. These terms are final, and if you do not accede to them no further communication will be attempted.

Two Desperate Men.

I addressed this letter to Dorset, and put it in my pocket. As I was about to start, the kid comes up to me and says:

"Aw, Snake-eye, you said I could play the Black Scout while you was gone."

"Play it, of course," says I. "Mr. Bill will play with you. What kind of a game is it?"

"I'm the Black Scout," says Red Chief, "and I have to ride to the stockade to warn the settlers that the Indians are coming. I'm tired of playing Indian myself. I want to be the Black Scout."

"All right," says I. "It sounds harmless to me. I guess Mr. Bill will help you foil the pesky savages."

"What am I to do?" asks Bill, looking at the kid suspiciously.

"You are the hoss," says Black Scout. "Get down on your hands and knees. How can I ride to the stockade without a hoss?"

"You'd better keep him interested," said I, "till we get the scheme going. Loosen up."

Bill gets down on his all fours, and a look comes in his eye like a rabbit's when you catch it in a trap.

"How far is it to the stockade, kid?" he asks, in a husky manner of voice.

"Ninety miles," says the Black Scout. "And you have to hump yourself to get there on time. Whoa, now!"

The Black Scout jumps on Bill's back and digs his heels in his side.

"For Heaven's sake," says Bill, "hurry back, Sam, as soon as you can. I wish we hadn't made the ransom more than a thousand. Say, you quit kicking me or I'll get up and warm you good."

I walked over to Poplar Cove and sat around the post-office and store, talking with the chawbacons that came in to trade. One whiskerando says that he hears Summit is all upset on account of Elder Ebenezer Dorset's boy having been lost or stolen. That was all I wanted to know. I bought some smoking tobacco, referred casually to the price of black-eyed peas, posted my letter surreptitiously and came away. The postmaster said the mail-carrier would come by in an hour to take the mail on to Summit.

When I got back to the cave Bill and the boy were not to be found. I explored the vicinity of the cave, and risked a yodel or two, but there was no response.

So I lighted my pipe and sat down on a mossy bank to await developments.

In about half an hour I heard the bushes rustle, and Bill wabbled out into the little glade in front of the cave. Behind him was the kid, stepping softly like a scout, with a broad grin on his face. Bill stopped, took off his hat and wiped his face with a red handkerchief. The kid stopped about eight feet behind him.

"Sam," says Bill, "I suppose you'll think I'm a renegade, but I couldn't help it. I'm a grown person with masculine proclivities and habits of self-defense, but there is a time when all systems of egotism and predominance fail. The boy is gone. I have sent him home. All is off. There was martyrs in old times," goes on Bill, "that suffered death rather than give up the particular graft they enjoyed. None of 'em ever was subjugated to such supernatural tortures as I have been. I tried to be faithful to our articles of depredation; but there came a limit."

"What's the trouble, Bill?" I asks him.

"I was rode," says Bill, "the ninety miles to the stockade, not barring an inch. Then, when the settlers was rescued, I was given oats. Sand ain't a palatable substitute. And then, for an hour I had to try to explain to him why there was nothin' in holes, how a road can run both ways and what makes the grass green. I tell you, Sam, a human can only stand so much. I takes him by the neck of his clothes and drags him down the mountain. On the way he kicks my legs black-and-blue from the knees down; and I've got to have two or three bites on my thumb and hand cauterized.

"But he's gone"—continues Bill—"gone home. I showed him the road to Summit and kicked him about eight feet nearer there at one kick. I'm sorry we lose the ransom; but it was either that or Bill Driscoll to the madhouse."

Bill is puffing and blowing, but there is a look of ineffable peace and growing content on his rose-pink features.

"Bill," says I, "there isn't any heart disease in your family, is there?"

"No," says Bill, "nothing chronic except malaria and accidents. Why?"

"Then you might turn around," says I, "and have a look behind you."

Bill turns and sees the boy, and loses his complexion and sits down plump on the ground and begins to pluck aimlessly at grass and little sticks. For an hour I was afraid for his mind. And then I told him that my scheme was to put the whole job through immediately and that we would get the ransom and be off with it by midnight if old Dorset fell in with our proposition. So Bill braced up enough to give the kid a weak sort of a smile and a promise to play the Russian in a Japanese war with him as soon as he felt a little better.

I had a scheme for collecting that ransom without danger of being caught by counterplots that ought to commend itself to professional kidnappers. The tree under which the answer was to be left—and the money later on—was close to the road fence with big, bare fields on all sides. If a gang of constables should be watching for any one to come for the note they could see him a long way off crossing the fields or in the road. But no, sirree! At half-past eight I was up in that tree as well hidden as a tree toad, waiting for the messenger to arrive.

Exactly on time, a half-grown boy rides up the road on a bicycle, locates the pasteboard box at the foot of the fence-post, slips a folded piece of paper into it and pedals away again back toward Summit.

I waited an hour and then concluded the thing was square. I slid down the tree, got the note, slipped along the fence till I struck the woods, and was back at the cave in another half an hour. I opened the note, got near the lantern and read it to Bill. It was written with a pen in a crabbed hand, and the sum and substance of it was this:

Two Desperate Men.
   Gentlemen: I received your letter to-day by post, in regard to the ransom you ask for the return of my son. I think you are a little high in your demands, and I hereby make you a counter-proposition, which I am inclined to believe you will accept. You bring Johnny home and pay me two hundred and fifty dollars in cash, and I agree to take him off your hands. You had better come at night, for the neighbours believe he is lost, and I couldn't be responsible for what they would do to anybody they saw bringing him back.   Very respectfully,
                                         EBENEZER DORSET.

"Great pirates of Penzance!" says I; "of all the impudent——"

But I glanced at Bill, and hesitated. He had the most appealing look in his eyes I ever saw on the face of a dumb or a talking brute.

"Sam," says he, "what's two hundred and fifty dollars, after all? We've got the money. One more night of this kid will send me to a bed in Bedlam. Besides being a thorough gentleman, I think Mr. Dorset is a spendthrift for making us such a liberal offer. You ain't going to let the chance go, are you?"

"Tell you the truth, Bill," says I, "this little he ewe lamb has somewhat got on my nerves too. We'll take him home, pay the ransom and make our get-away."

We took him home that night. We got him to go by telling him that his father had bought a silver-mounted rifle and a pair of moccasins for him, and we were going to hunt bears the next day.

It was just twelve o'clock when we knocked at Ebenezer's front door. Just at the moment when I should have been abstracting the fifteen hundred dollars from the box under the tree, according to the original proposition, Bill was counting out two hundred and fifty dollars into Dorset's hand.

When the kid found out we were going to leave him at home he started up a howl like a calliope and fastened himself as tight as a leech to Bill's leg. His father peeled him away gradually, like a porous plaster.

"How long can you hold him?" asks Bill.

"I'm not as strong as I used to be," says old Dorset, "but I think I can promise you ten minutes."

"Enough," says Bill. "In ten minutes I shall cross the Central, Southern and Middle Western States, and be legging it trippingly for the Canadian border."

And, as dark as it was, and as fat as Bill was, and as good a runner as I am, he was a good mile and a half out of Summit before I could catch up with him.

A Municipal Report

> The cities are full of pride,
>   Challenging each to each—
> This from her mountainside,
>   That from her burthened beach.
>
>   R. KIPLING.

Fancy a novel about Chicago or Buffalo, let us say, or Nashville, Tennessee! There are just three big cities in the United States that are "story cities"—New York, of course, New Orleans, and, best of the lot, San Francisco. —FRANK NORRIS.

EAST IS East, and West is San Francisco, according to Californians. Californians are a race of people; they are not merely inhabitants of a State. They are the Southerners of the West. Now, Chicagoans are no less loyal to their city; but when you ask them why, they stammer and speak of lake fish and the new Odd Fellows Building. But Californians go into detail.

Of course they have, in the climate, an argument that is good for half an hour while you are thinking of your coal bills and heavy underwear. But as soon as they come to mistake your silence for conviction, madness comes upon them, and they picture the city of the Golden Gate as the Bagdad of the New World. So far, as a matter of opinion, no refutation is necessary. But, dear cousins all (from Adam and Eve descended), it is a rash one who will lay his finger on the map and say: "In this town there can be no romance—what could happen here?" Yes, it is a bold and a rash deed to challenge in one sentence history, romance, and Rand and McNally.

> NASHVILLE.—A city, port of delivery, and the capital of the State of Tennessee, is on the Cumberland River and on the N. C. & St. L. and the L. & N. railroads. This city is regarded as the most important educational centre in the South.

I stepped off the train at 8 P.M. Having searched the thesaurus in vain for adjectives, I must, as a substitution, hie me to comparison in the form of a recipe.

Take of London fog 30 parts; malaria 10 parts; gas leaks 20 parts; dewdrops gathered in a brick yard at sunrise, 25 parts; odor of honeysuckle 15 parts. Mix.

The mixture will give you an approximate conception of a Nashville drizzle. It is not so fragrant as a moth-ball nor as thick as pea-soup; but 'tis enough—'twill serve.

I went to a hotel in a tumbril. It required strong self-suppression for me to keep from climbing to the top of it and giving an imitation of Sidney Carton. The vehicle was drawn by beasts of a bygone era and driven by something dark and emancipated.

I was sleepy and tired, so when I got to the hotel I hurriedly paid it the fifty cents it demanded (with approximate lagniappe, I assure you). I knew its habits; and I did not want to hear it prate about its old "marster" or anything that happened "befo' de wah."

The hotel was one of the kind described as "renovated." That means $20,000 worth of new marble pillars, tiling, electric lights and brass cuspidors in the lobby, and a new L. & N. time table and a lithograph of Lookout Mountain in each one of the great rooms above. The management was without reproach, the attention full of exquisite Southern courtesy, the service as slow as the progress of a snail and as good-humored as Rip Van Winkle. The food was worth traveling a thousand miles for. There is no other hotel in the world where you can get such chicken livers *en brochette*.

At dinner I asked a Negro waiter if there was anything doing in town. He pondered gravely for a minute, and then replied: "Well, boss, I don't really reckon there's anything at all doin' after sundown."

Sundown had been accomplished; it had been drowned in the drizzle long before. So that spectacle was denied me. But I went forth upon the streets in the drizzle to see what might be there.

> It is built on undulating grounds; and the streets are lighted by electricity at a cost of $32,470 per annum.

As I left the hotel there was a race riot. Down upon me charged a company of freedmen, or Arabs, or Zulus, armed with—no, I saw with relief that they were not rifles, but whips.

And I saw dimly a caravan of black, clumsy vehicles; and at the reassuring shouts, "Kyar you anywhere in the town, boss, fuh fifty cents," I reasoned that I was merely a "fare" instead of a victim.

I walked through long streets, all leading uphill. I wondered how those streets ever came down again. Perhaps they didn't until they were "graded." On a few of the "main streets" I saw lights in stores here and there; saw street cars go by conveying worthy burghers hither and yon; saw people pass engaged in the art of conversation, and heard a burst of semi-lively laughter issuing from a soda-water and ice-cream parlor. The streets other than "main" seemed to have enticed upon their borders houses consecrated to peace and domesticity. In many of them lights shone behind discreetly drawn window shades; in a few pianos tinkled orderly and irreproachable music. There was, indeed, little "doing." I wished I had come before sundown. So I returned to my hotel.

> In November, 1864, the Confederate General Hood advanced against Nashville, where he shut up a National force under General Thomas. The latter then sallied forth and defeated the Confederates in a terrible conflict.

All my life I have heard of, admired, and witnessed the fine marksmanship of the South in its peaceful conflicts in the tobacco-chewing regions. But in my hotel a surprise awaited me. There were twelve bright, new, imposing, capacious brass cuspidors in the great lobby, tall enough to be called urns and so wide-mouthed that the crack pitcher of a lady baseball team should have been able to throw a ball into one of them at five paces distant. But, although a terrible battle had raged and was still raging, the enemy had not suffered. Bright, new, imposing, capacious, untouched, they stood. But, shades of Jefferson Brick! the tile floor—the beautiful tile floor! I could not avoid thinking of the battle of Nashville, and trying to draw, as is my foolish habit, some deductions about hereditary marksmanship.

Here I first saw Major (by misplaced courtesy) Wentworth Caswell. I knew him for a type the moment my eyes suffered from the sight of him. A rat has no geographical habitat. My old friend, A. Tennyson, said, as he so well said almost everything:

Prophet, curse me the blabbing lip,
And curse me the British vermin, the rat.

Let us regard the word "British" as interchangeable *ad lib*.
A rat is a rat.

This man was hunting about the hotel lobby like a starved
dog that had forgotten where he had buried a bone. He had
a face of great acreage, red, pulpy, and with a kind of sleepy
massiveness like that of Buddha. He possessed one single
virtue—he was very smoothly shaven. The mark of the beast is
not indelible upon a man until he goes about with a stubble.
I think that if he had not used his razor that day I would have
repulsed his advances, and the criminal calendar of the world
would have been spared the addition of one murder.

I happened to be standing within five feet of a cuspidor
when Major Caswell opened fire upon it. I had been observant
enough to perceive that the attacking force was using Gatlings
instead of squirrel rifles; so I sidestepped so promptly that the
major seized the opportunity to apologize to a noncombatant.
He had the blabbing lip. In four minutes he had become my
friend and had dragged me to the bar.

I desire to interpolate here that I am a Southerner. But I
am not one by profession or trade. I eschew the string tie,
the slouch hat, the Prince Albert, the number of bales of
cotton destroyed by Sherman, and plug chewing. When the
orchestra plays Dixie I do not cheer. I slide a little lower on the
leather-cornered seat and, well, order another Würzburger and
wish that Longstreet had—but what's the use?

Major Caswell banged the bar with his fist, and the first
gun at Fort Sumter re-echoed. When he fired the last one at
Appomattox I began to hope. But then he began on family
trees, and demonstrated that Adam was only a third cousin of
a collateral branch of the Caswell family. Genealogy disposed
of, he took up, to my distaste, his private family matters. He
spoke of his wife, traced her descent back to Eve, and profanely
denied any possible rumor that she may have had relations in
the land of Nod.

By this time I began to suspect that he was trying to obscure
by noise the fact that he had ordered the drinks, on the chance
that I would be bewildered into paying for them. But when

they were down he crashed a silver dollar loudly upon the bar. Then, of course, another serving was obligatory. And when I had paid for that I took leave of him brusquely; for I wanted no more of him. But before I had obtained my release he had prated loudly of an income that his wife received, and showed a handful of silver money.

When I got my key at the desk the clerk said to me courteously: "If that man Caswell has annoyed you, and if you would like to make a complaint, we will have him ejected. He is a nuisance, a loafer, and without any known means of support, although he seems to have some money most the time. But we don't seem to be able to hit upon any means of throwing him out legally."

"Why, no," said I, after some reflection; "I don't see my way clear to making a complaint. But I would like to place myself on record as asserting that I do not care for his company. Your town," I continued, "seems to be a quiet one. What manner of entertainment, adventure, or excitement have you to offer to the stranger within your gates?"

"Well, sir," said the clerk, "there will be a show here next Thursday. It is—I'll look it up and have the announcement sent up to your room with the ice water. Good night."

After I went up to my room I looked out the window. It was only about ten o'clock, but I looked upon a silent town. The drizzle continued, spangled with dim lights, as far apart as currants in a cake sold at the Ladies' Exchange.

"A quiet place," I said to myself, as my first shoe struck the ceiling of the occupant of the room beneath mine. "Nothing of the life here that gives color and variety to the cities in the East and West. Just a good, ordinary, humdrum, business town."

Nashville occupies a foremost place among the manufacturing centres of the country. It is the fifth boot and shoe market in the United States, the largest candy and cracker manufacturing city in the South, and does an enormous wholesale drygoods, grocery, and drug business.

I must tell you how I came to be in Nashville, and I assure you the digression brings as much tedium to me as it does to you. I was traveling elsewhere on my own business, but I had a commission from a Northern literary magazine to stop over there and establish a personal connection between the publication and one of its contributors, Azalea Adair.

Adair (there was no clue to the personality except the handwriting) had sent in some essays (lost art!) and poems that had made the editors swear approvingly over their one o'clock luncheon. So they had commissioned me to round up said Adair and corner by contract his or her output at two cents a word before some other publisher offered her ten or twenty.

At nine o'clock the next morning, after my chicken livers *en brochette* (try them if you can find that hotel), I strayed out into the drizzle, which was still on for an unlimited run. At the first corner I came upon Uncle Cæsar. He was a stalwart Negro, older than the pyramids, with gray wool and a face that reminded me of Brutus, and a second afterwards of the late King Cettiwayo. He wore the most remarkable coat that I ever had seen or expect to see. It reached to his ankles and had once been a Confederate gray in colors. But rain and sun and age had so variegated it that Joseph's coat, beside it, would have faded to a pale monochrome. I must linger with that coat, for it has to do with the story—the story that is so long in coming, because you can hardly expect anything to happen in Nashville.

Once it must have been the military coat of an officer. The cape of it had vanished, but all adown its front it had been frogged and tasseled magnificently. But now the frogs and tassels were gone. In their stead had been patiently stitched (I surmised by some surviving "black mammy") new frogs made of cunningly twisted common hempen twine. This twine was frayed and disheveled. It must have been added to the coat as a substitute for vanished splendors, with tasteless but painstaking devotion, for it followed faithfully the curves of the long-missing frogs. And, to complete the comedy and pathos of the garment, all its buttons were gone save one. The second button from the top alone remained. The coat was fastened by other twine strings tied through the buttonholes and other holes rudely pierced in the opposite side. There was never such a weird garment so fantastically bedecked and of so many mottled hues. The lone button was the size of a half-dollar, made of yellow horn and sewed on with coarse twine.

This Negro stood by a carriage so old that Ham himself might have started a hack line with it after he left the ark with the two animals hitched to it. As I approached he threw open the door, drew out a feather duster, waved it without using it, and said in deep, rumbling tones:

"Step right in, suh; ain't a speck of dust in it—jus' got back from a funeral, suh."

I inferred that on such gala occasions carriages were given an extra cleaning. I looked up and down the street and perceived that there was little choice among the vehicles for hire that lined the curb. I looked in my memorandum book for the address of Azalea Adair.

"I want to go to 861 Jessamine Street," I said, and was about to step into the hack. But for an instant the thick, long, gorilla-like arm of the old Negro barred me. On his massive and saturnine face a look of sudden suspicion and enmity flashed for a moment. Then, with quickly returning conviction, he asked blandishingly: "What are you gwine there for, boss?"

"What is that to you?" I asked, a little sharply.

"Nothin', suh, jus' nothin'. Only it's a lonesome kind of part of town and few folks ever has business out there. Step right in. The seats is clean—jes' got back from a funeral, suh."

A mile and a half it must have been to our journey's end. I could hear nothing but the fearful rattle of the ancient hack over the uneven brick paving; I could smell nothing but the drizzle, now further flavored with coal smoke and something like a mixture of tar and oleander blossoms. All I could see through the streaming windows were two rows of dim houses.

The city has an area of 10 square miles; 181 miles of streets, of which 137 miles are paved; a system of waterworks that cost $2,000,000, with 77 miles of mains.

Eight-sixty-one Jessamine Street was a decayed mansion. Thirty yards back from the street it stood, outmerged in a splendid grove of trees and untrimmed shrubbery. A row of box bushes overflowed and almost hid the paling fence from sight; the gate was kept closed by a rope noose that encircled the gate post and the first paling of the gate. But when you got inside you saw that 861 was a shell, a shadow, a ghost of former grandeur and excellence. But in the story, I have not yet got inside.

When the hack had ceased from rattling and the weary

quadrupeds came to a rest I handed my jehu his fifty cents with an additional quarter, feeling a glow of conscious generosity, as I did so. He refused it.

"It's two dollars, suh," he said.

"How's that?" I asked. "I plainly heard you call out at the hotel: 'Fifty cents to any part of the town.'"

"It's two dollars, suh," he repeated obstinately. "It's a long ways from the hotel."

"It is within the city limits and well within them," I argued. "Don't think that you have picked up a greenhorn Yankee. Do you see those hills over there?" I went on, pointing toward the east (I could not see them, myself, for the drizzle); "well, I was born and raised on their other side. You old fool nigger, can't you tell people from other people when you see 'em?"

The grim face of King Cettiwayo softened. "Is you from the South, suh? I reckon it was them shoes of yourn fooled me. They is somethin' sharp in the toes for a Southern gen'l'man to wear."

"Then the charge is fifty cents, I suppose?" said I inexorably.

His former expression, a mingling of cupidity and hostility, returned, remained ten seconds, and vanished.

"Boss," he said, "fifty cents is right; but I *needs* two dollars, suh; I'm *obleeged* to have two dollars. I ain't *demandin'* it now, suh; after I knows whar you's from; I'm jus' sayin' that I *has* to have two dollars to-night, and business is mighty po'."

Peace and confidence settled upon his heavy features. He had been luckier than he had hoped. Instead of having picked up a greenhorn, ignorant of rates, he had come upon an inheritance.

"You confounded old rascal," I said, reaching down into my pocket, "you ought to be turned over to the police."

For the first time I saw him smile. He knew; *he knew*; HE KNEW.

I gave him two one-dollar bills. As I handed them over I noticed that one of them had seen parlous times. Its upper right-hand corner was missing, and it had been torn through in the middle, but joined again. A strip of blue tissue paper, pasted over the split, preserved its negotiability.

Enough of the African bandit for the present: I left him happy, lifted the rope and opened the creaky gate.

The house, as I said, was a shell. A paint brush had not

touched it in twenty years. I could not see why a strong wind should not have bowled it over like a house of cards until I looked again at the trees that hugged it close—the trees that saw the battle of Nashville and still drew their protecting branches around it against storm and enemy and cold.

Azalea Adair, fifty years old, white-haired, a descendant of the cavaliers, as thin and frail as the house she lived in, robed in the cheapest and cleanest dress I ever saw, with an air as simple as a queen's, received me.

The reception room seemed a mile square, because there was nothing in it except some rows of books, on unpainted white-pine bookshelves, a cracked marble-top table, a rag rug, a hairless horsehair sofa and two or three chairs. Yes, there was a picture on the wall, a colored crayon drawing of a cluster of pansies. I looked around for the portrait of Andrew Jackson and the pine-cone hanging basket but they were not there.

Azalea Adair and I had conversation, a little of which will be repeated to you. She was a product of the old South, gently nurtured in the sheltered life. Her learning was not broad, but was deep and of splendid originality in its somewhat narrow scope. She had been educated at home, and her knowledge of the world was derived from inference and by inspiration. Of such is the precious, small group of essayists made. While she talked to me I kept brushing my fingers, trying, unconsciously, to rid them guiltily of the absent dust from the half-calf backs of Lamb, Chaucer, Hazlitt, Marcus Aurelius, Montaigne and Hood. She was exquisite, she was a valuable discovery. Nearly everybody nowadays knows too much—oh, so much too much—of real life.

I could perceive clearly that Azalea Adair was very poor. A house and a dress she had, not much else, I fancied. So, divided between my duty to the magazine and my loyalty to the poets and essayists who fought Thomas in the valley of the Cumberland, I listened to her voice, which was like a harpsichord's, and found that I could not speak of contracts. In the presence of the nine Muses and the three Graces one hesitated to lower the topic to two cents. There would have to be another colloquy after I had regained my commercialism. But I spoke of my mission, and three o'clock of the next afternoon was set for the discussion of the business proposition.

"Your town," I said, as I began to make ready to depart (which is the time for smooth generalities), "seems to be a quiet, sedate place. A home town, I should say, where few things out of the ordinary ever happen."

> It carries on an extensive trade in stoves and hollow ware with the West and South, and its flouring mills have a daily capacity of more than 2,000 barrels.

Azalea Adair seemed to reflect.

"I have never thought of it that way," she said, with a kind of sincere intensity that seemed to belong to her. "Isn't it in the still, quiet places that things do happen? I fancy that when God began to create the earth on the first Monday morning one could have leaned out one's window and heard the drops of mud splashing from His trowel as He built up the everlasting hills. What did the noisiest project in the world—I mean the building of the tower of Babel—result in finally? A page and a half of Esperanto in the *North American Review*."

"Of course," said I platitudinously, "human nature is the same everywhere; but there is more color—er—more drama and movement and—er—romance in some cities than in others."

"On the surface," said Azalea Adair. "I have traveled many times around the world in a golden airship wafted on two wings—print and dreams. I have seen (on one of my imaginary tours) the Sultan of Turkey bowstring with his own hands one of his wives who had uncovered her face in public. I have seen a man in Nashville tear up his theatre tickets because his wife was going out with her face covered—with rice powder. In San Francisco's Chinatown I saw the slave girl Sing Yee dipped slowly, inch by inch, in boiling almond oil to make her swear she would never see her American lover again. She gave in when the boiling oil had reached three inches above her knee. At a euchre party in East Nashville the other night I saw Kitty Morgan cut dead by seven of her schoolmates and lifelong friends because she had married a house painter. The boiling oil was sizzling as high as her heart; but I wish you could have seen the fine little smile that she carried from table to table. Oh, yes, it is a humdrum town. Just a few miles of red brick houses and mud and stores and lumber yards."

Some one knocked hollowly at the back of the house. Azalea Adair breathed a soft apology and went to investigate the sound. She came back in three minutes with brightened eyes, a faint flush on her cheeks, and ten years lifted from her shoulders.

"You must have a cup of tea before you go," she said, "and a sugar cake."

She reached and shook a little iron bell. In shuffled a small Negro girl about twelve, barefoot, not very tidy, glowering at me with thumb in mouth and bulging eyes.

Azalea Adair opened a tiny, worn purse and drew out a dollar bill, a dollar bill with the upper right-hand corner missing, torn in two pieces and pasted together again with a strip of blue tissue paper. It was one of the bills I had given the piratical Negro—there was no doubt of it.

"Go up to Mr. Baker's store on the corner, Impy," she said, handing the girl the dollar bill, "and get a quarter of a pound of tea—the kind he always sends me—and ten cents worth of sugar cakes. Now, hurry. The supply of tea in the house happens to be exhausted," she explained to me.

Impy left by the back way. Before the scrape of her hard, bare feet had died away on the back porch, a wild shriek—I was sure it was hers—filled the hollow house. Then the deep, gruff tones of an angry man's voice mingled with the girl's further squeals and unintelligible words.

Azalea Adair rose without surprise or emotion and disappeared. For two minutes I heard the hoarse rumble of the man's voice; then something like an oath and a slight scuffle, and she returned calmly to her chair.

"This is a roomy house," she said, "and I have a tenant for part of it. I am sorry to have to rescind my invitation to tea. It was impossible to get the kind I always use at the store. Perhaps to-morrow Mr. Baker will be able to supply me."

I was sure that Impy had not had time to leave the house. I inquired concerning street-car lines and took my leave. After I was well on my way I remembered that I had not learned Azalea Adair's name. But to-morrow would do.

That same day I started in on the course of iniquity that this uneventful city forced upon me. I was in the town only two days, but in that time I managed to lie shamelessly by telegraph, and to be an accomplice—after the fact, if that is the correct legal term—to a murder.

As I rounded the corner nearest my hotel the Afrite coachman of the polychromatic, nonpareil coat seized me, swung open the dungeony door of his peripatetic sarcophagus, flirted his feather duster and began his ritual: "Step right in, boss. Carriage is clean—jus' got back from a funeral. Fifty cents to any——"

And then he knew me and grinned broadly. "'Scuse me, boss; you is de gen'l'man what rid out with me dis mawnin'. Thank you kindly, suh."

"I am going out to 861 again to-morrow afternoon at three," said I, "and if you will be here, I'll let you drive me. So you know Miss Adair?" I concluded, thinking of my dollar bill.

"I belonged to her father, Judge Adair, suh," he replied.

"I judge that she is pretty poor," I said. "She hasn't much money to speak of, has she?"

For an instant I looked again at the fierce countenance of King Cettiwayo, and then he changed back to an extortionate old Negro hack driver.

"She ain't gwine to starve, suh," he said slowly. "She has reso'ces, suh; she has reso'ces."

"I shall pay you fifty cents for the trip," said I.

"Dat is puffeckly correct, suh," he answered humbly. "I jus' *had* to have dat two dollars dis mawnin', boss."

I went to the hotel and lied by electricity. I wired the magazine: "A. Adair holds out for eight cents a word."

The answer that came back was: "Give it to her quick, you duffer."

Just before dinner "Major" Wentworth Caswell bore down upon me with the greetings of a long-lost friend. I have seen few men whom I have so instantaneously hated, and of whom it was so difficult to be rid. I was standing at the bar when he invaded me; therefore I could not wave the white ribbon in his face. I would have paid gladly for the drinks, hoping, thereby, to escape another; but he was one of those despicable, roaring, advertising bibbers who must have brass bands and fireworks attend upon every cent that they waste in their follies.

With an air of producing millions he drew two one-dollar bills from a pocket and dashed one of them upon the bar. I looked once more at the dollar bill with the upper right-hand corner missing, torn through the middle, and patched with a strip of blue tissue paper. It was my dollar bill again. It could have been no other.

I went up to my room. The drizzle and the monotony of a dreary, eventless Southern town had made me tired and listless. I remember that just before I went to bed I mentally disposed of the mysterious dollar bill (which might have formed the clew to a tremendously fine detective story of San Francisco) by saying to myself sleepily: "Seems as if a lot of people here own stock in the Hack-Driver's Trust. Pays dividends promptly, too. Wonder if——" Then I fell asleep.

King Cettiwayo was at his post the next day, and rattled my bones over the stones out to 861. He was to wait and rattle me back again when I was ready.

Azalea Adair looked paler and cleaner and frailer than she had looked on the day before. After she had signed the contract at eight cents per word she grew still paler and began to slip out of her chair. Without much trouble I managed to get her up on the antediluvian horsehair sofa and then I ran out to the sidewalk and yelled to the coffee-colored Pirate to bring a doctor. With a wisdom that I had not suspected in him, he abandoned his team and struck off up the street afoot, realizing the value of speed. In ten minutes he returned with a grave, gray-haired and capable man of medicine. In a few words (worth much less than eight cents each) I explained to him my presence in the hollow house of mystery. He bowed with stately understanding, and turned to the old Negro.

"Uncle Cæsar," he said calmly, "run up to my house and ask Miss Lucy to give you a cream pitcher full of fresh milk and half a tumbler of port wine. And hurry back. Don't drive—run. I want you to get back sometime this week."

It occurred to me that Dr. Merriman also felt a distrust as to the speeding powers of the land-pirate's steeds. After Uncle Cæsar was gone, lumberingly, but swiftly, up the street, the doctor looked me over with great politeness and as much careful calculation until he had decided that I might do.

"It is only a case of insufficient nutrition," he said. "In other words, the result of poverty, pride, and starvation. Mrs. Caswell has many devoted friends who would be glad to aid her, but she will accept nothing except from that old Negro, Uncle Cæsar, who was once owned by her family."

"Mrs. Caswell!" said I, in surprise. And then I looked at the contract and saw that she had signed it "Azalea Adair Caswell."

"I thought she was Miss Adair," I said.

"Married to a drunken, worthless loafer, sir," said the doctor. "It is said that he robs her even of the small sums that her old servant contributes toward her support."

When the milk and wine had been brought the doctor soon revived Azalea Adair. She sat up and talked of the beauty of the autumn leaves that were then in season, and their height of color. She referred lightly to her fainting seizure as the outcome of an old palpitation of the heart. Impy fanned her as she lay on the sofa. The doctor was due elsewhere, and I followed him to the door. I told him that it was within my power and intentions to make a reasonable advance of money to Azalea Adair on future contributions to the magazine, and he seemed pleased.

"By the way," he said, "perhaps you would like to know that you have had royalty for a coachman. Old Cæsar's grandfather was a king in Congo. Cæsar himself has royal ways, as you may have observed."

As the doctor was moving off I heard Uncle Cæsar's voice inside: "Did he git bofe of dem two dollars from you, Mis' Zalea?"

"Yes, Cæsar," I heard Azalea Adair answer weakly. And then I went in and concluded business negotiations with our contributor. I assumed the responsibility of advancing fifty dollars, putting it as a necessary formality in binding our bargain. And then Uncle Cæsar drove me back to the hotel.

Here ends all of the story as far as I can testify as a witness. The rest must be only bare statements of facts.

At about six o'clock I went out for a stroll. Uncle Cæsar was at his corner. He threw open the door of his carriage, flourished his duster and began his depressing formula: "Step right in, suh. Fifty cents to anywhere in the city—hack's puffickly clean, suh—jus' got back from a funeral——"

And then he recognized me. I think his eyesight was getting bad. His coat had taken on a few more faded shades of color, the twine strings were more frayed and ragged, the last remaining button—the button of yellow horn—was gone. A motley descendant of kings was Uncle Cæsar!

About two hours later I saw an excited crowd besieging the front of a drug store. In a desert where nothing happens this was manna; so I edged my way inside. On an extemporized couch of empty boxes and chairs was stretched the mortal corporeality of Major Wentworth Caswell. A doctor was testing him for the immortal ingredient. His decision was that it was conspicuous by its absence.

The erstwhile Major had been found dead on a dark street and brought by curious and ennuied citizens to the drug store. The late human being had been engaged in terrific battle—the details showed that. Loafer and reprobate though he had been, he had been also a warrior. But he had lost. His hands were yet clinched so tightly that his fingers would not be opened. The gentle citizens who had known him stood about and searched their vocabularies to find some good words, if it were possible, to speak of him. One kind-looking man said, after much thought: "When 'Cas' was about fo'teen he was one of the best spellers in school."

While I stood there the fingers of the right hand of "the man that was," which hung down the side of a white pine box, relaxed, and dropped something at my feet. I covered it with one foot quietly, and a little later on I picked it up and pocketed it. I reasoned that in his last struggle his hand must have seized that object unwittingly and held it in a death grip.

At the hotel that night the main topic of conversation, with the possible exceptions of politics and prohibition, was the demise of Major Caswell. I heard one man say to a group of listeners:

"In my opinion, gentlemen, Caswell was murdered by some of these no-account niggers for his money. He had fifty dollars this afternoon which he showed to several gentlemen in the hotel. When he was found the money was not on his person."

I left the city the next morning at nine, and as the train was crossing the bridge over the Cumberland River I took out of my pocket a yellow horn overcoat button the size of a fifty-cent piece, with frayed ends of coarse twine hanging from it, and cast it out of the window into the slow, muddy waters below.

I wonder what's doing in Buffalo!

WEST

A Fog in Santone

A METEOROLOGICAL SKETCH

THE DRUG clerk looks sharply at the white face half concealed by the high-turned overcoat collar.

"I would rather not supply you," he says doubtfully. "I sold you a dozen morphia tablets less than an hour ago."

The customer smiles wanly. "The fault is in your crooked streets. I did n't intend to call upon you twice, but I guess I got tangled up. Excuse me."

He draws his collar higher, and moves out, slowly. He stops under an electric light at the corner, and juggles absorbedly with three or four little pasteboard boxes. "Thirty-six," he announces to himself. "More than plenty."

For a gray mist had swooped upon Santone that night, an opaque terror that laid a hand to the throat of each of the city's guests. It was computed that three thousand invalids were hibernating in the town. They had come from by and wide, for here, among these contracted, river-sliced streets, the goddess Ozone has elected to linger.

Purest atmosphere, sir, on earth! You might think, from the river winding through our town, that we are malarial, but, no, sir! Repeated experiments made by both government and local experts show that our air contains nothing deleterious—nothing but ozone, sir, pure ozone. Litmus paper tests made all along the river show—but you can read it all in the prospectuses; or the Santonian will recite it for you, word by word.

We may achieve climate, but weather is thrust upon us. Santone, then, cannot be blamed for this cold, gray fog that came and kissed the lips of the three thousand, and then delivered them to the cross. That night the tubercles, whose ravages hope holds in check, multiplied. The writhing fingers of the pale mist did not go thence bloodless. Many of the wooers of ozone capitulated with the enemy that night, turning their faces to the wall in that dumb, isolated apathy that so terrifies their watchers. On the red stream of Hemorrhagia a few souls drifted away, leaving behind pathetic heaps, white and chill as the fog itself. Two or three came to view this atmospheric wraith as the ghost of impossible joys, sent to whisper to them of the egregious folly it is to inhale breath into the lungs, only to exhale it again, and these used whatever came handy to their relief, pistols, gas or the beneficent muriate.

The purchaser of the morphia wanders into the fog, and, at length, finds himself upon a little iron bridge, one of the score or more in the heart of the city under which the small, tortuous river flows. He leans on the rail and gasps, for here the mist has concentrated, lying like a footpad to garrote such of the Three Thousand as creep that way. The iron bridge guys rattle to the strain of his cough, a mocking, phthisical rattle, seeming to say to him: "Clackety—clack! just a little rusty cold, sir,—but not from our river. Lit—mus paper all along the banks and nothing but ozone. Clacket—y—clack!"

The Memphis man at last recovers sufficiently to be aware of another overcoated man ten feet away, leaning on the rail, and just coming out of a paroxysm. There is a freemasonry among the Three Thousand that does away with formalities and introductions. A cough is your card; a hemorrhage a letter of credit. The morphia man, being nearer recovered, speaks first.

"Goodall: Memphis—pulmonary tuberculosis—guess last stages." The Three Thousand economize on words. Words are breath, and they need breath to write checks for the doctors.

"Hurd," gasps the other. "Hurd; of T'leder. T'leder, Ah-hia. Catarrhal bronkeetis. Name's Dennis, too—doctor says. Says I 'll,—live four weeks if I—take care of myself. Got your walking papers yet?"

"My doctor," says Goodall, of Memphis, a little boastingly, "gives me three months."

"Oh," remarks the man from Toledo, filling up great gaps in his conversation with wheezes, "damn the difference. What's months! Expect to—cut mine down to one week—and die in a hack—a four wheeler, not a cough. Be considerable moanin' of the bars when I put out to sea. I 've patronized 'em—pretty freely since I struck my—present gait. Say, Goodall, of Memphis—if your doc has set your pegs so close—why don't you—get on a big spree and go—to the devil quick and easy—like I 'm doing?"

"A spree!" says Goodall, as one who entertains a new idea, "I never did such a thing. I was thinking of another way, but—"

"Come on," invites the Ohioan, "and have some drinks. I 've been at it—for two days, but the inf—ernal stuff won't bite like it used to. Goodall, of Memphis, what 's your respiration?"

"Twenty-four."

"Daily—temperature?"

"Hundred and four."

"You can do it in two days. It'll take me a—week. Tank up, friend Goodall—have all the fun you can, then—off you go, in the middle of a jag, and s-s-save trouble and expense. I 'm a s-son of a gun if this ain't a health resort—for your whiskers! A Lake Erie fog 'd get lost here in two minutes."

"You said something about a drink," says Goodall.

A few minutes later they line up at a glittering bar, and hang upon the arm rest. The bartender, blonde, heavy, well-groomed, sets out their drinks, instantly perceiving that he serves two of the Three Thousand. He observes that one is a middle-aged man, well dressed, with a lined and sunken face; the other a mere boy, who is chiefly eyes and overcoat. Disguised well the tedium begotten by many repetitions, the server of drinks begins to chant the sanitary saga of Santone. "Rather a moist night, gentlemen, for our town. A little fog from our river, but nothing to hurt. Repeated tests."

"Damn your litmus papers," gasps Toledo,—"without any—personal offence intended. We've heard of 'em before. Let 'em turn red, white and blue. What we want is a repeated test of that—whiskey. Come again. I paid for the last round, Goodall, of Memphis."

The bottle oscillates from one to the other, continues to do so, and is not removed from the counter. The bartender sees two emaciated invalids dispose of enough Kentucky Belle to floor a dozen cowboys, without displaying any emotion save a sad and contemplative interest in the peregrinations of the bottle. So he is moved to manifest a solicitude as to the consequences.

"Not on your Uncle Mark Hanna," responds Toledo, "will we get drunk. We've been—vaccinated with whiskey and—cod liver oil. What would send you to the police station—only gives us a thirst. S-s-set out another bottle."

It is slow work trying to meet death by that route. Some
quicker way must be found. They leave the saloon and plunge
again into the mist. The sidewalks are mere flanges at the base
of the houses; the street a cold ravine, the fog filling it like a
freshet. Not far away is the Mexican quarter. Conducted as if
by wires along the heavy air comes a guitar's tinkle, and the
demoralizing voice of some señorita singing:

> *"En las tardes sombrillos del invierno*
> *En el prado a Morar me reclino,*
> *Y maldigo mi fausto destino—*
> *Una vida la mas infeliz."*

The words of it they do not understand—neither Toledo nor
Memphis, but words are the least important things in life. The
music tears the breasts of the seekers after Nepenthe, inciting
Toledo to remark:

"Those kids of mine—I wonder—by God, Mr. Goodall, of
Memphis, we had too little of that whiskey! No slow music in
mine, if you please. It makes you disremember to forget."

Hurd, of Toledo, here pulls out his watch, and says:

"I'm a son of a gun! Got an engagement for a hack ride
out to San—Pedro Springs at eleven. Forgot it. A fellow from
Noo York, and me, and the Castillo sisters at Rhinegelder's
Garden. That Noo York chap's a lucky dog—Got one whole
lung—good for a year yet. Plenty of money, too. He pays for
everything. I can't afford—to miss the jamboree. Sorry you
ain't going along. Good-by, Goodall, of Memphis."

He rounds the corner and shuffles away, casting off thus
easily the ties of acquaintanceship as the moribund do, the
season of dissolution being man's supreme hour of egoism and
selfishness. But he turns and calls back through the fog to the
other: "I say, Goodall, of Memphis! If you get *there* before I
do, tell 'em Hurd 's a comin' too. Hurd, of T'leder, Ah-hia."

Thus Goodall's tempter deserts him. That youth, uncom-
plaining and uncaring, takes a spell at coughing, and, recovered,
wanders desultorily on down the street, the name of which he
neither knows nor recks. At a certain point he perceives swinging doors, and hears, filtering between them, a noise of wind
and string instruments. Two men enter from the street as he

arrives, and he follows them in. There is a kind of antechamber, plentifully set with palms and cactuses and oleanders. At little marble-topped tables some people sit, while soft-shod attendants bring the beer. All is orderly, clean, melancholy—gay; of the German method of pleasure. At his right is the foot of a stairway. A man standing there holds out his hand. Goodall extends his, full of silver, and the man selects therefrom a coin. Goodall goes upstairs, and sees there two galleries extending along the sides of a concert hall which he now perceives to lie below and beyond the anteroom he had first entered. These galleries are divided into boxes or stalls which bestow, with the aid of hanging lace curtains, a certain privacy upon their occupants.

Passing, with aimless feet, down the aisle contiguous to these saucy and discreet compartments, he is half checked by the sight, in one of them, of a young woman, alone and seated in an attitude of reflection. This young woman becomes aware of his approach. A smile from her brings him to a standstill, and her subsequent invitation draws him, though hesitating, to the other chair in the box, a little table between them.

Goodall is only nineteen. There are some whom, when the terrible god Phthisis wishes to destroy he first makes beautiful; and the boy is one of these. His face is wax, and an awful pulchritude is born of the menacing flame in his cheeks. His eyes reflect an unearthly vista engendered by the certainty of his doom. As it is forbidden man to guess accurately concerning his fate, it is inevitable that he shall tremble at the slightest lifting of the veil.

The young woman is well dressed, and exhibits a beauty of a distinctly feminine and tender sort; an Eve-like comeliness that seems scarcely predestined to fade.

It is immaterial, the steps by which the two mount to a certain plane of good understanding; they are short and few, as befits the occasion.

A button against the wall of the partition is frequently disturbed, and a waiter comes and goes at its signal. Pensive Beauty would nothing of wine; two thick plaits of her blonde hair hang almost to the floor; she is a lineal descendant of the Loreley. So the waiter brings the brew; effervescent, icy, greenish-golden. The orchestra on the stage is playing "Oh, Rachel." The two youngsters have exchanged a good bit of information. She calls him "Walter," and he calls her "Miss Rosa."

Goodall's tongue is loosened, and he has told her everything about himself. About his home in Tennessee, the old pillared mansion under the oaks, the stables, the hunting; the friends he has; down to the chickens, and the box bushes bordering the walks. About his coming South for the climate, hoping to escape the hereditary foe of his family. All about his three months on a ranch; the deer hunts, the rattlers, and the rollicking in the cow camps. Then of his advent to Santone, where he has indirectly learned from a great specialist that his life's calendar probably contains but two more leaves. And then of this death-white, choking night which has come and strangled his fortitude, and sent him out to seek a port amid its depressing billows.

"My weekly letter from home failed to come," he told her, "and I was pretty blue. I knew I had to go before long, and I was tired of waiting. I went out and began to buy morphine at every drug store where they would sell me a few tablets. I got thirty-six quarter-grains, and was going back to my room and take them, but I met a queer fellow on a bridge, who had a new idea."

Goodall fillips a little pasteboard box upon the table, "I put 'em all together in there."

Miss Rosa, being a woman, must raise the lid, and gave a slight shiver at the innocent-looking triturates. "Horrid things! but, those little, white bits—they could never kill one!"

Indeed they could. Walter knew better. Nine grains of morphia! Why, half the amount might.

Miss Rosa demands to know about Mr. Hurd, of Toledo, and is told. She laughs like a delighted child. "What a funny fellow! But tell me more about your home and your sisters, Walter. I know enough about Texas and tarantulas and cowboys."

The theme is dear, just now, to his mood, and he lays before her the simple details of a true home; the little ties and endearments that so fill the exile's heart. Of his sisters, one Alice furnishes him a theme he loves to dwell upon.

"She is like you, Miss Rosa," he says. "Maybe not quite so pretty, but just as nice, and good, and—"

"There! Walter," says Miss Rosa sharply, "now talk about something else."

But a shadow falls upon the wall outside, preceding a big, softly treading man, finely dressed, who pauses a second before the curtains and then passes on. Presently comes the waiter with a message: "Mr. Rolfe says—"

"Tell Rolfe I 'm engaged."

"I don't know why it is," says Goodall, of Memphis, "but I don't feel as bad as I did. An hour ago I wanted to die, but since I've met you, Miss Rosa, I'd like, so much, to live."

The young woman whirls around the table, lays an arm behind his neck, and kisses him on the cheek.

"You must, dear boy," she says. "I know what was the matter. It was this miserable foggy weather that has lowered your spirit and mine too—a little. But, look now!"

With a little spring she has drawn back the curtains. A window is in the wall opposite, and lo! the mist is cleared away. The indulgent moon is out again, revoyaging the plumbless sky. Roof and parapet and spire are softly pearl enamelled. Twice, thrice the retrieved river flashes back, between the houses, the light of the firmament. A tonic day will dawn, sweet and prosperous.

"Talk of death, when the world is so beautiful!" says Miss Rosa, laying her hand on his shoulder. "Do something to please me, Walter. Go home to your rest, and say: 'I mean to get better,' and do it."

"If you ask it," says the boy, with a smile, "I will."

The waiter brings full glasses. Did they ring? No; but it is well. He may leave them. A farewell glass. Miss Rosa says: "To your better health, Walter." He says: "To our next meeting."

His eyes look no longer into the void, but gaze upon the antithesis of death. His foot is set in an undiscovered country to-night. He is obedient, ready to go. "Good-night," she says.

"I never kissed a girl before," he confesses, "except my sisters."

"You didn't this time," she laughs, "I kissed you—good-night."

"When shall I see you again?" he persists.

"You promised me to go home," she frowns, "and get well. Perhaps we shall meet again—soon. Good-night." He hesitates, his hat in hand. She smiles broadly and kisses him once more, upon the forehead. She watches him far down the aisle, then sits again at the table.

The shadow falls once more against the wall. This time the big, softly stepping man parts the curtains and looks in. Miss Rosa's eye meets his, and for half a minute they remain thus, silent, fighting a battle with that king of weapons. Presently the big man drops the curtains and passes on.

The orchestra ceases playing suddenly, and an important voice can be heard loudly talking in one of the boxes farther down the aisle. No doubt some citizen entertains there some visitor to the town, and Miss Rosa leans back in her chair and smiles at some of the words she catches:

"Purest atmosphere—in the world—litmus paper all along— nothing hurtful—our city—nothing but pure ozone."

The waiter returns for the tray and glasses. As he enters, the girl crushes a little empty pasteboard box in her hand, and throws it in a corner. She is stirring something in her glass with her hat-pin.

"Why, Miss Rosa," says the waiter, with the civil familiarity he uses,—"putting salt in your beer this early in the night!"

Friends in San Rosario

THE WEST-BOUND stopped at San Rosario on time at 8.20 A.M. A man with a thick black-leather wallet under his arm left the train and walked rapidly up the main street of the town. There were other passengers who also got off at San Rosario, but they either slouched limberly over to the railroad eating-house or the Silver Dollar saloon, or joined the groups of idlers about the station.

Indecision had no part in the movements of the man with the wallet. He was short in stature, but strongly built, with very light, closely-trimmed hair, smooth, determined face, and aggressive, gold-rimmed nose glasses. He was well dressed in the prevailing Eastern style. His air denoted a quiet but conscious reserve force, if not actual authority.

After walking a distance of three squares he came to the centre of the town's business area. Here another street of importance crossed the main one, forming the hub of San Rosario's life and commerce. Upon one corner stood the post-office. Upon another Rubensky's Clothing Emporium. The other two diagonally opposing corners were occupied by the town's two banks, the First National and the Stockmen's National. Into the First National Bank of San Rosario the newcomer walked, never slowing his brisk step until he stood at the cashier's window. The bank opened for business at nine, and the working force was already assembled, each member preparing his department for the day's business. The cashier was examining the mail when he noticed the stranger standing at his window.

"Bank does n't open 'til nine," he remarked, curtly, but without feeling. He had had to make that statement so often to early birds since San Rosario adopted city banking hours.

"I am well aware of that," said the other man, in cool, brittle tones. "Will you kindly receive my card?"

The cashier drew the small, spotless parallelogram inside the bars of his wicket, and read:

J. F. C. NETTLEWICK

National Bank Examiner

"Oh—er—will you walk around inside, Mr.—er—Nettle-wick. Your first visit—did n't know your business, of course. Walk right around, please."

The examiner was quickly inside the sacred precincts of the bank, where he was ponderously introduced to each employee in turn by Mr. Edlinger, the cashier—a middle-aged gentleman of deliberation, discretion, and method.

"I was kind of expecting Sam Turner round again, pretty soon," said Mr. Edlinger. "Sam 's been examining us now, for about four years. I guess you 'll find us all right, though, considering the tightness in business. Not overly much money on hand, but able to stand the storms, sir, stand the storms."

"Mr. Turner and I have been ordered by the Comptroller to exchange districts," said the examiner, in his decisive, formal tones. "He is covering my old territory in Southern Illinois and Indiana. I will take the cash first, please."

Perry Dorsey, the teller, was already arranging his cash on the counter for the examiner's inspection. He knew it was right to a cent, and he had nothing to fear, but he was nervous and flustered. So was every man in the bank. There was something so icy and swift, so impersonal and uncompromising about this man that his very presence seemed an accusation. He looked to be a man who would never make nor overlook an error.

Mr. Nettlewick first seized the currency, and with a rapid, almost juggling motion, counted it by packages. Then he spun the sponge cup toward him and verified the count by bills. His thin, white fingers flew like some expert musician's upon the keys of a piano. He dumped the gold upon the counter with a crash, and the coins whined and sang as they skimmed across the marble slab from the tips of his nimble digits. The air was full of fractional currency when he came to the halves and quarters. He counted the last nickle and dime. He had the scales brought, and he weighed every sack of silver in the vault. He questioned Dorsey concerning each of the cash memoranda—certain checks, charge slips, etc., carried over from the previous day's work—with unimpeachable courtesy, yet with something so mysteriously momentous in his frigid manner, that the teller was reduced to pink cheeks and a stammering tongue.

This newly-imported examiner was so different from Sam Turner. It had been Sam's way to enter the bank with a shout, pass the cigars, and tell the latest stories he had picked up on his rounds. His customary greeting to Dorsey had been, "Hello, Perry! Have n't skipped out with the boodle yet, I see." Turner's way of counting the cash had been different, too. He would finger the packages of bills in a tired kind of way, and then go into the vault and kick over a few sacks of silver, and the thing was done. Halves and quarters and dimes? Not for Sam Turner. "No chicken feed for me," he would say when they were set before him. "I 'm not in the agricultural department." But, then, Turner was a Texan, an old friend of the bank's president, and had known Dorsey since he was a baby.

While the examiner was counting the cash, Major Thomas B. Kingman—known to every one as "Major Tom"—the president of the First National, drove up to the side door with his old dun horse and buggy, and came inside. He saw the examiner busy with the money, and, going into the little "pony corral," as he called it, in which his desk was railed off, he began to look over his letters.

Earlier, a little incident had occurred that even the sharp eyes of the examiner had failed to notice. When he had begun his work at the cash counter, Mr. Edlinger had winked significantly at Roy Wilson, the youthful bank messenger, and nodded his head slightly toward the front door. Roy understood, got his hat and walked leisurely out, with his collector's book under his arm. Once outside, he made a bee-line for the Stockmen's National. That bank was also getting ready to open. No customers had, as yet, presented themselves.

"Say, you people!" cried Roy, with the familiarity of youth and long acquaintance, "you want to get a move on you. There 's a new bank examiner over at the First, and he 's a stem-winder. He 's counting nickles on Perry, and he 's got the whole outfit bluffed. Mr. Edlinger gave me the tip to let you know."

Mr. Buckley, president of the Stockmen's National—a stout,

elderly man, looking like a farmer dressed for Sunday—heard Roy from his private office at the rear and called him.

"Has Major Kingman come down to the bank yet?" he asked of the boy.

"Yes, sir, he was just driving up as I left," said Roy.

"I want you to take him a note. Put it into his own hands as soon as you get back."

Mr. Buckley sat down and began to write.

Roy returned and handed to Major Kingman the envelope containing the note. The major read it, folded it, and slipped it into his vest pocket. He leaned back in his chair for a few moments as if he were meditating deeply, and then rose and went into the vault. He came out with the bulky, old-fashioned leather note case stamped on the back in gilt letters, "Bills Discounted." In this were the notes due the bank with their attached securities, and the major, in his rough way, dumped the lot upon his desk and began to sort them over.

By this time Nettlewick had finished his count of the cash. His pencil fluttered like a swallow over the sheet of paper on which he had set his figures. He opened his black wallet, which seemed to be also a kind of secret memorandum book, made a few rapid figures in it, wheeled and transfixed Dorsey with the glare of his spectacles. That look seemed to say: "You 're safe this time, but——"

"Cash all correct," snapped the examiner. He made a dash for the individual bookkeeper, and, for a few minutes there was a fluttering of ledger leaves and a sailing of balance sheets through the air.

"How often do you balance your pass-books?" he demanded, suddenly.

"Er—once a month," faltered the individual bookkeeper, wondering how many years they would give him.

"All right," said the examiner, turning and charging upon the general bookkeeper, who had the statements of his foreign banks and their reconcilement memoranda ready. Everything there was found to be all right. Then the stub book of the certificates of deposit. Flutter—flutter—zip—zip—check! All right. List of overdrafts, please. Thanks. H'm-m. Unsigned bills of the bank, next. All right.

Then came the cashier's turn, and easy-going Mr. Edlinger

rubbed his nose and polished his glasses nervously under the quick fire of questions concerning the circulation, undivided profits, bank real estate, and stock ownership.

Presently Nettlewick was aware of a big man towering above him at his elbow—a man sixty years of age, rugged and hale, with a rough, grizzled beard, a mass of gray hair, and a pair of penetrating blue eyes that confronted the formidable glasses of the examiner without a flicker.

"Er—Major Kingman, our president—er—Mr. Nettlewick," said the cashier.

Two men of very different types shook hands. One was a finished product of the world of straight lines, conventional methods, and formal affairs. The other was something freer, wider and nearer to nature. Tom Kingman had not been cut to any pattern. He had been mule-driver, cowboy, ranger, soldier, sheriff, prospector, and cattleman. Now, when he was bank president, his old comrades from the prairies, of the saddle, tent, and trail found no change in him. He had made his fortune when Texas cattle were at the high tide of value, and had organized the First National Bank of San Rosario. In spite of his largeness of heart and sometimes unwise generosity toward his old friends, the bank had prospered, for Major Tom Kingman knew men as well as he knew cattle. Of late years the cattle business had known a depression, and the major's bank was one of the few whose losses had not been great.

"And now," said the examiner, briskly, pulling out his watch, "the last thing is the loans. We will take them up now, if you please."

He had gone through the First National at almost record-breaking speed—but thoroughly, as he did everything. The running order of the bank was smooth and clean, and that had facilitated his work. There was but one other bank in the town. He received from the Government a fee of twenty-five dollars for each bank that he examined. He should be able to go over those loans and discounts in half an hour. If so, he could examine the other bank immediately afterward, and catch the 11.45, the only other train that day in the direction he was working. Otherwise, he would have to spend the night and Sunday in this uninteresting Western town. That was why Mr. Nettlewick was rushing matters.

"Come with me, sir," said Major Kingman, in his deep voice, that united the Southern drawl with the rhythmic twang of the West; "We will go over them together. Nobody in the bank knows those notes as I do. Some of 'em are a little wobbly on their legs, and some are mavericks without extra many brands on their backs, but they 'll most all pay out at the round-up."

The two sat down at the president's desk. First, the examiner went through the notes at lightning speed, and added up their total, finding it to agree with the amount of loans carried on the book of daily balances. Next, he took up the larger loans, inquiring scrupulously into the condition of their indorsers or securities. The new examiner's mind seemed to course and turn and make unexpected dashes hither and thither like a bloodhound seeking a trail. Finally he pushed aside all the notes except a few, which he arranged in a neat pile before him, and began a dry, formal little speech.

"I find, sir, the condition of your bank to be very good, considering the poor crops and the depression in the cattle interests of your state. The clerical work seems to be done accurately and punctually. Your past-due paper is moderate in amount, and promises only a small loss. I would recommend the calling in of your large loans, and the making of only sixty and ninety day or call loans until general business revives. And now, there is one thing more, and I will have finished with the bank. Here are six notes aggregating something like $40,000. They are secured, according to their faces, by various stocks, bonds, shares, etc., to the value of $70,000. Those securities are missing from the notes to which they should be attached. I suppose you have them in the safe or vault. You will permit me to examine them."

Major Tom's light-blue eyes turned unflinchingly toward the examiner.

"No, sir," he said, in a low but steady tone; "those securities are neither in the safe nor the vault. I have taken them. You may hold me personally responsible for their absence."

Nettlewick felt a slight thrill. He had not expected this. He had struck a momentous trail when the hunt was drawing to a close.

"Ah!" said the examiner. He waited a moment, and then continued: "May I ask you to explain more definitely?"

"The securities were taken by me," repeated the major. "It was not for my own use, but to save an old friend in trouble. Come in here, sir, and we 'll talk it over."

He led the examiner into the bank's private office at the rear, and closed the door. There was a desk, and a table, and half-a-dozen leather-covered chairs. On the wall was the mounted head of a Texas steer with horns five feet from tip to tip. Opposite hung the major's old cavalry saber that he had carried at Shiloh and Fort Pillow.

Placing a chair for Nettlewick, the major seated himself by the window, from which he could see the post-office and the carved limestone front of the Stockmen's National. He did not speak at once, and Nettlewick felt, perhaps, that the ice should be broken by something so near its own temperature as the voice of official warning.

"Your statement," he began, "since you have failed to modify it, amounts, as you must know, to a very serious thing. You are aware, also, of what my duty must compel me to do. I shall have to go before the United States Commissioner and make——"

"I know, I know," said Major Tom, with a wave of his hand. "You don't suppose I 'd run a bank without being posted on national banking laws and the revised statutes! Do your duty. I 'm not asking any favours. But, I spoke of my friend. I did want you to hear me tell you about Bob."

Nettlewick settled himself in his chair. There would be no leaving San Rosario for him that day. He would have to telegraph to the Comptroller of the Currency; he would have to swear out a warrant before the United States Commissioner for the arrest of Major Kingman; perhaps he would be ordered to close the bank on account of the loss of the securities. It was not the first crime the examiner had unearthed. Once or twice the terrible upheaval of human emotions that his investigations had loosed had almost caused a ripple in his official calm. He had seen bank men kneel and plead and cry like women for a chance—an hour's time—the overlooking of a single error. One cashier had shot himself at his desk before him. None of them had taken it with the dignity and coolness of this stern old Westerner. Nettlewick felt that he owed it to him at least to listen if he wished to talk. With his elbow on the arm of his chair, and his square chin resting upon the fingers of his right hand, the bank examiner waited to hear the confession of the president of the First National Bank of San Rosario.

"When a man's your friend," began Major Tom, somewhat didactically, "for forty years, and tried by water, fire, earth, and cyclones, when you can do him a little favour you feel like doing it."

("Embezzle for him $70,000 worth of securities," thought the examiner.)

"We were cowboys together, Bob and I," continued the major, speaking slowly, and deliberately, and musingly, as if his thoughts were rather with the past than the critical present, "and we prospected together for gold and silver over Arizona, New Mexico, and a good part of California. We were both in the war of 'sixty-one, but in different commands. We 've fought Indians and horse thieves side by side; we 've starved for weeks in a cabin in the Arizona mountains, buried twenty feet deep in snow; we 've ridden herd together when the wind blew so hard the lightning could n't strike——well, Bob and I have been through some rough spells since the first time we met in the branding camp of the old Anchor-Bar Ranch. And during that time we 've found it necessary more than once to help each other out of tight places. In those days it was expected of a man to stick to his friend, and he did n't ask any credit for it. Probably next day you 'd need him to get at your back and help stand off a band of Apaches, or put a tourniquet on your leg above a rattlesnake bite and ride for whisky. So, after all, it was give and take, and if you did n't stand square with your pardner, why, you might be shy one when you needed him. But Bob was a man who was willing to go further than that. He never played a limit.

"Twenty years ago I was sheriff of this county, and I made Bob my chief deputy. That was before the boom in cattle when we both made our stake. I was sheriff and collector, and it was a big thing for me then. I was married, and we had a boy and a girl—a four and a six year old. There was a comfortable house next to the courthouse, furnished by the county, rent free, and I was saving some money. Bob did most of the office work. Both of us had seen rough times and plenty of rustling and danger, and I tell you it was great to hear the rain and the sleet dashing against the windows of nights, and be warm and safe and comfortable, and know you could get up in the morning and be shaved and have folks call you 'mister.' And then, I had the finest wife and kids that ever struck the range, and my old friend with me enjoying the first fruits of prosperity and white shirts, and I guess I was happy. Yes, I was happy about that time."

The major sighed and glanced casually out of the window. The bank examiner changed his position, and leaned his chin upon his other hand.

"One winter," continued the major, "the money for the county taxes came pouring in so fast that I did n't have time to take the stuff to the bank for a week. I just shoved the checks into a cigar box and the money into a sack, and locked them in the big safe that belonged in the sheriff's office.

"I had been overworked that week, and was about sick, anyway. My nerves were out of order, and my sleep at night did n't seem to rest me. The doctor had some scientific name for it, and I was taking medicine. And so, added to the rest, I went to bed at night with that money on my mind. Not that there was much need of being worried, for the safe was a good one, and nobody but Bob and I knew the combination. On Friday night there was about $6,500 in cash in the bag. On Saturday morning I went to the office as usual. The safe was locked, and Bob was writing at his desk. I opened the safe, and the money was gone. I called Bob, and roused everybody in the court-house to announce the robbery. It struck me that Bob took it pretty quiet, considering how much it reflected upon both him and me.

"Two days went by and we never got a clew. It could n't have been burglars, for the safe had been opened by the combination in the proper way. People must have begun to talk, for one afternoon in comes Alice—that 's my wife—and the boy and girl, and Alice stamps her foot, and her eyes flash, and she cries out, 'The lying wretches—Tom, Tom!' and I catch her in a faint, and bring her 'round little by little, and she lays her head down and cries and cries for the first time since she took Tom Kingman's name and fortunes. And Jack and Zilla—the youngsters—they were always wild as tiger cubs to rush at Bob and climb all over him whenever they were allowed to come to the court-house—they stood and kicked their little shoes, and herded together like scared partridges. They were having their first trip down into the shadows of life. Bob was working at his desk, and he got up and went out without a word. The grand jury was in session then, and the next morning Bob went before them and confessed that he stole the money. He said he lost it in a poker game. In fifteen minutes they had found a true bill and sent me the warrant to arrest the man with whom I 'd been closer than a thousand brothers for many a year.

"I did it, and then I said to Bob, pointing: 'There 's my house, and here 's my office, and up there 's Maine, and out that way is California, and over there is Florida—and that 's your range 'til court meets. You 're in my charge, and I take the responsibility. You be here when you 're wanted.'

"'Thanks, Tom,' he said, kind of carelessly; 'I was sort of hoping you would n't lock me up. Court meets next Monday, so, if you don't object, I 'll just loaf around the office until then. I 've got one favour to ask, if it is n't too much. If you 'd let the kids come out in the yard once in a while and have a romp I 'd like it.'

"'Why not?' I answered him. 'They 're welcome, and so are you. And come to my house, the same as ever.' You see, Mr. Nettlewick, you can't make a friend of a thief, but neither can you make a thief of a friend, all at once."

The examiner made no answer. At that moment was heard the shrill whistle of a locomotive pulling into the depot. That was the train on the little, narrow-gauge road that struck into San Rosario from the south. The major cocked his ear and listened for a moment, and looked at his watch. The narrow-gauge was in on time—10.35. The major continued:

"So Bob hung around the office, reading the papers and smoking. I put another deputy to work in his place, and, after a while, the first excitement of the case wore off.

"One day when we were alone in the office Bob came over to where I was sitting. He was looking sort of grim and blue—the same look he used to get when he 'd been up watching for Indians all night or herd-riding.

"'Tom,' says he, 'it 's harder than standing off redskins; it 's harder than lying in the lava desert forty miles from water; but

I 'm going to stick it out to the end. You know that 's been my style. But if you 'd tip me the smallest kind of a sign—if you 'd just say, "Bob I understand," why, it would make it lots easier.'

"I was surprised. 'I don't know what you mean, Bob,' I said. "Of course, you know that I 'd do anything under the sun to help you that I could. But you 've got me guessing."

"'All right, Tom,' was all he said, and he went back to his newspaper and lit another cigar.

"It was the night before court met when I found out what he meant. I went to bed that night with that same old, light-headed, nervous feeling come back upon me. I dropped off to sleep about midnight. When I awoke I was standing half dressed in one of the court-house corridors. Bob was holding one of my arms, our family doctor the other, and Alice was shaking me and half crying. She had sent for the doctor without my knowing it, and when he came they had found me out of bed and missing, and had begun a search.

"'Sleep-walking,' said the doctor.

"All of us went back to the house, and the doctor told us some remarkable stories about the strange things people had done while in that condition. I was feeling rather chilly after my trip out, and, as my wife was out of the room at the time, I pulled open the door of an old wardrobe that stood in the room and dragged out a big quilt I had seen in there. With it tumbled out the bag of money for stealing which Bob was to be tried—and convicted—in the morning.

"'How the jumping rattlesnakes did that get there?' I yelled, and all hands must have seen how surprised I was. Bob knew in a flash.

"'You darned old snoozer,' he said, with the old-time look on his face, 'I saw you put it there. I watched you open the safe and take it out, and I followed you. I looked through the window and saw you hide it in that wardrobe.'

"'Then, you blankety-blank, flop-eared, sheep-headed coyote, what did you say you took it, for?'

"'Because,' said Bob, simply, 'I did n't know you were asleep.'

"I saw him glance toward the door of the room where Jack and Zilla were, and I knew then what it meant to be a man's friend from Bob's point of view."

Major Tom paused, and again directed his glance out of the window. He saw some one in the Stockmen's National Bank reach and draw a yellow shade down the whole length of its plate-glass, big front window, although the position of the sun did not seem to warrant such a defensive movement against its rays.

Nettlewick sat up straight in his chair. He had listened patiently, but without consuming interest, to the major's story. It had impressed him as irrelevant to the situation, and it could certainly have no effect upon the consequences. Those Western people, he thought, had an exaggerated sentimentality. They were not businesslike. They needed to be protected from their friends. Evidently the major had concluded. And what he had said amounted to nothing.

"May I ask," said the examiner, "if you have anything further to say that bears directly upon the question of those abstracted securities?"

"Abstracted securities, sir!" Major Tom turned suddenly in his chair, his blue eyes flashing upon the examiner. "What do you mean, sir?"

He drew from his coat pocket a batch of folded papers held together by a rubber band, tossed them into Nettlewick's hands, and rose to his feet.

"You 'll find those securities there, sir, every stock, bond, and share of 'em. I took them from the notes while you were counting the cash. Examine and compare them for yourself."

The major led the way back into the banking room. The examiner, astounded, perplexed, nettled, at sea, followed. He felt that he had been made the victim of something that was not exactly a hoax, but that left him in the shoes of one who had been played upon, used, and then discarded, without even an inkling of the game. Perhaps, also, his official position had been irreverently juggled with. But there was nothing he could take hold of. An official report of the matter would be an absurdity. And, somehow, he felt that he would never know anything more about the matter than he did then.

Frigidly, mechanically, Nettlewick examined the securities, found them to tally with the notes, gathered his black wallet, and rose to depart.

"I will say," he protested, turning the indignant glare of his glasses upon Major Kingman, "that your statements—your misleading statements, which you have not condescended to explain—do not appear to be quite the thing, regarded either as business or humour. I do not understand such motives or actions."

Major Tom looked down at him serenely and not unkindly.

"Son," he said, "there are plenty of things in the chaparral, and on the prairies, and up the cañons that you don't understand. But I want to thank you for listening to a garrulous old man's prosy story. We old Texans love to talk about our adventures and our old comrades, and the home folks have long ago learned to run when we begin with 'Once upon a time,' so we have to spin our yarns to the stranger within our gates."

The major smiled, but the examiner only bowed coldly, and abruptly quitted the bank. They saw him travel diagonally across the street in a straight line and enter the Stockmen's National Bank.

Major Tom sat down at his desk, and drew from his vest pocket the note Roy had given him. He had read it once, but hurriedly, and now, with something like a twinkle in his eyes, he read it again. These were the words he read:

DEAR TOM:

I hear there 's one of Uncle Sam's grayhound 's going through you, and that means that we 'll catch him inside of a couple of hours, maybe. Now, I want you to do something for me. We 've got just $2,200 in the bank, and the law requires that we have $20,000. I let Ross and Fisher have $18,000 late yesterday afternoon to buy up that Gibson bunch of cattle. They 'll realize $40,000 in less than thirty days on the transaction, but that won't make my cash on hand look any prettier to that bank examiner. Now, I can't show him those notes, for they 're just plain notes of hand without any security in sight, but you know very well that Pink Ross and Jim Fisher are two of the finest white men God ever made, and they 'll do the square thing. You remember Jim Fisher—he was the one who shot that faro dealer in El Paso. I wired Sam Bradshaw's bank to send me $20,000, and it will get in on the narrow-gauge at 10.35. You can't let a bank examiner in to count $2,200 and close your doors. Tom, you hold that examiner. Hold him. Hold him if you have to rope him and sit on his head. Watch our front window after the narrow-gauge gets in, and when we 've got the cash inside we 'll pull down the shade for a signal. Don't turn him loose till then. I 'm counting on you, Tom.

> Your Old Pard,
>> BOB BUCKLEY,
>> *Prest. Stockmen's National.*"

The major began to tear the note into small pieces and throw them into his waste basket. He gave a satisfied little chuckle as he did so.

"Confounded old reckless cowpuncher!" he growled, contentedly, "that pays him some on account for what he tried to do for me in the sheriff's office twenty years ago."

Round the Circle

"FIND YO' shirt all right, Sam?" asked Mrs. Webber, from her chair under the live-oak, where she was comfortably seated with a paper-back volume for company.

"It balances perfeckly, Marthy," answered Sam, with a suspicious pleasantness in his tone. "At first I was about ter be a little reckless and kick 'cause ther buttons was all off, but since I diskiver that the button holes is all busted out, why, I wouldn't go so fur as to say the buttons is any loss to speak of."

"Oh, well," said his wife carelessly, "put on your necktie—that'll keep it together."

Sam Webber's sheep ranch was situated in the loneliest part of the country between the Nueces and the Frio. The ranch house—a two-room, box structure, was on the rise of a gently swelling hill in the midst of a wilderness of high chaparral. In front of it was a small clearing where stood the sheep pens, shearing shed and wool house. Only a few feet back of it began the thorny jungle.

Sam was going to ride over to the Chapman ranch to see about buying some more improved merino rams. At length he came out, ready for his ride. This being a business trip of some importance, and the Chapman ranch being almost a small town in population and size, Sam had decided to "dress up" accordingly. The result was that he had transformed himself from a graceful, picturesque frontiersman into something much less pleasing to the sight. The tight white collar awkwardly constricted his muscular, mahogany-colored neck. The buttonless shirt bulged in stiff waves beneath his unbuttoned vest. The suit of "ready-made" effectually concealed the fine lines of his straight, athletic figure. His berry-brown face was set to the melancholy dignity befitting a prisoner of state. He gave Randy, his three-year old son, a pat on the head, and hurried out to where Mexico, his favorite saddlehorse, was standing.

Marthy, leisurely rocking in her chair, fixed her place in the book with her finger, and turned her head, smiling mischievously as she noted the havoc Sam had wrought with his appearance in trying to "fix up."

"Well, ef I must say it, Sam," she drawled, "you look jest like one of them hayseeds in the picture papers, 'stead of a free and independent sheepman of ther State o' Texas."

Sam climbed awkwardly into the saddle.

"You're the one ought to be 'shamed to say so," he replied hotly. "'Stead of 'tendin' to a man's clothes you al'ays settin' around a-readin' them billy-by-dam yaller-back novils."

"Oh, shet up and ride along," said Mrs. Webber, with a little jerk at the handles of her chair; "you al'ays fussin' 'bout my readin'. I do a-plenty; and I'll read when I wanter. I live in the bresh here like a varmint, never seein' nor hearin' nothin', and what other 'musement kin I have? Not in listenin' to you talk, for it's complain, complain, one day after another. Oh, go on, Sam, and leave me in peace."

Sam gave his pony a squeeze with his knees and "shoved" down the wagon trail that connected his ranch with the old, open Government road. It was eight o'clock, and already beginning to be very warm. He should have started three hours earlier. Chapman ranch was only eighteen miles away, but there was a road for only three miles of the distance. He had ridden over there once with one of the Half-Moon cowpunchers, and he had the direction well defined in his mind.

Sam turned off the old Government road at the split mesquite, and struck down the arroyo of the Quintanilla. Here was a narrow stretch of smiling valley, upholstered with a rich mat of green, curly mesquite grass; and Mexico consumed those few miles quickly with his long, easy lope. Again, upon reaching Wild Duck Waterhole, must he abandon well-defined ways. He turned now to his right up a little hill, pebble-covered, upon which grew only the tenacious and thorny prickly pear and chaparral. At the summit of this he paused to take his last general view of the landscape, for, from now on, he must wind through brakes and thickets of chaparral, pear and mesquite, for the most part seeing scarcely farther than twenty yards in any direction, choosing his way by the prairie-dweller's instinct, guided only by an occasional glimpse of a far-distant hilltop, a peculiarly shaped knot of trees, or the position of the sun.

Sam rode down the sloping hill and plunged into the great pear flat that lies between the Quintanilla and the Piedra.

In about two hours he discovered that he was lost. Then came the usual confusion of mind and the hurry to get somewhere. Mexico was anxious to redeem the situation, twisting with alacrity along the tortuous labyrinths of the jungle. At the moment his master's sureness of the route had failed his horse had divined the fact. There were no hills now that they could climb to obtain a view of the country. They came upon a few, but so dense and interlaced was the brush that scarcely could a rabbit penetrate the mass. They were in the great, lonely thicket of the Frio bottoms.

It was a mere nothing for a cattleman or a sheepman to be lost for a day or a night. The thing often happened. It was merely a matter of missing a meal or two and sleeping comfortably on your saddle blankets on a soft mattress of mesquite grass. But in Sam's case it was different. He had never been away from his ranch at night. Marthy was afraid of the country—afraid of Mexicans, of snakes, of panthers, even of sheep. So he had never left her alone.

It must have been about four in the afternoon when Sam's conscience awoke. He was limp and drenched—rather from anxiety than the heat or fatigue. Until now he had been hoping to strike the trail that led to the Frio crossing and the Chapman ranch. He must have crossed it at some dim part of it and ridden beyond. If so he was now something like fifty miles from home. If he could strike a ranch—a camp—any place where he could get a fresh horse and inquire the road, he would ride all night to get back to Marthy and the kid.

So, as I have hinted, Sam was seized by remorse. There was a big lump in his throat as he thought of the cross words he had spoken to his wife. Surely it was hard enough for her to live in that horrible country without having to bear the burden of his abuse. He cursed himself grimly, and felt a sudden flush of shame that overglowed the summer heat as he remembered the many times he had flouted and railed at her because she had a liking for reading fiction.

"Ther only so'ce ov amusement ther po' gal's got," said Sam aloud, with a sob, which unaccustomed sound caused Mexico to shy a bit. "A-livin' with a sore-headed kiote like me—a low-down skunk that ought to be licked to death with a saddle cinch—a-cookin' and a-washin' and a-livin' on mutton and beans—and me abusin' her fur takin' a squint or two in a little book!"

He thought of Marthy as she had been when he first met her in Dogtown—smart, pretty and saucy—before the sun had turned the roses in her cheeks brown and the silence of the chaparral had tamed her ambitions.

"Ef I ever speaks another hard word to ther little gal," muttered Sam, "or fails in the love and affection that's comin' to her in the deal, I hopes a wildcat'll t'ar me to pieces."

He knew what he would do. He would write to Garcia & Jones, his San Antonio merchants where he bought his supplies and sold his wool, and have them send down a big box of novels and reading matter for Marthy. Things were going to be different. He wondered whether a little piano could be placed in one of the rooms of the ranch house without the family having to move out of doors.

In nowise calculated to allay his self-reproach was the thought that Marthy and Randy would have to pass that night alone. In spite of their bickerings, when night came Marthy was wont to dismiss her fears of the country, and rest her head upon Sam's strong arm with a sigh of peaceful content and dependence. And were her fears so groundless? Sam thought of roving, marauding Mexicans, of stealthy cougars that sometimes invaded the ranches, of rattlesnakes, centipedes and a dozen possible dangers. Marthy would be frantic with fear. Randy would cry, and call for "dada" to come.

Still the interminable succession of stretches of brush, cactus and mesquite. Hollow after hollow, slope after slope—all exactly alike—all familiar by constant repetition, and yet all strange and new. If he could only arrive *somewhere*.

The straight line is Art. Nature moves in circles. A straightforward man is more an artificial product than a diplomatist is. Men lost in the snow travel in exact circles until they sink, exhausted, as their footprints have attested. Also, travelers in philosophy and other mental processes frequently wind up at their starting-point.

It was when Sam Webber was fullest of contrition and good resolves that Mexico, with a heavy sigh, subsided from his regular, brisk trot into a slow complacent walk. They were winding up an easy slope covered with brush ten or twelve feet high.

"I say now, Mex," demurred Sam, "this here won't do. I know you're plumb tired out, but we got ter git along. Oh, Lordy, ain't there no mo' houses in the world!" He gave Mexico a smart kick with his heels.

Mexico gave a protesting grunt as if to say: "What's the use of that, now we're so near?" He quickened his gait into a languid trot. Rounding a great clump of black chaparral, he stopped short. Sam dropped the bridle reins and sat, looking into the back door of his own house, not ten yards away.

Marthy, serene and comfortable, sat in her rocking-chair before the door in the shade of the house, with her feet resting luxuriously upon the steps. Randy, who was playing with a pair of spurs on the ground, looked up for a moment at his father and went on spinning the rowels and singing a little song. Marthy turned her head lazily against the back of the chair and considered the arrivals with emotionless eyes. She held a book in her lap with her finger holding the place.

Sam shook himself queerly, like a man coming out of a dream, and slowly dismounted. He moistened his dry lips.

"I see you are still a-settin'," he said, "a-readin' of them billy-by-dam yaller-back novils."

Sam had traveled round the circle and was himself again.

Hearts and Hands

A T DENVER there was an influx of passengers into the coaches on the eastbound B. & M. express. In one coach there sat a very pretty young woman dressed in elegant taste and surrounded by all the luxurious comforts of an experienced traveller. Among the newcomers were two young men, one of handsome presence, with a bold, frank countenance and manner; the other a ruffled, glum-faced person, heavily built and roughly dressed. The two were handcuffed together.

As they passed down the aisle of the coach the only vacant seat offered was a reversed one facing the attractive young woman. Here the linked couple seated themselves. The young woman's glance fell upon them with a distant, swift disinterest; then, with a lovely smile brightening her countenance and a tender pink tingeing her rounded cheeks, she held out a little gray-gloved hand. When she spoke her voice, full, sweet and deliberate, proclaimed that its owner was accustomed to speak and be heard.

"Well, Mr. Easton, if you *will* make me speak first, I suppose I must. Don't you ever recognize old friends when you meet them in the West?"

The younger man roused himself sharply at the sound of her voice, seemed to struggle with a slight embarrassment which he threw off instantly, and then clasped her fingers with his left hand.

"It's Miss Fairchild," he said, with a smile. "I'll ask you to excuse the other hand; it's otherwise engaged just at present."

He slightly raised his right hand, bound at the wrist by the shining "bracelet" to the left one of his companion. The glad look in the girl's eyes slowly changed to a bewildered horror. The glow faded from her cheeks. Her lips parted in a vague, relaxing distress. Easton, with a little laugh as if amused, was about to speak again when the other forestalled him. The glum-faced man had been watching the girl's countenance with veiled glances from his keen, shrewd eyes.

"You'll excuse me for speaking, miss, but I see you're ac-quainted with the marshal here. If you'll ask him to speak a word for me when we get to the pen he'll do it, and it'll make things easier for me there. He's taking me to Leavenworth prison. It's seven years for counterfeiting."

"Oh!" said the girl, with a deep breath and returning color. "So, that is what you are doing out here? A marshal!"

"My dear Miss Fairchild," said Easton calmly, "I had to do something. Money has a way of taking wings unto itself, and you know it takes money to keep step with our crowd in Washington. I saw this opening in the West, and—well, a marshalship isn't quite as high a position as that of ambassador, but——"

"The ambassador," said the girl warmly, "doesn't call any more. He needn't ever have done so. You ought to know that. And so now you are one of these dashing Western heroes, and you ride and shoot and go into all kinds of dangers. That's different from the Washington life. You have been missed from the old crowd."

The girl's eyes, fascinated, went back, widening a little, to rest upon the glittering handcuffs.

"Don't you worry about them, miss," said the other man. "All marshals handcuff themselves to their prisoners to keep them from getting away. Mr. Easton knows his business."

"Will we see you again soon in Washington?" asked the girl.

"Not soon, I think," said Easton. "My butterfly days are over, I fear."

"I love the West," said the girl, irrelevantly. Her eyes were shining softly. She looked away out the car window. She began to speak truly and simply, without the gloss of style and manner. "Mamma and I spent the Summer in Denver. She went home a week ago because father was slightly ill. I could live and be happy in the West. I think the air here agrees with me. Money isn't everything. But people always misunderstand things and remain stupid——"

"Say, Mr. Marshal," growled the glum-faced man, "This isn't quite fair. I'm needin' a drink, and haven't had a smoke all day. Haven't you talked long enough? Take me in the smoker now, won't you? I'm half dead for a pipe."

The bound travellers rose to their feet, Easton with the same slow smile on his face.

"I can't deny a petition for tobacco," he said lightly. "It's the one friend of the unfortunate. Good-bye, Miss Fairchild. Duty calls, you know." He held out his hand for a farewell.

"It's too bad you are not going East," she said, reclothing herself with manner and style. "But you must go on to Leavenworth, I suppose?"

"Yes," said Easton, "I must go on to Leavenworth."

The two men sidled down the aisle into the smoker.

Two passengers in a seat nearby had heard most of the conversation. Said one of them: "That's marshal's a good sort of chap. Some of these Western fellows are all right."

"Pretty young to hold an office like that, isn't he?" asked the other.

"Young!" exclaimed the first speaker, "why—— Oh! didn't you catch on? Say—did you ever know an officer to handcuff a prisoner to his *right* hand?"

The Lonesome Road

BROWN AS a coffee-berry, rugged, pistoled, spurred, wary, indefeasible, I saw my old friend, Deputy-Marshal Buck Caperton, stumble, with jingling rowels, into a chair in the marshal's outer office.

And because the court-house was almost deserted at that hour, and because Buck would sometimes relate to me things that were out of print, I followed him in and tricked him into talk through knowledge of a weakness he had. For, cigarettes rolled with sweet corn husk were as honey to Buck's palate; and though he could finger the trigger of a forty-five with skill and suddenness, he never could learn to roll a cigarette.

It was through no fault of mine (for I rolled the cigarettes tight and smooth), but the upshot of some whim of his own, that instead of to an Odyssey of the chaparral, I listened to—a dissertation upon matrimony! This from Buck Caperton! But I maintain that the cigarettes were impeccable, and crave absolution for myself.

"We just brought in Jim and Bud Granberry," said Buck. "Train robbing, you know. Held up the Aransas Pass last month. We caught 'em in the Twenty-Mile pear flat, south of the Nueces."

"Have much trouble corralling them?" I asked, for here was the meat that my hunger for epics craved.

"Some," said Buck; and then, during a little pause, his thoughts stampeded off the trail. "It 's kind of queer about women," he went on, "and the place they 're supposed to occupy in botany. If I was asked to classify them I 'd say they was a human loco weed. Ever see a bronc that had been chewing loco? Ride him up to a puddle of water two feet wide, and he 'll give a snort and fall back on you. It looks as big as the Mississippi River to him. Next trip he 'd walk into a cañon a thousand feet deep thinking it was a prairie-dog hole. Same way with a married man.

"I was thinking of Perry Rountree, that used to be my side-kicker before he committed matrimony. In them days me and Perry hated indisturbances of any kind. We roamed around considerable, stirring up the echoes and making 'em attend to business. Why, when me and Perry wanted to have some fun in a town it was a picnic for the census takers. They just counted the marshal's posse that it took to subdue us, and there was your population. But then there came along this Mariana Goodnight girl and looked at Perry sideways, and he was all bridle-wise and saddle-broke before you could skin a yearling.

"I was n't even asked to the wedding. I reckon the bride had my pedigree and the front elevation of my habits all mapped out, and she decided that Perry would trot better in double harness without any unconverted mustang like Buck Caperton whickering around on the matrimonial range. So it was six months before I saw Perry again.

"One day I was passing on the edge of town, and I see something like a man in a little yard by a little house with a sprinkling-pot squirting water on a rose-bush. Seemed to me, I 'd seen something like it before, and I stopped at the gate, trying to figure out its brands. 'Twas not Perry Rountree, but 'twas the kind of a curdled jellyfish matrimony had made out of him.

"Homicide was what that Mariana had perpetrated. He was looking well enough, but he had on a white collar and shoes, and you could tell in a minute that he 'd speak polite and pay taxes and stick his little finger out while drinking, just like a sheep man or a citizen. Great skyrockets! but I hated to see Perry all corrupted and Willie-ized like that.

"He came out to the gate, and shook hands; and I says, with scorn, and speaking like a paroquet with the pip: 'Beg pardon—Mr. Rountree, I believe. Seems to me I sagatiated in your associations once, if I am not mistaken.'

"'Oh, go to the devil, Buck,' says Perry, polite, as I was afraid he 'd be.

"'Well, then,' says I, 'you poor, contaminated adjunct of a sprinkling-pot and degraded household pet, what did you go and do it for? Look at you, all decent and unriotous, and only fit to sit on juries and mend the wood-house door. You was a man once. I have hostility for all such acts. Why don't you go in the house and count the tidies or set the clock, and not stand out here in the atmosphere? A jack-rabbit might come along and bite you.'

"'Now Buck,' says Perry, speaking mild, and some sorrowful, 'you don't understand. A married man has got to be different. He feels different from a tough old cloudburst like you. It 's sinful to waste time pulling up towns just to look at their roots, and playing faro and looking upon red liquor, and such restless policies as them.'

"'There was a time,' says I, and I expect I sighed when I mentioned it, 'when a certain domesticated little Mary's lamb I could name was some instructed himself in the line of pernicious sprightliness. I never expected, Perry, to see you reduced down from a full-grown pestilence to such a frivolous fraction of a man. Why,' says I, 'you 've got a necktie on; and you speak a senseless kind of indoor drivel that reminds me of a storekeeper or a lady. You look to me like you might tote an umbrella and wear suspenders, and go home of nights.'

"'The little woman,' says Perry, 'has made some improvements, I believe. You can't understand, Buck. I have n't been away from the house at night since we was married.'

"We talked on a while, me and Perry, and, as sure as I live, that man interrupted me in the middle of my talk to tell me about six tomato plants he had growing in his garden. Shoved his agricultural degradation right up under my nose while I was telling him about the fun we had tarring and feathering that faro dealer at California Pete's layout! But by and by Perry shows a flicker of sense.

"'Buck,' says he, 'I 'll have to admit that it is a little dull at times. Not that I 'm not perfectly happy with the little woman, but a man seems to require some excitement now and then. Now, I 'll tell you: Mariana's gone visiting this afternoon, and she won't be home till seven o'clock. That 's the limit for both of us—seven o'clock. Neither of us ever stays out a minute after that time unless we are together. Now, I 'm glad you came along, Buck,' says Perry, 'for I 'm feeling just like having one more rip-roaring razoo with you for the sake of old times. What you say to us putting in the afternoon having fun—I 'd like it fine,' says Perry.

"I slapped that old captive range-rider half across his little garden.

"'Get your hat, you old dried-up alligator,' I shouts, 'you ain't dead yet. You 're part human, anyhow, if you did get all bogged up in matrimony. We 'll take this town to pieces and see what makes it tick. We 'll make all kinds of profligate demands upon the science of cork pulling. You 'll grow horns yet, old muley cow,' says I, punching Perry in the ribs, 'if you trot around on the trail of vice with your Uncle Buck.'

"'I 'll have to be home by seven, you know,' says Perry again.

"'Oh, yes,' says I, winking to myself, for I knew the kind of seven o'clocks Perry Rountree got back by after he once got to passing repartee with the bartenders.

"We goes down to the Gray Mule saloon—that old 'dobe building by the depot.

"'Give it a name,' says I, as soon as we got one hoof on the foot-rest.

"'Sarsaparilla,' says Perry.

"You could have knocked me down with a lemon peeling.

"'Insult me as much as you want to,' I says to Perry, 'but don't startle the bartender. He may have heart-disease. Come on, now; your tongue got twisted. The tall glasses,' I orders, 'and the bottle in the left-hand corner of the ice-chest.'

"'Sarsaparilla,' repeats Perry, and then his eyes get animated, and I see he 's got some great scheme in his mind he wants to emit.

"'Buck,' he says, all interested, 'I 'll tell you what! I want to make this a red-letter day. I 've been keeping close at home, and I want to turn myself a-loose. We 'll have the highest old time you ever saw. We 'll go in the back room here and play checkers till half-past six.'

"I leaned against the bar, and I says to Gotch-eared Mike, who was on watch:

"'For God's sake don't mention this. You know what Perry used to be. He 's had the fever, and the doctor says we must humour him.'

"'Give us the checker-board and the men, Mike,' says Perry. 'Come on, Buck, I 'm just wild to have some excitement.'

"'I went in the back room with Perry. Before we closed the door, I says to Mike:

"'Don't ever let it straggle out from under your hat that you seen Buck Caperton fraternal with sarsaparilla or *persona grata* with a checker-board, or I 'll make a swallow-fork in your other ear.'

"I locked the door and me and Perry played checkers. To see that poor old humiliated piece of household bric-a-brac sitting there and sniggering out loud whenever he jumped a man, and all obnoxious with animation when he got into my king row, would have made a sheepdog sick with mortification. Him that was once satisfied only when he was pegging six boards at keno or giving the faro dealers nervous prostration—to see him pushing them checkers about like Sally Louisa at a school-children's party—why, I was all smothered up with mortification.

"And I sits there playing the black men, all sweating for fear somebody I knew would find it out. And I thinks to myself some about this marrying business, and how it seems to be the same kind of a game as that Mrs. Delilah played. She give her old man a hair cut, and everybody knows what a man's head looks like after a woman cuts his hair. And then when the Pharisees came around to guy him he was so 'shamed he went to work and kicked the whole house down on top of the whole outfit. 'Them married men,' thinks I, 'lose all their spirit and instinct for riot and foolishness. They won't drink, they won't buck the tiger, they won't even fight. What do they want to go and stay married for?' I asks myself.

"But Perry seems to be having hilarity in considerable quantities.

"'Buck old hoss,' says he, 'is n't this just the hell-roaringest time we ever had in our lives? I don't know when I 've been stirred up so. You see, I 've been sticking pretty close to home since I married, and I have n't been on a spree in a long time.'

"'Spree!' Yes, that 's what he called it. Playing checkers in the back room of the Gray Mule! I suppose it did seem to him a little more immoral and nearer to a prolonged debauch than standing over six tomato plants with a sprinkling-pot.

"Every little bit Perry looks at his watch and says:

"'I got to be home, you know, Buck, at seven.'

"'All right,' I 'd say. 'Romp along and move. This here excitement 's killing me. If I don't reform some, and loosen up the strain of this checkered dissipation I won't have a nerve left.'

"It might have been half-past six when commotions began to go on outside in the street. We heard a yelling and a six-shootering, and a lot of galloping and manœuvres.

"'What 's that?' I wonders.

"'Oh, some nonsense outside,' says Perry. 'It 's your move. We just got time to play this game.'

"'I 'll just take a peep through the window,' says I, 'and see. You can't expect a mere mortal to stand the excitement of having a king jumped and listen to an unidentified conflict going on at the same time.'

"The Gray Mule saloon was one of them old Spanish dobe buildings, and the back room only had two little windows a foot wide, with iron bars in 'em. I looked out one, and I see the cause of the rucus.

"There was the Trimble gang—ten of 'em—the worst outfit of desperadoes and horse-thieves in Texas, coming up the street shooting right and left. They was coming right straight for the Gray Mule. Then they got past the range of my sight, but we heard 'em ride up to the front door, and then they socked the place full of lead. We heard the big looking-glass behind the bar knocked all to pieces and the bottles crashing. We could see Gotch-eared Mike in his apron running across the plaza like a coyote, with the bullets puffing up the dust all around him. Then the gang went to work in the saloon, drinking what they wanted and smashing what they did n't.

"Me and Perry both knew that gang, and they knew us. The year before Perry married, him and me was in the same ranger company—and we fought that outfit down on the San Miguel, and brought back Ben Trimble and two others for murder.

"'We can't get out,' says I. 'We 'll have to stay in here till they leave.'

"Perry looked at his watch.

"'Twenty-five to seven,' says he. 'We can finish that game. I got two men on you. It 's your move, Buck. I got to be home at seven, you know.'

We sat down and went on playing. The Trimble gang had a roughhouse for sure. They were getting good and drunk. They 'd drink a while and holler a while, and then they 'd shoot up a few bottles and glasses. Two or three times they came and tried to open our door. Then there was some more shooting outside, and I looked out the window again. Ham Gossett, the town marshal, had a posse in the houses and stores across the street, and was trying to bag a Trimble or two through the windows.

"I lost that game of checkers. I 'm free in saying that I lost three kings that I might have saved if I had been corralled in a more peaceful pasture. But that drivelling married man sat there and cackled when he won a man like an unintelligent hen picking up a grain of corn.

"When the game was over Perry gets up and looks at his watch.

"'I 've had a glorious time, Buck,' says he, 'but I 'll have to be going now. It 's a quarter to seven, and I got to be home by seven, you know.'

"I thought he was joking.

"'They 'll clear out or be dead drunk in half an hour or an hour,' says I. 'You ain't that tired of being married that you want to commit any more sudden suicide, are you?' says I, giving him the laugh.

"'One time,' says Perry, 'I was half an hour late getting home. I met Mariana on the street looking for me. If you could have seen her, Buck—but you don't understand. She knows what a wild kind of a snoozer I 've been, and she 's afraid something will happen. I 'll never be late getting home again. I 'll say good-bye to you now, Buck.'

"I got between him and the door.

"'Married man,' says I, 'I know you was christened a fool the minute the preacher tangled you up, but don't you never sometimes think one little think on a human basis? There 's ten of that gang in there, and they 're pizen with whiskey and desire for murder. They 'll drink you up like a bottle of booze before you get half-way to the door. Be intelligent, now, and use at least wild-hog sense. Sit down and wait till we have some chance to get out without being carried in baskets.'

"'I got to be home by seven, Buck,' repeats this henpecked thing of little wisdom, like an unthinking poll parrot. 'Mariana,' says he, ''ll be looking out for me.' And he reaches down and pulls a leg out of the checker table. 'I 'll go through this Trimble outfit,' says he, 'like a cottontail through a brush corral. I 'm not pestered any more with a desire to engage in rucuses, but I got to be home by seven. You lock the door after me, Buck.

And don't you forget—I won three out of them five games. I 'd play longer, but Mariana——'

"'Hush up, you old locoed road runner,' I interrupts. Did you ever notice your Uncle Buck locking doors against trouble? I 'm not married,' says I, 'but I 'm as big a d——n fool as any Mormon. One from four leaves three,' says I, and I gathers out another leg of the table. 'We 'll get home by seven,' says I, 'whether it 's the heavenly one or the other. May I see you home?' says I, 'you sarsaparilla-drinking, checker-playing glutton for death and destruction.'

"We opened the door easy, and then stampeded for the front. Part of the gang was lined up at the bar; part of 'em was passing over the drinks, and two or three was peeping out the door and window taking shots at the marshal's crowd. The room was so full of smoke we got half-way to the front door before they noticed us. Then I heard Berry Trimble's voice somewhere yell out:

"How 'd that Buck Caperton get in here?' and he skinned the side of my neck with a bullet. I reckon he felt bad over that miss, for Berry's the best shot south of the Southern Pacific Railroad. But the smoke in the saloon was some too thick for good shooting.

"Me and Perry smashed over two of the gang with our table legs, which did n't miss like the guns did, and as we run out the door I grabbed a Winchester from a fellow who was watching the outside, and I turned and regulated the account of Mr. Berry.

"Me and Perry got out and around the corner all right. I never much expected to get out, but I was n't going to be intimidated by that married man. According to Perry's idea, checkers was the event of the day, but if I am any judge of gentle recreations that little table-leg parade through the Gray Mule saloon deserved the head-lines in the bill of particulars.

"'Walk fast,' says Perry, 'it 's two minutes to seven, and I got to be home by——'

"'Oh, shut up,' says I. 'I had an appointment as chief performer at an inquest at seven, and I 'm not kicking about not keeping it.'

"I had to pass by Perry's little house. His Mariana was standing at the gate. We got there at five minutes past seven. She had on a blue wrapper, and her hair was pulled back smooth like little girls do when they want to look grown-folksy. She did n't see us till we got close, for she was gazing up the other way. Then she backed around, and saw Perry, and a kind of a look scooted around over her face—danged if I can describe it. I heard her breathe long, just like a cow when you turn her calf in the lot, and she says: 'You 're late, Perry.'

"'Five minutes,' says Perry, cheerful. 'Me and old Buck was having a game of checkers.'

"Perry introduces me to Mariana, and they ask me to come in. No, sir-ee. I 'd had enough truck with married folks for that day. I says I 'll be going along, and that I 've spent a very pleasant afternoon with my old partner—'especially,' says I, just to jostle Perry, 'during that game when the table legs came all loose.' But I 'd promised him not to let her know anything.

"I 've been worrying over that business ever since it happened," continued Buck. "There 's one thing about it that 's got me all twisted up, and I can't figure it out."

"What was that?" I asked, as I rolled and handed Buck the last cigarette.

"Why, I 'll tell you: When I saw the look that little woman give Perry when she turned round and saw him coming back to the ranch safe—why was it I got the idea all in a minute that that look of hers was worth more than the whole caboodle of us—sarsaparilla, checkers, and all, and that the d—n fool in the game was n't named Perry Rountree at all?"

The Pimienta Pancakes

WHILE WE were rounding up a bunch of the Triangle-O cattle in the Frio bottoms a projecting branch of a dead mesquite caught my wooden stirrup and gave my ankle a wrench that laid me up in camp for a week.

On the third day of my compulsory idleness I crawled out near the grub wagon, and reclined helpless under the conversational fire of Judson Odom, the camp cook. Jud was a monologist by nature, whom Destiny, with customary blundering, had set in a profession wherein he was bereaved, for the greater portion of his time, of an audience.

Therefore, I was manna in the desert of Jud's obmutescence.

Betimes I was stirred by invalid longings for something to eat that did not come under the caption of "grub." I had visions of the maternal pantry "deep as first love, and wild with all regret," and then I asked:

"Jud, can you make pancakes?"

Jud laid down his six-shooter, with which he was preparing to pound an antelope steak, and stood over me in what I felt to be a menacing attitude. He further indorsed my impression that his pose was resentful by fixing upon me with his light blue eyes a look of cold suspicion.

"Say, you," he said, with candid, though not excessive, choler, "did you mean that straight, or was you trying to throw the gaff into me? Some of the boys been telling you about me and that pancake racket?"

"No, Jud," I said, sincerely, "I meant it. It seems to me I'd swap my pony and saddle for a stack of buttered brown pancakes with some first crop, open kettle, New Orleans sweetening. Was there a story about pancakes?"

Jud was mollified at once when he saw that I had not been dealing in allusions. He brought some mysterious bags and tin boxes from the grub wagon and set them in the shade of the hackberry where I lay reclined. I watched him as he began to arrange them leisurely and untie their many strings.

"No, not a story," said Jud, as he worked, "but just the

logical disclosures in the case of me and that pink-eyed snoozer from Mired Mule Cañada and Miss Willella Learight. I don't mind telling you.

"I was punching then for old Bill Toomey, on the San Miguel. One day I gets all ensnared up in aspirations for to eat some canned grub that hasn't ever mooed or baaed or grunted or been in peck measures. So, I gets on my bronc and pushes the wind for Uncle Emsley Telfair's store at the Pimienta Crossing on the Nueces.

"About three in the afternoon I threw my bridle rein over a mesquite limb and walked the last twenty yards into Uncle Emsley's store. I got up on the counter and told Uncle Emsley that the signs pointed to the devastation of the fruit crop of the world. In a minute I had a bag of crackers and a long-handled spoon, with an open can each of apricots and pineapples and cherries and greengages beside of me with Uncle Emsley busy chopping away with the hatchet at the yellow clings. I was feeling like Adam before the apple stampede, and was digging my spurs into the side of the counter and working with my twenty-four-inch spoon when I happened to look out of the window into the yard of Uncle Emsley's house, which was next to the store.

"There was a girl standing there—an imported girl with fixings on—philandering with a croquet maul and amusing herself by watching my style of encouraging the fruit canning industry.

"I slid off the counter and delivered up my shovel to Uncle Emsley.

"'That's my niece,' says he; 'Miss Willella Learight, down from Palestine on a visit. Do you want that I should make you acquainted?'

"'The Holy Land,' I says to myself, my thoughts milling some as I tried to run 'em into the corral. 'Why not? There was sure angels in Pales—— Why yes, Uncle Emsley,' I says out loud, 'I'd be awful edified to meet Miss Learight.'

"So Uncle Emsley took me out in the yard and gave us each other's entitlements.

"I never was shy about women. I never could understand why some men who can break a mustang before breakfast and shave in the dark, get all left-handed and full of perspiration and excuses when they see a bolt of calico draped around what belongs in it. Inside of eight minutes me and Miss Willella was aggravating the croquet balls around as amiable as second cousins. She gave me a dig about the quantity of canned fruit I had eaten, and I got back at her, flat-footed, about how a certain lady named Eve started the fruit trouble in the first free-grass pasture—'Over in Palestine, wasn' it?' says I, as easy and pat as roping a one-year-old.

"That was how I acquired cordiality for the proximities of Miss Willella Learight; and the disposition grew larger as time passed. She was stopping at Pimienta Crossing for her health, which was very good, and for the climate, which was forty per cent. hotter than Palestine. I rode over to see her once every week for a while; and then I figured it out that if I doubled the number of trips I would see her twice as often.

"One week I slipped in a third trip; and that's where the pancakes and the pink-eyed snoozer busted into the game.

"That evening, while I set on the counter with a peach and two damsons in my mouth, I asked Uncle Emsley how Miss Willella was.

"'Why,' says Uncle Emsley, 'she's gone riding with Jackson Bird, the sheep man from over at Mired Mule Cañada.'

"I swallowed the peach seed and the two damson seeds. I guess somebody held the counter by the bridle while I got off; and then I walked out straight ahead till I butted against the mesquite where my roan was tied.

"'She's gone riding,' I whisper in my bronc's ear, 'with Bird-stone Jack, the hired mule from Sheep Man's Cañada. Did you get that, old Leather-and-Gallops?'

"That bronc of mine wept, in his way. He'd been raised a cow pony and he didn't care for snoozers.

"I went back and said to Uncle Emsley: 'Did you say a sheep man?'

"'I said a sheep man,' says Uncle again. 'You must have heard tell of Jackson Bird. He's got eight sections of grazing and four thousand head of the finest Merinos south of the Arctic Circle.'

"I went out and sat on the ground in the shade of the store and leaned against a prickly pear. I sifted sand into my boots with unthinking hands while I soliloquised a quantity about this bird with the Jackson plumage to his name.

"I never had believed in harming sheep men. I see one, one day, reading a Latin grammar on hossback, and I never touched him! They never irritated me like they do most cowmen. You wouldn't go to work now, and impair and disfigure snoozers, would you, that eat on tables and wear little shoes and speak to you on subjects? I had always let 'em pass, just as you would a jack-rabbit; with a polite word and a guess about the weather, but no stopping to swap canteens. I never thought it was worth while to be hostile with a snoozer. And because I'd been lenient, and let 'em live, here was one going around riding with Miss Willella Learight!

"An hour by sun they come loping back, and stopped at Uncle Emsley's gate. The sheep person helped her off; and they stood throwing each other sentences all sprightful and sagacious for a while. And then this feathered Jackson flies up in his saddle and raises his little stewpot of a hat, and trots off in the direction of his mutton ranch. By this time I had turned the sand out of my boots and unpinned myself from the prickly pear; and by the time he gets half a mile out of Pimienta, I singlefoots up beside him on my bronc.

"I said that snoozer was pink-eyed, but he wasn't. His seeing arrangement was grey enough, but his eyelashes was pink and his hair was sandy, and that gave you the idea. Sheep man?—he wasn't more than a lamb man, anyhow—a little thing with his neck involved in a yellow silk handkerchief, and shoes tied up in bowknots.

"'Afternoon!' says I to him. 'You now ride with a equestrian who is commonly called Dead-Moral-Certainty Judson, on account of the way I shoot. When I want a stranger to know me I always introduce myself before the draw, for I never did like to shake hands with ghosts.'

"'Ah,' says he, just like that— 'Ah, I'm glad to know you, Mr. Judson. I'm Jackson Bird, from over at Mired Mule Ranch.'

"Just then one of my eyes saw a roadrunner skipping down the hill with a young tarantula in his bill, and the other eye noticed a rabbit-hawk sitting on a dead limb in a water-elm. I popped over one after the other with my forty-five, just to show him. 'Two out of three,' says I. 'Birds just naturally seem to draw my fire wherever I go.'

"'Nice shooting,' says the sheep man, without a flutter. 'But don't you sometimes ever miss the third shot? Elegant fine rain that was last week for the young grass, Mr. Judson?' says he.

"'Willie,' says I, riding over close to his palfrey, 'your infatuated parents may have denounced you by the name of Jackson, but you sure moulted into a twittering Willie—let us slough off this here analysis of rain and the elements, and get down to talk that is outside the vocabulary of parrots. That is a bad habit you have got of riding with young ladies over at Pimienta. I've known birds,' says I, 'to be served on toast for less than that. Miss Willella,' says I, 'don't ever want any nest made out of sheep's wool by a tomtit of the Jacksonian branch of ornithology. Now, are you going to quit, or do you wish for to gallop up against this Dead-Moral-Certainty attachment to my name, which is good for two hyphens and at least one set of funeral obsequies?'

"Jackson Bird flushed up some, and then he laughed.

"'Why, Mr. Judson,' says he, 'you've got the wrong idea. I've called on Miss Learight a few times; but not for the purpose you imagine. My object is purely a gastronomical one.'

"I reached for my gun.

"'Any coyote,' says I, 'that would boast of dishonourable——'

"'Wait a minute,' says this Bird, 'till I explain. What would I do with a wife? If you ever saw that ranch of mine! I do my own cooking and mending. Eating—that's all the pleasure I get out of sheep raising. Mr. Judson, did you ever taste the pancakes that Miss Learight makes?'

"'Me? No,' I told him. 'I never was advised that she was up to any culinary manœuvres.'

"'They're golden sunshine,' says he; 'honey-browned by the ambrosial fires of Epicurus. I'd give two years of my life to get the recipe for making them pancakes. That's what I went to see Miss Learight for,' says Jackson Bird, 'but I haven't been able to get it from her. It's an old recipe that's been in the family for seventy-five years. They hand it down from one generation to another, but they don't give it away to outsiders. If I could get that recipe, so I could make them pancakes for myself on my ranch, I'd be a happy man,' says Bird.

"'Are you sure,' I says to him, 'that it ain't the hand that mixes the pancakes that you're after?'

"'Sure,' says Jackson. 'Miss Learight is a mighty nice girl, but I can assure you my intentions go no further than the gastro——' but he seen my hand going down to my holster and he changed his similitude—'than the desire to procure a copy of the pancake recipe,' he finishes.

"'You ain't such a bad little man,' says I, trying to be fair. 'I was thinking some of making orphans of your sheep, but I'll let you fly away this time. But you stick to pancakes,' says I, 'as close as the middle one of a stack; and don't go and mistake sentiments for syrup, or there'll be singing at your ranch, and you won't hear it.'

"'To convince you that I am sincere,' says the sheep man, 'I'll ask you to help me. Miss Learight and you being closer friends, maybe she would do for you what she wouldn't for me. If you will get me a copy of that pancake recipe, I give you my word that I'll never call upon her again.'

"'That's fair,' I says, and I shook hands with Jackson Bird. 'I'll get it for you if I can, and glad to oblige.' And he turned off down the big pear flat on the Piedra, in the direction of Mired Mule; and I steered northwest for old Bill Toomey's ranch.

"It was five days afterward when I got another chance to ride over to Pimienta. Miss Willella and me passed a gratifying evening at Uncle Emsley's. She sang some, and exasperated the piano quite a lot with quotations from the operas. I gave imitations of a rattlesnake, and told her about Snaky McFee's new way of skinning cows, and described the trip I made to Saint Louis once. We was getting along in one another's estimations fine. Thinks I, if Jackson Bird can now be persuaded to migrate, I win. I recollect his promise about the pancake receipt, and I thinks I will persuade it from Miss Willella and give it to him; and then if I catches Birdie off of Mired Mule again, I'll make him hop the twig.

"So, along about ten o'clock, I put on a wheedling smile and says to Miss Willella: 'Now, if there's anything I do like better than the sight of a red steer on green grass it's the taste of a nice hot pancake smothered in sugar-house molasses.'

"Miss Willella gives a little jump on the piano stool, and looked at me curious.

"'Yes,' says she, 'they're real nice. What did you say was the name of that street in Saint Louis, Mr. Odom, where you lost your hat?'

"'Pancake Avenue,' says I, with a wink, to show her that I was on about the family receipt, and couldn't be side-corralled off of the subject. 'Come, now, Miss Willella,' I says; 'let's hear how you make 'em. Pancakes is just whirling in my head like wagon wheels. Start her off, now—pound of flour, eight dozen eggs, and so on. How does the catalogue of constituents run?'

"'Excuse me for a moment, please,' says Miss Willella, and she gives me a quick kind of sideways look, and slides off the stool. She ambled out into the other room, and directly Uncle Emsley comes in in his shirt sleeves, with a pitcher of water. He turns around to get a glass on the table, and I see a forty-five in his hip pocket. 'Great post-holes!' thinks I, 'but here's a family thinks a heap of cooking receipts, protecting it with firearms. I've known outfits that wouldn't do that much by a family feud.'

"'Drink this here down,' says Uncle Emsley, handing me the glass of water. 'You've rid too far to-day, Jud, and got yourself over-excited. Try to think about something else now.'

"'Do you know how to make them pancakes, Uncle Emsley?' I asked.

"'Well, I'm not as apprised in the anatomy of them as some,' says Uncle Emsley, 'but I reckon you take a sifter of plaster of paris and a little dough and saleratus and corn meal, and mix 'em with eggs and buttermilk as usual. Is old Bill going to ship beeves to Kansas City again this spring, Jud?'

"That was all the pancake specifications I could get that night. I didn't wonder that Jackson Bird found it uphill work. So I dropped the subject and talked with Uncle Emsley a while about hollow-horn and cyclones. And then Miss Willella came and said 'Good-night,' and I hit the breeze for the ranch.

"About a week afterward I met Jackson Bird riding out of Pimienta as I rode in, and we stopped in the road for a few frivolous remarks.

"'Got the bill of particulars for them flapjacks yet?' I asked him.

"'Well, no,' says Jackson. 'I don't seem to have any success in getting hold of it. Did you try?'

"'I did,' says I, 'and 'twas like trying to dig a prairie dog out of his hole with a peanut hull. That pancake receipt must be a jookalorum, the way they hold on to it.'

"'I'm most ready to give it up,' says Jackson, so discouraged in his pronunciations that I felt sorry for him; 'but I did want to know how to make them pancakes to eat on my lonely ranch,' says he. 'I lie awake of nights thinking how good they are.'

"'You keep on trying for it,' I tells him, 'and I'll do the same. One of us is bound to get a rope over its horns before long. Well, so-long, Jacksy.'

"You see, by this time we was on the peacefullest of terms. When I saw that he wasn't after Miss Willella I had more endurable contemplations of that sandy-haired snoozer. In order to help out the ambitions of his appetite I kept on trying to get that receipt from Miss Willella. But every time I would say 'pancakes' she would get sort of remote and fidgety about the eye, and try to change the subject. If I held her to it she would slide out and round up Uncle Emsley with his pitcher of water and hip-pocket howitzer.

"One day I galloped over to the store with a fine bunch of blue verbenas that I cut out of a herd of wild flowers over on Poisoned Dog Prairie. Uncle Emsley looked at 'em with one eye shut and says:

"'Haven't ye heard the news?'

"'Cattle up?' I asks.

"'Willella and Jackson Bird was married in Palestine yesterday,' says he. 'Just got a letter this morning.'

"I dropped them flowers in a cracker-barrel, and let the news trickle in my ears and down toward my upper left-hand shirt pocket until it got to my feet.

"'Would you mind saying that over again once more, Uncle Emsley?' says I. 'Maybe my hearing has got wrong, and you only said that prime heifers was 4.80 on the hoof, or something like that.'

"'Married yesterday,' says Uncle Emsley, 'and gone to Waco and Niagara Falls on a wedding tour. Why, didn't you see none of the signs all along? Jackson Bird has been courting Willella ever since that day he took her out riding.'

"'Then,' says I, in a kind of yell, 'what was all this zizzaparoola he gives me about pancakes? Tell me *that*.'

"When I said 'pancakes' Uncle Emsley sort of dodged and stepped back.

"'Somebody's been dealing me pancakes from the bottom of the deck,' I says, 'and I'll find out. I believe you know. Talk up,' says I, 'or we'll mix a panful of batter right here.'

"I slid over the counter after Uncle Emsley. He grabbed at his gun, but it was in a drawer, and he missed it two inches. I got him by the front of his shirt and shoved him in a corner.

"'Talk pancakes,' says I, 'or be made into one. Does Miss Willella make 'em?'

"'She never made one in her life and I never saw one,' says Uncle Emsley, soothing. 'Calm down now, Jud—calm down. You've got excited, and that wound in your head is contaminating your sense of intelligence. Try not to think about pancakes.'

"'Uncle Emsley,' says I, 'I'm not wounded in the head except so far as my natural cogitative instincts run to runts. Jackson Bird told me he was calling on Miss Willella for the purpose of finding out her system of producing pancakes, and he asked me to help him get the bill of lading of the ingredients. I done so, with the results as you see. Have I been sodded down with Johnson grass by a pink-eyed snoozer, or what?'

"'Slack up your grip on my dress shirt,' says Uncle Emsley, 'and I'll tell you. Yes, it looks like Jackson Bird has gone and humbugged you some. The day after he went riding with Willella he came back and told me and her to watch out for you whenever you got to talking about pancakes. He said you was in camp once where they was cooking flapjacks, and one of the fellows cut you over the head with a frying pan. Jackson said that whenever you got overhot or excited that wound hurt you and made you kind of crazy, and you went raving about pancakes. He told us to just get you worked off of the subject and soothed down, and you wouldn't be dangerous. So, me and Willella done the best by you we knew how. Well, well,' says Uncle Emsley, 'that Jackson Bird is sure a seldom kind of a snoozer.'"

During the progress of Jud's story he had been slowly but deftly combining certain portions of the contents of his sacks and cans. Toward the close of it he set before me the finished product—a pair of red-hot, rich-hued pancakes on a tin plate.

From some secret hoarding place he also brought a lump of excellent butter and a bottle of golden syrup.

"How long ago did these things happen?" I asked him.

"Three years," said Jud. "They're living on the Mired Mule Ranch now. But I haven't seen either of 'em since. They say Jackson Bird was fixing his ranch up fine with rocking chairs and window curtains all the time he was putting me up the pancake tree. Oh, I got over it after a while. But the boys kept the racket up."

"Did you make these cakes by the famous recipe?" I asked.

"Didn't I tell you there wasn't no receipt?" said Jud. "The boys hollered pancakes till they got pancake hungry, and I cut this recipe out of a newspaper. How does the truck taste?"

"They're delicious," I answered. "Why don't you have some, too, Jud?"

I was sure I heard a sigh.

"Me?" said Jud. "I don't never eat 'em."

Holding Up a Train

NOTE. The man who told me these things was for several years an outlaw in the Southwest and a follower of the pursuit he so frankly describes. His description of the *modus operandi* should prove interesting, his counsel of value to the potential passenger in some future "hold-up," while his estimate of the pleasures of train robbing will hardly induce any one to adopt it as a profession. I give the story in almost exactly his own words.   O. H.

MOST PEOPLE would say, if their opinion was asked for, that holding up a train would be a hard job. Well, it isn't; it's easy. I have contributed some to the uneasiness of railroads and the insomnia of express companies, and the most trouble I ever had about a hold-up was in being swindled by unscrupulous people while spending the money I got. The danger wasn't anything to speak of, and we didn't mind the trouble.

One man has come pretty near robbing a train by himself; two have succeeded a few times; three can do it if they are hustlers, but five is about the right number. The time to do it and the place depend upon several things.

The first "stick-up" I was ever in happened in 1890. Maybe the way I got into it will explain how most train robbers start in the business. Five out of six Western outlaws are just cowboys out of a job and gone wrong. The sixth is a tough from the East who dresses up like a bad man and plays some low-down trick that gives the boys a bad name. Wire fences and "nesters" made five of them; a bad heart made the sixth.

Jim S—— and I were working on the 101 Ranch in Colorado. The nesters had the cowman on the go. They had taken up the land and elected officers who were hard to get along with. Jim and I rode into La Junta one day, going south from a round-up. We were having a little fun without malice toward anybody when a farmer administration cut in and tried to harvest us. Jim shot a deputy marshal, and I kind of corroborated his side of the argument. We skirmished up and down the main street, the boomers having bad luck all the time. After a while we leaned forward and shoved for the ranch down on the Ceriso. We were riding a couple of horses that couldn't fly, but they could catch birds.

A few days after that, a gang of the La Junta boomers came to the ranch and wanted us to go back with them. Naturally, we declined. We had the house on them, and before we were done refusing, that old 'dobe was plumb full of lead. When dark came we fagged 'em a batch of bullets and shoved out the back door for the rocks. They sure smoked us as we went. We had to drift, which we did, and rounded up down in Oklahoma.

Well, there wasn't anything we could get there, and, being mighty hard up, we decided to transact a little business with the railroads. Jim and I joined forces with Tom and Ike Moore— two brothers who had plenty of sand they were willing to convert into dust. I can call their names, for both of them are dead. Tom was shot while robbing a bank in Arkansas; Ike was killed during the more dangerous pastime of attending a dance in the Creek Nation.

We selected a place on the Santa Fé where there was a bridge across a deep creek surrounded by heavy timber. All passenger trains took water at the tank close to one end of the bridge. It was a quiet place, the nearest house being five miles away. The day before it happened, we rested our horses and "made medicine" as to how we should get about it. Our plans were not at all elaborate, as none of us had ever engaged in a hold-up before.

The Santa Fé flyer was due at the tank at 11.15 P.M. At eleven, Tom and I lay down on one side of the track, and Jim and Ike took the other. As the train rolled up, the headlight flashing far down the track and the steam hissing from the engine, I turned weak all over. I would have worked a whole year on the ranch for nothing to have been out of that affair right then. Some of the nerviest men in the business have told me that they felt the same way the first time.

The engine had hardly stopped when I jumped on the running-board on one side, while Jim mounted the other. As soon as the engineer and fireman saw our guns they threw up their hands without being told, and begged us not to shoot, saying they would do anything we wanted them to.

"Hit the ground," I ordered, and they both jumped off. We

drove them before us down the side of the train. While this was happening, Tom and Ike had been blazing away, one on each side of the train, yelling like Apaches, so as to keep the passengers herded in the cars. Some fellow stuck a little twenty-two calibre out one of the coach windows and fired it straight up in the air. I let drive and smashed the glass just over his head. That settled everything like resistance from that direction.

By this time all my nervousness was gone. I felt a kind of pleasant excitement as if I were at a dance or a frolic of some sort. The lights were all out in the coaches, and, as Tom and Ike gradually quit firing and yelling, it got to be almost as still as a graveyard. I remember hearing a little bird chirping in a bush at the side of the track, as if it were complaining at being waked up.

I made the fireman get a lantern, and then I went to the express car and yelled to the messenger to open up or get perforated. He slid the door back and stood in it with his hands up. "Jump overboard, son," I said, and he hit the dirt like a lump of lead. There were two safes in the car—a big one and a little one. By the way, I first located the messenger's arsenal—a double-barrelled shot-gun with buckshot cartridges and a thirty-eight in a drawer. I drew the cartridges from the shot-gun, pocketed the pistol, and called the messenger inside. I shoved my gun against his nose and put him to work. He couldn't open the big safe, but he did the little one. There was only nine hundred dollars in it. That was mighty small winnings for our trouble, so we decided to go through the passengers. We took our prisoners to the smoking-car, and from there sent the engineer through the train to light up the coaches. Beginning with the first one, we placed a man at each door and ordered the passengers to stand between the seats with their hands up.

If you want to find out what cowards the majority of men are, all you have to do is rob a passenger train. I don't mean because they don't resist—I'll tell you later on why they can't do that—but it makes a man feel sorry for them the way they lose their heads. Big, burly drummers and farmers and ex-soldiers and high-collared dudes and sports that, a few moments before, were filling the car with noise and bragging, get so scared that their ears flop.

There were very few people in the day coaches at that time of night, so we made a slim haul until we got to the sleeper. The Pullman conductor met me at one door while Jim was going round to the other one. He very politely informed me that I could not go into that car, as it did not belong to the railroad company, and, besides, the passengers had already been greatly disturbed by the shouting and firing. Never in all my life have I met with a finer instance of official dignity and reliance upon the power of Mr. Pullman's great name. I jabbed my six-shooter so hard against Mr. Conductor's front that I afterward found one of his vest buttons so firmly wedged in the end of the barrel that I had to shoot it out. He just shut up like a weak-springed knife and rolled down the car steps.

I opened the door of the sleeper and stepped inside. A big, fat old man came wabbling up to me, puffing and blowing. He had one coat-sleeve on and was trying to put his vest on over that. I don't know who he thought I was.

"Young man, young man," says he, "you must keep cool and not get excited. Above everything, keep cool."

"I can't," says I. "Excitement's just eating me up." And then I let out a yell and turned loose my forty-five through the skylight.

That old man tried to dive into one of the lower berths, but a screech came out of it and a bare foot that took him in the bread-basket and landed him on the floor. I saw Jim coming in the other door, and I hollered for everybody to climb out and line up.

They commenced to scramble down, and for a while we had a three-ringed circus. The men looked as frightened and tame as a lot of rabbits in a deep snow. They had on, on an average, about a quarter of a suit of clothes and one shoe apiece. One chap was sitting on the floor of the aisle, looking as if he were working a hard sum in arithmetic. He was trying, very solemn, to pull a lady's number two shoe on his number nine foot.

The ladies didn't stop to dress. They were so curious to see a real, live train robber, bless 'em, that they just wrapped blankets and sheets around themselves and came out, squeaky and fidgety looking. They always show more curiosity and sand than the men do.

We got them all lined up and pretty quiet, and I went through the bunch. I found very little on them—I mean in the way of valuables. One man in the line was a sight. He was one of those big, overgrown, solemn snoozers that sit on the platform at lectures and look wise. Before crawling out he had managed to put on his long, frock-tailed coat and his high silk hat. The rest of him was nothing but pajamas and bunions. When I dug into that Prince Albert, I expected to drag out at least a block of gold mine stock or an armful of Government bonds, but all I found was a little boy's French harp about four inches long. What it was there for, I don't know. I felt a little mad because he had fooled me so. I stuck the harp up against his mouth.

"If you can't pay—play," I says.

"I can't play," says he.

"Then learn right off quick," says I, letting him smell the end of my gun-barrel.

He caught hold of the harp, turned red as a beet, and commenced to blow. He blew a dinky little tune I remembered hearing when I was a kid:

> Prettiest little gal in the country—oh!
> Mammy and Daddy told me so.

I made him keep on playing it all the time we were in the car. Now and then he'd get weak and off the key, and I'd turn my gun on him and ask what was the matter with that little gal, and whether he had any intention of going back on her, which would make him start up again like sixty. I think that old boy standing there in his silk hat and bare feet, playing his little French harp, was the funniest sight I ever saw. One little red-headed woman in the line broke out laughing at him. You could have heard her in the next car.

Then Jim held them steady while I searched the berths. I grappled around in those beds and filled a pillow-case with the strangest assortment of stuff you ever saw. Now and then I'd come across a little pop-gun pistol, just about right for plugging teeth with, which I'd throw out the window. When I finished with the collection, I dumped the pillow-case load in the middle of the aisle. There were a good many watches, bracelets, rings, and pocket-books, with a sprinkling of false teeth, whiskey flasks, face-powder boxes, chocolate caramels, and heads of hair of various colours and lengths. There were also about a dozen ladies' stockings into which jewellery, watches, and rolls of bills had been stuffed and then wadded up tight and stuck under the mattresses. I offered to return what I called the "scalps," saying that we were not Indians on the war-path, but none of the ladies seemed to know to whom the hair belonged.

One of the women—and a good-looker she was—wrapped in a striped blanket, saw me pick up one of the stockings that was pretty chunky and heavy about the toe, and she snapped out:

"That's mine, sir. You're not in the business of robbing women, are you?"

Now, as this was our first hold-up, we hadn't agreed upon any code of ethics, so I hardly knew what to answer. But, anyway, I replied: "Well, not as a specialty. If this contains your personal property you can have it back."

"It just does," she declared eagerly, and reached out her hand for it.

"You'll excuse my taking a look at the contents," I said, holding the stocking up by the toe. Out dumped a big gent's gold watch, worth two hundred, a gent's leather pocket-book that we afterward found to contain six hundred dollars, a 32-calibre revolver; and the only thing of the lot that could have been a lady's personal property was a silver bracelet worth about fifty cents.

I said: "Madame, here's your property," and handed her the bracelet. "Now," I went on, "how can you expect us to act square with you when you try to deceive us in this manner? I'm surprised at such conduct."

The young woman flushed up as if she had been caught doing something dishonest. Some other woman down the line called out: "The mean thing!" I never knew whether she meant the other lady or me.

When we finished our job we ordered everybody back to bed, told 'em good night very politely at the door, and left. We rode forty miles before daylight and then divided the stuff. Each one of us got $1,752.85 in money. We lumped the jewellery around. Then we scattered, each man for himself.

That was my first train robbery, and it was about as easily

done as any of the ones that followed. But that was the last and only time I ever went through the passengers. I don't like that part of the business. Afterward I stuck strictly to the express car. During the next eight years I handled a good deal of money.

The best haul I made was just seven years after the first one. We found out about a train that was going to bring out a lot of money to pay off the soldiers at a Government post. We stuck that train up in broad daylight. Five of us lay in the sand hills near a little station. Ten soldiers were guarding the money on the train, but they might just as well have been at home on a furlough. We didn't even allow them to stick their heads out the windows to see the fun. We had no trouble at all in getting the money, which was all in gold. Of course, a big howl was raised at the time about the robbery. It was Government stuff, and the Government got sarcastic and wanted to know what the convoy of soldiers went along for. The only excuse given was that nobody was expecting an attack among those bare sand hills in daytime. I don't know what the Government thought about the excuse, but I know that it was a good one. The surprise—that is the keynote of the train-robbing business. The papers published all kinds of stories about the loss, finally agreeing that it was between nine thousand and ten thousand dollars. The Government sawed wood. Here are the correct figures, printed for the first time—forty-eight thousand dollars. If anybody will take the trouble to look over Uncle Sam's private accounts for that little debit to profit and loss, he will find that I am right to a cent.

By that time we were expert enough to know what to do. We rode due west twenty miles, making a trail that a Broadway policeman could have followed, and then we doubled back, hiding our tracks. On the second night after the hold-up, while posses were scouring the country in every direction, Jim and I were eating supper in the second story of a friend's house in the town where the alarm started from. Our friend pointed out to us, in an office across the street, a printing press at work striking off handbills offering a reward for our capture.

I have been asked what we do with the money we get. Well, I never could account for a tenth part of it after it was spent. It goes fast and freely. An outlaw has to have a good many friends. A highly respected citizen may, and often does, get along with very few, but a man on the dodge has got to have "sidekickers." With angry posses and reward-hungry officers cutting out a hot trail for him, he must have a few places scattered about the country where he can stop and feed himself and his horse and get a few hours' sleep without having to keep both eyes open. When he makes a haul he feels like dropping some of the coin with these friends, and he does it liberally. Sometimes I have, at the end of a hasty visit at one of these havens of refuge, flung a handful of gold and bills into the laps of the kids playing on the floor, without knowing whether my contribution was a hundred dollars or a thousand.

When old-timers make a big haul they generally go far away to one of the big cities to spend their money. Green hands, however successful a hold-up they make, nearly always give themselves away by showing too much money near the place where they got it.

I was in a job in '94 where we got twenty thousand dollars. We followed our favourite plan for a get-away—that is, doubled on our trail—and laid low for a time near the scene of the train's bad luck. One morning I picked up a newspaper and read an article with big headlines stating that the marshal, with eight deputies and a posse of thirty armed citizens, had the train robbers surrounded in a mesquite thicket on the Cimarron, and that it was a question of only a few hours when they would be dead men or prisoners. While I was reading that article I was sitting at breakfast in one of the most elegant private residences in Washington City, with a flunky in knee pants standing behind my chair. Jim was sitting across the table talking to his half-uncle, a retired naval officer, whose name you have often seen in the accounts of doings in the capital. We had gone there and bought rattling outfits of good clothes, and were resting from our labours among the nabobs. We must have been killed in that mesquite thicket, for I can make an affidavit that we didn't surrender.

Now I propose to tell why it is easy to hold up a train, and, then, why no one should ever do it.

In the first place, the attacking party has all the advantage. That is, of course, supposing that they are old-timers with the necessary experience and courage. They have the outside and are protected by the darkness, while the others are in the light, hemmed into a small space, and exposed, the moment they show a head at a window or door, to the aim of a man who is a dead shot and who won't hesitate to shoot.

But, in my opinion, the main condition that makes train robbing easy is the element of *surprise* in connection with the imagination of the passengers. If you have ever seen a horse that has eaten loco weed you will understand what I mean when I say that the passengers get locoed. That horse gets the awfullest imagination on him in the world. You can't coax him to cross a little branch stream two feet wide. It looks as big to him as the Mississippi River. That's just the way with the passenger. He thinks there are a hundred men yelling and shooting outside, when maybe there are only two or three. And the muzzle of a forty-five looks like the entrance to a tunnel. The passenger is all right, although he may do mean little tricks, like hiding a wad of money in his shoe and forgetting to dig-up until you jostle his ribs some with the end of your six-shooter; but there's no harm in him.

As to the train crew, we never had any more trouble with them than if they had been so many sheep. I don't mean that they are cowards; I mean that they have got sense. They know they're not up against a bluff. It's the same way with the officers. I've seen secret service men, marshals, and railroad detectives fork over their change as meek as Moses. I saw one of the bravest marshals I ever knew hide his gun under his seat and dig up along with the rest while I was taking toll. He wasn't afraid; he simply knew that we had the drop on the whole outfit. Besides, many of those officers have families and they feel that they oughtn't to take chances; whereas death has no terrors for the man who holds up a train. He expects to get killed some day, and he generally does. My advice to you, if you should ever be in a hold-up, is to line up with the cowards and save your bravery for an occasion when it may be of some benefit to you. Another reason why officers are backward about mixing things with a train robber is a financial one. Every time there is a scrimmage and somebody gets killed, the officers lose money. If the train robber gets away they swear out a warrant against John Doe et al. and travel hundreds of miles and sign vouchers for thousands on the trail of the fugitives, and the

Government foots the bills. So, with them, it is a question of mileage rather than courage.

I will give one instance to support my statement that the surprise is the best card in playing for a hold-up.

Along in '92 the Daltons were cutting out a hot trail for the officers down in the Cherokee Nation. Those were their lucky days, and they got so reckless and sandy, that they used to announce before hand what job they were going to undertake. Once they gave it out that they were going to hold up the M. K. & T. flyer on a certain night at the station of Pryor Creek, in Indian Territory.

That night the railroad company got fifteen deputy marshals in Muscogee and put them on the train. Beside them they had fifty armed men hid in the depot at Pryor Creek.

When the Katy Flyer pulled in not a Dalton showed up. The next station was Adair, six miles away. When the train reached there, and the deputies were having a good time explaining what they would have done to the Dalton gang if they had turned up, all at once it sounded like an army firing outside. The conductor and brakeman came running into the car yelling, "Train robbers!"

Some of those deputies lit out of the door, hit the ground, and kept on running. Some of them hid their Winchesters under the seats. Two of them made a fight and were both killed.

It took the Daltons just ten minutes to capture the train and whip the escort. In twenty minutes more they robbed the express car of twenty-seven thousand dollars and made a clean get-away.

My opinion is that those deputies would have put up a stiff fight at Pryor Creek, where they were expecting trouble, but they were taken by surprise and "locoed" at Adair, just as the Daltons, who knew their business, expected they would.

I don't think I ought to close without giving some deductions from my experience of eight years "on the dodge." It doesn't pay to rob trains. Leaving out the question of right and morals, which I don't think I ought to tackle, there is very little to envy in the life of an outlaw. After a while money ceases to have any value in his eyes. He gets to looking upon the railroads and express companies as his bankers, and his six-shooter as a cheque book good for any amount. He throws away money right and left. Most of the time he is on the jump, riding day and night, and he lives so hard between times that he doesn't enjoy the taste of high life when he gets it. He knows that his time is bound to come to lose his life or liberty, and that the accuracy of his aim, the speed of his horse, and the fidelity of his "sider," are all that postpone the inevitable.

It isn't that he loses any sleep over danger from the officers of the law. In all my experience I never knew officers to attack a band of outlaws unless they outnumbered them at least three to one.

But the outlaw carries one thought constantly in his mind—and that is what makes him so sore against life, more than anything else—he knows where the marshals get their recruits of deputies. He knows that the majority of these upholders of the law were once lawbreakers, horse thieves, rustlers, highwaymen, and outlaws like himself, and that they gained their positions and immunity by turning state's evidence, by turning traitor and delivering up their comrades to imprisonment and death. He knows that some day—unless he is shot first—his Judas will set to work, the trap will be laid, and he will be the surprised instead of a surpriser at a stick-up.

That is why the man who holds up trains picks his company with a thousand times the care with which a careful girl chooses a sweetheart. That is why he raises himself from his blanket of nights and listens to the tread of every horse's hoofs on the distant road. That is why he broods suspiciously for days upon a jesting remark or an unusual movement of a tried comrade, or the broken mutterings of his closest friend, sleeping by his side.

And it is one of the reasons why the train-robbing profession is not so pleasant a one as either of its collateral branches—politics or cornering the market.

The Ransom of Mack

ME AND old Mack Lonsbury, we got out of that Little Hide-and-Seek gold mine affair with about $40,000 apiece. I say "old" Mack; but he wasn't old. Forty-one, I should say; but he always seemed old.

"Andy," he says to me, "I'm tired of hustling. You and me have been working hard together for three years. Say we knock off for a while, and spend some of this idle money we've coaxed our way."

"The proposition hits me just right," says I. "Let's be nabobs a while and see how it feels. What'll we do—take in the Niagara Falls, or buck at faro?"

"For a good many years," says Mack, "I've thought that if I ever had extravagant money I'd rent a two-room cabin somewhere, hire a Chinaman to cook, and sit in my stocking feet and read Buckle's History of Civilisation."

"That sounds self-indulgent and gratifying without vulgar ostentation," says I; "and I don't see how money could be better invested. Give me a cuckoo clock and a Sep Winner's Self-Instructor for the Banjo, and I'll join you."

A week afterward me and Mack hits this small town of Piña, about thirty miles out from Denver, and finds an elegant two-room house that just suits us. We deposited half-a-peck of money in the Piña bank and shook hands with every one of the 340 citizens in the town. We brought along the Chinaman and the cuckoo clock and Buckle and the Instructor with us from Denver; and they made the cabin seem like home at once.

Never believe it when they tell you riches don't bring happiness. If you could have seen old Mack sitting in his rocking-chair with his blue-yarn sock feet up in the window and absorbing in that Buckle stuff through his specs you'd have seen a picture of content that would have made Rockefeller jealous. And I was learning to pick out "Old Zip Coon" on the banjo, and the cuckoo was on time with his remarks, and Ah Sing was messing up the atmosphere with the handsomest smell of ham and eggs that ever laid the honeysuckle in the shade. When it got too dark to make out Buckle's nonsense and the notes in the Instructor, me and Mack would light our pipes and talk about science and pearl diving and sciatica and Egypt and spelling and fish and trade-winds and leather and gratitude and eagles, and a lot of subjects that we'd never had time to explain our sentiments about before.

One evening Mack spoke up and asked me if I was much apprised in the habits and policies of women folks.

"Why, yes," says I, in a tone of voice; "I know 'em from Alfred to Omaha. The feminine nature and similitude," says I, "is as plain to my sight as the Rocky Mountains is to a blue-eyed burro. I'm onto all their little side-steps and punctual discrepancies."

"I tell you, Andy," says Mack, with a kind of sigh, "I never had the least amount of intersection with their predispositions. Maybe I might have had a proneness in respect to their vicinity, but I never took the time. I made my own living since I was fourteen; and I never seemed to get my ratiocinations equipped with the sentiments usually depicted toward the sect. I sometimes wish I had," says old Mack.

"They're an adverse study," says I, "and adapted to points of view. Although they vary in rationale, I have found 'em quite often obviously differing from each other in divergences of contrast."

"It seems to me," goes on Mack, "that a man had better take 'em in and secure his inspirations of the sect when he's young and so preordained. I let my chance go by; and I guess I'm too old now to go hopping into the curriculum."

"Oh, I don't know," I tells him. "Maybe you better credit yourself with a barrel of money and a lot of emancipation from a quantity of uncontent. Still, I don't regret my knowledge of 'em," I says. "It takes a man who understands the symptoms and by-plays of women-folks to take care of himself in this world."

We stayed on in Piña because we liked the place. Some folks might enjoy their money with noise and rapture and locomotion; but me and Mack we had had plenty of turmoils and hotel towels. The people were friendly; Ah Sing got the swing of the grub we liked; Mack and Buckle were as thick as two body-snatchers, and I was hitting out a cordial resemblance to "Buffalo Gals, Can't You Come Out To-night," on the banjo.

One day I got a telegram from Speight, the man that was working a mine I had an interest in out in New Mexico. I had to go out there; and I was gone two months. I was anxious to get back to Piña and enjoy life once more.

When I struck the cabin I nearly fainted. Mack was standing in the door; and if angels ever wept, I saw no reason why they should be smiling then.

That man was a spectacle. Yes; he was worse; he was a spyglass; he was the great telescope in the Lick Observatory. He had on a coat and shiny shoes and a white vest and a high silk hat; and a geranium as big as an order of spinach was spiked onto his front. And he was smirking and warping his face like an infernal storekeeper or a kid with colic.

"Hello, Andy," says Mack, out of his face. "Glad to see you back. Things have happened since you went away."

"I know it," says I, "and a sacrilegious sight it is. God never made you that way, Mack Lonsbury. Why do you scarify His works with this presumptious kind of ribaldry?"

"Why, Andy," says he, "they've elected me justice of the peace since you left."

I looked at Mack close. He was restless and inspired. A justice of the peace ought to be diconsolate and assuaged.

Just then a young woman passed on the sidewalk; and I saw Mack kind of half snicker and blush, and then he raised up his hat and smiled and bowed, and she smiled and bowed, and went on by.

"No hope for you," says I, "if you've got the Mary-Jane infirmity at your age. I thought it wasn't going to take on you. And patent leather shoes! All this in two little short months!"

"I'm going to marry the young lady who just passed to-night," says Mack, in a kind of a flutter.

"I forgot something at the post-office," says I, and walked away quick.

I overtook that young woman a hundred yards away. I raised my hat and told her my name. She was about nineteen; and young for her age. She blushed, and then looked at me cool, like I was the snow scene from the "Two Orphans."

"I understand you are to be married to-night," I said.

"Correct," says she. "You got any objections?"

"Listen, sissy," I begins.

"My name is Miss Rebosa Redd," says she in a pained way.

"I know it," says I. "Now, Rebosa, I'm old enough to have owed money to your father. And that old, specious, dressed-up, garbled, sea-sick ptomaine prancing around avidiously like an irremediable turkey gobbler with patent leather shoes on is my best friend. Why did you go and get him invested in this marriage business?"

"Why, he was the only chance there was," answers Miss Rebosa.

"Nay," says I, giving a sickening look of admiration at her complexion and style of features; "with your beauty you might pick any kind of a man. Listen, Rebosa. Old Mack ain't the man you want. He was twenty-two when you was *née* Reed, as the papers say. This bursting into bloom won't last with him. He's all ventilated with oldness and rectitude and decay. Old Mack's down with a case of Indian summer. He overlooked his bet when he was young; and now he's suing Nature for the interest on the promissory note he took from Cupid instead of the cash. Rebosa, are you bent on having this marriage occur?"

"Why, sure I am," says she, oscillating the pansies on her hat, "and so is somebody else, I reckon."

"What time is it to take place?" I asks.

"At six o'clock," says she.

I made up my mind right away what to do. I'd save old Mack if I could. To have a good, seasoned, ineligible man like that turn chicken for a girl that hadn't quit eating slate pencils and buttoning in the back was more than I could look on with easiness.

"Rebosa," says I, earnest, drawing upon my display of knowledge concerning the feminine intuitions of reason—"ain't there a young man in Piña—a nice young man that you think a heap of?"

"Yep," says Rebosa, nodding her pansies—"Sure there is! What do you think! Gracious!"

"Does he like you?" I asks. "How does he stand in the matter?"

"Crazy," says Rebosa. "Ma has to wet down the front steps to keep him from sitting there all the time. But I guess that'll be all over after to-night," she winds up with a sigh.

"Rebosa," says I, "you don't really experience any of this adoration called love for old Mack, do you?"

"Lord! no," says the girl, shaking her head. "I think he's as dry as a lava bed. The idea!"

"Who is this young man that you like, Rebosa?" I inquires.

"It's Eddie Bayles," says she. "He clerks in Crosby's grocery. But he don't make but thirty-five a month. Ella Noakes was wild about him once."

"Old Mack tells me," I says, "that he's going to marry you at six o'clock this evening."

"That's the time," says she. "It's to be at our house."

"Rebosa," says I, "listen to me. If Eddie Bayles had a thousand dollars cash—a thousand dollars, mind you, would buy him a store of his own—if you and Eddie had that much to excuse matrimony on, would you consent to marry him this evening at five o'clock?"

The girl looks at me a minute; and I can see these inaudible cogitations going on inside of her, as women will.

"A thousand dollars?" says she. "Of course I would."

"Come on," says I. "We'll go and see Eddie."

We went up to Crosby's store and called Eddie outside. He looked to be estimable and freckled; and he had chills and fever when I made my proposition.

"At five o'clock?" says he, "for a thousand dollars? Please don't wake me up! Well, you *are* the rich uncle retired from the spice business in India! I'll buy out old Crosby and run the store myself."

We went inside and got old man Crosby apart and explained it. I wrote my check for a thousand dollars and handed it to him. If Eddie and Rebosa married each other at five he was to turn the money over to them.

And then I gave 'em my blessing, and went to wander in the wildwood for a season. I sat on a log and made cogitations on life and old age and the zodiac and the ways of women and all the disorder that goes with a lifetime. I passed myself congratulations that I had probably saved my old friend Mack from his attack of Indian summer. I knew when he got well of it and shed his infatuation and his patent leather shoes, he would feel grateful. "To keep old Mack disinvolved," thinks I, "from relapses like this, is worth more than a thousand dollars." And most of all I was glad that I'd made a study of women, and wasn't to be deceived any by their means of conceit and evolution.

It must have been half-past five when I got back home. I stepped in; and there sat old Mack on the back of his neck in his old clothes with his blue socks on the window and the History of Civilisation propped up on his knees.

"This don't look like getting ready for a wedding at six," I says, to seem innocent.

"Oh," says Mack, reaching for his tobacco, "that was postponed back to five o'clock. They sent me a note saying the hour had been changed. It's all over now. What made you stay away so long, Andy?"

"You heard about the wedding?" I asks.

"I operated it," says he. "I told you I was justice of the peace. The preacher is off East to visit his folks, and I'm the only one in town that can perform the dispensations of marriage. I promised Eddie and Rebosa a month ago I'd marry 'em. He's a busy lad; and he'll have a grocery of his own some day."

"He will," says I.

"There was lots of women at the wedding," says Mack, smoking up. "But I didn't seem to get any ideas from 'em. I wish I was informed in the structure of their attainments like you said you was."

"That was two months ago," says I, reaching up for the banjo.

Christmas by Injunction

CHEROKEE WAS the civic father of Yellowhammer. Yellowhammer was a new mining town constructed mainly of canvas and undressed pine. Cherokee was a prospector. One day while his burro was eating quartz and pine burrs Cherokee turned up with his pick a nugget weighing thirty ounces. He staked his claim and then, being a man of breadth and hospitality, sent out invitations to his friends in three States to drop in and share his luck.

Not one of the invited guests sent regrets. They rolled in from the Gila country, from Salt River, from the Pecos, from Albuquerque and Phœnix and Santa Fé, and from the camps intervening.

When a thousand citizens had arrived and taken up claims they named the town Yellowhammer, appointed a vigilance committee, and presented Cherokee with a watch-chain made of nuggets.

Three hours after the presentation ceremonies Cherokee's claim played out. He had located a pocket instead of a vein. He abandoned it and staked others one by one. Luck had kissed her hand to him. Never afterward did he turn up enough dust in Yellowhammer to pay his bar bill. But his thousand invited guests were mostly prospering, and Cherokee smiled and congratulated them.

Yellowhammer was made up of men who took off their hats to a smiling loser; so they invited Cherokee to say what he wanted.

"Me?" said Cherokee, "oh, grubstakes will be about the thing. I reckon I'll prospect along up in the Mariposas. If I strike it up there I will most certainly let you all know about the facts. I never was any hand to hold out cards on my friends."

In May Cherokee packed his burro and turned its thoughtful, mouse-coloured forehead to the north. Many citizens escorted him to the undefined limits of Yellowhammer and bestowed upon him shouts of commendation and farewells. Five pocket flasks without an air bubble between contents and cork were forced upon him; and he was bidden to consider Yellowhammer in perpetual commission for his bed, bacon and eggs, and hot water for shaving in the event that luck did not see fit to warm her hands by his campfire in the Mariposas.

The name of the father of Yellowhammer was given him by the gold hunters in accordance with their popular system of nomenclature. It was not necessary for a citizen to exhibit his baptismal certificate in order to acquire a cognomen. A man's name was his personal property. For convenience in calling him up to the bar and in designating him among other blue-shirted bipeds, a temporary appellation, title, or epithet was conferred upon him by the public. Personal peculiarities formed the source of the majority of such informal baptisms. Many were easily dubbed geographically from the regions from which they confessed to have hailed. Some announced themselves to be "Thompsons," and "Adamses," and the like, with a brazenness and loudness that cast a cloud upon their titles. A few vaingloriously and shamelessly uncovered their proper and indisputable names. This was held to be unduly arrogant, and did not win popularity. One man who said he was Chesterton L. C. Belmont, and proved it by letters, was given till sundown to leave the town. Such names as "Shorty," "Bow-legs," "Texas," "Lazy Bill," "Thirsty Rogers," "Limping Riley," "The Judge," and "California Ed" were in favour. Cherokee derived his title from the fact that he claimed to have lived for a time with that tribe in the Indian Nation.

On the twentieth day of December Baldy, the mail rider, brought Yellowhammer a piece of news.

"What do I see in Albuquerque," said Baldy, to the patrons of the bar, "but Cherokee all embellished and festooned up like the Czar of Turkey, and lavishin' money in bulk. Him and me seen the elephant and the owl, and we had specimens of this seidlitz powder wine; and Cherokee he audits all the bills, C. O. D. His pockets looked like a pool table's after a fifteen-ball run."

"Cherokee must have struck pay ore," remarked California Ed. "Well, he's white. I'm much obliged to him for his success."

"Seems like Cherokee would ramble down to Yellowhammer and see his friends," said another, slightly aggrieved. "But that's the way. Prosperity is the finest cure there is for lost forgetfulness."

"You wait," said Baldy; "I'm comin' to that. Cherokee strikes a three-foot vein up in the Mariposas that assays a trip to Europe to the ton, and he closes it out to a syndicate outfit for a hundred thousand hasty dollars in cash. Then he buys himself a baby sealskin overcoat and a red sleigh, and what do you think he takes it in his head to do next?"

"Chuck-a-luck," said Texas, whose ideas of recreation were the gamester's.

"Come and Kiss Me, Ma Honey," sang Shorty, who carried tintypes in his pocket and wore a red necktie while working on his claim.

"Bought a saloon?" suggested Thirsty Rogers.

"Cherokee took me to a room," continued Baldy, "and showed me. He's got that room full of drums and dolls and skates and bags of candy and jumping-jacks and toy lambs and whistles and such infantile truck. And what do you think he's goin' to do with them inefficacious knick-knacks? Don't surmise none—Cherokee told me. He's goin' to load 'em up in his red sleigh and—wait a minute, don't order no drinks yet—he's goin' to drive down here to Yellowhammer and give the kids—the kids of this here town—the biggest Christmas tree and the biggest cryin' doll and Little Giant Boys' Tool Chest blowout that was ever seen west of Cape Hatteras."

Two minutes of absolute silence ticked away in the wake of Baldy's words. It was broken by the House, who, happily conceiving the moment to be ripe for extending hospitality, sent a dozen whisky glasses spinning down the bar, with the slower travelling bottle bringing up the rear.

"Didn't you tell him?" asked the miner called Trinidad.

"Well, no," answered Baldy, pensively; "I never exactly seen my way to.

"You see, Cherokee had this Christmas mess already bought and paid for; and he was all flattered up with self-esteem over his idea; and we had in a way flew the flume with that fizzy wine I speak of; so I never let on."

"I cannot refrain from a certain amount of surprise," said the Judge, as he hung his ivory-handled cane on the bar, "that our friend Cherokee should possess such an erroneous conception of—ah—his, as it were, own town."

"Oh, it ain't the eighth wonder of the terrestrial world," said

Baldy. "Cherokee's been gone from Yellowhammer over seven months. Lots of things could happen in that time. How's he to know that there ain't a single kid in this town, and so far as emigration is concerned, none expected?"

"Come to think of it," remarked California Ed, "it's funny some ain't drifted in. Town ain't settled enough yet for to bring in the rubber-ring brigade, I reckon."

"To top off this Christmas-tree splurge of Cherokee's," went on Baldy, "he's goin' to give an imitation of Santa Claus. He's got a white wig and whiskers that disfigure him up exactly like the pictures of this William Cullen Longfellow in the books, and a red suit of fur-trimmed outside underwear, and eight-ounce gloves, and a stand-up, lay-down croshayed red cap. Ain't it a shame that a outfit like that can't get a chance to connect with a Annie and Willie's prayer layout?"

"When does Cherokee allow to come over with his truck?" inquired Trinidad.

"Mornin' before Christmas," said Baldy. "And he wants you folks to have a room fixed up and a tree hauled and ready. And such ladies to assist as can stop breathin' long enough to let it be a surprise for the kids."

The unblessed condition of Yellowhammer had been truly described. The voice of childhood had never gladdened its flimsy structures; the patter of restless little feet had never consecrated the one rugged highway between the two rows of tents and rough buildings. Later they would come. But now Yellowhammer was but a mountain camp, and nowhere in it were the roguish, expectant eyes, opening wide at dawn of the enchanting day; the eager, small hands to reach for Santa's bewildering hoard; the elated, childish voicings of the season's joy, such as the coming good things of the warm-hearted Cherokee deserved.

Of women there were five in Yellowhammer. The assayer's wife, the proprietress of the Lucky Strike Hotel, and a laundress whose washtub panned out an ounce of dust a day. These were the permanent feminines; the remaining two were the Spangler Sisters, Misses Fanchon and Erma, of the Transcontinental Comedy Company, then playing in repertoire at the (improvised) Empire Theatre. But of children there were none. Sometimes Miss Fanchon enacted with spirit and address the part of robustious childhood; but between her delineation and the visions of adolescence that the fancy offered as eligible recipients of Cherokee's holiday stores there seemed to be fixed a gulf.

Christmas would come on Thursday. On Tuesday morning Trinidad, instead of going to work, sought the Judge at the Lucky Strike Hotel.

"It'll be a disgrace to Yellowhammer," said Trinidad, "if it throws Cherokee down on his Christmas tree blowout. You might say that that man made this town. For one, I'm goin' to see what can be done to give Santa Claus a square deal."

"My co-operation," said the Judge, "would be gladly forthcoming. I am indebted to Cherokee for past favours. But, I do not see—I have heretofore regarded the absence of children rather as a luxury—but in this instance—still, I do not see——"

"Look at me," said Trinidad, "and you'll see old Ways and Means with the fur on. I'm goin' to hitch up a team and rustle a load of kids for Cherokee's Santa Claus act, if I have to rob an orphan asylum."

"Eureka!" cried the Judge, enthusiastically.

"No, you didn't," said Trinidad, decidedly. "I found it myself. I learned about that Latin word at school."

"I will accompany you," declared the Judge, waving his cane. "Perhaps such eloquence and gift of language as I may possess will be of benefit in persuading our young friends to lend themselves to our project."

Within an hour Yellowhammer was acquainted with the scheme of Trinidad and the Judge, and approved it. Citizens who knew of families with offspring within a forty-mile radius of Yellowhammer came forward and contributed their information. Trinidad made careful notes of all such, and then hastened to secure a vehicle and team.

The first stop scheduled was at a double log-house fifteen miles out from Yellowhammer. A man opened the door at Trinidad's hail, and then came down and leaned upon the rickety gate. The doorway was filled with a close mass of youngsters, some ragged, all full of curiosity and health.

"It's this way," explained Trinidad. "We're from Yellowhammer, and we come kidnappin' in a gentle kind of a way. One of our leading citizens is stung with the Santa Claus affliction, and he's due in town to-morrow with half the folderols that's painted red and made in Germany. The youngest kid we got in Yellowhammer packs a forty-five and a safety razor. Consequently we're mighty shy on anybody to say 'Oh' and 'Ah' when we light the candles on the Christmas tree. Now, partner, if you'll loan us a few kids we guarantee to return 'em safe and sound on Christmas Day. And they'll come back loaded down with a good time and Swiss Family Robinsons and cornucopias and red drums and similar testimonials. What do you say?"

"In other words," said the Judge, "we have discovered for the first time in our embryonic but progressive little city the inconveniences of the absence of adolescence. The season of the year having approximately arrived during which it is a custom to bestow frivolous but often appreciated gifts upon the young and tender——"

"I understand," said the parent, packing his pipe with a forefinger. "I guess I needn't detain you gentlemen. Me and the old woman have got seven kids, so to speak; and, runnin' my mind over the bunch, I don't appear to hit upon none that we could spare for you to take over to your doin's. The old woman has got some popcorn candy and rag dolls hid in the clothes chest, and we allow to give Christmas a little whirl of our own in a insignificant sort of style. No, I couldn't, with any degree of avidity, seem to fall in with the idea of lettin' none of 'em go. Thank you kindly, gentlemen."

Down the slope they drove and up another foothill to the ranch-house of Wiley Wilson. Trinidad recited his appeal and the Judge boomed out his ponderous antiphony. Mrs. Wiley gathered her two rosy-cheeked youngsters close to her skirts and did not smile until she had seen Wiley laugh and shake his head. Again a refusal.

Trinidad and the Judge vainly exhausted more than half their list before twilight set in among the hills. They spent the night at a stage road hostelry, and set out again early the next morning. The wagon had not acquired a single passenger.

"It's creepin' upon my faculties," remarked Trinidad, "that borrowin' kids at Christmas is somethin' like tryin' to steal butter from a man that's got hot pancakes a-comin'."

"It is undoubtedly an indisputable fact," said the Judge, "that the—ah—family ties seem to be more coherent and assertive at that period of the year."

On the day before Christmas they drove thirty miles, making four fruitless halts and appeals. Everywhere they found "kids" at a premium.

The sun was low when the wife of a section boss on a lonely railroad huddled her unavailable progeny behind her and said:

"There's a woman that's just took charge of the railroad eatin' house down at Granite Junction. I hear she's got a little boy. Maybe she might let him go."

Trinidad pulled up his mules at Granite Junction at five o'clock in the afternoon. The train had just departed with its load of fed and appeased passengers.

On the steps of the eating house they found a thin and glowering boy of ten smoking a cigarette. The dining-room had been left in chaos by the peripatetic appetites. A youngish woman reclined, exhausted, in a chair. Her face wore sharp lines of worry. She had once possessed a certain style of beauty that would never wholly leave her and would never wholly return. Trinidad set forth his mission.

"I'd count it a mercy if you'd take Bobby for a while," she said, wearily. "I'm on the go from morning till night, and I don't have time to 'tend to him. He's learning bad habits from the men. It'll be the only chance he'll have to get any Christmas."

The men went outside and conferred with Bobby. Trinidad pictured the glories of the Christmas tree and presents in lively colours.

"And, moreover, my young friend," added the Judge, "Santa Claus himself will personally distribute the offerings that will typify the gifts conveyed by the shepherds of Bethlehem to——"

"Aw, come off," said the boy, squinting his small eyes. "I ain't no kid. There ain't any Santa Claus. It's your folks that buys toys and sneaks 'em in when you're asleep. And they make marks in the soot in the chimney with the tongs to look like Santa's sleigh tracks."

"That might be so," argued Trinidad, "but Christmas trees ain't no fairy tale. This one's goin' to look like the ten-cent store in Albuquerque, all strung up in a redwood. There's tops and drums and Noah's arks and——"

"Oh, rats!" said Bobby, wearily. "I cut them out long ago. I'd like to have a rifle—not a target one—a real one, to shoot wildcats with; but I guess you won't have any of them on your old tree."

"Well, I can't say for sure," said Trinidad diplomatically; "it might be. You go along with us and see."

The hope thus held out, though faint, won the boy's hesitating consent to go. With this solitary beneficiary for Cherokee's holiday bounty, the canvassers spun along the homeward road.

In Yellowhammer the empty storeroom had been transformed into what might have passed as the bower of an Arizona fairy. The ladies had done their work well. A tall Christmas tree, covered to the topmost branch with candles, spangles, and toys sufficient for more than a score of children, stood in the centre of the floor. Near sunset anxious eyes had begun to scan the street for the returning team of the child-providers. At noon that day Cherokee had dashed into town with his new sleigh piled high with bundles and boxes and bales of all sizes and shapes. So intent was he upon the arrangements for his altruistic plans that the dearth of childhood did not receive his notice. No one gave away the humiliating state of Yellowhammer, for the efforts of Trinidad and the Judge were expected to supply the deficiency.

When the sun went down Cherokee, with many winks and arch grins on his seasoned face, went into retirement with the bundle containing the Santa Claus raiment and a pack containing special and undisclosed gifts.

"When the kids are rounded up," he instructed the volunteer arrangement committee, "light up the candles on the tree and set 'em to playin' 'Pussy Wants a Corner' and 'King William.' When they get good and at it, why—old Santa'll slide in the door. I reckon there'll be plenty of gifts to go 'round."

The ladies were flitting about the tree, giving it final touches that were never final. The Spangled Sisters were there in costume as Lady Violet de Vere and Marie, the maid, in their new drama, "The Miner's Bride." The theatre did not open until nine, and they were welcome assistants of the Christmas tree committee. Every minute heads would pop out the door to look and listen for the approach of Trinidad's team. And now this became an anxious function, for night had fallen and it would soon be necessary to light the candles on the tree, and Cherokee was apt to make an irruption at any time in his Kriss Kringle garb.

At length the wagon of the child "rustlers" rattled down the street to the door. The ladies, with little screams of excitement, flew to the lighting of the candles. The men of Yellowhammer passed in and out restlessly or stood about the room in embarrassed groups.

Trinidad and the Judge, bearing the marks of protracted travel, entered, conducting between them a single impish boy, who stared with sullen, pessimistic eyes at the gaudy tree.

"Where are the other children?" asked the assayer's wife, the acknowledged leader of all social functions.

"Ma'am," said Trinidad with a sigh, "prospectin' for kids at Christmas time is like huntin' in limestone for silver. This parental business is one that I haven't no chance to comprehend. It seems that fathers and mothers are willin' for their offsprings to be drownded, stole, fed on poison oak, and et by catamounts 364 days in the year; but on Christmas Day they insists on enjoyin' the exclusive mortification of their company. This here young biped, ma'am, is all that washes out of our two days' manœuvres."

"Oh, the sweet little boy!" cooed Miss Erma, trailing her De Vere robes to centre of stage.

"Aw, shut up," said Bobby, with a scowl. "Who's a kid? You ain't, you bet."

"Fresh brat!" breathed Miss Erma, beneath her enamelled smile.

"We done the best we could," said Trinidad. "It's tough on Cherokee, but it can't be helped."

Then the door opened and Cherokee entered in the conventional dress of Saint Nick. A white rippling beard and flowing hair covered his face almost to his dark and shining eyes. Over his shoulder he carried a pack.

No one stirred as he came in. Even the Spangler Sisters ceased their coquettish poses and stared curiously at the tall figure. Bobby stood with his hands in his pockets gazing gloomily at the effeminate and childish tree. Cherokee put down his pack and looked wonderingly about the room. Perhaps he fancied that a bevy of eager children were being herded somewhere, to be loosed upon his entrance. He went up to Bobby and extended his red-mittened hand.

"Merry Christmas, little boy," said Cherokee. "Anything on the tree you want they'll get it down for you. Won't you shake hands with Santa Claus?"

"There ain't any Santa Claus," whined the boy. "You've got old false billy goat's whiskers on your face. I ain't no kid. What do I want with dolls and tin horses? The driver said you'd have a rifle, and you haven't. I want to go home."

Trinidad stepped into the breach. He shook Cherokee's hand in warm greeting.

"I'm sorry, Cherokee," he explained. "There never was a kid in Yellowhammer. We tried to rustle a bunch of 'em for your swaree, but this sardine was all we could catch. He's a atheist, and he don't believe in Santa Claus. It's a shame for you to be out all this truck. But me and the Judge was sure we could round up a wagonful of candidates for your gimcracks."

"That's all right," said Cherokee gravely. "The expense don't amount to nothin' worth mentionin'. We can dump the stuff down a shaft or throw it away. I don't know what I was thinkin' about; but it never occurred to my cogitations that there wasn't any kids in Yellowhammer."

Meanwhile the company had relaxed into a hollow but praiseworthy imitation of a pleasure gathering.

Bobby had retreated to a distant chair, and was coldly regarding the scene with ennui plastered thick upon him. Cherokee, lingering with his original idea, went over and sat beside him.

"Where do you live, little boy?" he asked respectfully.

"Granite Junction," said Bobby without emphasis.

The room was warm. Cherokee took off his cap, and then removed his beard and wig.

"Say!" exclaimed Bobby, with a show of interest, "I know your mug, all right."

"Did you ever see me before?" asked Cherokee.

"I don't know; but I've seen your picture lots of times."

"Where?"

The boy hesitated. "On the bureau at home," he answered.

"Let's have your name, if you please, buddy."

"Robert Lumsden. The picture belongs to my mother. She

puts it under her pillow of nights. And once I saw her kiss it. I wouldn't. But women are that way."

Cherokee rose and beckoned to Trinidad.

"Keep this boy by you till I come back," he said. "I'm goin' to shed these Christmas duds, and hitch up my sleigh. I'm goin' to take this kid home."

"Well, infidel," said Trinidad, taking Cherokee's vacant chair, "and so you are too superannuated and effete to yearn for such mockeries as candy and toys, it seems."

"I don't like you," said Bobby, with acrimony. "You said there would be a rifle. A fellow can't even smoke. I wish I was at home."

Cherokee drove his sleigh to the door, and they lifted Bobby in beside him. The team of fine horses sprang away prancingly over the hard snow. Cherokee had on his $500 overcoat of baby sealskin. The laprobe that he drew about them was as warm as velvet.

Bobby slipped a cigarette from his pocket and was trying to snap a match.

"Throw that cigarette away," said Cherokee, in a quiet but new voice.

Bobby hesitated, and then dropped the cylinder overboard.

"Throw the box, too," commanded the new voice.

More reluctantly the boy obeyed.

"Say," said Bobby, presently, "I like you. I don't know why. Nobody never made me do anything I didn't want to do before."

"Tell me, kid," said Cherokee, not using his new voice, "are you sure your mother kissed that picture that looks like me?"

"Dead sure. I seen her do it."

"Didn't you remark somethin' a while ago about wanting a rifle?"

"You bet I did. Will you get me one?"

"To-morrow—silver-mounted."

Cherokee took out his watch.

"Half-past nine. We'll hit the Junction plumb on time with Christmas Day. Are you cold? Sit closer, son."

The Handbook of Hymen

'Tɪs ᴛʜᴇ opinion of myself, Sanderson Pratt, who sets this down, that the educational system of the United States should be in the hands of the weather bureau. I can give you good reasons for it; and you can't tell me why our college professors shouldn't be transferred to the meteorological department. They have been learned to read; and they could very easily glance at the morning papers and then wire in to the main office what kind of weather to expect. But there's the other side of the proposition. I am going on to tell you how the weather furnished me and Idaho Green with an elegant education.

We was up in the Bitter Root Mountains over the Montana line prospecting for gold. A chin-whiskered man in Walla-Walla, carrying a line of hope as excess baggage, had grubstaked us; and there we was in the foothills pecking away, with enough grub on hand to last an army through a peace conference.

Along one day comes a mail-rider over the mountains from Carlos, and stops to eat three cans of greengages, and leave us a newspaper of modern date. This paper prints a system of premonitions of the weather, and the card it dealt Bitter Root Mountains from the bottom of the deck was "warmer and fair, with light westerly breezes."

That evening it began to snow, with the wind strong in the east. Me and Idaho moved camp into an old empty cabin higher up the mountain, thinking it was only a November flurry. But after falling three foot on a level it went to work in earnest; and we knew we was snowed in. We got in plenty of firewood before it got deep, and we had grub enough for two months, so we let the elements rage and cut up all they thought proper.

If you want to instigate the art of manslaughter just shut two men up in an eighteen by twenty-foot cabin for a month. Human nature won't stand it.

When the first snowflakes fell me and Idaho Green laughed at each other's jokes and praised the stuff we turned out of a skillet and called bread. At the end of three weeks Idaho makes this kind of an edict to me. Says he:

"I never exactly heard sour milk dropping out of a balloon on the bottom of a tin pan, but I have an idea it would be music of the spears compared to this attenuated stream of asphyxiated thought that emanates out of your organs of conversation. The kind of half-masticated noises that you emit every day puts me in mind of a cow's cud, only she's lady enough to keep hers to herself, and you ain't."

"Mr. Green," says I, "you having been a friend of mine once, I have some hesitations in confessing to you that if I had my choice for society between you and a common yellow, three-legged cur pup, one of the inmates of this here cabin would be wagging a tail just at present."

This way we goes on for two or three days, and then we quits speaking to one another. We divides up the cooking implements, and Idaho cooks his grub on one side of the fireplace, and me on the other. The snow is up to the windows, and we have to keep a fire all day.

You see me and Idaho never had any education beyond reading and doing "if John had three apples and James five" on a slate. We never felt any special need for a university degree, though we had acquired a species of intrinsic intelligence in knocking around the world that we could use in emergencies. But, snowbound in that cabin in the Bitter Roots, we felt for the first time that if we had studied Homer or Greek and fractions and the higher branches of information, we'd have had some resources in the line of meditation and private thought. I've seen them Eastern college fellows working in camps all through the West, and I never noticed but what education was less of a drawback to 'em than you would think. Why, once over on Snake River, when Andrew McWilliams' saddle horse got the botts, he sent a buckboard ten miles for one of these strangers that claimed to be a botanist. But that horse died.

One morning Idaho was poking around with a stick on top of a little shelf that was too high to reach. Two books fell down to the floor. I started toward 'em, but caught Idaho's eye. He speaks for the first time in a week.

"Don't burn your fingers," says he. "In spite of the fact that you're only fit to be the companion of a sleeping mud-turtle, I'll give you a square deal. And that's more than your parents did when they turned you loose in the world with the sociability of a rattlesnake and the bedside manner of a frozen turnip. I'll play you a game of seven-up, the winner to pick up his choice of the books, the loser to take the other."

We played; and Idaho won. He picked up his book; and I took mine. Then each of us got on his side of the house and went to reading.

I never was as glad to see a ten-ounce nugget as I was that book. And Idaho looked at his like a kid looks at a stick of candy.

Mine was a little book about five by six inches called "Herkimer's Handbook of Indispensable Information." I may be wrong, but I think that was the greatest book that ever was written. I've got it to-day; and I can stump you or any man fifty times in five minutes with the information in it. Talk about Solomon or the New York *Tribune*! Herkimer had cases on both of 'em. That man must have put in fifty years and travelled a million miles to find out all that stuff. There was the population of all cities in it, and the way to tell a girl's age, and the number of teeth a camel has. It told you the longest tunnel in the world, the number of the stars, how long it takes for chicken pox to break out, what a lady's neck ought to measure, the veto powers of Governors, the dates of the Roman aqueducts, how many pounds of rice going without three beers a day would buy, the average annual temperature of Augusta, Maine, the quantity of seed required to plant an acre of carrots in drills, antidotes for poisons, the number of hairs on a blond lady's head, how to preserve eggs, the height of all the mountains in the world, and the dates of all wars and battles, and how to restore drowned persons, and sunstroke, and the number of tacks in a pound, and how to make dynamite and flowers and beds, and what to do before the doctor comes—and a hundred times as many things besides. If there was anything Herkimer didn't know I didn't miss it out of the book.

I sat and read that book for four hours. All the wonders of education was compressed in it. I forgot the snow, and I forgot that me and old Idaho was on the outs. He was sitting still on a stool reading away with a kind of partly soft and partly mysterious look shining through his tan-bark whiskers.

"Idaho," says I, "what kind of a book is yours?"

Idaho must have forgot, too, for he answered moderate, without any slander or malignity.

"Why," says he, "this here seems to be a volume by Homer K. M."

"Homer K. M. what?" I asks.

"Why, just Homer K. M.," says he.

"You're a liar," says I, a little riled that Idaho should try to put me up a tree. "No man is going 'round signing books with his initials. If it's Homer K. M. Spoopendyke, or Homer K. M. McSweeney, or Homer K. M. Jones, why don't you say so like a man instead of biting off the end of it like a calf chewing off the tail of a shirt on a clothes-line?"

"I put it to you straight, Sandy," says Idaho, quiet. "It's a poem book," says he, "by Homer K. M. I couldn't get colour out of it at first, but there's a vein if you follow it up. I wouldn't have missed this book for a pair of red blankets."

"You're welcome to it," says I. "What I want is a disinterested statement of facts for the mind to work on, and that's what I seem to find in the book I've drawn."

"What you've got," says Idaho, "is statistics, the lowest grade of information that exists. They'll poison your mind. Give me old K. M.'s system of surmises. He seems to be a kind of a wine agent. His regular toast is 'nothing doing,' and he seems to have a grouch, but he keeps it so well lubricated with booze that his worst kicks sound like an invitation to split a quart. But it's poetry," says Idaho, "and I have sensations of scorn for that truck of yours that tries to convey sense in feet and inches. When it comes to explaining the instinct of philosophy through the art of nature, old K. M. has got your man beat by drills, rows, paragraphs, chest measurement, and average annual rainfall."

So that's the way me and Idaho had it. Day and night all the excitement we got was studying our books. That snowstorm sure fixed us with a fine lot of attainments apiece. By the time the snow melted, if you had stepped up to me suddenly and said: "Sanderson Pratt, what would it cost per square foot to lay a roof with twenty by twenty-eight tin at nine dollars and fifty cents per box?" I'd have told you as quick as light could travel the length of a spade handle at the rate of one hundred and ninety-two thousand miles per second. How many can do it? You wake up 'most any man you know in the middle of the night, and ask him quick to tell you the number of bones in the human skeleton exclusive of the teeth, or what percentage of the vote of the Nebraska Legislature overrules a veto. Will he tell you? Try him and see.

About what benefit Idaho got out of his poetry book I didn't exactly know. Idaho boosted the wine-agent every time he opened his mouth; but I wasn't so sure.

This Homer K. M., from what leaked out of his libretto through Idaho, seemed to me to be a kind of a dog who looked at life like it was a tin can tied to his tail. After running himself half to death, he sits down, hangs his tongue out, and looks at the can and says:

"Oh, well, since we can't shake the growler, let's get it filled at the corner, and all have a drink on me."

Besides that, it seems he was a Persian; and I never hear of Persia producing anything worth mentioning unless it was Turkish rugs and Maltese cats.

That spring me and Idaho struck pay ore. It was a habit of ours to sell out quick and keep moving. We unloaded on our grubstaker for eight thousand dollars apiece; and then we drifted down to this little town of Rosa, on the Salmon River, to rest up, and get some human grub, and have our whiskers harvested.

Rosa was no mining-camp. It laid in the valley, and was as free of uproar and pestilence as one of them rural towns in the country. There was a three-mile trolley line champing its bit in the environs; and me and Idaho spent a week riding on one of the cars, dropping off of nights at the Sunset View Hotel. Being now well read as well as travelled, we was soon *pro re nata* with the best society in Rosa, and was invited out to the most dressed-up and high-toned entertainments. It was at a piano recital and quail-eating contest in the city hall, for the benefit of the fire company, that me and Idaho first met Mrs. De Ormond Sampson, the queen of Rosa society.

Mrs. Sampson was a widow, and owned the only two-story house in town. It was painted yellow, and whichever way you looked from you could see it as plain as egg on the chin of an

O'Grady on a Friday. Twenty-two men in Rosa besides me and Idaho was trying to stake a claim on that yellow house.

There was a dance after the song books and quail bones had been raked out of the Hall. Twenty-three of the bunch galloped over to Mrs. Sampson and asked for a dance. I side-stepped the two-step, and asked permission to escort her home. That's where I made a hit.

On the way home says she:

"Ain't the stars lovely and bright to-night, Mr. Pratt?"

"For the chance they've got," says I, "they're humping themselves in a mighty creditable way. That big one you see is sixty-six billions of miles distant. It took thirty-six years for its light to reach us. With an eighteen-foot telescope you can see forty-three millions of 'em, including them of the thirteenth magnitude, which, if one was to go out now, you would keep on seeing it for twenty-seven hundred years."

"My!" says Mrs. Sampson. "I never knew that before. How warm it is! I'm as damp as I can be from dancing so much."

"That's easy to account for," says I, "when you happen to know that you've got two million sweat-glands working all at once. If every one of your perspiratory ducts, which are a quarter of an inch long, was placed end to end, they would reach a distance of seven miles."

"Lawsy!" says Mrs. Sampson. "It sounds like an irrigation ditch you was describing, Mr. Pratt. How do you get all this knowledge of information?"

"From observation, Mrs. Sampson," I tells her. "I keep my eyes open when I go about the world."

"Mr. Pratt," says she, "I always did admire a man of education. There are so few scholars among the sap-headed plug-uglies of this town that it is a real pleasure to converse with a gentleman of culture. I'd be gratified to have you call at my house whenever you feel so inclined."

And that was the way I got the goodwill of the lady in the yellow house. Every Tuesday and Friday evenings I used to go there and tell her about the wonders of the universe as discovered, tabulated, and compiled from nature by Herkimer. Idaho and the other gay Lutherans of the town got every minute of the rest of the week that they could.

I never imagined that Idaho was trying to work on Mrs. Sampson with old K. M.'s rules of courtship till one afternoon when I was on my way over to take her a basket of wild hog-plums. I met the lady coming down the lane that led to her house. Her eyes was snapping, and her hat made a dangerous dip over one eye.

"Mr. Pratt," she opens up, "this Mr. Green is a friend of yours, I believe."

"For nine years," says I.

"Cut him out," says she. "He's no gentleman!"

"Why ma'am," says I, "he's a plain incumbent of the mountains, with asperities and the usual failings of a spendthrift and a liar, but I never on the most momentous occasion had the heart to deny that he was a gentleman. It may be that in haberdashery and the sense of arrogance and display Idaho offends the eye, but inside, ma'am, I've found him impervious to the lower grades of crime and obesity. After nine years of Idaho's society, Mrs. Sampson," I winds up, "I should hate to impute him, and I should hate to see him imputed."

"It's right plausible of you, Mr. Pratt," says Mrs. Sampson, "to take up the curmudgeons in your friend's behalf; but it don't alter the fact that he has made proposals to me sufficiently obnoxious to ruffle the ignominy of any lady."

"Why, now, now, now!" says I. "Old Idaho do that! I could believe it of myself sooner. I never knew but one thing to deride in him; and a blizzard was responsible for that. Once while we was snowbound in the mountains he became a prey to a kind of spurious and uneven poetry, which may have corrupted his demeanour."

"It has," says Mrs. Sampson. "Ever since I knew him he has been reciting to me a lot of irreligious rhymes by some person he calls Ruby Ott, and who is no better than she should be, if you judge by her poetry."

"Then Idaho has struck a new book," says I, "for the one he had was by a man who writes under the *nom de plume* of K. M."

"He'd better have stuck to it," says Mrs. Sampson, "whatever it was. And to-day he caps the vortex. I get a bunch of flowers from him, and on 'em is pinned a note. Now, Mr. Pratt, you know a lady when you see her; and you know how I stand in

Rosa society. Do you think for a moment that I'd skip out to the woods with a man along with a jug of wine and a loaf of bread, and go singing and cavorting up and down under the trees with him? I take a little claret with my meals, but I'm not in the habit of packing a jug of it into the brush and raising Cain in any such style as that. And of course he'd bring his book of verses along too. He said so. Let him go on his scandalous picnics alone! Or let him take his Ruby Ott with him. I reckon she wouldn't kick unless it was on account of there being too much bread along. And what do you think of your gentleman friend now, Mr. Pratt?"

"Well, 'm," says I, "it may be that Idaho's invitation was a kind of poetry, and meant no harm. May be it belonged to the class of rhymes they call figurative. They offend law and order, but they get sent through the mails on the grounds that they mean something that they don't say. I'd be glad on Idaho's account if you'd overlook it," says I, "and let us extricate our minds from the low regions of poetry to the higher planes of fact and fancy. On a beautiful afternoon like this, Mrs. Sampson," I goes on, "we should let our thoughts dwell accordingly. Though it is warm here, we should remember that at the equator the line of perpetual frost is at an altitude of fifteen thousand feet. Between the latitudes of forty degrees and forty-nine degrees it is from four thousand to nine thousand feet."

"Oh, Mr. Pratt," says Mrs. Sampson, "it's such a comfort to hear you say them beautiful facts after getting such a jar from that minx of a Ruby's poetry!"

"Let us sit on this log at the roadside," says I, "and forget the inhumanity and ribaldry of the poets. It is in the glorious columns of ascertained facts and legalised measures that beauty is to be found. In this very log we sit upon, Mrs. Sampson," says I, "is statistics more wonderful than any poem. The rings show it was sixty years old. At the depth of two thousand feet it would become coal in three thousand years. The deepest coal mine in the world is at Killingworth, near Newcastle. A box four feet long, three feet wide, and two feet eight inches deep will hold one ton of coal. If an artery is cut, compress it above the wound. A man's leg contains thirty bones. The Tower of London was burned in 1841."

"Go on, Mr. Pratt," says Mrs. Sampson. "Them ideas is so original and soothing. I think statistics are just as lovely as they can be."

But it wasn't till two weeks later that I got all that was coming to me out of Herkimer.

One night I was waked up by folks hollering "Fire!" all around. I jumped up and dressed and went out of the hotel to enjoy the scene. When I seen it was Mrs. Sampson's house, I gave forth a kind of yell, and I was there in two minutes.

The whole lower story of the yellow house was in flames, and every masculine, feminine, and canine in Rosa was there, screeching and barking and getting in the way of the firemen. I saw Idaho trying to get away from six firemen who were holding him. They was telling him the whole place was on fire downstairs, and no man could go in it and come out alive.

"Where's Mrs. Sampson?" I asks.

"She hasn't been seen," says one of the firemen. "She sleeps up-stairs. We've tried to get in, but we can't, and our company hasn't got any ladders yet."

I runs around to the light of the big blaze, and pulls the Handbook out of my inside pocket. I kind of laughed when I felt it in my hands—I reckon I was some daffy with the sensation of excitement.

"Herky, old boy," I says to it, as I flipped over the pages, "you ain't ever lied to me yet, and you ain't ever throwed me down at a scratch yet. Tell me what, old boy, tell me what!" says I.

I turned to "What to do in Case of Accidents," on page 117. I run my finger down the page, and struck it. Good old Herkimer, he never overlooked anything! It said:

SUFFOCATION FROM INHALING SMOKE OR GAS.—There is nothing better than flaxseed. Place a few seed in the outer corner of the eye.

I shoved the Handbook back in my pocket, and grabbed a boy that was running by.

"Here," says I, giving him some money, "run to the drug store and bring a dollar's worth of flaxseed. Hurry, and you'll get another one for yourself. Now," I sings out to the crowd, "we'll have Mrs. Sampson!" And I throws away my coat and hat.

Four of the firemen and citizens grabs hold of me. It's sure death, they say, to go in the house, for the floors was beginning to fall through.

"How in blazes," I sings out, kind of laughing yet, but not feeling like it, "do you expect me to put flaxseed in a eye without the eye?"

I jabbed each elbow in a fireman's face, kicked the bark off of one citizen's shin, and tripped the other one with a side hold. And then I busted into the house. If I die first I'll write you a letter and tell you if it's any worse down there than the inside of that yellow house was; but don't believe it yet. I was a heap more cooked than the hurry-up orders of broiled chicken that you get in restaurants. The fire and smoke had me down on the floor twice, and was about to shame Herkimer, but the firemen helped me with their little stream of water, and I got to Mrs. Sampson's room. She'd lost conscientiousness from the smoke, so I wrapped her in the bed clothes and got her on my shoulder. Well, the floors wasn't as bad as they said, or I never could have done it—not by no means.

I carried her out fifty yards from the house and laid her on the grass. Then, of course, every one of them other twenty-two plaintiffs to the lady's hand crowded around with tin dippers of water ready to save her. And up runs the boy with the flaxseed.

I unwrapped the covers from Mrs. Sampson's head. She opened her eyes and says:

"Is that you, Mr. Pratt?"

"S-s-sh," says I. "Don't talk till you've had the remedy."

I runs my arm around her neck and raises her head, gentle, and breaks the bag of flaxseed with the other hand; and as easy as I could I bends over and slips three or four of the seeds in the outer corner of her eye.

Up gallops the village doc by this time, and snorts around, and grabs at Mrs. Sampson's pulse, and wants to know what I mean by any such sandblasted nonsense.

"Well, old Jalap and Jerusalem oakseed," says I, "I'm no regular practitioner, but I'll show you my authority, anyway."

They fetched my coat, and I gets out the Handbook.

"Look on page 117," says I, "at the remedy for suffocation by smoke or gas. Flaxseed in the outer corner of the eye, it says. I don't know whether it works as a smoke consumer or whether it hikes the compound gastro-hippopotamus nerve into action, but Herkimer says it, and he was called to the case first. If you want to make it a consultation, there's no objection."

Old doc takes the book and looks at it by means of his specs and a fireman's lantern.

"Well, Mr. Pratt," says he, "you evidently got on the wrong line in reading your diagnosis. The recipe for suffocation says: 'Get the patient into fresh air as quickly as possible, and place in a reclining position.' The flaxseed remedy is for 'Dust and Cinders in the Eye,' on the line above. But, after all——"

"See here," interrupts Mrs. Sampson, "I reckon I've got something to say in this consultation. That flaxseed done me more good than anything I ever tried." And then she raises up her head and lays it back on my arm again, and says: "Put some in the other eye, Sandy dear."

And so if you was to stop off at Rosa to-morrow, or any other day, you'd see a fine new yellow house with Mrs. Pratt, that was Mrs. Sampson, embellishing and adorning it. And if you was to step inside you'd see on the marble-top centre table in the parlour "Herkimer's Handbook of Indispensable Information," all rebound in red morocco, and ready to be consulted on any subject pertaining to human happiness and wisdom.

The Caballero's Way

THE CISCO Kid had killed six men in more or less fair scrimmages, had murdered twice as many (mostly Mexicans), and had winged a larger number whom he modestly forbore to count. Therefore a woman loved him.

The Kid was twenty-five, looked twenty; and a careful insurance company would have estimated the probable time of his demise at, say, twenty-six. His habitat was anywhere between the Frio and the Rio Grande. He killed for the love of it—because he was quick-tempered—to avoid arrest—for his own amusement—any reason that came to his mind would suffice. He had escaped capture because he could shoot five-sixths of a second sooner than any sheriff or ranger in the service, and because he rode a speckled roan horse that knew every cow-path in the mesquite and pear thickets from San Antonio to Matamoras.

Tonia Perez, the girl who loved the Cisco Kid, was half Carmen, half Madonna, and the rest—oh, yes, a woman who is half Carmen and half Madonna can always be something more—the rest, let us say, was humming-bird. She lived in a grass-roofed *jacal* near a little Mexican settlement at the Lone Wolf Crossing of the Frio. With her lived a father or grandfather, a lineal Aztec, somewhat less than a thousand years old, who herded a hundred goats and lived in a continuous drunken dream from drinking *mescal*. Back of the *jacal* a tremendous forest of bristling pear, twenty feet high at its worst, crowded almost to its door. It was along the bewildering maze of this spinous thicket that the speckled roan would bring the Kid to see his girl. And once, clinging like a lizard to the ridge-pole, high up under the peaked grass roof, he had heard Tonia, with her Madonna face and Carmen beauty and humming-bird soul, parley with the sheriff's posse, denying knowledge of her man in her soft *mélange* of Spanish and English.

One day the adjutant-general of the State, who is, *ex officio*, commander of the ranger forces, wrote some sarcastic lines to Captain Duval of Company X, stationed at Laredo, relative to the serene and undisturbed existence led by murderers and desperadoes in the said captain's territory.

The captain turned the colour of brick dust under his tan, and forwarded the letter, after adding a few comments, per ranger Private Bill Adamson, to ranger Lieutenant Sandridge, camped at a water hole on the Nueces with a squad of five men in preservation of law and order.

Lieutenant Sandridge turned a beautiful *couleur de rose* through his ordinary strawberry complexion, tucked the letter in his hip pocket, and chewed off the ends of his gamboge moustache.

The next morning he saddled his horse and rode alone to the Mexican settlement at the Lone Wolf Crossing of the Frio, twenty miles away.

Six feet two, blond as a Viking, quiet as a deacon, dangerous as a machine gun, Sandridge moved among the *Jacales*, patiently seeking news of the Cisco Kid.

Far more than the law, the Mexicans dreaded the cold and certain vengeance of the lone rider that the ranger sought. It had been one of the Kid's pastimes to shoot Mexicans "to see them kick": if he demanded from them moribund Terpsichorean feats, simply that he might be entertained, what terrible and extreme penalties would be certain to follow should they anger him! One and all they lounged with upturned palms and shrugging shoulders, filling the air with "*quien sabes*" and denials of the Kid's acquaintance.

But there was a man named Fink who kept a store at the Crossing—a man of many nationalities, tongues, interests, and ways of thinking.

"No use to ask them Mexicans," he said to Sandridge. "They're afraid to tell. This *hombre* they call the Kid—Goodall is his name, ain't it?—he's been in my store once or twice. I have an idea you might run across him at—but I guess I don't keer to say, myself. I'm two seconds later in pulling a gun than I used to be, and the difference is worth thinking about. But this Kid's got a half-Mexican girl at the Crossing that he comes to see. She lives in that *jacal* a hundred yards down the arroyo at the edge of the pear. Maybe she—no, I don't suppose she would, but that *jacal* would be a good place to watch, anyway."

Sandridge rode down to the *jacal* of Perez. The sun was low, and the broad shade of the great pear thicket already covered the grass-thatched hut. The goats were enclosed for the night in a brush corral near by. A few kids walked the top of it, nibbling the chaparral leaves. The old Mexican lay upon a blanket on the grass, already in a stupor from his mescal, and dreaming, perhaps, of the nights when he and Pizarro touched glasses to their New World fortunes—so old his wrinkled face seemed to proclaim him to be. And in the door of the *jacal* stood Tonia. And Lieutenant Sandridge sat in his saddle staring at her like a gannet agape at a sailorman.

The Cisco Kid was a vain person, as all eminent and successful assassins are, and his bosom would have been ruffled had he known that at a simple exchange of glances two persons, in whose minds he had been looming large, suddenly abandoned (at least for the time) all thought of him.

Never before had Tonia seen such a man as this. He seemed to be made of sunshine and blood-red tissue and clear weather. He seemed to illuminate the shadow of the pear when he smiled, as though the sun were rising again. The men she had known had been small and dark. Even the Kid, in spite of his achievements, was a stripling no larger than herself, with black, straight hair and a cold, marble face that chilled the noonday.

As for Tonia, though she sends description to the poorhouse, let her make a millionaire of your fancy. Her blue-black hair, smoothly divided in the middle and bound close to her head, and her large eyes full of the Latin melancholy, gave her the Madonna touch. Her motions and air spoke of the concealed fire and the desire to charm that she had inherited from the *gitanas* of the Basque province. As for the humming-bird part of her, that dwelt in her heart; you could not perceive it unless her bright red skirt and dark blue blouse gave you a symbolic hint of the vagarious bird.

The newly lighted sun-god asked for a drink of water. Tonia brought it from the red jar hanging under the brush shelter. Sandridge considered it necessary to dismount so as to lessen the trouble of her ministrations.

I play no spy; nor do I assume to master the thoughts of any human heart; but I assert, by the chronicler's right, that before a quarter of an hour had sped Sandridge was teaching her how to plait a six-strand rawhide stake-rope, and Tonia had explained to him that were it not for her little English book that the peripatetic *padre* had given her and the little crippled *chivo*, that she fed from a bottle, she would be very, very lonely indeed.

Which leads to a suspicion that the Kid's fences needed repairing, and that the adjutant-general's sarcasm had fallen upon unproductive soil.

In his camp by the water hole Lieutenant Sandridge announced and reiterated his intention of either causing the Cisco Kid to nibble the black loam of the Frio country prairies or of haling him before a judge and jury. That sounded business-like. Twice a week he rode over to the Lone Wolf Crossing of the Frio, and directed Tonia's slim, slightly lemon-tinted fingers among the intricacies of the slowly growing lariata. A six-strand plait is hard to learn and easy to teach.

The ranger knew that he might find the Kid there at any visit. He kept his armament ready, and had a frequent eye for the pear thicket at the rear of the *jacal*. Thus he might bring down the kite and the humming-bird with one stone.

While the sunny-haired ornithologist was pursuing his studies the Cisco Kid was also attending to his professional duties. He moodily shot up a saloon in a small cow village on Quintana Creek, killed the town marshal (plugging him neatly in the centre of his tin badge), and then rode away, morose and unsatisfied. No true artist is uplifted by shooting an aged man carrying an old-style .38 bulldog.

On his way the Kid suddenly experienced the yearning that all men feel when wrong-doing loses its keen edge of delight. He yearned for the woman he loved to reassure him that she was his in spite of it. He wanted her to call his bloodthirstiness bravery and his cruelty devotion. He wanted Tonia to bring him water from the red jar under the brush shelter, and tell him how the *chivo* was thriving on the bottle.

The Kid turned the speckled roan's head up the ten-mile pear flat that stretches along the Arroyo Hondo until it ends at the Lone Wolf Crossing of the Frio. The roan whickered; for he had a sense of locality and direction equal to that of a belt-line street-car horse; and he knew he would soon be nibbling the rich mesquite grass at the end of a forty-foot stake-rope while Ulysses rested his head in Circe's straw-roofed hut.

More weird and lonesome than the journey of an Amazonian explorer is the ride of one through a Texas pear flat. With dismal monotony and startling variety the uncanny and multiform shapes of the cacti lift their twisted trunks, and fat, bristly hands to encumber the way. The demon plant, appearing to live without soil or rain, seems to taunt the parched traveller with its lush grey greenness. It warps itself a thousand times about what look to be open and inviting paths, only to lure the rider into blind and impassable spine-defended "bottoms of the bag," leaving him to retreat, if he can, with the points of the compass whirling in his head.

To be lost in the pear is to die almost the death of the thief on the cross, pierced by nails and with grotesque shapes of all the fiends hovering about.

But it was not so with the Kid and his mount. Winding, twisting, circling, tracing the most fantastic and bewildering trail ever picked out, the good roan lessened the distance to the Lone Wolf Crossing with every coil and turn that he made.

While they fared the Kid sang. He knew but one tune and sang it, as he knew but one code and lived it, and but one girl and loved her. He was a single-minded man of conventional ideas. He had a voice like a coyote with bronchitis, but whenever he chose to sing his song he sang it. It was a conventional song of the camps and trail, running at its beginning as near as may be to these words:

> Don't you monkey with my Lulu girl
> Or I'll tell you what I'll do—

and so on. The roan was inured to it, and did not mind.

But even the poorest singer will, after a certain time, gain his own consent to refrain from contributing to the world's noises. So the Kid, by the time he was within a mile or two of Tonia's *jacal*, had reluctantly allowed his song to die away—not because his vocal performance had become less charming to his own ears, but because his laryngeal muscles were aweary.

As though he were in a circus ring the speckled roan wheeled and danced through the labyrinth of pear until at length his rider knew by certain landmarks that the Lone Wolf Crossing was close at hand. Then, where the pear was thinner, he caught sight of the grass roof of the *jacal* and the hackberry tree on the edge of the arroyo. A few yards farther the Kid stopped the roan and gazed intently through the prickly openings. Then he dismounted, dropped the roan's reins, and proceeded on foot, stooping and silent, like an Indian. The roan, knowing his part, stood still, making no sound.

The Kid crept noiselessly to the very edge of the pear thicket and reconnoitered between the leaves of a clump of cactus.

Ten yards from his hiding-place, in the shade of the *jacal*, sat his Tonia calmly plaiting a rawhide lariat. So far she might surely escape condemnation; women have been known, from time to time, to engage in more mischievous occupations. But if all must be told, there is to be added that her head reposed against the broad and comfortable chest of a tall red-and-yellow man, and that his arm was about her, guiding her nimble small fingers that required so many lessons at the intricate six-strand plait.

Sandridge glanced quickly at the dark mass of pear when he heard a slight squeaking sound that was not altogether unfamiliar. A gun-scabbard will make that sound when one grasps the handle of a six-shooter suddenly. But the sound was not repeated; and Tonia's fingers needed close attention.

And then, in the shadow of death, they began to talk of their love; and in the still July afternoon every word they uttered reached the ears of the Kid.

"Remember, then," said Tonia, "you must not come again until I send for you. Soon he will be here. A *vaquero* at the *tienda* said to-day he saw him on the Guadalupe three days ago. When he is that near he always comes. If he comes and finds you here he will kill you. So, for my sake, you must come no more until I send you the word."

"All right," said the ranger. "And then what?"

"And then," said the girl, "you must bring your men here and kill him. If not, he will kill you."

"He ain't a man to surrender, that's sure," said Sandridge. "It's kill or be killed for the officer that goes up against Mr. Cisco Kid."

"He must die," said the girl. "Otherwise there will not be any peace in the world for thee and me. He has killed many. Let him so die. Bring your men, and give him no chance to escape."

"You used to think right much of him," said Sandridge.

Tonia dropped the lariat, twisted herself around, and curved a lemon-tinted arm over the ranger's shoulder.

"But then," she murmured in liquid Spanish, "I had not beheld thee, thou great, red mountain of a man! And thou art kind and good, as well as strong. Could one choose him, knowing thee? Let him die; for then I will not be filled with fear by day and night lest he hurt thee or me."

"How can I know when he comes?" asked Sandridge.

"When he comes," said Tonia, "he remains two days, sometimes three. Gregorio, the small son of old Luisa, the *lavandera*, has a swift pony. I will write a letter to thee and send it by him, saying how it will be best to come upon him. By Gregorio will the letter come. And bring many men with thee, and have much care, oh, dear red one, for the rattlesnake is not quicker to strike than is '*El Chivato*,' as they call him, to send a ball from his *pistola*."

"The Kid's handy with his gun, sure enough," admitted Sandridge, "but when I come for him I shall come alone. I'll get him by myself or not at all. The Cap wrote one or two things to me that make me want to do the trick without any help. You let me know when Mr. Kid arrives, and I'll do the rest."

"I will send you the message by the boy Gregorio," said the girl. "I knew you were braver than that small slayer of men who never smiles. How could I ever have thought I cared for him?"

It was time for the ranger to ride back to his camp on the water hole. Before he mounted his horse he raised the slight form of Tonia with one arm high from the earth for a parting salute. The drowsy stillness of the torpid summer air still lay thick upon the dreaming afternoon. The smoke from the fire in the *jacal*, where the *frijoles* blubbered in the iron pot, rose straight as a plumb-line above the clay-daubed chimney. No sound or movement disturbed the serenity of the dense pear thicket ten yards away.

When the form of Sandridge had disappeared, loping his big dun down the steep banks of the Frio crossing, the Kid crept back to his own horse, mounted him, and rode back along the tortuous trail he had come.

But not far. He stopped and waited in the silent depths of the pear until half an hour had passed. And then Tonia heard the high, untrue notes of his unmusical singing coming nearer and nearer; and she ran to the edge of the pear to meet him.

The Kid seldom smiled; but he smiled and waved his hat when he saw her. He dismounted, and his girl sprang into his arms. The Kid looked at her fondly. His thick, black hair clung to his head like a wrinkled mat. The meeting brought a slight ripple of some undercurrent of feeling to his smooth, dark face that was usually as motionless as a clay mask.

"How's my girl?" he asked, holding her close.

"Sick of waiting so long for you, dear one," she answered. "My eyes are dim with always gazing into that devil's pincushion through which you come. And I can see into it such a little way, too. But you are here, beloved one, and I will not scold. *Que mal muchacho!* not to come to see your *alma* more often. Go in and rest, and let me water your horse and stake him with the long rope. There is cool water in the jar for you."

The Kid kissed her affectionately.

"Not if the court knows itself do I let a lady stake my horse for me," said he. "But if you'll run in, *chica*, and throw a pot of coffee together while I attend to the *caballo*, I'll be a good deal obliged."

Besides his marksmanship the Kid had another attribute for which he admired himself greatly. He was *muy caballero*, as the Mexicans express it, where the ladies were concerned. For them he had always gentle words and consideration. He could not have spoken a harsh word to a woman. He might ruthlessly slay their husbands and brothers, but he could not have laid the weight of a finger in anger upon a woman. Wherefore many of that interesting division of humanity who had come under the spell of his politeness declared their disbelief in the stories circulated about Mr. Kid. One shouldn't believe everything one heard, they said. When confronted by their indignant men folk with proof of the *caballero*'s deeds of infamy, they said maybe he had been driven to it, and that he knew how to treat a lady, anyhow.

Considering this extremely courteous idiosyncrasy of the Kid and the pride that he took in it, one can perceive that the solution of the problem that was presented to him by what he

saw and heard from his hiding-place in the pear that afternoon
(at least as to one of the actors) must have been obscured by
difficulties. And yet one could not think of the Kid overlooking
little matters of that kind.

At the end of the short twilight they gathered around a
supper of *frijoles*, goat steaks, canned peaches, and coffee, by
the light of a lantern in the *jacal*. Afterward, the ancestor, his
flock corralled, smoked a cigarette and became a mummy in a
grey blanket. Tonia washed the few dishes while the Kid dried
them with the flour-sacking towel. Her eyes shone; she chatted
volubly of the inconsequent happenings of her small world
since the Kid's last visit; it was as all his other home-comings
had been.

Then outside Tonia swung in a grass hammock with her
guitar and sang sad *canciones de amor*.

"Do you love me just the same, old girl?" asked the Kid,
hunting for his cigarette papers.

"Always the same, little one," said Tonia, her dark eyes lingering upon him.

"I must go over to Fink's," said the Kid, rising, "for some
tobacco. I thought I had another sack in my coat. I'll be back
in a quarter of an hour."

"Hasten," said Tonia, "and tell me—how long shall I call you
my own this time? Will you be gone again to-morrow, leaving
me to grieve, or will you be longer with your Tonia?"

"Oh, I might stay two or three days this trip," said the Kid,
yawning. "I've been on the dodge for a month, and I'd like to
rest up."

He was gone half an hour for his tobacco. When he returned
Tonia was still lying in the hammock.

"It's funny," said the Kid, "how I feel. I feel like there was
somebody lying behind every bush and tree waiting to shoot
me. I never had mullygrubs like them before. Maybe it's one
of them presumptions. I've got half a notion to light out in
the morning before day. The Guadalupe country is burning up
about that old Dutchman I plugged down there."

"You are not afraid—no one could make my brave little one
fear."

"Well, I haven't been usually regarded as a jackrabbit when
it comes to scrapping; but I don't want a posse smoking me

out when I'm in your *jacal*. Somebody might get hurt that oughtn't to."

"Remain with your Tonia; no one will find you here."

The Kid looked keenly into the shadows up and down the arroyo and toward the dim lights of the Mexican village.

"I'll see how it looks later on," was his decision.

At midnight a horseman rode into the rangers' camp, blazing his way by noisy "halloes" to indicate a pacific mission. Sandridge and one or two others turned out to investigate the row. The rider announced himself to be Domingo Sales, from the Lone Wolf Crossing. He bore a letter for Señor Sandridge. Old Luisa, the *lavandera*, had persuaded him to bring it, he said, her son Gregorio being too ill of a fever to ride.

Sandridge lighted the camp lantern and read the letter. These were its words:

Dear One: He has come. Hardly had you ridden away when he came out of the pear. When he first talked he said he would stay three days or more. Then as it grew later he was like a wolf or a fox, and walked about without rest, looking and listening. Soon he said he must leave before daylight when it is dark and stillest. And then he seemed to suspect that I be not true to him. He looked at me so strange that I am frightened. I swear to him that I love him, his own Tonia. Last of all he said I must prove to him I am true. He thinks that even now men are waiting to kill him as he rides from my house. To escape he says he will dress in my clothes, my red skirt and the blue waist I wear and the brown mantilla over the head, and thus ride away. But before that he says that I must put on his clothes, his *pantalones* and *camisa* and hat, and ride away on his horse from the *jacal* as far as the big road beyond the crossing and back again. This before he goes, so he can tell if I am true and if men are hidden to shoot him. It is a terrible thing. An hour before daybreak this is to be. Come, my dear one, and kill this man and take me for your Tonia. Do not try to take hold of him alive, but kill him quickly. Knowing all, you should do that. You must come long before the time and hide yourself in the little shed near the *jacal* where the wagon and saddles are kept. It is dark in there. He will wear my red skirt and blue waist and brown mantilla. I send you a hundred kisses. Come surely and shoot quickly and straight.

THINE OWN TONIA.

Sandridge quickly explained to his men the official part of the missive. The rangers protested against his going alone.

"I'll get him easy enough," said the lieutenant. "The girl's got him trapped. And don't even think he'll get the drop on me."

Sandridge saddled his horse and rode to the Lone Wolf Crossing. He tied his big dun in a clump of brush on the arroyo, took his Winchester from its scabbard, and carefully approached the Perez *jacal*. There was only the half of a high moon drifted over by ragged, milk-white gulf clouds.

The wagon-shed was an excellent place for ambush; and the ranger got inside it safely. In the black shadow of the brush shelter in front of the *jacal* he could see a horse tied and hear him impatiently pawing the hard-trodden earth.

He waited almost an hour before two figures came out of the *jacal*. One, in man's clothes, quickly mounted the horse and galloped past the wagon-shed toward the crossing and village. And then the other figure, in skirt, waist, and mantilla over its head, stepped out into the faint moonlight, gazing after the rider. Sandridge thought he would take his chance then before Tonia rode back. He fancied she might not care to see it.

"Throw up your hands," he ordered loudly, stepping out of the wagon-shed with his Winchester at his shoulder.

There was a quick turn of the figure, but no movement to obey, so the ranger pumped in the bullets—one—two—three—and then twice more; for you never could be too sure of bringing down the Cisco Kid. There was no danger of missing at ten paces, even in that half moonlight.

The old ancestor, asleep on his blanket, was awakened by the shots. Listening further, he heard a great cry from some man in mortal distress or anguish, and rose up grumbling at the disturbing ways of moderns.

The tall, red ghost of a man burst into the *jacal*, reaching one hand, shaking like a *tule* reed, for the lantern hanging on its nail. The other spread a letter on the table.

"Look at this letter, Perez," cried the man. "Who wrote it?"

"*Ah, Dios!* it is Señor Sandridge," mumbled the old man, approaching. "*Pues, señor*, that letter was written by '*El Chivato*,' as he is called—by the man of Tonia. They say he is a bad man; I do not know. While Tonia slept he wrote the letter and sent it by this old hand of mine to Domingo Sales to be brought to you. Is there anything wrong in the letter? I am very old; and I did not know. *Valgame Dios!* it is a very foolish world; and there is nothing in the house to drink—nothing to drink."

Just then all that Sandridge could think of to do was to go outside and throw himself face downward in the dust by the side of his humming-bird, of whom not a feather fluttered. He was not a *caballero* by instinct, and he could not understand the niceties of revenge.

A mile away the rider who had ridden past the wagon-shed struck up a harsh, untuneful song, the words of which began:

> Don't you monkey with my Lulu girl,
> Or I'll tell you what I'll do—

The Moment of Victory

BEN GRANGER is a war veteran aged twenty-nine—which should enable you to guess the war. He is also principal merchant and postmaster of Cadiz, a little town over which the breezes from the Gulf of Mexico perpetually blow.

Ben helped to hurl the Don from his stronghold in the Greater Antilles; and then, hiking across half the world, he marched as a corporal-usher up and down the blazing tropic aisles of the open-air college in which the Filipino was schooled. Now, with his bayonet beaten into a cheese-slicer, he rallies his corporal's guard of cronies in the shade of his well-whittled porch, instead of in the matted jungles of Mindanao. Always have his interest and choice been for deeds rather than for words; but the consideration and digestion of motives is not beyond him, as this story, which is his, will attest.

"What is it," he asked me one moonlit eve, as we sat among his boxes and barrels, "that generally makes men go through dangers, and fire, and trouble, and starvation, and battle, and such rucouses? What does a man do it for? Why does he try to outdo his fellow-humans, and be braver and stronger and more daring and showy than even his best friends are? What's his game? What does he expect to get out of it? He don't do it just for the fresh air and exercise. What would you say, now, Bill, that an ordinary man expects, generally speaking, for his efforts along the line of ambition and extraordinary hustling in the marketplaces, forums, shooting-galleries, lyceums, battle-fields, links, cinder-paths, and arenas of the civilized and *vice versa* places of the world?"

"Well, Ben," said I, with judicial seriousness, "I think we might safely limit the number of motives of a man who seeks fame to three—to ambition, which is a desire for popular applause; to avarice, which looks to the material side of success; and to love of some woman whom he either possesses or desires to possess."

Ben pondered over my words while a mocking-bird on the top of a mesquite by the porch trilled a dozen bars.

"I reckon," said he, "that your diagnosis about covers the

257

case according to the rules laid down in the copy-books and historical readers. But what I had in my mind was the case of Willie Robbins, a person I used to know. I'll tell you about him before I close up the store, if you don't mind listening.

"Willie was one of our social set up in San Augustine. I was clerking there then for Brady & Murchison, wholesale dry-goods and ranch supplies. Willie and I belonged to the same german club and athletic association and military company. He played the triangle in our serenading and quartet crowd that used to ring the welkin three nights a week somewhere in town.

"Willie jibed with his name considerable. He weighed about as much as a hundred pounds of veal in his summer suitings, and he had a 'Where-is-Mary?' expression on his features so plain that you could almost see the wool growing on him.

"And yet you couldn't fence him away from the girls with barbed wire. You know that kind of young fellows—a kind of a mixture of fools and angels—they rush in and fear to tread at the same time; but they never fail to tread when they get the chance. He was always on hand when 'a joyful occasion was had,' as the morning paper would say, looking as happy as a king full, and at the same time as uncomfortable as a raw oyster served with sweet pickles. He danced like he had hind hobbles on; and he had a vocabulary of about three hundred and fifty words that he made stretch over four germans a week, and plagiarized from to get him through two ice-cream suppers and a Sunday-night call. He seemed to me to be a sort of a mixture of Maltese kitten, sensitive plant, and a member of a stranded *Two Orphans* company.

"I'll give you an estimate of his physiological and pictorial make-up, and then I'll stick spurs into the sides of my narrative.

"Willie inclined to the Caucasian in his coloring and manner of style. His hair was opalescent and his conversation fragmentary. His eyes were the same blue shade as the china dog's on the right-hand corner of your Aunt Ellen's mantelpiece. He took things as they come, and I never felt any hostility against him. I let him live, and so did others.

"But what does this Willie do but coax his heart out of his boots and lose it to Myra Allison, the liveliest, brightest, keenest, smartest, and prettiest girl in San Augustine. I tell you, she had the blackest eyes, the shiniest curls, and the most tantalizing— Oh, no, you're off—I wasn't a victim. I might have been, but I knew better. I kept out. Joe Granberry was It from the start. He had everybody else beat a couple of leagues and thence east to a stake and mound. But, anyhow, Myra was a nine-pound, full-merino, fall-clip fleece, sacked and loaded on a four-horse team for San Antone.

"One night there was an ice-cream sociable at Mrs. Colonel Spraggins', in San Augustine. We fellows had a big room up-stairs opened up for us to put our hats and things in, and to comb our hair and put on the clean collars we brought along inside the sweat-bands of our hats—in short, a room to fix up in just like they have everywhere at high-toned doings. A little farther down the hall was the girls' room, which they used to powder up in, and so forth. Downstairs we—that is, the San Augustine Social Cotillion and Merrymakers' Club— had a stretcher put down in the parlor where our dance was going on.

"Willie Robbins and me happened to be up in our— cloak-room, I believe we called it—when Myra Allison skipped through the hall on her way down-stairs from the girls' room. Willie was standing before the mirror, deeply interested in smoothing down the blond grass-plot on his head, which seemed to give him lots of trouble. Myra was always full of life and devilment. She stopped and stuck her head in our door. She certainly was good-looking. But I knew how Joe Granberry stood with her. So did Willie; but he kept on ba-a-a-ing after her and following her around. He had a system of persistence that didn't coincide with pale hair and light eyes.

"'Hello, Willie!' says Myra. 'What are you doing to yourself in the glass?'

"'I'm trying to look fly,' says Willie.

"'Well, you never could *be* fly,' says Myra, with her special laugh, which was the provokingest sound I ever heard except the rattle of an empty canteen against my saddle-horn.

"I looked around at Willie after Myra had gone. He had a kind of a lily-white look on him which seemed to show that her remark had, as you might say, disrupted his soul. I never noticed anything in what she said that sounded particularly destructive to a man's ideas of self-consciousness; but he was set back to an extent you could scarcely imagine.

"After we went down-stairs with our clean collars on, Willie never went near Myra again that night. After all, he seemed to be a diluted kind of a skim-milk sort of a chap, and I never wondered that Joe Granberry beat him out.

"The next day the battleship *Maine* was blown up, and then pretty soon somebody—I reckon it was Joe Bailey, or Ben Tillman, or maybe the Government—declared war against Spain.

"Well, everybody south of Mason & Hamlin's line knew that the North by itself couldn't whip a whole country the size of Spain. So the Yankees commenced to holler for help, and the Johnny Rebs answered the call. 'We're coming, Father William, a hundred thousand strong—and then some,' was the way they sang it. And the old party lines drawn by Sherman's march and the Kuklux and nine-cent cotton and the Jim Crow street-car ordinances faded away. We became one undivided country, with no North, very little East, a good-sized chunk of West, and a South that loomed up as big as the first foreign label on a new eight-dollar suit-case.

"Of course the dogs of war weren't a complete pack without a yelp from the San Augustine Rifles, Company D, of the Fourteenth Texas Regiment. Our company was among the first to land in Cuba and strike terror into the hearts of the foe. I'm not going to give you a history of the war; I'm just dragging it in to fill out my story about Willie Robbins, just as the Republican party dragged it in to help out the election in 1898.

"If anybody ever had heroitis, it was that Willie Robbins. From the minute he set foot on the soil of the tyrants of Castile he seemed to engulf danger as a cat laps up cream. He certainly astonished every man in our company, from the captain up. You'd have expected him to gravitate naturally to the job of an orderly to the colonel, or typewriter in the commissary—but not any. He created the part of the flaxen-haired boy hero who lives and gets back home with the goods, instead of dying with an important despatch in his hands at his colonel's feet.

"Our company got into a section of Cuban scenery where one of the messiest and most unsung portions of the campaign occurred. We were out every day capering around in the bushes, and having little skirmishes with the Spanish troops that looked more like kind of tired-out feuds than anything else. The war was a joke to us, and of no interest to them. We never could see it any other way than as a howling farce-comedy that the San Augustine Rifles were actually fighting to uphold the Stars and Stripes. And the blamed little señors didn't get enough pay to make them care whether they were patriots or traitors. Now and then somebody would get killed. It seemed like a waste of life to me. I was at Coney Island when I went to New York once, and one of them down-hill skidding apparatuses they call 'roller-coasters' flew the track and killed a man in a brown sack-suit. Whenever the Spaniards shot one of our men, it struck me as just about as unnecessary and regrettable as that was.

"But I'm dropping Willie Robbins out of the conversation.

"He was out for bloodshed, laurels, ambition, medals, recommendations, and all other forms of military glory. And he didn't seem to be afraid of any of the recognized forms of military danger, such as Spaniards, cannon-balls, canned beef, gunpowder, or nepotism. He went forth with his pallid hair and china-blue eyes and ate up Spaniards like you would sardines *à la* canopy. Wars and rumbles of wars never flustered him. He would stand guard-duty, mosquitoes, hardtack, treat, and fire with equally perfect unanimity. No blondes in history ever come in comparison distance of him except the Jack of Diamonds and Queen Catherine of Russia.

"I remember, one time, a little *caballard* of Spanish men sauntered out from behind a patch of sugar-cane and shot Bob Turner, the first sergeant of our company, while we were eating dinner. As required by the army regulations, we fellows went through the usual tactics of falling into line, saluting the enemy, and loading and firing, kneeling.

"That wasn't the Texas way of scrapping; but, being a very important addendum and annex to the regular army, the San Augustine Rifles had to conform to the red-tape system of getting even.

"By the time we had got out our 'Upton's Tactics,' turned to page fifty-seven, said 'one—two—three—one—two—three' a couple of times, and got blank cartridges into our Springfields, the Spanish outfit had smiled repeatedly, rolled and lit cigarettes by squads, and walked away contemptuously.

"I went straight to Captain Floyd, and says to him: 'Sam, I don't think this war is a straight game. You know as well as I do that Bob Turner was one of the whitest fellows that ever threw a leg over a saddle, and now these wire-pullers in Washington have fixed his clock. He's politically and ostensibly dead. It ain't fair. Why should they keep this thing up? If they want Spain licked, why don't they turn the San Augustine Rifles and Joe Seely's ranger company and a car-load of West Texas deputy-sheriffs onto these Spaniards, and let us exonerate them from the face of the earth? I never did,' says I, 'care much about fighting by the Lord Chesterfield ring rules. I'm going to hand in my resignation and go home if anybody else I am personally acquainted with gets hurt in this war. If you can get somebody in my place, Sam,' says I, 'I'll quit the first of next week. I don't want to work in an army that don't give its help a chance. Never mind my wages,' says I; 'let the Secretary of the Treasury keep 'em.'

"'Well, Ben,' says the captain to me, 'your allegations and estimations of the tactics of war, government, patriotism, guard-mounting, and democracy are all right. But I've looked into the system of international arbitration and the ethics of justifiable slaughter a little closer, maybe, than you have. Now, you can hand in your resignation the first of next week if you are so minded. But if you do,' says Sam, 'I'll order a corporal's guard to take you over by that limestone bluff on the creek and shoot enough lead into you to ballast a submarine air-ship. I'm captain of this company, and I've swore allegiance to the Amalgamated States regardless of sectional, secessional, and Congressional differences. Have you got any smoking-tobacco?' winds up Sam. 'Mine got wet when I swum the creek this morning.'

"The reason I drag all this *non ex parte* evidence in is because Willie Robbins was standing there listening to us. I was a second sergeant and he was a private then, but among us Texans and Westerners there never was as much tactics and subordination as there was in the regular army. We never called our captain anything but 'Sam' except when there was a lot of major-generals and admirals around, so as to preserve the discipline.

"And says Willie Robbins to me, in a sharp construction of voice much unbecoming to his light hair and previous record:

"'You ought to be shot, Ben, for emitting any such sentiments. A man that won't fight for his country is worse than a horse-thief. If I was the cap, I'd put you in the guard-house for thirty days on round steak and tamales. War,' says Willie, 'is great and glorious. I didn't know you were a coward.'

"'I'm not,' says I. 'If I was, I'd knock some of the pallidness off of your marble brow. I'm lenient with you,' I says, 'just as I am with the Spaniards, because you have always reminded me of something with mushrooms on the side. Why, you little Lady of Shalott,' says I, 'you underdone leader of cotillions, you glassy fashion and moulded form, you white-pine soldier made in the Cisalpine Alps in Germany for the late New-Year trade, do you know of whom you are talking to? We've been in the same social circle,' say I, 'and I've put up with you because you seemed so meek and self-unsatisfying. I don't understand why you have so sudden taken a personal interest in chivalrousness and murder. Your nature's undergone a complete revelation. Now, how is it?'

"'Well, you wouldn't understand, Ben,' says Willie, giving one of his refined smiles and turning away.

"'Come back here!' says I, catching him by the tail of his khaki coat. 'You've made me kind of mad, in spite of the aloofness in which I have heretofore held you. You are out for making a success in this hero business, and I believe I know what for. You are doing it either because you are crazy or because you expect to catch some girl by it. Now, if it's a girl, I've got something here to show you.'

"I wouldn't have done it, but I was plumb mad. I pulled a San Augustine paper out of my hip-pocket, and showed him an item. It was a half a column about the marriage of Myra Allison and Joe Granberry.

"Willie laughed, and I saw I hadn't touched him.

"'Oh,' says he, 'everybody knew that was going to happen. I heard about that a week ago.' And then he gave me the laugh again.

"'All right,' says I. 'Then why do you so recklessly chase the bright rainbow of fame? Do you expect to be elected President, or do you belong to a suicide club?'

"And then Captain Sam interferes.

"'You gentlemen quit jawing and go back to your quarters,' says he, 'or I'll have you escorted to the guard-house. Now, scat, both of you! Before you go, which one of you has got any chewing-tobacco?'

"'We're off, Sam,' says I. 'It's supper-time, anyhow. But what do you think of what we was talking about? I've noticed you throwing out a good many grappling-hooks for this here balloon called fame— What's ambition, anyhow? What does a man risk his life day after day for? Do you know of anything he gets in the end that can pay him for the trouble? I want to go back home,' says I. 'I don't care whether Cuba sinks or swims, and I don't give a pipeful of rabbit tobacco whether Queen Sophia Christina or Charlie Culberson rules these fairy isles; and I don't want my name on any list except the list of survivors. But I've noticed you, Sam,' says I, 'seeking the bubble notoriety in the cannon's larynx a number of times. Now, what do you do it for? Is it ambition, business, or some freckle-faced Phœbe at home that you are heroing for?'

"'Well, Ben,' says Sam, kind of hefting his sword out from between his knees, 'as your superior officer I could court-martial you for attempted cowardice and desertion. But I won't. And I'll tell you why I'm trying for promotion and the usual honors of war and conquest. A major gets more pay than a captain, and I need the money.'

"'Correct for you!' says I. 'I can understand that. Your system of fame-seeking is rooted in the deepest soil of patriotism. But I can't comprehend,' says I, 'why Willie Robbins, whose folks at home are well off, and who used to be as meek and undesirous of notice as a cat with cream on his whiskers, should all at once develop into a warrior bold with the most fire-eating kind of proclivities. And the girl in his case seems to have been eliminated by marriage to another fellow. I reckon,' says I, 'it's a plain case of just common ambition. He wants his name, maybe, to go thundering down the coroners of time. It must be that.'

"Well, without itemizing his deeds, Willie sure made good as a hero. He simply spent most of his time on his knees begging our captain to send him on forlorn hopes and dangerous scouting expeditions. In every fight he was the first man to mix it at close quarters with the Don Alfonsos. He got three or four bullets planted in various parts of his autonomy. Once he went off with a detail of eight men and captured a whole company of

Spanish. He kept Captain Floyd busy writing out recommendations of his bravery to send in to headquarters; and he began to accumulate medals for all kinds of things—heroism and target-shooting and valor and tactics and uninsubordination, and all the little accomplishments that look good to the third assistant secretaries of the War Department.

"Finally, Cap Floyd got promoted to be a major-general, or a knight commander of the main herd, or something like that. He pounded around on a white horse, all desecrated up with gold-leaf and hen-feathers and a Good Templar's hat, and wasn't allowed by the regulations to speak to us. And Willie Robbins was made captain of our company.

"And maybe he didn't go after the wreath of fame then! As far as I could see it was him that ended the war. He got eighteen of us boys—friends of his, too—killed in battles that he stirred up himself, and that didn't seem to me necessary at all. One night he took twelve of us and waded through a little rill about a hundred and ninety yards wide, and climbed a couple of mountains, and sneaked through a mile of neglected shrubbery and a couple of rock-quarries and into a rye-straw village, and captured a Spanish general named, as they said, Benny Veedus. Benny seemed to me hardly worth the trouble, being a blackish man without shoes or cuffs, and anxious to surrender and throw himself on the commissary of his foe.

"But that job gave Willie the big boost he wanted. The San Augustine *News* and the Galveston, St. Louis, New York, and Kansas City papers printed his picture and columns of stuff about him. Old San Augustine simply went crazy over its 'gallant son.' The *News* had an editorial tearfully begging the Government to call off the regular army and the national guard, and let Willie carry on the rest of the war single-handed. It said that a refusal to do so would be regarded as a proof that the Northern jealousy of the South was still as rampant as ever.

"If the war hadn't ended pretty soon, I don't know to what heights of gold braid and encomiums Willie would have climbed; but it did. There was a secession of hostilities just three days after he was appointed a colonel, and got in three more medals by registered mail, and shot two Spaniards while they were drinking lemonade in an ambuscade.

"Our company went back to San Augustine when the war

was over. There wasn't anywhere else for it to go. And what do you think? The old town notified us in print, by wire cable, special delivery, and a nigger named Saul sent on a gray mule to San Antone, that they was going to give us the biggest blow-out, complimentary, alimentary, and elementary, that ever disturbed the kildees on the sand-flats outside of the immediate contiguity of the city.

"I say 'we,' but it was all meant for ex-Private, Captain *de facto*, and Colonel-elect Willie Robbins. The town was crazy about him. They notified us that the reception they were going to put up would make the Mardi Gras in New Orleans look like an afternoon tea in Bury St. Edmunds with a curate's aunt.

"Well, the San Augustine Rifles got back home on schedule time. Everybody was at the depot giving forth Roosevelt-Democrat—they used to be called Rebel—yells. There was two brass-bands, and the mayor, and schoolgirls in white frightening the street-car horses by throwing Cherokee roses in the streets, and—well, maybe you've seen a celebration by a town that was inland and out of water.

"They wanted Brevet-Colonel Willie to get into a carriage and be drawn by prominent citizens and some of the city aldermen to the armory, but he stuck to his company and marched at the head of it up Sam Houston Avenue. The buildings on both sides was covered with flags and audiences, and everybody hollered 'Robbins!' or 'Hello, Willie!' as we marched up in files of fours. I never saw a illustriouser-looking human in my life than Willie was. He had at least seven or eight medals and diplomas and decorations on the breast of his khaki coat; he was sunburnt the color of a saddle, and he certainly done himself proud.

"They told us at the depot that the court-house was to be illuminated at half-past seven, and there would be speeches and chili-con-carne at the Palace Hotel. Miss Delphine Thompson was to read an original poem by James Whitcomb Ryan, and Constable Hooker had promised us a salute of nine guns from Chicago that he had arrested that day.

"After we had disbanded in the armory, Willie says to me:

"'Want to walk out a piece with me?'

"'Why, yes,' says I, 'if it ain't so far that we can't hear the tumult and the shouting die away. I'm hungry myself,' says I, 'and I'm pining for some home grub, but I'll go with you.'

"Willie steered me down some side streets till we came to a little white cottage in a new lot with a twenty-by-thirty-foot lawn decorated with brickbats and old barrel-staves.

"'Halt and give the countersign,' says I to Willie. 'Don't you know this dugout? It's the bird's-nest that Joe Granberry built before he married Myra Allison. What you going there for?'

"But Willie already had the gate open. He walked up the brick walk to the steps, and I went with him. Myra was sitting in a rocking-chair on the porch, sewing. Her hair was smoothed back kind of hasty and tied in a knot. I never noticed till then that she had freckles. Joe was at one side of the porch, in his shirt-sleeves, with no collar on, and no signs of a shave, trying to scrape out a hole among the brickbats and tin cans to plant a little fruit-tree in. He looked up but never said a word, and neither did Myra.

"Willie was sure dandy-looking in his uniform, with medals strung on his breast and his new gold-handled sword. You'd never have taken him for the little white-headed snipe that the girls used to order about and make fun of. He just stood there for a minute, looking at Myra with a peculiar little smile on his face; and then he says to her, slow, and kind of holding on to his words with his teeth:

"*Oh, I don't know! Maybe I could if I tried!*'

"That was all that was said. Willie raised his hat, and we walked away.

"And, somehow, when he said that, I remembered, all of a sudden, the night of that dance and Willie brushing his hair before the looking-glass, and Myra sticking her head in the door to guy him.

"When we got back to Sam Houston Avenue, Willie says:

"'Well, so long, Ben. I'm going down home and get off my shoes and take a rest.'

"'You?' says I. 'What's the matter with you? Ain't the court-house jammed with everybody in town waiting to honor the hero? And two brass-bands, and recitations and flags and jags and grub to follow waiting for you?'

"Willie sighs.

"'All right, Ben,' says he. 'Darned if I didn't forget all about that.'

"And that's why I say," concluded Ben Granger, "that you can't tell where ambition begins any more than you can where it is going to wind up."

Buried Treasure

THERE ARE many kinds of fools. Now, will everybody please sit still until they are called upon specifically to rise?

I had been every kind of fool except one. I had expended my patrimony, pretended my matrimony, played poker, lawn-tennis, and bucket-shops—parted soon with my money in many ways. But there remained one rôle of the wearer of cap and bells that I had not played. That was the Seeker after Buried Treasure. To few does the delectable furor come. But of all the would-be followers in the hoof-prints of King Midas none has found a pursuit so rich in pleasurable promise.

But, going back from my theme a while—as lame pens must do—I was a fool of the sentimental sort. I saw May Martha Mangum, and was hers. She was eighteen, the color of the white ivory keys of a new piano, beautiful, and possessed by the exquisite solemnity and pathetic witchery of an unsophisticated angel doomed to live in a small, dull, Texas prairie-town. She had a spirit and charm that could have enabled her to pluck rubies like raspberries from the crown of Belgium or any other sporty kingdom, but she did not know it, and I did not paint the picture for her.

You see, I wanted May Martha Mangum for to have and to hold. I wanted her to abide with me, and put my slippers and pipe away every day in places where they cannot be found of evenings.

May Martha's father was a man hidden behind whiskers and spectacles. He lived for bugs and butterflies and all insects that fly or crawl or buzz or get down your back or in the butter. He was an etymologist, or words to that effect. He spent his life seining the air for flying fish of the June-bug order, and then sticking pins through 'em and calling 'em names.

He and May Martha were the whole family. He prized her highly as a fine specimen of the *racibus humanus* because she saw that he had food at times, and put his clothes on right side before, and kept his alcohol-bottles filled. Scientists, they say, are apt to be absent-minded.

There was another besides myself who thought May Martha

Mangum one to be desired. That was Goodloe Banks, a young man just home from college. He had all the attainments to be found in books—Latin, Greek, philosophy, and especially the higher branches of mathematics and logic.

If it hadn't been for his habit of pouring out this information and learning on every one that he addressed, I'd have liked him pretty well. But, even as it was, he and I were, you would have thought, great pals.

We got together every time we could because each of us wanted to pump the other for whatever straws we could to find which way the wind blew from the heart of May Martha Mangum—rather a mixed metaphor; Goodloe Banks would never have been guilty of that. That is the way of rivals.

You might say that Goodloe ran to books, manners, culture, rowing, intellect, and clothes. I would have put you in mind more of baseball and Friday-night debating societies—by way of culture—and maybe of a good horseback rider.

But in our talks together, and in our visits and conversation with May Martha, neither Goodloe Banks nor I could find out which one of us she preferred. May Martha was a natural-born non-committal, and knew in her cradle how to keep people guessing.

As I said, old man Mangum was absent-minded. After a long time he found out one day—a little butterfly must have told him—that two young men were trying to throw a net over the head of the young person, a daughter, or some such technical appendage, who looked after his comforts.

I never knew scientists could rise to such occasions. Old Mangum orally labelled and classified Goodloe and myself easily among the lowest orders of the vertebrates; and in English, too, without going any further into Latin than the simple references to *Orgetorix, Rex Helvetii*—which is as far as I ever went, myself. And he told us that if he ever caught us around his house again he would add us to his collection.

Goodloe Banks and I remained away five days, expecting the storm to subside. When we dared to call at the house again May Martha Mangum and her father were gone. Gone! The house they had rented was closed. Their little store of goods and chattels was gone also.

And not a word of farewell to either of us from May Martha

—not a white, fluttering note pinned to the hawthorn-bush; not a chalk-mark on the gate-post nor a post-card in the post-office to give us a clew.

For two months Goodloe Banks and I—separately—tried every scheme we could think of to track the runaways. We used our friendship and influence with the ticket-agent, with livery-stable men, railroad conductors, and our one lone, lorn constable, but without results.

Then we became better friends and worse enemies than ever. We forgathered in the back room of Snyder's saloon every afternoon after work, and played dominoes, and laid conversational traps to find out from each other if anything had been discovered. That is the way of rivals.

Now, Goodloe Banks had a sarcastic way of displaying his own learning and putting me in the class that was reading "Poor Jane Ray, her bird is dead, she cannot play." Well, I rather liked Goodloe, and I had a contempt for his college learning, and I was always regarded as good-natured, so I kept my temper. And I was trying to find out if he knew anything about May Martha, so I endured his society.

In talking things over one afternoon he said to me:

"Suppose you do find her, Ed, whereby would you profit? Miss Mangum has a mind. Perhaps it is yet uncultured, but she is destined for higher things than you could give her. I have talked with no one who seemed to appreciate more the enchantment of the ancient poets and writers and the modern cults that have assimilated and expended their philosophy of life. Don't you think you are wasting your time looking for her?"

"My idea," said I, "of a happy home is an eight-room house in a grove of live-oaks by the side of a *charco* on a Texas prairie. A piano," I went on, "with an automatic player in the sitting-room, three thousand head of cattle under fence for a starter, a buckboard and ponies always hitched at a post for 'the missus'—and May Martha Mangum to spend the profits of the ranch as she pleases, and to abide with me, and put my slippers and pipe away every day in places where they cannot be found of evenings. That," said I, "is what is to be; and a fig—a dried, Smyrna, dago-stand fig—for your curriculums, cults, and philosophy."

"She is meant for higher things," repeated Goodloe Banks.

"Whatever she is meant for," I answered, "just now she is out of pocket. And I shall find her as soon as I can without aid of the colleges."

"The game is blocked," said Goodloe, putting down a domino; and we had the beer.

Shortly after that a young farmer whom I knew came into town and brought me a folded blue paper. He said his grandfather had just died. I concealed a tear, and he went on to say that the old man had jealously guarded this paper for twenty years. He left it to his family as part of his estate, the rest of which consisted of two mules and a hypotenuse of non-arable land.

The sheet of paper was of the old, blue kind used during the rebellion of the abolitionists against the secessionists. It was dated June 14, 1863, and it described the hiding-place of ten burro-loads of gold and silver coin valued at three hundred thousand dollars. Old Rundle—grandfather of his grandson, Sam—was given the information by a Spanish priest who was in on the treasure-burying, and who died many years before—no, afterward—in old Rundle's house. Old Rundle wrote it down from dictation.

"Why didn't your father look this up?" I asked young Rundle.

"He went blind before he could do so," he replied.

"Why didn't you hunt for it yourself?" I asked.

"Well," said he, "I've only known about the paper for ten years. First there was the spring ploughin' to do, and then choppin' the weeds out of the corn; and then come takin' fodder; and mighty soon winter was on us. It seemed to run along that way year after year."

That sounded perfectly reasonable to me, so I took it up with young Lee Rundle at once.

The directions on the paper were simple. The whole burro cavalcade laden with the treasure started from an old Spanish mission in Dolores County. They travelled due south by the compass until they reached the Alamito River. They forded this, and buried the treasure on the top of a little mountain shaped like a pack-saddle standing in a row between two higher ones. A heap of stones marked the place of the buried treasure. All the party except the Spanish priest were killed by Indians a few days later. The secret was a monopoly. It looked good to me.

Lee Rundle suggested that we rig out a camping outfit, hire a surveyor to run out the line from the Spanish mission, and then spend the three hundred thousand dollars seeing the sights in Fort Worth. But, without being highly educated, I knew a way to save time and expense.

We went to the State land-office and had a practical, what they call a "working," sketch made of all the surveys of land from the old mission to the Alamito River. On this map I drew a line due southward to the river. The length of lines of each survey and section of land was accurately given on the sketch. By these we found the point on the river and had a "connection" made with it and an important, well-identified corner of the Los Animos five-league survey—a grant made by King Philip of Spain.

By doing this we did not need to have the line run out by a surveyor. It was a great saving of expense and time.

So, Lee Rundle and I fitted out a two-horse wagon team with all the accessories, and drove a hundred and forty-nine miles to Chico, the nearest town to the point we wished to reach. There we picked up a deputy county surveyor. He found the corner of the Los Animos survey for us, ran out the five thousand seven hundred and twenty varas west that our sketch called for, laid a stone on the spot, had coffee and bacon, and caught the mail-stage back to Chico.

I was pretty sure we would get that three hundred thousand dollars. Lee Rundle's was to be only one-third, because I was paying all the expenses. With that two hundred thousand dollars I knew I could find May Martha Mangum if she was on earth. And with it I could flutter the butterflies in old man Mangum's dove-cot, too. If I could find that treasure!

But Lee and I established camp. Across the river were a dozen little mountains densely covered by cedar-brakes, but not one shaped like a pack-saddle. That did not deter us. Appearances are deceptive. A pack-saddle, like beauty, may exist only in the eye of the beholder.

I and the grandson of the treasure examined those cedar-covered hills with the care of a lady hunting for the wicked flea. We explored every side, top, circumference, mean elevation, angle, slope, and concavity of every one for two miles up and down the river. We spent four days doing so. Then we hitched up the roan and the dun, and hauled the remains of the coffee and bacon the one hundred and forty-nine miles back to Concho City.

Lee Rundle chewed much tobacco on the return trip. I was busy driving, because I was in a hurry.

As shortly as could be after our empty return Goodloe Banks and I forgathered in the back room of Snyder's saloon to play dominoes and fish for information. I told Goodloe about my expedition after the buried treasure.

"If I could have found that three hundred thousand dollars," I said to him, "I could have scoured and sifted the surface of the earth to find May Martha Mangum."

"She is meant for higher things," said Goodloe. "I shall find her myself. But, tell me how you went about discovering the spot where this unearthed increment was imprudently buried."

I told him in the smallest detail. I showed him the draughtsman's sketch with the distances marked plainly upon it.

After glancing over it in a masterly way, he leaned back in his chair and bestowed upon me an explosion of sardonic, superior, collegiate laughter.

"Well, you *are* a fool, Jim," he said, when he could speak.

"It's your play," said I, patiently, fingering my double-six.

"Twenty," said Goodloe, making two crosses on the table with his chalk.

"Why am I a fool?" I asked. "Buried treasure has been found before in many places."

"Because," said he, "in calculating the point on the river where your line would strike you neglected to allow for the variation. The variation there would be nine degrees west. Let me have your pencil."

Goodloe Banks figured rapidly on the back of an envelope.

"The distance, from north to south, of the line run from the Spanish mission," said he, "is exactly twenty-two miles. It was run by a pocket-compass, according to your story. Allowing for the variation, the point on the Alamito River where you should have searched for your treasure is exactly six miles and nine hundred and forty-five varas farther west than the place you hit upon. Oh, what a fool you are, Jim!"

"What is this variation that you speak of?" I asked. "I thought figures never lied."

"The variation of the magnetic compass," said Goodloe, "from the true meridian."

He smiled in his superior way; and then I saw come out in his face the singular, eager, consuming cupidity of the seeker after buried treasure.

"Sometimes," he said with the air of the oracle, "these old traditions of hidden money are not without foundation. Suppose you let me look over that paper describing the location. Perhaps together we might—"

The result was that Goodloe Banks and I, rivals in love, became companions in adventure. We went to Chico by stage from Huntersburg, the nearest railroad town. In Chico we hired a team drawing a covered spring-wagon and camping paraphernalia. We had the same surveyor run out our distance, as revised by Goodloe and his variations, and then dismissed him and sent him on his homeward road.

It was night when we arrived. I fed the horses and made a fire near the bank of the river and cooked supper. Goodloe would have helped, but his education had not fitted him for practical things.

But while I worked he cheered me with the expression of great thoughts handed down from the dead ones of old. He quoted some translations from the Greek at much length.

"Anacreon," he explained. "That was a favorite passage with Miss Mangum—as I recited it."

"She is meant for higher things," said I, repeating his phrase.

"Can there be anything higher," asked Goodloe, "than to dwell in the society of the classics, to live in the atmosphere of learning and culture? You have often decried education. What of your wasted efforts through your ignorance of simple mathematics? How soon would you have found your treasure if my knowledge had not shown you your error?"

"We'll take a look at those hills across the river first," said I, "and see what we find. I am still doubtful about variations. I have been brought up to believe that the needle is true to the pole."

The next morning was a bright June one. We were up early and had breakfast. Goodloe was charmed. He recited—Keats,

I think it was, and Kelly or Shelley—while I broiled the bacon. We were getting ready to cross the river, which was little more than a shallow creek there, and explore the many sharp-peaked cedar-covered hills on the other side.

"My good Ulysses," said Goodloe, slapping me on the shoulder while I was washing the tin breakfast-plates, "let me see the enchanted document once more. I believe it gives directions for climbing the hill shaped like a pack-saddle. I never saw a pack-saddle. What is it like, Jim?"

"Score one against culture," said I. "I'll know it when I see it."

Goodloe was looking at old Rundle's document when he ripped out a most uncollegiate swear-word.

"Come here," he said, holding the paper up against the sunlight. "Look at that," he said, laying his finger against it.

On the blue paper—a thing I had never noticed before—I saw stand out in white letters the word and figures: "Malvern, 1898."

"What about it?" I asked.

"It's the water-mark," said Goodloe. "The paper was manufactured in 1898. The writing on the paper is dated 1863. This is a palpable fraud."

"Oh, I don't know," said I. "The Rundles are pretty reliable, plain, uneducated country people. Maybe the paper manufacturers tried to perpetrate a swindle."

And then Goodloe Banks went as wild as his education permitted. He dropped the glasses off his nose and glared at me.

"I've often told you you were a fool," he said. "You have let yourself be imposed upon by a clodhopper. And you have imposed upon me."

"How," I asked, "have I imposed upon you?"

"By your ignorance," said he. "Twice I have discovered serious flaws in your plans that a common-school education should have enabled you to avoid. And," he continued, "I have been put to expense that I could ill afford in pursuing this swindling quest. I am done with it."

I rose and pointed a large pewter spoon at him, fresh from the dish-water.

"Goodloe Banks," I said, "I care not one parboiled navy bean for your education. I always barely tolerated it in any one, and I despised it in you. What has your learning done for you? It is a curse to yourself and a bore to your friends. Away," I said—"away with your water-marks and variations! They are nothing to me. They shall not deflect me from the quest."

I pointed with my spoon across the river to a small mountain shaped like a pack-saddle.

"I am going to search that mountain," I went on, "for the treasure. Decide now whether you are in it or not. If you wish to let a water-mark or a variation shake your soul, you are no true adventurer. Decide."

A white cloud of dust began to rise far down the river road. It was the mail-wagon from Hesperus to Chico. Goodloe flagged it.

"I am done with the swindle," said he, sourly. "No one but a fool would pay any attention to that paper now. Well, you always were a fool, Jim. I leave you to your fate."

He gathered his personal traps, climbed into the mail-wagon, adjusted his glasses nervously, and flew away in a cloud of dust.

After I had washed the dishes and staked the horses on new grass, I crossed the shallow river and made my way slowly through the cedar-brakes up to the top of the hill shaped like a pack-saddle.

It was a wonderful June day. Never in my life had I seen so many birds, so many butterflies, dragon-flies, grasshoppers, and such winged and stinged beasts of the air and fields.

I investigated the hill shaped like a pack-saddle from base to summit. I found an absolute absence of signs relating to buried treasure. There was no pile of stones, no ancient blazes on the trees, none of the evidences of the three hundred thousand dollars, as set forth in the document of old man Rundle.

I came down the hill in the cool of the afternoon. Suddenly, out of the cedar-brake I stepped into a beautiful green valley where a tributary small stream ran into the Alamito River.

And there I was startled to see what I took to be a wild man, with unkempt beard and ragged hair, pursuing a giant butterfly with brilliant wings.

"Perhaps he is an escaped madman," I thought; and wondered how he had strayed so far from seats of education and learning.

And then I took a few more steps and saw a vine-covered

cottage near the small stream. And in a little grassy glade I saw May Martha Mangum plucking wild flowers.

She straightened up and looked at me. For the first time since I knew her I saw her face—which was the color of the white keys of a new piano—turn pink. I walked toward her without a word. She let the gathered flowers trickle slowly from her hand to the grass.

"I knew you would come, Jim," she said clearly. "Father wouldn't let me write, but I knew you would come."

What followed you may guess—there was my wagon and team just across the river.

I've often wondered what good too much education is to a man if he can't use it for himself. If all the benefits of it are to go to others, where does it come in?

For May Martha Mangum abides with me. There is an eight-room house in a live-oak grove, and a piano with an automatic player, and a good start toward the three thousand head of cattle is under fence.

And when I ride home at night my pipe and slippers are put away in places where they cannot be found.

But who cares for that? Who cares—who cares?

The Last of the Troubadours

INEXORABLY SAM Galloway saddled his pony. He was going away from the Rancho Altito at the end of a three-months' visit. It is not to be expected that a guest should put up with wheat coffee and biscuits yellow-streaked with saleratus for longer than that. Nick Napoleon, the big Negro man cook, had never been able to make good biscuits: Once before, when Nick was cooking at the Willow Ranch, Sam had been forced to fly from his *cuisine*, after only a six-weeks' sojourn.

On Sam's face was an expression of sorrow, deepened with regret and slightly tempered by the patient forgiveness of a connoisseur who cannot be understood. But very firmly and inexorably he buckled his saddle-cinches, looped his stake-rope and hung it to his saddle-horn, tied his slicker and coat on the cantle, and looped his quirt on his right wrist. The Merrydews (householders of the Rancho Altito), men, women, children, and servants, vassals, visitors, employés, dogs, and casual callers were grouped in the "gallery" of the ranch house, all with faces set to the tune of melancholy and grief. For, as the coming of Sam Galloway to any ranch, camp, or cabin between the rivers Frio or Bravo del Norte aroused joy, so his departure caused mourning and distress.

And then, during absolute silence, except for the bumping of a hind elbow of a hound dog as he pursued a wicked flea, Sam tenderly and carefully tied his guitar across his saddle on top of his slicker and coat. The guitar was in a green duck bag; and if you catch the significance of it, it explains Sam.

Sam Galloway was the Last of the Troubadours. Of course you know about the troubadours. The encyclopædia says they flourished between the eleventh and the thirteenth centuries. What they flourished doesn't seem clear—you may be pretty sure it wasn't a sword: maybe it was a fiddlebow, or a forkful of spaghetti, or a lady's scarf. Anyhow, Sam Galloway was one of 'em.

Sam put on a martyred expression as he mounted his pony. But the expression on his face was hilarious compared with the one on his pony's. You see, a pony gets to know his rider mighty well, and it is not unlikely that cow ponies in pastures and at hitching racks had often guyed Sam's pony for being ridden by a guitar player instead of by a rollicking, cussing, all-wool cowboy. No man is a hero to his saddle-horse. And even an escalator in a department store might be excused for tripping up a troubadour.

Oh, I know I'm one; and so are you. You remember the stories you memorize and the card tricks you study and that little piece on the piano—how does it go?—ti-tum-te-tum-ti-tum—those little Arabian Ten Minute Entertainments that you furnish when you go up to call on your rich Aunt Jane. You should know that *omnæ personæ in tres partes divisæ sunt.* Namely: Barons, Troubadours, and Workers. Barons have no inclination to read such folderol as this; and Workers have no time: so I know you must be a Troubadour, and that you will understand Sam Galloway. Whether we sing, act, dance, write, lecture, or paint, we are only troubadours; so let us make the worst of it.

The pony with the Dante Alighieri face, guided by the pressure of Sam's knees, bore that wandering minstrel sixteen miles southeastward. Nature was in her most benignant mood. League after league of delicate, sweet flowerets made fragrant the gently undulating prairie. The east wind tempered the spring warmth; wool-white clouds flying in from the Mexican Gulf hindered the direct rays of the April sun. Sam sang songs as he rode. Under his pony's bridle he had tucked some sprigs of chaparral to keep away the deer flies. Thus crowned, the long-faced quadruped looked more Dantesque than before, and, judging by his countenance, seemed to think of Beatrice.

Straight as topography permitted, Sam rode to the sheep ranch of old man Ellison. A visit to a sheep ranch seemed to him desirable just then. There had been too many people, too much noise, argument, competition, confusion, at Rancho Altito. He had never conferred upon old man Ellison the favour of sojourning at his ranch; but he knew he would be welcome. The troubadour is his own passport everywhere. The Workers in the castle let down the drawbridge to him, and the Baron sets him at his left hand at table in the banquet hall. There ladies smile upon him and applaud his songs and stories, while the Workers bring boars' heads and flagons. If the Baron nods once or twice in his carved oaken chair, he does not do it maliciously.

Old man Ellison welcomed the troubadour flatteringly. He had often heard praises of Sam Galloway from other ranchmen who had been complimented by his visits, but had never aspired to such an honour for his own humble barony. I say barony because old man Ellison was the Last of the Barons. Of course, Mr. Bulwer-Lytton lived too early to know him, or he wouldn't have conferred that sobriquet upon Warwick. In life it is the duty and the function of the Baron to provide work for the Workers and lodging and shelter for the Troubadours.

Old man Ellison was a shrunken old man, with a short, yellow-white beard and a face lined and seamed by past-and-gone smiles. His ranch was a little two-room box house in a grove of hackberry trees in the lonesomest part of the sheep country. His household consisted of a Kiowa Indian man cook, four hounds, a pet sheep, and a half-tamed coyote chained to a fence-post. He owned 3,000 sheep, which he ran on two sections of leased land and many thousands of acres neither leased nor owned. Three or four times a year some one who spoke his language would ride up to his gate and exchange a few bald ideas with him. Those were red-letter days to old man Ellison. Then in what illuminated, embossed, and gorgeously decorated capitals must have been written the day on which a troubadour—a troubadour who, according to the encyclopædia, should have flourished between the eleventh and the thirteenth centuries—drew rein at the gates of his baronial castle!

Old man Ellison's smiles came back and filled his wrinkles when he saw Sam. He hurried out of the house in his shuffling, limping way to greet him.

"Hello, Mr. Ellison," called Sam cheerfully. "Thought I'd drop over and see you a while. Notice you've had fine rains on your range. They ought to make good grazing for your spring lambs."

"Well, well, well," said old man Ellison. "I'm mighty glad to see you, Sam. I never thought you'd take the trouble to ride over to as out-of-the-way an old ranch as this. But you're mighty welcome. 'Light. I've got a sack of new oats in the kitchen—shall I bring out a feed for your hoss?"

"Oats for him?" said Sam, derisively. "No, sir-ee. He's as fat as a pig now on grass. He don't get rode enough to keep him in condition. I'll just turn him in the horse pasture with a drag rope on if you don't mind."

I am positive that never during the eleventh and thirteenth centuries did Baron, Troubadour, and Worker amalgamate as harmoniously as their parallels did that evening at old man Ellison's sheep ranch. The Kiowa's biscuits were light and tasty and his coffee strong. Ineradicable hospitality and appreciation glowed on old man Ellison's weather-tanned face. As for the troubadour, he said to himself that he had stumbled upon pleasant places indeed. A well-cooked, abundant meal, a host whom his lightest attempt to entertain seemed to delight far beyond the merits of the exertion, and the reposeful atmosphere that his sensitive soul at that time craved united to confer upon him a satisfaction and luxurious ease that he had seldom found on his tours of the ranches.

After the delectable supper, Sam untied the green duck bag and took out his guitar. Not by way of payment, mind you—neither Sam Galloway nor any other of the true troubadours are lineal descendants of the late Tommy Tucker. You have read of Tommy Tucker in the works of the esteemed but often obscure Mother Goose. Tommy Tucker sang for his supper. No true troubadour would do that. He would have his supper, and then sing for Art's sake.

Sam Galloway's repertoire comprised about fifty funny stories and between thirty and forty songs. He by no means stopped there. He could talk through twenty cigarettes on any topic that you brought up. And he never sat up when he could lie down; and never stood when he could sit. I am strongly disposed to linger with him, for I am drawing a portrait as well as a blunt pencil and a tattered thesaurus will allow.

I wish you could have seen him: he was small and tough and inactive beyond the power of imagination to conceive. He wore an ultramarine-blue woollen shirt laced down the front with a pearl-gray, exaggerated sort of shoestring, indestructible brown duck clothes, inevitable high-heeled boots with Mexican spurs, and a Mexican straw sombrero.

That evening Sam and old man Ellison dragged their chairs out under the hackberry trees. They lighted cigarettes; and the troubadour gaily touched his guitar. Many of the songs he sang were the weird, melancholy, minor-keyed *canciones* that he had learned from the Mexican sheep herders and *vaqueros*. One, in particular, charmed and soothed the soul of the lonely baron. It was a favourite song of the sheep herders, beginning: "*Huile, huile, palomita*," which being translated means, "Fly, fly, little dove." Sam sang it for old man Ellison many times that evening.

The troubadour stayed on at the old man's ranch. There was peace and quiet and appreciation there, such as he had not found in the noisy camps of the cattle kings. No audience in the world could have crowned the work of poet, musician, or artist with more worshipful and unflagging approval than that bestowed upon his efforts by old man Ellison. No visit by a royal personage to a humble woodchopper or peasant could have been received with more flattering thankfulness and joy.

On a cool, canvas-covered cot in the shade of the hackberry trees Sam Galloway passed the greater part of his time. There he rolled his brown paper cigarettes, read such tedious literature as the ranch afforded, and added to his repertoire of improvisations that he played so expertly on his guitar. To him, as a slave ministering to a great lord, the Kiowa brought cool water from the red jar hanging under the brush shelter, and food when he called for it. The prairie zephyrs fanned him mildly; mocking-birds at morn and eve competed with but scarce equalled the sweet melodies of his lyre; a perfumed stillness seemed to fill all his world. While old man Ellison was pottering among his flocks of sheep on his mile-an-hour pony, and while the Kiowa took his siesta in the burning sunshine at the end of the kitchen, Sam would lie on his cot thinking what a happy world he lived in, and how kind it is to the ones whose mission in life it is to give entertainment and pleasure. Here he had food and lodging as good as he had ever longed for; absolute immunity from care or exertion or strife; an endless welcome, and a host whose delight at the sixteenth repetition of a song or a story was as keen as at its initial giving. Was there ever a troubadour of old who struck upon as royal a castle in his wanderings? While he lay thus, meditating upon his blessings, little brown cottontails would shyly frolic through the yard; a covey of white-topknotted blue quail would run past, in single file, twenty yards away; a *paisano* bird, out hunting for taran-tulas, would hop upon the fence and salute him with sweeping flourishes of its long tail. In the eighty-acre horse pasture the pony with the Dantesque face grew fat and almost smiling. The troubadour was at the end of his wanderings.

Old man Ellison was his own *vaciero*. That means that he supplied his sheep camps with wood, water, and rations by his own labours instead of hiring a *vaciero*. On small ranches it is often done.

One morning he started for the camp of Incarnación Felipe de la Cruz y Monte Piedras (one of his sheep herders) with the week's usual rations of brown beans, coffee, meal, and sugar. Two miles away on the trail from old Fort Ewing he met, face to face, a terrible being called King James, mounted on a fiery, prancing, Kentucky-bred horse.

King James's real name was James King; but people reversed it because it seemed to fit him better, and also because it seemed to please his majesty. King James was the biggest cattleman between the Alamo plaza in San Antone and Bill Hopper's sa-loon in Brownsville. Also he was the loudest and most offensive bully and braggart and bad man in southwest Texas. And he always made good whenever he bragged; and the more noise he made the more dangerous he was. In the story papers it is always the quiet, mild-mannered man with light blue eyes and a low voice who turns out to be really dangerous; but in real life and in this story such is not the case. Give me my choice between assaulting a large, loud-mouthed rough-houser and an inoffensive stranger with blue eyes sitting quietly in a corner, and you will see something doing in the corner every time.

King James, as I intended to say earlier, was a fierce, two-hundred-pound, sunburned, blond man, as pink as an October strawberry, and with two horizontal slits under shaggy red eyebrows for eyes. On that day he wore a flannel shirt that was tan-coloured, with the exception of certain large areas which were darkened by transudations due to the summer sun. There seemed to be other clothing and garnishings about him, such as brown duck trousers stuffed into immense boots, and red handkerchiefs and revolvers; and a shotgun laid across his saddle and a leather belt with millions of cartridges shining in it—but your mind skidded off such accessories; what held your gaze was just the two little horizontal slits that he used for eyes.

This was the man that old man Ellison met on the trail; and when you count up in the baron's favour that he was sixty-five and weighed ninety-eight pounds and had heard of King James's record and that he (the baron) had a hankering for the *vita simplex* and had no gun with him and wouldn't have used it if he had, you can't censure him if I tell you that the smiles with which the troubadour had filled his wrinkles went out of them and left them plain wrinkles again. But he was not the kind of baron that flies from danger. He reined in the mile-an-hour pony (no difficult feat), and saluted the formidable monarch.

King James expressed himself with royal directness.

"You're that old snoozer that's running sheep on this range, ain't you?" said he. "What right have you got to do it? Do you own any land, or lease any?"

"I have two sections leased from the state," said old man Ellison, mildly.

"Not by no means you haven't," said King James. "Your lease expired yesterday; and I had a man at the land office on the minute to take it up. You don't control a foot of grass in Texas. You sheep men have got to git. Your time's up. It's a cattle country, and there ain't any room in it for snoozers. This range you've got your sheep on is mine. I'm putting up a wire fence, forty by sixty miles; and if there's a sheep inside of it when it's done it'll be a dead one. I'll give you a week to move yours away. If they ain't gone by then, I'll send six men over here with Winchesters to make mutton out of the whole lot. And if I find you here at the same time this is what you'll get."

King James patted the breech of his shot-gun warningly.

Old man Ellison rode on to the camp of Incarnación. He sighed many times, and the wrinkles in his face grew deeper. Rumours that the old order was about to change had reached him before. The end of Free Grass was in sight. Other troubles, too, had been accumulating upon his shoulders. His flocks were decreasing instead of growing; the price of wool was declining at every clip; even Bradshaw, the storekeeper at Frio City, at whose store he bought his ranch supplies, was dunning him for his last six months' bill and threatening to cut him off. And so this last greatest calamity suddenly dealt out to him by the terrible King James was a crusher.

When the old man got back to the ranch at sunset he found Sam Galloway lying on his cot, propped against a roll of blankets and wool sacks, fingering his guitar.

"Hello, Uncle Ben," the troubadour called, cheerfully. "You rolled in early this evening. I been trying a new twist on the Spanish Fandango to-day. I just about got it. Here's how she goes—listen."

"That's fine, that's mighty fine," said old man Ellison, sitting on the kitchen step and rubbing his white, Scotch-terrier whiskers. "I reckon you've got all the musicians beat east and west, Sam, as far as the roads are cut out."

"Oh, I don't know," said Sam, reflectively. "But I certainly do get there on variations. I guess I can handle anything in five flats about as well as any of 'em. But you look kind of fagged out, Uncle Ben—ain't you feeling right well this evening?"

"Little tired; that's all, Sam. If you ain't played yourself out, let's have that Mexican piece that starts off with: '*Huile, huile, palomita.*' It seems that that song always kind of soothes and comforts me after I've been riding far or anything bothers me."

"Why, *seguramente, señor*," said Sam. "I'll hit her up for you as often as you like. And before I forget about it, Uncle Ben, you want to jerk Bradshaw up about them last hams he sent us. They're just a little bit strong."

A man sixty-five years old, living on a sheep ranch and beset by a complication of disasters, cannot successfully and continuously dissemble. Moreover, a troubadour has eyes quick to see unhappiness in others around him—because it disturbs his own ease. So, on the next day, Sam again questioned the old man about his air of sadness and abstraction. Then old man Ellison told him the story of King James's threats and orders and that pale melancholy and red ruin appeared to have marked him for their own. The troubadour took the news thoughtfully. He had heard much about King James.

On the third day of the seven days of grace allowed him by the autocrat of the range, old man Ellison drove his buckboard to Frio City to fetch some necessary supplies for the ranch. Bradshaw was hard but not implacable. He divided the old man's order by two, and let him have a little more time. One article secured was a new, fine ham for the pleasure of the troubadour.

Five miles out of Frio City on his way home the old man met King James riding into town. His majesty could never look anything but fierce and menacing, but to-day his slits of eyes appeared to be a little wider than they usually were.

"Good day," said the king, gruffly. "I've been wanting to see you. I hear it said by a cowman from Sandy yesterday that you was from Jackson County, Mississippi, originally. I want to know if that's a fact."

"Born there," said old man Ellison, "and raised there till I was twenty-one."

"This man says," went on King James, "that he thinks you was related to the Jackson County Reeveses. Was he right?"

"Aunt Caroline Reeves," said the old man, "was my half-sister."

"She was my aunt," said King James. "I run away from home when I was sixteen. Now, let's re-talk over some things that we discussed a few days ago. They call me a bad man; and they're only half right. There's plenty of room in my pasture for your bunch of sheep and their increase for a long time to come. Aunt Caroline used to cut out sheep in cake dough and bake 'em for me. You keep your sheep where they are, and use all the range you want. How's your finances?"

The old man related his woes in detail, dignifiedly, with restraint and candour.

"She used to smuggle extra grub into my school basket—I'm speaking of Aunt Caroline," said King James. "I'm going over to Frio City to-day, and I'll ride back by your ranch to-morrow. I'll draw $2,000 out of the bank there and bring it over to you; and I'll tell Bradshaw to let you have everything you want on credit. You are bound to have heard the old saying at home, that the Jackson County Reeveses and Kings would stick closer by each other than chestnut burrs. Well, I'm a King yet whenever I run across a Reeves. So you look out for me along about sundown to-morrow, and don't worry about nothing. Shouldn't wonder if the dry spell don't kill out the young grass."

Old man Ellison drove happily ranchward. Once more the smiles filled out his wrinkles. Very suddenly, by the magic of kinship and the good that lies somewhere in all hearts, his troubles had been removed.

On reaching the ranch he found that Sam Galloway was not there. His guitar hung by its buckskin string to a hackberry limb, moaning as the gulf breeze blew across its masterless strings.

The Kiowa endeavoured to explain.

"Sam, he catch pony," said he, "and say he ride to Frio City. What for no can damn sabe. Say he come back to-night. Maybe so. That all."

As the first stars came out the troubadour rode back to his haven. He pastured his pony and went into the house, his spurs jingling martially.

Old man Ellison sat at the kitchen table, having a tin cup of before-supper coffee. He looked contented and pleased.

"Hello, Sam," said he, "I'm darned glad to see ye back. I don't know how I managed to get along on this ranch, anyhow, before ye dropped in to cheer things up. I'll bet ye've been skylarking around with some of them Frio City gals, now, that's kept ye so late."

And then old man Ellison took another look at Sam's face and saw that the minstrel had changed to the man of action.

And while Sam is unbuckling from his waist old man Ellison's six-shooter, that the latter had left behind when he drove to town, we may well pause to remark that anywhere and whenever a troubadour lays down the guitar and takes up the sword trouble is sure to follow. It is not the expert thrust of Athos nor the cold skill of Aramis nor the iron wrist of Porthos that we have to fear—it is the Gascon's fury—the wild and unacademic attack of the troubadour—the sword of D'Artagnan.

"I done it," said Sam. "I went over to Frio City to do it. I couldn't let him put the skibunk on you, Uncle Ben. I met him in Summers's saloon. I knowed what to do. I said a few things to him that nobody else heard. He reached for his gun first— half a dozen fellows saw him do it—but I got mine unlimbered first. Three doses I gave him—right around the lungs, and a saucer could have covered up all of 'em. He won't bother you no more."

"This—is—King—James—you speak—of?" asked old man Ellison, while he sipped his coffee.

"You bet it was. And they took me before the county judge; and the witnesses what saw him draw his gun first was all there. Well, of course, they put me under $300 bond to appear before the court, but there was four or five boys on the spot ready to sign the bail. He won't bother you no more, Uncle Ben. You ought to have seen how close them bullet holes was together. I reckon playing a guitar as much as I do must kind of limber a fellow's trigger finger up a little, don't you think, Uncle Ben?"

Then there was a little silence in the castle except for the spluttering of a venison steak that the Kiowa was cooking.

"Sam," said old man Ellison, stroking his white whiskers with a tremulous hand, "would you mind getting the guitar and playing that '*Huile, huile, palomita*' piece once or twice? It always seems to be kind of soothing and comforting when a man's tired and fagged out."

There is no more to be said, except that the title of the story is wrong. It should have been called "The Last of the Barons." There never will be an end to the troubadours; and now and then it does seem that the jingle of their guitars will drown the sound of the muffled blows of the pickaxes and trip hammers of all the Workers in the world.

The Hiding of Black Bill

A LANK, strong, red-faced man with a Wellington beak and small, fiery eyes tempered by flaxen lashes, sat on the station platform at Los Pinos swinging his legs to and fro. At his side sat another man, fat, melancholy, and seedy, who seemed to be his friend. They had the appearance of men to whom life had appeared as a reversible coat—seamy on both sides.

"Ain't seen you in about four years, Ham," said the seedy man. "Which way you been travelling?"

"Texas," said the red-faced man. "It was too cold in Alaska for me. And I found it warm in Texas. I'll tell you about one hot spell I went through there.

"One morning I steps off the International at a water-tank and lets it go on without me. 'Twas a ranch country, and fuller of spite-houses than New York City. Only out there they build 'em twenty miles away so you can't smell what they've got for dinner, instead of running 'em up two inches from their neighbors' windows.

"There wasn't any roads in sight, so I footed it 'cross country. The grass was shoe-top deep, and the mesquite timber looked just like a peach orchard. It was so much like a gentleman's private estate that every minute you expected a kennelful of bulldogs to run out and bite you. But I must have walked twenty miles before I came in sight of a ranch-house. It was a little one, about as big as an elevated-railroad station.

"There was a little man in a white shirt and brown overalls and a pink handkerchief around his neck rolling cigarettes under a tree in front of the door.

"'Greetings,' says I. 'Any refreshment, welcome, emoluments, or even work for a comparative stranger?'

"'Oh, come in,' says he, in a refined tone. 'Sit down on that stool, please. I didn't hear your horse coming.'

"'He isn't near enough yet,' says I. 'I walked. I don't want to be a burden, but I wonder if you have three or four gallons of water handy.'

"'You do look pretty dusty,' says he; 'but our bathing arrangements—'

"'It's a drink I want,' says I. 'Never mind the dust that's on the outside.'

"He gets me a dipper of water out of a red jar hanging up, and then goes on:

"'Do you want work?'

"'For a time,' says I. 'This is a rather quiet section of the country, isn't it?'

"'It is,' says he. 'Sometimes—so I have been told—one sees no human being pass for weeks at a time. I've been here only a month. I bought the ranch from an old settler who wanted to move farther west.'

"'It suits me,' says I. 'Quiet and retirement are good for a man sometimes. And I need a job. I can tend bar, salt mines, lecture, float stock, do a little middle-weight slugging, and play the piano.'

"'Can you herd sheep?' asks the little ranchman.

"'Do you mean *have* I heard sheep?' says I.

"'Can you herd 'em—take charge of a flock of 'em?' says he.

"'Oh,' says I, 'now I understand. You mean chase 'em around and bark at 'em like collie dogs. Well, I might,' says I. 'I've never exactly done any sheep-herding, but I've often seen 'em from car windows masticating daisies, and they don't look dangerous.'

"'I'm short a herder,' says the ranchman. 'You never can depend on the Mexicans. I've only got two flocks. You may take out my bunch of muttons—there are only eight hundred of 'em—in the morning, if you like. The pay is twelve dollars a month and your rations furnished. You camp in a tent on the prairie with your sheep. You do your own cooking, but wood and water are brought to your camp. It's an easy job.'

"'I'm on,' says I. 'I'll take the job even if I have to garland my brow and hold on to a crook and wear a loose-effect and play on a pipe like the shepherds do in pictures.'

"So the next morning the little ranchman helps me drive the flock of muttons from the corral to about two miles out and let 'em graze on a little hillside on the prairie. He gives me a lot of instructions about not letting bunches of them stray off from the herd, and driving 'em down to a water-hole to drink at noon.

"'I'll bring out your tent and camping outfit and rations in the buckboard before night,' says he.

"'Fine,' says I. 'And don't forget the rations. Nor the camping outfit. And be sure to bring the tent. Your name's Zollicoffer, ain't it?'

"'My name,' says he, 'is Henry Ogden.'

"'All right, Mr. Ogden,' says I. 'Mine is Mr. Percival Saint Clair.'

"I herded sheep for five days on the Rancho Chiquito; and then the wool entered my soul. That getting next to Nature certainly got next to me. I was lonesomer than Crusoe's goat. I've seen a lot of persons more entertaining as companions than those sheep were. I'd drive 'em to the corral and pen 'em every evening, and then cook my corn-bread and mutton and coffee, and lie down in a tent the size of a tablecloth, and listen to the coyotes and whippoorwills singing around the camp.

"The fifth evening, after I had corralled my costly but uncongenial muttons, I walked over to the ranch-house and stepped in the door.

"'Mr. Ogden,' says I, 'you and me have got to get sociable. Sheep are all very well to dot the landscape and furnish eight-dollar cotton suitings for man, but for table-talk and fireside companions they rank along with five-o'clock teazers. If you've got a deck of cards, or a parcheesi outfit, or a game of authors, get 'em out, and let's get on a mental basis. I've got to do something in an intellectual line, if it's only to knock somebody's brains out.'

"This Henry Ogden was a peculiar kind of ranchman. He wore finger-rings and a big gold watch and careful neckties. And his face was calm, and his nose-spectacles was kept very shiny. I saw once, in Muscogee, an outlaw hung for murdering six men, who was a dead ringer for him. But I knew a preacher in Arkansas that you would have taken to be his brother. I didn't care much for him either way; what I wanted was some fellowship and communion with holy saints or lost sinners—anything sheepless would do.

"'Well, Saint Clair,' says he, laying down the book he was reading, 'I guess it must be pretty lonesome for you at first. And I don't deny that it's monotonous for me. Are you sure you corralled your sheep so they won't stray out?'

"'They're shut up as tight as the jury of a millionaire murderer,' says I. 'And I'll be back with them long before they'll need their trained nurse.'

"So Ogden digs up a deck of cards, and we play casino. After five days and nights of my sheep-camp it was like a toot on Broadway. When I caught big casino I felt as excited as if I had made a million in Trinity. And when H. O. loosened up a little and told the story about the lady in the Pullman car I laughed for five minutes.

"That showed what a comparative thing life is. A man may see so much that he'd be bored to turn his head to look at a $3,000,000 fire or Joe Weber or the Adriatic Sea. But let him herd sheep for a spell, and you'll see him splitting his ribs laughing at 'Curfew Shall Not Ring To-night,' or really enjoying himself playing cards with ladies.

"By-and-by Ogden gets out a decanter of Bourbon, and then there is a total eclipse of sheep.

"'Do you remember reading in the papers, about a month ago,' says he, 'about a train hold-up on the M. K. & T.? The express agent was shot through the shoulder, and about $15,000 in currency taken. And it's said that only one man did the job.'

"'Seems to me I do,' says I. 'But such things happen so often they don't linger long in the human Texas mind. Did they overtake, overhaul, seize, or lay hands upon the despoiler?'

"'He escaped,' says Ogden. 'And I was just reading in a paper to-day that the officers have tracked him down into this part of the country. It seems the bills the robber got were all the first issue of currency to the Second National Bank of Espinosa City. And so they've followed the trail where they've been spent, and it leads this way.'

"Ogden pours out some more Bourbon, and shoves me the bottle.

"'I imagine,' says I, after ingurgitating another modicum of the royal boose, 'that it wouldn't be at all a disingenuous idea for a train robber to run down into this part of the country to hide for a spell. A sheep-ranch, now,' says I, 'would be the finest kind of a place. Who'd ever expect to find such a desperate character among these song-birds and muttons and wild flowers? And, by the way,' says I, kind of looking H. Ogden over, 'was there any description mentioned of this single-handed terror?

Was his lineaments or height and thickness or teeth fillings or style of habiliments set forth in print?'

"'Why, no,' says Ogden; 'they say nobody got a good sight of him because he wore a mask. But they know it was a train-robber called Black Bill, because he always works alone and because he dropped a handkerchief in the express-car that had his name on it.'

"'All right,' says I. 'I approve of Black Bill's retreat to the sheep-ranges. I guess they won't find him.'

"'There's one thousand dollars reward for his capture,' says Ogden.

"'I don't need that kind of money,' says I, looking Mr. Sheep-man straight in the eye. 'The twelve dollars a month you pay me is enough. I need a rest, and I can save up until I get enough to pay my fare to Texarkana, where my widowed mother lives. If Black Bill,' I goes on, looking significantly at Ogden, 'was to have come down this way—say, a month ago—and bought a little sheep-ranch and—'

"'Stop,' says Ogden, getting out of his chair and looking pretty vicious. 'Do you mean to insinuate—'

"'Nothing,' says I; 'no insinuations. I'm stating a hypo-dermical case. I say, if Black Bill had come down here and bought a sheep-ranch and hired me to Little-Boy-Blue 'em and treated me square and friendly, as you've done, he'd never have anything to fear from me. A man is a man, regardless of any complications he may have with sheep or railroad trains. Now you know where I stand.'

"Ogden looks black as camp-coffee for nine seconds, and then he laughs, amused.

"'You'll do, Saint Clair,' says he. 'If I *was* Black Bill I wouldn't be afraid to trust you. Let's have a game or two of seven-up to-night. That is, if you don't mind playing with a train-robber.'

"'I've told you,' says I, 'my oral sentiments, and there's no strings to 'em.'

"While I was shuffling after the first hand, I asks Ogden, as if the idea was a kind of a casualty, where he was from.

"'Oh,' says he, 'from the Mississippi Valley.'

"'That's a nice little place,' says I. 'I've often stopped over there. But didn't you find the sheets a little damp and the food poor? Now, I hail,' says I, 'from the Pacific Slope. Ever put up there?'

"'Too draughty,' says Ogden. 'But if you're ever in the Middle West just mention my name, and you'll get foot-warmers and dripped coffee.'

"'Well,' says I, 'I wasn't exactly fishing for your private telephone number and the middle name of your aunt that carried off the Cumberland Presbyterian minister. It don't matter. I just want you to know you are safe in the hands of your shepherd. Now, don't play hearts on spades, and don't get nervous.'

"'Still harping,' says Ogden, laughing again. 'Don't you suppose that if I was Black Bill and thought you suspected me, I'd put a Winchester bullet into you and stop my nervousness, if I had any?'

"'Not any,' says I. 'A man who's got the nerve to hold up a train single-handed wouldn't do a trick like that. I've knocked about enough to know that them are the kind of men who put a value on a friend. Not that I can claim being a friend of yours, Mr. Ogden,' says I, 'being only your sheep-herder; but under more expeditious circumstances we might have been.'

"'Forget the sheep temporarily, I beg,' says Ogden, 'and cut for deal.'

"About four days afterward, while my muttons was nooning on the water-hole and I deep in the interstices of making a pot of coffee, up rides softly on the grass a mysterious person in the garb of the being he wished to represent. He was dressed somewhere between a Kansas City detective, Buffalo Bill, and the town dog-catcher of Baton Rouge. His chin and eye wasn't molded on fighting lines, so I knew he was only a scout.

"'Herdin' sheep?' he asks me.

"'Well,' says I, 'to a man of your evident gumptional endowments, I wouldn't have the nerve to state that I am engaged in decorating old bronzes or oiling bicycle sprockets.'

"'You don't talk or look like a sheep-herder to me,' says he.

"'But you talk like what you look like to me,' says I.

"And then he asks me who I was working for, and I shows him Rancho Chiquito, two miles away, in the shadow of a low hill, and he tells me he's a deputy sheriff.

"'There's a train-robber called Black Bill supposed to be

somewhere in these parts,' says the scout. 'He's been traced as far as San Antonio, and maybe farther. Have you seen or heard of any strangers around here during the past month?'

"'I have not,' says I, 'except a report of one over at the Mexican quarters of Loomis' ranch, on the Frio.'

"'What do you know about him?' asks the deputy.

"'He's three days old,' says I.

"'What kind of a looking man is the man you work for?' he asks. 'Does old George Ramey own this place yet? He's run sheep here for the last ten years, but never had no success.'

"'The old man has sold out and gone West,' I tells him. 'Another sheep-fancier bought him out about a month ago.'

"'What kind of a looking man is he?' asks the deputy again.

"'Oh,' says I, 'a big, fat kind of a Dutchman with long whiskers and blue specs. I don't think he knows a sheep from a ground-squirrel. I guess old George soaked him pretty well on the deal,' says I.

"After indulging himself in a lot more non-communicative information and two-thirds of my dinner, the deputy rides away.

"That night I mentions the matter to Ogden.

"'They're drawing the tendrils of the octopus around Black Bill,' says I. And then I told him about the deputy sheriff, and how I'd described him to the deputy, and what the deputy said about the matter.

"'Oh, well,' says Ogden, 'let's don't borrow any of Black Bill's troubles. We've a few of our own. Get the Bourbon out of the cupboard and we'll drink to his health—unless,' says he, with his little cackling laugh, 'you're prejudiced against train-robbers.'

"'I'll drink,' says I, 'to any man who's a friend to a friend. And I believe that Black Bill,' I goes on, 'would be that. So here's to Black Bill, and may he have good luck.'

"And both of us drank.

"About two weeks later comes shearing-time. The sheep had to be driven up to the ranch, and a lot of frowzy-headed Mexicans would snip the fur off of them with back-action scissors. So the afternoon before the barbers were to come I hustled my underdone muttons over the hill, across the dell, down by the winding brook, and up to the ranch-house, where I penned 'em in a corral and bade 'em my nightly adieus.

"I went from there to the ranch-house. I find H. Ogden, Esquire, lying asleep on his little cot bed. I guess he had been overcome by anti-insomnia or diswakefulness or some of the diseases peculiar to the sheep business. His mouth and vest were open, and he breathed like a second-hand bicycle pump. I looked at him and gave vent to just a few musings. 'Imperial Cæsar,' says I, 'asleep in such a way, might shut his mouth and keep the wind away.'

"A man asleep is certainly a sight to make angels weep. What good is all his brain, muscle, backing, nerve, influence, and family connections? He's at the mercy of his enemies, and more so of his friends. And he's about as beautiful as a cab-horse leaning against the Metropolitan Opera House at 12.30 A.M. dreaming of the plains of Arabia. Now, a woman asleep you regard as different. No matter how she looks, you know it's better for all hands for her to be that way.

"Well, I took a drink of Bourbon and one for Ogden, and started in to be comfortable while he was taking his nap. He had some books on his table on indigenous subjects, such as Japan and drainage and physical culture—and some tobacco, which seemed more to the point.

"After I'd smoked a few, and listened to the sartorial breathing of H. O., I happened to look out the window toward the shearing-pens, where there was a kind of a road coming up from a kind of a road across a kind of a creek farther away.

"I saw five men riding up to the house. All of 'em carried guns across their saddles, and among 'em was the deputy that had talked to me at my camp.

"They rode up careful, in open formation, with their guns ready. I set apart with my eye the one I opinionated to be the boss muck-raker of this law-and-order cavalry.

"'Good-evening, gents,' says I. 'Won't you 'light, and tie your horses?'

"The boss rides up close, and swings his gun over till the opening in it seems to cover my whole front elevation.

"'Don't you move your hands none,' says he, 'till you and me indulge in a adequate amount of necessary conversation.'

"'I will not,' says I. 'I am no deaf-mute, and therefore will not have to disobey your injunctions in replying.'

"'We are on the lookout,' says he, 'for Black Bill, the man that held up the Katy for $15,000 in May. We are searching the ranches and everybody on 'em. What is your name, and what do you do on this ranch?'

"'Captain,' says I, 'Percival Saint Clair is my occupation, and my name is sheep-herder. I've got my flock of veals—no, muttons—penned here to-night. The shearers are coming to-morrow to give them a hair-cut—with baa-a-rum, I suppose.'

"'Where's the boss of this ranch?' the captain of the gang asks me.

"'Wait just a minute, cap'n,' says I. 'Wasn't there a kind of a reward offered for the capture of this desperate character you have referred to in your preamble?'

"'There's a thousand dollars reward offered,' says the captain, 'but it's for his capture and conviction. There don't seem to be no provision made for an informer.'

"'It looks like it might rain in a day or so,' says I, in a tired way, looking up at the cerulean blue sky.

"'If you know anything about the locality, disposition, or secretiveness of this here Black Bill,' says he, in a severe dialect, 'you are amiable to the law in not reporting it.'

"'I heard a fence-rider say,' says I, in a desultory kind of voice, 'that a Mexican told a cowboy named Jake over at Pidgin's store on the Nueces that he heard that Black Bill had been seen in Matamoros by a sheepman's cousin two weeks ago.'

"'Tell you what I'll do, Tight Mouth,' says the captain, after looking me over for bargains. 'If you put us on so we can scoop Black Bill, I'll pay you a hundred dollars out of my own—out of our own—pockets. That's liberal,' says he. 'You ain't entitled to anything. Now, what do you say?'

"'Cash down now?' I asks.

"The captain has a sort of discussion with his helpmates, and they all produce the contents of their pockets for analysis. Out of the general results they figured up $102.30 in cash and $31 worth of plug tobacco.

"'Come nearer, capitan meeo,' says I, 'and listen.' He so did.

"'I am mighty poor and low down in the world,' says I. 'I am working for twelve dollars a month trying to keep a lot of animals together whose only thought seems to be to get asunder. Although,' says I, 'I regard myself as some better than the State of South Dakota, it's a come-down to a man who has heretofore regarded sheep only in the form of chops. I'm pretty far reduced in the world on account of foiled ambitions and rum and a kind of cocktail they make along the P. R. R. all the way from Scranton to Cincinnati—dry gin, French vermouth, one squeeze of a lime, and a good dash of orange bitters. If you're ever up that way, don't fail to let one try you. And, again,' says I, 'I have never yet went back on a friend. I've stayed by 'em when they had plenty, and when adversity's overtaken me I've never forsook 'em.

"'But,' I goes on, 'this is not exactly the case of a friend. Twelve dollars a month is only bowing-acquaintance money. And I do not consider brown beans and corn-bread the food of friendship. I am a poor man,' says I, 'and I have a widowed mother in Texarkana. You will find Black Bill,' says I, 'lying asleep in this house on a cot in the room to your right. He's the man you want, as I know from his words and conversation. He was in a way a friend,' I explains, 'and if I was the man I once was the entire product of the mines of Gondola would not have tempted me to betray him. But,' says I, 'every week half of the beans was wormy, and not nigh enough wood in camp.

"'Better go in careful, gentlemen,' says I. 'He seems impatient at times, and when you think of his late professional pursuits one would look for abrupt actions if he was come upon sudden.'

"So the whole posse unmounts and ties their horses, and unlimbers their ammunition and equipments, and tiptoes into the house. And I follows, like Delilah when she set the Philip Steins on to Samson.

"The leader of the posse shakes Ogden and wakes him up. And then he jumps up, and two more of the reward-hunters grab him. Ogden was mighty tough with all his slimness, and he gives 'em as neat a single-footed tussle against odds as I ever see.

"'What does this mean?' he says, after they had him down.

"'You're scooped in, Mr. Black Bill,' says the captain. 'That's all.'

"'It's an outrage,' says H. Ogden, madder yet.

"'It was,' says the peace-and-good-will man. 'The Katy wasn't bothering you, and there's a law against monkeying with express packages.'

"And he sits on H. Ogden's stomach and goes through his pockets symptomatically and careful.

"'I'll make you perspire for this,' says Ogden, perspiring some himself. 'I can prove who I am.'

"'So can I,' says the captain, as he draws from H. Ogden's inside coat-pocket a handful of new bills of the Second National Bank of Espinosa City. 'Your regular engraved Tuesdays-and-Fridays visiting-card wouldn't have a louder voice in proclaiming your indemnity than this here currency. You can get up now and prepare to go with us and expatriate your sins.'

"H. Ogden gets up and fixes his necktie. He says no more after they have taken the money off of him.

"'A well-greased idea,' says the sheriff captain, admiring, 'to slip off down here and buy a little sheep-ranch where the hand of man is seldom heard. It was the slickest hide-out I ever see,' says the captain.

"So one of the men goes to the shearing-pen and hunts up the other herder, a Mexican they call John Sallies, and he saddles Ogden's horse, and the sheriffs all ride up close around him with their guns in hand, ready to take their prisoner to town.

"Before starting, Ogden puts the ranch in John Sallies' hands and gives him orders about the shearing and where to graze the sheep, just as if he intended to be back in a few days. And a couple of hours afterward one Percival Saint Clair, an ex-sheepherder of the Rancho Chiquito, might have been seen, with a hundred and nine dollars—wages and blood-money—in his pocket, riding south on another horse belonging to said ranch."

The red-faced man paused and listened. The whistle of a coming freight-train sounded far away among the low hills.

The fat, seedy man at his side sniffed, and shook his frowzy head slowly and disparagingly.

"What is it, Snipy?" asked the other. "Got the blues again?"

"No, I ain't," said the seedy one, sniffing again. "But I don't like your talk. You and me have been friends, off and on, for fifteen year; and I never yet knew or heard of you giving anybody up to the law—not no one. And here was a man whose saleratus you had et and at whose table you had played games of cards—if casino can be so called. And yet you inform him to the law and take money for it. It never was like you, I say."

"This H. Ogden," resumed the red-faced man, "through a lawyer, proved himself free by alibis and other legal terminalities, as I so heard afterward. He never suffered no harm. He did me favors, and I hated to hand him over."

"How about the bills they found in his pocket?" asked the seedy man.

"I put 'em there," said the red-faced man, "while he was asleep, when I saw the posse riding up. I was Black Bill. Look out, Snipy, here she comes! We'll board her on the bumpers when she takes water at the tank."

A Technical Error

I NEVER cared especially for feuds, believing them to be even more overrated products of our country than grapefruit, scrapple, or honeymoons. Nevertheless, if I may be allowed, I will tell you of an Indian Territory feud of which I was press-agent, camp-follower, and inaccessory during the fact.

I was on a visit to Sam Durkee's ranch, where I had a great time falling off unmanicured ponies and waving my bare hand at the lower jaws of wolves about two miles away. Sam was a hardened person of about twenty-five, with a reputation for going home in the dark with perfect equanimity, though often with reluctance.

Over in the Creek Nation was a family bearing the name of Tatum. I was told that the Durkees and Tatums had been feuding for years. Several of each family had bitten the grass, and it was expected that more Nebuchadnezzars would follow. A younger generation of each family was growing up, and the grass was keeping pace with them. But I gathered that they had fought fairly; that they had not lain in cornfields and aimed at the division of their enemies' suspenders in the back—partly, perhaps, because there were no cornfields, and nobody wore more than one suspender. Nor had any woman or child of either house ever been harmed. In those days—and you will find it so yet—their women were safe.

Sam Durkee had a girl. (If it were an all-fiction magazine that I expect to sell this story to, I should say, "Mr. Durkee rejoiced in a fiancée.") Her name was Ella Baynes. They appeared to be devoted to each other, and to have perfect confidence in each other, as all couples do who are and have or aren't and haven't. She was tolerably pretty, with a heavy mass of brown hair that helped her along. He introduced me to her, which seemed not to lessen her preference for him; so I reasoned that they were surely soul-mates.

Miss Baynes lived in Kingfisher, twenty miles from the ranch. Sam lived on a gallop between the two places.

One day there came to Kingfisher a courageous young man, rather small, with smooth face and regular features. He made many inquiries about the business of the town, and especially of the inhabitants cognominally. He said he was from Muscogee, and he looked it, with his yellow shoes and crocheted four-in-hand. I met him once when I rode in for the mail. He said his name was Beverly Travers, which seemed rather improbable.

There were active times on the ranch, just then, and Sam was too busy to go to town often. As an incompetent and generally worthless guest, it devolved upon me to ride in for little things such as post cards, barrels of flour, baking-powder, smoking-tobacco, and—letters from Ella.

One day, when I was messenger for half a gross of cigarette papers and a couple of wagon tires, I saw the alleged Beverly Travers in a yellow-wheeled buggy with Ella Baynes, driving about town as ostentatiously as the black, waxy mud would permit. I knew that this information would bring no balm of Gilead to Sam's soul, so I refrained from including it in the news of the city that I retailed on my return. But on the next afternoon an elongated ex-cowboy of the name of Simmons, an old-time pal of Sam's, who kept a feed store in Kingfisher, rode out to the ranch and rolled and burned many cigarettes before he would talk. When he did make oration, his words were these:

"Say, Sam, there's been a description of a galoot miscallin' himself Bevel-edged Travels impairing the atmospheric air of Kingfisher for the past two weeks. You know who he was? He was not otherwise than Ben Tatum, from the Creek Nation, son of old Gopher Tatum that your Uncle Newt shot last February. You know what he done this morning? He killed your brother Lester—shot him in the co't-house yard."

I wondered if Sam had heard. He pulled a twig from a mesquite bush, chewed it gravely, and said:

"He did, did he? He killed Lester?"

"The same," said Simmons. "And he did more. He run away with your girl, the same as to say Miss Ella Baynes. I thought you might like to know, so I rode out to impart the information."

"I am much obliged, Jim," said Sam, taking the chewed twig from his mouth. "Yes, I'm glad you rode out. Yes, I'm right glad."

"Well, I'll be ridin' back, I reckon. That boy I left in the feed store don't know hay from oats. He shot Lester in the *back*."

"Shot him in the back?"

"Yes, while he was hitchin' his hoss."

"I'm much obliged, Jim."

"I kind of thought you'd like to know as soon as you could."

"Come in and have some coffee before you ride back, Jim?"

"Why, no, I reckon not; I must get back to the store."

"And you say——"

"Yes, Sam. Everybody seen 'em drive away together in a buckboard, with a big bundle, like clothes, tied up in the back of it. He was drivin' the team he brought over with him from Muscogee. They'll be hard to overtake right away."

"And which——"

"I was goin' on to tell you. They left on the Guthrie road; but there's no tellin' which forks they'll take—you know that."

"All right, Jim; much obliged."

"You're welcome, Sam."

Simmons rolled a cigarette and stabbed his pony with both heels. Twenty yards away he reined up and called back:

"You don't want no—assistance, as you might say?"

"Not any, thanks."

"I didn't think you would. Well, so long!"

Sam took out and opened a bone-handled pocket-knife and scraped a dried piece of mud from his left boot. I thought at first he was going to swear a vendetta on the blade of it, or recite "The Gipsy's Curse." The few feuds I had ever seen or read about usually opened that way. This one seemed to be presented with a new treatment. Thus offered on the stage, it would have been hissed off, and one of Belasco's thrilling melodramas demanded instead.

"I wonder," said Sam, with a profoundly thoughtful expression, "if the cook has any cold beans left over!"

He called Wash, the Negro cook, and finding that he had some, ordered him to heat up the pot and make some strong coffee. Then we went into Sam's private room, where he slept, and kept his armoury, dogs, and the saddles of his favourite mounts. He took three or four six-shooters out of a bookcase and began to look them over, whistling "The Cowboy's

Lament" abstractedly. Afterward he ordered the two best horses on the ranch saddled and tied to the hitching-post.

Now, in the feud business, in all sections of the country, I have observed that in one particular there is a delicate but strict etiquette belonging. You must not mention the word or refer to the subject in the presence of a feudist. It would be more reprehensible than commenting upon the mole on the chin of your rich aunt. I found, later on, that there is another unwritten rule, but I think that belongs solely to the West.

It yet lacked two hours to supper-time; but in twenty minutes Sam and I were plunging deep into the reheated beans, hot coffee, and cold beef.

"Nothing like a good meal before a long ride," said Sam. "Eat hearty."

I had a sudden suspicion.

"Why did you have two horses saddled?" I asked.

"One, two—one, two," said Sam. "You can count, can't you?"

His mathematics carried with it a momentary qualm and a lesson. The thought had not occurred to him that the thought could possibly occur to me not to ride at his side on that red road to revenge and justice. It was the higher calculus. I was booked for the trail. I began to eat more beans.

In an hour we set forth at a steady gallop eastward. Our horses were Kentucky-bred, strengthened by the mesquite grass of the west. Ben Tatum's steeds may have been swifter, and he had a good lead; but if he had heard the punctual thuds of the hoofs of those trailers of ours, born in the heart of feudland, he might have felt that retribution was creeping up on the hoof-prints of his dapper nags.

I knew that Ben Tatum's card to play was flight—flight until he came within the safer territory of his own henchmen and supporters. He knew that the man pursuing him would follow the trail to any end where it might lead.

During the ride Sam talked of the prospect for rain, of the price of beef, and of the musical glasses. You would have thought he had never had a brother or a sweetheart or an enemy on earth. There are some subjects too big even for the words in the "Unabridged." Knowing this phase of the feud code, but not having practised it sufficiently, I overdid the thing by telling some slightly funny anecdotes. Sam laughed at exactly the right place—laughed with his mouth. When I caught sight of his mouth, I wished I had been blessed with enough sense of humour to have suppressed those anecdotes.

Our first sight of them we had in Guthrie. Tired and hungry, we stumbled, unwashed, into a little yellow-pine hotel and sat at a table. In the opposite corner we saw the fugitives. They were bent upon their meal, but looked around at times uneasily.

The girl was dressed in brown—one of these smooth, half-shiny, silky-looking affairs with lace collar and cuffs, and what I believe they call an accordion-plaited skirt. She wore a thick brown veil down to her nose, and a broad-brimmed straw hat with some kind of feathers adorning it. The man wore plain, dark clothes, and his hair was trimmed very short. He was such a man as you might see anywhere.

There they were—the murderer and the woman he had stolen. There we were—the rightful avenger, according to the code, and the supernumerary who writes these words.

For one time, at least, in the heart of the supernumerary there rose the killing instinct. For one moment he joined the force of combatants—orally.

"What are you waiting for, Sam?" I said in a whisper. "Let him have it now!"

Sam gave a melancholy sigh.

"You don't understand; but *he* does," he said. "*He* knows. Mr. Tenderfoot, there's a rule out here among white men in the Nation that you can't shoot a man when he's with a woman. I never knew it to be broke yet. You *can't* do it. You've got to get him in a gang of men or by himself. That's why. He knows it, too. We all know. So, that's Mr. Ben Tatum! One of the 'pretty men'! I'll cut him out of the herd before they leave the hotel, and regulate his account!"

After supper the flying pair disappeared quickly. Although Sam haunted lobby and stairway and halls half the night, in some mysterious way the fugitives eluded him; and in the morning the veiled lady in the brown dress with the accordion-plaited skirt and the dapper young man with the close-clipped hair, and the buckboard with the prancing nags, were gone.

It is a monotonous story, that of the ride; so it shall be curtailed. Once again we overtook them on a road. We were about fifty yards behind. They turned in the buckboard and looked at us; then drove on without whipping up their horses. Their safety no longer lay in speed. Ben Tatum knew. He knew that the only rock of safety left to him was the code. There is no doubt that, had he been alone, the matter would have been settled quickly with Sam Durkee in the usual way; but he had something at his side that kept still the trigger-finger of both. It seemed likely that he was no coward.

So, you may perceive that woman, on occasions, may postpone instead of precipitating conflict between man and man. But not willingly or consciously. She is oblivious of codes.

Five miles farther, we came upon the future great Western city of Chandler. The horses of pursuers and pursued were starved and weary. There was one hotel that offered danger to man and entertainment to beast; so the four of us met again in the dining room at the ringing of a bell so resonant and large that it had cracked the welkin long ago. The dining room was not as large as the one at Guthrie.

Just as we were eating apple pie—how Ben Davises and tragedy impinge upon each other!—I noticed Sam looking with keen intentness at our quarry where they were seated at a table across the room. The girl still wore the brown dress with lace collar and cuffs, and the veil drawn down to her nose. The man bent over his plate, with his close cropped head held low.

"There's a code," I heard Sam say, either to me or to himself, "that won't let you shoot a man in the company of a woman; but, by thunder, there ain't one to keep you from killing a woman in the company of a man!"

And, quicker than my mind could follow his argument, he whipped a Colt's automatic from under his left arm and pumped six bullets into the body that the brown dress covered—the brown dress with the lace collar and cuffs and the accordion-plaited skirt.

The young person in the dark sack suit, from whose head and from whose life a woman's glory had been clipped, laid her head on her arms stretched upon the table; while people came running to raise Ben Tatum from the floor in his feminine masquerade that had given Sam the opportunity to set aside, technically, the obligations of the code.

The Friendly Call

W HEN I used to sell hardware in the West, I often "made" a little town called Saltillo, in Colorado. I was always certain of securing a small or a large order from Simon Bell, who kept a general store there. Bell was one of those six-foot, low-voiced products, formed from a union of the West and the South. I liked him. To look at him you would think he should be robbing stage coaches or juggling gold mines with both hands; but he would sell you a paper of tacks or a spool of thread, with ten times more patience and courtesy than any saleslady in a city department store.

I had a twofold object in my last visit to Saltillo. One was to sell a bill of goods; the other to advise Bell of a chance that I knew of by which I was certain he could make a small fortune.

In Mountain City, a town on the Union Pacific, five times larger than Saltillo, a mercantile firm was about to go to the wall. It had a lively and growing custom, but was on the edge of dissolution and ruin. Mismanagement and the gambling habits of one of the partners explained it. The condition of the firm was not yet public property. I had my knowledge of it from a private source. I knew that, if the ready cash were offered, the stock and good will could be bought for about one fourth their value.

On arriving in Saltillo I went to Bell's store. He nodded to me, smiled his broad, lingering smile, went on leisurely selling some candy to a little girl, then came around the counter and shook hands.

"Well," he said (his invariable preliminary jocosity at every call I made), "I suppose you are out here making kodak pictures of the mountains. It's the wrong time of the year to buy any hardware, of course."

I told Bell about the bargain in Mountain City. If he wanted to take advantage of it, I would rather have missed a sale than have him overstocked in Saltillo.

"It sounds good," he said, with enthusiasm. "I'd like to branch out and do a bigger business, and I'm obliged to you

308

for mentioning it. But—well, you come and stay at my house to-night and I'll think about it."

It was then after sundown and time for the larger stores in Saltillo to close. The clerks in Bell's put away their books, whirled the combination of the safe, put on their coats and hats and left for their homes. Bell padlocked the big, double wooden front doors, and we stood, for a moment, breathing the keen, fresh mountain air coming across the foothills.

A big man walked down the street and stopped in front of the high porch of the store. His long, black moustache, black eyebrows, and curly black hair contrasted queerly with his light, pink complexion, which belonged, by rights, to a blonde. He was about forty, and wore a white vest, white hat, a watch chain made of five-dollar gold pieces linked together, and a rather well-fitting two-piece gray suit of the cut that college boys of eighteen are wont to affect. He glanced at me distrustfully, and then at Bell with coldness and, I thought, something of enmity in his expression.

"Well," asked Bell, as if he were addressing a stranger, "did you fix up that matter?"

"Did I!" the man answered, in a resentful tone. "What do you suppose I've been here two weeks for? The business is to be settled to-night. Does that suit you, or have you got something to kick about?"

"It's all right," said Bell. "I knew you'd do it."

"Of course, you did," said the magnificent stranger. "Haven't I done it before?"

"You have," admitted Bell. "And so have I. How do you find it at the hotel?"

"Rocky grub. But I ain't kicking. Say—can you give me any pointers about managing that—affair? It's my first deal in that line of business, you know."

"No, I can't," answered Bell, after some thought. "I've tried all kinds of ways. You'll have to try some of your own."

"Tried soft soap?"

"Barrels of it."

"Tried a saddle girth with a buckle on the end of it?"

"Never none. Started to once; and here's what I got."

Bill held out his right hand. Even in the deepening twilight,

I could see on the back of it a long, white scar, that might have been made by a claw or a knife or some sharp-edged tool.

"Oh, well," said the florid man, carelessly, "I'll know what to do later on."

He walked away without another word. When he had gone ten steps he turned and called to Bell:

"You keep well out of the way when the goods are delivered, so there won't be any hitch in the business."

"All right," anwered Bell, "I'll attend to my end of the line."

This talk was scarcely clear in its meaning to me; but as it did not concern me, I did not let it weigh upon my mind. But the singularity of the other man's appearance lingered with me for a while; and as we walked toward Bell's house I remarked to him:

"Your customer seems to be a surly kind of fellow—not one that you'd like to be snowed in with in a camp on a hunting trip."

"He is that," assented Bell, heartily. "He reminds me of a rattlesnake that's been poisoned by the bite of a tarantula."

"He doesn't look like a citizen of Saltillo," I went on.

"No," said Bell, "he lives in Sacramento. He's down here on a little business trip. His name is George Ringo, and he's been my best friend—in fact the only friend I ever had—for twenty years."

I was too surprised to make any further comment.

Bell lived in a comfortable, plain, square, two-story white house on the edge of the little town. I waited in the parlor—a room depressingly genteel—furnished with red plush, straw matting, looped-up lace curtains, and a glass case large enough to contain a mummy, full of mineral specimens.

While I waited, I heard, upstairs, that unmistakable sound instantly recognized the world over—a bickering woman's voice, rising as her anger and fury grew. I could hear, between the gusts, the temperate rumble of Bell's tones, striving to oil the troubled waters.

The storm subsided soon; but not before I had heard the woman say, in a lower, concentrated tone, rather more carrying than her high-pitched railings: "This is the last time. I tell you—the last time. Oh, you *will* understand."

The household seemed to consist of only Bell and his wife and a servant or two. I was introduced to Mrs. Bell at supper.

At first sight she seemed to be a handsome woman, but I soon perceived that her charm had been spoiled. An uncontrolled petulance, I thought, an emotional egotism, an absence of poise and a habitual dissatisfaction had marred her womanhood. During the meal, she showed that false gayety, spurious kindliness and reactionary softness that mark the woman addicted to tantrums. Withal, she was a woman who might be attractive to many men.

After supper, Bell and I took our chairs outside, set them on the grass in the moonlight and smoked. The full moon is a witch. In her light, truthful men dig up for you nuggets of purer gold; while liars squeeze out brighter colors from the tubes of their invention. I saw Bell's broad, slow smile come out upon his face and linger there.

"I reckon you think George and me are a funny kind of friends," he said. "The fact is we never did take much interest in each other's company. But his idea and mine, of what a friend should be, was always synonymous and we lived up to it, strict, all these years. Now, I'll give you an idea of what our idea is.

"A man don't need but one friend. The fellow who drinks your liquor and hangs around you, slapping you on the back and taking up your time, telling you how much he likes you, ain't a friend, even if you did play marbles at school and fish in the same creek with him. As long as you don't need a friend one of that kind may answer. But a friend, to my mind, is one you can deal with on a strict reciprocity basis like me and George have always done.

"A good many years ago, him and me was connected in a number of ways. We put our capital together and run a line of freight wagons in New Mexico, and we mined some and gambled a few. And then, we got into trouble of one or two kinds; and I reckon that got us on a better understandable basis than anything else did, unless it was the fact that we never had much personal use for each other's ways. George is the vainest man I ever see, and the biggest brag. He could blow the biggest geyser in the Yosemite valley back into its hole with one whisper. I am a quiet man, and fond of studiousness and thought. The more we used to see each other, personally, the less we seemed to like to be together. If he ever had slapped me on the back and snivelled over me like I've seen men do to what they called their friends, I know I'd have had a rough-and-tumble with him on the spot. Same way with George. He hated my ways as bad as I did his. When we were mining, we lived in separate tents, so as not to intrude our obnoxiousness on each other.

"But after a long time, we begun to know each of us could depend on the other when we were in a pinch, up to his last dollar, word of honor or perjury, bullet, or drop of blood we had in the world. We never even spoke of it to each other, because that would have spoiled it. But we tried it out, time after time, until we came to know. I've grabbed my hat and jumped a freight and rode 200 miles to identify him when he was about to be hung by mistake, in Idaho, for a train robber. Once, I laid sick of typhoid in a tent in Texas, without a dollar or a change of clothes, and sent for George in Boise City. He came on the next train. The first thing he did before speaking to me, was to hang up a little looking glass on the side of the tent and curl his moustache and rub some hair dye on his head. His hair is naturally a light reddish. Then he gave me the most scientific cussing I ever had, and took off his coat.

"'If you wasn't a Moses-meek little Mary's lamb, you wouldn't have been took down this way,' says he. 'Haven't you got gumption enough not to drink swamp water or fall down and scream whenever you have a little colic or feel a mosquito bite you?' He made me a little mad.

"'You've got the bedside manners of a Piute medicine man,' says I. 'And I wish you'd go away and let me die a natural death. I'm sorry I sent for you.'

"'I've a mind to,' says George, 'for nobody cares whether you live or die. But now I've been tricked into coming, I might as well stay until this little attack of indigestion or nettle rash or whatever it is, passes away.'

"Two weeks afterward, when I was beginning to get around again, the doctor laughed and said he was sure that my friend's keeping me mad all the time did more than his drugs to cure me.

"So that's the way George and me was friends. There wasn't any sentiment about it—it was just give and take, and each of us knew that the other was ready for the call at any time.

"I remember, once, I played a sort of joke on George, just to try him. I felt a little mean about it afterward, because I never ought to have doubted he'd do it.

"We was both living in a little town in the San Luis valley, running some flocks of sheep and a few cattle. We were partners, but, as usual, we didn't live together. I had an old aunt, out from the East, visiting for the summer, so I rented a little cottage. She soon had a couple of cows and some pigs and chickens to make the place look like home. George lived alone in a little cabin half a mile out of town.

"One day a calf that we had, died. That night I broke its bones, dumped it into a coarse sack and tied it up with wire. I put on an old shirt, tore a sleeve 'most out of it, and the collar half off, tangled up my hair, put some red ink on my hands and splashed some of it over my shirt and face. I must have looked like I'd been having the fight of my life. I put the sack in a wagon and drove out to George's cabin. When I halloed, he came out in a yellow dressing-gown, a Turkish cap and patent leather shoes. George always was a great dresser.

"I dumped the bundle to the ground.

"'Sh-sh!' says I, kind of wild in my way. 'Take that and bury it, George, out somewhere behind your house—bury it just like it is. And don——'

"'Don't get excited,' says George. 'And for the Lord's sake go and wash your hands and face and put on a clean shirt.'

"And he lights his pipe, while I drive away at a gallop. The next morning he drops around to our cottage, where my aunt was fiddling with her flowers and truck in the front yard. He bends himself and bows and makes compliments as he could do, when so disposed, and begs a rose bush from her, saying he had turned up a little land back of his cabin, and wanted to plant something on it by way of usefulness and ornament. So my aunt, flattered, pulls up one of her biggest by the roots and gives it to him. Afterward I see it growing where he planted it, in a place where the grass had been cleared off and the dirt levelled. But neither George nor me ever spoke of it to each other again."

The moon rose higher, possibly drawing water from the sea, pixies from their dells and certainly more confidences from Simms Bell, the friend of a friend.

"There come a time, not long afterward," he went on, "when

I was able to do a good turn for George Ringo. George had made a little pile of money in beeves and he was up in Denver, and he showed up when I saw him, wearing deer-skin vests, yellow shoes, clothes like the awnings in front of drug stores, and his hair dyed so blue that it looked black in the dark. He wrote me to come up there, quick—that he needed me, and to bring the best outfit of clothes I had. I had 'em on when I got the letter, so I left on the next train. George was——"

Bell stopped for half a minute, listening intently.

"I thought I heard a team coming down the road," he explained. "George was at a summer resort on a lake near Denver and was putting on as many airs as he knew how. He had rented a little two-room cottage, and had a Chihuahua dog and a hammock and eight different kinds of walking sticks.

"'Simms,' he says to me, 'there's a widow woman here that's pestering the soul out of me with her intentions. I can't get out of her way. It ain't that she ain't handsome and agreeable, in a sort of style, but her attentions is serious, and I ain't ready for to marry nobody and settle down. I can't go to no festivity nor sit on the hotel piazza or mix in any of the society round-ups, but what she cuts me out of the herd and puts her daily brand on me. I like this here place,' goes on George, 'and I'm making a hit here in the most censorious circles, so I don't want to have to run away from it. So I sent for you.'

"'What do you want me to do?' I asks George.

"'Why,' says he, 'I want you to head her off. I want you to cut me out. I want you to come to the rescue. Suppose you seen a wildcat about for to eat me, what would you do?'

"'Go for it,' says I.

"'Correct,' says George. 'Then go for this Mrs. De Clinton the same.'

"'How am I to do it?' I asks. 'By force and awfulness or in some gentler and less lurid manner?'

"'Court her,' George says, 'get her off my trail. Feed her. Take her out in boats. Hang around her and stick to her. Get her mashed on you if you can. Some women are pretty big fools. Who knows but what she might take a fancy to you.'

"'Had you ever thought,' I asks, 'of repressing your fatal fascinations in her presence; of squeezing a harsh note in the melody of your siren voice, of veiling your beauty—in other words, of giving her the bounce yourself?'

"George sees no essence of sarcasm in my remark. He twists his moustache and looks at the points of his shoes.

"'Well, Simms,' he said, 'you know how I am about the ladies. I can't hurt none of their feelings. I'm, by nature, polite and esteemful of their intents and purposes. This Mrs. De Clinton don't appear to be the suitable sort for me. Besides, I ain't a marrying man by all means.'

"'All right,' said I, 'I'll do the best I can in the case.'

"So I bought a new outfit of clothes and a book on etiquette and made a dead set for Mrs. De Clinton. She was a fine-looking woman, cheerful and gay. At first, I almost had to hobble her to keep her from loping around at George's heels; but finally I got her so she seemed glad to go riding with me and sailing on the lake; and she seemed real hurt on the mornings when I forgot to send her a bunch of flowers. Still, I didn't like the way she looked at George, sometimes, out of the corner of her eye. George was having a fine time now, going with the whole bunch just as he pleased. Yes'm," continued Bell, "she certainly was a fine-looking woman at that time. She's changed some since, as you might have noticed at the supper table."

"What!" I exclaimed.

"I married Mrs. De Clinton," went on Bell. "One evening while we were up at the lake. When I told George about it, he opened his mouth and I thought he was going to break our traditions and say something grateful, but he swallowed it back.

"'All right,' says he, playing with his dog. 'I hope you won't have too much trouble. Myself, I'm not never going to marry.'

"That was three years ago," said Bell. "We came here to live. For a year we got along medium fine. And then everything changed. For two years I've been having something that rhymes first-class with my name. You heard the row upstairs this evening? That was a merry welcome compared to the usual average. She's tired of me and of this little town life and she rages all day, like a panther in a cage. I stood it until two weeks ago and then I had to send out The Call. I located George in Sacramento. He started the day he got my wire."

Mrs. Bell came out of the house swiftly toward us. Some

strong excitement or anxiety seemed to possess her, but she smiled a faint hostess smile, and tried to keep her voice calm.

"The dew is falling," she said, "and it's growing rather late. Wouldn't you gentlemen rather come into the house?"

Bell took some cigars from his pocket and answered: "It's most too fine a night to turn in yet. I think Mr. Ames and I will walk out along the road a mile or so and have another smoke. I want to talk with him about some goods that I want to buy."

"Up the road or down the road?" asked Mrs. Bell.

"Down," said Bell.

I thought she breathed a sigh of relief.

When we had gone a hundred yards and the house became concealed by trees, Bell guided me into the thick grove that lined the road and back through them toward the house again. We stopped within twenty yards of the house, concealed by the dark shadows. I wondered at this maneuver. And then I heard in the distance coming down the road beyond the house, the regular hoofbeats of a team of horses. Bell held his watch in a ray of moonlight.

"On time, within a minute," he said. "That's George's way."

The team slowed up as it drew near the house and stopped in a patch of black shadows. We saw the figure of a woman carrying a heavy valise move swiftly from the other side of the house, and hurry to the waiting vehicle. Then it rolled away briskly in the direction from which it had come.

I looked at Bell inquiringly, I suppose. I certainly asked him no question.

"She's running away with George," said Bell, simply. "He's kept me posted about the progress of the scheme all along. She'll get a divorce in six months and then George will marry her. He never helps anybody halfway. It's all arranged between them."

I began to wonder what friendship was, after all.

When we went into the house, Bell began to talk easily on other subjects; and I took his cue. By and by the big chance to buy out the business in Mountain City came back to my mind and I began to urge it upon him. Now that he was free, it would be easier for him to make the move; and he was sure of a splendid bargain.

Bell was silent for some minutes, but when I looked at him

I fancied that he was thinking of something else—that he was not considering the project.

"Why, no, Mr. Ames," he said, after a while, "I can't make that deal. I'm awful thankful to you, though, for telling me about it. But I've got to stay here. I can't go to Mountain City."

"Why?" I asked.

"Missis Bell," he replied, "won't live in Mountain City. She hates the place and wouldn't go there. I've got to keep right on here in Saltillo."

"Mrs. Bell!" I exclaimed, too puzzled to conjecture what he meant.

"I ought to explain," said Bell. "I know George and I know Mrs. Bell. He's impatient in his ways. He can't stand things that fret him, long, like I can. Six months, I give them—six months of married life, and there'll be another disunion. Mrs. Bell will come back to me. There's no other place for her to go. I've got to stay here and wait. At the end of six months, I'll have to grab a satchel and catch the first train. For George will be sending out The Call."

TROPICS

Shoes

JOHN DE Graffenreid Atwood ate of the lotus, root, stem, and flower. The tropics gobbled him up. He plunged enthusiastically into his work, which was to try to forget Rosine.

Now, they who dine on the lotus rarely consume it plain. There is a sauce *au diable* that goes with it; and the distillers are the chefs who prepare it. And on Johnny's menu card it read "brandy." With a bottle between them, he and Billy Keogh would sit on the porch of the little consulate at night and roar out great, indecorous songs, until the natives, slipping hastily past, would shrug a shoulder and mutter things to themselves about the "*Americanos diablos.*"

One day Johnny's *mozo* brought the mail and dumped it on the table. Johnny leaned from his hammock, and fingered the four or five letters dejectedly. Keogh was sitting on the edge of the table chopping lazily with a paper knife at the legs of a centipede that was crawling among the stationery. Johnny was in that phase of lotus-eating when all the world tastes bitter in one's mouth.

"Same old thing!" he complained. "Fool people writing for information about the country. They want to know all about raising fruit, and how to make a fortune without work. Half of 'em don't even send stamps for a reply. They think a consul hasn't anything to do but write letters. Slit those envelopes for me, old man, and see what they want. I'm feeling too rocky to move."

Keogh, acclimated beyond all possibility of ill-humour, drew his chair to the table with smiling compliance on his rose-pink countenance, and began to slit open the letters. Four of them were from citizens in various parts of the United States who seemed to regard the consul at Coralio as a cyclopædia of information. They asked long lists of questions, numerically arranged, about the climate, products, possibilities, laws, business chances, and statistics of the country in which the consul had the honour of representing his own government.

"Write 'em, please, Billy," said that inert official, "just a line, referring them to the latest consular report. Tell 'em the State

Department will be delighted to furnish the literary gems. Sign my name. Don't let your pen scratch, Billy; it'll keep me awake."

"Don't snore," said Keogh, amiably, "and I'll do your work for you. You need a corps of assistants, anyhow. Don't see how you ever get out a report. Wake up a minute!—here's one more letter—it's from your own town, too—Dalesburg."

"That so?" murmured Johnny showing a mild and obligatory interest. "What's it about?"

"Postmaster writes," explained Keogh. "Says a citizen of the town wants some facts and advice from you. Says the citizen has an idea in his head of coming down where you are and opening a shoe store. Wants to know if you think the business would pay. Says he's heard of the boom along this coast, and wants to get in on the ground floor."

In spite of the heat and his bad temper, Johnny's hammock swayed with his laughter. Keogh laughed too; and the pet monkey on the top shelf of the bookcase chattered in shrill sympathy with the ironical reception of the letter from Dalesburg.

"Great bunions!" exclaimed the consul. "Shoe store! What'll they ask about next, I wonder? Overcoat factory, I reckon. Say, Billy—of our 3,000 citizens, how many do you suppose ever had on a pair of shoes?"

Keogh reflected judicially.

"Let's see—there's you and me and—"

"Not me," said Johnny, promptly and incorrectly, holding up a foot encased in a disreputable deerskin *zapato*. "I haven't been a victim to shoes in months."

"But you've got 'em, though," went on Keogh. "And there's Goodwin and Blanchard and Geddie and old Lutz and Doc Gregg and that Italian that's agent for the banana company, and there's old Delgado—no; he wears sandals. And, oh, yes; there's Madama Ortiz, 'what kapes the hotel'—she had on a pair of red kid slippers at the *baile* the other night. And Miss Pasa, her daughter, that went to school in the States—she brought back some civilized notions in the way of footgear. And there's the *comandante*'s sister that dresses up her feet on feast-days—and Mrs. Geddie, who wears a two with a Castilian instep—and that's about all the ladies. Let's see—don't some of the soldiers at the *cuartel*—no: that's so; they're allowed shoes only when on the march. In barracks they turn their little toeses out to grass."

"'Bout right," agreed the consul. "Not over twenty out of the three thousand ever felt leather on their walking arrangements. Oh, yes; Coralio is just the town for an enterprising shoe store—that doesn't want to part with its goods. Wonder if old Patterson is trying to jolly me! He always was full of things he called jokes. Write him a letter, Billy. I'll dictate it. We'll jolly him back a few."

Keogh dipped his pen, and wrote at Johnny's dictation. With many pauses, filled in with smoke and sundry travellings of the bottle and glasses, the following reply to the Dalesburg communication was perpetrated:

Mr. OBADIAH PATTERSON,
        Dalesburg, Ala.
    Dear Sir: In reply to your favour of July 2d, I have the honour to inform you that, according to my opinion, there is no place on the habitable globe that presents to the eye stronger evidence of the need of a first-class shoe store than does the town of Coralio. There are 3,000 inhabitants in the place, and not a single shoe store! The situation speaks for itself. This coast is rapidly becoming the goal of enterprising business men, but the shoe business is one that has been sadly overlooked or neglected. In fact, there are a considerable number of our citizens actually without shoes at present.
    Besides the want above mentioned, there is also a crying need for a brewery, a college of higher mathematics, a coal yard, and a clean and intellectual Punch and Judy show. I have the honour to be, sir,
                                Your Obt. Servant,
                        JOHN DE GRAFFENREID ATWOOD,
                                U. S. Consul at Coralio.

    P. S.—Hello! Uncle Obadiah. How's the old burg racking along? What would the government do without you and me? Look out for a green-headed parrot and a bunch of bananas soon, from your old friend   JOHNNY.

"I throw in that postscript," explained the consul, "so Uncle Obadiah won't take offence at the official tone of the letter!

Now, Billy, you get that correspondence fixed up, and send Pancho to the post-office with it. The *Ariadne* takes the mail out to-morrow if they make up that load of fruit to-day."

The night programme in Coralio never varied. The recreations of the people were soporific and flat. They wandered about, barefoot and aimless, speaking lowly and smoking cigar or cigarette. Looking down on the dimly lighted ways one seemed to see a threading maze of brunette ghosts tangled with a procession of insane fireflies. In some houses the thrumming of lugubrious guitars added to the depression of the *triste* night. Giant tree-frogs rattled in the foliage as loudly as the end man's "bones" in a minstrel troupe. By nine o'clock the streets were almost deserted.

Nor at the consulate was there often a change of bill. Keogh would come there nightly, for Coralio's one cool place was the little seaward porch of that official residence.

The brandy would be kept moving; and before midnight sentiment would begin to stir in the heart of the self-exiled consul. Then he would relate to Keogh the story of his ended romance. Each night Keogh would listen patiently to the tale, and be ready with untiring sympathy.

"But don't you think for a minute"—thus Johnny would always conclude his woeful narrative—"that I'm grieving about that girl, Billy. I've forgotten her. She never enters my mind. If she were to enter that door right now, my pulse wouldn't gain a beat. That's all over long ago."

"Don't I know it?" Keogh would answer. "Of course you've forgotten her. Proper thing to do. Wasn't quite O. K. of her to listen to the knocks that—er—Dink Pawson kept giving you."

"Pink Dawson!"—a world of contempt would be in Johnny's tones—"Poor white trash! That's what he was. Had five hundred acres of farming land, though; and that counted. Maybe I'll have a chance to get back at him some day. The Dawsons weren't anybody. Everybody in Alabama knows the Atwoods. Say, Billy—did you know my mother was a De Graffenreid?"

"Why, no," Keogh would say; "is that so?" He had heard it some three hundred times.

"Fact. The De Graffenreids of Hancock County. But I never think of that girl any more, do I, Billy?"

"Not for a minute, my boy," would be the last sounds heard by the conqueror of Cupid.

At this point Johnny would fall into a gentle slumber, and Keogh would saunter out to his own shack under the calabash tree at the edge of the plaza.

In a day or two the letter from the Dalesburg postmaster and its answer had been forgotten by the Coralio exiles. But on the 26th day of July the fruit of the reply appeared upon the tree of events.

The *Andador*, a fruit steamer that visited Coralio regularly, drew into the offing and anchored. The beach was lined with spectators while the quarantine doctor and the custom-house crew rowed out to attend to their duties.

An hour later Billy Keogh lounged into the consulate, clean and cool in his linen clothes, and grinning like a pleased shark.

"Guess what?" he said to Johnny, lounging in his hammock.

"Too hot to guess," said Johnny, lazily.

"Your shoe-store man's come," said Keogh, rolling the sweet morsel on his tongue, "with a stock of goods big enough to supply the continent as far down as Terra del Fuego. They're carting his cases over to the custom-house now. Six barges full they brought ashore and have paddled back for the rest. Oh, ye saints in glory! won't there be regalements in the air when he gets onto the joke and has an interview with Mr. Consul? It'll be worth nine years in the tropics just to witness that one joyful moment."

Keogh loved to take his mirth easily. He selected a clean place on the matting and lay upon the floor. The walls shook with his enjoyment. Johnny turned half over and blinked.

"Don't tell me," he said, "that anybody was fool enough to take that letter seriously."

"Four-thousand-dollar stock of goods!" gasped Keogh, in ecstasy. "Talk about coals to Newcastle! Why didn't he take a ship-load of palm-leaf fans to Spitzbergen while he was about it? Saw the old codger on the beach. You ought to have been there when he put on his specs and squinted at the five hundred or so barefooted citizens standing around."

"Are you telling the truth, Billy?" asked the consul, weakly.

"Am I? You ought to see the buncoed gentleman's daughter

he brought along. Looks! She makes the brick-dust señoritas here look like tar-babies."

"Go on," said Johnny, "if you can stop that asinine giggling. I hate to see a grown man make a laughing hyena of himself."

"Name is Hemstetter," went on Keogh. "He's a— Hello! what's the matter now?"

Johnny's moccasined feet struck the floor with a thud as he wriggled out of his hammock.

"Get up, you idiot," he said, sternly, "or I'll brain you with this inkstand. That's Rosine and her father. Gad! what a drivelling idiot old Patterson is! Get up, here, Billy Keogh, and help me. What the devil are we going to do? Has all the world gone crazy?"

Keogh rose and dusted himself. He managed to regain a decorous demeanour.

"Situation has got to be met, Johnny," he said, with some success at seriousness. "I didn't think about its being your girl until you spoke. First thing to do is to get them comfortable quarters. You go down and face the music, and I'll trot out to Goodwin's and see if Mrs. Goodwin won't take them in. They've got the decentest house in town."

"Bless you, Billy!" said the consul. "I knew you wouldn't desert me. The world's bound to come to an end, but maybe we can stave it off for a day or two."

Keogh hoisted his umbrella and set out for Goodwin's house. Johnny put on his coat and hat. He picked up the brandy bottle, but set it down again without drinking, and marched bravely down to the beach.

In the shade of the custom-house walls he found Mr. Hemstetter and Rosine surrounded by a mass of gaping citizens. The customs officers were ducking and scraping, while the captain of the *Andador* interpreted the business of the new arrivals. Rosine looked healthy and very much alive. She was gazing at the strange scenes around her with amused interest. There was a faint blush upon her round cheek as she greeted her old admirer. Mr. Hemstetter shook hands with Johnny in a very friendly way. He was an oldish, impractical man—one of that numerous class of erratic business men who are forever dissatisfied, and seeking a change.

"I am very glad to see you, John—may I call you John?"

he said. "Let me thank you for your prompt answer to our postmaster's letter of inquiry. He volunteered to write to you on my behalf. I was looking about for something different in the way of a business in which the profits would be greater. I had noticed in the papers that this coast was receiving much attention from investors. I am extremely grateful for your advice to come. I sold out everything that I possess, and invested the proceeds in as fine a stock of shoes as could be bought in the North. You have a picturesque town here, John. I hope business will be as good as your letter justifies me in expecting."

Johnny's agony was abbreviated by the arrival of Keogh, who hurried up with the news that Mrs. Goodwin would be much pleased to place rooms at the disposal of Mr. Hemstetter and his daughter. So there Mr. Hemstetter and Rosine were at once conducted and left to recuperate from the fatigue of the voyage, while Johnny went down to see that the cases of shoes were safely stored in the customs warehouse pending their examination by the officials. Keogh, grinning like a shark, skirmished about to find Goodwin, to instruct him not to expose to Mr. Hemstetter the true state of Coralio as a shoe market until Johnny had been given a chance to redeem the situation, if such a thing were possible.

That night the consul and Keogh held a desperate consultation on the breezy porch of the consulate.

"Send 'em back home," began Keogh, reading Johnny's thoughts.

"I would," said Johnny, after a little silence; "but I've been lying to you, Billy."

"All right about that," said Keogh, affably.

"I've told you hundreds of times," said Johnny, slowly, "that I had forgotten that girl, haven't I?"

"About three hundred and seventy-five," admitted the monument of patience.

"I lied," repeated the consul, "every time. I never forgot her for one minute. I was an obstinate ass for running away just because she said 'No' once. And I was too proud a fool to go back. I talked with Rosine a few minutes this evening up at Goodwin's. I found out one thing. You remember that farmer fellow who was always after her?"

"Dink Pawson?" asked Keogh.

"Pink Dawson. Well, he wasn't a hill of beans to her. She says she didn't believe a word of the things he told her about me. But I'm sewed up now, Billy. That tomfool letter we sent ruined whatever chance I had left. She'll despise me when she finds out that her old father has been made the victim of a joke that a decent school boy wouldn't have been guilty of. Shoes! Why he couldn't sell twenty pairs of shoes in Coralio if he kept store here for twenty years. You put a pair of shoes on one of these Caribs or Spanish brown boys and what'd he do? Stand on his head and squeal until he'd kicked 'em off. None of 'em ever wore shoes and they never will. If I send 'em back home I'll have to tell the whole story, and what'll she think of me? I want that girl worse than ever, Billy, and now when she's in reach I've lost her forever because I tried to be funny when the thermometer was at 102."

"Keep cheerful," said the optimistic Keogh. "And let 'em open the store. I've been busy myself this afternoon. We can stir up a temporary boom in foot-gear anyhow. I'll buy six pairs when the doors open. I've been around and seen all the fellows and explained the catastrophe. They'll all buy shoes like they was centipedes. Frank Goodwin will take cases of 'em. The Geddies want about eleven pairs between 'em. Clancy is going to invest the savings of weeks, and even old Doc Gregg wants three pairs of alligator-hide slippers if they've got any tens. Blanchard got a look at Miss Hemstetter; and as he's a Frenchman, no less than a dozen pairs will do for him."

"A dozen customers," said Johnny, "for a $4,000 stock of shoes! It won't work. There's a big problem here to figure out. You go home, Billy, and leave me alone. I've got to work at it all by myself. Take that bottle of Three-star along with you—no, sir; not another ounce of booze for the United States consul. I'll sit here to-night and pull out the think stop. If there's a soft place on this proposition anywhere I'll land on it. If there isn't there'll be another wreck to the credit of the gorgeous tropics."

Keogh left, feeling that he could be of no use. Johnny laid a handful of cigars on a table and stretched himself in a steamer chair. When the sudden daylight broke, silvering the harbour ripples, he was still sitting there. Then he got up, whistling a little tune, and took his bath.

At nine o'clock he walked down to the dingy little cable

office and hung for half an hour over a blank. The result of his application was the following message, which he signed and had transmitted at a cost of $33:

To PINKNEY DAWSON,
        Dalesburg, Ala.
    Draft for $100 comes to you next mail. Ship me immediately 500 pounds stiff, dry cockleburrs. New use here in arts. Market price twenty cents pound. Further orders likely. Rush.

Ships

WITHIN A week a suitable building had been secured in the Calle Grande, and Mr. Hemstetter's stock of shoes arranged upon their shelves. The rent of the store was moderate; and the stock made a fine showing of neat white boxes, attractively displayed.

Johnny's friends stood by him loyally. On the first day Keogh strolled into the store in a casual kind of way about once every hour, and bought shoes. After he had purchased a pair each of extension soles, congress gaiters, button kids, low-quartered calfs, dancing pumps, rubber boots, tans of various hues, tennis shoes and flowered slippers, he sought out Johnny to be prompted as to the names of other kinds that he might inquire for. The other English-speaking residents also played their parts nobly by buying often and liberally. Keogh was grand marshal, and made them distribute their patronage, thus keeping up a fair run of custom for several days.

Mr. Hemstetter was gratified by the amount of business done thus far; but expressed surprise that the natives were so backward with their custom.

"Oh, they're awfully shy," explained Johnny, as he wiped his forehead nervously. "They'll get the habit pretty soon. They'll come with a rush when they do come."

One afternoon Keogh dropped into the consul's office, chewing an unlighted cigar thoughtfully.

"Got anything up your sleeve?" he inquired of Johnny. "If you have it's about time to show it. If you can borrow some gent's hat in the audience, and make a lot of customers for an idle stock of shoes come out of it, you'd better spiel. The boys have all laid in enough footwear to last 'em ten years; and there's nothing doing in the shoe store but dolcy far nienty. I just came by there. Your venerable victim was standing in the door, gazing through his specs at the bare toes passing by his emporium. The natives here have got the true artistic temperament. Me and Clancy took eighteen tintypes this morning in two hours. There's been but one pair of shoes sold all day.

Blanchard went in and bought a pair of fur-lined house-slippers because he thought he saw Miss Hemstetter go into the store. I saw him throw the slippers into the lagoon afterwards."

"There's a Mobile fruit steamer coming in to-morrow or next day," said Johnny. "We can't do anything until then."

"What are you going to do—try to create a demand?"

"Political economy isn't your strong point," said the consul, impudently. "You can't create a demand. But you can create a necessity for a demand. That's what I am going to do."

Two weeks after the consul sent his cable, a fruit steamer brought him a huge, mysterious brown bale of some unknown commodity. Johnny's influence with the custom-house people was sufficiently strong for him to get the goods turned over to him without the usual inspection. He had the bale taken to the consulate and snugly stowed in the back room.

That night he ripped open a corner of it and took out a handful of the cockleburrs. He examined them with the care with which a warrior examines his arms before he goes forth to battle for his lady-love and life. The burrs were the ripe August product, as hard as filberts, and bristling with spines as tough and sharp as needles. Johnny whistled softly a little tune, and went out to find Billy Keogh.

Later in the night, when Coralio was steeped in slumber, he and Billy went forth into the deserted streets with their coats bulging like balloons. All up and down the Calle Grande they went, sowing the sharp burrs carefully in the sand, along the narrow sidewalks, in every foot of grass between the silent houses. And then they took the side streets and byways, missing none. No place where the foot of man, woman or child might fall was slighted. Many trips they made to and from the prickly hoard. And then, nearly at the dawn, they laid themselves down to rest calmly, as great generals do after planning a victory according to the revised tactics, and slept, knowing that they had sowed with the accuracy of Satan sowing tares and the perseverance of Paul planting.

With the rising sun came the purveyors of fruits and meats, and arranged their wares in and around the little market-house. At one end of the town near the seashore the market-house stood; and the sowing of the burrs had not been carried that far. The dealers waited long past the hour when their sales usually began. None came to buy. "*Qué hay?*" they began to exclaim, one to another.

At their accustomed time, from every 'dobe and palm hut and grass-thatched shack and dim *patio* glided women—black women, brown women, lemon-colored women, women dun and yellow and tawny. They were the marketers starting to purchase the family supply of cassava, plantains, meat, fowls, and tortillas. Décolleté they were and bare-armed and bare-footed, with a single skirt reaching below the knee. Stolid and ox-eyed, they stepped from their doorways into the narrow paths or upon the soft grass of the streets.

The first to emerge uttered ambiguous squeals, and raised one foot quickly. Another step and they sat down, with shrill cries of alarm, to pick at the new and painful insects that had stung them upon the feet. "*Qué picadores diablos!*" they screeched to one another across the narrow ways. Some tried the grass instead of the paths, but there they were also stung and bitten by the strange little prickly balls. They plumped down in the grass, and added their lamentations to those of their sisters in the sandy paths. All through the town was heard the plaint of the feminine jabber. The venders in the market still wondered why no customers came.

Then men, lords of the earth, came forth. They, too, began to hop, to dance, to limp, and to curse. They stood stranded and foolish, or stooped to pluck at the scourge that attacked their feet and ankles. Some loudly proclaimed the pest to be poisonous spiders of an unknown species.

And then the children ran out for their morning romp. And now to the uproar was added the howls of limping infants and cockleburred childhood. Every minute the advancing day brought forth fresh victims.

Doña Maria Castillas y Buenventura de las Casas stepped from her honoured doorway, as was her daily custom, to procure fresh bread from the *panaderia* across the street. She was clad in a skirt of flowered yellow satin, a chemise of ruffled linen, and wore a purple mantilla from the looms of Spain. Her lemon-tinted feet, alas! were bare. Her progress was majestic, for were not her ancestors hidalgos of Aragon? Three steps she made across the velvety grass, and set her aristocratic sole upon a bunch of Johnny's burrs. Doña Maria Castillas y Buenventura de las Casas emitted a yowl even as a wild-cat. Turning about, she fell upon hands and knees, and crawled—ay, like a beast of the field she crawled back to her honourable door-sill.

Don Señor Ildefonso Federico Valdazar, *Juez de la Paz*, weighing twenty stone, attempted to convey his bulk to the *pulperia* at the corner of the plaza in order to assuage his matutinal thirst. The first plunge of his unshod foot into the cool grass struck a concealed mine. Don Ildefonso fell like a crumbled cathedral, crying out that he had been fatally bitten by a deadly scorpion. Everywhere were the shoeless citizens hopping, stumbling, limping, and picking from their feet the venomous insects that had come in a single night to harass them.

The first to perceive the remedy was Estebán Delgado, the barber, a man of travel and education. Sitting upon a stone, he plucked burrs from his toes, and made oration:

"Behold, my friends, these bugs of the devil! I know them well. They soar through the skies in swarms like pigeons. These are dead ones that fell during the night. In Yucatan I have seen them as large as oranges. Yes! There they hiss like serpents, and have wings like bats. It is the shoes—the shoes that one needs! *Zapatos—zapatos para mi!*"

Estebán hobbled to Mr. Hemstetter's store, and bought shoes. Coming out, he swaggered down the street with impunity, reviling loudly the bugs of the devil. The suffering ones sat up or stood upon one foot and beheld the immune barber. Men, women and children took up the cry: "*Zapatos! zapatos!*"

The necessity for the demand had been created. The demand followed. That day Mr. Hemstetter sold three hundred pairs of shoes.

"It is really surprising," he said to Johnny, who came up in the evening to help him straighten out the stock, "how trade is picking up. Yesterday I made but three sales."

"I told you they'd whoop things up when they got started," said the consul.

"I think I shall order a dozen more cases of goods, to keep the stock up," said Mr. Hemstetter, beaming through his spectacles.

"I wouldn't send in any orders yet," advised Johnny. "Wait till you see how the trade holds up."

Each night Johnny and Keogh sowed the crop that grew dollars by day. At the end of ten days two-thirds of the stock of shoes had been sold; and the stock of cockleburrs was exhausted. Johnny cabled to Pink Dawson for another 500 pounds, paying twenty cents per pound as before. Mr. Hemstetter carefully made up an order for $1500 worth of shoes from Northern firms. Johnny hung about the store until this order was ready for the mail, and succeeded in destroying it before it reached the postoffice.

That night he took Rosine under the mango tree by Goodwin's porch, and confessed everything. She looked him in the eye, and said: "You are a very wicked man. Father and I will go back home. You say it was a joke? I think it is a very serious matter."

But at the end of half an hour's argument the conversation had been turned upon a different subject. The two were considering the respective merits of pale blue and pink wall paper with which the old colonial mansion of the Atwoods in Dalesburg was to be decorated after the wedding.

On the next morning Johnny confessed to Mr. Hemstetter. The shoe merchant put on his spectacles, and said through them: "You strike me as being a most extraordinary young scamp. If I had not managed this enterprise with good business judgment my entire stock of goods might have been a complete loss. Now, how do you propose to dispose of the rest of it?"

When the second invoice of cockleburrs arrived Johnny loaded them and the remainder of the shoes into a schooner, and sailed down the coast to Alazan.

There, in the same dark and diabolical manner, he repeated his success: and came back with a bag of money and not so much as a shoestring.

And then he besought his great Uncle of the waving goatee and starred vest to accept his resignation, for the lotus no longer lured him. He hankered for the spinach and cress of Dalesburg.

The services of Mr. William Terence Keogh as acting consul, *pro tem.*, were suggested and accepted, and Johnny sailed with the Hemstetters back to his native shores.

Keogh slipped into the sinecure of the American consulship with the ease that never left him even in such high places. The tintype establishment was soon to become a thing of the past, although its deadly work along the peaceful and helpless Spanish Main was never effaced. The restless partners were about to be off again, scouting ahead of the slow ranks of Fortune. But now they would take different ways. There were rumours of a promising uprising in Peru; and thither the martial Clancy would turn his adventurous steps. As for Keogh, he was figuring in his mind and on quires of Government letter-heads a scheme that dwarfed the art of misrepresenting the human countenance upon tin.

"What suits me," Keogh used to say, "in the way of a business proposition is something diversified that looks like a longer shot than it is—something in the way of a genteel graft that isn't worked enough for the correspondence schools to be teaching it by mail. I take the long end; but I like to have at least as good a chance to win as a man learning to play poker on an ocean steamer, or running for governor of Texas on the Republican ticket. And when I cash in my winnings I don't want to find any widows' and orphans' chips in my stack."

The grass-grown globe was the green table on which Keogh gambled. The games he played were of his own invention. He was no grubber after the diffident dollar. Nor did he care to follow it with horn and hounds. Rather he loved to coax it with egregious and brilliant flies from its habitat in the waters of strange streams. Yet Keogh was a business man; and his schemes, in spite of their singularity, were as solidly set as the plans of a building contractor. In Arthur's time Sir William Keogh would have been a Knight of the Round Table. In these modern days he rides abroad, seeking the Graft instead of the Grail.

Three days after Johnny's departure, two small schooners appeared off Coralio. After some delay a boat put off from one of them, and brought a sunburned young man ashore. This young man had a shrewd and calculating eye; and he gazed with amazement at the strange things that he saw. He found on the beach some one who directed him to the consul's office; and thither he made his way at a nervous gait.

Keogh was sprawled in the official chair, drawing caricatures of his Uncle's head on an official pad of paper. He looked up at his visitor.

"Where's Johnny Atwood?" inquired the sunburned young man, in a business tone.

"Gone," said Keogh, working carefully at Uncle Sam's necktie.

"That's just like him," remarked the nut-brown one, leaning against the table. "He always was a fellow to gallivant around instead of 'tending to business. Will he be in soon?"

"Don't think so," said Keogh, after a fair amount of deliberation.

"I s'pose he's out at some of his tomfoolery," conjectured the visitor, in a tone of virtuous conviction. "Johnny never would stick to anything long enough to succeed. I wonder how he manages to run his business here, and never be 'round to look after it."

"I'm looking after the business just now," admitted the *pro tem.* consul.

"Are you?—then, say!—where's the factory?"

"What factory?" asked Keogh, with mildly polite interest.

"Why, the factory where they use them cockleburrs. Lord knows what they use 'em for, anyway! I've got the basements of both them ships out there loaded with 'em. I'll give you a bargain in this lot. I've had every man, woman and child around Dalesburg that wasn't busy pickin' 'em for a month. I hired these ships to bring 'em over. Everybody thought I was crazy. Now, you can have this lot for fifteen cents a pound, delivered on land. And if you want more I guess old Alabam' can come up to the demand. Johnny told me when he left home that if he struck anything down here that there was any money in he'd let me in on it. Shall I drive the ships in and hitch?"

A look of supreme, almost incredulous, delight dawned in Keogh's ruddy countenance. He dropped his pencil. His eyes turned upon the sunburned young man with joy in them mingled with fear lest his ecstasy should prove a dream.

"For God's sake tell me," said Keogh, earnestly, "are you Dink Pawson?"

"My name is Pinkney Dawson," said the cornerer of the cockleburr market.

Billy Keogh slid rapturously and gently from his chair to his favourite strip of matting on the floor.

There were not many sounds in Coralio on that sultry

afternoon. Among those that were may be mentioned a noise of enraptured and unrighteous laughter from a prostrate Irish-American, while a sunburned young man, with a shrewd eye, looked on him with wonder and amazement. Also the "tramp, tramp, tramp" of many well-shod feet in the streets outside. Also the lonesome wash of the waves that beat along the historic shores of the Spanish Main.

A Ruler of Men

I WALKED the streets of the City of Insolence, thirsting for the sight of a stranger face. For the City is a desert of familiar types as thick and alike as the grains in a sand-storm; and you grow to hate them as you do a friend who is always by you, or one of your own kin.

And my desire was granted, for I saw, near a corner of Broadway and Twenty-ninth Street, a little flaxen-haired man with a face like a scaly-bark hickory-nut, selling to a fast-gathering crowd a tool that omnigeneously proclaimed itself a can-opener, a screw-driver, a button-hook, a nail-file, a shoe-horn, a watch-guard, a potato-peeler, and an ornament to any gentleman's key-ring.

And then a stall-fed cop shoved himself through the congregation of customers. The vender, plainly used to having his seasons of trade thus abruptly curtailed, closed his satchel and slipped like a weasel through the opposite segment of the circle. The crowd scurried aimlessly away like ants from a disturbed crumb. The cop, suddenly becoming oblivious of the earth and its inhabitants, stood still, swelling his bulk and putting his club through an intricate drill of twirls. I hurried after Kansas Bill Bowers, and caught him by an arm.

Without his looking at me or slowing his pace, I found a five-dollar bill crumpled neatly into my hand.

"I wouldn't have thought, Kansas Bill," I said, "that you'd hold an old friend that cheap."

Then he turned his head, and the hickory-nut cracked into a wide smile.

"Give back the money," said he, "or I'll have the cop after you for false pretenses. I thought you was the cop."

"I want to talk to you, Bill," I said. "When did you leave Oklahoma? Where is Reddy McGill now? Why are you selling those impossible contraptions on the street? How did your Big Horn gold-mine pan out? How did you get so badly sunburned? What will you drink?"

"A year ago," answered Kansas Bill systematically. "Putting

up windmills in Arizona. For pin money to buy etceteras with. Salted. Been down in the tropics. Beer."

We foregathered in a propitious place and became Elijahs, while a waiter of dark plumage played the raven to perfection. Reminiscence needs must be had before I could steer Bill into his epic mood.

"Yes," said he, "I mind the time Timoteo's rope broke on that cow's horns while the calf was chasing you. You and that cow! I'd never forget it."

"The tropics," said I, "are a broad territory. What part of Cancer or Capricorn have you been honoring with a visit?"

"Down along China or Peru—or maybe the Argentine Con-federacy," said Kansas Bill. "Anyway 'twas among a great race of people, off-colored but progressive. I was there three months."

"No doubt you are glad to be back among the truly great race," I surmised. "Especially among New Yorkers, the most progressive and independent citizens of any country in the world," I continued, with the fatuity of the provincial who has eaten the Broadway lotus.

"Do you want to start an argument?" asked Bill.

"Can there be one?" I answered.

"Has an Irishman humor, do you think?" asked he.

"I have an hour or two to spare," said I, looking at the café clock.

"Not that the Americans aren't a great commercial nation," conceded Bill. "But the fault laid with the people who wrote lies for fiction."

"What was this Irishman's name?" I asked.

"Was that last beer cold enough?" said he.

"I see there is talk of further outbreak among the Russian peasants," I remarked.

"His name was Barney O'Connor," said Bill.

Thus, because of our ancient prescience of each other's trail of thought, we traveled ambiguously to the point where Kansas Bill's story began:

"I met O'Connor in a boarding-house on the West Side. He invited me to his hall-room to have drink, and we became like a dog and a cat that had been raised together. There he sat, a tall, fine, handsome man, with his feet against one wall and his back against the other, looking over a map. On the bed and sticking three feet out of it was a beautiful gold sword with tassels on it and rhinestones in the handle.

"'What is this?' says I (for by that time we were well acquainted). 'The annual parade in vilification of the ex-snakes of Ireland? And what's the line of march? Up Broadway to Forty-second; thence east to McCarty's café; thence——'

"'Sit down on the wash-stand,' says O'Connor, 'and listen. And cast no perversions on the sword. 'Twas me father's in old Munster. And this map, Bowers, is no diagram of a holiday procession. If ye look again ye'll see that it's the continent known as South America, comprising fourteen green, blue, red, and yellow countries, all crying out from time to time to be liberated from the yoke of the oppressor.'

"'I know,' says I to O'Connor. 'The idea is a literary one. The ten-cent magazines stole it from "Ridpath's History of the World from the Sandstone Period to the Equator." You'll find it in every one of 'em. It's a continued story of a soldier of fortune, generally named O'Keefe, who gets to be dictator while the Spanish-American populace cries "*Cospetto!*" and other Italian maledictions. I misdoubt if it's ever been done. You're not thinking of trying that, are you, Barney?' I asks.

"'Bowers,' says he, 'you're a man of education and courage.'

"'How can I deny it?' says I. 'Education runs in my family; and I have acquired courage by a hard struggle with life.'

"'The O'Connors,' says he, 'are a warlike race. There is me father's sword; and here is the map. A life of inaction is not for me. The O'Connors were born to rule. 'Tis a ruler of men I must be.'

"'Barney,' I says to him, 'why don't you get on the force and settle down to a quiet life of carnage and corruption instead of roaming off to foreign parts? In what better way can you indulge your desire to subdue and maltreat the oppressed?'

"'Look again at the map,' says he, 'at the country I have the point of me knife on. 'Tis that one I have selected to aid and overthrow with me father's sword.'

"'I see,' says I. 'It's the green one; and that does credit to your patriotism. And it's the smallest one; and that does credit to your judgment.'

"'Do ye accuse me of cowardice?' says Barney, turning pink.

"'No man,' says I, 'who attacks and confiscates a country single-handed could be called a coward. The worst you can be charged with is plagiarism or imitation. If Anthony Hope and Roosevelt let you get away with it, nobody else will have any right to kick.'

"'I'm not joking,' says O'Connor. 'And I've got $1,500 cash to work the scheme with. I've taken a liking to you. Do you want in, or not?'

"'I'm not working,' I told him; 'but how is it to be? Do I eat during the fomentation of the insurrection, or am I only to be Secretary of War after the country is conquered? Is it to be a pay envelope or only a portfolio?'

"'I'll pay all expenses,' says O'Connor. 'I want a man I can trust. If we succeed you may pick out any appointment you want in the gift of the government.'

"'All right, then,' says I. 'You can get me a bunch of draying contracts and then a quick-action consignment to a seat on the Supreme Court bench so I won't be in line for the presidency. I wouldn't mind Uncle Joe, but the kind of cannon they chasten their presidents with in that country hurt too much. You can consider me on the payroll.'

"Two weeks afterward O'Connor and me took a steamer for the small, green, doomed country. We were three weeks on the trip. O'Connor said he had his plans all figured out in advance; but being the commanding general, it consorted with his dignity to keep the details concealed from his army and cabinet, commonly known as William T. Bowers. Three dollars a day was the price for which I joined the cause of liberating an undiscovered country from the ills that threatened or sustained it. Every Saturday night on the steamer I stood in line at parade rest, and O'Connor handed over the twenty-one dollars.

"The town we landed at was named Guayaquerita, so they told me. 'Not for me,' says I. 'It'll be little old Hilldale or Tompkinsville or Cherry Tree Corners when I speak of it. It's a clear case where Brander Matthews and Andy ought to butt in and disenvowel it.'

"But the town looked fine from the bay when we sailed in. It was white, with green ruching, and lace ruffles on the skirt when the surf slashed up on the sand. It looked as tropical and *dolce far ultra* as the pictures of Lake Ronkonkoma in the brochure of the passenger department of the Long Island Railroad.

"We went through the quarantine and custom-house indignities; and then O'Connor leads me to a 'dobe house on a street called 'The Avenue of the Dolorous Butterflies of the Individual and Collective Saints.' Ten feet wide it was, and knee-deep in alfalfa and cigar stumps.

"'Hooligan Alley,' says I, rechristening it.

"''Twill be our headquarters,' says O'Connor. 'My agent here, Don Fernando Pacheco, secured it for us.'

"So in that house O'Connor and me established the revolutionary center. In the front room we had ostensible things such as fruit, a guitar, and a table with a conch shell on it. In the back room O'Connor had his desk and a large looking-glass and his sword hid in a roll of straw matting. We slept on hammocks that we hung to hooks in the wall; and took our meals at the Hotel Ingles, a beanery run on the American plan by a German proprietor with Chinese cooking served *à la* Kansas City, Clinton & Springfield Railroad lunch-counter *table d'hôte*.

"It seems that O'Connor really did have some sort of system planned out beforehand. He wrote plenty of letters; and every day or two some native gent would stroll around to headquarters and be shut up in the back room for half an hour with O'Connor and the interpreter. I noticed that when they went in they were always smoking eight-inch cigars and at peace with the world; but when they came out they would be folding up a ten- or twenty-dollar bill and cursing the government horribly.

"One evening after we had been in Guaya—in this town of Smellville-by-the-Sea—about a month, and me and O'Connor were sitting outside the door helping along old *tempus fugit* with rum and ice and limes, I says to him:

"'If you'll excuse a patriot that don't exactly know what he's patronizing, for the question—what is your scheme for subjugating this country? Do you intend to plunge it into bloodshed, or do you mean to buy its votes peacefully and honorably at the polls?'

"'Bowers,' says he, 'ye're a fine little man and I intend to make great use of ye after the conflict. But ye do not understand statecraft. Already by now we have a network of strategy clutching with invisible fingers at the throat of the tyrant Calderas. We have agents at work in every town in the republic. The Liberal party is bound to win. On our secret lists we have the names of enough sympathizers to crush the administration forces at a single blow.'

"'A straw vote,' says I, 'only shows which way the hot air blows.'

"'Who has accomplished this?' goes on O'Connor. 'I have. I have directed everything. The time was ripe when we came, so my agents inform me. The people are groaning under their burden of taxes and levies. Who will be their natural leader when they rise? Could it be any one but meself? 'Twas only yesterday that Zaldas, our representative in the province of Durasnas, tells me that the people, in secret, already call me "El Library Door," which is the Spanish manner of saying "the Liberator."'

"'Was Zaldas that maroon-colored old Aztec with a paper collar on and unbleached domestic shoes?' I asked.

"'He was,' says O'Connor.

"'I saw him tucking a yellow-back in his vest pocket as he came out,' says I. 'It may be,' says I, 'that they call you a library door, but they treat you more like the side door of a bank. But let us hope for the worst.'

"'It has cost money, of course,' says O'Connor; 'but we'll have the country in our hands inside of a month.'

"In the evenings we walked about in the plaza and listened to the band playing and mingled with the populace at its distressing and obnoxious pleasures. There were thirteen vehicles belonging to the upper classes, mostly rockaways and old-style barouches, such as the mayor rides in at the unveiling of the new poorhouse at Milledgeville, Alabama. Round and round the desiccated fountain in the middle of the plaza they drove, and lifted their high silk hats to their friends. The common people walked around in barefooted bunches, puffing stogies that a Pittsburg millionaire wouldn't have chewed for a dry smoke on Ladies' Day at his club. And the grandest figure in the whole turnout was Barney O'Connor. Six foot two he stood in his Fifth Avenue clothes, with his eagle eye and his black mustache that tickled his ears. He was a born dictator and czar and hero and harrier of the human race. It looked to me that all eyes were turned upon O'Connor, and that every woman there loved him and every man feared him. Once or twice I looked at him and thought of funnier things that had happened than his winning out in his game; and I began to feel like a Hidalgo de Officio de Grafto de South America myself. And then I would come down again to solid bottom and let my imagination gloat, as usual, upon the twenty-one American dollars due me on Saturday night.

"'Take note,' says O'Connor to me as thus we walked, 'of the mass of the people. Observe their oppressed and melancholy air. Can ye not see that they are ripe for revolt? Do ye not perceive that they are disaffected?'

"'I do not,' says I. 'Nor disinfected either. I'm beginning to understand these people. When they look unhappy they're enjoying themselves. When they feel unhappy they go to sleep. They're not the kind of people to take an interest in revolutions.'

"'They'll flock to our standard,' says O'Connor. 'Three thousand men in this town alone will spring to arms when the signal is given. I am assured of that. But everything is in secret. There is no chance for us to fail.'

"On Hooligan Alley, as I prefer to call the street our headquarters was on, there was a row of flat 'dobe houses with red tile roofs, some straw shacks full of Indians and dogs, and one two-story wooden house with balconies a little farther down. That was where General Tumbalo, the comandante and commander of the military forces, lived. Right across the street was a private residence built like a combination bake-oven and folding-bed. One day O'Connor and me were passing it, single file, on the flange they called a sidewalk, when out of the window flies a big red rose. O'Connor, who is ahead, picks it up, presses it to his fifth rib, and bows to the ground. By *carrambos!* that man certainly had the Irish drama chauncey-ized. I looked around expecting to see the little boy and girl in white sateen ready to jump on his shoulder while he jolted their spinal columns and ribs together through a breakdown and sang: 'Sleep, Little One, Sleep.'

"As I passed the window I glanced inside and caught a glimpse of a white dress and a pair of big, flashing black eyes and gleaming teeth under a dark lace mantilla.

"When we got back to our house O'Connor began to walk up and down the floor and twist his mustaches.

"'Did ye see her eyes, Bowers?' he asks me.

"'I did,' says I, 'and I can see more than that. It's all coming out according to the story-books. I knew there was something missing. 'Twas the love interest. What is it that comes in Chapter VII to cheer the gallant Irish adventurer? Why, Love, of course—Love that makes the hat go round. At last we have the eyes of midnight hue and the rose flung from the barred window. Now, what comes next? The underground passage—the intercepted letter—the traitor in camp—the hero thrown into a dungeon—the mysterious message from the señorita—then the outburst—the fighting on the plaza—the——'

"'Don't be a fool,' says O'Connor, interrupting. 'But that's the only woman in the world for me, Bowers. The O'Connors are as quick to love as they are to fight. I shall wear that rose over me heart when I lead me men into action. For a good battle to be fought there must be some woman to give it power.'

"'Every time,' I agreed. 'If you want to have a good, lively scrap. There's only one thing bothering me. In the novels the light-haired friend of the hero always gets killed. Think 'em all over that you've read, and you'll see that I'm right. I think I'll step down to the Botica Española and lay in a bottle of walnut stain before war is declared.'

"'How will I find out her name?' says O'Connor, laying his chin in his hand.

"'Why don't you go across the street and ask her?' says I.

"'Will ye never regard anything in life seriously?' says O'Connor, looking down at me like a schoolmaster.

"'Maybe she meant the rose for me,' I said, whistling the Spanish Fandango.

"For the first time since I'd known O'Connor, he laughed. He got up and roared and clapped his knees, and leaned against the wall till the tiles on the roof clattered to the noise of his lungs. He went into the back room and looked at himself in the glass and began and laughed all over from the beginning again. Then he looked at me and repeated himself. That's why I asked you if you thought an Irishman had any humor. He'd been doing farce comedy from the day I saw him without knowing it; and the first time he had an idea advanced to him with any intelligence in it he acted like two twelfths of the sextet in a 'Florodora' road company.

"The next afternoon he comes in with a triumphant smile, and begins to pull something like ticker tape out of his pocket.

"'Great!' says I. 'This is something like home. How is Amalgamated Copper to-day?'

"'I've got her name,' says O'Connor, and he reads off something like this: 'Doña Isabel Antonia Inez Lolita Carreras y Buencaminos y Monteleon.' 'She lives with her mother,' explains O'Connor. 'Her father was killed in the last revolution. She is sure to be in sympathy with our cause.'

"And sure enough the next day she flung a little bunch of roses clear across the street into our door. O'Connor dived for it and found a piece of paper curled around a stem with a line in Spanish on it. He dragged the interpreter out of his corner and got him busy. The interpreter scratched his head, and gave us as a translation three best bets: 'Fortune has got a face like the man fighting'; 'Fortune looks like a brave man'; and 'Fortune favors the brave.' We put our money on the last one.

"'Do ye see?' said O'Connor. 'She intends to encourage me sword to save her country.'

"'It looks to me like an invitation to supper,' says I.

"So, every day this señorita sits behind the barred windows and exhausts a conservatory or two, one posy at a time. And O'Connor walks like a Dominecker rooster and swells his chest and swears to me he will win her by feats of arms and big deeds on the gory field of battle.

"By and by the revolution began to get ripe. One day O'Connor takes me into the back room and tells me all.

"'Bowers,' says he, 'at twelve o'clock one week from to-day the struggle will take place. It has pleased ye to find amusement and diversion in this project because ye have not sense enough to perceive that it is easily accomplished by a man of courage, intelligence, and historical superiority, such as meself. The whole world over,' says he, 'the O'Connors have ruled men, women, and nations. To subdue a small and indifferent country like this is a trifle. Ye see what little, barefooted manikins the men of it are. I could lick four of 'em, single-handed.'

"'No doubt,' says I. 'But could you lick six? And suppose they hurled an army of seventeen against you?'

"'Listen,' says O'Connor, 'to what will occur. At noon next Tuesday 25,000 patriots will rise up in the towns of the republic. The government will be absolutely unprepared. The public buildings will be taken, the regular army made prisoners, and the new administration set up. In the capital it will not be so easy on account of most of the army being stationed there. They will occupy the president's palace and the strongly fortified government buildings and stand a siege. But on the very day of the outbreak a body of our troops will begin a march to the capital from every town as soon as the local victory has been won. The thing is so well planned that it is an impossibility for us to fail. I meself will lead the troops from here. The new president will be Señor Espadas, now Minister of Finance in the present cabinet.'

"'What do you get?' I asked.

"''Twill be strange,' said O'Connor, smiling, 'if I don't have all the jobs handed to me on a silver salver to pick what I choose. I've been the brains of the scheme, and when the fighting opens I guess I won't be in the rear rank. Who managed it so our troops could get arms smuggled into this country? Didn't I arrange it with a New York firm before I left there? Our financial agents inform me that 20,000 stands of Winchester rifles have been delivered a month ago at a secret place up coast and distributed among the towns. I tell you, Bowers, the game is already won.'

"Well, that kind of talk kind of shook my disbelief in the infallibility of the serious Irish gentleman soldier of fortune. It certainly seemed that the patriotic grafters had gone about the thing in a business way. I looked upon O'Connor with more respect, and began to figure on what kind of uniform I might wear as Secretary of War.

"Tuesday, the day set for the revolution, came around according to schedule. O'Connor said that a signal had been agreed upon for the uprising. There was an old cannon on the beach near the national warehouse. That had been secretly loaded, and promptly at twelve o'clock was to be fired off. Immediately the revolutionists would seize their concealed arms, attack the comandante's troops in the *cuartel*, and capture the custom-house and all government property and supplies.

"I was nervous all the morning. And about eleven o'clock

O'Connor became infused with the excitement and martial spirit of murder. He geared his father's sword around him, and walked up and down in the back room like a lion in the Zoo suffering from corns. I smoked a couple of dozen cigars, and decided on yellow stripes down the trousers legs of my uniform.

"At half-past eleven O'Connor asks me to take a short stroll through the streets to see if I could notice any signs of the uprising. I was back in fifteen minutes.

"'Did you hear anything?' he asks.

"'I did,' says I. 'At first I thought it was drums. But it wasn't; it was snoring. Everybody in town's asleep.'

"O'Connor tears out his watch.

"'Fools!' says he. 'They've set the time right at the siesta hour when everybody takes a nap. But the cannon will wake 'em up. Everything will be all right, depend upon it.'

"Just at twelve o'clock we heard the sound of a cannon— BOOM!—shaking the whole town.

"O'Connor loosens his sword in its scabbard and jumps for the door. I went as far as the door and stood in it.

"People were sticking their heads out of doors and windows. But there was one grand sight that made the landscape look tame.

"General Tumbalo, the comandante, was rolling down the steps of his residential dugout, waving a five-foot saber in his hand. He wore his cocked and plumed hat and his dress-parade coat covered with gold braid and buttons. Sky-blue pajamas, one rubber boot, and one red-plush slipper completed his make-up.

"The general had heard the cannon, and he puffed down the sidewalk toward the soldiers' barracks as fast as his rudely awakened two hundred pounds could travel.

"O'Connor sees him and lets out a battle-cry, and draws his father's sword and rushes across the street and tackles the enemy.

"Right there in the street he and the general gave an exhibition of blacksmithing and butchery that put Kyrle Bellew and Phil Armour in the shade. Sparks flew from their blades, the general roared, and O'Connor gave the slogan of his race and proclivities.

"Then the general's saber broke in two; and he took to

his ginger-colored heels crying out '*Policios*' at every jump. O'Connor chased him a block, imbued with the sentiment of manslaughter, and slicing buttons off the general's coat tails with the paternal weapon. At the corner five barefooted policemen in cotton undershirts and straw hats climbed over O'Connor and subjugated him according to the municipal statutes.

"They brought him past the late revolutionary headquarters on the way to jail. I stood in the door. A policeman had him by each hand and foot, and they dragged him on his back through the grass like a turtle. Twice they stopped, and the odd policeman took another's place while he rolled a cigarette. The great soldier of fortune turned his head and looked at me as they passed. I blushed, and lit another cigar. The procession passed on, and at ten minutes past twelve everybody had gone back to sleep again.

"In the afternoon the interpreter came around, and smiled as he laid his hand on the big red jar we usually kept ice-water in.

"'The ice man didn't call to-day,' says I. 'What's the matter with everything, Sancho?'

"'Ah, yes,' says the liver-colored linguist. 'They just tell me in the town. Verree bad act that Señor O'Connor make fight with General Tumbola. Yes. General Tumbola great soldier and big mans.'

"'What'll they do to Mr. O'Connor?' I asks.

"'I talk little while presently with the *Juez de la Paz*—what you call Justice-with-the-peace,' says Sancho. 'He tell me it verree bad crime that one señor Americano try kill General Tumbola. He say they keep Señor O'Connor in jail six month; then have trial and shoot him with guns. Verree sorree.'

"'How about this revolution that was to be pulled off?' I asks.

"'Oh,' says this Sancho, 'I think too hot weather for revolution. Revolution better in winter-time. Maybe so next winter. *Quien sabe?*'

"'But the cannon went off,' says I. 'The signal was given.'

"'That big sound?' says Sancho, grinning. 'The boiler in ice factory he blow up—BOOM! Wake everybody up from siesta. Verree sorree. No ice. *Mucho* hot day.'

"About sunset I went over to the jail, and they let me talk to O'Connor through the bars.

"'What's the news, Bowers?' says he. 'Have we taken the town? I've been expecting a rescue party all the afternoon. I haven't heard any firing. Has any word been received from the capital?'

"'Take it easy, Barney,' says I. 'I think there's been a change of plans. There's something more important to talk about. Have you any money?'

"'I have not,' says O'Connor. 'The last dollar went to pay our hotel bill yesterday. Did our troops capture the custom-house? There ought to be plenty of government money there.'

"'Segregate your mind from battles,' says I. 'I've been making inquiries. You're to be shot six months from date for assault and battery. I'm expecting to receive fifty years at hard labor for vagrancy. All they furnish you while you're a prisoner is water. You depend on your friends for food. I'll see what I can do.'

"I went away and found a silver Chile dollar in an old vest of O'Connor's. I took him some fried fish and rice for his supper. In the morning I went down to a lagoon and had a drink of water, and then went back to the jail. O'Connor had a porterhouse-steak look in his eye.

"'Barney,' says I, 'I've found a pond full of the finest kind of water. It's the grandest, sweetest, purest water in the world. Say the word and I'll go fetch you a bucket of it, and you can throw this vile government stuff out the window. I'll do anything I can for a friend.'

"'Has it come to this?' says O'Connor, raging up and down his cell. 'Am I to be starved to death and then shot? I'll make those traitors feel the weight of an O'Connor's hand when I get out of this.' And then he comes to the bars and speaks softer. 'Has nothing been heard from Doña Isabel?' he asks. 'Though every one else in the world fail,' says he, 'I trust those eyes of hers. She will find a way to effect me release. Do ye think ye could communicate with her? One word from her—even a rose would make me sorrows light. But don't let her know except with the utmost delicacy, Bowers. These high-bred Castilians are sensitive and proud.'

"'Well said, Barney,' says I. 'You've given me an idea. I'll report later. Something's got to be pulled off quick, or we'll both starve.'

"I walked out, and down to Hooligan Alley, and then on

the other side of the street. As I went past the window of Doña Isabel Antonia Concha Regalia, out flies the rose as usual and hits me on the ear.

"The door was open, and I took off my hat and walked in. It wasn't very light inside, but there she sat in a rocking-chair by the window smoking a black cheroot. And when I got closer I saw that she was about thirty-nine, and had never seen a straight front in her life. I sat down on the arm of her chair, and took the cheroot out of her mouth and stole a kiss.

"'Hullo, Izzy,' I says. 'Excuse my unconventionality, but I feel like I have known you for a month. Whose Izzy is oo?'

"The lady ducked her head under her mantilla, and drew in a long breath. I thought she was going to scream, but with all that intake of air she only came out with: 'Me likee Americanos.'

"As soon as she said that I knew that O'Connor and me would be doing things with a knife and fork before the day was over. I drew a chair beside her, and inside of half an hour we were engaged. Then I took my hat and said I must go out for a while.

"'You come back?' says Izzy, in alarm.

"'Me go bring preacher,' says I. 'Come back twenty minutes. We marry now. How you likee?'

"'Marry to-day?' says Izzy. 'Good!'

"I went down on the beach to the United States consul's shack. He was a grizzly man, eighty-two pounds, smoked glasses, five foot eleven, pickled. He was playing chess with an india-rubber man in white clothes.

"'Excuse me for interrupting,' says I, 'but can you tell me how a man could get married quick?'

"The consul gets up and fingers in a pigeonhole.

"'I believe I had a license to perform the ceremony myself, a year or two ago,' he said. 'I'll look, and——'

"I caught hold of his arm.

"'Don't look it up,' says I. 'Marriage is a lottery anyway. I'm willing to take the risk about the license if you are.'

"The consul went back to Hooligan Alley with me. Izzy called her ma to come in, but the old lady was picking a chicken in the patio and begged to be excused. So we stood up, and the consul performed the ceremony.

"That evening Mrs. Bowers cooked a great supper of stewed

goat, tamales, baked bananas, fricasseed red peppers, and coffee. Afterward I sat in the rocking-chair by the front window,
and she sat on the floor plunking at a guitar and happy, as she
should be, as Mrs. William T. B.

"All at once I sprang up in a hurry. I'd forgotten all about
O'Connor. I asked Izzy to fix up a lot of truck for him to eat.

"'That big, oogly man?' says Izzy. 'But all right—he your
friend.'

"I pulled a rose out of a bunch in a jar, and took the
grub-basket around to the jail. O'Connor ate like a wolf. Then
he wiped his face with a banana peel and said: 'Have you heard
nothing from Doña Isabel yet?'

"'Hist!' says I, slipping the rose between the bars. 'She sends
you this. She bids you take courage. At nightfall two masked
men brought it to the ruined château in the orange grove.
How did you like that goat hash, Barney?'

"O'Connor pressed the rose to his lips.

"'This is more to me than all the food in the world,' says he.
'But the supper was fine. Where did you raise it?'

"'I've negotiated a stand-off at a delicatessen hut down-town,'
I tells him. 'Rest easy. If there's anything to be done I'll do it.'

"So things went along that way for some weeks. Izzy was a
great cook; and if she had had a little more poise of character
and smoked a little better brand of tobacco we might have
drifted into some sense of responsibility for the honor I'd
conferred on her. But as time went on I began to hunger for
the sight of a real lady standing before me in a street-car. All
I was staying in that land of bilk and money for was because I
couldn't get away, and I thought it no more than decent to stay
and see O'Connor shot.

"One day our old interpreter drops around and after smoking an hour says that the judge of the peace sent him to request
me to call on him. I went to his office in a lemon grove on a
hill at the edge of town; and there I had a surprise. I expected
to see one of the usual cinnamon-colored natives in congress
gaiters and one of Pizarro's cast-off hats. What I saw was an
elegant gentleman of a slightly claybank complexion sitting
in an upholstered leather chair, sipping a highball and reading
Mrs. Humphry Ward. I had smuggled into my brain a few

words of Spanish by the help of Izzy, and I began to remark in a rich Andalusian brogue:

"*'Buenas dias, señor. Yo tengo—y tengo—*'

"'Oh, sit down, Mr. Bowers,' says he. 'I spent eight years in your country in colleges and law schools. Let me mix you a highball. Lemon peel, or not?'

"Thus we got along. In about half an hour I was beginning to tell him about the scandal in our family when Aunt Elvira ran away with a Cumberland Presbyterian preacher. Then he says to me:

"'I sent for you, Mr. Bowers, to let you know that you can have your friend Mr. O'Connor now. Of course we had to make a show of punishing him on account of his attack on General Tumbalo. It is arranged that he shall be released to-morrow night. You and he will be conveyed on board the fruit steamer Voyager, bound for New York, which lies in the harbor. Your passage will be arranged for.'

"'One moment, judge,' says I; 'that revolution——'

"The judge lays back in his chair and howls.

"'Why,' says he presently, 'that was all a little joke fixed up by the boys around the court-room, and one or two of our cut-ups, and a few clerks in the stores. The town is bursting its sides with laughing. The boys made themselves up to be conspirators, and they—what you call it?—stick Señor O'Connor for his money. It is very funny.'

"'It was,' says I. 'I saw the joke all along. I'll take another highball, if your Honor don't mind.'

"The next evening, just at dark, a couple of soldiers brought O'Connor down to the beach where I was waiting under a cocoanut-tree.

"'Hist!' says I in his ear; 'Doña Isabel has arranged our escape. Not a word!'

"They rowed us in a boat out to a little steamer that smelled of *table d'hôte* salad oil and bone phosphate.

"The great, mellow, tropical moon was rising as we steamed away. O'Connor leaned on the taffrail or rear balcony of the ship and gazed silently at Guaya—at Buncoville-on-the-Beach. He had the red rose in his hand.

"'She will wait,' I heard him say. 'Eyes like hers never deceive.

But I shall see her again. Traitors cannot keep an O'Connor down forever.'

"'You talk like a sequel,' says I. 'But in Volume II please omit the light-haired friend who totes the grub to the hero in his dungeon cell.'

"And thus reminiscing, we came back to New York."

There was a little silence broken only by the familiar roar of the streets after Kansas Bill Bowers ceased talking.

"Did O'Connor ever go back?" I asked.

"He attained his heart's desire," said Bill. "Can you walk two blocks? I'll show you."

He led me eastward and down a flight of stairs that was covered by a curious-shaped, glowing, pagoda-like structure. Signs and figures on the tiled walls and supporting columns attested that we were in the Grand Central station of the subway. Hundreds of people were on the midway platform.

An up-town express dashed up and halted. It was crowded. There was a rush for it by a still larger crowd.

Towering above every one there a magnificent, broad-shouldered, athletic man leaped into the center of the struggle. Men and women he seized in either hand and hurled them like manikins toward the open gates of the train.

Now and then some passenger with a shred of soul and self-respect left to him turned to offer remonstrance; but the blue uniform on the towering figure, the fierce and conquering glare of his eye, and the ready impact of his ham-like hands glued together the lips that would have spoken complaint.

When the train was full, then he exhibited to all who might observe and admire his irresistible genius as a ruler of men. With his knees, with his elbows, with his shoulders, with his resistless feet he shoved, crushed, slammed, heaved, kicked, flung, pounded the overplus of passengers aboard. Then with the sounds of its wheels drowned by the moans, shrieks, prayers, and curses of its unfortunate crew, the express dashed away.

"That's him. Ain't he a wonder?" said Kansas Bill admiringly. "That tropical country wasn't the place for him. I wish the distinguished traveler, writer, war correspondent, and playwright, Richmond Hobson Davis, could see him now. O'Connor ought to be dramatized."

"Next to Reading Matter"

HE COMPELLED my interest as he stepped from the ferry at Desbrosses Street. He had the air of being familiar with hemispheres and worlds, and of entering New York as the lord of a demesne who revisited it after years of absence. But I thought that, with all his air, he had never before set foot on the slippery cobblestones of the City of Too Many Caliphs.

He wore loose clothes of a strange bluish drab colour, and a conservative, round Panama hat without the cock-a-hoop indentations and cants with which Northern fanciers disfigure the tropic head-gear. Moreover, he was the homeliest man I have ever seen. His ugliness was less repellent than startling—arising from a sort of Lincolnian ruggedness and irregularity of feature that spellbound you with wonder and dismay. So may have looked afrites or the shapes metamorphosed from the vapour of the fisherman's vase. As he afterward told me, his name was Judson Tate; and he may as well be called so at once. He wore his green silk tie through a topaz ring; and he carried a cane made of the vertebræ of a shark.

Judson Tate accosted me with some large and casual inquiries about the city's streets and hotels, in the manner of one who had but for the moment forgotten the trifling details. I could think of no reason for dispraising my own quiet hotel in the downtown district; so the mid-morning of the night found us already victualed and drinked (at my expense), and ready to be chaired and tobaccoed in a quiet corner of the lobby.

There was something on Judson Tate's mind, and, such as it was, he tried to convey it to me. Already he had accepted me as his friend; and when I looked at his great, snuff-brown first-mate's hand, with which he brought emphasis to his periods, within six inches of my nose, I wondered if, by any chance, he was as sudden in conceiving enmity against strangers.

When this man began to talk I perceived in him a certain power. His voice was a persuasive instrument, upon which he played with a somewhat specious but effective art. He did not try to make you forget his ugliness; he flaunted it in your face and made it part of the charm of his speech. Shutting your eyes,

you would have trailed after this rat-catcher's pipes at least to
the walls of Hamelin. Beyond that you would have had to be
more childish to follow. But let him play his own tune to the
words set down, so that if all is too dull, the art of music may
bear the blame.

"Women," said Judson Tate, "are mysterious creatures."

My spirits sank. I was not there to listen to such a world-old
hypothesis—to such a time-worn, long-ago-refuted, bald, feeble, illogical, vicious, patent sophistry—to an ancient, baseless,
wearisome, ragged, unfounded, insidious falsehood originated
by women themselves, and by them insinuated, foisted, thrust,
spread, and ingeniously promulgated into the ears of mankind
by underhanded, secret, and deceptive methods, for the
purpose of augmenting, furthering, and reinforcing their own
charms and designs.

"Oh, I don't know!" said I, vernacularly.

"Have you ever heard of Oratama?" he asked.

"Possibly," I answered. "I seem to recall a toe dancer—or a
suburban addition—or was it a perfume?—of some such name."

"It is a town," said Judson Tate, "on the coast of a foreign
country of which you know nothing and could understand less.
It is a country governed by a dictator and controlled by revolutions and insubordination. It was there that a great life-drama
was played, with Judson Tate, the homeliest man in America,
and Fergus McMahan, the handsomest adventurer in history or
fiction, and Señorita Anahela Zamora, the beautiful daughter
of the alcalde of Oratama, as chief actors. And, another thing—
nowhere else on the globe except in the department of Trienta
y tres in Uruguay does the *chuchula* plant grow. The products
of the country I speak of are valuable woods, dyestuffs, gold,
rubber, ivory, and cocoa."

"I was not aware," said I, "that South America produced
any ivory."

"There you are twice mistaken," said Judson Tate, distributing the words over at least an octave of his wonderful voice. "I
did not say that the country I spoke of was in South America—I
must be careful, my dear man; I have been in politics there, you
know. But, even so—I have played chess against its president
with a set carved from the nasal bones of the tapir—one of
our native specimens of the order of *perissodactyle ungulates*

inhabiting the Cordilleras—which was as pretty ivory as you would care to see.

"But it was of romance and adventure and the ways of woman that I was going to tell you, and not of zoölogical animals.

"For fifteen years I was the ruling power behind old Sancho Benavides, the Royal High Thumbscrew of the republic. You 've seen his picture in the papers—a mushy black man with whiskers like the notes on a Swiss music-box cylinder, and a scroll in his right hand like the ones they write births on in the family Bible. Well, that chocolate potentate used to be the biggest item of interest anywhere between the colour line and the parallels of latitude. It was three throws, horses, whether he was to wind up in the Hall of Fame or the Bureau of Combustibles. He 'd have been sure called the Roosevelt of the Southern Continent if it had n't been that Grover Cleveland was President at the time. He 'd hold office a couple of terms, then he 'd sit out for a hand—always after appointing his own successor for the interims.

"But it was not Benavides, the Liberator, who was making all this fame for himself. Not him. It was Judson Tate. Benavides was only the chip over the bug. I gave him the tip when to declare war and increase import duties and wear his state trousers. But that was n't what I wanted to tell you. How did I get to be It? I 'll tell you. Because I 'm the most gifted talker that ever made vocal sounds since Adam first opened his eyes, pushed aside the smelling-salts, and asked: 'Where am I?'

"As you observe, I am about the ugliest man you ever saw outside of the gallery of photographs of the New England early Christian Scientists. So, at an early age, I perceived that what I lacked in looks I must make up in eloquence. That I 've done. I get what I go after. As the back-stop and still small voice of old Benavides I made all the great historical powers-behind-the-throne, such as Talleyrand, Mrs. de Pompadour, and Loeb, look as small as the minority report of a Duma. I could talk nations into or out of debt, harangue armies to sleep on the battlefield, reduce insurrections, inflammations, taxes, appropriations, or surpluses with a few words, and call up the dogs of war or the dove of peace with the same bird-like whistle. Beauty and epaulettes and curly moustaches and Grecian profiles in other men were never in my way. When people first look at me they shudder. Unless they are in the last stages of *angina pectoris* they are mine in ten minutes after I begin to talk. Women and men—I win 'em as they come. Now, you would n't think women would fancy a man with a face like mine, would you?"

"Oh, yes, Mr. Tate," said I. "History is bright and fiction dull with homely men who have charmed women. There seems——"

"Pardon me," interrupted Judson Tate, "but you don't quite understand. You have yet to hear my story.

"Fergus McMahan was a friend of mine in the capital. For a handsome man I 'll admit he was the duty-free merchandize. He had blond curls and laughing blue eyes and was featured regular. They said he was a ringer for the statue they call Herr Mees, the god of speech and eloquence resting in some museum at Rome. Some German anarchist, I suppose. They are always resting and talking.

"But Fergus was no talker. He was brought up with the idea that to be beautiful was to make good. His conversation was about as edifying as listening to a leak dropping in a tin dish-pan at the head of the bed when you want to go to sleep. But he and me got to be friends—maybe because we was so opposite, don't you think? Looking at the Hallowe'en mask that I call my face when I 'm shaving seemed to give Fergus pleasure; and I 'm sure that whenever I heard the feeble output of throat noises that he called conversation I felt contented to be a gargoyle with a silver tongue.

"One time I found it necessary to go down to this coast town of Oratama to straighten out a lot of political unrest and chop off a few heads in the customs and military departments. Fergus, who owned the ice and sulphur-match concessions of the republic, says he 'll keep me company.

"So, in a jangle of mule-train bells, we gallops into Oratama, and the town belonged to us as much as Long Island Sound does n't belong to Japan when T. R. is at Oyster Bay. I say us; but I mean me. Everybody for four nations, two oceans, one bay and isthmus, and five archipelagoes around had heard of Judson Tate. Gentleman adventurer, they called me. I had been written up in five columns of the yellow journals, 40,000 words (with marginal decorations) in a monthly magazine, and a stickful on the twelfth page of the New York *Times*. If the beauty of Fergus McMahan gained any part of our reception in Oratama, I 'll eat the price-tag in my Panama. It was me that they hung out paper flowers and palm branches for. I am not a jealous man; I am stating facts. The people were Nebuchadnez-zars; they bit the grass before me; there was no dust in the town for them to bite. They bowed down to Judson Tate. They knew that I was the power behind Sancho Benavides. A word from me was more to them than a whole deckle-edged library from East Aurora in sectional bookcases was from anybody else. And yet there are people who spend hours fixing their faces—rub-bing in cold cream and massaging the muscles (always toward the eyes) and taking in the slack with tincture of benzoin and electrolyzing moles—to what end? Looking handsome. Oh, what a mistake! It 's the larynx that the beauty doctors ought to work on. It 's words more than warts, talk more than talcum, palaver more than powder, blarney more than bloom that counts—the phonograph instead of the photograph. But I was going to tell you.

"The local Astors put me and Fergus up at the Centipede Club, a frame building built on posts sunk in the surf. The tide 's only nine inches. The Little Big High Low Jacks-in-the-game of the town came around and kowtowed. Oh, it was n't to Herr Mees. They had heard about Judson Tate.

"One afternoon me and Fergus McMahan was sitting on the seaward gallery of the Centipede, drinking iced rum and talking.

"'Judson,' says Fergus, 'there 's an angel in Oratama.'

"'So long,' says I, 'as it ain't Gabriel, why talk as if you had heard a trump blow?'

"'It 's the Señorita Anabela Zamora,' says Fergus. 'She 's—she 's—she 's as lovely as—as hell!'

"'Bravo!' says I, laughing heartily. 'You have a true lover's eloquence to paint the beauties of your inamorata. You remind me,' says I, 'of Faust's wooing of Marguerite—that is, if he wooed her after he went down the trap-door of the stage.'

"'Judson,' says Fergus, 'you know you are as beautiless as a rhinoceros. You can't have any interest in women. I 'm awfully gone on Miss Anabela. And that 's why I 'm telling you."

"'Oh, *seguramente*,' says I. 'I know I have a front elevation like an Aztec god that guards a buried treasure that never did exist in Jefferson County, Yucatan. But there are compensations. For instance, I am It in this country as far as the eye can reach, and then a few perches and poles. And again,' says I, 'when I engage people in a set-to of oral, vocal, and laryngeal utterances, I do not usually confine my side of the argument to what may be likened to a cheap phonographic reproduction of the ravings of a jellyfish.'

"'Oh, I know,' says Fergus, amiable, 'that I 'm not handy at small talk. Or large, either. That 's why I 'm telling you. I want you to help me.'

"'How can I do it?' I asked.

"'I have subsidized,' says Fergus, 'the services of Señorita Anabela's duenna, whose name is Francesca. You have a reputation in this country, Judson,' says Fergus, 'of being a great man and a hero.'

"'I have,' says I. 'And I deserve it.'

"'And I,' says Fergus, 'am the best-looking man between the arctic circle and the antarctic ice pack.'

"'With limitations,' says I, 'as to physiognomy and geography, I freely concede you to be.'

"'Between the two of us,' says Fergus, 'we ought to land the Señorita Anabela Zamora. The lady, as you know, is of an old Spanish family, and further than looking at her driving in the family *carruaje* of afternoons around the plaza, or catching a glimpse of her through a barred window of evenings, she is as unapproachable as a star.'

"'Land her for which one of us?' says I.

"'For me, of course,' says Fergus. 'You 've never seen her. Now, I 've had Francesca point me out to her as being you on several occasions. When she sees me on the plaza, she thinks she 's looking at Don Judson Tate, the greatest hero, statesman, and romantic figure in the country. With your reputation and my looks combined in one man, how can she resist him? She 's heard all about your thrilling history, of course. And she 's seen me. Can any woman want more?' asks Fergus McMahan.

"'Can she do with less?' I ask. 'How can we separate our mutual attractions, and how shall we apportion the proceeds?'

"Then Fergus tells me his scheme.

"The house of the alcalde, Don Luis Zamora, he says, has a *patio*, of course—a kind of inner courtyard opening from the street. In an angle of it is his daughter's window—as dark a place as you could find. And what do you think he wants me to do? Why, knowing my freedom, charm, and skilfulness of tongue, he proposes that I go into that *patio* at midnight, when the hobgoblin face of me cannot be seen, and make love to her for him—for the pretty man that she has seen on the plaza, thinking him to be Don Judson Tate.

"Why should n't I do it for him—for my friend, Fergus McMahan? For him to ask me was a compliment—an acknowledgment of his own shortcomings.

"'You little, lily-white, fine-haired, highly polished piece of dumb sculpture,' says I, 'I 'll help you. Make your arrangements and get me in the dark outside her window and my stream of conversation opened up with the moonlight tremolo stop turned on, and she 's yours.'

"'Keep your face hid, Jud,' says Fergus. 'For heaven's sake, keep your face hid. I 'm a friend of yours in all kinds of sentiment, but this is a business deal. If I could talk I would n't ask you. But seeing me and listening to you I don't see why she can't be landed.'

"'By you?' says I.

"'By me,' says Fergus.

"Well, Fergus and the duenna, Francesca, attended to the details. And one night they fetched me a long black cloak with a high collar, and led me to the house at midnight. I stood by the window in the *patio* until I heard a voice as soft and sweet as an angel's whisper on the other side of the bars. I could see only a faint, white clad shape inside; and, true to Fergus, I pulled the collar of my cloak high up, for it was July in the wet season, and the nights were chilly. And, smothering a laugh as I thought of the tongue-tied Fergus, I began to talk.

"Well, sir, I talked an hour at the Señorita Anabela. I say 'at' because it was not 'with.' Now and then she would say: 'Oh, Señor,' or 'Now, ain't you foolin'?' or 'I know you don't mean that,' and such things as women will when they are being rightly courted. Both of us knew English and Spanish; so in two languages I tried to win the heart of the lady for my friend

Fergus. But for the bars to the window I could have done it in one. At the end of the hour she dismissed me and gave me a big, red rose. I handed it over to Fergus when I got home.

"For three weeks every third or fourth night I impersonated my friend in the *patio* at the window of Señorita Anabela. At last she admitted that her heart was mine, and spoke of having seen me every afternoon when she drove in the plaza. It was Fergus she had seen, of course. But it was my talk that won her. Suppose Fergus had gone there and tried to make a hit in the dark with his beauty all invisible, and not a word to say for himself!

"On the last night she promised to be mine—that is, Fergus's. And she put her hand between the bars for me to kiss. I bestowed the kiss and took the news to Fergus.

"'You might have left that for me to do,' says he.

"'That 'll be your job hereafter,' says I. 'Keep on doing that and don't try to talk. Maybe after she thinks she 's in love she won't notice the difference between real conversation and the inarticulate sort of droning that you give forth.'

"Now, I had never seen Señorita Anabela. So, the next day Fergus asks me to walk with him through the plaza and view the daily promenade and exhibition of Oratama society, a sight that had no interest for me. But I went; and children and dogs took to the banana groves and mangrove swamps as soon as they had a look at my face.

"'Here she comes,' said Fergus, twirling his moustache—'the one in white, in the open carriage with the black horse.'

"I looked, and felt the ground rock under my feet. For Señorita Anabela Zamora was the most beautiful woman in the world, and the only one from that moment on, so far as Judson Tate was concerned. I saw at a glance that I must be hers and she mine forever. I thought of my face and nearly fainted; and then I thought of my other talents and stood upright again. And I had been wooing her for three weeks for another man!

"As Señorita Anabela's carriage rolled slowly past, she gave Fergus a long, soft glance from the corners of her night-black eyes, a glance that would have sent Judson Tate up into heaven in a rubber-tired chariot. But she never looked at me. And that handsome man only ruffles his curls and smirks and prances like a lady-killer at my side.

"'What do you think of her, Judson?' asks Fergus, with an air.

"'This much,' says I. 'She is to be Mrs. Judson Tate. I am no man to play tricks on a friend. So take your warning.'

"I thought Fergus would die laughing.

"'Well, well, well,' said he, 'you old doughface! Struck too, are you? That 's great! But you 're too late. Francesca tells me that Anabela talks of nothing but me, day and night. Of course, I 'm awfully obliged to you for making that chin-music to her of evenings. But, do you know, I 've an idea that I could have done it as well myself.'

"'Mrs. Judson Tate,' says I. 'Don't forget the name. You 've had the use of my tongue to go with your good looks, my boy. You can't lend me your looks; but hereafter my tongue is my own. Keep your mind on the name that 's to be on the visiting cards two inches by three and a half—"Mrs. Judson Tate." That 's all.'

"'All right,' says Fergus, laughing again. 'I 've talked with her father, the alcalde, and he 's willing. He 's to give a *baile* to-morrow evening in his new warehouse. If you were a dancing man, Jud, I 'd expect you around to meet the future Mrs. McMahan.'

"But on the next evening, when the music was playing loudest at the Alcalde Zamora's *baile*, into the room steps Judson Tate in new white linen clothes as if he were the biggest man in the whole nation, which he was.

"Some of the musicians jumped off the key when they saw my face, and one or two of the timidest señoritas let out a screech or two. But up prances the alcalde and almost wipes the dust off my shoes with his forehead. No mere good looks could have won me that sensational entrance.

"'I hear much, Señor Zamora,' says I, 'of the charm of your daughter. It would give me great pleasure to be presented to her.'

"There were about six dozen willow rocking-chairs, with pink tidies tied on to them, arranged against the walls. In one of them sat Señorita Anabela in white Swiss and red slippers, with pearls and fireflies in her hair. Fergus was at the other end of the room trying to break away from two maroons and a claybank girl.

"The alcalde leads me up to Anabela and presents me. When she took the first look at my face she dropped her fan and nearly turned her chair over from the shock. But I 'm used to that.

"I sat down by her and began to talk. When she heard me speak she jumped, and her eyes got as big as alligator pears. She could n't strike a balance between the tones of my voice and the face I carried. But I kept on talking in the key of C, which is the ladies' key; and presently she sat still in her chair and a dreamy look came into her eyes. She was coming my way. She knew of Judson Tate, and what a big man he was, and the big things he had done; and that was in my favour. But, of course, it was some shock to her to find out that I was not the pretty man that had been pointed out to her as the great Judson. And then I took the Spanish language, which is better than English for certain purposes, and played on it like a harp of a thousand strings. I ranged from the second G below the staff up to F-sharp above it. I set my voice to poetry, art, romance, flowers, and moonlight. I repeated some of the verses that I had murmured to her in the dark at her window; and I knew from a sudden soft sparkle in her eye that she recognized in my voice the tones of her midnight mysterious wooer.

"Anyhow, I had Fergus McMahan going. Oh, the vocal is the true art—no doubt about that. Handsome is as handsome palavers. That 's the renovated proverb.

"I took Señorita Anabela for a walk in the lemon grove while Fergus, disfiguring himself with an ugly frown, was waltzing with the claybank girl. Before we returned I had permission to come to her window in the *patio* the next evening at midnight and talk some more.

"Oh, it was easy enough. In two weeks Anabela was engaged to me, and Fergus was out. He took it calm, for a handsome man, and told me he was n't going to give in.

"'Talk may be all right in its place, Judson,' he says to me, 'although I 've never thought it worth cultivating. But,' says he, 'to expect mere words to back up successfully a face like yours in a lady's good graces is like expecting a man to make a square meal on the ringing of a dinner-bell.'

"But I have n't begun on the story I was going to tell you yet.

"One day I took a long ride in the hot sunshine, and then

took a bath in the cold waters of a lagoon on the edge of the town before I 'd cooled off.

"That evening after dark I called at the alcalde's to see Anabela. I was calling regular every evening then, and we were to be married in a month. She was looking like a bulbul, a gazelle, and a tea-rose, and her eyes were as soft and bright as two quarts of cream skimmed off from the Milky Way. She looked at my rugged features without any expression of fear or repugnance. Indeed, I fancied that I saw a look of deep admiration and affection, such as she had cast at Fergus on the plaza.

"I sat down, and opened my mouth to tell Anabela what she loved to hear—that she was a trust, monopolizing all the loveliness of earth. I opened my mouth, and instead of the usual vibrating words of love and compliment, there came forth a faint wheeze such as a baby with croup might emit. Not a word—not a syllable—not an intelligible sound. I had caught cold in my laryngeal regions when I took my injudicious bath.

"For two hours I sat trying to entertain Anabela. She talked a certain amount, but it was perfunctory and diluted. The nearest approach I made to speech was to formulate a sound like a clam trying to sing 'A Life on the Ocean Wave' at low tide. It seemed that Anabela's eyes did not rest upon me as often as usual. I had nothing with which to charm her ears. We looked at pictures and she played the guitar occasionally, very badly. When I left, her parting manner seemed cool—or at least thoughtful.

"This happened for five evenings consecutively.

"On the sixth day she ran away with Fergus McMahan.

"It was known that they fled in a sailing yacht bound for Belize. I was only eight hours behind them in a small steam launch belonging to the Revenue Department.

"Before I sailed, I rushed into the *botica* of old Manuel Iquito, a half-breed Indian druggist. I could not speak, but I pointed to my throat and made a sound like escaping steam. He began to yawn. In an hour, according to the customs of the country, I would have been waited on. I reached across the counter, seized him by the throat, and pointed again to my own. He yawned once more, and thrust into my hand a small bottle containing a black liquid.

"'Take one small spoonful every two hours,' says he.

"I threw him a dollar and skinned for the steamer.

"I steamed into the harbour at Belize thirteen seconds behind the yacht that Anabela and Fergus were on. They started for the shore in a dory just as my skiff was lowered over the side. I tried to order my sailormen to row faster, but the sounds died in my larynx before they came to the light. Then I thought of old Iquito's medicine, and I got out his bottle and took a swallow of it.

"The two boats landed at the same moment. I walked straight up to Anabela and Fergus. Her eyes rested upon me for an instant; then she turned them, full of feeling and confidence, upon Fergus. I knew I could not speak, but I was desperate. In speech lay my only hope. I could not stand beside Fergus and challenge comparison in the way of beauty. Purely involuntarily, my larynx and epiglottis attempted to reproduce the sounds that my mind was calling upon my vocal organs to send forth.

"To my intense surprise and delight the words rolled forth beautifully clear, resonant, exquisitely modulated, full of power, expression, and long-repressed emotion.

"'Señorita Anabela,' says I, 'may I speak with you aside for a moment?'

"You don't want details about that, do you? Thanks. The old eloquence had come back all right. I led her under a cocoanut palm and put my old verbal spell on her again.

"'Judson,' says she, 'when you are talking to me I can hear nothing else—I can see nothing else—there is nothing and nobody else in the world for me.'

"Well, that 's about all of the story. Anabela went back to Oratama in the steamer with me. I never heard what became of Fergus. I never saw him any more. Anabela is now Mrs. Judson Tate. Has my story bored you much?"

"No," said I. "I am always interested in psychological studies. A human heart—and especially a woman's—is a wonderful thing to contemplate."

"It is," said Judson Tate. "And so are the trachea and the bronchial tubes of man. And the larynx, too. Did you ever make a study of the windpipe?"

"Never," said I. "But I have taken much pleasure in your story. May I ask after Mrs Tate, and inquire of her present health and whereabouts?"

"Oh, sure," said Judson Tate. "We are living in Bergen Avenue, Jersey City. The climate down in Oratama did n't suit Mrs. T. I don't suppose you ever dissected the arytenoid cartilages of the epiglottis, did you?"

"Why, no," said I, "I am no surgeon."

"Pardon me," said Judson Tate, "but every man should know enough of anatomy and therapeutics to safeguard his own health. A sudden cold may set up capillary bronchitis or inflammation of the pulmonary vesicles, which may result in a serious affection of the vocal organs."

"Perhaps so," said I, with some impatience; "but that is neither here nor there. Speaking of the strange manifestations of the affection of women, I——"

"Yes, yes," interrupted Judson Tate, "they have peculiar ways. But, as I was going to tell you: when I went back to Oratama I found out from Manuel Iquito what was in that mixture he gave me for my lost voice. I told you how quick it cured me. He made that stuff from the *chuchula* plant. Now, look here."

Judson Tate drew an oblong, white pasteboard box from his pocket.

"For any cough," he said, "or cold, or hoarseness, or bronchial affection whatsoever, I have here the greatest remedy in the world. You see the formula printed on the box. Each tablet contains licorice, 2 grains; balsam tolu, $\frac{1}{10}$ grain; oil of anise, $\frac{1}{20}$ minim; oil of tar, $\frac{1}{60}$ minim; oleo-resin of cubebs, $\frac{1}{60}$ minim; fluid extract of *chuchula*, $\frac{1}{10}$ minim.

"I am in New York," went on Judson Tate, "for the purpose of organizing a company to market the greatest remedy for throat affections ever discovered. At present I am introducing the lozenges in a small way. I have here a box containing four dozen, which I am selling for the small sum of fifty cents. If you are suffering——"

I got up and went away without a word. I walked slowly up to the little park near my hotel, leaving Judson Tate alone with his conscience. My feelings were lacerated. He had poured gently upon me a story that I might have used. There was a little of the breath of life in it, and some of the synthetic atmosphere that passes, when cunningly tinkered, in the marts. And, at the last it had proven to be a commercial pill, deftly coated with the sugar of fiction. The worst of it was that I could not offer it for sale. Advertising departments and counting-rooms look down upon me. And it would never do for the literary. Therefore I sat upon a bench with other disappointed ones until my eyelids drooped.

I went to my room, and, as my custom is, read for an hour stories in my favourite magazines. This was to get my mind back to art again.

And as I read each story, I threw the magazines sadly and hopelessly, one by one, upon the floor. Each author, without one exception to bring balm to my heart, wrote liltingly and sprightly a story of some particular make of motor-car that seemed to control the sparking plug of his genius.

And when the last one was hurled from me I took heart.

"If readers can swallow so many proprietary automobiles," I said to myself, "they ought not to strain at one of Tate's Compound Magic Chuchula Bronchial Lozenges."

And so if you see this story in print you will understand that business is business, and that if Art gets very far ahead of Commerce, she will have to get up and hustle.

I may as well add, to make a clean job of it, that you can't buy the *chuchula* plant in the drug stores.

THE GENTLE GRAFTER

The Atavism of John Tom Little Bear

I SAW a light in Jeff Peters's room over the Red Front Drug Store. I hastened toward it, for I had not known that Jeff was in town. He is a man of the Hadji breed, of a hundred occupations, with a story to tell (when he will) of each one.

I found Jeff repacking his grip for a run down to Florida to look at an orange grove for which he had traded, a month before, his mining claim on the Yukon. He kicked me a chair, with the same old humorous, profound smile on his seasoned countenance. It had been eight months since we had met, but his greeting was such as men pass from day to day. Time is Jeff Peters's servant, and the continent is a big lot across which he cuts to his many roads.

For a while we skirmished along the edges of unprofitable talk which culminated in that unquiet problem of the Philippines.

"All them tropical races," said Jeff, "could be run out better with their own jockeys up. The tropical man knows what he wants. All he wants is a season ticket to the cock-fights and a pair of Western Union climbers to go up the bread-fruit tree. The Anglo-Saxon man wants him to learn to conjugate and wear suspenders. He'll be happiest in his own way."

I was shocked.

"Education, man," I said, "is the watchword. In time they will rise to our standard of civilization. Look what education has done for the Indian."

"O-ho!" sang Jeff, lighting his pipe (which was a good sign). "Yes, the Indian! I'm looking. I hasten to contemplate the Red Man as a standard bearer of progress. He's the same as the other brown boys. You can't make an Anglo-Saxon of him. Did I ever tell you about the time my friend John Tom Little Bear bit off the right ear of the arts of culture and education and spun the teetotum back round to where it was when Columbus was a boy? I did not?

"John Tom Little Bear was an educated Cherokee Indian and an old friend of mine when I was in the Territories. He was a graduate of one of them Eastern football colleges that have been so successful in teaching the Indian to use the gridiron instead of burning his victims at the stake. As an Anglo-Saxon, John Tom was copper-colored in spots. As an Indian, he was one of the whitest men I ever knew. As a Cherokee, he was a gentleman on the first ballot. As a ward of the nation, he was mighty hard to carry at the primaries.

"John Tom and me got together and began to make medicine—how to get up some lawful, genteel swindle which we might work in a quiet way so as not to excite the stupidity of the police or the cupidity of the larger corporations. We had close upon $500 between us, and we pined to make it grow, as all respectable capitalists do.

"So we figures out a proposition which seems to be as honorable as a gold mine prospectus and as profitable as a church raffle. And inside of thirty days you find us swarming into Kansas with a pair of fluent horses and a red camping wagon on the European plan. John Tom is Chief Wish-Heap-Dough, the famous Indian medicine man and Samaritan Sachem of the Seven Tribes. Mr. Peters is business manager and half owner. We needed a third man, so we looked around and found J. Conyngham Binkly leaning against the want column of a newspaper. This Binkly had a disease for Shakespearean rôles, and an hallucination about a 200 nights' run on the New York stage. But he confesses that he never could earn the butter to spread on his William S. rôles, so he is willing to drop to the ordinary baker's kind, and be satisfied with a 200-mile run behind the medicine ponies. Besides Richard III., he could do twenty-seven coon songs and banjo specialties, and was willing to cook, and curry the horses. We carried a fine line of excuses for taking money. One was a magic soap for removing grease spots and quarters from clothes. One was Sum-wah-tah, the great Indian Remedy, made from a prairie herb revealed by the Great Spirit in a dream to his favorite medicine men, the great chiefs McGarrity and Silberstein, bottlers, Chicago. And the other was a frivolous system of pickpocketing the Kansasters that had the department stores reduced to a decimal fraction. Look ye! A pair of silk garters, a dream book, one dozen clothes-pins, a gold tooth, and 'When Knighthood Was in Flower,' all wrapped up in a genuine Japanese silkarina handkerchief and handed to the handsome lady by Mr. Peters for the trivial sum of fifty cents, while Professor Binkly entertains us in a three-minute round with the banjo.

"'Twas an eminent graft we had. We ravaged peacefully through the State, determined to remove all doubt as to why 'twas called bleeding Kansas. John Tom Little Bear, in full Indian chief's costume, drew crowds away from the parchesi sociables and government ownership conversaziones. While at the football college in the East he had acquired quantities of rhetoric and the arts of calisthenics and sophistry in his classes, and when he stood up in the red wagon and explained to the farmers, eloquent, about chilblains and hyperæsthesia of the cranium, Jeff couldn't hand out the Indian Remedy fast enough for 'em.

"One night we was camped on the edge of a little town out west of Salina. We always camped near a stream, and put up a little tent. Sometimes we sold out of the Remedy unexpected, and then Chief Wish-Heap-Dough would have a dream in which the Manitou commanded him to fill up a few bottles of Sum-wah-tah at the most convenient place. 'Twas about ten o'clock, and we'd just got in from a street performance. I was in the tent with the lantern, figuring up the day's profits. John Tom hadn't taken off his Indian make-up, and was sitting by the camp-fire minding a fine sirloin steak in the pan for the Professor till he finished his hair-raising scene with the trained horses.

"All at once out of the dark bushes comes a pop like a fire-cracker, and John Tom gives a grunt and digs out of his bosom a little bullet that has dented itself against his collarbone. John Tom makes a dive in the direction of the fireworks, and comes back dragging by the collar a kid about nine or ten years young, in a velveteen suit, with a little nickel-mounted rifle in his hand about as big as a fountain-pen.

"'Here, you pappoose,' says John Tom, 'what are you gunning for with that howitzer? You might hit somebody in the eye. Come out, Jeff, and mind the steak. Don't let it burn, while I investigate this demon with the pea-shooter.'

"'Cowardly redskin,' says the kid, like he was quoting from a favorite author. 'Dare to burn me at the stake and the paleface will sweep you from the prairies like—like everything. Now, you lemme go, or I'll tell mamma.'

"John Tom plants the kid on a camp-stool, and sits down by him. 'Now, tell the big chief,' he says, 'why you try to shoot pellets into your Uncle John's system. Didn't you know it was loaded?'

"'Are you a Indian?' asks the kid, looking up, cute as you please, at John Tom's buckskin and eagle feathers. 'I am,' says John Tom. 'Well, then, that's why,' answers the boy, swinging his feet. I nearly let the steak burn watching the nerve of that youngster.

"'O-ho!' says John Tom, 'I see. You're the Boy Avenger. And you've sworn to rid the continent of the savage Red Man. Is that about the way of it, son?'

"The kid half-way nodded his head. And then he looked glum. 'Twas indecent to wring his secret from his bosom before a single brave had fallen before his parlor-rifle.

"'Now, tell us where your wigwam is, pappoose,' says John Tom—'where you live? Your mamma will be worrying about you being out so late. Tell me, and I'll take you home.' The kid grins. 'I guess not,' he says. 'I live thousands and thousands of miles over there.' He gyrated his hand toward the horizon. 'I come on the train,' he says, 'by myself. I got off here because the conductor said my ticket had ex-pirated.' He looks at John Tom with sudden suspicion. 'I bet you ain't a Indian,' he says. 'You don't talk like a Indian. You look like one, but all a Indian can say is "heap good" and "paleface die." Say, I bet you are one of them make-believe Indians that sell medicine on the streets. I saw one once in Quincy.'

"'You never mind,' says John Tom, 'whether I'm a cigar-sign or a Tammany cartoon. The question before the council is what's to be done with you. You've run away from home. You've been reading Howells. You've disgraced the profession of boy avengers by trying to shoot a tame Indian, and never saying: "Die, dog of a redskin! You have crossed the path of the Boy Avenger nineteen times too often." What do you mean by it?'

"The kid thought for a minute. 'I guess I made a mistake,' he says. 'I ought to have gone farther west. They find 'em wild out there in the cañons.' He holds out his hand to John Tom, the little rascal. 'Please excuse me, sir,' says he, 'for shooting at you. I hope it didn't hurt you. But you ought to be more careful. When a scout sees a Indian in his war-dress, his rifle must speak.' Little Bear give a big laugh with a whoop at the end of it, and swings the kid ten feet high and sets him on his shoulder. And the runaway fingers the fringe and the eagle feathers, and is full of the joy the white man knows when he dangles his heels against an inferior race. It is plain that Little Bear and that kid are chums from that on. The little renegade has already smoked the pipe of peace with the savage; and you can see in his eye that he is figuring on a tomahawk and a pair of moccasins, children's size.

"We have supper in the tent. The youngster looks upon me and the Professor as ordinary braves, only intended as a background to the camp scene. When he is seated on a box of Sum-wah-tah, with the edge of the table sawing his neck, and his mouth full of beefsteak, Little Bear calls for his name. 'Roy,' says the kid, with a sirloiny sound to it. But when the rest of it and his post-office address is referred to, he shakes his head. 'I guess not,' he says. 'You'll send me back. I want to stay with you. I like this camping out. At home, we fellows had a camp in our back yard. They called me Roy, the Red Wolf. I guess that'll do for a name. Gimme another piece of beefsteak, please.'

"We had to keep that kid. We knew there was a hallabaloo about him somewheres, and that Mamma and Uncle Harry and Aunt Jane and the Chief of Police were hot after finding his trail, but not another word would he tell us. In two days he was the mascot of the Big Medicine outfit, and all of us had a sneaking hope that his owners wouldn't turn up. When the red wagon was doing business he was in it, and passed up the bottles to Mr. Peters as proud and satisfied as a prince that's abjured a two-hundred-dollar crown for a million-dollar parvenuess. Once John Tom asked him something about his papa. 'I ain't got any papa,' he says. 'He runned away and left us. He made my mamma cry. Aunt Lucy says he's a shape.' 'A what?' somebody asks him. 'A shape,' says the kid; 'some kind of a shape—lemme see—oh, yes, a feendenuman shape. I don't know what it means.' John Tom was for putting our brand on him, and dressing him up like a little chief, with wampum and beads, but I vetoes it. 'Somebody's lost that kid, is my view of it, and they may want him. You let me try him with a few stratagems, and see if I can't get a look at his visiting card.'

"So that night I goes up to Mr. Roy Blank by the camp-fire, and looks at him contemptuous and scornful. 'Snickenwitzel!' says I, like the word made me sick; 'Snickenwitzel!' Bah! Before I'd be named Snickenwitzel!

"'What's the matter with you, Jeff?' says the kid, opening his eyes wide.

"'Snickenwitzel!' I repeats, and I spat the word out. 'I saw a man to-day from your town, and he told me your name. I'm not surprised you was ashamed to tell it. Snickenwitzel! Whew!'

"'Ah, here, now,' says the boy, indignant and wriggling all over, 'what's the matter with you? That ain't my name. It's Conyers. What's the matter with you?'

"'And that's not the worst of it,' I went on quick, keeping him hot and not giving him time to think. 'We thought you was from a nice, well-to-do family. Here's Mr. Little Bear, a chief of the Cherokees, entitled to wear nine otter tails on his Sunday blanket, and Professor Binkly, who plays Shakespeare and the banjo, and me, that's got hundreds of dollars in that black tin box in the wagon, and we've got to be careful about the company we keep. That man tells me your folks live 'way down in little old Hencoop Alley, where there's no sidewalks, and the goats eat off the table with you.'

"That kid was almost crying now. ''Tain't so,' he splutters. 'He—he don't know what he's talking about. We live on Poplar Av'noo. I don't 'sociate with goats. What's the matter with you?'

"'Poplar Avenue,' says I, sarcastic, 'Poplar Avenue! That's a street to live on! It only runs two blocks and then falls off a bluff. You can throw a keg of nails the whole length of it. Don't talk to me about Poplar Avenue.'

"'Aw, it's—it's miles long,' says the kid. 'Our number's 862, and there's lots of houses after that. What's the matter with—aw, you make me tired, Jeff.'

"'Well, well, now,' says I, 'I guess that man made a mistake. Maybe it was some other boy he was talking about. If I catch him I'll teach him to go around slandering people.' And after supper I goes uptown and telegraphs to Mrs. Conyers, 862 Poplar Avenue, Quincy, Ill., that the kid is safe and sassy with us, and will be held for further orders. In two hours an answer comes to hold him tight, and she'll start for him by next train.

"The next train was due at 6 P.M. the next day, and me and John Tom was at the depot with the kid. You might scour the plains in vain for the big chief Wish-Heap-Dough. In his place is Mr. Little Bear in the human habiliments of the Anglo-Saxon sect; and the leather of his shoes is patented and the loop of his necktie is copyrighted. For these things John Tom has had grafted on him at college along with metaphysics and the knockout guard for the low tackle. But for his complexion, which is some yellowish, and the black mop of his straight hair, you might have thought here was an ordinary man out of the city directory that subscribes for *Harper's Weekly* and pushes the lawn-mower in his shirt-sleeves of evenings.

"Then the train rolled in, and a little woman in a gray dress, with sort of illuminating hair, slides off and looks around quick. And the Boy Avenger sees her, and yells 'Mamma,' and she cries 'Oh!' and they meet in a clinch, and now the pesky redskins can come forth from their caves on the plains without fear any more of the rifle of Roy, the Red Wolf. Mrs. Conyers comes up and thanks me and John Tom without the usual extremities you always look for in a woman. She says just enough, in a way to convince, and there is no incidental music by the orchestra. I made a few illiterate requisitions upon the art of conversation, at which the lady smiles friendly, as if she had known me a week. And then Mr. Little Bear adorns the atmosphere with the various idioms into which education can fracture the wind of speech. I could see the kid's mother didn't quite place John Tom; but it seemed she was apprised in his dialects, and she played up to his lead in the science of making three words do the work of one.

"That kid introduced us, with some footnotes and explanations that made things plainer than a week of rhetoric. He danced around, and punched us in the back, and tried to climb John Tom's leg. 'This is John Tom, mamma,' says he. 'He's a Indian. He sells medicine in a red wagon. I shot him, but he wasn't wild. The other one's Jeff. He's a fakir, too. Come on and see the camp where we live, won't you, mamma?'

"It is plain to see that the life of the woman is in that boy. She has got him again where her arms can gather him, and that's enough. She's ready to do anything to please him. She hesitates the eighth of a second and takes another look at these men. I imagine she says to herself about John Tom, 'Seems to be a gentleman, if his hair *don't* curl.' And Mr. Peters she disposes of as follows: 'No ladies' man, but a man who knows a lady.' So we all ramble down to the camp as neighborly as coming from a wake. And there she inspects the wagon, and pats the place with her hand where the kid used to sleep, and dabs around her eyewinkers with her handkerchief. And Professor Binkly gives us 'Trovatore' on one string of the banjo, and is about to slide off into *Hamlet*'s monologue when one of the horses gets tangled in his rope and he must go look after him, and says something about 'foiled again.'

"When it got dark me and John Tom walked back up to the Corn Exchange Hotel, and the four of us had supper there. I think the trouble started at that supper, for then was when Mr. Little Bear made an intellectual balloon ascension. I held on to the tablecloth, and listened to him soar. That Red Man, if I could judge, had the gift of information. He took language, and did with it all a Roman can do with macaroni. His vocal remarks was all embroidered over with the most scholarly verbs and prefixes. And his syllables was smooth, and fitted nicely to the joints of his ideas. I thought I'd heard him talk before, but I hadn't. And it wasn't the size of his words, but the way they come; and 'twasn't his subjects, for he spoke of common things like cathedrals and football and poems and catarrh and souls and freight rates and sculpture. Mrs. Conyers understood his accents, and the elegant sounds went back and forth between 'em. And now and then Jefferson D. Peters would intervene a few shop-worn, senseless words to have the butter passed or another leg of the chicken.

"Yes, John Tom Little Bear appeared to be inveigled some in his bosom about that Mrs. Conyers. She was of the kind that pleases. She had the good looks and more, I'll tell you. You take one of these cloak models in a big store. They strike you as being on the impersonal system. They are adapted for the eye. What they run to is inches-around and complexion, and the art of fanning the delusion that the sealskin would look just as well on the lady with the warts and the pocket-book. Now, if one of them models was off duty, and you took it, and it would say 'Charlie' when you pressed it, and sit up at the table, why, then, you would have something similar to Mrs. Conyers. I could see how John Tom could resist any inclination to hate that white squaw.

"The lady and the kid stayed at the hotel. In the morning, they say, they will start home. Me and Little Bear left at eight o'clock, and sold Indian Remedy on the court-house square till nine. He leaves me and the Professor to drive down to camp, while he stays up town. I am not enamored with that plan, for it shows John Tom is uneasy in his composures, and that leads to firewater, and sometimes to the green corn dance and costs. Not often does Chief Wish-Heap-Dough get busy with the firewater, but whenever he does there is heap much doing in the lodges of the palefaces who wear blue and carry the club.

"At half-past nine Professor Binkly is rolled in his quilt, snoring in blank verse, and I am sitting by the fire listening to the frogs. Mr. Little Bear slides into camp and sits down against a tree. There is no symptoms of firewater.

"'Jeff,' says he, after a long time, 'a little boy came West to hunt Indians.'

"'Well, then?' says I, for I wasn't thinking as he was.

"'And he bagged one,' says John Tom, 'and 'twas not with a gun, and he never had on a velveteen suit of clothes in his life.' And then I began to catch his smoke.

"'I know it,' says I. 'And I'll bet you his pictures are on valentines, and fool men are his game, red and white.'

"'You win on the red,' says John Tom, calm. 'Jeff, for how many ponies do you think I could buy Mrs. Conyers?'

"'Scandalous talk!' I replies. ''Tis not a paleface custom.' John Tom laughs loud and bites into a cigar. 'No,' he answers; ''tis the savage equivalent for the dollars of the white man's marriage settlement. Oh, I know. There's an eternal wall between the races. If I could do it, Jeff, I'd put a torch to every white college that a red man has ever set foot inside. Why don't you leave us alone,' says he, 'to our own ghost-dances and dog-feasts, and our dingy squaws to cook our grasshopper soup and darn our moccasins?'

"'Now, you sure don't mean disrespect to the perennial blossom entitled education?' says I, scandalized, 'because I wear it in the bosom of my own intellectual shirtwaist. I've had education,' says I, 'and never took any harm from it.'

"'You lasso us,' goes on Little Bear, not noticing my prose

insertions, 'and teach us what is beautiful in literature and life, and how to appreciate what is fine in men and women. What have you done to me?' says he. 'You've made me a Cherokee Moses. You've taught me to hate the wigwams and love the white man's ways. I can look over into the promised land and see Mrs. Conyers, but my place is—on the reservation.'

"Little Bear stands up in his chief's dress, and laughs again. 'But, white man Jeff,' he goes on, 'the paleface provides a recourse. 'Tis a temporary one, but it gives a respite; and the name of it is whiskey.' And straight off he walks up the path to town again. 'Now,' says I in my mind, 'may the Manitou move him to do only bailable things this night!' For I perceive that John Tom is about to avail himself of the white man's solace.

"Maybe it was 10.30, as I sat, smoking, when I hear pit-a-pats on the path, and here comes Mrs. Conyers running, her hair twisted up any way, and a look on her face that says burglars and mice and the flour's-all-out rolled into one. 'Oh, Mr. Peters,' she calls out, as they will, 'Oh, oh!' I made a quick think, and I spoke the gist of it out loud. 'Now,' says I, 'we've been brothers, me and that Indian, but I'll make a good one of him in two minutes if——'

"'No, no,' she says, wild, and cracking her knuckles, 'I haven't seen Mr. Little Bear. 'Tis my—husband. He's stolen my boy. Oh,' she says, 'just when I had him back in my arms again! That heartless villain! Every bitterness life knows,' she says, 'he's made me drink. My poor little lamb, that ought to be warm in his bed, carried off by that fiend!'

"'How did all this happen?' I ask. 'Let's have the facts.'

"'I was fixing his bed,' she explains, 'and Roy was playing on the hotel porch. And *he* drives up to the steps. I heard Roy scream, and ran out. My husband had him in the buggy then. I begged him for my child. This is what he gave me.' She turns her face to the light. There is a crimson streak running across her cheek and mouth. 'He did that with his whip,' she says.

"'Come back to the hotel,' I says, 'and we'll see what can be done.'

"On the way she tells me some of the wherefores. When he slashed her with the whip he told her he found out she was coming for the kid, and he was on the same train. Mrs. Conyers had been living with her brother, and they'd watched the boy always, as her husband had tried to steal him before. I judge that man was worse than a street railway promoter. It seems he had spent her money and slugged her and killed her canary bird, and told it around that she had cold feet.

"At the hotel we found a mass meeting of five infuriated citizens chewing tobacco and denouncing the outrage. Most of the town was asleep by ten o'clock. I talks the lady some quiet, and tells her I will take the one o'clock train for the next town, forty miles east, for it is likely that the esteemed Mr. C. will drive there to take the cars. 'I don't know,' I tell her, 'but what he has legal rights; but if I find him I can give him an illegal left in the eye, and tie him up for a day or two, anyhow, on a disturbal of the peace proposition.'

"Mrs. Conyers goes inside and cries with the landlord's wife, who is fixing some catnip tea that will make everything all right for the poor dear. The landlord comes out on the porch, thumbing his one suspender, and says to me:

"'Ain't had so much excitements in town since Bedford Steegall's wife swallered a spring lizard. I seen him through the winder hit her with the buggy whip, and everything. What'd that suit of clothes cost you got on? 'Pears like we'd have some rain, don't it? Say, doc, that Indian of yourn's on a kind of a whizz to-night, ain't he? He come along just before you did, and I told him about this here occurrence. He give a cur'us kind of a hoot, and trotted off. I guess our constable'll have him in the lock-up 'fore morning.'

"I thought I'd sit out on the porch and wait for the one o'clock train. I wasn't feeling saturated with mirth. Here was John Tom on one of his sprees, and this kidnapping business losing sleep for me. But then, I'm always having trouble with other people's troubles. Every few minutes Mrs. Conyers would come out on the porch and look down the road the way the buggy went, like she expected to see that kid coming back on a white pony with a red apple in his hand. Now, wasn't that like a woman? And that brings up cats. 'I saw a mouse go in this hole,' says Mrs. Cat; 'you can go prize up a plank over there if you like; I'll watch this hole.'

"About a quarter to one o'clock the lady comes out again, restless, and crying easy, as females do for their own amusement, and she looks down that road again and listens. 'Now, ma'am,' says I, 'there's no use watching cold wheel-tracks. By this time they're half-way to —— ' 'Hush,' says she, holding up her hand. And I do hear something coming 'flip-flap' in the dark; and then there is the awfulest warwhoop ever heard outside of Madison Square Garden at a Buffalo Bill matinée. And up the steps and onto the porch jumps the disrespectable Indian. The lamp in the hall shines on him, and I fail to recognize Mr. J. T. Little Bear, alumnus of the class of '91. What I see is a Cherokee brave, and the warpath is what he has been travelling. Firewater and other things have got him going. His buckskin is hanging in strings, and his feathers are mixed up like a frizzly hen's. The dust of miles is on his moccasins, and the light in his eye is the kind the aborigines wear. But in his arms he brings that kid, his eyes half closed, with his little shoes dangling and one hand fast around the Indian's collar.

"'Pappoose!' says John Tom, and I notice that the flowers of the white man's syntax has left his tongue. He is the original proposition in bear's claws and copper color. 'Me bring,' says he, and he lays the kid in his mother's arms. 'Run fifteen mile,' says John Tom—'Ugh! Catch white man. Bring pappoose.'

"The little woman is in extremities of gladness. She must wake up that stir-up-trouble youngster and hug him and make proclamation that he is mamma's own precious treasure. I was about to ask questions, but I looked at Mr. Little Bear, and my eye caught sight of something in his belt. 'Now go to bed, ma'am,' says I, 'and this gadabout youngster likewise, for there's no more danger, and the kidnapping business is not what it was earlier in the night.'

"I inveigled John Tom down to camp quick, and when he tumbled over asleep I got that thing out of his belt and disposed of it where the eye of education can't see it. For even the football colleges disapprove of the art of scalp-taking in their curriculums.

"It is ten o'clock next day when John Tom wakes up and looks around. I am glad to see the nineteenth century in his eye again.

"'What was it, Jeff?' he asks.

"'Heap firewater,' says I.

"John Tom frowns, and thinks a little. 'Combined,' says he, directly, 'with the interesting little physiological shake-up known as reversion to type. I remember now. Have they gone yet?'

"'On the 7.30 train,' I answers.

"'Ugh!' says John Tom; 'better so. Paleface, bring big Chief Wish-Heap-Dough a little bromo-seltzer, and then he'll take up the Red Man's burden again.'"

Conscience in Art

"I NEVER could hold my partner, Andy Tucker, down to legitimate ethics of pure swindling," said Jeff Peters to me one day.

"Andy had too much imagination to be honest. He used to devise schemes of money-getting so fraudulent and high-financial that they wouldn't have been allowed in the bylaws of a railroad rebate system.

"Myself, I never believed in taking any man's dollars unless I gave him something for it—something in the way of rolled gold jewelry, garden seeds, lumbago lotion, stock certificates, stove polish or a crack on the head to show for his money. I guess I must have had New England ancestors away back and inherited some of their stanch and rugged fear of the police.

"But Andy's family tree was in different kind. I don't think he could have traced his descent any further back than a corporation.

"One summer while we was in the middle West, working down the Ohio valley with a line of family albums, headache powders and roach destroyer, Andy takes one of his notions of high and actionable financiering.

"'Jeff,' says he, 'I've been thinking that we ought to drop these rutabaga fanciers and give our attention to something more nourishing and prolific. If we keep on snapshooting these hinds for their egg money we'll be classed as nature fakers. How about plunging into the fastnesses of the skyscraper country and biting some big bull caribous in the chest?'

"'Well,' says I, 'you know my idiosyncrasies. I prefer a square, non-illegal style of business such as we are carrying on now. When I take money I want to leave some tangible object in the other fellow's hands for him to gaze at and to distract his attention from my spoor, even if it's only a Komical Kuss Trick Finger Ring for Squirting Perfume in a Friend's Eye. But if you've got a fresh idea, Andy,' says I, 'let's have a look at it. I'm not so wedded to petty graft that I would refuse something better in the way of a subsidy.'

"'I was thinking,' says Andy, 'of a little hunt without horn, hound or camera among the great herd of the Midas Americanus, commonly known as the Pittsburg millionaires.'

"'In New York?' I asks.

"'No, sir,' says Andy, 'in Pittsburg. That's their habitat. They don't like New York. They go there now and then just because it's expected of 'em.'

"'A Pittsburg millionaire in New York is like a fly in a cup of hot coffee—he attracts attention and comment, but he don't enjoy it. New York ridicules him for "blowing" so much money in that town of sneaks and snobs, and sneers. The truth is, he don't spend anything while he is there. I saw a memorandum of expenses for a ten days trip to Bunkum Town made by a Pittsburg man worth $15,000,000 once. Here's the way he set it down:

R. R. fare to and from	$21 00
Cab fare to and from hotel	2 00
Hotel bill @ $5 per day	50 00
Tips	5,750 00
Total	$5,823 00

"'That's the voice of New York,' goes on Andy. 'The town's nothing but a head waiter. If you tip it too much it'll go and stand by the door and make fun of you to the hat check boy. When a Pittsburger wants to spend money and have a good time he stays at home. That's where we'll go to catch him.'

"Well, to make a dense story more condensed, me and Andy cached our paris green and antipyrine powders and albums in a friend's cellar, and took the trail to Pittsburg. Andy didn't have any especial prospectus of chicanery and violence drawn up, but he always had plenty of confidence that his immoral nature would rise to any occasion that presented itself.

"As a concession to my ideas of self-preservation and rectitude he promised that if I should take an active and incriminating part in any little business venture that we might work up there should be something actual and cognizant to the senses of touch, sight, taste or smell to transfer to the victim for the money so my conscience might rest easy. After that I felt better and entered more cheerfully into the foul play.

"'Andy,' says I, as we strayed through the smoke along the cinderpath they call Smithfield street, 'had you figured out how we are going to get acquainted with these coke kings and pig iron squeezers? Not that I would decry my own worth or system of drawing room deportment, and work with the olive fork and pie knife,' says I, 'but isn't the entree nous into the salons of the stogie smokers going to be harder than you imagined?'

"'If there's any handicap at all,' says Andy, 'it's our own refinement and inherent culture. Pittsburg millionaires are a fine body of plain, wholehearted, unassuming, democratic men.

"'They are rough but uncivil in their manners, and though their ways are boisterous and unpolished, under it all they have a great deal of impoliteness and discourtesy. Nearly every one of 'em rose from obscurity,' says Andy, 'and they'll live in it till the town gets to using smoke consumers. If we act simple and unaffected and don't go too far from the saloons and keep making a noise like an import duty on steel rails we won't have any trouble in meeting some of 'em socially.'

"Well Andy and me drifted about town three or four days getting our bearings. We got to knowing several millionaires by sight.

"One used to stop his automobile in front of our hotel and have a quart of champagne brought out to him. When the waiter opened it he'd turn it up to his mouth and drink it out of the bottle. That showed he used to be a glassblower before he made his money.

"One evening Andy failed to come to the hotel for dinner. About 11 o'clock he came into my room.

"'Landed one, Jeff,' says he. 'Twelve millions. Oil, rolling mills, real estate and natural gas. He's a fine man; no airs about him. Made all his money in the last five years. He's got professors posting him up now in education—art and literature and haberdashery and such things.

"'When I saw him he'd just won a bet of $10,000 with a Steel Corporation man that there'd be four suicides in the Allegheny rolling mills to-day. So everybody in sight had to walk up and have drinks on him. He took a fancy to me and asked me to dinner with him. We went to a restaurant in Diamond alley and sat on stools and had sparkling Moselle and clam chowder and apple fritters.

"'Then he wanted to show me his bachelor apartment on Liberty street. He's got ten rooms over a fish market with privilege of the bath on the next floor above. He told me it cost him $18,000 to furnish his apartment, and I believe it.

"'He's got $40,000 worth of pictures in one room, and $20,000 worth of curios and antiques in another. His name's Scudder, and he's 45, and taking lessons on the piano and 15,000 barrels of oil a day out of his wells.

"'All right,' says I. 'Preliminary canter satisfactory. But, kay vooly, voo? What good is the art junk to us? And the oil?'

"'Now, that man,' says Andy, sitting thoughtfully on the bed, 'ain't what you would call an ordinary scutt. When he was showing me his cabinet of art curios his face lighted up like the door of a coke oven. He says that if some of his big deals go through he'll make J. P. Morgan's collection of sweatshop tapestry and Augusta, Me., beadwork look like the contents of an ostrich's craw thrown on a screen by a magic lantern.

"'And then he showed me a little carving,' went on Andy, 'that anybody could see was a wonderful thing. It was something like 2,000 years old, he said. It was a lotus flower with a woman's face in it carved out of a solid piece of ivory.

"'Scudder looks it up in a catalogue and describes it. An Egyptian carver named Khafra made two of 'em for King Rameses II. about the year B.C. The other one can't be found. The junkshops and antique bugs have rubbered all Europe for it, but it seems to be out of stock. Scudder paid $2,000 for the one he has.'

"'Oh, well,' says I, 'this sounds like the purling of a rill to me. I thought we came here to teach the millionaires business, instead of learning art from 'em?'

"'Be patient,' says Andy, kindly. 'Maybe we will see a rift in the smoke ere long.'

"All the next morning Andy was out. I didn't see him until about noon. He came to the hotel and called me into his room across the hall. He pulled a roundish bundle about as big as a goose egg out of his pocket and unwrapped it. It was an ivory carving just as he had described the millionaire's to me.

"'I went in an old second hand store and pawnshop a while ago,' says Andy, 'and I see this half hidden under a lot of old daggers and truck. The pawnbroker said he'd had it several years and thinks it was soaked by some Arabs or Turks or some foreign dubs that used to live down by the river.

"'I offered him $2 for it, and I must have looked like I wanted it, for he said it would be taking the pumpernickel out of his children's mouths to hold any conversation that did not lead up to a price of $35. I finally got it for $25.

"'Jeff,' goes on Andy, 'this is the exact counterpart of Scudder's carving. It's absolutely a dead ringer for it. He'll pay $2,000 for it as quick as he'd tuck a napkin under his chin. And why shouldn't it be the genuine other one, anyhow, that the old gypsy whittled out?'

"'Why not, indeed?' says I. 'And how shall we go about compelling him to make a voluntary purchase of it?'

"Andy had his plan all ready, and I'll tell you how we carried it out.

"I got a pair of blue spectacles, put on my black frock coat, rumpled my hair up and became Prof. Pickleman. I went to another hotel, registered, and sent a telegram to Scudder to come to see me at once on important art business. The elevator dumped him on me in less than an hour. He was a foggy man with a clarion voice, smelling of Connecticut wrappers and naphtha.

"'Hello, Profess!' he shouts. 'How's your conduct?'

"I rumpled my hair some more and gave him a blue glass stare.

"'Sir,' says I. 'Are you Cornelius T. Scudder? Of Pittsburg, Pennsylvania?'

"'I am,' says he. 'Come out and have a drink.'

"'I have neither the time nor the desire,' says I, 'for such harmful and deleterious amusements. I have come from New York,' says I, 'on a matter of busi— on a matter of art.

"'I learned there that you are the owner of an Egyptian ivory carving of the time of Rameses II., representing the head of Queen Isis in a lotus flower. There were only two of such carvings made. One has been lost for many years. I recently discovered and purchased the other in a pawn— in an obscure museum in Vienna. I wish to purchase yours. Name your price.'

"'Well, the great ice jams, Profess!' says Scudder. 'Have you found the other one? Me sell? No. I don't guess Cornelius

Scudder needs to sell anything that he wants to keep. Have you got the carving with you, Profess?'

"I shows it to Scudder. He examines it careful all over.

"'It's the article,' says he. 'It's a duplicate of mine, every line and curve of it. Tell you what I'll do,' he says. 'I won't sell, but I'll buy. Give you $2,500 for yours.'

"'Since you won't sell, I will,' says I. 'Large bills, please. I'm a man of few words. I must return to New York to-night. I lecture to-morrow at the aquarium.'

"Scudder sends a check down and the hotel cashes it. He goes off with his piece of antiquity and I hurry back to Andy's hotel, according to arrangement.

"Andy is walking up and down the room looking at his watch.

"'Well?' he says.

"'Twenty-five hundred,' says I. 'Cash.'

"'We've got just eleven minutes,' says Andy, 'to catch the B. & O. westbound. Grab your baggage.'

"'What's the hurry,' says I. 'It was a square deal. And even if it was only an imitation of the original carving it'll take him some time to find it out. He seemed to be sure it was the genuine article.'

"'It was,' says Andy. 'It was his own. When I was looking at his curios yesterday he stepped out of the room for a moment and I pocketed it. Now, will you pick up your suit case and hurry?'

"'Then,' says I, 'why was that story about finding another one in the pawn—'

"'Oh,' says Andy, 'out of respect for that conscience of yours. Come on.'"

The Man Higher Up

ACROSS OUR two dishes of spaghetti, in a corner of Provenzano's restaurant, Jeff Peters was explaining to me the three kinds of graft.

Every winter Jeff comes to New York to eat spaghetti, to watch the shipping in East River from the depths of his chinchilla overcoat, and to lay in a supply of Chicago-made clothing at one of the Fulton street stores. During the other three seasons he may be found further west—his range is from Spokane to Tampa. In his profession he takes a pride which he supports and defends with a serious and unique philosophy of ethics. His profession is no new one. He is an incorporated, uncapitalized, unlimited asylum for the reception of the restless and unwise dollars of his fellowmen.

In the wilderness of stone in which Jeff seeks his annual lonely holiday he is glad to palaver of his many adventures, as a boy will whistle after sundown in a wood. Wherefore, I mark on my calendar the time of his coming, and open a question of privilege at Provenzano's concerning the little wine-stained table in the corner between the rakish rubber plant and the framed palazzio della something on the wall.

"There are two kinds of grafts," said Jeff, "that ought to be wiped out by law. I mean Wall Street speculation, and burglary."

"Nearly everybody will agree with you as to one of them," said I, with a laugh.

"Well, burglary ought to be wiped out, too," said Jeff; and I wondered whether the laugh had been redundant.

"About three months ago," said Jeff, "it was my privilege to become familiar with a sample of each of the aforesaid branches of illegitimate art. I was *sine qua grata* with a member of the housebreakers' union and one of the John D. Napoleons of finance at the same time."

"Interesting combination," said I, with a yawn. "Did I tell you I bagged a duck and a ground-squirrel at one shot last week over in the Ramapos?" I knew well how to draw Jeff's stories.

"Let me tell you first about these barnacles that clog the

wheels of society by poisoning the springs of rectitude with their upas-like eye," said Jeff, with the pure gleam of the muck-raker in his own.

"As I said, three months ago I got into bad company. There are two times in a man's life when he does this—when he's dead broke, and when he's rich.

"Now and then the most legitimate business runs out of luck. It was out in Arkansas I made the wrong turn at a cross-road, and drives into this town of Peavine by mistake. It seems I had already assaulted and disfigured Peavine the spring of the year before. I had sold $600 worth of young fruit trees there—plums, cherries, peaches and pears. The Peaviners were keeping an eye on the country road and hoping I might pass that way again. I drove down Main street as far as the Crystal Palace drugstore before I realized I had committed ambush upon myself and my white horse Bill.

"The Peaviners took me by surprise and Bill by the bridle and began a conversation that wasn't entirely disassociated with the subject of fruit trees. A committee of 'em ran some trace-chains through the armholes of my vest, and escorted me through their gardens and orchards.

"Their fruit trees hadn't lived up to their labels. Most of 'em had turned out to be persimmons and dogwoods, with a grove or two of blackjacks and poplars. The only one that showed any signs of bearing anything was a fine young cottonwood that had put forth a hornet's nest and half of an old corset-cover.

"The Peaviners protracted our fruitless stroll to the edge of town. They took my watch and money on account; and they kept Bill and the wagon as hostages. They said the first time one of them dogwood trees put forth an Amsden's June peach I might come back and get my things. Then they took off the trace-chains and jerked their thumbs in the direction of the Rocky Mountains; and I struck a Lewis and Clark lope for the swollen rivers and impenetrable forests.

"When I regained intellectualness I found myself walking into an unidentified town on the A., T. & S. F. railroad. The Peaviners hadn't left anything in my pockets except a plug of chewing—they wasn't after my life—and that saved it. I bit off a chunk and sits down on a pile of ties by the track to recogitate my sensations of thought and perspicacity.

"And then along comes a fast freight which slows up a little at the town; and off of it drops a black bundle that rolls for twenty yards in a cloud of dust and then gets up and begins to spit soft coal and interjections. I see it is a young man broad across the face, dressed more for Pullmans than freights, and with a cheerful kind of smile in spite of it all that made Phœbe Snow's job look like a chimney-sweep's.

"'Fall off?' says I.

"'Nunk,' says he. 'Got off. Arrived at my destination. What town is this?'

"'Haven't looked it up on the map yet,' says I. 'I got in about five minutes before you did. How does it strike you?'

"'Hard,' says he, twisting one of his arms around. 'I believe that shoulder—no, it's all right.'

"He stoops over to brush the dust off his clothes, when out of his pocket drops a fine, nine-inch burglar's steel jimmy. He picks it up and looks at me sharp, and then grins and holds out his hand.

"'Brother,' says he, 'greetings. Didn't I see you in Southern Missouri last summer selling colored sand at half-a-dollar a teaspoonful to put into lamps to keep the oil from exploding?'

"'Oil,' says I, 'never explodes. It's the gas that forms that explodes.' But I shakes hands with him, anyway.

"'My name's Bill Bassett,' says he to me, 'and if you'll call it professional pride instead of conceit, I'll inform you that you have the pleasure of meeting the best burglar that ever set a gum-shoe on ground drained by the Mississippi River.'

"Well, me and this Bill Bassett sits on the ties and exchanges brags as artists in kindred lines will do. It seems he didn't have a cent, either, and we went into close caucus. He explained why an able burglar sometimes had to travel on freights by telling me that a servant girl had played him false in Little Rock, and he was making a quick get-away.

"'It's part of my business,' says Bill Bassett, 'to play up to the ruffles when I want to make a riffle as Raffles. 'Tis loves that makes the bit go 'round. Show me a house with the swag in it and a pretty parlor-maid, and you might as well call the silver melted down and sold, and me spilling truffles and that Château stuff on the napkin under my chin, while the police are calling it an inside job just because the old lady's nephew teaches a Bible class. I first make an impression on the girl,' says Bill, 'and when she lets me inside I make an impression on the locks. But this one in Little Rock done me,' says he. 'She saw me taking a trolley ride with another girl, and when I came 'round on the night she was to leave the door open for me it was fast. And I had keys made for the doors upstairs. But, no sir. She had sure cut off my locks. She was a Delilah,' says Bill Bassett.

"It seems that Bill tried to break in anyhow with his jimmy, but the girl emitted a succession of bravura noises like the top-riders of a tally-ho, and Bill had to take all the hurdles between there and the depot. As he had no baggage they tried hard to check his departure, but he made a train that was just pulling out.

"'Well,' says Bill Bassett, when we had exchanged memoirs of our dead lives, 'I could eat. This town don't look like it was kept under a Yale lock. Suppose we commit some mild atrocity that will bring in temporary expense money. I don't suppose you've brought along any hair tonic or rolled gold watch-chains, or similar law-defying swindles that you could sell on the plaza to the pikers of the paretic populace, have you?'

"'No,' says I, 'I left an elegant line of Patagonian diamond earrings and rainy-day sunbursts in my valise at Peavine. But they're to stay there till some of them black-gum trees begin to glut the market with yellow clings and Japanese plums. I reckon we can't count on them unless we take Luther Burbank in for a partner.'

"'Very well,' says Bassett, 'we'll do the best we can. Maybe after dark I'll borrow a hairpin from some lady, and open the Farmers and Drovers Marine Bank with it.'

"While we were talking, up pulls a passenger train to the depot near by. A person in a high hat gets off on the wrong side of the train and comes tripping down the track towards us. He was a little, fat man with a big nose and rat's eyes, but dressed expensive, and carrying a hand-satchel careful, as if it had eggs or railroad bonds in it. He passes by us and keeps on down the track, not appearing to notice the town.

"'Come on,' says Bill Bassett to me, starting after him.

"'Where?' I asks.

"'Lordy!' says Bill, 'had you forgot you was in the desert? Didn't you see Colonel Manna drop down right before your eyes? Don't you hear the rustling of General Raven's wings? I'm surprised at you, Elijah.'

"We overtook the stranger in the edge of some woods, and, as it was after sun-down and in a quiet place, nobody saw us stop him. Bill takes the silk hat off the man's head and brushes it with his sleeve and puts it back.

"'What does this mean, sir?' says the man.

"'When I wore one of these,' says Bill, 'and felt embarrassed, I always done that. Not having one now I had to use yours. I hardly know how to begin, sir, in explaining our business with you, but I guess we'll try your pockets first.'

"Bill Bassett felt in all of them, and looked disgusted.

"'Not even a watch,' he says. 'Ain't you ashamed of yourself, you whited sculpture? Going about dressed like a head-waiter, and financed like a Count! You haven't even got carfare. What did you do with your transfer?'

"The man speaks up and says he has no assets or valuables of any sort. But Bassett takes his hand-satchel and opens it. Out comes some collars and socks and a half a page of a newspaper clipped out. Bill reads the clipping careful, and holds out his hand to the held-up party.

"'Brother,' says he, 'greetings! Accept the apologies of friends. I am Bill Bassett, the burglar. Mr. Peters, you must make the acquaintance of Mr. Alfred E. Ricks. Shake hands. Mr. Peters,' says Bill, 'stands about halfway between me and you, Mr. Ricks, in the line of havoc and corruption. He always gives something for the money he gets. I'm glad to meet you, Mr. Ricks—you and Mr. Peters. This is the first time I ever attended a full gathering of the National Synod of Sharks— housebreaking, swindling, and financiering all represented. Please examine Mr. Ricks's credentials, Mr. Peters.'

"The piece of newspaper that Bill Bassett handed me had a good picture of this Ricks on it. It was a Chicago paper, and it had obloquies of Ricks in every paragraph. By reading it over I harvested the intelligence that said alleged Ricks had laid off all that portion of the State of Florida that lies under water into town lots and sold 'em to alleged innocent investors from his magnificently furnished offices in Chicago. After he had taken in a hundred thousand or so dollars one of these fussy purchasers that are always making trouble (I've had 'em actually try gold watches I've sold 'em with acid) took a cheap excursion down to the land where it is always just before supper to look at his lot and see if it didn't need a new paling or two on the fence, and market a few lemons in time for the Christmas present trade. He hires a surveyor to find his lot for him. They run the line out and find the flourishing town of Paradise Hollow, so advertised, to be about 40 rods and 16 poles S., 27° E. of the middle of Lake Okeechobee. This man's lot was under thirty-six feet of water, and, besides, had been preëmpted so long by the alligators and gars that his title looked fishy.

"Naturally, the man goes back to Chicago and makes it as hot for Alfred E. Ricks as the morning after a prediction of snow by the weather bureau. Ricks defied the allegation, but he couldn't deny the alligators. One morning the papers came out with a column about it, and Ricks come out by the fire-escape. It seems the alleged authorities had beat him to the safe-deposit box where he kept his winnings, and Ricks has to westward ho! with only feetwear and a dozen 15½ English pokes in his shopping bag. He happened to have some mileage left in his book, and that took him as far as the town in the wilderness where he was spilled out on me and Bill Bassett as Elijah III. with not a raven in sight for any of us.

"Then this Alfred E. Ricks lets out a squeak that he is hungry, too, and denies the hypothesis that he is good for the value, let alone the price, of a meal. And so, there was the three of us, representing, if we had a mind to draw syllogisms and parabolas, labor and trade and capital. Now, when trade has no capital there isn't a dicker to be made. And when capital has no money there's a stagnation in steak and onions. That put it up to the man with the jimmy.

"'Brother bushrangers,' says Bill Bassett, 'never yet, in trouble, did I desert a pal. Hard by, in yon wood, I seem to see unfurnished lodgings. Let us go there and wait till dark.'

"There was an old, deserted cabin in the grove, and we three took possession of it. After dark Bill Bassett tells us to wait, and goes out for half an hour. He comes back with an armful of bread and spareribs and pies.

"'Panhandled 'em at a farmhouse on Washita Avenue,' says he. 'Eat, drink and be leary.'

"The full moon was coming up bright, so we sat on the floor of the cabin and ate in the light of it. And this Bill Bassett begins to brag.

"'Sometimes,' says he, with his mouth full of country produce, 'I lose all patience with you people that think you are higher up in the profession than I am. Now, what could either of you have done in the present emergency to set us on our feet again? Could you do it, Ricksy?'

"'I must confess, Mr. Bassett,' says Ricks, speaking nearly inaudible out of a slice of pie. 'that at this immediate juncture I could not, perhaps, promote an enterprise to relieve the situation. Large operations, such as I direct, naturally require careful preparation in advance. I—'

"'I know, Ricksy,' breaks in Bill Bassett. 'You needn't finish. You need $500 to make the first payment on a blond typewriter, and four roomsful of quartered oak furniture. And you need $500 more for advertising contracts. And you need two weeks' time for the fish to begin to bite. Your line of relief would be about as useful in an emergency as advocating municipal ownership to cure a man suffocated by eighty-cent gas. And your graft ain't much swifter, Brother Peters,' he winds up.

"'Oh,' says I, 'I haven't seen you turn anything into gold with your wand yet, Mr. Good Fairy. 'Most anybody could rub the magic ring for a little left-over victuals.'

"'That was only getting the pumpkin ready,' says Bassett, braggy and cheerful. 'The coach and six'll drive up to the door before you know it, Miss Cinderella. Maybe you've got some scheme under your sleeve-holders that will give us a start.'

"'Son,' says I, 'I'm fifteen years older than you are, and young enough yet to take out an endowment policy. I've been broke before. We can see the lights of that town not half a mile away. I learned under Montague Silver, the greatest street man that ever spoke from a wagon. There are hundreds of men walking those streets this moment with grease spots on their clothes. Give me a gasoline lamp, a dry-goods box, and a two-dollar bar of white castile soap, cut into little—'

"'Where's your two dollars?' snickered Bill Bassett into my discourse. There was no use arguing with that burglar.

"'No,' he goes on; 'you're both babes-in-the-wood. Finance has closed the mahogany desk, and trade has put the shutters up. Both of you look to labor to start the wheels going. All right. You admit it. To-night I'll show you what Bill Bassett can do.'

"'Bassett tells me and Ricks not to leave the cabin till he comes back, even if it's daylight, and then he starts off toward town, whistling gay.

"This Alfred E. Ricks pulls off his shoes and his coat, lays a silk handkerchief over his hat, and lays down on the floor.

"'I think I will endeavor to secure a little slumber,' he squeaks. 'The day has been fatiguing. Good-night, my dear Mr. Peters.'

"'My regards to Morpheus,' says I. 'I think I'll sit up a while.'

"About two o'clock, as near as I could guess by my watch in Peavine, home comes our laboring man and kicks up Ricks, and calls us to the streak of bright moonlight shining in the cabin door. Then he spreads out five packages of one thousand dollars each on the floor, and begins to cackle over the nest-egg like a hen.

"'I'll tell you a few things about that town,' says he. 'It's named Rocky Springs, and they're building a Masonic temple, and it looks like the Democratic candidate for mayor is going to get soaked by a Pop, and Judge Tucker's wife, who has been down with pleurisy, is some better. I had a talk on these liliputian thesises before I could get a siphon in the fountain of knowledge that I was after. And there's a bank there called the Lumberman's Fidelity and Plowman's Savings Institution. It closed for business yesterday with $23,000 cash on hand. It will open this morning with $18,000—all silver—that's the reason I didn't bring more. There you are, trade and capital. Now, will you be bad?'

"'My young friend,' says Alfred E. Ricks, holding up his hands, 'have you robbed this bank? Dear me, dear me!'

"'You couldn't call it that,' says Bassett. '"Robbing" sounds harsh. All I had to do was to find out what street it was on. That town is so quiet that I could stand on the corner and hear the tumblers clicking in that safe lock—"right to 45; left twice to 80; right once to 60; left to 15"—as plain as the Yale captain giving orders in the football dialect. Now, boys,' says Bassett, 'this is an early rising town. They tell me the citizens are all up and stirring before daylight. I asked what for, and they said because breakfast was ready at that time. And what of merry Robin Hood? It must be Yoicks! and away with the tinkers' chorus. I'll stake you. How much do you want? Speak up. Capital.'

"'My dear young friend,' says this ground squirrel of a Ricks, standing on his hind legs and juggling nuts in his paws, 'I have friends in Denver who would assist me. If I had a hundred dollars I—'

"Bassett unpins a package of the currency and throws five twenties to Ricks.

"'Trade, how much?' he says to me.

"'Put your money up, Labor,' says I. 'I never yet drew upon honest toil for its hard-earned pittance. The dollars I get are surplus ones that are burning the pockets of damfools and greenhorns. When I stand on a street corner and sell a solid gold diamond ring to a yap for $3.00, I make just $2.60. And I know he's going to give it to a girl in return for all the benefits accruing from a $125.00 ring. His profits are $122.00. Which of us is the biggest fakir?'

"'And when you sell a poor woman a pinch of sand for fifty cents to keep her lamp from exploding,' says Bassett, 'what do you figure her gross earnings to be, with sand at forty cents a ton?'

"'Listen,' says I. 'I instruct her to keep her lamp clean and well filled. If she does that it can't burst. And with the sand in it she knows it can't, and she don't worry. It's a kind of Industrial Christian Science. She pays fifty cents, and gets both Rockefeller and Mrs. Eddy on the job. It ain't everybody that can let the gold-dust twins do their work.'

"Alfred E. Ricks all but licks the dust off of Bill Bassett's shoes.

"'My dear young friend,' says he, 'I will never forget your generosity. Heaven will reward you. But let me implore you to turn from your ways of violence and crime.'

"'Mousie,' says Bill, 'the hole in the wainscoting for yours. Your dogmas and inculcations sound to me like the last words of a bicycle pump. What has your high moral, elevator-service system of pillage brought you to? Penuriousness and want. Even Brother Peters, who insists upon contaminating the art of robbery with theories of commerce and trade, admitted he was on the lift. Both of you live by the gilded rule. Brother Peters,' says Bill, 'you'd better choose a slice of this embalmed currency. You're welcome.'

"I told Bill Bassett once more to put his money in his pocket. I never had the respect for burglary that some people have. I always gave something for the money I took, even if it was only some little trifle for a souvenir to remind 'em not to get caught again.

"And then Alfred E. Ricks grovels at Bill's feet again, and bids us adieu. He says he will have a team at a farmhouse, and drive to the station below, and take the train for Denver. It salubrified the atmosphere when that lamentable boll-worm took his departure. He was a disgrace to every non-industrial profession in the country. With all his big schemes and fine offices he had wound up unable even to get an honest meal except by the kindness of a strange and maybe unscrupulous burglar. I was glad to see him go, though I felt a little sorry for him, now that he was ruined forever. What could such a man do without a big capital to work with? Why, Alfred E. Ricks, as we left him, was as helpless as a turtle on its back. He couldn't have worked a scheme to beat a little girl out of a penny slate-pencil.

"When me and Bill Bassett was left alone I did a little sleight-of-mind turn in my head with a trade secret at the end of it. Thinks I, I'll show this Mr. Burglar Man the difference between business and labor. He had hurt some of my professional self-adulation by casting his Persians upon commerce and trade.

"'I won't take any of your money as a gift, Mr. Bassett,' says I to him, 'but if you'll pay my expenses as a traveling companion until we get out of the danger zone of the immoral deficit you have caused in this town's finances to-night, I'll be obliged.'

"Bill Bassett agreed to that, and we hiked westward as soon as we could catch a safe train.

"When we got to a town in Arizona called Los Perros I suggested that we once more try our luck on terra-cotta. That was the home of Montague Silver, my old instructor, now retired from business. I knew Monty would stake me to web money if I could show him a fly buzzing 'round in the locality. Bill Bassett said all towns looked alike to him as he worked mainly in the dark. So we got off the train in Los Perros, a fine little town in the silver region.

"I had an elegant little sure thing in the way of a commercial slungshot that I intended to hit Bassett behind the ear with. I wasn't going to take his money while he was asleep, but I was going to leave him with a lottery ticket that would represent in experience to him $4,755—I think that was the amount he had when we got off the train. But the first time I hinted to him about an investment, he turns on me and disencumbers himself of the following terms and expressions.

"'Brother Peters,' says he, 'it ain't a bad idea to go into an enterprise of some kind, as you suggest. I think I will. But if I do it will be such a cold proposition that nobody but Robert E. Peary and Charlie Fairbanks will be able to sit on the board of directors.'

"'I thought you might want to turn your money over,' says I.

"'I do,' says he, 'frequently. I can't sleep on one side all night. I'll tell you, Brother Peters,' says he, 'I'm going to start a poker room. I don't seem to care for the humdrum in swindling, such as peddling egg-beaters and working off breakfast food on Barnum and Bailey for sawdust to strew in their circus rings. But the gambling business,' says he, 'from the profitable side of the table is a good compromise between swiping silver spoons and selling penwipers at a Waldorf-Astoria charity bazar.'

"'Then,' says I, 'Mr. Bassett, you don't care to talk over my little business proposition?'

"'Why,' says he, 'do you know, you can't get a Pasteur institute to start up within fifty miles of where I live. I bite so seldom.'

"So, Bassett rents a room over a saloon and looks around for some furniture and chromos. The same night I went to Monty Silver's house, and he let me have $200 on my prospects. Then I went to the only store in Los Perros that sold playing cards and bought every deck in the house. The next morning when the store opened I was there bringing all the cards back with me. I said that my partner that was going to back me in the game had changed his mind; and I wanted to sell the cards back again. The storekeeper took 'em at half price.

"Yes, I was seventy-five dollars loser up to that time. But while I had the cards that night I marked every one in every deck. That was labor. And then trade and commerce had their innings, and the bread I had cast upon the waters began to come back in the form of cottage pudding with wine sauce.

"Of course I was among the first to buy chips at Bill Bassett's game. He had bought the only cards there was to be had in town; and I knew the back of every one of them better than I know the back of my head when the barber shows me my haircut in the two mirrors.

"When the game closed I had the five thousand and a few odd dollars, and all Bill Bassett had was the wanderlust and a black cat he had bought for a mascot. Bill shook hands with me when I left.

"'Brother Peters,' says he, 'I have no business being in business. I was preordained to labor. When a No. 1 burglar tries to make a James out of his jimmy he perpetrates an improfundity. You have a well-oiled and efficacious system of luck at cards,' says he. 'Peace go with you.' And I never afterward sees Bill Bassett again."

"Well, Jeff," said I, when the Autolycan adventurer seemed to have divulged the gist of his tale, "I hope you took care of the money. That would be a respecta—that is a considerable working capital if you should choose some day to settle down to some sort of regular business."

"Me?" said Jeff, virtuously. "You can bet I've taken care of that five thousand."

He tapped his coat over the region of his chest exultantly.

"Gold mining stock," he explained, "every cent of it. Shares par value one dollar. Bound to go up 500 per cent. within a year. Non-assessable. The Blue Gopher Mine. Just discovered a month ago. Better get in yourself if you've any spare dollars on hand."

"Sometimes," said I, "these mines are not—"

"Oh, this one's solid as an old goose," said Jeff. "Fifty thousand dollars' worth of ore in sight, and 10 per cent. monthly earnings guaranteed."

He drew a long envelope from his pocket and cast it on the table.

"Always carry it with me," said he. "So the burglar can't corrupt or the capitalist break in and water it."

I looked at the beautifully engraved certificate of stock.

"In Colorado, I see," said I. "And, by the way, Jeff, what was the name of the little man who went to Denver—the one you and Bill met at the station?"

"Alfred E. Ricks," said Jeff, "was the toad's designation."

"I see," said I, "the president of this mining company signs himself A. L. Fredericks. I was wondering—"

"Let me see that stock," said Jeff quickly, almost snatching it from me.

To mitigate, even though slightly, the embarrassment I summoned the waiter and ordered another bottle of the Barbera. I thought it was the least I could do.

NEW YORK

The Social Triangle

A<small>T THE</small> stroke of six Ikey Snigglefritz laid down his goose. Ikey was a tailor's apprentice. Are there tailor's apprentices nowadays?

At any rate, Ikey toiled and snipped and basted and pressed and patched and sponged all day in the steamy fetor of a tailor-shop. But when work was done Ikey hitched his wagon to such stars as his firmament let shine.

It was Saturday night, and the boss laid twelve begrimed and begrudged dollars in his hand. Ikey dabbled discreetly in water, donned coat, hat and collar with its frazzled tie and chalcedony pin, and set forth in pursuit of his ideals.

For each of us, when our day's work is done, must seek our ideal, whether it be love or pinochle or lobster à la Newburg, or the sweet silence of the musty bookshelves.

Behold Ikey as he ambles up the street beneath the roaring "El" between the rows of reeking sweatshops. Pallid, stooping, insignificant, squalid, doomed to exist forever in penury of body and mind, yet, as he swings his cheap cane and projects the noisome inhalations from his cigarette, you perceive that he nurtures in his narrow bosom the bacillus of society.

Ikey's legs carried him to and into that famous place of entertainment known as the Café Maginnis—famous because it was the rendezvous of Billy McMahan, the greatest man, the most wonderful man, Ikey thought, that the world had ever produced.

Billy McMahan was the district leader. Upon him the Tiger purred, and his hand held manna to scatter. Now, as Ikey entered, McMahan stood, flushed and triumphant and mighty, the centre of a huzzaing concourse of his lieutenants and constituents. It seems there had been an election; a signal victory had been won; the city had been swept back into line by a resistless besom of ballots.

Ikey slunk along the bar and gazed, breath-quickened, at his idol.

How magnificent was Billy McMahan, with his great, smooth, laughing face; his gray eye, shrewd as a chicken hawk's;

his diamond ring, his voice like a bugle call, his prince's air, his plump and active roll of money, his clarion call to friend and comrade—oh, what a king of men he was! How he obscured his lieutenants, though they themselves loomed large and serious, blue of chin and important of mien, with hands buried deep in the pockets of their short overcoats! But Billy—oh, what small avail are words to paint for you his glory as seen by Ikey Snigglefritz!

The Café Maginnis rang to the note of victory. The white-coated bartenders threw themselves featfully upon bottle, cork and glass. From a score of clear Havanas the air received its paradox of clouds. The leal and the hopeful shook Billy McMahan's hand. And there was born suddenly in the worshipful soul of Ikey Snigglefritz an audacious, thrilling impulse.

He stepped forward into the little cleared space in which majesty moved, and held out his hand.

Billy McMahan grasped it unhesitatingly, shook it and smiled.

Made mad now by the gods who were about to destroy him, Ikey threw away his scabbard and charged upon Olympus.

"Have a drink with me, Billy," he said familiarly, "you and your friends?"

"Don't mind if I do, old man," said the great leader, "just to keep the ball rolling."

The last spark of Ikey's reason fled.

"Wine," he called to the bartender, waving a trembling hand.

The corks of three bottles were drawn; the champagne bubbled in the long row of glasses set upon the bar. Billy McMahan took his and nodded, with his beaming smile, at Ikey. The lieutenants and satellites took theirs and growled "Here's to you." Ikey took his nectar in delirium. All drank.

Ikey threw his week's wages in a crumpled roll upon the bar.

"C'rect," said the bartender, smoothing the twelve one-dollar notes. The crowd surged around Billy McMahan again. Some one was telling how Brannigan fixed 'em over in the Eleventh. Ikey leaned against the bar a while, and then went out.

He went down Hester street and up Chrystie, and down Delancey to where he lived. And there his women folk, a bibulous mother and three dingy sisters, pounced upon him for his wages. And at his confession they shrieked and objurgated him in the pithy rhetoric of the locality.

But even as they plucked at him and struck him Ikey remained in his ecstatic trance of joy. His head was in the clouds; the star was drawing his wagon. Compared with what he had achieved the loss of wages and the bray of women's tongues were slight affairs.

He had shaken the hand of Billy McMahan.

Billy McMahan had a wife, and upon her visiting cards was engraved the name "Mrs. William Darragh McMahan." And there was a certain vexation attendant upon these cards; for, small as they were, there were houses in which they could not be inserted. Billy McMahan was a dictator in politics, a four-walled tower in business, a mogul, dreaded, loved and obeyed among his own people. He was growing rich; the daily papers had a dozen men on his trail to chronicle his every word of wisdom; he had been honored in caricature holding the Tiger cringing in leash.

But the heart of Billy was sometimes sore within him. There was a race of men from which he stood apart but that he viewed with the eye of Moses looking over into the promised land. He, too, had ideals, even as had Ikey Snigglefritz; and sometimes, hopeless of attaining them, his own solid success was as dust and ashes in his mouth. And Mrs. William Darragh McMahan wore a look of discontent upon her plump but pretty face, and the very rustle of her silks seemed a sigh.

There was a brave and conspicuous assemblage in the dining salon of a noted hostelry where Fashion loves to display her charms. At one table sat Billy McMahan and his wife. Mostly silent they were, but the accessories they enjoyed little needed the indorsement of speech. Mrs. McMahan's diamonds were outshone by few in the room. The waiter bore the costliest brands of wine to their table. In evening dress, with an expression of gloom upon his smooth and massive countenance, you would look in vain for a more striking figure than Billy's.

Four tables away sat alone a tall, slender man, about thirty, with thoughtful, melancholy eyes, a Van Dyke beard and peculiarly white, thin hands. He was dining on filet mignon, dry toast and appollinaris. That man was Cortlandt Van Duyckink, a man worth eighty millions, who inherited and held a sacred seat in the exclusive inner circle of society.

Billy McMahan spoke to no one around him, because he knew no one. Van Duyckink kept his eyes on his plate because he knew that every eye present was hungry to catch his. He could bestow knighthood and prestige by a nod, and he was chary of creating a too extensive nobility.

And then Billy McMahan conceived and accomplished the most startling and audacious act of his life. He rose deliberately and walked over to Cortlandt Van Duyckink's table and held out his hand.

"Say, Mr. Van Duyckink," he said, "I've heard you was talking about starting some reforms among the poor people down in my district. I'm McMahan, you know. Say, now, if that's straight I'll do all I can to help you. And what I says goes in that neck of the woods, don't it? Oh, say, I rather guess it does."

Van Duyckink's rather sombre eyes lighted up. He rose to his lank height and grasped Billy McMahan's hand.

"Thank you, Mr. McMahan," he said, in his deep, serious tones. "I have been thinking of doing some work of that sort. I shall be glad of your assistance. It pleases me to have become acquainted with you."

Billy walked back to his seat. His shoulder was tingling from the accolade bestowed by royalty. A hundred eyes were now turned upon him in envy and new admiration. Mrs. William Darragh McMahan trembled with ecstasy, so that her diamonds smote the eye almost with pain. And now it was apparent that at many tables there were those who suddenly remembered that they enjoyed Mr. McMahan's acquaintance. He saw smiles and bows about him. He became enveloped in the aura of dizzy greatness. His campaign coolness deserted him.

"Wine for that gang!" he commanded the waiter, pointing with his finger. "Wine over there. Wine to those three gents by that green bush. Tell 'em it's on me. D——n it! Wine for everybody!"

The waiter ventured to whisper that it was perhaps inexpedient to carry out the order, in consideration of the dignity of the house and its custom.

"All right," said Billy, "if it's against the rules. I wonder if 'twould do to send my friend Van Duyckink a bottle. No? Well, it'll flow all right at the caffy to-night, just the same. It'll be rubber boots for anybody who comes in there any time up to 2 A.M."

Billy McMahan was happy.

He had shaken the hand of Cortlandt Van Duyckink.

The big pale-gray auto with its shining metal work looked out of place moving slowly among the pushcarts and trash-heaps on the lower east side. So did Cortlandt Van Duyckink, with his aristocratic face and white, thin hands, as he steered carefully between the groups of ragged, scurrying youngsters in the streets. And so did Miss Constance Schuyler, with her dim, ascetic beauty, seated at his side.

"Oh, Cortlandt," she breathed, "isn't it sad that human beings have to live in such wretchedness and poverty? And you—how noble it is of you to think of them, to give your time and money to improve their condition!"

Van Duyckink turned his solemn eyes upon her.

"It is little," he said, sadly, "that I can do. The question is a large one, and belongs to society. But even individual effort is not thrown away. Look, Constance! On this street I have arranged to build soup kitchens, where no one who is hungry will be turned away. And down this other street are the old buildings that I shall cause to be torn down and there erect others in place of those death-traps of fire and disease."

Down Delancey slowly crept the pale-gray auto. Away from it toddled coveys of wondering, tangle-haired, barefooted, unwashed children. It stopped before a crazy brick structure, foul and awry.

Van Duyckink alighted to examine at a better perspective one of the leaning walls. Down the steps of the building came a young man who seemed to epitomize its degradation, squalor and infelicity—a narrow-chested, pale, unsavory young man, puffing at a cigarette.

Obeying a sudden impulse, Van Duyckink stepped out and warmly grasped the hand of what seemed to him a living rebuke.

"I want to know you people," he said, sincerely. "I am going to help you as much as I can. We shall be friends."

As the auto crept carefully away Cortlandt Van Duyckink felt an unaccustomed glow about his heart. He was near to being a happy man.

He had shaken the hand of Ikey Snigglefritz.

A Little Local Colour

I MENTIONED to Rivington that I was in search of characteristic New York scenes and incidents—something typical, I told him, without necessarily having to spell the first syllable with an "i."

"Oh, for your writing business," said Rivington; "you couldn't have applied to a better shop. What I don't know about little old New York wouldn't make a sonnet to a sunbonnet. I'll put you right in the middle of so much local colour that you won't know whether you are a magazine cover or in the erysipelas ward. When do you want to begin?"

Rivington is a young-man-about-town and a New Yorker by birth, preference and incommutability.

I told him that I would be glad to accept his escort and guardianship so that I might take notes of Manhattan's grand, gloomy and peculiar idiosyncrasies, and that the time of so doing would be at his own convenience.

"We'll begin this very evening," said Rivington, himself interested, like a good fellow. "Dine with me at seven, and then I'll steer you up against metropolitan phases so thick you'll have to have a kinetoscope to record 'em."

So I dined with Rivington pleasantly at his club, in Forty-eleventh street, and then we set forth in pursuit of the elusive tincture of affairs.

As we came out of the club there stood two men on the sidewalk near the steps in earnest conversation.

"And by what process of ratiocination," said one of them, "do you arrive at the conclusion that the division of society into producing and non-possessing classes predicates failure when compared with competitive systems that are monopolizing in tendency and result inimically to industrial evolution?"

"Oh, come off your perch!" said the other man, who wore glasses. "Your premises won't come out in the wash. You wind-jammers who apply bandy-legged theories to concrete categorical syllogisms send logical conclusions skallybootin' into the infinitesimal ragbag. You can't pull my leg with an old sophism with whiskers on it. You quote Marx and Hyndman and Kautsky—what are they?—shines! Tolstoi?—his garret is full of rats. I put it to you over the home-plate that the idea of a coöperative commonwealth and an abolishment of competitive systems simply takes the rag off the bush and gives me hyperesthesia of the roopteetoop! The skookum house for yours!"

I stopped a few yards away and took out my little notebook.

"Oh, come ahead," said Rivington, somewhat nervously; "you don't want to listen to that."

"Why man," I whispered, "this is just what I do want to hear. These slang types are among your city's most distinguishing features. Is this the Bowery variety? I really must hear more of it."

"If I follow you," said the man who had spoken first, "you do not believe it possible to reorganize society on the basis of common interest?"

"Shinny on your own side!" said the man with glasses. "You never heard any such music from my foghorn. What I said was that I did not believe it practicable just now. The guys with wads are not in the frame of mind to slack up on the mazuma, and the man with the portable tin banqueting canister isn't exactly ready to join the Bible class. You can bet your variegated socks that the situation is all spifflicated up from the Battery to breakfast! What the country needs is for some bully old bloke like Cobden or some wise guy like old Ben Franklin to sashay up to the front and biff the nigger's head with the baseball. Do you catch my smoke? What?"

Rivington pulled me by the arm impatiently.

"Please come on," he said. "Let's go see something. This isn't what you want."

"Indeed, it is," I said resisting. "This tough talk is the very stuff that counts. There is a picturesqueness about the speech of the lower order of people that is quite unique. Did you say that this is the Bowery variety of slang?"

"Oh, well," said Rivington, giving it up, "I'll tell you straight. That's one of our college professors talking. He ran down for a day or two at the club. It's a sort of fad with him lately to use slang in his conversation. He thinks it improves language. The man he is talking to is one of New York's famous social economists. Now will you come on? You can't use that, you know."

"No," I agreed; "I can't use that. Would you call that typical of New York?"

"Of course not," said Rivington, with a sigh of relief. "I'm glad you see the difference. But if you want to hear the real old tough Bowery slang I'll take you down where you'll get your fill of it."

"I would like it," I said; "that is, if it's the real thing. I've often read it in books, but I never heard it. Do you think it will be dangerous to go unprotected among those characters?"

"Oh, no," said Rivington; "not at this time of night. To tell the truth, I haven't been along the Bowery in a long time, but I know it as well as I do Broadway. We'll look up some of the typical Bowery boys and get them to talk. It'll be worth your while. They talk a peculiar dialect that you won't hear anywhere else on earth."

Rivington and I went east in a Forty-second street car and then south on the Third avenue line.

At Houston street we got off and walked.

"We are now on the famous Bowery," said Rivington; "the Bowery celebrated in song and story."

We passed block after block of "gents'" furnishing stores—the windows full of shirts with prices attached and cuffs inside. In other windows were neckties and no shirts. People walked up and down the sidewalks.

"In some ways," said I, "this reminds me of Kokomono, Ind., during the peach-crating season."

Rivington was nettled.

"Step into one of these saloons or vaudeville shows," said he, "with a large roll of money, and see how quickly the Bowery will sustain its reputation."

"You make impossible conditions," said I, coldly.

By and by Rivington stopped and said we were in the heart of the Bowery. There was a policeman on the corner whom Rivington knew.

"Hallo, Donahue!" said my guide. "How goes it? My friend and I are down this way looking up a bit of local colour. He's anxious to meet one of the Bowery types. Can't you put us on to something genuine in that line—something that's got the colour, you know?"

Policeman Donahue turned himself about ponderously, his

florid face full of good-nature. He pointed with his club down the street.

"Sure!" he said huskily. "Here comes a lad now that was born on the Bowery and knows every inch of it. If he's ever been above Bleecker street he's kept it to himself."

A man about twenty-eight or twenty-nine, with a smooth face, was sauntering toward us with his hands in his coat pockets. Policeman Donahue stopped him with a courteous wave of his club.

"Evening, Kerry," he said. "Here's a couple of gents, friends of mine, that want to hear you spiel something about the Bowery. Can you reel 'em off a few yards?"

"Certainly, Donahue," said the young man, pleasantly. "Good evening, gentlemen," he said to us, with a pleasant smile. Donahue walked off on his beat.

"This is the goods," whispered Rivington, nudging me with his elbow. "Look at his jaw!"

"Say, cull," said Rivington, pushing back his hat, "wot's doin'? Me and my friend's taking a look down de old line—see? De copper tipped us off dat you was wise to de Bowery. Is dat right?"

I could not help admiring Rivington's power of adapting himself to his surroundings.

"Donahue was right," said the young man, frankly; "I was brought up on the Bowery. I have been newsboy, teamster, pugilist, member of an organized band of 'toughs,' bartender, and a 'sport' in various meanings of the word. The experience certainly warrants the supposition that I have at least a passing acquaintance with a few phases of Bowery life. I will be pleased to place whatever knowledge and experience I have at the service of my friend Donahue's friends."

Rivington seemed ill at ease.

"I say," he said—somewhat entreatingly, "I thought—you're not stringing us, are you? It isn't just the kind of talk we expected. You haven't even said 'Hully gee!' once. Do you really belong on the Bowery?"

"I am afraid," said the Bowery boy, smilingly, "that at some time you have been enticed into one of the dives of literature and had the counterfeit coin of the Bowery passed upon you. The 'argot' to which you doubtless refer was the invention of certain of your literary 'discoverers' who invaded the unknown wilds below Third avenue and put strange sounds into the mouths of the inhabitants. Safe in their homes far to the north and west, the credulous readers who were beguiled by this new 'dialect' perused and believed. Like Marco Polo and Mungo Park—pioneers indeed, but ambitious souls who could not draw the line of demarcation between discovery and invention—the literary bones of these explorers are dotting the trackless wastes of the subway. While it is true that after the publication of the mythical language attributed to the dwellers along the Bowery certain of its pat phrases and apt metaphors were adopted and, to a limited extent, used in this locality, it was because our people are prompt in assimilating whatever is to their commercial advantage. To the tourists who visited our newly discovered clime, and who expected a realization of their literary guide books, they supplied the demands of the market.

"But perhaps I am wandering from the question. In what way can I assist you, gentlemen? I beg you will believe that the hospitality of the street is extended to all. There are, I regret to say, many catchpenny places of entertainment, but I cannot conceive that they would entice you."

I felt Rivington lean somewhat heavily against me.

"Say!" he remarked, with uncertain utterance; "come and have a drink with us."

"Thank you, but I never drink. I find that alcohol, even in the smallest quantities, alters the perspective. And I must preserve my perspective, for I am studying the Bowery. I have lived in it nearly thirty years, and I am just beginning to understand its heartbeats. It is like a great river fed by a hundred alien streams. Each influx brings strange seeds on its flood, strange silt and weeds, and now and then a flower of rare promise. To construe this river requires a man who can build dykes against the overflow, who is a naturalist, a geologist, a humanitarian, a diver and a strong swimmer. I love my Bowery. It was my cradle and is my inspiration. I have published one book. The critics have been kind. I put my heart in it. I am writing another, into which I hope to put both heart and brain. Consider me your guide, gentlemen. Is there anything I can take you to see, any place to which I can conduct you?"

I was afraid to look at Rivington except with one eye.

"Thanks," said Rivington. "We were looking up . . . that is . . . my friend . . . confound it; it's against all precedent, you know . . . awfully obliged . . . just the same."

"In case," said our friend, "you would like to meet some of our Bowery young men I would be pleased to have you visit the quarters of our East Side Kappa Delta Phi Society, only two blocks east of here."

"Awfully sorry," said Rivington, "but my friend's got me on the jump to-night. He's a terror when he's out after local colour. Now, there's nothing I would like better than to drop in at the Kappa Delta Phi, but—some other time!"

We said our farewells and boarded a home-bound car. We had a rabbit on upper Broadway, and then I parted with Rivington on a street corner.

"Well, anyhow," said he, braced and recovered, "it couldn't have happened anywhere but in little old New York."

Which to say the least, was typical of Rivington.

A Newspaper Story

AT 8 A.M. it lay on Giuseppi's news-stand, still damp from the presses. Giuseppi, with the cunning of his ilk, philandered on the opposite corner, leaving his patrons to help themselves, no doubt on a theory related to the hypothesis of the watched pot.

This particular newspaper was, according to its custom and design, an educator, a guide, a monitor, a champion and a household counsellor and *vade mecum*.

From its many excellencies might be selected three editorials. One was in simple and chaste but illuminating language directed to parents and teachers, deprecating corporal punishment for children.

Another was an accusive and significant warning addressed to a notorious labour leader who was on the point of instigating his clients to a troublesome strike.

The third was an eloquent demand that the police force be sustained and aided in everything that tended to increase its efficiency as public guardians and servants.

Besides these more important chidings and requisitions upon the store of good citizenship was a wise prescription or form of procedure laid out by the editor of the heart-to-heart column in the specific case of a young man who had complained of the obduracy of his lady love, teaching him how he might win her.

Again, there was, on the beauty page, a complete answer to a young lady inquirer who desired admonition toward the securing of bright eyes, rosy cheeks and a beautiful countenance.

One other item requiring special cognizance was a brief "personal," running thus:

DEAR JACK:—Forgive me. You were right. Meet me corner Madison and —th at 8.30 this morning. We leave at noon.
PENITENT.

At 8 o'clock a young man with a haggard look and the feverish gleam of unrest in his eye dropped a penny and picked up the top paper as he passed Giuseppi's stand. A sleepless night had left him a late riser. There was an office to be reached by nine, and a shave and a hasty cup of coffee to be crowded into the interval.

He visited his barber shop and then hurried on his way. He pocketed his paper, meditating a belated perusal of it at the luncheon hour. At the next corner it fell from his pocket, carrying with it his pair of new gloves. Three blocks he walked, missed the gloves and turned back fuming.

Just on the half-hour he reached the corner where lay the gloves and the paper. But he strangely ignored that which he had come to seek. He was holding two little hands as tightly as ever he could and looking into two penitent brown eyes, while joy rioted in his heart.

"Dear Jack," she said, "I knew you would be here on time."

"I wonder what she means by that," he was saying to himself; "but it's all right, it's all right."

A big wind puffed out of the west, picked up the paper from the sidewalk, opened it out and sent it flying and whirling down a side street. Up that street was driving a skittish bay to a spider-wheel buggy, the young man who had written to the heart-to-heart editor for a recipe that he might win her for whom he sighed.

The wind, with a prankish flurry, flapped the flying newspaper against the face of the skittish bay. There was a lengthened streak of bay mingled with the red of running gear that stretched itself out for four blocks. Then a water-hydrant played its part in the cosmogony, the buggy became matchwood as foreordained, and the driver rested very quietly where he had been flung on the asphalt in front of a certain brownstone mansion.

They came out and had him inside very promptly. And there was one who made herself a pillow for his head, and cared for no curious eyes, bending over and saying, "Oh, it was you; it was you all the time, Bobby! Couldn't you see it? And if you die, why, so must I, and——"

But in all this wind we must hurry to keep in touch with our paper.

Policeman O'Brine arrested it as a character dangerous to traffic. Straightening its dishevelled leaves with his big, slow fingers, he stood a few feet from the family entrance of the Shandon Bells Café. One headline he spelled out ponderously: "The Papers to the Front in a Move to Help the Police."

But, whisht! The voice of Danny, the head bartender, through the crack of the door: "Here's a nip for ye, Mike, ould man."

Behind the widespread, amicable columns of the press Policeman O'Brine receives swiftly his nip of the real stuff. He moves away, stalwart, refreshed, fortified, to his duties. Might not the editor man view with pride the early, the spiritual, the literal fruit that had blessed his labours.

Policeman O'Brine folded the paper and poked it playfully under the arm of a small boy that was passing. That boy was named Johnny, and he took the paper home with him. His sister was named Gladys, and she had written to the beauty editor of the paper asking for the practicable touchstone of beauty. That was weeks ago, and she had ceased to look for an answer. Gladys was a pale girl, with dull eyes and a discontented expression. She was dressing to go up to the avenue to get some braid. Beneath her skirt she pinned two leaves of the paper Johnny had brought. When she walked the rustling sound was an exact imitation of the real thing.

On the street she met the Brown girl from the flat below and stopped to talk. The Brown girl turned green. Only silk at $5 a yard could make the sound that she heard when Gladys moved. The Brown girl, consumed by jealousy, said something spiteful and went her way, with pinched lips.

Gladys proceeded toward the avenue. Her eyes now sparkled like jagerfonteins. A rosy bloom visited her cheeks; a triumphant, subtle, vivifying smile transfigured her face. She was beautiful. Could the beauty editor have seen her then! There was something in her answer in the paper, I believe, about cultivating kind feelings toward others in order to make plain features attractive.

The labour leader against whom the paper's solemn and weighty editorial injunction was laid was the father of Gladys and Johnny. He picked up the remains of the journal from which Gladys had ravished a cosmetic of silken sounds. The editorial did not come under his eye, but instead it was greeted by one of those ingenious and specious puzzle problems that enthrall alike the simpleton and the sage.

The labour leader tore off half of the page, provided himself with table, pencil and paper and glued himself to his puzzle.

Three hours later, after waiting vainly for him at the appointed place, other more conservative leaders declared and ruled in favour of arbitration, and the strike with its attendant dangers was averted. Subsequent editions of the paper referred, in coloured inks, to the clarion tone of its successful denunciation of the labour leader's intended designs.

The remaining leaves of the active journal also went loyally to the proving of its potency.

When Johnny returned from school he sought a secluded spot and removed the missing columns from the inside of his clothing, where they had been artfully distributed so as to successfully defend such areas as are generally attacked during scholastic castigations. Johnny attended a private school and had had trouble with his teacher. As has been said, there was an excellent editorial against corporal punishment in that morning's issue, and no doubt it had its effect.

After this can any one doubt the power of the press?

After Twenty Years

THE POLICEMAN on the beat moved up the avenue impressively. The impressiveness was habitual and not for show, for spectators were few. The time was barely 10 o'clock at night, but chilly gusts of wind with a taste of rain in them had well nigh depeopled the streets.

Trying doors as he went, twirling his club with many intricate and artful movements, turning now and then to cast his watchful eye adown the pacific thoroughfare, the officer, with his stalwart form and slight swagger, made a fine picture of a guardian of the peace. The vicinity was one that kept early hours. Now and then you might see the lights of a cigar store or of an all-night lunch counter; but the majority of the doors belonged to business places that had long since been closed.

When about midway of a certain block the policeman suddenly slowed his walk. In the doorway of a darkened hardware store a man leaned, with an unlighted cigar in his mouth. As the policeman walked up to him the man spoke up quickly.

"It's all right, officer," he said, reassuringly. "I'm just waiting for a friend. It's an appointment made twenty years ago. Sounds a little funny to you, doesn't it? Well, I'll explain if you'd like to make certain it's all straight. About that long ago there used to be a restaurant where this store stands—'Big Joe' Brady's restaurant."

"Until five years ago," said the policeman. "It was torn down then."

The man in the doorway struck a match and lit his cigar. The light showed a pale, square-jawed face with keen eyes, and a little white scar near his right eyebrow. His scarfpin was a large diamond, oddly set.

"Twenty years ago to-night," said the man. "I dined here at 'Big Joe' Brady's with Jimmy Wells, my best chum, and the finest chap in the world. He and I were raised here in New York, just like two brothers, together. I was eighteen and Jimmy was twenty. The next morning I was to start for the West to make my fortune. You couldn't have dragged Jimmy out of New York; he thought it was the only place on earth.

Well, we agreed that night that we would meet here again exactly twenty years from that date and time, no matter what our conditions might be or from what distance we might have to come. We figured that in twenty years each of us ought to have our destiny worked out and our fortunes made, whatever they were going to be."

"It sounds pretty interesting," said the policeman. "Rather a long time between meets, though, it seems to me. Haven't you heard from your friend since you left?"

"Well, yes, for a time we corresponded," said the other. "But after a year or two we lost track of each other. You see, the West is a pretty big proposition, and I kept hustling around over it pretty lively. But I know Jimmy will meet me here if he's alive, for he always was the truest, stanchest old chap in the world. He'll never forget. I came a thousand miles to stand in this door to-night, and it's worth it if my old partner turns up."

The waiting man pulled out a handsome watch, the lids of it set with small diamonds.

"Three minutes to ten," he announced. "It was exactly ten o'clock when we parted here at the restaurant door."

"Did pretty well out West, didn't you?" asked the policeman.

"You bet! I hope Jimmy has done half as well. He was a kind of plodder, though, good fellow as he was. I've had to compete with some of the sharpest wits going to get my pile. A man gets in a groove in New York. It takes the West to put a razor-edge on him."

The policeman twirled his club and took a step or two.

"I'll be on my way. Hope your friend comes around all right. Going to call time on him sharp?"

"I should say not!" said the other. "I'll give him half an hour at least. If Jimmy is alive on earth he'll be here by that time. So long, officer."

"Good-night, sir," said the policeman, passing on along his beat, trying doors as he went.

There was now a fine, cold drizzle falling, and the wind had risen from its uncertain puffs into a steady blow. The few foot passengers astir in that quarter hurried dismally and silently along with coat collars turned high and pocketed hands. And in the door of the hardware store the man who had come a thousand miles to fill an appointment, uncertain almost to absurdity, with the friend of his youth, smoked his cigar and waited.

About twenty minutes he waited, and then a tall man in a long overcoat, with collar turned up to his ears, hurried across from the opposite side of the street. He went directly to the waiting man.

"Is that you, Bob?" he asked, doubtfully.

"Is that you, Jimmy Wells?" cried the man in the door.

"Bless my heart!" exclaimed the new arrival, grasping both the other's hands with his own. "It's Bob, sure as fate. I was certain I'd find you here if you were still in existence. Well, well, well!—twenty years is a long time. The old restaurant's gone, Bob; I wish it had lasted, so we could have had another dinner there. How has the West treated you, old man?"

"Bully; it has given me everything I asked it for. You've changed lots, Jimmy. I never thought you were so tall by two or three inches."

"Oh, I grew a bit after I was twenty."

"Doing well in New York, Jimmy?"

"Moderately. I have a position in one of the city departments. Come on, Bob; we'll go around to a place I know of, and have a good long talk about old times."

The two men started up the street, arm in arm. The man from the West, his egotism enlarged by success, was beginning to outline the history of his career. The other, submerged in his overcoat, listened with interest.

At the corner stood a drug store, brilliant with electric lights. When they came into this glare each of them turned simultaneously to gaze upon the other's face.

The man from the West stopped suddenly and released his arm.

"You're not Jimmy Wells," he snapped. "Twenty years is a long time, but not long enough to change a man's nose from a Roman to a pug."

"It sometimes changes a good man into a bad one," said the tall man. "You've been under arrest for ten minutes, 'Silky' Bob. Chicago thinks you may have dropped over our way and wires us she wants to have a chat with you. Going quietly, are you? That's sensible. Now, before we go on to the station here's a note I was asked to hand you. You may read it here at the window. It's from Patrolman Wells."

The man from the West unfolded the little piece of paper handed him. His hand was steady when he began to read, but it trembled a little by the time he had finished. The note was rather short.

"Bob: I was at the appointed place on time. When you struck the match to light your cigar I saw it was the face of the man wanted in Chicago. Somehow I couldn't do it myself, so I went around and got a plain clothes man to do the job.

"JIMMY."

Lost on Dress Parade

M R. TOWERS Chandler was pressing his evening suit in his hall bedroom. One iron was heating on a small gas stove; the other was being pushed vigorously back and forth to make the desirable crease that would be seen later on extending in straight lines from Mr. Chandler's patent leather shoes to the edge of his low-cut vest. So much of the hero's toilet may be intrusted to our confidence. The remainder may be guessed by those whom genteel poverty has driven to ignoble expedient. Our next view of him shall be as he descends the steps of his lodging-house immaculately and correctly clothed; calm, assured, handsome—in appearance the typical New York young clubman setting out, slightly bored, to inaugurate the pleasures of the evening.

Chandler's honorarium was $18 per week. He was employed in the office of an architect. He was twenty-two years old; he considered architecture to be truly an art; and he honestly believed—though he would not have dared to admit it in New York—that the Flatiron Building was inferior in design to the great cathedral in Milan.

Out of each week's earnings Chandler set aside $1. At the end of each ten weeks with the extra capital thus accumulated, he purchased one gentleman's evening from the bargain counter of stingy old Father Time. He arrayed himself in the regalia of millionaires and presidents; he took himself to the quarter where life is brightest and showiest, and there dined with taste and luxury. With ten dollars a man may, for a few hours, play the wealthy idler to perfection. The sum is ample for a well-considered meal, a bottle bearing a respectable label, commensurate tips, a smoke, cab fare and the ordinary etceteras.

This one delectable evening culled from each dull seventy was to Chandler a source of renascent bliss. To the society bud comes but one début; it stands alone sweet in her memory when her hair has whitened; but to Chandler each ten weeks brought a joy as keen, as thrilling, as new as the first had been. To sit among *bon vivants* under palms in the swirl of concealed music, to look upon the *habitués* of such a paradise and to be looked upon by them—what is a girl's first dance and short-sleeved tulle compared with this?

Up Broadway Chandler moved with the vespertine dress parade. For this evening he was an exhibit as well as a gazer. For the next sixty-nine evenings he would be dining in cheviot and worsted at dubious *table d'hôtes*, at whirlwind lunch counters, on sandwiches and beer in his hall bedroom. He was willing to do that, for he was a true son of the great city of razzle-dazzle, and to him one evening in the limelight made up for many dark ones.

Chandler protracted his walk until the Forties began to intersect the great and glittering primrose way, for the evening was yet young, and when one is of the *beau monde* only one day in seventy, one loves to protract the pleasure. Eyes bright, sinister, curious, admiring, provocative, alluring were bent upon him, for his garb and air proclaimed him a devotee to the hour of solace and pleasure.

At a certain corner he came to a standstill, proposing to himself the question of turning back toward the showy and fashionable restaurant in which he usually dined on the evenings of his especial luxury. Just then a girl scudded lightly around the corner, slipped on a patch of icy snow and fell plump upon the sidewalk.

Chandler assisted her to her feet with instant and solicitous courtesy. The girl hobbled to the wall of the building, leaned against it, and thanked him demurely.

"I think my ankle is strained," she said. "It twisted when I fell."

"Does it pain you much?" inquired Chandler.

"Only when I rest my weight upon it. I think I will be able to walk in a minute or two."

"If I can be of any further service," suggested the young man, "I will call a cab, or——"

"Thank you," said the girl, softly but heartily. "I am sure you need not trouble yourself any further. It was so awkward of me. And my shoe heels are horridly common-sense; I can't blame them at all."

Chandler looked at the girl and found her swiftly drawing his interest. She was pretty in a refined way; and her eye was both merry and kind. She was inexpensively clothed in a plain black dress that suggested a sort of uniform such as shop girls wear. Her glossy dark-brown hair showed its coils beneath a cheap hat of black straw whose only ornament was a velvet ribbon and bow. She could have posed as a model for the self-respecting working girl of the best type.

A sudden idea came into the head of the young architect. He would ask this girl to dine with him. Here was the element that his splendid but solitary periodic feasts had lacked. His brief season of elegant luxury would be doubly enjoyable if he could add to it a lady's society. This girl was a lady, he was sure—her manner and speech settled that. And in spite of her extremely plain attire he felt that he would be pleased to sit at table with her.

These thoughts passed swiftly through his mind, and he decided to ask her. It was a breach of etiquette, of course, but oftentimes wage-earning girls waived formalities in matters of this kind. They were generally shrewd judges of men; and thought better of their own judgment than they did of useless conventions. His ten dollars, discreetly expended, would enable the two to dine very well indeed. The dinner would no doubt be a wonderful experience thrown into the dull routine of the girl's life; and her lively appreciation of it would add to his own triumph and pleasure.

"I think," he said to her, with frank gravity, "that your foot needs a longer rest than you suppose. Now, I am going to suggest a way in which you can give it that and at the same time do me a favour. I was on my way to dine all by my lonely self when you came tumbling around the corner. You come with me and we'll have a cozy dinner and a pleasant talk together, and by that time your game ankle will carry you home very nicely, I am sure."

The girl looked quickly up into Chandler's clear, pleasant countenance. Her eyes twinkled once very brightly, and then she smiled ingenuously.

"But we don't know each other—it wouldn't be right, would it?" she said, doubtfully.

"There is nothing wrong about it," said the young man, candidly. "I'll introduce myself—permit me—Mr. Towers

Chandler. After our dinner, which I will try to make as pleasant as possible, I will bid you good-evening, or attend you safely to your door, whichever you prefer."

"But, dear me!" said the girl, with a glance at Chandler's faultless attire. "In this old dress and hat!"

"Never mind that," said Chandler, cheerfully. "I'm sure you look more charming in them than any one we shall see in the most elaborate dinner toilette."

"My ankle does hurt yet," admitted the girl, attempting a limping step. "I think I will accept your invitation, Mr. Chandler. You may call me—Miss Marian."

"Come, then, Miss Marian," said the young architect, gaily, but with perfect courtesy; "you will not have far to walk. There is a very respectable and good restaurant in the next block. You will have to lean on my arm—so—and walk slowly. It is lonely dining all by one's self. I'm just a little bit glad that you slipped on the ice."

When the two were established at a well-appointed table, with a promising waiter hovering in attendance, Chandler began to experience the real joy that his regular outing always brought to him.

The restaurant was not so showy or pretentious as the one further down Broadway, which he always preferred, but it was nearly so. The tables were well filled with prosperous-looking diners, there was a good orchestra, playing softly enough to make conversation a possible pleasure, and the cuisine and service were beyond criticism. His companion, even in her cheap hat and dress, held herself with an air that added distinction to the natural beauty of her face and figure. And it is certain that she looked at Chandler, with his animated but self-possessed manner and his kindling and frank blue eyes, with something not far from admiration in her own charming face.

Then it was that the Madness of Manhattan, the Frenzy of Fuss and Feathers, the Bacillus of Brag, the Provincial Plague of Pose seized upon Towers Chandler. He was on Broadway, surrounded by pomp and style, and there were eyes to look at him. On the stage of that comedy he had assumed to play the one-night part of a butterfly of fashion and an idler of means and taste. He was dressed for the part, and all his good angels had not the power to prevent him from acting it.

So he began to prate to Miss Marian of clubs, of teas, of golf and riding and kennels and cotillions and tours abroad and threw out hints of a yacht lying at Larchmont. He could see that she was vastly impressed by this vague talk, so he endorsed his pose by random insinuations concerning great wealth, and mentioned familiarly a few names that are handled reverently by the proletariat. It was Chandler's short little day, and he was wringing from it the best that could be had, as he saw it. And yet once or twice he saw the pure gold of this girl shine through the mist that his egotism had raised between him and all objects.

"This way of living that you speak of," she said, "sounds so futile and purposeless. Haven't you any work to do in the world that might interest you more?"

"My dear Miss Marian," he exclaimed—"work! Think of dressing every day for dinner, of making half a dozen calls in an afternoon—with a policeman at every corner ready to jump into your auto and take you to the station, if you get up any greater speed than a donkey cart's gait. We do-nothings are the hardest workers in the land."

The dinner was concluded, the waiter generously feed, and the two walked out to the corner where they had met. Miss Marian walked very well now; her limp was scarcely noticeable.

"Thank you for a nice time," she said, frankly. "I must run home now. I liked the dinner very much, Mr. Chandler."

He shook hands with her, smiling cordially, and said something about a game of bridge at his club. He watched her for a moment, walking rather rapidly eastward, and then he found a cab to drive him slowly homeward.

In his chilly bedroom Chandler laid away his evening clothes for a sixty-nine days' rest. He went about it thoughtfully.

"That was a stunning girl," he said to himself. "She's all right, too, I'd be sworn, even if she does have to work. Perhaps if I'd told her the truth instead of all that razzle-dazzle we might—but, confound it! I had to play up to my clothes."

Thus spoke the brave who was born and reared in the wigwams of the tribe of the Manhattans.

The girl, after leaving her entertainer, sped swiftly cross-town until she arrived at a handsome and sedate mansion two squares to the east, facing on that avenue which is the highway of Mammon and the auxiliary gods. Here she entered hurriedly and ascended to a room where a handsome young lady in an elaborate house dress was looking anxiously out the window.

"Oh, you madcap!" exclaimed the elder girl, when the other entered. "When will you quit frightening us this way? It is two hours since you ran out in that rag of an old dress and Marie's hat. Mamma has been so alarmed. She sent Louis in the auto to try to find you. You are a bad, thoughtless Puss."

The elder girl touched a button, and a maid came in a moment.

"Marie, tell mamma that Miss Marian has returned."

"Don't scold, sister. I only ran down to Mme. Theo's to tell her to use mauve insertion instead of pink. My costume and Marie's hat were just what I needed. Every one thought I was a shopgirl, I am sure."

"Dinner is over, dear; you stayed so late."

"I know. I slipped on the sidewalk and turned my ankle. I could not walk, so I hobbled into a restaurant and sat there until I was better. That is why I was so long."

The two girls sat in the window seat, looking out at the lights and the stream of hurrying vehicles in the avenue. The younger one cuddled down with her head in her sister's lap.

"We will have to marry some day," she said dreamily—"both of us. We have so much money that we will not be allowed to disappoint the public. Do you want me to tell you the kind of a man I could love, Sis?"

"Go on, you scatterbrain," smiled the other.

"I could love a man with dark and kind blue eyes, who is gentle and respectful to poor girls, who is handsome and good and does not try to flirt. But I could love him only if he had an ambition, an object, some work to do in the world. I would not care how poor he was if I could help him build his way up. But, sister dear, the kind of man we always meet—the man who lives an idle life between society and his clubs—I could not love a man like that, even if his eyes were blue and he were ever so kind to poor girls whom he met in the street."

The Complete Life of John Hopkins

THERE IS a saying that no man has tasted the full flavor of
life until he has known poverty, love and war. The just-
ness of this reflection commends it to the lover of condensed
philosophy. The three conditions embrace about all there is in
life worth knowing. A surface thinker might deem that wealth
should be added to the list. Not so. When a poor man finds a
long-hidden quarter-dollar that has slipped through a rip into
his vest lining, he sounds the pleasure of life with a deeper
plummet than any millionaire can hope to cast.

It seems that the wise executive power that rules life has
thought best to drill man in these three conditions; and none
may escape all three. In rural places the terms do not mean so
much. Poverty is less pinching; love is temperate; war shrinks to
contests about boundary lines and the neighbors' hens. It is in
the cities that our epigram gains in truth and vigor; and it has
remained for one John Hopkins to crowd the experience into
a rather small space of time.

The Hopkins flat was like a thousand others. There was a
rubber plant in one window; a flea-bitten terrier sat in the
other, wondering when he was to have his day.

John Hopkins was like a thousand others. He worked at $20
per week in a nine-story, red-brick building at either Insurance,
Buckle's Hoisting Engines, Chiropody, Loans, Pulleys, Boas
Renovated, Waltz Guaranteed in Five Lessons, or Artificial
Limbs. It is not for us to wring Mr. Hopkins's avocation from
these outward signs that be.

Mrs. Hopkins was like a thousand others. The auriferous
tooth, the sedentary disposition, the Sunday afternoon wanderlust, the draught upon the delicatessen store for home-made
comforts, the furor for department store marked-down sales,
the feeling of superiority to the lady in the third-floor front
who wore genuine ostrich tips and had two names over her
bell, the mucilaginous hours during which she remained glued
to the window sill, the vigilant avoidance of the instalment
man, the tireless patronage of the acoustics of the dumb-waiter
shaft—all the attributes of the Gotham flat-dweller were hers.

One moment yet of sententiousness and the story moves.

In the Big City large and sudden things happen. You round a corner and thrust the rib of your umbrella into the eye of your old friend from Kootenai Falls. You stroll out to pluck a Sweet William in the park—and lo! bandits attack you—you are ambulanced to the hospital—you marry your nurse; are divorced—get squeezed while short on U. P. S. and D. O. W. N. S.—stand in the bread line—marry an heiress, take out your laundry and pay your club dues—seemingly all in the wink of an eye. You travel the streets, and a finger beckons to you, a handkerchief is dropped for you, a brick is dropped upon you, the elevator cable or your bank breaks, a table d'hôte or your wife disagrees with you, and Fate tosses you about like cork crumbs in wine opened by an un-feed waiter. The City is a sprightly youngster, and you are red paint upon its toy, and you get licked off.

John Hopkins sat, after a compressed dinner, in his glove-fitting straight-front flat. He sat upon a hornblende couch and gazed, with satiated eyes, at Art Brought Home to the People in the shape of "The Storm" tacked against the wall. Mrs. Hopkins discoursed droningly of the dinner smells from the flat across the hall. The flea-bitten terrier gave Hopkins a look of disgust, and showed a man-hating tooth.

Here was neither poverty, love, nor war; but upon such barren stems may be grafted those essentials of a complete life.

John Hopkins sought to inject a few raisins of conversation into the tasteless dough of existence. "Putting a new elevator in at the office," he said, discarding the nominative noun, "and the boss has turned out his whiskers."

"You don't mean it!" commented Mrs. Hopkins.

"Mr. Whipples," continued John, "wore his new spring suit down to-day. I liked it fine. It's a gray with——" He stopped, suddenly stricken by a need that made itself known to him. "I believe I'll walk down to the corner and get a five-cent cigar," he concluded.

John Hopkins took his hat and picked his way down the musty halls and stairs of the flat-house.

The evening air was mild, and the streets shrill with the care-less cries of children playing games controlled by mysterious rhythms and phrases. Their elders held the doorways and steps with leisurely pipe and gossip. Paradoxically, the fire-escapes supported lovers in couples who made no attempt to fly the mounting conflagration they were there to fan.

The corner cigar store aimed at by John Hopkins was kept by a man named Freshmayer, who looked upon the earth as a sterile promontory.

Hopkins, unknown in the store, entered and called genially for his "bunch of spinach, car-fare grade." This imputation deepened the pessimism of Freshmayer; but he set out a brand that came perilously near to filling the order. Hopkins bit off the roots of his purchase, and lighted up at the swinging gas jet. Feeling in his pockets to make payment, he found not a penny there.

"Say, my friend," he explained, frankly, "I've come out without any change. Hand you that nickel first time I pass."

Joy surged in Freshmayer's heart. Here was corroboration of his belief that the world was rotten and man a peripatetic evil. Without a word he rounded the end of his counter and made earnest onslaught upon his customer. Hopkins was no man to serve as a punching-bag for a pessimistic tobacconist. He quickly bestowed upon Freshmayer a colorado-maduro eye in return for the ardent kick that he received from that dealer in goods for cash only.

The impetus of the enemy's attack forced the Hopkins line back to the sidewalk. There the conflict raged; the pacific wooden Indian, with his carven smile, was overturned, and those of the street who delighted in carnage pressed round to view the zealous joust.

But then came the inevitable cop and imminent inconvenience for both the attacker and attacked. John Hopkins was a peaceful citizen, who worked at rebuses of nights in a flat, but he was not without the fundamental spirit of resistance that comes with the battle-rage. He knocked the policeman into a grocer's sidewalk display of goods and gave Freshmayer a punch that caused him temporarily to regret that he had not made it a rule to extend a five-cent line of credit to certain customers. Then Hopkins took spiritedly to his heels down the sidewalk, closely followed by the cigar-dealer and the policeman, whose uniform testified to the reason in the grocer's sign that read: "Eggs cheaper than anywhere else in the city."

As Hopkins ran he became aware of a big, low, red, racing automobile that kept abreast of him in the street. This auto steered in to the side of the sidewalk, and the man guiding it motioned to Hopkins to jump into it. He did so without slackening his speed, and fell into the turkey-red upholstered seat beside the chauffeur. The big machine, with a diminuendo cough, flew away like an albatross down the avenue into which the street emptied.

The driver of the auto sped his machine without a word. He was masked beyond guess in the goggles and diabolic garb of the chauffeur.

"Much obliged, old man," called Hopkins, gratefully. "I guess you've got sporting blood in you, all right, and don't admire the sight of two men trying to soak one. Little more and I'd have been pinched."

The chauffeur made no sign that he had heard. Hopkins shrugged a shoulder and chewed at his cigar, to which his teeth had clung grimly throughout the mêlée.

Ten minutes and the auto turned into the open carriage entrance of a noble mansion of brown stone, and stood still. The chauffeur leaped out, and said:

"Come quick. The lady, she will explain. It is the great honor you will have, monsieur. Ah, that milady could call upon Armand to do this thing! But, no, I am only one chauffeur."

With vehement gestures the chauffeur conducted Hopkins into the house. He was ushered into a small but luxurious reception chamber. A lady, young, and possessing the beauty of visions, rose from a chair. In her eyes smouldered a becoming anger. Her high-arched, thread-like brows were ruffled into a delicious frown.

"Milady," said the chauffeur, bowing low, "I have the honor to relate to you that I went to the house of Monsieur Long and found him to be not at home. As I came back I see this gentleman in combat against—how you say—greatest odds. He is fighting with five—ten—thirty men—gendarmes, *aussi*. Yes, milady, he what you call 'swat' one—three—eight policemans. If that Monsieur Long is out I say to myself this gentleman he will serve milady so well, and I bring him here."

"Very well, Armand," said the lady, "you may go." She turned to Hopkins.

"I sent my chauffeur," she said, "to bring my cousin, Walter Long. There is a man in this house who has treated me with insult and abuse. I have complained to my aunt, and she laughs at me. Armand says you are brave. In these prosaic days men who are both brave and chivalrous are few. May I count upon your assistance?"

John Hopkins thrust the remains of his cigar into his coat pocket. He looked upon this winning creature and felt his first thrill of romance. It was a knightly love, and contained no disloyalty to the flat with the flea-bitten terrier and the lady of his choice. He had married her after a picnic of the Lady Label Stickers' Union, Lodge No. 2, on a dare and a bet of new hats and chowder all around with his friend, Billy McManus. This angel who was begging him to come to her rescue was something too heavenly for chowder, and as for hats—golden, jewelled crowns for her!

"Say," said John Hopkins, "just show me the guy that you've got the grouch at. I've neglected my talents as a scrapper heretofore, but this is my busy night."

"He is in there," said the lady, pointing to a closed door. "Come. Are you sure that you do not falter or fear?"

"Me?" said John Hopkins. "Just give me one of those roses in the bunch you are wearing, will you?"

The lady gave him a red, red rose. John Hopkins kissed it, stuffed it into his vest pocket, opened the door and walked into the room. It was a handsome library, softly but brightly lighted. A young man was there, reading.

"Books on etiquette is what you want to study," said John Hopkins, abruptly. "Get up here, and I'll give you some lessons. Be rude to a lady, will you?"

The young man looked mildly surprised. Then he arose languidly, dextrously caught the arms of John Hopkins and conducted him irresistibly to the front door of the house.

"Beware, Ralph Branscombe," cried the lady, who had followed, "what you do to the gallant man who has tried to protect me."

The young man shoved John Hopkins gently out the door and then closed it.

"Bess," he said, calmly, "I wish you would quit reading historical novels. How in the world did that fellow get in here?"

"Armand brought him," said the young lady. "I think you are awfully mean not to let me have that St. Bernard. I sent Armand for Walter. I was so angry with you."

"Be sensible, Bess," said the young man, taking her arm. "That dog isn't safe. He has bitten two or three people around the kennels. Come now, let's go tell auntie we are in good humor again."

Arm in arm, they moved away.

John Hopkins walked to his flat. The janitor's five-year-old daughter was playing on the steps. Hopkins gave her a nice, red rose and walked upstairs.

Mrs. Hopkins was philandering with curl-papers.

"Get your cigar?" she asked, disinterestedly.

"Sure," said Hopkins, "and I knocked around a while outside. It's a nice night."

He sat upon the hornblende sofa, took out the stump of his cigar, lighted it, and gazed at the graceful figures in "The Storm" on the opposite wall.

"I was telling you," said he, "about Mr. Whipple's suit. It's a gray, with an invisible check, and it looks fine."

The Rubber Plant's Story

WE RUBBER plants form the connecting link between the vegetable kingdom and the decorations of a Waldorf-Astoria scene in a Third Avenue theatre. I haven't looked up our family tree, but I believe we were raised by grafting a gum overshoe on to a 30-cent table d'hôte stalk of asparagus. You take a white bulldog with a Bourke Cockran air of independence about him and a rubber plant and there you have the fauna and flora of a flat. What the shamrock is to Ireland the rubber plant is to the dweller in flats and furnished rooms. We get moved from one place to another so quickly that the only way we can get our picture taken is with a kinetoscope. We are the vagrant vine and the flitting fig tree. You know the proverb: "Where the rubber plant sits in the window the moving van backs up to the door."

We are the city equivalent to the woodbine and the honeysuckle. No other vegetable except the Pittsburg stogie can withstand as much handling as we can. When the family to which we belong moves into a flat they set us in the front window and we become lares and penates, fly-paper and the peripatetic emblem of "Home, Sweet Home." We aren't as green as we look. I guess we are about what you would call the soubrettes of the conservatory. You try sitting in the front window of a $40 flat in Manhattan and looking out into the street all day, and back into the flat at night, and see whether you get wise or not—hey? Talk about the tree of knowledge of good and evil in the garden of Eden—say! suppose there had been a rubber plant there when Eve—but I was going to tell you a story.

The first thing I can remember I had only three leaves and belonged to a member of the pony ballet. I was kept in a sunny window, and was generally watered with seltzer and lemon. I had plenty of fun in those days. I got cross-eyed trying to watch the numbers of the automobiles in the street and the dates on the labels inside at the same time.

Well, then the angel that was moulting for the musical comedy lost his last feather and the company broke up. The ponies trotted away and I was left in the window ownerless. The janitor gave me to a refined comedy team on the eighth floor, and in six weeks I had been set in the window of five different flats. I took on experience and put out two more leaves.

Miss Carruthers, of the refined comedy team—did you ever see her cross both feet back of her neck?—gave me to a friend of hers who had made an unfortunate marriage with a man in a store. Consequently I was placed in the window of a furnished room, rent in advance, water two flights up, gas extra after 10 o'clock at night. Two of my leaves withered off here. Also, I was moved from one room to another so many times that I got to liking the odor of the pipes the expressmen smoked.

I don't think I ever had so dull a time as I did with this lady. There was never anything amusing going on inside—she was devoted to her husband, and, besides leaning out the window and flirting with the iceman, she never did a thing towards breaking the monotony.

When the couple broke up they left me with the rest of their goods at a second-hand store. I was put out in front for sale along with the jobbiest lot you ever heard of being lumped into one bargain. Think of this little cornucopia of wonders, all for $1.89: Henry James's works, six talking machine records, one pair of tennis shoes, two bottles of horse radish and a rubber plant—that was me!

One afternoon a girl came along and stopped to look at me. She had dark hair and eyes, and she looked slim and sad around the mouth.

"Oh, oh!" she says to herself. "I never thought to see one up here."

She pulls out a little purse about as thick as one of my leaves and fingers over some small silver in it. Old Koen, always on the lookout, is ready, rubbing his hands. This girl proceeds to turn down Mr. James and the other commodities. Rubber plants or nothing is the burden of her song. And at last Koen and she come together at 39 cents, and away she goes with me in her arms.

She was a nice girl, but not my style. Too quiet and sober looking. Thinks I to myself: "I'll just about land on the fire-escape of a tenement, six stories up. And I'll spend the next six months looking at clothes on the line."

But she carried me to a nice little room only three flights

up in quite a decent street. And she put me in the window, of course. And then she went to work and cooked dinner for herself. And what do you suppose she had? Bread and tea and a little dab of jam! Nothing else. Not a single lobster, nor so much as one bottle of champagne. The Carruthers comedy team had both every evening, except now and then when they took a notion for pig's knuckle and kraut.

After she had finished her dinner my new owner came to the window and leaned down close to my leaves and cried softly to herself for a while. It made me feel funny. I never knew anybody to cry that way over a rubber plant before. Of course, I've seen a few of 'em turn on the tears for what they could get out of it, but she seemed to be crying just for the pure enjoyment of it. She touched my leaves like she loved 'em, and she bent down her head and kissed each one of 'em. I guess I'm about the toughest specimen of a peripatetic orchid on earth, but I tell you it made me feel sort of queer. Home never was like that to me before. Generally I used to get chewed by poodles and have shirt-waists hung on me to dry, and get watered with coffee grounds and peroxide of hydrogen.

This girl had a piano in the room, and she used to disturb it with both hands while she made noises with her mouth for hours at a time. I suppose she was practising vocal music.

One day she seemed very much excited and kept looking at the clock. At 11 somebody knocked and she let in a stout, dark man with towsled black hair. He sat down at once at the piano and played while she sang for him. When she finished she laid one hand on her bosom and looked at him. He shook his head, and she leaned against the piano.

"Two years already," she said, speaking slowly—"do you think in two more—or even longer?"

The man shook his head again. "You waste your time," he said, roughly I thought. "The voice is not there." And then he looked at her in a peculiar way. "But the voice is not everything," he went on. "You have looks. I can place you, as I told you if,——"

The girl pointed to the door without saying anything, and the dark man left the room. And then she came over and cried around me again. It's a good thing I had enough rubber in me to be waterproof.

About that time somebody else knocked at the door. "Thank goodness," I said to myself. "Here's a chance to get the water-works turned off. I hope it's somebody that's game enough to stand a bird and a bottle to liven things up a little." Tell you the truth, this little girl made me tired. A rubber plant likes to see a little sport now and then. I don't suppose there's another green thing in New York that sees as much of gay life unless it's the chartreuse or the sprigs of parsley around the dish.

When the girl opens the door in steps a young chap in a travelling cap and picks her up in his arms, and she sings out "Oh, Dick!" and stays there long enough to—well, you've been a rubber plant, too, sometimes, I suppose.

"Good thing!" says I to myself. "This is livelier than scales and weeping. Now there'll be something doing."

"You've got to go back with me," says the young man. "I've come two thousand miles for you. Aren't you tired of it yet, Bess? You've kept all of us waiting so long. Haven't you found out yet what is best?"

"The bubble burst only to-day," says the girl. "Come here, Dick, and see what I found the other day on the sidewalk for sale." She brings him by the hand and exhibits yours truly. "How one ever got away up here who can tell? I bought it with almost the last money I had."

He looked at me, but he couldn't keep his eyes off her for more than a second.

"Do you remember the night, Bess," he said, "when we stood under one of those on the bank of the bayou and what you told me then?"

"Geewillikins!" I said to myself. "Both of them stand under a rubber plant! Seems to me they are stretching matters somewhat."

"Do I not," says she, looking up at him and sneaking close to his vest, "and now I say it again, and it is to last forever. Look, Dick, at its leaves, how wet they are. Those are my tears, and it was thinking of you that made them fall."

"The dear old magnolias!" says the young man, pinching one of my leaves. "I love them all."

Magnolia! Well, wouldn't that—say! those innocents thought I was a magnolia! What the—well, wasn't that tough on a genuine little old New York rubber plant?

A Dinner at ——————*

THE ADVENTURES OF AN AUTHOR
WITH HIS OWN HERO

ALL THAT day—in fact from the moment of his creation—
Van Sweller had conducted himself fairly well in my eyes.
Of course I had had to make many concessions; but in return
he had been no less considerate. Once or twice we had had
sharp, brief contentions over certain points of behavior; but,
prevailingly, give and take had been our rule.

His morning toilet provoked our first tilt. Van Sweller went
about it confidently.

"The usual thing, I suppose, old chap," he said, with a smile
and a yawn. "I ring for a b. and s., and then I have my tub. I
splash a good deal in the water, of course. You are aware that
there are two ways in which I can receive Tommy Carmichael
when he looks in to have a chat about polo. I can talk to him
through the bathroom door, or I can be picking at a grilled
bone which my man has brought in. Which would you prefer?"

I smiled with diabolic satisfaction at his coming discomfiture.

"Neither," I said. "You will make your appearance on the
scene when a gentleman should—after you are fully dressed,
which indubitably private function shall take place behind
closed doors. And I will feel indebted to you if, after you do
appear, your deportment and manners are such that it will
not be necessary to inform the public, in order to appease its
apprehension, that you have taken a bath."

Van Sweller slightly elevated his brows.

"Oh, very well," he said, a trifle piqued. "I rather imagine it
concerns you more than it does me. Cut the 'tub' by all means,
if you think best. But it has been the usual thing, you know."

This was my victory; but after Van Sweller emerged from
his apartments in the "Beaujolie" I was vanquished in a dozen
small but well-contested skirmishes. I allowed him a cigar;
but routed him on the question of naming its brand. But he
worsted me when I objected to giving him a "coat unmistakably

---

*See advertising column, "Where to Dine Well," in the daily newspapers.

English in its cut." I allowed him to "stroll down Broadway,"
and even permitted "passers by" (God knows there's nowhere
to pass but by) to "turn their heads and gaze with evident
admiration at his erect figure." I demeaned myself, and, as a
barber, gave him a "smooth, dark face with its keen, frank eye,
and firm jaw."

Later on he looked in at the club and saw Freddy Vavasour,
the polo team captain, dawdling over grilled bone No. 1.

"Dear old boy," began Van Sweller; but in an instant I had
seized him by the collar and dragged him aside with the scant-
iest courtesy.

"For heaven's sake talk like a man," I said, sternly. "Do you
think it is manly to use those mushy and inane forms of address?
That man is neither dear nor old nor a boy."

To my surprise Van Sweller turned upon me a look of frank
pleasure.

"I am glad to hear you say that," he said, heartily. "I used
those words because I have been forced to say them so often.
They really are contemptible. Thanks for correcting me, dear
old boy."

Still I must admit that Van Sweller's conduct in the park
that morning was almost without flaw. The courage, the dash,
the modesty, the skill, and fidelity that he displayed atoned for
everything.

This is the way the story runs.

Van Sweller has been a gentleman member of the "Rugged
Riders," the company that made a war with a foreign country
famous. Among his comrades was Lawrence O'Roon, a man
whom Van Sweller liked. A strange thing—and a hazardous
one in fiction—was that Van Sweller and O'Roon resembled
each other mightily in face, form, and general appearance. After
the war Van Sweller pulled wires, and O'Roon was made a
mounted policeman.

Now, one night in New York there are commemorations and
libations by old comrades, and in the morning mounted policeman O'Roon, unused to potent liquids,—another premise
hazardous in fiction,—finds the earth bucking and bounding
like a bronco, with no stirrup into which he may insert foot and
save his honor and his badge.

Noblesse oblige? Surely. So out along the driveways and bridle

paths trots Hudson Van Sweller in the uniform of his incapac-
itated comrade, as like unto him as one French pea is unto a
petit pois.

It is, of course, jolly larks for Van Sweller, who has wealth and
social position enough for him to masquerade safely even as a
police commissioner doing his duty, if he wished to do so. But
society, not given to scanning the countenances of mounted
policemen, sees nothing unusual in the officer on the beat.

And then comes the runaway.

That is a fine scene—the swaying victoria, the impetuous,
daft horses plunging through the line of scattering vehicles, the
driver stupidly holding his broken reins, and the ivory-white
face of Amy Ffolliott, as she clings desperately with each slender
hand. Fear has come and gone: it has left her expression pensive
and just a little pleading, for life is not so bitter.

And then the clatter and swoop of mounted policeman Van
Sweller! Oh, it was—but the story has not yet been printed.
When it is you shall learn how he sent his bay like a bullet after
the imperilled victoria. A Crichton, a Crœsus, and a Centaur in
one, he hurls the invincible combination into the chase.

When the story is printed you will admire the breathless
scene where Van Sweller checks the headlong team. And then
he looks into Amy Ffolliott's eyes and sees two things—the
possibilities of a happiness he has long sought, and a nascent
promise of it. He is unknown to her; but he stands in her sight
illuminated by the hero's potent glory, she his and he hers by all
the golden, fond, unreasonable laws of love and light literature.

Ay, that is a rich moment. And it will stir you to find Van
Sweller in that fruitful nick of time thinking of his comrade
O'Roon, who is cursing his gyrating bed and incapable legs in
an unsteady room in a West Side hotel while Van Sweller holds
his badge and his honor.

Van Sweller hears Miss Ffolliott's voice thrillingly asking the
name of her preserver. If Hudson Van Sweller, in policeman's
uniform, has saved the life of palpitating beauty in the park—
where is mounted policeman O'Roon, in whose territory the
deed is done? How quickly by a word can the hero reveal
himself, thus discarding his masquerade of ineligibility and
doubling the romance! But there is his friend!

Van Sweller touches his cap. "It 's nothing, Miss," he says,

sturdily; "that 's what we are paid for—to do our duty." And
away he rides. But the story does not end there.

As I have said, Van Sweller carried off the park scene to my
decided satisfaction. Even to me he was a hero when he fore-
swore, for the sake of his friend, the romantic promise of his
adventure. It was later in the day, amongst the more exacting
conventions that encompass the society hero, when we had our
liveliest disagreement. At noon he went to O'Roon's room and
found him far enough recovered to return to his post, which
he at once did.

At about six o'clock in the afternoon Van Sweller fingered
his watch, and flashed at me a brief look full of such shrewd
cunning that I suspected him at once.

"Time to dress for dinner, old man," he said, with exaggerated carelessness.

"Very well," I answered, without giving him a clew to my
suspicions; "I will go with you to your rooms and see that you
do the thing properly. I suppose that every author must be a
valet to his own hero."

He affected cheerful acceptance of my somewhat officious
proposal to accompany him. I could see that he was annoyed
by it, and that fact fastened deeper in my mind the conviction
that he was meditating some act of treachery.

When he had reached his apartments he said to me, with a
too patronizing air: "There are, as you perhaps know, quite a
number of little distinguishing touches to be had out of the
dressing process. Some writers rely almost wholly upon them.
I suppose that I am to ring for my man, and that he is to enter
noiselessly, with an expressionless countenance."

"He may enter," I said, with decision, "and only enter. Valets
do not usually enter a room shouting college songs or with St.
Vitus's dance in their faces; so the contrary may be assumed
without fatuous or gratuitous asseveration."

"I must ask you to pardon me," continued Van Sweller,
gracefully, "for annoying you with questions, but some of your
methods are a little new to me. Shall I don a full-dress suit
with an immaculate white tie—or is there another tradition to
be upset?"

"You will wear," I replied, "evening dress, such as a gentleman wears. If it is full, your tailor should be responsible for

its bagginess. And I will leave it to whatever erudition you are supposed to possess whether a white tie is rendered any whiter by being immaculate. And I will leave it to the consciences of you and your man whether a tie that is not white, and therefore not immaculate, could possibly form any part of a gentleman's evening dress. If not, then the perfect tie is included and understood in the term 'dress,' and its expressed addition predicates either a redundancy of speech or the spectacle of a man wearing two ties at once."

With this mild but deserved rebuke I left Van Sweller in his dressing-room, and waited for him in his library.

About an hour later his valet came out, and I heard him telephone for an electric cab. Then out came Van Sweller, smiling, but with that sly, secretive design in his eye that was puzzling me.

"I believe," he said easily, as he smoothed a glove, "that I will drop in at ——* for dinner."

I sprang up, angrily, at his words. This, then, was the paltry trick he had been scheming to play upon me. I faced him with a look so grim that even his patrician poise was flustered.

"You will never do so," I exclaimed, "with my permission. What kind of a return is this," I continued, hotly, "for the favors I have granted you? I gave you a 'Van' to your name when I might have called you 'Perkins' or 'Simpson.' I have humbled myself so far as to brag of your polo ponies, your automobiles, and the iron muscles that you acquired when you were stroke-oar of your 'varsity eight,' or 'eleven,' whichever it is. I created you for the hero of this story; and I will not submit to having you queer it. I have tried to make you a typical young New York gentleman of the highest social station and breeding. You have no reason to complain of my treatment of you. Amy Ffolliott, the girl you are to win, is a prize for any man to be thankful for, and cannot be equalled for beauty—provided the story is illustrated by the right artist. I do not understand why you should try to spoil everything. I had thought you were a gentleman."

"What is it you are objecting to, old man?" asked Van Sweller, in a surprised tone.

---

*See advertising column, "Where to Dine Well," in the daily newspapers.

"To your dining at ——,*" I answered. "The pleasure would be yours, no doubt, but the responsibility would fall upon me. You intend deliberately to make me out a tout for a restaurant. Where you dine to-night has not the slightest connection with the thread of our story. You know very well that the plot requires that you be in front of the Alhambra Opera House at 11.30 where you are to rescue Miss Ffolliott a second time as the fire engine crashes into her cab. Until that time your movements are immaterial to the reader. Why can't you dine out of sight somewhere, as many a hero does, instead of insisting upon an inapposite and vulgar exhibition of yourself?"

"My dear fellow," said Van Sweller, politely, but with a stubborn tightening of his lips, "I 'm sorry it does n't please you, but there 's no help for it. Even a character in a story has rights that an author cannot ignore. The hero of a story of New York social life must dine at ——* at least once during its action."

"'Must,'" I echoed, disdainfully; "why 'must'? Who demands it?"

"The magazine editors," answered Van Sweller, giving me a glance of significant warning.

"But why?" I persisted.

"To please subscribers around Kankakee, Ill.," said Van Sweller, without hesitation.

"How do you know these things?" I inquired, with sudden suspicion. "You never came into existence until this morning. You are only a character in fiction, anyway. I, myself, created you. How is it possible for you to know anything?"

"Pardon me for referring to it," said Van Sweller, with a sympathetic smile, "but I have been the hero of hundreds of stories of this kind."

I felt a slow flush creeping into my face.

"I thought . . ." I stammered; "I was hoping . . . that is . . . Oh, well, of course an absolutely original conception in fiction is impossible in these days."

"Metropolitan types," continued Van Sweller, kindly, "do not offer a hold for much originality. I 've sauntered through every story in pretty much the same way. Now and then the women writers have made me cut some rather strange capers,

*See advertising column, "Where to Dine Well," in the daily newspapers.

for a gentleman; but the men generally pass me along from one to another without much change. But never yet, in any story, have I failed to dine at ——.*"

"You will fail this time," I said, emphatically.

"Perhaps so," admitted Van Sweller, looking out of the window into the street below, "but if so it will be for the first time. The authors all send me there. I fancy that many of them would have liked to accompany me, but for the little matter of the expense."

"I say I will be touting for no restaurant," I repeated, loudly. "You are subject to my will, and I declare that you shall not appear of record this evening until the time arrives for you to rescue Miss Ffolliott again. If the reading public cannot conceive that you have dined during that interval at some one of the thousands of establishments provided for that purpose that do not receive literary advertisement it may suppose, for aught I care, that you have gone fasting."

"Thank you," said Van Sweller, rather coolly, "you are hardly courteous. But take care! it is at your own risk that you attempt to disregard a fundamental principle in metropolitan fiction— one that is dear alike to author and reader. I shall, of course attend to my duty when it comes time to rescue your heroine; but I warn you that it will be your loss if you fail to send me to-night to dine at ——.*"

"I will take the consequences if there are to be any," I replied. "I am not yet come to be sandwich man for an eating-house."

I walked over to a table where I had left my cane and gloves. I heard the whirr of the electric alarm in the cab below, and I turned quickly. Van Sweller was gone.

I rushed down the stairs and out to the curb. An empty hansom was just passing. I hailed the driver excitedly.

"See that auto cab half-way down the block?" I shouted. "Follow it. Don't lose sight of it for an instant, and I will give you two dollars!"

If I only had been one of the characters in my story instead of myself I could easily have offered $10 or $25 or even $100. But $2 was all I felt justified in expending, with fiction at its present rates.

---

*See advertising column, "Where to Dine Well," in the daily newspapers.

The cab driver, instead of lashing his animal into a foam, proceeded at a deliberate trot that suggested a by-the-hour arrangement.

But I suspected Van Sweller's design; and when we lost sight of his cab I ordered my driver to proceed at once to ——.*

I found Van Sweller at a table under a palm, just glancing over the menu, with a hopeful waiter hovering at his elbow.

"Come with me," I said, inexorably. "You will not give me the slip again. Under my eye you shall remain until 11.30."

Van Sweller countermanded the order for his dinner, and arose to accompany me. He could scarcely do less. A fictitious character is but poorly equipped for resisting a hungry but live author who comes to drag him forth from a restaurant. All he said was: "You were just in time; but I think you are making a mistake. You cannot afford to ignore the wishes of the great reading public."

I took Van Sweller to my own rooms—to my room. He had never seen anything like it before.

"Sit on that trunk," I said to him, "while I observe whether the landlady is stalking us. If she is not, I will get things at a delicatessen store below, and cook something for you in a pan over the gas jet. It will not be so bad. Of course nothing of this will appear in the story."

"Jove! old man!" said Van Sweller, looking about him with interest, "this is a jolly little closet you live in! Where the devil do you sleep?—Oh, that pulls down! And I say—what is this under the corner of the carpet?—Oh, a frying-pan! I see—clever idea! Fancy cooking over the gas! What larks it will be!"

"Think of anything you could eat?" I asked; "try a chop, or what?"

"Anything," said Van Sweller, enthusiastically, "except a grilled bone."

Two weeks afterward the postman brought me a large, fat envelope. I opened it, and took out something that I had seen before, and this typewritten letter from a magazine that encourages society fiction:

---

*See advertising column, "Where to Dine Well," in the daily newspapers.

Your short story, "The Badge of Policeman O'Roon," is herewith returned.

We are sorry that it has been unfavorably passed upon; but it seems to lack in some of the essential requirements of our publication.

The story is splendidly constructed; its style is strong and inimitable, and its action and character-drawing deserve the highest praise. As a story *per se* it has merit beyond anything that we have read for some time. But, as we have said, it fails to come up to some of the standards we have set.

Could you not re-write the story, and inject into it the social atmosphere, and return it to us for further consideration? It is suggested to you that you have the hero, Van Sweller, drop in for luncheon or dinner once or twice at ————* or at the ————,* which will be in line with the changes desired.

Very truly yours,

THE EDITORS.

*See advertising column, "Where to Dine Well," in the daily newspapers.

A Comedy in Rubber

ONE MAY hope, in spite of the metaphorists, to avoid the breath of the deadly upas tree; one may, by great good fortune, succeed in blacking the eye of the basilisk; one might even dodge the attentions of Cerberus and Argus, but no man, alive or dead, can escape the gaze of the Rubberer.

New York is the Caoutchouc City. There are many, of course, who go their ways, making money, without turning to the right or the left, but there is a tribe abroad wonderfully composed, like the Martians, solely of eyes and means of locomotion.

These devotees of curiosity swarm, like flies, in a moment in a struggling, breathless circle about the scene of an unusual occurrence. If a workman opens a manhole, if a street car runs over a man from North Tarrytown, if a little boy drops an egg on his way home from the grocery, if a casual house or two drops into the subway, if a lady loses a nickel through a hole in the lisle thread, if the police drag a telephone and a racing chart forth from an Ibsen Society reading-room, if Senator Depew or Mr. Chuck Connors walks out to take the air—if any of these incidents or accidents takes place, you will see the mad, irresistible rush of the "rubber" tribe to the spot.

The importance of the event does not count. They gaze with equal interest and absorption at a chorus girl or at a man painting a liver pill sign. They will form as deep a cordon around a man with a clubfoot as they will around a balked automobile. They have the furor rubberendi. They are optical gluttons, feasting and fattening on the misfortunes of their fellow beings. They gloat and pore and glare and squint and stare with their fishy eyes like goggle-eyed perch at the hook baited with calamity.

It would seem that Cupid would find these ocular vampires too cold game for his calorific shafts, but have we not yet to discover an immune even among the Protozoa? Yes, beautiful Romance descended upon two of this tribe, and love came into their hearts as they crowded about the prostrate form of a man who had been run over by a brewery wagon.

William Pry was the first on the spot. He was an expert at

such gatherings. With an expression of intense happiness on his features, he stood over the victim of the accident, listening to his groans as if to the sweetest music. When the crowd of spectators had swelled to a closely packed circle William saw a violent commotion in the crowd opposite him. Men were hurled aside like ninepins by the impact of some moving body that clove them like the rush of a tornado. With elbows, umbrella, hat-pin, tongue, and fingernails doing their duty, Violet Seymour forced her way through the mob of onlookers to the first row. Strong men who even had been able to secure a seat on the 5.30 Harlem express staggered back like children as she bucked centre. Two large lady spectators who had seen the Duke of Roxburgh married and had often blocked traffic on Twenty-third Street fell back into the second row with ripped shirt-waists when Violet had finished with them. William Pry loved her at first sight.

The ambulance removed the unconscious agent of Cupid. William and Violet remained after the crowd had dispersed. They were true Rubberers. People who leave the scene of an accident with the ambulance have not genuine caoutchouc in the cosmogony of their necks. The delicate, fine flavor of the affair is to be had only in the after-taste—in gloating over the spot, in gazing fixedly at the houses opposite, in hovering there in a dream more exquisite than the opium-eater's ecstasy. William Pry and Violet Seymour were connoisseurs in casualties. They knew how to extract full enjoyment from every incident.

Presently they looked at each other. Violet had a brown birthmark on her neck as large as a silver half-dollar. William fixed his eyes upon it. William Pry had inordinately bowed legs. Violet allowed her gaze to linger unswervingly upon them. Face to face they stood thus for moments, each staring at the other. Etiquette would not allow them to speak; but in the Caoutchouc City it is permitted to gaze without stint at the trees in the parks and at the physical blemishes of a fellow creature.

At length with a sigh they parted. But Cupid had been the driver of the brewery wagon, and the wheel that broke a leg united two fond hearts.

The next meeting of the hero and heroine was in front of a board fence near Broadway. The day had been a disappointing one. There had been no fights on the street, children had kept from under the wheels of the street cars, cripples and fat men in negligée shirts were scarce; nobody seemed to be inclined to slip on banana peels or fall down with heart disease. Even the sport from Kokomo, Ind., who claims to be a cousin of ex-Mayor Low and scatters nickels from a cab window, had not put in his appearance. There was nothing to stare at, and William Pry had premonitions of ennui.

But he saw a large crowd scrambling and pushing excitedly in front of a billboard. Sprinting for it, he knocked down an old woman and a child carrying a bottle of milk, and fought his way like a demon into the mass of spectators. Already in the inner line stood Violet Seymour with one sleeve and two gold fillings gone, a corset steel puncture and a sprained wrist, but happy. She was looking at what there was to see. A man was painting upon the fence: "Eat Bricklets—They Fill Your Face."

Violet blushed when she saw William Pry. William jabbed a lady in a black silk raglan in the ribs, kicked a boy in the shin, hit an old gentleman on the left ear and managed to crowd nearer to Violet. They stood for an hour looking at the man paint the letters. Then William's love could be repressed no longer. He touched her on the arm.

"Come with me," he said. "I know where there is a bootblack without an Adam's apple."

She looked up at him shyly, yet with unmistakable love transfiguring her countenance.

"And you have saved it for me?" she asked, trembling with the first dim ecstasy of a woman beloved.

Together they hurried to the bootblack's stand. An hour they spent there gazing at the malformed youth.

A window-cleaner fell from the fifth story to the sidewalk beside them. As the ambulance came clanging up William pressed her hand joyously. "Four ribs at least and a compound fracture," he whispered, swiftly. "You are not sorry that you met me, are you, dearest?"

"Me?" said Violet, returning the pressure. "Sure not. I could stand all day rubbering with you."

The climax of the romance occurred a few days later. Perhaps the reader will remember the intense excitement into which the city was thrown when Eliza Jane, a colored woman, was served with a subpœna. The Rubber Tribe encamped on the spot. With his own hands William Pry placed a board upon two beer kegs in the street opposite Eliza Jane's residence. He and Violet sat there for three days and nights. Then it occurred to a detective to open the door and serve the subpœna. He sent for a kinetoscope and did so.

Two souls with such congenial tastes could not long remain apart. As a policeman drove them away with his night stick that evening they plighted their troth. The seeds of love had been well sown, and had grown up, hardy and vigorous, into a—let us call it a rubber plant.

The wedding of William Pry and Violet Seymour was set for June 10. The Big Church in the Middle of the Block was banked high with flowers. The populous tribe of Rubberers the world over is rampant over weddings. They are the pessimists of the pews. They are the guyers of the groom and the banterers of the bride. They come to laugh at your marriage, and should you escape from Hymen's tower on the back of death's pale steed they will come to the funeral and sit in the same pew and cry over your luck. Rubber will stretch.

The church was lighted. A grosgrain carpet lay over the asphalt to the edge of the sidewalk. Bridesmaids were patting one another's sashes awry and speaking of the Bride's freckles. Coachmen tied white ribbons on their whips and bewailed the space of time between drinks. The minister was musing over his possible fee, essaying conjecture whether it would suffice to purchase a new broadcloth suit for himself and a photograph of Laura Jean Libbey for his wife. Yea, Cupid was in the air.

And outside the church, oh, my brothers, surged and heaved the rank and file of the tribe of Rubberers. In two bodies they were, with the grosgrain carpet and cops with clubs between. They crowded like cattle, they fought, they pressed and surged and swayed and trampled one another to see a bit of a girl in a white veil acquire license to go through a man's pockets while he sleeps.

But the hour for the wedding came and went, and the bride and bridegroom came not. And impatience gave way to alarm and alarm brought about search, and they were not found. And then two big policemen took a hand and dragged out of the furious mob of onlookers a crushed and trampled thing, with a wedding ring in its vest pocket and a shredded and hysterical woman beating her way to the carpet's edge, ragged, bruised and obstreperous.

William Pry and Violet Seymour, creatures of habit, had joined in the seething game of the spectators, unable to resist the overwhelming desire to gaze upon themselves entering, as bride and bridegroom, the rose-decked church.

Rubber will out.

The Pride of the Cities

SAID MR. Kipling, "The cities are full of pride, challenging each to each." Even so.

New York was empty. Two hundred thousand of its people were away for the summer. Three million eight hundred thousand remained as caretakers and to pay the bills of the absentees. But the two hundred thousand are an expensive lot.

The New Yorker sat at a roof-garden table, ingesting solace through a straw. His panama lay upon a chair. The July audience was scattered among vacant seats as widely as outfielders when the champion batter steps to the plate. Vaudeville happened at intervals. The breeze was cool from the bay; around and above—everywhere except on the stage—were stars. Glimpses were to be had of waiters, always disappearing, like startled chamois. Prudent visitors who had ordered refreshments by 'phone in the morning were now being served. The New Yorker was aware of certain drawbacks to his comfort, but content beamed softly from his rimless eyeglasses. His family was out of town. The drinks were warm; the ballet was suffering from lack of both tune and talcum—but his family would not return until September.

Then up into the garden stumbled the man from Topaz City, Nevada. The gloom of the solitary sightseer enwrapped him. Bereft of joy through loneliness, he stalked with a widower's face through the halls of pleasure. Thirst for human companionship possessed him as he panted in the metropolitan draught. Straight to the New Yorker's table he steered.

The New Yorker, disarmed and made reckless by the lawless atmosphere of a roof garden, decided upon utter abandonment of his life's traditions. He resolved to shatter with one rash, dare-devil, impulsive, hair-brained act the conventions that had hitherto been woven into his existence. Carrying out this radical and precipitous inspiration he nodded slightly to the stranger as he drew nearer the table.

The next moment found the man from Topaz City in the list of the New Yorker's closest friends. He took a chair at the table, he gathered two others for his feet, he tossed his broad-brimmed hat upon a fourth, and told his life's history to his new-found pard.

The New Yorker warmed a little, as an apartment-house furnace warms when the strawberry season begins. A waiter who came within hail in an unguarded moment was captured and paroled on an errand to the Doctor Wiley experimental station. The ballet was now in the midst of a musical vagary, and danced upon the stage programmed as Bolivian peasants, clothed in some portions of its anatomy as Norwegian fisher maidens, in others as ladies-in-waiting of Marie Antoinette, historically denuded in other portions so as to represent sea nymphs, and presenting the *tout ensemble* of a social club of Central Park West housemaids at a fish fry.

"Been in the city long?" inquired the New Yorker, getting ready the exact tip against the waiter's coming with large change from the bill.

"Me?" said the man from Topaz City. "Four days. Never in Topaz City, was you?"

"I!" said the New Yorker. "I was never farther west than Eighth Avenue. I had a brother who died on Ninth, but I met the cortege at Eighth. There was a bunch of violets on the hearse, and the undertaker mentioned the incident to avoid mistake. I cannot say that I am familiar with the West."

"Topaz City," said the man who occupied four chairs, "is one of the finest towns in the world."

"I presume that you have seen the sights of the metropolis," said the New Yorker. "Four days is not a sufficient length of time in which to view even our most salient points of interest, but one can possibly form a general impression. Our architectural supremacy is what generally strikes visitors to our city most forcibly. Of course you have seen our Flatiron Building. It is considered——"

"Saw it," said the man from Topaz City. "But you ought to come out our way. It's mountainous, you know, and the ladies all wear short skirts for climbing and——"

"Excuse me," said the New Yorker, "but that isn't exactly the point. New York must be a wonderful revelation to a visitor from the West. Now, as to our hotels——"

"Say," said the man from Topaz City, "that reminds me—

there were sixteen stage robbers shot last year within twenty miles of——"

"I was speaking of hotels," said the New Yorker. "We lead Europe in that respect. And as far as our leisure class is concerned we are far——"

"Oh, I don't know," interrupted the man from Topaz City. "There were twelve tramps in our jail when I left home. I guess New York isn't so——"

"Beg pardon, you seem to misapprehend the idea. Of course, you visited the Stock Exchange and Wall Street, where the——"

"Oh, yes," said the man from Topaz City, as he lighted a Pennsylvania stogie, "and I want to tell you that we've got the finest town marshal west of the Rockies. Bill Rainer he took in five pickpockets out of the crowd when Red Nose Thompson laid the cornerstone of his new saloon. Topaz City don't allow——"

"Have another Rhine wine and seltzer," suggested the New Yorker. "I've never been West, as I said; but there can't be any place out there to compare with New York. As to the claims of Chicago I——"

"One man," said the Topazite—"one man only has been murdered and robbed in Topaz City in the last three——"

"Oh, I know what Chicago is," interposed the New Yorker. "Have you been up Fifth Avenue to see the magnificent residences of our mil——"

"Seen 'em all. You ought to know Reub Stegall, the assessor of Topaz. When old man Tilbury, that owns the only two-story house in town, tried to swear his taxes from $6,000 down to $450.75, Reub buckled on his forty-five and went down to see——"

"Yes, yes, but speaking of our great city—one of its greatest features is our superb police department. There is no body of men in the world that can equal it for——"

"That waiter gets around like a Langley flying machine," remarked the man from Topaz City, thirstily. "We've got men in our town, too, worth $400,000. There's old Bill Withers and Colonel Metcalf and——"

"Have you seen Broadway at night?" asked the New Yorker, courteously. "There are few streets in the world that can compare with it. When the electrics are shining and the pavements are alive with two hurrying streams of elegantly clothed men and beautiful women attired in the costliest costumes that wind in and out in a close maze of expensively——"

"Never knew but one case in Topaz City," said the man from the West. "Jim Bailey, our mayor, had his watch and chain and $235 in cash taken from his pocket while——"

"That's another matter," said the New Yorker. "While you are in our city you should avail yourself of every opportunity to see its wonders. Our rapid transit system——"

"If you was out in Topaz," broke in the man from there, "I could show you a whole cemetery full of people that got killed accidentally. Talking about mangling folks up! why, when Berry Rogers turned loose that old double-barrelled shot-gun of his loaded with slugs at anybody——"

"Here, waiter!" called the New Yorker. "Two more of the same. It is acknowledged by every one that our city is the centre of art, and literature, and learning. Take, for instance, our after-dinner speakers. Where else in the country would you find such wit and eloquence as emanate from Depew and Ford, and——"

"If you take the papers," interrupted the Westerner, "you must have read of Pete Webster's daughter. The Websters live two blocks north of the court-house in Topaz City. Miss Tillie Webster, she slept forty days and nights without waking up. The doctors said that——"

"Pass the matches, please," said the New Yorker. "Have you observed the expedition with which new buildings are being run up in New York? Improved inventions in steel framework and——"

"I noticed," said the Nevadian, "that the statistics of Topaz City showed only one carpenter crushed by falling timbers last year and he was caught in a cyclone."

"They abuse our sky line," continued the New Yorker, "and it is likely that we are not yet artistic in the construction of our buildings. But I can safely assert that we lead in pictorial and decorative art. In some of our houses can be found masterpieces in the way of paintings and sculpture. One who has the entrée to our best galleries will find——"

"Back up," exclaimed the man from Topaz City. "There was

a game last month in our town in which $90,000 changed hands on a pair of——"

"Ta-romt-tara!" went the orchestra. The stage curtain, blushing pink at the name "Asbestos" inscribed upon it, came down with a slow midsummer movement. The audience trickled leisurely down the elevator and stairs.

On the sidewalk below, the New Yorker and the man from Topaz City shook hands with alcoholic gravity. The elevated crashed raucously, surface cars hummed and clanged, cabmen swore, newsboys shrieked, wheels clattered ear-piercingly. The New Yorker conceived a happy thought, with which he aspired to clinch the pre-eminence of his city.

"You must admit," said he, "that in the way of noise New York is far ahead of any other——"

"Back to the everglades!" said the man from Topaz City. "In 1900, when Sousa's band and the repeating candidate were in our town you couldn't——"

The rattle of an express wagon drowned the rest of the words.

The Foreign Policy of Company 99

JOHN BYRNES, hose-cart driver of Engine Company No. 99, was afflicted with what his comrades called Japanitis.

Byrnes had a war map spread permanently upon a table in the second story of the engine-house, and he could explain to you at any hour of the day or night the exact positions, conditions and intentions of both the Russian and Japanese armies. He had little clusters of pins stuck in the map which represented the opposing forces, and these he moved about from day to day in conformity with the war news in the daily papers.

Whenever the Japs won a victory John Byrnes would shift his pins, and then he would execute a war dance of delight, and the other firemen would hear him yell: "Go it, you blamed little, sawed-off, huckleberry-eyed, monkey-faced hot tamales! Eat 'em up, you little sleight-o'-hand, bow-legged bull terriers—give 'em another of them Yalu looloos, and you'll eat rice in St. Petersburg. Talk about your Russians—say, wouldn't they give you a painsky when it comes to a scrapovitch?"

Not even on the fair island of Nippon was there a more enthusiastic champion of the Mikado's men. Supporters of the Russian cause did well to keep clear of Engine-House No. 99.

Sometimes all thoughts of the Japs left John Byrnes's head. That was when the alarm of fire had sounded and he was strapped in his driver's seat on the swaying cart, guiding Erebus and Joe, the finest team in the whole department—according to the crew of 99.

Of all the codes adopted by man for regulating his actions toward his fellow-mortals, the greatest are these—the code of King Arthur's Knights of the Round Table, the Constitution of the United States and the unwritten rules of the New York Fire Department. The Round Table methods are no longer practicable since the invention of street cars and breach-of-promise suits, and our Constitution is being found more and more unconstitutional every day, so the code of our firemen must be considered in the lead, with the Golden Rule and Jeffries's new punch trying for place and show.

The Constitution says that one man is as good as another;

but the Fire Department says he is better. This is a too generous theory, but the law will not allow itself to be construed otherwise. All of which comes perilously near to being a paradox, and commends itself to the attention of the S. P. C. A.

One of the transatlantic liners dumped out at Ellis Island a lump of protozoa which was expected to evolve into an American citizen. A steward kicked him down the gangway, a doctor pounced upon his eyes like a raven, seeking for trachoma or ophthalmia; he was hustled ashore and ejected into the city in the name of Liberty—perhaps, theoretically, thus inoculating against kingocracy with a drop of its own virus. This hypodermic injection of Europeanism wandered happily into the veins of the city with the broad grin of a pleased child. It was not burdened with baggage, cares or ambitions. Its body was lithely built and clothed in a sort of foreign fustian; its face was brightly vacant, with a small, flat nose, and was mostly covered by a thick, ragged, curling beard like the coat of a spaniel. In the pocket of the imported Thing were a few coins—denarii—scudi—kopecks—pfennigs—pilasters—whatever the financial nomenclature of his unknown country may have been.

Prattling to himself, always broadly grinning, pleased by the roar and movement of the barbarous city into which the steamship cut-rates had shunted him, the alien strayed away from the sea, which he hated, as far as the district covered by Engine Company No. 99. Light as a cork, he was kept bobbing along by the human tide, the crudest atom in all the silt of the stream that emptied into the reservoir of Liberty.

While crossing Third avenue he slowed his steps, enchanted by the thunder of the elevated trains above him and the soothing crash of the wheels on the cobbles. And then there was a new, delightful chord in the uproar—the musical clanging of a gong and a great shining juggernaut belching fire and smoke, that people were hurrying to see.

This beautiful thing, entrancing to the eye, dashed past, and the protoplasmic immigrant stepped into the wake of it with his broad, enraptured, uncomprehending grin. And so stepping, stepped into the path of No. 99's flying hose-cart, with John Byrnes gripping, with arms of steel, the reins over the plunging backs of Erebus and Joe.

The unwritten constitutional code of the firemen has no

exceptions or amendments. It is a simple thing—as simple as the rule of three. There was the heedless unit in the right of way; there was the hose-cart and the iron pillar of the elevated railroad.

John Byrnes swung all his weight and muscle on the left rein. The team and cart swerved that way and crashed like a torpedo into the pillar. The men on the cart went flying like skittles. The driver's strap burst, the pillar rang with the shock, and John Byrnes fell on the car track with a broken shoulder twenty feet away, while Erebus—beautiful, raven-black, best-loved Erebus—lay whickering in his harness with a broken leg.

In consideration for the feelings of Engine Company No. 99 the details will be lightly touched. The company does not like to be reminded of that day. There was a great crowd, and hurry calls were sent in; and while the ambulance gong was clearing the way the men of No. 99 heard the crack of the S. P. C. A. agent's pistol, and turned their heads away, not daring to look toward Erebus again.

When the firemen got back to the engine-house they found that one of them was dragging by the collar the cause of their desolation and grief. They set it in the middle of the floor and gathered grimly about it. Through its whiskers the calamitous object chattered effervescently and waved its hands.

"Sounds like a seidlitz powder," said Mike Dowling, disgustedly, "and it makes me sicker than one. Call that a man!—that hoss was worth a steamer full of such two-legged animals. It's a immigrant—that's what it is."

"Look at the doctor's chalk mark on its coat," said Reilly, the desk man. "It's just landed. It must be a kind of a Dago or a Hun or one of them Finns, I guess. That's the kind of truck that Europe unloads onto us."

"Think of a thing like that getting in the way and laying John up in hospital and spoiling the best fire team in the city," groaned another fireman. "It ought to be taken down to the dock and drowned."

"Somebody go around and get Sloviski," suggested the engine driver, "and let's see what nation is responsible for this conglomeration of hair and head noises."

Sloviski kept a delicatessen store around the corner on Third avenue, and was reputed to be a linguist.

One of the men fetched him—a fat, cringing man, with a discursive eye and the odors of many kinds of meats upon him.

"Take a whirl at this importation with your jaw-breakers, Sloviski," requested Mike Dowling. "We can't quite figure out whether he's from the Hackensack bottoms or Hongkong-on-the-Ganges."

Sloviski addressed the stranger in several dialects, that ranged in rhythm and cadence from the sounds produced by a tonsilitis gargle to the opening of a can of tomatoes with a pair of scissors. The immigrant replied in accents resembling the uncorking of a bottle of ginger ale.

"I have you his name," reported Sloviski. "You shall not pronounce it. Writing of it in paper is better." They gave him paper, and he wrote. "Demetre Svangvsk."

"Looks like short hand," said the desk man.

"He speaks some language," continued the interpreter, wiping his forehead, "of Austria and mixed with a little Turkish. And, den, he have some Magyar words and a Polish or two, and many like the Roumanian, but not without talk of one tribe in Bessarabia. I do not him quite understand."

"Would you call him a Dago or a Polocker, or what?" asked Mike, frowning at the polyglot description.

"He is a"—answered Sloviski—"he is a—I dink he come from—I dink he is a fool," he concluded, impatient at his linguistic failure, "and if you pleases I will go back at mine delicatessen."

"Whatever he is, he's a bird," said Mike Dowling; "and you want to watch him fly."

Taking by the wing the alien fowl that had fluttered into the nest of Liberty, Mike led him to the door of the engine-house and bestowed upon him a kick hearty enough to convey the entire animus of Company 99. Demetre Svangvsk hustled away down the sidewalk, turning once to show his ineradicable grin to the aggrieved firemen.

In three weeks John Byrnes was back at his post from the hospital. With great gusto he proceeded to bring his war map up to date. "My money on the Japs every time," he declared. "Why, look at them Russians—they're nothing but wolves. Wipe 'em out, I say—and the little old jiu jitsu gang are just the cherry blossoms to do the trick, and don't you forget it!"

The second day after Byrne's reappearance came Demetre Svangvsk, the unidentified, to the engine-house, with a broader grin than ever. He managed to convey the idea that he wished to congratulate the hose-cart driver on his recovery and to apologize for having caused the accident. This he accomplished by so many extravagant gestures and explosive noises that the company was diverted for half an hour. Then they kicked him out again, and on the next day he came back grinning. How or where he lived no one knew. And then John Byrnes's nine-year-old son, Chris, who brought him convalescent delicacies from home to eat, took a fancy to Svangvsk, and they allowed him to loaf about the door of the engine-house occasionally.

One afternoon the big drab automobile of the Deputy Fire Commissioner buzzed up to the door of No. 99 and the Deputy stepped inside for an informal inspection. The men kicked Svangvsk out a little harder than usual and proudly escorted the Deputy around 99, in which everything shone like my lady's mirror.

The Deputy respected the sorrow of the company concerning the loss of Erebus, and he had come to promise it another mate for Joe that would do him credit. So they let Joe out of his stall and showed the Deputy how deserving he was of the finest mate that could be in horsedom.

While they were circling around Joe confabbing, Chris climbed into the Deputy's auto and threw the power full on. The men heard a monster puffing and a shriek from the lad, and sprang out too late. The big auto shot away, luckily taking a straight course down the street. The boy knew nothing of its machinery; he sat clutching the cushions and howling. With the power on nothing could have stopped that auto except a brick house, and there was nothing for Chris to gain by such a stoppage.

Demetre Svankvsk was just coming in again with a grin for another kick when Chris played his merry little prank. While the others sprang for the door Demetre sprang for Joe. He glided upon the horse's bare back like a snake and shouted something at him like the crack of a dozen whips. One of the firemen afterward swore that Joe answered him back in the same language. Ten seconds after the auto started the big horse was eating up the asphalt behind it like a strip of macaroni.

Some people two blocks and a half away saw the rescue. They said that the auto was nothing but a drab noise with a black speck in the middle of it for Chris, when a big bay horse with a lizard lying on its back cantered up alongside of it, and the lizard reached over and picked the black speck out of the noise.

Only fifteen minutes after Svangvsk's last kicking at the hands—or rather the feet—of Engine Company No. 99 he rode Joe back through the door with the boy safe, but acutely conscious of the licking he was going to receive.

Svangvsk slipped to the floor, leaned his head against Joe's and made a noise like a clucking hen. Joe nodded and whistled loudly through his nostrils, putting to shame the knowledge of Sloviski, of the delicatessen.

John Byrnes walked up to Svangvsk, who grinned, expecting to be kicked. Byrnes gripped the outlander so strongly by the hand that Demetre grinned anyhow, conceiving it to be a new form of punishment.

"The heathen rides like a Cossack," remarked a fireman who had seen a Wild West show—"they're the greatest riders in the world."

The word seemed to electrify Svankvsk. He grinned wider than ever.

"Yas—yas—me Cossack," he spluttered, striking his chest.

"Cossack!" repeated John Byrnes, thoughtfully, "ain't that a kind of a Russian?"

"They're one of the Russian tribes, sure," said the desk man, who read books between fire alarms.

Just then Alderman Foley, who was on his way home and did not know of the runaway, stopped at the door of the engine-house and called to Byrnes:

"Hello there, Jimmy, me boy—how's the war coming along? Japs still got the bear on the trot, have they?"

"Oh, I don't know," said John Byrnes, argumentatively, "them Japs haven't got any walkover. You wait till Kuropatkin gets a good whack at 'em and they won't be knee-high to a puddle-ducksky."

The Furnished Room

RESTLESS, SHIFTING, fugacious as time itself is a certain vast bulk of the population of the red brick district of the lower West Side. Homeless, they have a hundred homes. They flit from furnished room to furnished room, transients forever—transients in abode, transients in heart and mind. They sing "Home, Sweet Home" in ragtime; they carry their *lares et penates* in a bandbox; their vine is entwined about a picture hat; a rubber plant is their fig tree.

Hence the houses of this district, having had a thousand dwellers, should have a thousand tales to tell, mostly dull ones, no doubt; but it would be strange if there could not be found a ghost or two in the wake of all these vagrant guests.

One evening after dark a young man prowled among these crumbling red mansions, ringing their bells. At the twelfth he rested his lean hand-baggage upon the step and wiped the dust from his hat-band and forehead. The bell sounded faint and far away in some remote, hollow depths.

To the door of this, the twelfth house whose bell he had rung, came a housekeeper who made him think of an unwholesome, surfeited worm that had eaten its nut to a hollow shell and now sought to fill the vacancy with edible lodgers.

He asked if there was a room to let.

"Come in," said the housekeeper. Her voice came from her throat; her throat seemed lined with fur. "I have the third floor back, vacant since a week back. Should you wish to look at it?"

The young man followed her up the stairs. A faint light from no particular source mitigated the shadows of the halls. They trod noiselessly upon a stair carpet that its own loom would have forsworn. It seemed to have become vegetable; to have degenerated in that rank, sunless air to lush lichen or spreading moss that grew in patches to the staircase and was viscid under the foot like organic matter. At each turn of the stairs were vacant niches in the wall. Perhaps plants had once been set within them. If so they had died in that foul and tainted air. It may be that statues of the saints had stood there, but it was not difficult to conceive that imps and devils had dragged them forth in the darkness and down to the unholy depths of some furnished pit below.

"This is the room," said the housekeeper, from her furry throat. "It's a nice room. It ain't often vacant. I had some most elegant people in it last summer—no trouble at all, and paid in advance to the minute. The water's at the end of the hall. Sprowls and Mooney kept it three months. They done a vaudeville sketch. Miss B'retta Sprowls—you may have heard of her—Oh, that was just the stage names—right there over the dresser is where the marriage certificate hung, framed. The gas is here, and you see there is plenty of closet room. It's a room everybody likes. It never stays idle long."

"Do you have many theatrical people rooming here?" asked the young man.

"They comes and goes. A good proportion of my lodgers is connected with the theatres. Yes, sir, this is the theatrical district. Actor people never stays long anywhere. I get my share. Yes, they comes and they goes."

He engaged the room, paying for a week in advance. He was tired, he said, and would take possession at once. He counted out the money. The room had been made ready, she said, even to towels and water. As the housekeeper moved away he put, for the thousandth time, the question that he carried at the end of his tongue.

"A young girl—Miss Vashner—Miss Eloise Vashner—do you remember such a one among your lodgers? She would be singing on the stage, most likely. A fair girl, of medium height and slender, with reddish, gold hair and a dark mole near her left eyebrow."

"No, I don't remember the name. Them stage people has names they change as often as their rooms. They comes and they goes. No, I don't call that one to mind."

No. Always no. Five months of ceaseless interrogation and the inevitable negative. So much time spent by day in questioning managers, agents, schools and choruses; by night among the audiences of theatres from all-star casts down to music halls so low that he dreaded to find what he most hoped for. He who had loved her best had tried to find her. He was sure that since her disappearance from home this great, water-girt city held her somewhere, but it was like a monstrous quicksand, shifting its particles constantly, with no foundation, its upper granules of to-day buried to-morrow in ooze and slime.

The furnished room received its latest guest with a first glow of pseudo-hospitality, a hectic, haggard, perfunctory welcome like the specious smile of a demirep. The sophistical comfort came in reflected gleams from the decayed furniture, the ragged brocade upholstery of a couch and two chairs, a foot-wide cheap pier glass between the two windows, from one or two gilt picture frames and a brass bedstead in a corner.

The guest reclined, inert, upon a chair, while the room, confused in speech as though it were an apartment in Babel, tried to discourse to him of its divers tenantry.

A polychromatic rug like some brilliant-flowered rectangular, tropical islet lay surrounded by a billowy sea of soiled matting. Upon the gay-papered wall were those pictures that pursue the homeless one from house to house—The Huguenot Lovers, The First Quarrel, The Wedding Breakfast, Psyche at the Fountain. The mantel's chastely severe outline was ingloriously veiled behind some pert drapery drawn rakishly askew like the sashes of the Amazonian ballet. Upon it was some desolate flotsam cast aside by the room's marooned when a lucky sail had borne them to a fresh port—a trifling vase or two, pictures of actresses, a medicine bottle, some stray cards out of a deck.

One by one, as the characters of a cryptograph become explicit, the little signs left by the furnished room's procession of guests developed a significance. The threadbare space in the rug in front of the dresser told that lovely women had marched in the throng. Tiny finger prints on the wall spoke of little prisoners trying to feel their way to sun and air. A splattered stain, raying like the shadow of a bursting bomb, witnessed where a hurled glass or bottle had splintered with its contents against the wall. Across the pier glass had been scrawled with a diamond in staggering letters the name "Marie." It seemed that the succession of dwellers in the furnished room had turned in fury—perhaps tempted beyond forbearance by its garish coldness—and wreaked upon it their passions. The furniture was chipped and bruised; the couch, distorted by bursting springs, seemed a horrible monster that had been slain during the stress of some grotesque convulsion. Some more potent upheaval had cloven a great slice from the marble mantel. Each plank in the floor owned its particular cant and shriek as from a separate and individual agony. It seemed incredible that all this malice and injury had been wrought upon the room by those who had called it for a time their home; and yet it may have been the cheated home instinct surviving blindly, the resentful rage at false household gods that had kindled their wrath. A hut that is our own we can sweep and adorn and cherish.

The young tenant in the chair allowed these thoughts to file, soft-shod, through his mind, while there drifted into the room furnished sounds and furnished scents. He heard in one room a tittering and incontinent, slack laughter; in others the monologue of a scold, the rattling of dice, a lullaby, and one crying dully; above him a banjo tinkled with spirit. Doors banged somewhere; the elevated trains roared intermittently; a cat yowled miserably upon a back fence. And he breathed the breath of the house—a dank savour rather than a smell—a cold, musty effluvium as from underground vaults mingled with the reeking exhalations of linoleum and mildewed and rotten woodwork.

Then, suddenly, as he rested there, the room was filled with the strong, sweet odour of mignonette. It came as upon a single buffet of wind with such sureness and fragrance and emphasis that it almost seemed a living visitant. And the man cried aloud: "What, dear?" as if he had been called, and sprang up and faced about. The rich odour clung to him and wrapped him around. He reached out his arms for it, all his senses for the time confused and commingled. How could one be peremptorily called by an odour? Surely it must have been a sound. But, was it not the sound that had touched, that had caressed him?

"She has been in this room," he cried, and he sprang to wrest from it a token, for he knew he would recognise the smallest thing that had belonged to her or that she had touched. This enveloping scent of mignonette, the odour that she had loved and made her own—whence came it?

The room had been but carelessly set in order. Scattered upon the flimsy dresser scarf were half a dozen hairpins—those discreet, indistinguishable friends of womankind, feminine of gender, infinite of mood and uncommunicative of tense. These he ignored, conscious of their triumphant lack of identity. Ransacking the drawers of the dresser he came upon a discarded, tiny, ragged handkerchief. He pressed it to his face. It was racy and insolent with heliotrope; he hurled it to the floor. In another drawer he found odd buttons, a theatre programme, a pawnbroker's card, two lost marshmallows, a book on the divination of dreams. In the last was a woman's black satin hair bow, which halted him, poised between ice and fire. But the black satin hair-bow also is femininity's demure, impersonal, common ornament, and tells no tales.

And then he traversed the room like a hound on the scent, skimming the walls, considering the corners of the bulging matting on his hands and knees, rummaging mantel and tables, the curtains and hangings, the drunken cabinet in the corner, for a visible sign, unable to perceive that she was there beside, around, against, within, above him, clinging to him, wooing him, calling him so poignantly through the finer senses that even his grosser ones became cognisant of the call. Once again he answered loudly: "Yes, dear!" and turned, wild-eyed, to gaze on vacancy, for he could not yet discern form and colour and love and outstretched arms in the odour of mignonette. Oh, God! whence that odour, and since when have odours had a voice to call? Thus he groped.

He burrowed in crevices and corners, and found corks and cigarettes. These he passed in passive contempt. But once he found in a fold of the matting a half-smoked cigar, and this he ground beneath his heel with a green and trenchant oath. He sifted the room from end to end. He found dreary and ignoble small records of many a peripatetic tenant; but of her whom he sought, and who may have lodged there, and whose spirit seemed to hover there, he found no trace.

And then he thought of the housekeeper.

He ran from the haunted room downstairs and to a door that showed a crack of light. She came out to his knock. He smothered his excitement as best he could.

"Will you tell me, madam," he besought her, "who occupied the room I have before I came?"

"Yes, sir. I can tell you again. 'Twas Sprowls and Mooney, as I said. Miss B'retta Sprowls it was in the theatres, but Missis Mooney she was. My house is well known for respectability. The marriage certificate hung, framed, on a nail over——"

"What kind of a lady was Miss Sprowls—in looks, I mean?"

"Why, black-haired, sir, short, and stout, with a comical face. They left a week ago Tuesday."

"And before they occupied it?"

"Why, there was a single gentleman connected with the draying business. He left owing me a week. Before him was Missis Crowder and her two children, that stayed four months; and back of them was old Mr. Doyle, whose sons paid for him. He kept the room six months. That goes back a year, sir, and further I do not remember."

He thanked her and crept back to his room. The room was dead. The essence that had vivified it was gone. The perfume of mignonette had departed. In its place was the old, stale odour of mouldy house furniture, of atmosphere in storage.

The ebbing of his hope drained his faith. He sat staring at the yellow, singing gaslight. Soon he walked to the bed and began to tear the sheets into strips. With the blade of his knife he drove them tightly into every crevice around windows and door. When all was snug and taut he turned out the light, turned the gas full on again and laid himself gratefully upon the bed.

It was Mrs. McCool's night to go with the can for beer. So she fetched it and sat with Mrs. Purdy in one of those subterranean retreats where house-keepers foregather and the worm dieth seldom.

"I rented out my third floor, back, this evening," said Mrs. Purdy, across a fine circle of foam. "A young man took it. He went up to bed two hours ago."

"Now, did ye, Mrs. Purdy, ma'am?" said Mrs. McCool, with intense admiration. "You do be a wonder for rentin' rooms of that kind. And did ye tell him, then?" she concluded in a husky whisper, laden with mystery.

"Rooms," said Mrs. Purdy, in her furriest tones, "are furnished for to rent. I did not tell him, Mrs. McCool."

"'Tis right ye are, ma'am; 'tis by renting rooms we kape alive. Ye have the rale sense for business, ma'am. There be many people will rayjict the rentin' of a room if they be tould a suicide has been after dyin' in the bed of it."

"As you say, we has our living to be making," remarked Mrs. Purdy.

"Yis, ma'am; 'tis true. 'Tis just one wake ago this day I helped ye lay out the third floor, back. A pretty slip of a colleen she was to be killin' herself wid the gas—a swate little face she had, Mrs. Purdy, ma'am."

"She'd a-been called handsome, as you say," said Mrs. Purdy, assenting but critical, "but for that mole she had a-growin' by her left eyebrow. Do fill up your glass again, Mrs. McCool."

The Love-Philtre of Ikey Schoenstein

THE BLUE Light Drug Store is downtown, between the Bowery and First Avenue, where the distance between the two streets is the shortest. The Blue Light does not consider that pharmacy is a thing of bric-a-brac, scent and ice-cream soda. If you ask it for pain-killer it will not give you a bonbon.

The Blue Light scorns the labour-saving arts of modern pharmacy. It macerates its opium and percolates its own laudanum and paregoric. To this day pills are made behind its tall prescription desk—pills rolled out on its own pill-tile, divided with a spatula, rolled with the finger and thumb, dusted with calcined magnesia and delivered in little round pasteboard pill-boxes. The store is on a corner about which coveys of ragged-plumed, hilarious children play and become candidates for the cough drops and soothing syrups that wait for them inside.

Ikey Schoenstein was the night clerk of the Blue Light and the friend of his customers. Thus it is on the East Side, where the heart of pharmacy is not glacé. There, as it should be, the druggist is a counsellor, a confessor, an adviser, an able and willing missionary and mentor whose learning is respected, whose occult wisdom is venerated and whose medicine is often poured, untasted, into the gutter. Therefore Ikey's corniform, be-spectacled nose and narrow, knowledge-bowed figure was well known in the vicinity of the Blue Light, and his advice and notice were much desired.

Ikey roomed and breakfasted at Mrs. Riddle's two squares away. Mrs. Riddle had a daughter named Rosy. The circumlocution has been in vain—you must have guessed it—Ikey adored Rosy. She tinctured all his thoughts; she was the compound extract of all that was chemically pure and officinal—the dispensatory contained nothing equal to her. But Ikey was timid, and his hopes remained insoluble in the menstruum of his backwardness and fears. Behind his counter he was a superior being, calmly conscious of special knowledge and worth; outside he was a weak-kneed, purblind, motorman-cursed rambler, with ill-fitting clothes stained with chemicals and smelling of socotrine aloes and valerianate of ammonia.

The fly in Ikey's ointment (thrice welcome, pat trope!) was Chunk McGowan.

Mr. McGowan was also striving to catch the bright smiles tossed about by Rosy. But he was no outfielder as Ikey was; he picked them off the bat. At the same time he was Ikey's friend and customer, and often dropped in at the Blue Light Drug Store to have a bruise painted with iodine or get a cut rubber-plastered after a pleasant evening spent along the Bowery.

One afternoon McGowan drifted in in his silent, easy way, and sat, comely, smooth-faced, hard, indomitable, good-natured, upon a stool.

"Ikey," said he, when his friend had fetched his mortar and sat opposite, grinding gum benzoin to a powder, "get busy with your ear. It's drugs for me if you've got the line I need."

Ikey scanned the countenance of Mr. McGowan for the usual evidences of conflict, but found none.

"Take your coat off," he ordered. "I guess already that you have been stuck in the ribs with a knife. I have many times told you those Dagoes would do you up."

Mr. McGowan smiled. "Not them," he said. "Not any Dagoes. But you've located the diagnosis all right enough—it's under my coat, near the ribs. Say! Ikey—Rosy and me are goin' to run away and get married to-night."

Ikey's left forefinger was doubled over the edge of the mortar, holding it steady. He gave it a wild rap with the pestle, but felt it not. Meanwhile Mr. McGowan's smile faded to a look of perplexed gloom.

"That is," he continued, "if she keeps in the notion until the time comes. We've been layin' pipes for the getaway for two weeks. One day she says she will; the same evenin' she says nixy. We've agreed on to-night, and Rosy's stuck to the affirmative this time for two whole days. But it's five hours yet till the time, and I'm afraid she'll stand me up when it comes to the scratch."

"You said you wanted drugs," remarked Ikey.

Mr. McGowan looked ill at ease and harassed—a condition opposed to his usual line of demeanour. He made a patent-medicine almanac into a roll and fitted it with unprofitable carefulness about his finger.

"I wouldn't have this double handicap make a false start to-night for a million," he said. "I've got a little flat up in Harlem all ready, with chrysanthemums on the table and a kettle ready to boil. And I've engaged a pulpit pounder to be ready at his house for us at 9:30. It's got to come off. And if Rosy don't change her mind again!"—Mr. McGowan ceased, a prey to his doubts.

"I don't see then yet," said Ikey, shortly, "what makes it that you talk of drugs, or what I can be doing about it."

"Old man Riddle don't like me a little bit," went on the uneasy suitor, bent upon marshalling his arguments. "For a week he hasn't let Rosy step outside the door with me. If it wasn't for losin' a boarder they'd have bounced me long ago. I'm makin' $20 a week and she'll never regret flyin' the coop with Chunk McGowan."

"You will excuse me, Chunk," said Ikey. "I must make a prescription that is to be called for soon."

"Say," said McGowan, looking up suddenly, "say, Ikey, ain't there a drug of some kind—some kind of powders that'll make a girl like you better if you give 'em to her?"

Ikey's lip beneath his nose curled with the scorn of superior enlightenment; but before he could answer, McGowan continued:

"Tim Lacy told me he got some once from a croaker uptown and fed 'em to his girl in soda water. From the very first dose he was ace-high and everybody else looked like thirty cents to her. They was married in less than two weeks."

Strong and simple was Chunk McGowan. A better reader of men than Ikey was could have seen that his tough frame was strung upon fine wires. Like a good general who was about to invade the enemy's territory he was seeking to guard every point against possible failure.

"I thought," went on Chunk hopefully, "that if I had one of them powders to give Rosy when I see her at supper to-night it might brace her up and keep her from reneging on the proposition to skip. I guess she don't need a mule team to drag her away, but women are better at coaching than they are at running bases. If the stuff'll work just for a couple hours it'll do the trick."

"When is this foolishness of running away to be happening?" asked Ikey.

"Nine o'clock," said Mr. McGowan. "Supper's at seven. At eight Rosy goes to bed with a headache. At nine old Parvenzano lets me through to his back yard, where there's a board off Riddle's fence, next door. I go under her window and help her down the fire-escape. We've got to make it early on the preacher's account. It's all dead easy if Rosy don't balk when the flag drops. Can you fix me one of them powders, Ikey?"

Ikey Schoenstein rubbed his nose slowly.

"Chunk," said he, "it is of drugs of that nature that pharmaceutists must have much carefulness. To you alone of my acquaintance would I intrust a powder like that. But for you I shall make it, and you shall see how it makes Rosy to think of you."

Ikey went behind the prescription desk. There he crushed to a powder two soluble tablets, each containing a quarter of a grain of morphia. To them he added a little sugar of milk to increase the bulk, and folded the mixture neatly in a white paper. Taken by an adult this powder would insure several hours of heavy slumber without danger to the sleeper. This he handed to Chunk McGowan, telling him to administer it in a liquid if possible, and received the hearty thanks of the backyard Lochinvar.

The subtlety of Ikey's action becomes apparent upon recital of his subsequent move. He sent a messenger for Mr. Riddle and disclosed the plans of Mr. McGowan for eloping with Rosy. Mr. Riddle was a stout man, brick-dusty of complexion and sudden in action.

"Much obliged," he said, briefly, to Ikey. "The lazy Irish loafer! My own room's just above Rosy's. I'll just go up there myself after supper and load the shot-gun and wait. If he comes in my back yard he'll go away in a ambulance instead of a bridal chaise."

With Rosy held in the clutches of Morpheus for a many-hours deep slumber, and the bloodthirsty parent waiting, armed and forewarned, Ikey felt that his rival was close, indeed, upon discomfiture.

All night in the Blue Light Drug Store he waited at his duties for chance news of the tragedy, but none came.

At eight o'clock in the morning the day clerk arrived and Ikey started hurriedly for Mrs. Riddle's to learn the outcome. And, lo! as he stepped out of the store who but Chunk McGowan sprang from a passing street car and grasped his hand—Chunk McGowan with a victor's smile and flushed with joy.

"Pulled it off," said Chunk with Elysium in his grin. "Rosy hit the fire-escape on time to a second, and we was under the wire at the Reverend's at 9.30¼. She's up at the flat—she cooked eggs this mornin' in a blue kimono—Lord! how lucky I am! You must pace up some day, Ikey, and feed with us. I've got a job down near the bridge, and that's where I'm heading for now."

"The—the—powder?" stammered Ikey.

"Oh, that stuff you gave me!" said Chunk, broadening his grin; "well, it was this way. I sat down at the supper table last night at Riddle's, and I looked at Rosy, and I says to myself, 'Chunk, if you get the girl get her on the square—don't try any hocus-pocus with a thoroughbred like her.' And I keeps the paper you give me in my pocket. And then my lamps fall on another party present, who, I says to myself, is failin' in a proper affection toward his comin' son-in-law, so I watches my chance and dumps that powder in old man Riddle's coffee—see?"

The Rathskeller and the Rose

Miss Posie Carrington had earned her success. She began life handicapped by the family name of "Boggs," in the small town known as Cranberry Corners. At the age of eighteen she had acquired the name of "Carrington" and a position in the chorus of a metropolitan burlesque company. Thence upward she had ascended by the legitimate and delectable steps of "broiler," member of the famous "Dickey-bird" octette, in the successful musical comedy, "Fudge and Fellows," leader of the potato-bug dance in "Fol-de-Rol," and at length to the part of the maid "'Toinette" in "The King's Bath-Robe," which captured the critics and gave her her chance. And when we come to consider Miss Carrington she is in the heyday of flattery, fame and fizz; and that astute manager, Herr Timothy Goldstein, has her signature to iron-clad papers that she will star the coming season in Dyde Rich's new play, "Paresis by Gaslight."

Promptly there came to Herr Timothy a capable twentieth-century young character actor by the name of Highsmith, who besought engagement as "Sol Haytosser," the comic and chief male character part in "Paresis by Gaslight."

"My boy," said Goldstein, "take the part if you can get it. Miss Carrington won't listen to any of my suggestions. She has turned down half a dozen of the best imitators of the rural dub in the city. She declares she won't set a foot on the stage unless 'Haytosser' is the best that can be raked up. She was raised in a village, you know, and when a Broadway orchid sticks a straw in his hair and tries to call himself a clover blossom she's on, all right. I asked her, in a sarcastic vein, if she thought Denman Thompson would make any kind of a show in the part. 'Oh, no,' says she. 'I don't want him or John Drew or Jim Corbett or any of these swell actors that don't know a turnip from a turnstile. I want the real article.' So, my boy, if you want to play 'Sol Haytosser' you will have to convince Miss Carrington. Luck be with you."

Highsmith took the train the next day for Cranberry Corners. He remained in that forsaken and inanimate village three days. He found the Boggs family and corkscrewed their history unto the third and fourth generation. He amassed the facts and the local color of Cranberry Corners. The village had not grown as rapidly as had Miss Carrington. The actor estimated that it had suffered as few actual changes since the departure of its solitary follower of Thespis as had a stage upon which "four years is supposed to have elapsed." He absorbed Cranberry Corners and returned to the city of chameleon changes.

It was in the rathskeller that Highsmith made the hit of his histrionic career. There is no need to name the place; there is but one rathskeller where you could hope to find Miss Posie Carrington after a performance of "The King's Bath-Robe."

There was a jolly small party at one of the tables that drew many eyes. Miss Carrington, petite, marvellous, bubbling, electric, fame-drunken, shall be named first. Herr Goldstein follows, sonorous, curly-haired, heavy, a trifle anxious, as some bear that had caught, somehow, a butterfly in his claws. Next, a man condemned to a newspaper, sad, courted, armed, analyzing for press agent's dross every sentence that was poured over him, eating his à la Newburg in the silence of greatness. To conclude, a youth with parted hair, a name that is ochre to red journals and gold on the back of a supper check. These sat at a table while the musicians played, while waiters moved in the mazy performance of their duties with their backs toward all who desired their service, and all was bizarre and merry because it was nine feet below the level of the sidewalk.

At 11.45 a being entered the rathskeller. The first violin perceptibly flatted a C that should have been natural; the clarionet blew a bubble instead of a grace note; Miss Carrington giggled and the youth with parted hair swallowed an olive seed.

Exquisitely and irreproachably rural was the new entry. A lank, disconcerted, hesitating young man it was, flaxen-haired, gaping of mouth, awkward, stricken to misery by the lights and company. His clothing was butternut, with bright blue tie, showing four inches of bony wrist and white-socked ankle. He upset a chair, sat in another one, curled a foot around a table leg and cringed at the approach of a waiter.

"You may fetch me a glass of lager beer," he said, in response to the discreet questioning of the servitor.

The eyes of the rathskeller were upon him. He was as fresh as a collard and as ingenuous as a hay rake. He let his eye rove about the place as one who regards, big-eyed, hogs in the potato patch. His gaze rested at length upon Miss Carrington. He rose and went to her table with a lateral, shining smile and a blush of pleased trepidation.

"How're ye, Miss Posie?" he said in accents not to be doubted. "Don't ye remember me—Bill Summers—the Summerses that lived back of the blacksmith shop? I reckon I've growed up some since ye left Cranberry Corners.

"'Liza Perry 'lowed I might see ye in the city while I was here. You know 'Liza married Benny Stanfield, and she says——"

"Ah, say!" interrupted Miss Carrington, brightly, "Lize Perry is never married—what! Oh, the freckles of her!"

"Married in June," grinned the gossip, "and livin' in the old Tatum Place. Ham Riley perfessed religion; old Mrs. Blithers sold her place to Cap'n Spooner; the youngest Waters girl run away with a music teacher; the court-house burned up last March; your uncle Wiley was elected constable; Matilda Hoskins died from runnin' a needle in her hand, and Tom Beedle is courtin' Sallie Lathrop—they say he don't miss a night but what he's settin' on their porch."

"The wall-eyed thing!" exclaimed Miss Carrington, with asperity. "Why, Tom Beedle once—say, you folks, excuse me a while—this is an old friend of mine—Mr.—what was it? Yes, Mr. Summers—Mr. Goldstein, Mr. Ricketts, Mr.—— Oh, what's yours? 'Johnny' 'll do—come on over here and tell me some more."

She swept him to an isolated table in a corner. Herr Goldstein shrugged his fat shoulders and beckoned to the waiter. The newspaper man brightened a little and mentioned absinthe. The youth with parted hair was plunged into melancholy. The guests of the rathskeller laughed, clinked glasses and enjoyed the comedy that Posie Carrington was treating them to after her regular performance. A few cynical ones whispered "press agent" and smiled wisely.

Posie Carrington laid her dimpled and desirable chin upon her hands, and forgot her audience—a faculty that had won her laurels for her.

"I don't seem to recollect any Bill Summers," she said, thoughtfully gazing straight into the innocent blue eyes of the rustic young man. "But I know the Summerses, all right. I guess there ain't many changes in the old town. You see any of my folks lately?"

And then Highsmith played his trump. The part of "Sol Haytosser" called for pathos as well as comedy. Miss Carrington should see that he could do that as well.

"Miss Posie," said "Bill Summers," "I was up to your folkeses house jist two or three days ago. No, there ain't many changes to speak of. The lilac bush by the kitchen window is over a foot higher, and the elm in the front yard died and had to be cut down. And yet it don't seem the same place that it used to be."

"How's ma?" asked Miss Carrington.

"She was settin' by the front door, crocheting a lamp-mat when I saw her last," said "Bill." "She's older'n she was, Miss Posie. But everything in the house looked jest the same. Your ma asked me to set down. 'Don't touch that willow rocker, William,' says she. 'It ain't been moved since Posie left; and that's the apron she was hemmin', layin' over the arm of it, jist as she flung it. I'm in hopes,' she goes on, 'that Posie'll finish runnin' out that hem some day.'"

Miss Carrington beckoned peremptorily to a waiter.

"A pint of extra dry," she ordered, briefly; "and give the check to Goldstein."

"The sun was shinin' in the door," went on the chronicler from Cranberry, "and your ma was settin' right in it. I asked her if she hadn't better move back a little. 'William,' says she, 'when I get sot down and lookin' down the road, I can't bear to move. Never a day,' says she, 'but what I set here every minute that I can spare and watch over them palin's for Posie. She went away down that road in the night, for we seen her little shoe tracks in the dust, and somethin' tells me she'll come back that way ag'in when she's weary of the world and begins to think about her old mother.'

"When I was comin' away," concluded "Bill," "I pulled this off'n the bush by the front steps. I thought maybe I might see you in the city, and I knowed you'd like somethin' from the old home."

He took from his coat pocket a rose—a drooping, yellow, velvet, odorous rose, that hung its head in the foul atmosphere of that tainted rathskeller like a virgin bowing before the hot breath of the lions in a Roman arena.

Miss Carrington's penetrating but musical laugh rose above the orchestra's rendering of "Bluebells."

"Oh, say!" she cried, with glee, "aint't those poky places the limit? I just know that two hours at Cranberry Corners would give me the horrors now. Well, I'm awful glad to have seen you, Mr. Summers. I guess I'll hustle around to the hotel now and get my beauty sleep."

She thrust the yellow rose into the bosom of her wonderful, dainty, silken garments, stood up and nodded imperiously at Herr Goldstein.

Her three companions and "Bill Summers" attended her to her cab. When her flounces and streamers were all safely tucked inside she dazzled them with au revoirs from her shining eyes and teeth.

"Come around to the hotel and see me, Bill, before you leave the city," she called as the glittering cab rolled away.

Highsmith, still in his make-up, went with Herr Goldstein to a café booth.

"Bright idea, eh?" asked the smiling actor. "Ought to land 'Sol Haytosser' for me, don't you think? The little lady never once tumbled."

"I didn't hear your conversation," said Goldstein, "but your make-up and acting was O. K. Here's to your success. You'd better call on Miss Carrington early to-morrow and strike her for the part. I don't see how she can keep from being satisfied with your exhibition of ability."

At 11.45 A.M. on the next day Highsmith, handsome, dressed in the latest mode, confident, with a fuchsia in his button-hole, sent up his card to Miss Carrington in her select apartment hotel.

He was shown up and received by the actress's French maid.

"I am sorree," said Mlle. Hortense, "but I am to say this to all. It is with great regret. Mees Carrington have cancelled all engagements on the stage and have returned to live in that—how you call that town? Cranberry Cornaire!"

A Sacrifice Hit

THE EDITOR of the *Hearthstone Magazine* has his own ideas about the selection of manuscript for his publication. His theory is no secret; in fact, he will expound it to you willingly sitting at his mahogany desk, smiling benignantly and tapping his knee gently with his gold-rimmed eyeglasses.

"The *Hearthstone*," he will say, "does not employ a staff of readers. We obtain opinions of the manuscripts submitted to us directly from types of the various classes of our readers."

That is the editor's theory; and this is the way he carries it out:

When a batch of MSS. is received the editor stuffs every one of his pockets full of them and distributes them as he goes about during the day. The office employees, the hall porter, the janitor, the elevator man, messenger boys, the waiters at the café where the editor has luncheon, the man at the news-stand where he buys his evening paper, the grocer and milkman, the guard on the 5.30 uptown elevated train, the ticket-chopper at Sixty —th street, the cook and maid at his home—these are the readers who pass upon MSS. sent in to the *Hearthstone Magazine*. If his pockets are not entirely emptied by the time he reaches the bosom of his family the remaining ones are handed over to his wife to read after the baby goes to sleep. A few days later the editor gathers in the MSS. during his regular rounds and considers the verdict of his assorted readers.

This system of making up a magazine has been very successful; and the circulation, paced by the advertising rates, is making a wonderful record of speed.

The *Hearthstone* Company also publishes books, and its imprint is to be found on several successful works—all recommended, says the editor, by the *Hearthstone*'s army of volunteer readers. Now and then (according to talkative members of the editorial staff) the *Hearthstone* has allowed manuscripts to slip through its fingers on the advice of its heterogeneous readers, that afterward proved to be famous sellers when brought out by other houses.

For instance (the gossips say), "The Rise and Fall of Silas Latham" was unfavourably passed upon by the elevator-man; the office-boy unanimously rejected "The Boss"; "In the Bishop's Carriage" was contemptuously looked upon by the street-car conductor; "The Deliverance" was turned down by a clerk in the subscription department whose wife's mother had just begun a two-months' visit at his home; "The Queen's Quair" came back from the janitor with the comment: "So is the book."

But nevertheless the *Hearthstone* adheres to its theory and system, and it will never lack volunteer readers; for each one of the widely scattered staff, from the young lady stenographer in the editorial office to the man who shovels in coal (whose adverse decision lost to the *Hearthstone* Company the manuscript of "The Under World"), has expectations of becoming editor of the magazine some day.

This method of the *Hearthstone* was well known to Allen Slayton when he wrote his novelette entitled "Love Is All." Slayton had hung about the editorial offices of all the magazines so persistently that he was acquainted with the inner workings of every one in Gotham.

He knew not only that the editor of the *Hearthstone* handed his MSS. around among different types of people for reading, but that the stories of sentimental love-interest went to Miss Puffkin, the editor's stenographer. Another of the editor's peculiar customs was to conceal invariably the name of the writer from his readers of MSS. so that a glittering name might not influence the sincerity of their reports.

Slayton made "Love Is All" the effort of his life. He gave it six months of the best work of his heart and brain. It was a pure love-story, fine, elevated, romantic, passionate—a prose poem that set the divine blessing of love (I am transposing from the manuscript) high above all earthly gifts and honours, and listed it in the catalogue of heaven's choicest rewards. Slayton's literary ambition was intense. He would have sacrificed all other worldly possessions to have gained fame in his chosen art. He would almost have cut off his right hand, or have offered himself to the knife of the appendicitis fancier to have realized his dream of seeing one of his efforts published in the *Hearthstone*.

Slayton finished "Love Is All," and took it to the *Hearthstone* in person. The office of the magazine was in a large, conglomerate building, presided under by a janitor.

As the writer stepped inside the door on his way to the elevator a potato masher flew through the hall, wrecking Slayton's hat, and smashing the glass of the door. Closely following in the wake of the utensil flew the janitor, a bulky, unwholesome man, suspenderless and sordid, panic-stricken and breathless. A frowsy, fat woman with flying hair followed the missile. The janitor's foot slipped on the tiled floor, he fell in a heap with an exclamation of despair. The woman pounced upon him and seized his hair. The man bellowed lustily.

Her vengeance wreaked, the virago rose and stalked, triumphant as Minerva, back to some cryptic domestic retreat at the rear. The janitor got to his feet, blown and humiliated.

"This is married life," he said to Slayton, with a certain bruised humour. "That's the girl I used to lay awake of nights thinking about. Sorry about your hat, mister. Say, don't snitch to the tenants about this, will yer? I don't want to lose me job."

Slayton took the elevator at the end of the hall and went up to the offices of the *Hearthstone*. He left the MS. of "Love Is All" with the editor, who agreed to give him an answer as to its availability at the end of a week.

Slayton formulated his great winning scheme on his way down. It struck him with one brilliant flash, and he could not refrain from admiring his own genius in conceiving the idea. That very night he set about carrying it into execution.

Miss Puffkin, the *Hearthstone* stenographer, boarded in the same house with the author. She was an oldish, thin, exclusive, languishing, sentimental maid; and Slayton had been introduced to her some time before.

The writer's daring and self-sacrificing project was this: He knew that the editor of the *Hearthstone* relied strongly upon Miss Puffkin's judgment in the manuscript of romantic and sentimental fiction. Her taste represented the immense average of mediocre women who devour novels and stories of that type. The central idea and keynote of "Love Is All" was love at first sight—the enrapturing, irresistible, soul-thrilling feeling that compels a man or a woman to recognize his or her spirit-mate as soon as heart speaks to heart. Suppose he should impress this divine truth upon Miss Puffkin personally!—would she not surely indorse her new and rapturous sensations by recommending highly to the editor of the *Hearthstone* the novelette "Love Is All"?

Slayton thought so. And that night he took Miss Puffkin to the theatre. The next night he made vehement love to her in the dim parlour of the boarding-house. He quoted freely from "Love Is All"; and he wound up with Miss Puffkin's head on his shoulder, and visions of literary fame dancing in his head.

But Slayton did not stop at love-making. This, he said to himself, was the turning point of his life; and, like a true sportsman, he "went the limit." On Thursday night he and Miss Puffkin walked over to the Big Church in the Middle of the Block and were married.

Brave Slayton! Châteaubriand died in a garret, Byron courted a widow, Keats starved to death, Poe mixed his drinks, De Quincey hit the pipe, Ade lived in Chicago, James kept on doing it, Dickens wore white socks, De Maupassant wore a strait-jacket, Tom Watson became a Populist, Jeremiah wept, all these authors did these things, for the sake of literature, but thou didst cap them all; thou marriedst a wife for to carve for thyself a niche in the temple of fame!

On Friday morning Mrs. Slayton said she would go over to the *Hearthstone* office, hand in one or two manuscripts that the editor had given to her to read, and resign her position as stenographer.

"Was there anything—er—that—er—you particularly fancied in the stories you are going to turn in?" asked Slayton with a thumping heart.

"There was one—a novelette, that I liked so much," said his wife. "I haven't read anything in years that I thought was half as nice and true to life."

That afternoon Slayton hurried down to the *Hearthstone* office. He felt that his reward was close at hand. With a novelette in the *Hearthstone*, literary reputation would soon be his.

The office boy met him at the railing in the outer office. It was not for unsuccessful authors to hold personal colloquy with the editor except at rare intervals.

Slayton, hugging himself internally, was nursing in his heart the exquisite hope of being able to crush the office boy with his forthcoming success.

He inquired concerning his novelette. The office boy went into the sacred precincts and brought forth a large envelope, thick with more than the bulk of a thousand checks.

"The boss told me to tell you he's sorry," said the boy, "but your manuscript ain't available for the magazine."

Slayton stood, dazed. "Can you tell me," he stammered, "whether or no Miss Puff—that is my—I mean Miss Puffkin—handed in a novelette this morning that she had been asked to read?"

"Sure she did," answered the office boy wisely. "I heard the old man say that Miss Puffkin said it was a daisy. The name of it was, 'Married for the Mazuma, or a Working Girl's Triumph.'

"Say, you!" said the office boy confidentially, "your name's Slayton, ain't it? I guess I mixed cases on you without meanin' to do it. The boss give me some manuscript to hand around the other day and I got the ones for Miss Puffkin and the janitor mixed. I guess it's all right, though."

And then Slayton looked closer and saw on the cover of his manuscript, under the title "Love Is All," the janitor's comment scribbled with a piece of charcoal:

"The — you say!"

The Coming-Out of Maggie

EVERY SATURDAY night the Clover Leaf Social Club gave a hop in the hall of the Give and Take Athletic Association on the East Side. In order to attend one of these dances you must be a member of the Give and Take—or, if you belong to the division that starts off with the right foot in waltzing, you must work in Rhinegold's paper-box factory. Still, any Clover Leaf was privileged to escort or be escorted by an outsider to a single dance. But mostly each Give and Take brought the paper-box girl that he affected; and few strangers could boast of having shaken a foot at the regular hops.

Maggie Toole, on account of her dull eyes, broad mouth and left-handed style of footwork in the two-step, went to the dances with Anna McCarty and her "fellow." Anna and Maggie worked side by side in the factory, and were the greatest chums ever. So Anna always made Jimmy Burns take her by Maggie's house every Saturday night so that her friend could go to the dance with them.

The Give and Take Athletic Association lived up to its name. The hall of the association in Orchard street was fitted out with muscle-making inventions. With the fibres thus builded up the members were wont to engage the police and rival social and athletic organisations in joyous combat. Between these more serious occupations the Saturday night hops with the paper-box factory girls came as a refining influence and as an efficient screen. For sometimes the tip went 'round, and if you were among the elect that tiptoed up the dark back stairway you might see as neat and satisfying a little welter-weight affair to a finish as ever happened inside the ropes.

On Saturdays Rhinegold's paper-box factory closed at 3 P.M. On one such afternoon Anna and Maggie walked homeward together. At Maggie's door Anna said, as usual: "Be ready at seven, sharp, Mag; and Jimmy and me'll come by for you."

But what was this? Instead of the customary humble and grateful thanks from the non-escorted one there was to be perceived a high-poised head, a prideful dimpling at the corners of a broad mouth, and almost a sparkle in a dull brown eye.

"Thanks, Anna," said Maggie; "but you and Jimmy needn't bother to-night. I've a gentleman friend that's coming 'round to escort me to the hop."

The comely Anna pounced upon her friend, shook her, chided and beseeched her. Maggie Toole catch a fellow! Plain, dear, loyal, unattractive Maggie, so sweet as a chum, so unsought for a two-step or a moonlit bench in the little park. How was it? When did it happen? Who was it?

"You'll see to-night," said Maggie, flushed with the wine of the first grapes she had gathered in Cupid's vineyard. "He's swell all right. He's two inches taller than Jimmy, and an up-to-date dresser. I'll introduce him, Anna, just as soon as we get to the hall."

Anna and Jimmy were among the first Clover Leafs to arrive that evening. Anna's eyes were brightly fixed upon the door of the hall to catch the first glimpse of her friend's "catch."

At 8.30 Miss Toole swept into the hall with her escort. Quickly her triumphant eye discovered her chum under the wing of her faithful Jimmy.

"Oh, gee!" cried Anna, "Mag ain't made a hit—oh, no! Swell fellow? well, I guess! Style? Look at 'um."

"Go as far as you like," said Jimmy, with sandpaper in his voice. "Cop him out if you want him. These new guys always win out with the push. Don't mind me. He don't squeeze all the limes, I guess. Huh!"

"Shut up, Jimmy. You know what I mean. I'm glad for Mag. First fellow she ever had. Oh, here they come."

Across the floor Maggie sailed like a coquettish yacht convoyed by a stately cruiser. And truly, her companion justified the encomiums of the faithful chum. He stood two inches taller than the average Give and Take athlete; his dark hair curled; his eyes and his teeth flashed whenever he bestowed his frequent smiles. The young men of the Clover Leaf Club pinned not their faith to the graces of person as much as they did to its prowess, its achievements in hand-to-hand conflicts, and its preservation from the legal duress that constantly menaced it. The member of the association who would bind a paper-box maiden to his conquering chariot scorned to employ Beau Brummel airs. They were not considered honourable methods of warfare. The swelling biceps, the coat straining at its buttons over the chest, the air of conscious conviction of the super-eminence of the male in the cosmogony of creation, even a calm display of bow legs as subduing and enchanting agents in the gentle tourneys of Cupid—these were the approved arms and ammunition of the Clover Leaf gallants. They viewed, then, the genuflexions and alluring poses of this visitor with their chins at a new angle.

"A friend of mine, Mr. Terry O'Sullivan," was Maggie's formula of introduction. She led him around the room, presenting him to each new-arriving Clover Leaf. Almost was she pretty now, with the unique luminosity in her eyes that comes to a girl with her first suitor and a kitten with its first mouse.

"Maggie Toole's got a fellow at last," was the word that went round among the paper-box girls. "Pipe Mag's floor-walker"—thus the Give and Takes expressed their indifferent contempt.

Usually at the weekly hops Maggie kept a spot on the wall warm with her back. She felt and showed so much gratitude whenever a self-sacrificing partner invited her to dance that his pleasure was cheapened and diminished. She had even grown used to noticing Anna joggle the reluctant Jimmy with her elbow as a signal for him to invite her chum to walk over his feet through a two-step.

But to-night the pumpkin had turned to a coach and six. Terry O'Sullivan was a victorious Prince Charming, and Maggie Toole winged her first butterfly flight. And though our tropes of fairyland be mixed with those of entomology they shall not spill one drop of ambrosia from the rose-crowned melody of Maggie's one perfect night.

The girls besieged her for introductions to her "fellow." The Clover Leaf young men, after two years of blindness, suddenly perceived charms in Miss Toole. They flexed their compelling muscles before her and bespoke her for the dance.

Thus she scored; but to Terry O'Sullivan the honours of the evening fell thick and fast. He shook his curls; he smiled and went easily through the seven motions for acquiring grace in your own room before an open window ten minutes each day. He danced like a faun; he introduced manner and style and atmosphere; his words came trippingly upon his tongue, and—he waltzed twice in succession with the paper-box girl that Dempsey Donovan brought.

Dempsey was the leader of the association. He wore a dress suit, and could chin the bar twice with one hand. He was one of "Big Mike" O'Sullivan's lieutenants, and was never troubled by trouble. No cop dared to arrest him. Whenever he broke a pushcart man's head or shot a member of the Heinrick B. Sweeney Outing and Literary Association in the kneecap, an officer would drop around and say:

"The Cap'n 'd like to see ye a few minutes round to the office whin ye have time, Dempsey, me boy."

But there would be sundry gentlemen there with large gold fob chains and black cigars; and somebody would tell a funny story, and then Dempsey would go back and work half an hour with the six-pound dumbbells. So, doing a tight-rope act on a wire stretched across Niagara was a safe terpsichorean performance compared with waltzing twice with Dempsey Donovan's paper-box girl. At 10 o'clock the jolly round face of "Big Mike" O'Sullivan shone at the door for five minutes upon the scene. He always looked in for five minutes, smiled at the girls and handed out real perfectos to the delighted boys.

Dempsey Donovan was at his elbow instantly, talking rapidly. "Big Mike" looked carefully at the dancers, smiled, shook his head and departed.

The music stopped. The dancers scattered to the chairs along the walls. Terry O'Sullivan, with his entrancing bow, relinquished a pretty girl in blue to her partner and started back to find Maggie. Dempsey intercepted him in the middle of the floor.

Some fine instinct that Rome must have bequeathed to us caused nearly every one to turn and look at them—there was a subtle feeling that two gladiators had met in the arena. Two or three Give and Takes with tight coat sleeves drew nearer.

"One moment, Mr. O'Sullivan," said Dempsey. "I hope you're enjoying yourself. Where did you say you lived?"

The two gladiators were well matched. Dempsey had, perhaps, ten pounds of weight to give away. The O'Sullivan had breadth with quickness. Dempsey had a glacial eye, a dominating slit of a mouth, an indestructible jaw, a complexion like a belle's and the coolness of a champion. The visitor showed more fire in his contempt and less control over his conspicuous sneer. They were enemies by the law written when the rocks were molten. They were each too splendid, too mighty, too incomparable to divide pre-eminence. One only must survive.

"I live on Grand," said O'Sullivan, insolently; "and no trouble to find me at home. Where do you live?"

Dempsey ignored the question.

"You say your name's O'Sullivan," he went on. "Well, 'Big Mike' says he never saw you before."

"Lots of things he never saw," said the favourite of the hop.

"As a rule," went on Dempsey, huskily sweet, "O'Sullivans in this district know one another. You escorted one of our lady members here, and we want a chance to make good. If you've got a family tree let's see a few historical O'Sullivan buds come out on it. Or do you want us to dig it out of you by the roots?"

"Suppose you mind your own business," suggested O'Sullivan, blandly.

Dempsey's eye brightened. He held up an inspired forefinger as though a brilliant idea had struck him.

"I've got it now," he said cordially. "It was just a little mistake. You ain't no O'Sullivan. You are a ring-tailed monkey. Excuse us for not recognising you at first."

O'Sullivan's eye flashed. He made a quick movement, but Andy Geoghan was ready and caught his arm.

Dempsey nodded at Andy and William McMahan, the secretary of the club, and walked rapidly toward a door at the rear of the hall. Two other members of the Give and Take Association swiftly joined the little group. Terry O'Sullivan was now in the hands of the Board of Rules and Social Referees. They spoke to him briefly and softly, and conducted him out through the same door at the rear.

This movement on the part of the Clover Leaf members requires a word of elucidation. Back of the association hall was a smaller room rented by the club. In this room personal difficulties that arose on the ballroom floor were settled, man to man, with the weapons of nature, under the supervision of the board. No lady could say that she had witnessed a fight at a Clover Leaf hop in several years. Its gentlemen members guaranteed that.

So easily and smoothly had Dempsey and the board done their preliminary work that many in the hall had not noticed the checking of the fascinating O'Sullivan's social triumph. Among these was Maggie. She looked about for her escort.

"Smoke up!" said Rose Cassidy. "Wasn't you on? Demps Donovan picked a scrap with your Lizzie-boy, and they've waltzed out to the slaughter room with him. How's my hair look done up this way, Mag?"

Maggie laid a hand on the bosom of her cheesecloth waist.

"Gone to fight with Dempsey!" she said, breathlessly. "They've got to be stopped. Dempsey Donovan can't fight him. Why, he'll—he'll kill him!"

"Ah, what do you care?" said Rosa. "Don't some of 'em fight every hop?"

But Maggie was off, darting her zig-zag way through the maze of dancers. She burst through the rear door into the dark hall and then threw her solid shoulder against the door of the room of single combat. It gave way, and in the instant that she entered her eye caught the scene—the Board standing about with open watches; Dempsey Donovan in his shirt sleeves dancing, light-footed, with the wary grace of the modern pugilist, within easy reach of his adversary; Terry O'Sullivan standing with arms folded and a murderous look in his dark eyes. And without slacking the speed of her entrance she leaped forward with a scream—leaped in time to catch and hang upon the arm of O'Sullivan that was suddenly uplifted, and to whisk from it the long, bright stiletto that he had drawn from his bosom.

The knife fell and rang upon the floor. Cold steel drawn in the rooms of the Give and Take Association! Such a thing had never happened before. Every one stood motionless for a minute. Andy Geoghan kicked the stiletto with the toe of his shoe curiously, like an antiquarian who has come upon some ancient weapon unknown to his learning.

And then O'Sullivan hissed something unintelligible between his teeth. Dempsey and the board exchanged looks. And then Dempsey looked at O'Sullivan without anger, as one looks at a stray dog, and nodded his head in the direction of the door.

"The back stairs, Giuseppi," he said, briefly. "Somebody 'll pitch your hat down after you."

Maggie walked up to Dempsey Donovan. There was a brilliant spot of red in her cheeks, down which slow tears were running. But she looked him bravely in the eye.

"I knew it, Dempsey," she said, as her eyes grew dull even in their tears. "I knew he was a Guinea. His name's Tony Spinelli. I hurried in when they told me you and him was scrappin'. Them Guineas always carries knives. But you don't understand, Dempsey. I never had a fellow in my life. I got tired of comin' with Anna and Jimmy every night, so I fixed it with him to call himself O'Sullivan, and brought him along. I knew there'd be nothin' doin' for him if he came as a Dago. I guess I'll resign from the club now."

Dempsey turned to Andy Geoghan.

"Chuck that cheese slicer out of the window," he said, "and tell 'em inside that Mr. O'Sullivan has had a telephone message to go down to Tammany Hall."

And then he turned back to Maggie.

"Say, Mag," he said, "I'll see you home. And how about next Saturday night? Will you come to the hop with me if I call around for you?"

It was remarkable how quickly Maggie's eyes could change from dull to a shining brown.

"With you, Dempsey?" she stammered. "Say—will a duck swim?"

The Cop and the Anthem

O N HIS bench in Madison Square Soapy moved uneasily. When wild geese honk high of nights, and when women without sealskin coats grow kind to their husbands, and when Soapy moves uneasily on his bench in the park, you may know that winter is near at hand.

A dead leaf fell in Soapy's lap. That was Jack Frost's card. Jack is kind to the regular denizens of Madison Square, and gives fair warning of his annual call. At the corners of four streets he hands his pasteboard to the North Wind, footman of the mansion of All Outdoors, so that the inhabitants thereof may make ready.

Soapy's mind became cognisant of the fact that the time had come for him to resolve himself into a singular Committee of Ways and Means to provide against the coming rigour. And therefore he moved uneasily on his bench.

The hihernatorial ambitions of Soapy were not of the highest. In them there were no considerations of Mediterranean cruises, of soporific Southern skies or drifting in the Vesuvian Bay. Three months on the Island was what his soul craved. Three months of assured board and bed and congenial company, safe from Boreas and bluecoats, seemed to Soapy the essence of things desirable.

For years the hospitable Blackwell's had been his winter quarters. Just as his more fortunate fellow New Yorkers had bought their tickets to Palm Beach and the Riviera each winter, so Soapy had made his humbler arrangements for his annual hegira to the Island. And now the time was come. On the previous night three Sabbath newspapers, distributed beneath his coat, about his ankles and over his lap, had failed to repulse the cold as he slept on his bench near the spurting fountain in the ancient square. So the Island loomed big and timely in Soapy's mind. He scorned the provisions made in the name of charity for the city's dependents. In Soapy's opinion the Law was more benign than Philanthropy. There was an endless round of institutions, municipal and eleemosynary, on which he might set out and receive lodging and food accordant with the simple

life. But to one of Soapy's proud spirit the gifts of charity are
encumbered. If not in coin you must pay in humiliation of
spirit for every benefit received at the hands of philanthropy.
As Cæsar had his Brutus, every bed of charity must have its
toll of a bath, every loaf of bread its compensation of a private
and personal inquisition. Wherefore it is better to be a guest
of the law, which though conducted by rules, does not meddle
unduly with a gentleman's private affairs.

Soapy, having decided to go to the Island, at once set about
accomplishing his desire. There were many easy ways of doing
this. The pleasantest was to dine luxuriously at some expensive
restaurant; and then, after declaring insolvency, be handed over
quietly and without uproar to a policeman. An accommodating
magistrate would do the rest.

Soapy left his bench and strolled out of the square and across
the level sea of asphalt, where Broadway and Fifth Avenue flow
together. Up Broadway he turned, and halted at a glittering
café, where are gathered together nightly the choicest products
of the grape, the silkworm and the protoplasm.

Soapy had confidence in himself from the lowest button of
his vest upward. He was shaven, and his coat was decent and his
neat black, ready-tied four-in-hand had been presented to him
by a lady missionary on Thanksgiving Day. If he could reach a
table in the restaurant unsuspected success would be his. The
portion of him that would show above the table would raise no
doubt in the waiter's mind. A roasted mallard duck, thought
Soapy, would be about the thing—with a bottle of Chablis,
and then Camembert, a demi-tasse and a cigar. One dollar for
the cigar would be enough. The total would not be so high as
to call forth any supreme manifestation of revenge from the
café management; and yet the meat would leave him filled and
happy for the journey to his winter refuge.

But as Soapy set foot inside the restaurant door the head
waiter's eye fell upon his frayed trousers and decadent shoes.
Strong and ready hands turned him about and conveyed him
in silence and haste to the sidewalk and averted the ignoble fate
of the menaced mallard.

Soapy turned off Broadway. It seemed that his route to the
coveted island was not to be an epicurean one. Some other way
of entering limbo must be thought of.

At a corner of Sixth Avenue electric lights and cunningly displayed wares behind plate-glass made a shop window conspicuous. Soapy took a cobblestone and dashed it through the glass. People came running around the corner, a policeman in the lead. Soapy stood still, with his hands in his pockets, and smiled at the sight of brass buttons.

"Where's the man that done that?" inquired the officer excitedly.

"Don't you figure out that I might have had something to do with it?" said Soapy, not without sarcasm, but friendly, as one greets good fortune.

The policeman's mind refused to accept Soapy even as a clue. Men who smash windows do not remain to parley with the law's minions. They take to their heels. The policeman saw a man half way down the block running to catch a car. With drawn club he joined in the pursuit. Soapy, with disgust in his heart, loafed along, twice unsuccessful.

On the opposite side of the street was a restaurant of no great pretensions. It catered to large appetites and modest purses. Its crockery and atmosphere were thick; its soup and napery thin. Into this place Soapy took his accusive shoes and telltale trousers without challenge. At a table he sat and consumed beefsteak, flapjacks, doughnuts and pie. And then to the waiter he betrayed the fact that the minutest coin and himself were strangers.

"Now, get busy and call a cop," said Soapy. "And don't keep a gentleman waiting."

"No cop for youse," said the waiter, with a voice like butter cakes and an eye like the cherry in a Manhattan cocktail. "Hey, Con!"

Neatly upon his left ear on the callous pavement two waiters pitched Soapy. He arose, joint by joint, as a carpenter's rule opens, and beat the dust from his clothes. Arrest seemed but a rosy dream. The Island seemed very far away. A policeman who stood before a drug store two doors away laughed and walked down the street.

Five blocks Soapy travelled before his courage permitted him to woo capture again. This time the opportunity presented what he fatuously termed to himself a "cinch." A young woman of a modest and pleasing guise was standing before a show window gazing with sprightly interest at its display of shaving mugs and inkstands, and two yards from the window a large policeman of severe demeanour leaned against a water plug.

It was Soapy's design to assume the rôle of the despicable and execrated "masher." The refined and elegant appearance of his victim and the contiguity of the conscientious cop encouraged him to believe that he would soon feel the pleasant official clutch upon his arm that would insure his winter quarters on the right little, tight little isle.

Soapy straightened the lady missionary's ready-made tie, dragged his shrinking cuffs into the open, set his hat at a killing cant and sidled toward the young woman. He made eyes at her, was taken with sudden coughs and "hems," smiled, smirked and went brazenly through the impudent and contemptible litany of the "masher." With half an eye Soapy saw that the policeman was watching him fixedly. The young woman moved away a few steps, and again bestowed her absorbed attention upon the shaving mugs. Soapy followed, boldly stepping to her side, raised his hat and said:

"Ah there, Bedelia! Don't you want to come and play in my yard?"

The policeman was still looking. The persecuted young woman had but to beckon a finger and Soapy would be practically en route for his insular haven. Already he imagined he could feel the cozy warmth of the station-house. The young woman faced him and, stretching out a hand, caught Soapy's coat sleeve.

"Sure, Mike," she said joyfully, "if you'll blow me to a pail of suds. I'd have spoke to you sooner, but the cop was watching."

With the young woman playing the clinging ivy to his oak Soapy walked past the policeman overcome with gloom. He seemed doomed to liberty.

At the next corner he shook off his companion and ran. He halted in the district where by night are found the lightest streets, hearts, vows and librettos. Women in furs and men in greatcoats moved gaily in the wintry air. A sudden fear seized Soapy that some dreadful enchantment had rendered him immune to arrest. The thought brought a little of panic upon it, and when he came upon another policeman lounging grandly in front of a transplendent theatre he caught at the immediate straw of "disorderly conduct."

On the sidewalk Soapy began to yell drunken gibberish at the top of his harsh voice. He danced, howled, raved and otherwise disturbed the welkin.

The policeman twirled his club, turned his back to Soapy and remarked to a citizen.

"'Tis one of them Yale lads celebratin' the goose egg they give to the Hartford College. Noisy; but no harm. We've instructions to lave them be."

Disconsolate, Soapy ceased his unavailing racket. Would never a policeman lay hands on him? In his fancy the Island seemed an unattainable Arcadia. He buttoned his thin coat against the chilling wind.

In a cigar store he saw a well-dressed man lighting a cigar at a swinging light. His silk umbrella he had set by the door on entering. Soapy stepped inside, secured the umbrella and sauntered off with it slowly. The man at the cigar light followed hastily.

"My umbrella," he said, sternly.

"Oh, is it?" sneered Soapy, adding insult to petit larceny. "Well, why don't you call a policeman? I took it. Your umbrella! Why don't you call a cop? There stands one on the corner."

The umbrella owner slowed his steps. Soapy did likewise, with a presentiment that luck would again run against him. The policeman looked at the two curiously.

"Of course," said the umbrella man—"that is—well, you know how these mistakes occur—I—if it's your umbrella I hope you'll excuse me—I picked it up this morning in a restaurant—If you recognise it as yours, why—I hope you'll——"

"Of course it's mine," said Soapy, viciously.

The ex-umbrella man retreated. The policeman hurried to assist a tall blonde in an opera cloak across the street in front of a street car that was approaching two blocks away.

Soapy walked eastward through a street damaged by improvements. He hurled the umbrella wrathfully into an excavation. He muttered against the men who wear helmets and carry clubs. Because he wanted to fall into their clutches, they seemed to regard him as a king who could do no wrong.

At length Soapy reached one of the avenues to the east where the glitter and turmoil was but faint. He set his face down this toward Madison Square, for the homing instinct survives even when the home is a park bench.

But on an unusually quiet corner Soapy came to a standstill. Here was an old church, quaint and rambling and gabled. Through one violet-stained window a soft light glowed, where, no doubt, the organist loitered over the keys, making sure of his mastery of the coming Sabbath anthem. For there drifted out to Soapy's ears sweet music that caught and held him transfixed against the convolutions of the iron fence.

The moon was above, lustrous and serene; vehicles and pedestrians were few; sparrows twittered sleepily in the eaves—for a little while the scene might have been a country churchyard. And the anthem that the organist played cemented Soapy to the iron fence, for he had known it well in the days when his life contained such things as mothers and roses and ambitions and friends and immaculate thoughts and collars.

The conjunction of Soapy's receptive state of mind and the influences about the old church wrought a sudden and wonderful change in his soul. He viewed with swift horror the pit into which he had tumbled, the degraded days, unworthy desires, dead hopes, wrecked faculties and base motives that made up his existence.

And also in a moment his heart responded thrillingly to this novel mood. An instantaneous and strong impulse moved him to battle with his desperate fate. He would pull himself out of the mire; he would make a man of himself again; he would conquer the evil that had taken possession of him. There was time; he was comparatively young yet; he would resurrect his old eager ambitions and pursue them without faltering. Those solemn but sweet organ notes had set up a revolution in him. Tomorrow he would go into the roaring downtown district and find work. A fur importer had once offered him a place as driver. He would find him to-morrow and ask for the position. He would be somebody in the world. He would——

Soapy felt a hand laid on his arm. He looked quickly around into the broad face of a policeman.

"What are you doin' here?" asked the officer.

"Nothin'," said Soapy.

"Then come along," said the policeman.

"Three months on the Island," said the Magistrate in the Police Court the next morning.

The Green Door

S UPPOSE YOU should be walking down Broadway after dinner, with ten minutes allotted to the consummation of your
cigar while you are choosing between a diverting tragedy and
something serious in the way of vaudeville. Suddenly a hand is
laid upon your arm. You turn to look into the thrilling eyes of
a beautiful woman, wonderful in diamonds and Russian sables.
She thrusts hurriedly into your hand an extremely hot buttered roll, flashes out a tiny pair of scissors, snips off the second
button of your overcoat, meaningly ejaculates the one word,
"parallelogram!" and swiftly flies down a cross street, looking
back fearfully over her shoulder.

That would be pure adventure. Would you accept it? Not
you. You would flush with embarrassment; you would sheep-
ishly drop the roll and continue down Broadway, fumbling
feebly for the missing button. This you would do unless you
are one of the blessed few in whom the pure spirit of adventure
is not dead.

True adventurers have never been plentiful. They who are
set down in print as such have been mostly business men with
newly invented methods. They have been out after the things
they wanted—golden fleeces, holy grails, lady loves, treasure,
crowns and fame. The true adventurer goes forth aimless and
uncalculating to meet and greet unknown fate. A fine example
was the Prodigal Son—when he started back home.

Half-adventurers—brave and splendid figures—have been
numerous. From the Crusades to the Palisades they have enriched the arts of history and fiction and the trade of historical
fiction. But each of them had a prize to win, a goal to kick, an
axe to grind, a race to run, a new thrust in tierce to deliver, a
name to carve, a crow to pick—so they were not followers of
true adventure.

In the big city the twin spirits Romance and Adventure are
always abroad seeking worthy wooers. As we roam the streets
they slyly peep at us and challenge us in twenty different guises.
Without knowing why, we look up suddenly to see in a window
a face that seems to belong to our gallery of intimate portraits;

in a sleeping thoroughfare we hear a cry of agony and fear coming from an empty and shuttered house; instead of at our familiar curb a cab-driver deposits us before a strange door, which one, with a smile, opens for us and bids us enter; a slip of paper, written upon, flutters down to our feet from the high lattices of Chance; we exchange glances of instantaneous hate, affection and fear with hurrying strangers in the passing crowds; a sudden souse of rain—and our umbrella may be sheltering the daughter of the Full Moon and first cousin of the Sidereal System; at every corner handkerchiefs drop, fingers beckon, eyes besiege, and the lost, the lonely, the rapturous, the mysterious, the perilous, changing clues of adventure are slipped into our fingers. But few of us are willing to hold and follow them. We are grown stiff with the ramrod of convention down our backs. We pass on; and some day we come, at the end of a very dull life, to reflect that our romance has been a pallid thing of a marriage or two, a satin rosette kept in a safe-deposit drawer, and a lifelong feud with a steam radiator.

Rudolf Steiner was a true adventurer. Few were the evenings on which he did not go forth from his hall bedchamber in search of the unexpected and the egregious. The most interesting thing in life seemed to him to be what might lie just around the next corner. Sometimes his willingness to tempt fate led him into strange paths. Twice he had spent the night in a station-house; again and again he had found himself the dupe of ingenious and mercenary tricksters; his watch and money had been the price of one flattering allurement. But with undiminished ardour he picked up every glove cast before him into the merry lists of adventure.

One evening Rudolf was strolling along a crosstown street in the older central part of the city. Two streams of people filled the sidewalks—the home-hurrying, and that restless contingent that abandons home for the specious welcome of the thousand-candle-power *table d'hôte*.

The young adventurer was of pleasing presence, and moved serenely and watchfully. By daylight he was a salesman in a piano store. He wore his tie drawn through a topaz ring instead of fastened with a stick pin; and once he had written to the editor of a magazine that "Junie's Love Test," by Miss Libbey, had been the book that had most influenced his life.

During his walk a violent chattering of teeth in a glass case on the sidewalk seemed at first to draw his attention (with a qualm), to a restaurant before which it was set; but a second glance revealed the electric letters of a dentist's sign high above the next door. A giant negro, fantastically dressed in a red embroidered coat, yellow trousers and a military cap, discreetly distributed cards to those of the passing crowd who consented to take them.

This mode of dentistic advertising was a common sight to Rudolf. Usually he passed the dispenser of the dentist's cards without reducing his store; but to-night the African slipped one into his hand so deftly that he retained it there smiling a little at the successful feat.

When he had travelled a few yards further he glanced at the card indifferently. Surprised, he turned it over and looked again with interest. One side of the card was blank; on the other was written in ink three words, "The Green Door." And then Rudolf saw, three steps in front of him, a man throw down the card the negro had given him as he passed. Rudolf picked it up. It was printed with the dentist's name and address and the usual schedule of "plate work "and "bridge work" and "crowns," and specious promises of "painless" operations.

The adventurous piano salesman halted at the corner and considered. Then he crossed the street, walked down a block, recrossed and joined the upward current of people again. Without seeming to notice the negro as he passed the second time, he carelessly took the card that was handed him. Ten steps away he inspected it. In the same handwriting that appeared on the first card "The Green Door" was inscribed upon it. Three or four cards were tossed to the pavement by pedestrians both following and leading him. These fell blank side up. Rudolf turned them over. Every one bore the printed legend of the dental "parlours."

Rarely did the arch sprite Adventure need to beckon twice to Rudolf Steiner, his true follower. But twice it had been done, and the quest was on.

Rudolf walked slowly back to where the giant negro stood by the case of rattling teeth. This time as he passed he received no card. In spite of his gaudy and ridiculous garb, the Ethiopian displayed a natural barbaric dignity as he stood, offering the cards suavely to some, allowing others to pass unmolested. Every half minute he chanted a harsh, unintelligible phrase akin to the jabber of car conductors and grand opera. And not only did he withhold a card this time, but it seemed to Rudolf that he received from the shining and massive black countenance a look of cold, almost contemptuous disdain.

The look stung the adventurer. He read in it a silent accusation that he had been found wanting. Whatever the mysterious written words on the cards might mean, the black had selected him twice from the throng for their recipient; and now seemed to have condemned him as deficient in the wit and spirit to engage the enigma.

Standing aside from the rush, the young man made a rapid estimate of the building in which he conceived that his adventure must lie. Five stories high it rose. A small restaurant occupied the basement.

The first floor, now closed, seemed to house millinery or furs. The second floor, by the winking electric letters, was the dentist's. Above this a polyglot babel of signs struggled to indicate the abodes of palmists, dressmakers, musicians and doctors. Still higher up draped curtains and milk bottles white on the window sills proclaimed the regions of domesticity.

After concluding his survey Rudolf walked briskly up the high flight of stone steps into the house. Up two flights of the carpeted stairway he continued; and at its top paused. The hallway there was dimly lighted by two pale jets of gas—one far to his right, the other nearer, to his left. He looked toward the nearer light and saw, within its wan halo, a green door. For one moment he hesitated; then he seemed to see the contumelious sneer of the African juggler of cards; and then he walked straight to the green door and knocked against it.

Moments like those that passed before his knock was answered measure the quick breath of true adventure. What might not be behind those green panels! Gamesters at play; cunning rogues baiting their traps with subtle skill; beauty in love with courage, and thus planning to be sought by it; danger, death, love, disappointment, ridicule—any of these might respond to that temerarious rap.

A faint rustle was heard inside, and the door slowly opened. A girl not yet twenty stood there, white-faced and tottering.

She loosed the knob and swayed weakly, groping with one hand. Rudolf caught her and laid her on a faded couch that stood against the wall. He closed the door and took a swift glance around the room by the light of a flickering gas jet. Neat, but extreme poverty was the story that he read.

The girl lay still, as if in a faint. Rudolf looked around the room excitedly for a barrel. People must be rolled upon a barrel who—no, no; that was for drowned persons. He began to fan her with his hat. That was successful, for he struck her nose with the brim of his derby and she opened her eyes. And then the young man saw that hers, indeed, was the one missing face from his heart's gallery of intimate portraits. The frank, grey eyes, the little nose, turning pertly outward; the chestnut hair, curling like the tendrils of a pea vine, seemed the right end and reward of all his wonderful adventures. But the face was wofully thin and pale.

The girl looked at him calmly, and then smiled.

"Fainted, didn't I?" she asked, weakly. "Well, who wouldn't? You try going without anything to eat for three days and see!"

"Himmel!" exclaimed Rudolf, jumping up. "Wait till I come back."

He dashed out the green door and down the stairs. In twenty minutes he was back again, kicking at the door with his toe for her to open it. With both arms he hugged an array of wares from the grocery and the restaurant. On the table he laid them—bread and butter, cold meats, cakes, pies, pickles, oysters, a roasted chicken, a bottle of milk and one of red-hot tea.

"This is ridiculous," said Rudolf, blusteringly, "to go without eating. You must quit making election bets of this kind. Supper is ready." He helped her to a chair at the table and asked: "Is there a cup for the tea?" "On the shelf by the window," she answered. When he turned again with the cup he saw her, with eyes shining rapturously, beginning upon a huge Dill pickle that she had rooted out from the paper bags with a woman's unerring instinct. He took it from her, laughingly, and poured the cup full of milk. "Drink that first," he ordered, "and then you shall have some tea, and then a chicken wing. If you are very good you shall have a pickle to-morrow. And now, if you'll allow me to be your guest we'll have supper."

He drew up the other chair. The tea brightened the girl's eyes and brought back some of her colour. She began to eat with a sort of dainty ferocity like some starved wild animal. She seemed to regard the young man's presence and the aid he had rendered her as a natural thing—not as though she undervalued the conventions; but as one whose great stress gave her the right to put aside the artificial for the human. But gradually, with the return of strength and comfort, came also a sense of the little conventions that belong; and she began to tell him her little story. It was one of a thousand such as the city yawns at every day—the shop girl's story of insufficient wages, further reduced by "fines" that go to swell the store's profits; of time lost through illness; and then of lost positions, lost hope, and—the knock of the adventurer upon the green door.

But to Rudolf the history sounded as big as the Iliad or the crisis in "Junie's Love Test."

"To think of you going through all that," he exclaimed.

"It was something fierce," said the girl, solemnly.

"And you have no relatives or friends in the city?"

"None whatever."

"I am all alone in the world, too," said Rudolf, after a pause.

"I am glad of that," said the girl, promptly; and somehow it pleased the young man to hear that she approved of his bereft condition.

Very suddenly her eyelids dropped and she sighed deeply.

"I'm awfully sleepy," she said, "and I feel so good."

Rudolf rose and took his hat.

"Then I'll say good-night. A long night's sleep will be fine for you."

He held out his hand, and she took it and said "good-night." But her eyes asked a question so eloquently, so frankly and pathetically that he answered it with words.

"Oh, I'm coming back to-morrow to see how you are getting along. You can't get rid of me so easily."

Then, at the door, as though the way of his coming had been so much less important than the fact that he had come, she asked: "How did you come to knock at my door?"

He looked at her for a moment, remembering the cards, and felt a sudden jealous pain. What if they had fallen into other hands as adventurous as his? Quickly he decided that she must never know the truth. He would never let her know that he was aware of the strange expedient to which she had been driven by her great distress.

"One of our piano tuners lives in this house," he said. "I knocked at your door by mistake."

The last thing he saw in the room before the green door closed was her smile.

At the head of the stairway he paused and looked curiously about him. And then he went along the hallway to its other end; and, coming back, ascended to the floor above and continued his puzzled explorations. Every door that he found in the house was painted green.

Wondering, he descended to the sidewalk. The fantastic African was still there. Rudolf confronted him with his two cards in his hand.

"Will you tell me why you gave me these cards and what they mean?" he asked.

In a broad, good-natured grin the negro exhibited a splendid advertisement of his master's profession.

"Dar it is, boss," he said, pointing down the street. "But I 'spect you is a little late for de fust act."

Looking the way he pointed Rudolf saw above the entrance to a theatre the blazing electric sign of its new play, "The Green Door."

"I'm informed dat it's a fust-rate show, sah," said the negro. "De agent what represents it pussented me with a dollar, sah, to distribute a few of his cards along with de doctah's. May I offer you one of de doctah's cards, sah?"

At the corner of the block in which he lived Rudolf stopped for a glass of beer and a cigar. When he had come out with his lighted weed he buttoned his coat, pushed back his hat and said, stoutly, to the lamp post on the corner:

"All the same, I believe it was the hand of Fate that doped out the way for me to find her."

Which conclusion, under the circumstances, certainly admits Rudolf Steiner to the ranks of the true followers of Romance and Adventure.

The Badge of Policeman O'Roon

IT CANNOT be denied that men and women have looked upon one another for the first time and become instantly enamored. It is a risky process, this love at first sight, before she has seen him in Bradstreet or he has seen her in curl papers. But these things do happen; and one instance must form a theme for this story—though not, thank Heaven, to the overshadowing of more vital and important subjects, such as drink, policemen, horses and earldoms.

During a certain war a troop calling itself the Gentle Riders rode into history and one or two ambuscades. The Gentle Riders were recruited from the aristocracy of the wild men of the West and the wild men of the aristocracy of the East. In khaki there is little telling them one from another, so they became good friends and comrades all around.

Ellsworth Remsen, whose old Knickerbocker descent atoned for his modest rating at only ten millions, ate his canned beef gayly by the campfires of the Gentle Riders. The war was a great lark to him, so that he scarcely regretted polo and planked shad.

One of the troopers was a well set up, affable, cool young man, who called himself O'Roon. To this young man Remsen took an especial liking. The two rode side by side during the famous mooted up-hill charge that was disputed so hotly at the time by the Spaniards and afterward by the Democrats.

After the war Remsen came back to his polo and shad. One day a well set up, affable, cool young man disturbed him at his club, and he and O'Roon were soon pounding each other and exchanging opprobrious epithets after the manner of long-lost friends. O'Roon looked seedy and out of luck and perfectly contented. But it seemed that his content was only apparent.

"Get me a job, Remsen," he said. "I've just handed a barber my last shilling."

"No trouble at all," said Remsen. "I know a lot of men who have banks and stores and things downtown. Any particular line you fancy?"

"Yes," said O'Roon, with a look of interest. "I took a walk

in your Central Park this morning. I'd like to be one of those
bobbies on horseback. That would be about the ticket. Besides,
it's the only thing I could do. I can ride a little and the fresh air
suits me. Think you could land that for me?"

Remsen was sure that he could. And in a very short time
he did. And they who were not above looking at mounted
policemen might have seen a well set up, affable, cool young
man on a prancing chestnut steed attending to his duties along
the driveways of the park.

And now at the extreme risk of wearying old gentlemen
who carry leather fob chains, and elderly ladies who—but no!
grandmother herself yet thrills at foolish, immortal Romeo—
there must be a hint of love at first sight.

It came just as Remsen was strolling into Fifth avenue from
his club a few doors away.

A motor car was creeping along foot by foot, impeded
by a freshet of vehicles that filled the street. In the car was a
chauffeur and an old gentleman with snowy side whiskers and a
Scotch plaid cap which could not be worn while automobiling
except by a personage. Not even a wine agent would dare to
do it. But these two were of no consequence—except, perhaps,
for the guiding of the machine and the paying for it. At the old
gentleman's side sat a young lady more beautiful than pomegranate blossoms, more exquisite than the first quarter moon
viewed at twilight through the tops of oleanders. Remsen saw
her and knew his fate. He could have flung himself under the
very wheels that conveyed her, but he knew that would be
the last means of attracting the attention of those who ride in
motor cars. Slowly the auto passed, and, if we place the poets
above the autoists, carried the heart of Remsen with it. Here
was a large city of millions, and many women who at a certain
distance appear to resemble pomegranate blossoms. Yet he
hoped to see her again; for each one fancies that his romance
has its own tutelary guardian and divinity.

Luckily for Remsen's peace of mind there came a diversion
in the guise of a reunion of the Gentle Riders of the city. There
were not many of them—perhaps a score—and there was
wassail, and things to eat, and speeches and the Spaniard was
bearded again in recapitulation. And when daylight threatened

them the survivors prepared to depart. But some remained upon the battlefield. One of these was Trooper O'Roon, who was not seasoned to potent liquids. His legs declined to fulfil the obligations they had sworn to the police department.

"I'm stewed, Remsen," said O'Roon to his friend. "Why do they built hotels that go round and round like catherine wheels? They'll take away my shield and break me. I can think and talk con-con-consec-sec-secutively, but I s-s-stammer with my feet. I've got to go on duty in three hours. The jig is up, Remsen. The jig is up, I tell you."

"Look at me," said Remsen, who was his smiling self, pointing to his own face; "whom do you see here?"

"Goo' fellow," said O'Roon, dizzily, "Goo' old Remsen."

"Not so," said Remsen. "You see Mounted Policeman O'Roon. Look at your face—no; you can't do that without a glass—but look at mine, and think of yours. How much alike are we? As two French *table d'hôte* dinners. With your badge, on your horse, in your uniform, will I charm nurse-maids and prevent the grass from growing under people's feet in the Park this day. I will save your badge and your honor, besides having the jolliest lark I've been blessed with since we licked Spain."

Promptly on time the counterfeit presentment of Mounted Policeman O'Roon single-footed into the Park on his chestnut steed. In a uniform two men who are unlike will look alike; two who somewhat resemble each other in feature and figure will appear as twin brothers. So Remsen trotted down the bridle paths, enjoying himself hugely, so few real pleasures do ten-millionaires have.

Along the driveway in the early morning spun a victoria drawn by a pair of fiery bays. There was something foreign about the affair, for the Park is rarely used in the morning except by unimportant people who love to be healthy, poor and wise. In the vehicle sat an old gentleman with snowy side-whiskers and a Scotch plaid cap which could not be worn while driving except by a personage. At his side sat the lady of Remsen's heart—the lady who looked like pomegranate blossoms and the gibbous moon.

Remsen met them coming. At the instant of their passing her eyes looked into his, and but for the ever coward heart of a true lover he could have sworn that she flushed a faint pink. He trotted on for twenty yards, and then wheeled his horse at the sound of runaway hoofs. The bays had bolted.

Remsen sent his chestnut after the victoria like a shot. There was work cut out for the impersonator of Policeman O'Roon. The chestnut ranged alongside the off bay thirty seconds after the chase began, rolled his eye back at Remsen, and said in the only manner open to policemen's horses:

"Well, you duffer, are you going to do your share? You're not O'Roon, but it seems to me if you'd lean to the right you could reach the reins of that foolish, slow-running bay—ah! you're all right; O'Roon couldn't have done it more neatly!"

The runaway team was tugged to an inglorious halt by Remsen's tough muscles. The driver released his hands from the wrapped reins, jumped from his seat and stood at the heads of the team. The chestnut, approving his new rider, danced and pranced, reviling equinely the subdued bays. Remsen, lingering, was dimly conscious of a vague, impossible, unnecessary old gentleman in a Scotch cap who talked incessantly about something. And he was acutely conscious of a pair of violet eyes that would have drawn Saint Pyrites from his iron pillar—or whatever the allusion is—and of the lady's smile and look—a little frightened, but a look that, with the ever coward heart of a true lover, he could not yet construe. They were asking his name and bestowing upon him well-bred thanks for his heroic deed, and the Scotch cap was especially babbling and insistent. But the eloquent appeal was in the eyes of the lady.

A little thrill of satisfaction ran through Remsen, because he had a name to give which, without undue pride, was worthy of being spoken in high places, and a small fortune which, with due pride, he could leave at his end without disgrace.

He opened his lips to speak, and closed them again.

Who was he? Mounted Policeman O'Roon. The badge and the honor of his comrade were in his hands. If Ellsworth Remsen, ten-millionaire and Knickerbocker, had just rescued pomegranate blossoms and Scotch cap from possible death, where was Policeman O'Roon? Off his beat, exposed, disgraced, discharged. Love had come, but before that there had been something that demanded precedence—the fellowship of men on battlefields fighting an alien foe.

Remsen touched his cap, looked between the chestnut's ears, and took refuge in vernacularity.

"Don't mention it," he said stolidly. "We policemen are paid to do these things. It's our duty."

And he rode away—rode away cursing *noblesse oblige*, but knowing he could never have done anything else.

At the end of the day Remsen sent the chestnut to his stable and went to O'Roon's room. The policeman was again a well set up, affable, cool young man who sat by the window smoking cigars.

"I wish you and the rest of the police force and all badges, horses, brass buttons and men who can't drink two glasses of *brut* without getting upset were at the devil," said Remsen feelingly.

O'Roon smiled with evident satisfaction.

"Good old Remsen," he said, affably, "I know all about it. They trailed me down and cornered me here two hours ago. There was a little row at home, you know, and I cut sticks just to show them. I don't believe I told you that my Governor was the Earl of Ardsley. Funny you should bob against them in the Park. If you damaged that horse of mine I'll never forgive you. I'm going to buy him and take him back with me. Oh, yes, and I think my sister—Lady Angela, you know—wants particularly for you to come up to the hotel with me this evening. Didn't lose my badge, did you, Remsen? I've got to turn that in at Headquarters when I resign."

The Making of a New Yorker

BESIDES MANY other things, Raggles was a poet. He was called a tramp; but that was only an elliptical way of saying that he was a philosopher, an artist, a traveller, a naturalist and a discoverer. But most of all he was a poet. In all his life he never wrote a line of verse; he lived his poetry. His Odyssey would have been a Limerick, had it been written. But, to linger with the primary proposition, Raggles was a poet.

Raggles's specialty, had he been driven to ink and paper, would have been sonnets to the cities. He studied cities as women study their reflections in mirrors; as children study the glue and sawdust of a dislocated doll; as the men who write about wild animals study the cages in the zoo. A city to Raggles was not merely a pile of bricks and mortar, peopled by a certain number of inhabitants; it was a thing with a soul characteristic and distinct; an individual conglomeration of life, with its own peculiar essence, flavor and feeling. Two thousand miles to the north and south, east and west, Raggles wandered in poetic fervor, taking the cities to his breast. He footed it on dusty roads, or sped magnificently in freight cars, counting time as of no account. And when he had found the heart of a city and listened to its secret confession, he strayed on, restless, to another. Fickle Raggles!—but perhaps he had not met the civic corporation that could engage and hold his critical fancy.

Through the ancient poets we have learned that the cities are feminine. So they were to poet Raggles; and his mind carried a concrete and clear conception of the figure that symbolized and typified each one that he had wooed.

Chicago seemed to swoop down upon him with a breezy suggestion of Mrs. Partington, plumes and patchouli, and to disturb his rest with a soaring and beautiful song of future promise. But Raggles would awake to a sense of shivering cold and a haunting impression of ideals lost in a depressing aura of potato salad and fish.

Thus Chicago affected him. Perhaps there is a vagueness and inaccuracy in the description; but that is Raggles's fault. He should have recorded his sensations in magazine poems.

Pittsburg impressed him as the play of "Othello" performed in the Russian language in a railroad station by Dockstader's minstrels. A royal and generous lady this Pittsburg, though—homely, hearty, with flushed face, washing the dishes in a silk dress and white kid slippers, and bidding Raggles sit before the roaring fireplace and drink champagne with his pigs' feet and fried potatoes.

New Orleans had simply gazed down upon him from a balcony. He could see her pensive, starry eyes and catch the flutter of her fan, and that was all. Only once he came face to face with her. It was at dawn, when she was flushing the red bricks of the banquette with a pail of water. She laughed and hummed a chansonette and filled Raggles's shoes with ice-cold water. Allons!

Boston construed herself to the poetic Raggles in an erratic and singular way. It seemed to him that he had drunk cold tea and that the city was a white, cold cloth that had been bound tightly around his brow to spur him to some unknown but tremendous mental effort. And, after all, he came to shovel snow for a livelihood; and the cloth, becoming wet, tightened its knots and could not be removed.

Indefinite and unintelligible ideas, you will say; but your disapprobation should be tempered with gratitude, for these are poets' fancies—and suppose you had come upon them in verse!

One day Raggles came and laid siege to the heart of the great city of Manhattan. She was the greatest of all; and he wanted to learn her note in the scale; to taste and appraise and classify and solve and label her and arrange her with the other cities that had given him up the secret of their individuality. And here we cease to be Raggles's translator and become his chronicler.

Raggles landed from a ferry-boat one morning and walked into the core of the town with the blasé air of a cosmopolite. He was dressed with care to play the role of an "unidentified man." No country, race, class, clique, union, party, clan or bowling association could have claimed him. His clothing, which had been donated to him piece-meal by citizens of different height, but same number of inches around the heart, was not yet as uncomfortable to his figure as those specimens of raiment, self-measured, that are railroaded to you by transcontinental tailors

with a suit case, suspenders, silk handkerchief and pearl studs as
a bonus. Without money—as a poet should be—but with the
ardor of an astronomer discovering a new star in the chorus of
the milky way, or a man who has seen ink suddenly flow from
his fountain pen, Raggles wandered into the great city.

Late in the afternoon he drew out of the roar and commotion with a look of dumb terror on his countenance. He was
defeated, puzzled, discomfited, frightened. Other cities had
been to him as long primer to read; as country maidens quickly
to fathom; as send-price-of-subscription-with-answer rebuses
to solve; as oyster cocktails to swallow; but here was one as
cold, glittering, serene, impossible as a four-carat diamond in
a window to a lover outside fingering damply in his pocket his
ribbon-counter salary.

The greetings of the other cities he had known—their homespun kindliness, their human gamut of rough charity, friendly
curses, garrulous curiosity and easily estimated credulity or
indifference. This city of Manhattan gave him no clue; it was
walled against him. Like a river of adamant it flowed past him in
the streets. Never an eye was turned upon him; no voice spoke
to him. His heart yearned for the clap of Pittsburg's sooty hand
on his shoulder; for Chicago's menacing but social yawp in his
ear; for the pale and eleemosynary stare through the Bostonian
eyeglass—even for the precipitate but unmalicious boot-toe of
Louisville or St. Louis.

On Broadway Raggles, successful suitor of many cities,
stood, bashful, like any country swain. For the first time he
experienced the poignant humiliation of being ignored. And
when he tried to reduce this brilliant, swiftly changing, ice-
cold city to a formula he failed utterly. Poet though he was, it
offered him no color, no similes, no points of comparison, no
flaw in its polished facets, no handle by which he could hold it
up and view its shape and structure, as he familiarly and often
contemptuously had done with other towns. The houses were
interminable ramparts loopholed for defense; the people were
bright but bloodless spectres passing in sinister and selfish array.

The thing that weighed heaviest on Raggles's soul and
clogged his poet's fancy was the spirit of absolute egotism that
seemed to saturate the people as toys are saturated with paint.

Each one that he considered appeared a monster of abominable and insolent conceit. Humanity was gone from them; they were toddling idols of stone and varnish, worshipping themselves and greedy for though oblivious of worship from their fellow graven images. Frozen, cruel, implacable, impervious, cut to an identical pattern, they hurried on their ways like statues brought by some miracles to motion, while soul and feeling lay unaroused in the reluctant marble.

Gradually Raggles became conscious of certain types. One was an elderly gentleman with a snow-white, short beard, pink, unwrinkled face and stony, sharp blue eyes, attired in the fashion of a gilded youth, who seemed to personify the city's wealth, ripeness and frigid unconcern. Another type was a woman, tall, beautiful, clear as a steel engraving, goddess-like, calm, clothed like the princesses of old, with eyes as coldly blue as the reflection of sunlight on a glacier. And another was a by-product of this town of marionettes—a broad, swaggering, grim, threateningly sedate fellow, with a jowl as large as a harvested wheat field, the complexion of a baptized infant and the knuckles of a prize-fighter. This type leaned against cigar signs and viewed the world with frappéd contumely.

A poet is a sensitive creature, and Raggles soon shrivelled in the bleak embrace of the undecipherable. The chill, sphynx-like, ironical, illegible, unnatural, ruthless expression of the city left him downcast and bewildered. Had it no heart? Better the woodpile, the scolding of vinegar-faced housewives at back doors, the kindly spleen of bartenders behind provincial free-lunch counters, the amiable truculence of rural constables, the kicks, arrests and happy-go-lucky chances of the other vulgar, loud, crude cities than this freezing heartlessness.

Raggles summoned his courage and sought alms from the populace. Unheeding, regardless, they passed on without the wink of an eyelash to testify that they were conscious of his existence. And then he said to himself that this fair but pitiless city of Manhattan was without a soul; that its inhabitants were manikins moved by wires and springs, and that he was alone in a great wilderness.

Raggles started to cross the street. There was a blast, a roar, a hissing and a crash as something struck him and hurled him over and over six yards from where he had been. As he was coming down like the stick of a rocket the earth and all the cities thereof turned to a fractured dream.

Raggles opened his eyes. First an odor made itself known to him—an odor of the earliest spring flowers of Paradise. And then a hand soft as a falling petal touched his brow. Bending over him was the woman clothed like the princess of old, with blue eyes, now soft and humid with human sympathy. Under his head on the pavement were silks and furs. With Raggles's hat in his hand and with his face pinker than ever from a vehement burst of oratory against reckless driving, stood the elderly gentleman who personified the city's wealth and ripeness. From a nearby café hurried the by-product with the vast jowl and baby complexion, bearing a glass full of a crimson fluid that suggested delightful possibilities.

"Drink dis, sport," said the by-product, holding the glass to Raggles's lips.

Hundreds of people huddled around in a moment, their faces wearing the deepest concern. Two flattering and gorgeous policemen got into the circle and pressed back the overplus of Samaritans. An old lady in a black shawl spoke loudly of camphor; a newsboy slipped one of his papers beneath Raggles's elbow, where it lay on the muddy pavement. A brisk young man with a notebook was asking for names.

A bell clanged importantly, and the ambulance cleaned a lane through the crowd. A cool surgeon slipped into the midst of affairs.

"How do you feel, old man?" asked the surgeon, stooping easily to his task. The princess of silks and satins wiped a red drop or two from Raggles's brow with a fragrant cobweb.

"Me?" said Raggles, with a seraphic smile, "I feel fine."

He had found the heart of his new city.

In three days they let him leave his cot for the convalescent ward in the hospital. He had been in there an hour when the attendants heard sounds of conflict. Upon investigation they found that Raggles had assaulted and damaged a brother convalescent—a glowering transient whom a freight train collision had sent in to be patched up.

"What's all this about?" inquired the head nurse.

"He was runnin' down me town," said Raggles.

"What town?" asked the nurse.

"Noo York," said Raggles.

Psyche and the Pskyscraper

IF YOU are a philosopher you can do this thing: you can go to the top of a high building, look down upon your fellow-men 300 feet below, and despise them as insects. Like the irresponsible black waterbugs on summer ponds, they crawl and circle and hustle about idiotically without aim or purpose. They do not even move with the admirable intelligence of ants, for ants always know when they are going home. The ant is of a lowly station, but he will often reach home and get his slippers on while you are left at your elevated station.

Man, then, to the housetopped philosopher, appears to be but a creeping, contemptible beetle. Brokers, poets, millionaires, bootblacks, beauties, hod-carriers and politicians become little black specks dodging bigger black specks in streets no wider than your thumb.

From this high view the city itself becomes degraded to an unintelligible mass of distorted buildings and impossible perspectives; the revered ocean is a duck pond; the earth itself a lost golf ball. All the minutiæ of life are gone. The philosopher gazes into the infinite heavens above him, and allows his soul to expand to the influence of his new view. He feels that he is the heir to Eternity and the child of Time. Space, too, should be his by the right of his immortal heritage, and he thrills at the thought that some day his kind shall traverse those mysterious aerial roads between planet and planet. The tiny world beneath his feet upon which this towering structure of steel rests as a speck of dust upon a Himalayan mountain—it is but one of a countless number of such whirling atoms. What are the ambitions, the achievements, the paltry conquests and loves of those restless black insects below compared with the serene and awful immensity of the universe that lies above and around their insignificant city?

It is guaranteed that the philosopher will have these thoughts. They have been expressly compiled from the philosophies of the world and set down with the proper interrogation point at the end of them to represent the invariable musings of deep thinkers on high places. And when the philosopher takes the elevator down his mind is broader, his heart is at peace, and his conception of the cosmogony of creation is as wide as the buckle of Orion's summer belt.

But if your name happened to be Daisy, and you worked in an Eighth Avenue candy store and lived in a little cold hall bedroom, five feet by eight, and earned $6 per week, and ate ten-cent lunches and were nineteen years old, and got up at 6.30 and worked till 9, and never had studied philosophy, maybe things wouldn't look that way to you from the top of a skyscraper.

Two sighed for the hand of Daisy, the unphilosophical. One was Joe, who kept the smallest store in New York. It was about the size of a tool-box of the D. P. W., and was stuck like a swallow's nest against a corner of a downtown skyscraper. Its stock consisted of fruit, candies, newspapers, song books, cigarettes, and lemonade in season. When stern winter shook his congealed locks and Joe had to move himself and the fruit inside, there was exactly room in the store for the proprietor, his wares, a stove the size of a vinegar cruet, and one customer.

Joe was not of the nation that keeps us forever in a furore with fugues and fruit. He was a capable American youth who was laying by money, and wanted Daisy to help him spend it. Three times he had asked her.

"I got money saved up, Daisy," was his love song; "and you know how bad I want you. That store of mine ain't very big, but——"

"Oh, ain't it?" would be the antiphony of the unphilosophical one. "Why, I heard Wanamaker's was trying to get you to sublet part of your floor space to them for next year."

Daisy passed Joe's corner every morning and evening.

"Hello, Two-by-Four!" was her usual greeting. "Seems to me your store looks emptier. You must have sold a package of chewing gum."

"Ain't much room in here, sure," Joe would answer, with his slow grin, "except for you, Daise. Me and the store are waitin' for you whenever you'll take us. Don't you think you might before long?"

"Store!"—a fine scorn was expressed by Daisy's uptilted

nose—"sardine box! Waitin' for me, you say? Gee! you'd have to throw out about a hundred pounds of candy before I could get inside of it, Joe."

"I wouldn't mind an even swap like that," said Joe, complimentary.

Daisy's existence was limited in every way. She had to walk sideways between the counter and the shelves in the candy store. In her own hall bedroom coziness had been carried close to cohesiveness. The walls were so near to one another that the paper on them made a perfect Babel of noise. She could light the gas with one hand and close the door with the other without taking her eyes off the reflection of her brown pompadour in the mirror. She had Joe's picture in a gilt frame on the dresser, and sometimes—but her next thought would always be of Joe's funny little store tacked like a soap box to the corner of that great building, and away would go her sentiment in a breeze of laughter.

Daisy's other suitor followed Joe by several months. He came to board in the house where she lived. His name was Dabster, and he was a philosopher. Though young, attainments stood out upon him like continental labels on a Passaic (N. J.) suit-case. Knowledge he had kidnapped from cyclopedias and handbooks of useful information; but as for wisdom, when she passed he was left sniffing in the road without so much as the number of her motor car. He could and would tell you the proportion of water and muscle-making properties of peas and veal, the shortest verse in the Bible, the number of pounds of shingle nails required to fasten 256 shingles laid four inches to the weather, the population of Kankakee, Ill., the theories of Spinoza, the name of Mr. H. McKay Twombly's second hall footman, the length of the Hoosac Tunnel, the best time to set a hen, the salary of the railway post-office messenger between Driftwood and Red Bank Furnace, Pa., and the number of bones in the foreleg of a cat.

This weight of learning was no handicap to Dabster. His statistics were the sprigs of parsley with which he garnished the feast of small talk that he would set before you if he conceived that to be your taste. And again he used them as breastworks in foraging at the boarding-house. Firing at you a volley of figures concerning the weight of a lineal foot of bar-iron 5 x 2¾ inches, and the average annual rainfall at Fort Snelling, Minn., he would transfix with his fork the best piece of chicken on the dish while you were trying to rally sufficiently to ask him weakly why does a hen cross the road.

Thus, brightly armed, and further equipped with a measure of good looks, of a hair-oily, shopping-district-at-three-in-the-afternoon kind, it seems that Joe, of the Lilliputian emporium, had a rival worthy of his steel. But Joe carried no steel. There wouldn't have been room in his store to draw it if he had.

One Saturday afternoon, about four o'clock, Daisy and Mr. Dabster stopped before Joe's booth. Dabster wore a silk hat, and—well, Daisy was a woman, and that hat had no chance to get back in its box until Joe had seen it. A stick of pineapple chewing gum was the ostensible object of the call. Joe supplied it through the open side of his store. He did not pale or falter at sight of the hat.

"Mr. Dabster's going to take me on top of the building to observe the view," said Daisy, after she had introduced her admirers. "I never was on a skyscraper. I guess it must be awful nice and funny up there."

"H'm!" said Joe.

"The panorama," said Mr. Dabster, "exposed to the gaze from the top of a lofty building is not only sublime, but instructive. Miss Daisy has a decided pleasure in store for her."

"It's windy up there, too, as well as here," said Joe. "Are you dressed warm enough, Daisy?"

"Sure thing! I'm all lined," said Daisy, smiling slyly at his clouded brow. "You look just like a mummy in a case, Joe. Ain't you just put in an invoice of a pint of peanuts or another apple? Your store looks awful overstocked."

Daisy giggled at her favorite joke; and Joe had to smile with her.

"Your quarters are somewhat limited, Mr.—er—er," remarked Dabster, "in comparison with the size of this building. I understand the area of its side to be about 340 by 100 feet. That would make you occupy a proportionate space as if half of Beloochistan were placed upon a territory as large as the United States east of the Rocky Mountains, with the Province of Ontario and Belgium added."

"Is that so, sport?" said Joe, genially. "You are Weisenheimer

on figures, all right. How many square pounds of baled hay do
you think a jackass could eat if he stopped brayin' long enough
to keep still a minute and five eighths?"

A few minutes later Daisy and Mr. Dabster stepped from an
elevator to the top floor of the skyscraper. Then up a short,
steep stairway and out upon the roof. Dabster led her to the
parapet so she could look down at the black dots moving in
the street below.

"What are they?" she asked, trembling. She had never before
been on a height like this before.

And then Dabster must needs play the philosopher on the
tower, and conduct her soul forth to meet the immensity of
space.

"Bipeds," he said, solemnly. "See what they become even at
the small elevation of 340 feet—mere crawling insects going to
and fro at random."

"Oh, they ain't anything of the kind," exclaimed Daisy,
suddenly—"they're folks! I saw an automobile. Oh, gee! are
we that high up?"

"Walk over this way," said Dabster.

He showed her the great city lying like an orderly array of
toys far below, starred here and there, early as it was, by the first
beacon lights of the winter afternoon. And then the bay and
sea to the south and east vanishing mysteriously into the sky.

"I don't like it," declared Daisy, with troubled blue eyes.
"Say we go down."

But the philosopher was not to be denied his opportunity. He
would let her behold the grandeur of his mind, the half-nelson
he had on the infinite, and the memory he had for statistics.
And then she would nevermore be content to buy chewing
gum at the smallest store in New York. And so he began to
prate of the smallness of human affairs, and how that even so
slight a removal from earth made man and his works look like
the tenth part of a dollar thrice computed. And that one should
consider the sidereal system and the maxims of Epictetus and
be comforted.

"You don't carry me with you," said Daisy. "Say, I think it's
awful to be up so high that folks look like fleas. One of them
we saw might have been Joe. Why, Jiminy! we might as well be
in New Jersey! Say, I'm afraid up here!"

The philosopher smiled fatuously.

"The earth," said he, "is itself only as a grain of wheat in space. Look up there."

Daisy gazed upward apprehensively. The short day was spent and the stars were coming out above.

"Yonder star," said Dabster, "is Venus, the evening star. She is 66,000,000 miles from the sun."

"Fudge!" said Daisy, with a brief flash of spirit, "where do you think I come from—Brooklyn? Susie Price, in our store— her brother sent her a ticket to go to San Francisco—that's only three thousand miles."

The philosopher smiled indulgently.

"Our world," he said, "is 91,000,000 miles from the sun. There are eighteen stars of the first magnitude that are 211,000 times further from us than the sun is. If one of them should be extinguished it would be three years before we would see its light go out. There are six thousand stars of the sixth magnitude. It takes thirty-six years for the light of one of them to reach the earth. With an eighteen-foot telescope we can see 43,000,000 stars, including those of the thirteenth magnitude, whose light takes 2,700 years to reach us. Each of these stars——"

"You're lyin'," cried Daisy, angrily. "You're tryin' to scare me. And you have; I want to go down!"

She stamped her foot.

"Arcturus——" began the philosopher, soothingly, but he was interrupted by a demonstration out of the vastness of the nature that he was endeavoring to portray with his memory instead of his heart. For to the heart-expounder of nature the stars were set in the firmament expressly to give soft light to lovers wandering happily beneath them; and if you stand tiptoe some September night with your sweetheart on your arm you can almost touch them with your hand. Three years for their light to reach us, indeed!

Out of the west leaped a meteor, lighting the roof of the skyscraper almost to midday. Its fiery parabola was limned against the sky toward the east. It hissed as it went, and Daisy screamed.

"Take me down," she cried vehemently, "you—you mental arithmetic!"

Dabster got her to the elevator, and inside of it. She was

wild-eyed, and she shuddered when the express made its de-
bilitating drop.

Outside the revolving door of the skyscraper the philosopher
lost her. She vanished; and he stood, bewildered, without figures or statistics to aid him.

Joe had a lull in trade, and by squirming among his stock
succeeded in lighting a cigarette and getting one cold foot
against the attenuated stove.

The door was burst open, and Daisy, laughing, crying, scattering fruit and candies, tumbled into his arms.

"Oh, Joe, I've been up on the skyscraper. Ain't it cozy and
warm and homelike in here! I'm ready for you, Joe, whenever
you want me."

Man About Town

THERE WERE two or three things that I wanted to know. I do not care about a mystery. So I began to inquire.

It took me two weeks to find out what women carry in dress suit cases. And then I began to ask why a mattress is made in two pieces. This serious query was at first received with suspicion because it sounded like a conundrum. I was at last assured that its double form of construction was designed to make lighter the burden of woman, who makes up beds. I was so foolish as to persist, begging to know why, then, they were not made in two equal pieces; whereupon I was shunned.

The third draught that I craved from the fount of knowledge was enlightenment concerning the character known as A Man About Town. He was more vague in my mind than a type should be. We must have a concrete idea of anything, even if it be an imaginary idea, before we can comprehend it. Now, I have a mental picture of John Doe that is as clear as a steel engraving. His eyes are weak blue; he wears a brown vest and a shiny black serge coat. He stands always in the sunshine chewing something; and he keeps half-shutting his pocket knife and opening it again with his thumb. And, if the Man Higher Up is ever found, take my assurance for it, he will be a large, pale man with blue wristlets showing under his cuffs, and he will be sitting to have his shoes polished within sound of a bowling alley, and there will be somewhere about him turquoises.

But the canvas of my imagination, when it came to limning the Man About Town, was blank. I fancied that he had a detachable sneer (like the smile of the Cheshire cat) and attached cuffs; and that was all. Whereupon I asked a newspaper reporter about him.

"Why," said he, "a 'Man About Town' is something between a 'rounder' and a 'clubman.' He isn't exactly—well, he fits in between Mrs. Fish's receptions and private boxing bouts. He doesn't—well, he doesn't belong either to the Lotos Club or to the Jerry McGeogheghan Galvanised Iron Workers' Apprentices' Left Hook Chowder Association. I don't exactly know how to describe him to you. You'll see him everywhere there's anything doing. Yes, I suppose he's a type. Dress clothes every evening; knows the ropes; calls every policeman and waiter in town by their first names. No; he never travels with the hydrogen derivatives. You generally see him alone or with another man."

My friend the reporter left me, and I wandered further afield. By this time the 3126 electric lights on the Rialto were alight. People passed, but they held me not. Paphian eyes rayed upon me, and left me unscathed. Diners, heimgangers, shop-girls, confidence men, panhandlers, actors, highwaymen, millionaires and outlanders hurried, skipped, strolled, sneaked, swaggered and scurried by me; but I took no note of them. I knew them all; I had read their hearts; they had served. I wanted my Man About Town. He was a type, and to drop him would be an error—a typograph—but no! let us continue.

Let us continue with a moral digression. To see a family reading the Sunday paper gratifies. The sections have been separated. Papa is earnestly scanning the page that pictures the young lady exercising before an open window, and bending—but there, there! Mamma is interested in trying to guess the missing letters in the word N—w Yo—k. The oldest girls are eagerly perusing the financial reports, for a certain young man remarked last Sunday night that he had taken a flyer in Q., X. & Z. Willie, the eighteen-year-old son, who attends the New York public school, is absorbed in the weekly article describing how to make over an old skirt, for he hopes to take a prize in sewing on graduation day.

Grandma is holding to the comic supplement with a two-hours' grip; and little Tottie, the baby, is rocking along the best she can with the real estate transfers. This view is intended to be reassuring, for it is desirable that a few lines of this story be skipped. For it introduces strong drink.

I went into a café to—and while it was being mixed I asked the man who grabs up your hot Scotch spoon as soon as you lay it down what he understood by the term, epithet, description, designation, characterisation or appellation, viz.: a "Man About Town."

"Why," said he, carefully, "it means a fly guy that's wise to the all-night push—see? It's a hot sport that you can't bump to the rail anywhere between the Flatirons—see? I guess that's about what it means."

I thanked him and departed.

On the sidewalk a Salvation lassie shook her contribution receptacle gently against my waistcoat pocket.

"Would you mind telling me," I asked her, "if you ever meet with the character commonly denominated as 'A Man About Town' during your daily wanderings?"

"I think I know whom you mean," she answered, with a gentle smile. "We see them in the same places night after night. They are the devil's body guard, and if the soldiers of any army are as faithful as they are, their commanders are well served. We go among them, diverting a few pennies from their wickedness to the Lord's service."

She shook the box again and I dropped a dime into it.

In front of a glittering hotel a friend of mine, a critic, was climbing from a cab. He seemed at leisure; and I put my question to him. He answered me conscientiously, as I was sure he would.

"There is a type of 'Man About Town' in New York," he answered. "The term is quite familiar to me, but I don't think I was ever called upon to define the character before. It would be difficult to point you out an exact specimen. I would say, offhand, that it is a man who had a hopeless case of the peculiar New York disease of wanting to see and know. At 6 o'clock each day life begins with him. He follows rigidly the conventions of dress and manners; but in the business of poking his nose into places where he does not belong he could give pointers to a civet cat or a jackdaw. He is the man who has chased Bohemia about the town from rathskeller to roof garden and from Hester street to Harlem until you can't find a place in the city where they don't cut their spaghetti with a knife. Your 'Man About Town' has done that. He is always on the scent of something new. He is curiosity, impudence and omnipresence. Hansoms were made for him, and gold-banded cigars; and the curse of music at dinner. There are not so many of him; but his minority report is adopted everywhere.

"I'm glad you brought up the subject; I've felt the influence of this nocturnal blight upon our city, but I never thought to analyse it before. I can see now that your 'Man About Town' should have been classified long ago. In his wake spring up wine agents and cloak models; and the orchestra plays 'Let's All Go Up to Maud's' for him, by request, instead of Händel. He makes his rounds every evening; while you and I see the elephant once a week. When the cigar store is raided, he winks at the officer, familiar with his ground, and walks away immune, while you and I search among the Presidents for names, and among the stars for addresses to give the desk sergeant."

My friend, the critic, paused to acquire breath for fresh eloquence. I seized my advantage.

"You have classified him," I cried with joy. "You have painted his portrait in the gallery of city types. But I must meet one face to face. I must study the Man About Town at first hand. Where shall I find him? How shall I know him?"

Without seeming to hear me, the critic went on. And his cab-driver was waiting for his fare, too.

"He is the sublimated essence of Butt-in; the refined, intrinsic extract of Rubber; the concentrated, purified, irrefutable, unavoidable spirit of Curiosity and Inquisitiveness. A new sensation is the breath in his nostrils; when his experience is exhausted he explores new fields with the indefatigability of a——"

"Excuse me," I interrupted, "but can you produce one of this type? It is a new thing to me. I must study it. I will search the town over until I find one. Its habitat must be here on Broadway."

"I am about to dine here," said my friend. "Come inside, and if there is a Man About Town present I will point him out to you. I know most of the regular patrons here."

"I am not dining yet," I said to him. "You will excuse me. I am going to find my Man About Town this night if I have to rake New York from the Battery to Little Coney Island."

I left the hotel and walked down Broadway. The pursuit of my type gave a pleasant savour of life and interest to the air I breathed. I was glad to be in a city so great, so complex and diversified. Leisurely and with something of an air I strolled along with my heart expanding at the thought that I was a citizen of great Gotham, a sharer in its magnificence and pleasures, a partaker in its glory and prestige.

I turned to cross the street. I heard something buzz like a bee, and then I took a long, pleasant ride with Santos-Dumont.

When I opened my eyes I remembered a smell of gasoline, and I said aloud: "Hasn't it passed yet?"

A hospital nurse laid a hand that was not particularly soft upon my brow that was not at all fevered. A young doctor came along, grinned, and handed me a morning newspaper.

"Want to see how it happened?" he asked cheerily. I read the article. Its headlines began where I heard the buzzing leave off the night before. It closed with these lines:

"——Bellevue Hospital, where it was said that his injuries were not serious. He appeared to be a typical Man About Town."

Springtime À La Carte

I T WAS a day in March.

Never, never begin a story this way when you write one. No opening could possibly be worse. It is unimaginative, flat, dry and likely to consist of mere wind. But in this instance it is allowable. For the following paragraph, which should have inaugurated the narrative, is too wildly extravagant and preposterous to be flaunted in the face of the reader without preparation.

Sarah was crying over her bill of fare.

Think of a New York girl shedding tears on the menu card!

To account for this you will be allowed to guess that the lobsters were all out, or that she had sworn ice-cream off during Lent, or that she had ordered onions, or that she had just come from a Hackett matinee. And then, all these theories being wrong, you will please let the story proceed.

The gentleman who announced that the world was an oyster which he with his sword would open made a larger hit than he deserved. It is not difficult to open an oyster with a sword. But did you ever notice any one try to open the terrestrial bivalve with a typewriter? Like to wait for a dozen raw opened that way?

Sarah had managed to pry apart the shells with her unhandy weapon far enough to nibble a wee bit at the cold and clammy world within. She knew no more shorthand than if she had been a graduate in stenography just let slip upon the world by a business college. So, not being able to stenog, she could not enter that bright galaxy of office talent. She was a free-lance typewriter and canvassed for odd jobs of copying.

The most brilliant and crowning feat of Sarah's battle with the world was the deal she made with Schulenberg's Home Restaurant. The restaurant was next door to the old red brick in which she hall-roomed. One evening after dining at Schulenberg's 40-cent, five-course *table d'hôte* (served as fast as you throw the five baseballs at the coloured gentleman's head) Sarah took away with her the bill of fare. It was written in an almost unreadable script neither English nor German, and so arranged that if you were not careful you began with a toothpick and rice pudding and ended with soup and the day of the week.

The next day Sarah showed Schulenberg a neat card on which the menu was beautifully typewritten with the viands temptingly marshalled under their right and proper heads from "hors d'œuvre" to "not responsible for overcoats and umbrellas."

Schulenberg became a naturalised citizen on the spot. Before Sarah left him she had him willingly committed to an agreement. She was to furnish typewritten bills of fare for the twenty-one tables in the restaurant—a new bill for each day's dinner, and new ones for breakfast and lunch as often as changes occurred in the food or as neatness required.

In return for this Schulenberg was to send three meals per diem to Sarah's hall room by a waiter—an obsequious one if possible—and furnish her each afternoon with a pencil draft of what Fate had in store for Schulenberg's customers on the morrow.

Mutual satisfaction resulted from the agreement. Schulenberg's patrons now knew what the food they ate was called even if its nature sometimes puzzled them. And Sarah had food during a cold, dull winter, which was the main thing with her.

And then the almanac lied, and said that spring had come. Spring comes when it comes. The frozen snows of January still lay like adamant in the crosstown streets. The hand-organs still played "In the Good Old Summertime," with their December vivacity and expression. Men began to make thirty-day notes to buy Easter dresses. Janitors shut off steam. And when these things happen one may know that the city is still in the clutches of winter.

One afternoon Sarah shivered in her elegant hall bedroom; "house heated; scrupulously clean; conveniences; seen to be appreciated." She had no work to do except Schulenberg's menu cards. Sarah sat in her squeaky willow rocker, and looked out the window. The calendar on the wall kept crying to her: "Springtime is here, Sarah—springtime is here, I tell you. Look at me, Sarah, my figures show it. You've got a neat figure yourself, Sarah—a—nice springtime figure—why do you look out the window so sadly?"

Sarah's room was at the back of the house. Looking out the

window she could see the windowless rear brick wall of the box factory on the next street. But the wall was clearest crystal; and Sarah was looking down a grassy lane shaded with cherry trees and elms and bordered with raspberry bushes and Cherokee roses.

Spring's real harbingers are too subtle for the eye and ear. Some must have the flowering crocus, the wood-starring dogwood, the voice of bluebird—even so gross a reminder as the farewell handshake of the retiring buckwheat and oyster before they can welcome the Lady in Green to their dull bosoms. But to old earth's choicest kin there come straight, sweet messages from his newest bride, telling them they shall be no stepchildren unless they choose to be.

On the previous summer Sarah had gone into the country and loved a farmer.

(In writing your story never hark back thus. It is bad art, and cripples interest. Let it march, march.)

Sarah stayed two weeks at Sunnybrook Farm. There she learned to love old Farmer Franklin's son Walter. Farmers have been loved and wedded and turned out to grass in less time. But young Walter Franklin was a modern agriculturist. He had a telephone in his cow house, and he could figure up exactly what effect next year's Canada wheat crop would have on potatoes planted in the dark of the moon.

It was in this shaded and raspberried lane that Walter had wooed and won her. And together they had sat and woven a crown of dandelions for her hair. He had immoderately praised the effect of the yellow blossoms against her brown tresses; and she had left the chaplet there, and walked back to the house swinging her straw sailor in her hands.

They were to marry in the spring—at the very first signs of spring, Walter said. And Sarah came back to the city to pound her typewriter.

A knock at the door dispelled Sarah's visions of that happy day. A waiter had brought the rough pencil draft of the Home Restaurant's next day fare in old Schulenberg's angular hand.

Sarah sat down to her typewriter and slipped a card between the rollers. She was a nimble worker. Generally in an hour and a half the twenty-one menu cards were written and ready.

To-day there were more changes on the bill of fare than usual. The soups were lighter; pork was eliminated from the entrees, figuring only with Russian turnips among the roasts. The gracious spirit of spring pervaded the entire menu. Lamb, that lately capered on the greening hillsides, was becomingly exploited with the sauce that commemorated its gambols. The song of the oyster, though not silenced, was *diminuendo con amore*. The frying-pan seemed to be held, inactive, behind the beneficent bars of the broiler. The pie list swelled; the richer puddings had vanished; the sausage, with his drapery wrapped about him, barely lingered in a pleasant thanatopsis with the buckwheats and the sweet but doomed maple.

Sarah's fingers danced like midgets above a summer stream. Down through the courses she worked, giving each item its position according to its length with an accurate eye.

Just above the desserts came the list of vegetables. Carrots and peas, asparagus on toast, the perennial tomatoes and corn and succotash, lima beans, cabbage—and then——

Sarah was crying over her bill of fare. Tears from the depths of some divine despair rose in her heart and gathered to her eyes. Down went her head on the little typewriter stand; and the keyboard rattled a dry accompaniment to her moist sobs.

For she had received no letter from Walter in two weeks, and the next item on the bill of fare was dandelions—dandelions with some kind of egg—but bother the egg!—dandelions, with whose golden blooms Walter had crowned her his queen of love and future bride—dandelions, the harbingers of spring, her sorrow's crown of sorrow—reminder of her happiest days.

Madam, I dare you to smile until you suffer this test: Let the Marechal Niel roses that Percy brought you on the night you gave him your heart be served as a salad with French dressing before your eyes at a Schulenberg *table d'hôte*. Had Juliet so seen her love tokens dishonoured the sooner would she have sought the lethean herbs of the good apothecary.

But what a witch is Spring! Into the great cold city of stone and iron a message had to be sent. There was none to convey it but the little hardy courier of the fields with his rough green coat and modest air. He is a true soldier of fortune, this *dent-de-lion*—this lion's tooth, as the French chefs call him. Flowered, he will assist at love-making, wreathed in my lady's nut-brown hair; young and callow and unblossomed, he goes into the boiling pot and delivers the word of his sovereign mistress.

By and by Sarah forced back her tears. The cards must be written. But, still in a faint, golden glow from her dandeleonine dream, she fingered the typewriter keys absently for a little while, with her mind and heart in the meadow lane with her young farmer. But soon she came swiftly back to the rock-bound lanes of Manhattan, and the typewriter began to rattle and jump like a strike-breaker's motor car.

At 6 o'clock the waiter brought her dinner and carried away the typewritten bill of fare. When Sarah ate she set aside, with a sigh, the dish of dandelions with its crowning ovarious accompaniment. As this dark mass had been transformed from a bright and love-indorsed flower to be an ignominious vegetable, so had her summer hopes wilted and perished. Love may, as Shakespeare said, feed on itself: but Sarah could not bring herself to eat the dandelions that had graced, as ornaments, the first spiritual banquet of her heart's true affection.

At 7.30 the couple in the next room began to quarrel: the man in the room above sought for A on his flute; the gas went a little lower; three coal wagons started to unload—the only sound of which the phonograph is jealous; cats on the back fences slowly retreated toward Mukden. By these signs Sarah knew that it was time for her to read. She got out "The Cloister and the Hearth," the best non-selling book of the month, settled her feet on her trunk, and began to wander with Gerard.

The front door bell rang. The landlady answered it. Sarah left Gerard and Denys treed by a bear and listened. Oh, yes; you would, just as she did!

And then a strong voice was heard in the hall below, and Sarah jumped for her door, leaving the book on the floor and the first round easily the bear's.

You have guessed it. She reached the top of the stairs just as her farmer came up, three at a jump, and reaped and garnered her, with nothing left for the gleaners.

"Why haven't you written—oh, why?" cried Sarah.

"New York is a pretty large town," said Walter Franklin. "I came in a week ago to your old address. I found that you went away on a Thursday. That consoled some; it eliminated the possible Friday bad luck. But it didn't prevent my hunting for you with police and otherwise ever since!"

"I wrote!" said Sarah, vehemently.

"Never got it!"

"Then how did you find me?"

The young farmer smiled a springtime smile.

"I dropped into that Home Restaurant next door this evening," said he. "I don't care who knows it; I like a dish of some kind of greens at this time of the year. I ran my eye down that nice typewritten bill of fare looking for something in that line. When I got below cabbage I turned my chair over and hollered for the proprietor. He told me where you lived."

"I remember," sighed Sarah, happily. "That was dandelions below cabbage."

"I'd know that cranky capital W 'way above the line that your typewriter makes anywhere in the world," said Franklin.

"Why, there's no W in dandelions," said Sarah, in surprise.

The young man drew the bill of fare from his pocket, and pointed to a line.

Sarah recognised the first card she had typewritten that afternoon. There was still the rayed splotch in the upper right-hand corner where a tear had fallen. But over the spot where one should have read the name of the meadow plant, the clinging memory of their golden blossoms had allowed her fingers to strike strange keys.

Between the red cabbage and the stuffed green peppers was the item:

"DEAREST WALTER, WITH HARD-BOILED EGG."

Extradited from Bohemia

FROM NEAR the village of Harmony, at the foot of the Green Mountains, came Miss Medora Martin to New York with her color-box and easel.

Miss Medora resembled the rose which the autumnal frosts had spared the longest of all her sister blossoms. In Harmony, when she started alone to the wicked city to study art, they said she was a mad, reckless, headstrong girl. In New York, when she first took her seat at a West Side boarding-house table, the boarders asked: "Who is the nice-looking old maid?"

Medora took heart, a cheap hall bedroom and two art lessons a week from Professor Angelini, a retired barber who had studied his profession in a Harlem dancing academy. There was no one to set her right, for here in the big city they do it unto all of us. How many of us are badly shaved daily and taught the two-step imperfectly by ex-pupils of Bastien Le Page and Gérôme? The most pathetic sight in New York—except the manners of the rush-hour crowds—is the dreary march of the hopeless army of Mediocrity. Here Art is no benignant goddess, but a Circe who turns her wooers into mewing Toms and Tabbies who linger about the doorsteps of her abode, unmindful of the flying brickbats and boot-jacks of the critics. Some of us creep back to our native villages to the skim-milk of "I told you so"; but most of us prefer to remain in the cold courtyard of our mistress's temple, snatching the scraps that fall from her divine table d'hôte. But some of us grow weary at last of the fruitless service. And then there are two fates open to us. We can get a job driving a grocer's wagon, or we can get swallowed up in the Vortex of Bohemia. The latter sounds good; but the former really pans out better. For, when the grocer pays us off we can rent a dress suit and—the capitalized system of humor describes it best—Get Bohemia On the Run.

Miss Medora chose the Vortex and thereby furnishes us with our little story.

Professor Angelini praised her sketches excessively. Once when she had made a neat study of a horse-chestnut tree in the park he declared she would become a second Rosa Bonheur.

Again—a great artist has his moods—he would say cruel and cutting things. For example, Medora had spent an afternoon patiently sketching the statue and the architecture at Columbus Circle. Tossing it aside with a sneer, the professor informed her that Giotto had once drawn a perfect circle with one sweep of his hand.

One day it rained, the weekly remittance from Harmony was overdue, Medora had a headache, the professor had tried to borrow two dollars from her, her art dealer had sent back all her water-colors unsold, and—Mr. Binkley asked her out to dinner.

Mr. Binkley was the gay boy of the boarding-house. He was forty-nine, and owned a fishstall in a downtown market. But after six o'clock he wore an evening suit and whooped things up connected with the beaux arts. The young men said he was an "Indian." He was supposed to be an accomplished habitué of the inner circles of Bohemia. It was no secret that he had once loaned $10 to a young man who had had a drawing printed in *Puck*. Often has one thus obtained his entrée into the charmed circle, while the other obtained both his entrée and roast.

The other boarders enviously regarded Medora as she left at Mr. Binkley's side at nine o'clock. She was as sweet as a cluster of dried autumn grasses in her pale blue—oh—er—that very thin stuff—in her pale blue Comstockized silk waist and box-pleated voile skirt, with a soft pink glow on her thin cheeks and the tiniest bit of rouge powder on her face, with her handkerchief and room key in her brown walrus, pebble-grain hand-bag.

And Mr. Binkley looked imposing and dashing with his red face and gray mustache, and his tight dress coat, that made the back of his neck roll up just like a successful novelist's.

They drove in a cab to the Café Terence, just off the most glittering part of Broadway, which, as every one knows, is one of the most popular and widely patronized, jealously exclusive Bohemian resorts in the city.

Down between the rows of little tables tripped Medora, of the Green Mountains, after her escort. Thrice in a lifetime may woman walk upon clouds—once when she trippeth to the altar, once when she first enters Bohemian halls, the last when she marches back across her first garden with the dead hen of her neighbor in her hand.

There was a table set, with three or four about it. A waiter buzzed around it like a bee, and silver and glass shone upon it. And, preliminary to the meal, as the prehistoric granite strata heralded the protozoa, the bread of Gaul, compounded after the formula of the recipe for the eternal hills, was there set forth to the hand and tooth of a long-suffering city, while the gods lay beside their nectar and home-made biscuits and smiled, and the dentists leaped for joy in their gold-leafy dens.

The eye of Binkley fixed a young man at his table with the Bohemian gleam, which is a compound of the look of the basilisk, the shine of a bubble of Würzburger, the inspiration of genius and the pleading of a panhandler.

The young man sprang to his feet. "Hello, Bink, old boy!" he shouted. "Don't tell me you were going to pass our table. Join us—unless you've another crowd on hand."

"Don't mind, old chap," said Binkley, of the fishstall. "You know how I like to butt up against the fine arts. Mr. Van-dyke—Mr. Madder—er—Miss Martin, one of the elect also in art—er——"

The introduction went around. There were also Miss Elise and Miss 'Toinette. Perhaps they were models, for they chattered of the St. Regis decorations and Henry James—and they did it not badly.

Medora sat in transport. Music—wild, intoxicating music made by troubadours direct from a rear basement room in Elysium—set her thoughts to dancing. Here was a world never before penetrated by her warmest imagination or any of the lines controlled by Harriman. With the Green Mountains' external calm upon her she sat, her soul flaming in her with the fire of Andalusia. The tables were filled with Bohemia. The room was full of the fragrance of flowers—both mille and cauli. Questions and corks popped; laughter and silver rang; champagne flashed in the pail, wit flashed in the pan.

Vandyke ruffled his long, black locks, disarranged his careless tie and leaned over to Madder.

"Say, Maddy," he whispered, feelingly, "sometimes I'm tempted to pay this Philistine his ten dollars and get rid of him."

Madder ruffled his long, sandy locks and disarranged his careless tie.

"Don't think of it, Vandy," he replied. "We are short, and Art is long."

Medora ate strange viands and drank elderberry wine that they poured in her glass. It was just the color of that in the Vermont home. The waiter poured something in another glass that seemed to be boiling, but when she tasted it it was not hot. She had never felt so light-hearted before. She thought lovingly of the Green Mountain farm and its fauna. She leaned, smiling, to Miss Elise.

"If I were at home," she said, beamingly, "I could show you the cutest little calf!"

"Nothing for you in the White Lane," said Miss Elise. "Why don't you pad?"

The orchestra played a wailing waltz that Medora had learned from the hand-organs. She followed the air with nodding head in a sweet soprano hum. Madder looked across the table at her, and wondered in what strange waters Binkley had caught her in his seine. She smiled at him, and they raised glasses and drank of the wine that boiled when it was cold. Binkley had abandoned art and was prating of the unusual spring catch of shad. Miss Elise arranged the palette-and-maul-stick tie pin of Mr. Vandyke. A Philistine at some distant table was maundering volubly either about Jerome or Gérôme. A famous actress was discoursing excitably about monogrammed hosiery. A hose clerk from a department store was loudly proclaiming his opinions of the drama. A writer was abusing Dickens. A magazine editor and a photographer were drinking a dry brand at a reserved table. A 36-25-42 young lady was saying to an eminent sculptor: "Fudge for your Prax Italys! Bring one of your Venus Anno Dominis down to Cohen's and see how quick she'd be turned down for a cloak model. Back to the quarries with your Greeks and Dagos!"

Thus went Bohemia.

At eleven Mr. Binkley took Medora to the boarding-house and left her, with a society bow, at the foot of the hall stairs. She went up to her room and lit the gas.

And then, as suddenly as the dreadful genie arose in vapor from the copper vase of the fisherman, arose in that room the formidable shape of the New England Conscience. The terrible thing that Medora had done was revealed to her in its full enormity. She had sat in the presence of the ungodly and looked upon the wine both when it was red and effervescent.

At midnight she wrote this letter:

"Mr. BERIAH HOSKINS, Harmony, Vermont.

"Dear Sir: Henceforth, consider me as dead to you forever. I have loved you too well to blight your career by bringing into it my guilty and sin-stained life. I have succumbed to the insidious wiles of this wicked world and have been drawn into the vortex of Bohemia. There is scarcely any depth of glittering iniquity that I have not sounded. It is hopeless to combat my decision. There is no rising from the depths to which I have sunk. Endeavor to forget me. I am lost forever in the fair but brutal maze of awful Bohemia. Farewell.

"ONCE YOUR MEDORA."

On the next day Medora formed her resolutions. Beelzebub, flung from heaven, was no more cast down. Between her and the apple blossoms of Harmony there was a fixed gulf. Flaming cherubim warded her from the gates of her lost paradise. In one evening, by the aid of Binkley and Mumm, Bohemia had gathered her into its awful midst.

There remained to her but one thing—a life of brilliant, but irremediable error. Vermont was a shrine that she never would dare to approach again. But she would not sink—there were great and compelling ones in history upon whom she would model her meteoric career—Camille, Lola Montez, Royal Mary, Zaza—such a name as one of these would that of Medora Martin be to future generations.

For two days Medora kept her room. On the third she opened a magazine at the portrait of the King of Belgium, and laughed sardonically. If that far-famed breaker of women's hearts should cross her path, he would have to bow before her cold and imperious beauty. She would not spare the old or the young. All America—all Europe should do homage to her sinister, but compelling charm.

As yet she could not bear to think of the life she had once desired—a peaceful one in the shadow of the Green Mountains with Beriah at her side, and orders for expensive oil paintings coming in by each mail from New York. Her one fatal misstep had shattered that dream.

On the fourth day Medora powdered her face and rouged her lips. Once she had seen Carter in "Zaza." She stood before the mirror in a reckless attitude and cried: "*Zut! zut!*" She rhymed it with "nut," but with the lawless word Harmony seemed to pass away forever. The Vortex had her. She belonged to Bohemia for evermore. And never would Beriah——

The door opened and Beriah walked in.

"'Dory," said he, "what's all that chalk and pink stuff on your face, honey?"

Medora extended an arm.

"Too late," she said, solemnly. "The die is cast. I belong in another world. Curse me if you will—it is your right. Go, and leave me in the path I have chosen. Bid them all at home never to mention my name again. And sometimes, Beriah, pray for me when I am revelling in the gaudy, but hollow, pleasures of Bohemia."

"Get a towel, 'Dory," said Beriah, "and wipe that paint off your face. I came as soon as I got your letter. Them pictures of yours ain't amounting to anything. I've got tickets for both of us back on the evening train. Hurry and get your things in your trunk."

"Fate was too strong for me, Beriah. Go while I am strong to bear it."

"How do you fold this easel, 'Dory?—now begin to pack, so we have time to eat before train time. The maples is all out in full-grown leaves, 'Dory—you just ought to see 'em!"

"Not this early, Beriah?"

"You ought to see 'em, 'Dory; they're like an ocean of green in the morning sunlight."

"Oh, Beriah!"

On the train she said to him suddenly:

"I wonder why you came when you got my letter."

"Oh, shucks!" said Beriah. "Did you think you could fool me? How could you be run away to that Bohemia country like you said when your letter was postmarked New York as plain as day?"

Tommy's Burglar

At ten o'clock p.m. Felicia, the maid, left by the basement door with the policeman to get a raspberry phosphate around the corner. She detested the policeman and objected earnestly to the arrangement. She pointed out, not unreasonably, that she might have been allowed to fall asleep over one of St. George Rathbone's novels on the third floor, but she was overruled. Raspberries and cops were not created for nothing.

The burglar got into the house without much difficulty; because we must have action and not too much description in a 2,000-word story.

In the dining room he opened the slide of his dark lantern. With a brace and centrebit he began to bore into the lock of the silver-closet.

Suddenly a click was heard. The room was flooded with electric light. The dark velvet portières parted to admit a fair-haired boy of eight in pink pajamas, bearing a bottle of olive oil in his hand.

"Are you a burglar?" he asked, in a sweet, childish voice.

"Listen to that," exclaimed the man, in a hoarse voice. "Am I a burglar? Wot do you suppose I have a three-days' growth of bristly beard on my face for, and a cap with flaps? Give me the oil, quick, and let me grease the bit, so I won't wake up your mamma, who is lying down with a headache, and left you in charge of Felicia, who has been faithless to her trust."

"Oh, dear," said Tommy, with a sigh. "I thought you would be more up-to-date. This oil is for the salad when I bring lunch from the pantry for you. And mamma and papa have gone to the Metropolitan to hear De Reszke. But that isn't my fault. It only shows how long the story has been knocking around among the editors. If the author had been wise he'd have changed it to Caruso in the proofs."

"Be quiet," hissed the burglar, under his breath. "If you raise an alarm I'll wring your neck like a rabbit's."

"Like a chicken's," corrected Tommy. "You had that wrong. You don't wring rabbits' necks."

"Aren't you afraid of me?" asked the burglar.

"You know I'm not," answered Tommy. "Don't you suppose I know fact from fiction. If this wasn't a story I'd yell like an Indian when I saw you; and you'd probably tumble downstairs and get pinched on the sidewalk."

"I see," said the burglar, "that you're on to your job. Go on with the performance."

Tommy seated himself in an armchair and drew his toes up under him.

"Why do you go around robbing strangers, Mr. Burglar? Have you no friends?"

"I see what you're driving at," said the burglar, with a dark frown. "It's the same old story. Your innocence and childish insouciance is going to lead me back into an honest life. Every time I crack a crib where there's a kid around, it happens."

"Would you mind gazing with wolfish eyes at the plate of cold beef that the butler has left on the dining table?" said Tommy. "I'm afraid it's growing late."

The burglar accommodated.

"Poor man," said Tommy. "You must be hungry. If you will please stand in a listless attitude I will get you something to eat."

The boy brought a roast chicken, a jar of marmalade and a bottle of wine from the pantry. The burglar seized a knife and fork sullenly.

"It's only been an hour," he grumbled, "since I had a lobster and a pint of musty ale up on Broadway. I wish these story writers would let a fellow have a pepsin tablet, anyhow, between feeds."

"My papa writes books," remarked Tommy.

The burglar jumped to his feet quickly.

"You said he had gone to the opera," he hissed, hoarsely and with immediate suspicion.

"I ought to have explained," said Tommy. "He didn't buy the tickets." The burglar sat again and toyed with the wishbone.

"Why do you burgle houses?" asked the boy, wonderingly.

"Because," replied the burglar, with a sudden flow of tears. "God bless my little brown-haired boy Bessie at home."

"Ah," said Tommy, wrinkling his nose, "you got that answer in the wrong place. You want to tell your hard-luck story before you pull out the child stop."

"Oh, yes," said the burglar, "I forgot. Well, once I lived in Milwaukee, and——"

"Take the silver," said Tommy, rising from his chair.

"Hold on," said the burglar. "But I moved away. I could find no other employment. For a while I managed to support my wife and child by passing confederate money; but, alas! I was forced to give that up because it did not belong to the union. I became desperate and a burglar."

"Have you ever fallen into the hands of the police?" asked Tommy.

"I said 'burglar,' not 'beggar,'" answered the cracksman.

"After you finish your lunch," said Tommy, "and experience the usual change of heart, how shall we wind up the story?"

"Suppose," said the burglar, thoughtfully, "that Tony Pastor turns out earlier than usual to-night, and your father gets in from 'Parsifal' at 10.30. I am thoroughly repentant because you have made me think of my own little boy Bessie, and——"

"Say," said Tommy, "haven't you got that wrong?"

"Not on your coloured crayon drawings by B. Cory Kilvert," said the burglar. "It's always a Bessie that I have at home, artlessly prattling to the pale-cheeked burglar's bride. As I was saying, your father opens the front door just as I am departing with admonitions and sandwiches that you have wrapped up for me. Upon recognizing me as an old Harvard classmate he starts back in——"

"Not in surprise?" interrupted Tommy, with wide-open eyes.

"He starts back in the doorway," continued the burglar. And then he rose to his feet and began to shout: "Rah, rah, rah! rah, rah, rah! rah, rah, rah!"

"Well," said Tommy, wonderingly, "that's the first time I ever knew a burglar to give a college yell when he was burglarizing a house, even in a story."

"That's one on you," said the burglar, with a laugh. "I was practising the dramatization. If this is put on the stage that college touch is about the only thing that will make it go."

Tommy looked his admiration.

"You're on, all right," he said.

"And there's another mistake you've made," said the burglar. "You should have gone some time ago and brought me the $9 gold piece your mother gave you on your birthday to take to Bessie."

"But she didn't give it to me to take to Bessie," said Tommy, pouting.

"Come, come!" said the burglar, sternly. "It's not nice of you to take advantage because the story contains an ambiguous sentence. You know what I mean. It's mighty little I get out of these fictional jobs, anyhow. I lose all the loot, and I have to reform every time; and all the swag I'm allowed is the blamed little fol-de-rols and luck-pieces that you kids hand over. Why, in one story, all I got was a kiss from a little girl who came in on me when I was opening a safe. And it tasted of molasses candy, too. I've a good notion to tie this table cover over your head and keep on into the silver-closet."

"Oh, no, you haven't," said Tommy, wrapping his arms around his knees. "Because if you did no editor would buy the story. You know you've got to preserve the unities."

"So've you," said the burglar, rather glumly. "Instead of sitting here talking impudence and taking the bread out of a poor man's mouth, what you'd like to be doing is hiding under the bed and screeching at the top of your voice."

"You're right, old man," said Tommy, heartily. "I wonder what they make us do it for? I think the S. P. C. C. ought to interfere. I'm sure it's neither agreeable nor usual for a kid of my age to butt in when a full-grown burglar is at work and offer him a red sled and a pair of skates not to awaken his sick mother. And look how they make the burglars act! You'd think editors would know—but what's the use?"

The burglar wiped his hands on the tablecloth and arose with a yawn.

"Well, let's get through with it," he said. "God bless you, my little boy! you have saved a man from committing a crime this night. Bessie shall pray for you as soon as I get home and give her her orders. I shall never burglarize another house—at least not until the June magazines are out. It'll be your little sister's turn then to run in on me while I am abstracting the U. S. 4 per cent. from the tea urn and buy me off with her coral necklace and a falsetto kiss."

"You haven't got all the kicks coming to you," sighed Tommy, crawling out of his chair. "Think of the sleep I'm losing. But it's tough on both of us, old man. I wish you could get out of the story and really rob somebody. Maybe you'll have the chance if they dramatize us."

"Never!" said the burglar, gloomily. "Between the box office and my better impulses that your leading juveniles are supposed to awaken and the magazines that pay on publication, I guess I'll always be broke."

"I'm sorry," said Tommy, sympathetically. "But I can't help myself any more than you can. It's one of the canons of household fiction that no burglar shall be successful. The burglar must be foiled by a kid like me, or by a young lady heroine, or at the last moment by his old pal, Red Mike, who recognizes the house as one in which he used to be the coachman. You have got the worst end of it in any kind of a story."

"Well, I suppose I must be clearing out now," said the burglar, taking up his lantern and bracebit.

"You have to take the rest of this chicken and the bottle of wine with you for Bessie and her mother," said Tommy, calmly.

"But confound it," exclaimed the burglar, in an annoyed tone, "they don't want it. I've got five cases of Château de Beychsvelle at home that was bottled in 1853. That claret of yours is corked. And you couldn't get either of them to look at a chicken unless it was stewed in champagne. You know, after I get out of the story I don't have so many limitations. I make a turn now and then."

"Yes, but you must take them," said Tommy, loading his arms with the bundles.

"Bless you, young master!" recited the burglar, obedient. "Second-Story Saul will never forget you. And now hurry and let me out, kid. Our 2,000 words must be nearly up."

Tommy led the way through the hall toward the front door. Suddenly the burglar stopped and called to him softly: "Ain't there a cop out there in front somewhere sparking the girl?"

"Yes," said Tommy, "but what——"

"I'm afraid he'll catch me," said the burglar. "You mustn't forget that this is fiction."

"Great head!" said Tommy, turning. "Come out by the back door."

The Girl and the Graft

THE OTHER day I ran across my old friend Ferguson Pogue. Pogue is a conscientious grafter of the highest type. His headquarters is the Western Hemisphere, and his line of business is anything from speculating in town lots on the Great Staked Plains to selling wooden toys in Connecticut, made by hydraulic pressure from nutmegs ground to a pulp.

Now and then when Pogue has made a good haul he comes to New York for a rest. He says the jug of wine and loaf of bread and Thou in the wilderness business is about as much rest and pleasure to him as sliding down the bumps at Coney would be to President Taft. "Give me," says Pogue, "a big city for my vacation. Especially New York. I'm not much fond of New Yorkers, and Manhattan is about the only place on the globe where I don't find any."

While in the metropolis Pogue can always be found at one of two places. One is a little second-hand bookshop on Fourth Avenue, where he reads books about his hobbies, Mahometanism and taxidermy. I found him at the other—his hall bedroom in Eighteenth Street—where he sat in his stocking feet trying to pluck "The Banks of the Wabash" out of a small zither. Four years he has practised this tune without arriving near enough to cast the longest trout line to the water's edge. On the dresser lay a blued-steel Colt's forty-five and a tight roll of tens and twenties large enough around to belong to the spring rattlesnake-story class. A chambermaid with a room-cleaning air fluttered nearby in the hall, unable to enter or to flee, scandalized by the stocking feet, aghast at the Colt's, yet powerless, with her metropolitan instincts, to remove herself beyond the magic influence of the yellow-hued roll.

I sat on his trunk while Ferguson Pogue talked. No one could be franker or more candid in his conversation. Beside his expression the cry of Henry James for lacteal nourishment at the age of one month would have seemed like a Chaldean cryptogram. He told me stories of his profession with pride, for he considered it an art. And I was curious enough to ask him whether he had known any women who followed it.

"Ladies?" said Pogue, with Western chivalry. "Well, not to any great extent. They don't amount to much in special lines of graft, because they're all so busy in general lines. What? Why, they have to. Who's got the money in the world? The men. Did you ever know a man to give a woman a dollar without any consideration? A man will shell out his dust to another man free and easy and gratis. But if he drops a penny in one of the machines run by the Madam Eve's Daughters' Amalgamated Association and the pineapple chewing gum don't fall out when he pulls the lever you can hear him kick to the superintendent four blocks away. Man is the hardest proposition a woman has to go up against. He's a low-grade one, and she has to work overtime to make him pay. Two times out of five she's salted. She can't put in crushers and costly machinery. He'd notice 'em and be onto the game. They have to pan out what they get, and it hurts their tender hands. Some of 'em are natural sluice troughs and can carry out $1,000 to the ton. The dry-eyed ones have to depend on signed letters, false hair, sympathy, the kangaroo walk, cowhide whips, ability to cook, sentimental juries, conversational powers, silk underskirts, ancestry, rouge, anonymous letters, violet sachet powders, witnesses, revolvers, pneumatic forms, carbolic acid, moonlight, cold cream and the evening newspapers."

"You are outrageous, Ferg," I said. "Surely there is none of this 'graft,' as you call it, in a perfect and harmonious matrimonial union!"

"Well," said Pogue, "nothing that would justify you every time in calling up Police Headquarters and ordering out the reserves and a vaudeville manager on a dead run. But it's this way: Suppose you're a Fifth Avenue millionaire, soaring high, on the right side of copper and cappers.

"You come home at night and bring a $9,000,000 diamond brooch to the lady who's staked you for a claim. You hand it over. She says, 'Oh, George!' and looks to see if it's backed. She comes up and kisses you. You've waited for it. You get it. All right. It's graft.

"But I'm telling you about Artemisia Blye. She was from Kansas and she suggested corn in all of its phases. Her hair was as yellow as the silk; her form was as tall and graceful as a stalk in the low grounds during a wet summer; her eyes were as big and startling as bunions, and green was her favorite color.

"On my last trip into the cool recesses of your sequestered city I met a human named Vaucross. He was worth—that is, he had a million. He told me he was in business on the street. 'A sidewalk merchant?' says I, sarcastic. 'Exactly,' says he. 'Senior partner of a paving concern.'

"I kind of took to him. For this reason, I met him on Broadway one night when I was out of heart, luck, tobacco and place. He was all silk hat, diamonds and front. He was all front. If you had gone behind him you would have only looked yourself in the face. I looked like a cross between Count Tolstoy and a June lobster. I was out of luck. I had—but let me lay my eyes on that dealer again.

"Vaucross stopped and talked to me a few minutes and then he took me to a high-toned restaurant to eat dinner. There was music, and then some Beethoven, and Bordelaise sauce, and cussing in French, and frangipangi, and some hauteur and cigarettes. When I am flush I know them places.

"I declare, I must have looked as bad as a magazine artist sitting there without any money and my hair all rumpled like I was booked to read a chapter from 'Elsie's School Days' at a Brooklyn Bohemian smoker. But Vaucross treated me like a bear hunter's guide. He wasn't afraid of hurting the waiter's feelings.

"'Mr. Pogue,' he explains to me, 'I am using you.'

"'Go on,' says I; 'I hope you don't wake up.'

"And then he tells me, you know, the kind of man he was. He was a New Yorker. His whole ambition was to be noticed. He wanted to be conspicuous. He wanted people to point him out and bow to him, and tell others who he was. He said it had been the desire of his life always. He didn't have but a million, so he couldn't attract attention by spending money. He said he tried to get into public notice one time by planting a little public square on the east side with garlic for free use of the poor; but Carnegie heard of it, and covered it over at once with a library in the Gælic language. Three times he had jumped in the way of automobiles; but the only result was five broken ribs and a notice in the papers that an unknown man, five feet ten, with four amalgam-filled teeth, supposed to be the last of the famous Red Leary gang had been run over.

"'Ever try the reporters?' I asked him.

"'Last month,' says Mr. Vaucross, 'my expenditure for lunches to reporters was $124.80.'

"'Get anything out of that?' I asks.

"'That reminds me,' says he; 'add $8.50 for pepsin. Yes, I got indigestion.'

"'How am I supposed to push along your scramble for prominence?' I inquires. 'Contrast?'

"'Something of that sort to-night,' says Vaucross. 'It grieves me; but I am forced to resort to eccentricity.' And here he drops his napkin in his soup and rises up and bows to a gent who is devastating a potato under a palm across the room.

"'The Police Commissioner,' says my climber, gratified.

"'Friend,' says I, in a hurry, 'have ambitions but don't kick a rung out of your ladder. When you use me as a stepping stone to salute the police you spoil my appetite on the grounds that I may be degraded and incriminated. Be thoughtful.'

"At the Quaker City squab en casserole the idea about Artemisia Blye comes to me.

"'Suppose I can manage to get you in the papers,' says I—'a column or two every day in all of 'em and your picture in most of 'em for a week. How much would it be worth to you?'

"'Ten thousand dollars,' says Vaucross, warm in a minute. 'But no murder,' says he; 'and I won't wear pink pants at a cotillon.'

"'I wouldn't ask you to,' says I. 'This is honorable, stylish and uneffeminate. Tell the waiter to bring a demi tasse and some other beans, and I will disclose to you the opus moderandi.'

"We closed the deal an hour later in the rococo rouge et noise room. I telegraphed that night to Miss Artemisia in Salina. She took a couple of photographs and an autograph letter to an elder in the Fourth Presbyterian Church in the morning, and got some transportation and $80. She stopped in Topeka long enough to trade a flashlight interior and a valentine to the vice-president of a trust company for a mileage book and a package of five-dollar notes with $250 scrawled on the band.

"The fifth evening after she got my wire she was waiting, all décolletée and dressed up, for me and Vaucross to take her to dinner in one of these New York feminine apartment houses where a man can't get in unless he plays bezique and smokes depilatory powder cigarettes.

"'She's a stunner,' says Vaucross when he saw her. 'They'll give her a two-column cut sure.'

"This was the scheme the three of us concocted. It was business straight through. Vaucross was to rush Miss Blye with all the style and display and emotion he could for a month. Of course, that amounted to nothing as far as his ambitions were concerned. The sight of a man in a white tie and patent leather pumps pouring greenbacks through the large end of a cornucopia to purchase nutriment and heartsease for tall, willowy blondes in New York is as common a sight as blue turtles in delirium tremens. But he was to write her love letters—the worst kind of love letters, such as your wife publishes after you are dead—every day. At the end of the month he was to drop her, and she would bring suit for $100,000 for breach of promise.

"Miss Artemisia was to get $10,000. If she won the suit that was all; and if she lost she was to get it anyhow. There was a signed contract to that effect.

"Sometimes they had me out with 'em, but not often. I couldn't keep up to their style. She used to pull out his notes and criticize them like bills of lading.

"'Say, you!' she'd say. 'What do you call this—Letter to a Hardware Merchant from His Nephew on Learning that His Aunt Has Nettlerash? You Eastern duffers know as much about writing love letters as a Kansas grasshopper does about tugboats. "My dear Miss Blye!"—wouldn't that put pink icing and a little red sugar bird on your bridal cake? How long do you expect to hold an audience in a court-room with that kind of stuff? You want to get down to business, and call me "Tweedlums Babe" and "Honeysuckle," and sign yourself "Mama's Own Big Bad Puggy Wuggy Boy" if you want any limelight to concentrate upon your sparse gray hairs. Get sappy.'

"After that Vaucross dipped his pen in the indelible tabasco. His notes read like something or other in the original. I could see a jury sitting up, and women tearing one another's hats to hear 'em read. And I could see piling up for Mr. Vaucross as much notoriousness as Archbishop Cranmer or the Brooklyn

Bridge or cheese-on-salad ever enjoyed. He seemed mighty pleased at the prospects.

"They agreed on a night; and I stood on Fifth Avenue outside a solemn restaurant and watched 'em. A process-server walked in and handed Vaucross the papers at his table. Everybody looked at 'em; and he looked as proud as Cicero. I went back to my room and lit a five-cent cigar, for I knew the $10,000 was as good as ours.

"About two hours later somebody knocked at my door. There stood Vaucross and Miss Artemisia, and she was clinging—yes, sir, clinging—to his arm. And they tells me they'd been out and got married. And they articulated some trivial cadences about love and such. And they laid down a bundle on the table and said 'Good night' and left.

"And that's why I say," concluded Ferguson Pogue, "that a woman is too busy occupied with her natural vocation and instinct of graft such as is given her for self-preservation and amusement to make any great success in special lines."

"What was in the bundle that they left?" I asked, with my usual curiosity.

"Why," said Ferguson, "there was a scalper's railroad ticket as far as Kansas City and two pairs of Mr. Vaucross's old pants."

Sisters of the Golden Circle

THE RUBBERNECK Auto was about ready to start. The merry top-riders had been assigned to their seats by the gentlemanly conductor. The sidewalk was blockaded with sightseers who had gathered to stare at sightseers, justifying the natural law that every creature on earth is preyed upon by some other creature.

The megaphone man raised his instrument of torture; the inside of the great automobile began to thump and throb like the heart of a coffee drinker. The top-riders nervously clung to the seats; the old lady from Valparaiso, Indiana, shrieked to be put ashore. But, before a wheel turns, listen to a brief preamble through the cardiaphone, which shall point out to you an object of interest on life's sightseeing tour.

Swift and comprehensive is the recognition of white man for white man in African wilds; instant and sure is the spiritual greeting between mother and babe; unhesitatingly do master and dog commune across the slight gulf between animal and man; immeasurably quick and sapient are the brief messages between one and one's beloved. But all these instances set forth only slow and groping interchange of sympathy and thought beside one other instance which the Rubberneck coach shall disclose. You shall learn (if you have not learned already) what two beings of all earth's living inhabitants most quickly look into each other's hearts and souls when they meet face to face.

The gong whirred, and the Glaring-at-Gotham car moved majestically upon its instructive tour.

On the highest, rear seat was James Williams, of Cloverdale, Missouri, and his Bride.

Capitalise it, friend typo—that last word—word of words in the epiphany of life and love. The scent of the flowers, the booty of the bee, the primal drip of spring waters, the overture of the lark, the twist of lemon peel on the cocktail of creation—such is the bride. Holy is the wife; revered the mother; galliptious is the summer girl—but the bride is the certified check among the wedding presents that the gods send in when man is married to mortality.

The car glided up the Golden Way. On the bridge of the great cruiser the captain stood, trumpeting the sights of the big city to his passengers. Wide-mouthed and open-eared, they heard the sights of the metropolis thundered forth to their eyes. Confused, delirious with excitement and provincial longings, they tried to make ocular responses to the megaphonic ritual. In the solemn spires of spreading cathedrals they saw the home of the Vanderbilts; in the busy bulk of the Grand Central depot they viewed, wonderingly, the frugal cot of Russell Sage. Bidden to observe the highlands of the Hudson, they gaped, unsuspecting, at the upturned mountains of a new-laid sewer. To many the elevated railroad was the Rialto, on the stations of which uniformed men sat and made chop suey of your tickets. And to this day in the outlying districts many have it that Chuck Connors, with his hand on his heart, leads reform; and that but for the noble municipal efforts of one Parkhurst, a district attorney, the notorious "Bishop" Potter gang would have destroyed law and order from the Bowery to the Harlem River.

But I beg you to observe Mrs. James Williams—Hattie Chalmers that was—once the belle of Cloverdale. Pale-blue is the bride's, if she will; and this colour she had honoured. Willingly had the moss rosebud loaned to her cheeks of its pink—and as for the violet!—her eyes will do very well as they are, thank you. A useless strip of white chaf—oh, no, he was guiding the auto car—of white chiffon—or perhaps it was grenadine or tulle—was tied beneath her chin, pretending to hold her bonnet in place. But you know as well as I do that the hatpins did the work.

And on Mrs. James Williams's face was recorded a little library of the world's best thoughts in three volumes. Volume No. 1 contained the belief that James Williams was about the right sort of thing. Volume No. 2 was an essay on the world, declaring it to be a very excellent place. Volume No. 3 disclosed the belief that in occupying the highest seat in a Rubberneck auto they were travelling the pace that passes all understanding.

James Williams, you would have guessed, was about twenty-four. It will gratify you to know that your estimate was so accurate. He was exactly twenty-three years, eleven months and twenty-nine days old. He was well built, active, strong-jawed, good-natured and rising. He was on his wedding trip.

Dear kind fairy, please cut out those orders for money and 40 H.P. touring cars and fame and a new growth of hair and the presidency of the boat club. Instead of any of them turn backward—oh, turn backward and give us just a teeny-weeny bit of our wedding trip over again. Just an hour, dear fairy, so we can remember how the grass and poplar trees looked, and the bow of those bonnet strings tied beneath her chin—even if it was the hatpins that did the work. Can't do it? Very well; hurry up with that touring car and the oil stock, then.

Just in front of Mrs. James Williams sat a girl in a loose tan jacket and a straw hat adorned with grapes and roses. Only in dreams and milliners' shops do we, alas! gather grapes and roses at one swipe. This girl gazed with large blue eyes, credulous, when the megaphone man roared his doctrine that millionaires were things about which we should be concerned. Between blasts she resorted to Epictetian philosophy in the form of pepsin chewing gum.

At this girl's right hand sat a young man about twenty-four. He was well-built, active, strong-jawed and good-natured. But if his description seems to follow that of James Williams, divest it of anything Cloverdalian. This man belonged to hard streets and sharp corners. He looked keenly about him, seeming to begrudge the asphalt under the feet of those upon whom he looked down from his perch.

While the megaphone barks at a famous hostelry, let me whisper you through the low-tuned cardiaphone to sit tight; for now things are about to happen, and the great city will close over them again as over a scrap of ticker tape floating down from the den of a Broad street bear.

The girl in the tan jacket twisted around to view the pilgrims on the last seat. The other passengers she had absorbed; the seat behind her was her Bluebeard's chamber.

Her eyes met those of Mrs. James Williams. Between two ticks of a watch they exchanged their life's experiences, histories, hopes and fancies. And all, mind you, with the eye, before two men could have decided whether to draw steel or borrow a match.

The bride leaned forward low. She and the girl spoke rapidly together, their tongues moving quickly like those of two serpents—a comparison that is not meant to go further. Two smiles and a dozen nods closed the conference.

And now in the broad, quiet avenue in front of the Rubberneck car a man in dark clothes stood with uplifted hand. From the sidewalk another hurried to join him.

The girl in the fruitful hat quickly seized her companion by the arm and whispered in his ear. That young man exhibited proof of ability to act promptly. Crouching low, he slid over the edge of the car, hung lightly for an instant, and then disappeared. Half a dozen of the top-riders observed his feat, wonderingly, but made no comment, deeming it prudent not to express surprise at what might be the conventional manner of alighting in this bewildering city. The truant passenger dodged a hansom and then floated past, like a leaf on a stream between a furniture van and a florist's delivery wagon.

The girl in the tan jacket turned again, and looked in the eyes of Mrs. James Williams. Then she faced about and sat still while the Rubberneck auto stopped at the flash of the badge under the coat of the plainclothes man.

"What's eatin' you?" demanded the megaphonist, abandoning his professional discourse for pure English.

"Keep her at anchor for a minute," ordered the officer. "There's a man on board we want—a Philadelphia burglar called 'Pinky' McGuire. There he is on the back seat. Look out for the side, Donovan."

Donovan went to the hind wheel and looked up at James Williams.

"Come down, old sport," he said, pleasantly. "We've got you. Back to Sleepytown for yours. It ain't a bad idea, hidin' on a Rubberneck, though. I'll remember that."

Softly through the megaphone came the advice of the conductor:

"Better step off, sir, and explain. The car must proceed on its tour."

James Williams belonged among the level heads. With necessary slowness he picked his way through the passengers down to the steps at the front of the car. His wife followed, but she first turned her eyes and saw the escaped tourist glide from behind the furniture van and slip behind a tree on the edge of the little park, not fifty feet away.

Descended to the ground, James Williams faced his captors with a smile. He was thinking what a good story he would have to tell in Cloverdale about having been mistaken for a burglar. The Rubberneck coach lingered, out of respect for its patrons. What could be a more interesting sight than this?

"My name is James Williams, of Cloverdale, Missouri," he said kindly, so that they would not be too greatly mortified. "I have letters here that will show——"

"You'll come with us, please," announced the plainclothes man. "'Pinky' McGuire's description fits you like flannel washed in hot suds. A detective saw you on the Rubberneck up at Central Park and 'phoned down to take you in. Do your explaining at the station-house."

James Williams's wife—his bride of two weeks—looked him in the face with a strange, soft radiance in her eyes and a flush on her cheeks, looked him in the face and said:

"Go with 'em quietly, 'Pinky,' and maybe it'll be in your favour."

And then as the Glaring-at-Gotham car rolled away she turned and threw a kiss—his wife threw a kiss—at some one high up on the seats of the Rubberneck.

"Your girl gives you good advice, McGuire," said Donovan. "Come on, now."

And then madness descended upon and occupied James Williams. He pushed his hat far upon the back of his head.

"My wife seems to think I am a burglar," he said, recklessly. "I never heard of her being crazy; therefore I must be. And if I'm crazy, they can't do anything to me for killing you two fools in my madness."

Whereupon he resisted arrest so cheerfully and industriously that cops had to be whistled for, and afterwards the reserves, to disperse a few thousand delighted spectators.

At the station-house the desk sergeant asked for his name.

"McDoodle, the Pink, or Pinky the Brute, I forget which," was James Williams's answer. "But you can bet I'm a burglar; don't leave that out. And you might add that it took five of 'em to pluck the Pink. I'd especially like to have that in the records."

In an hour came Mrs. James Williams, with Uncle Thomas,

of Madison Avenue, in a respect-compelling motor car and proofs of the hero's innocence—for all the world like the third act of a drama backed by an automobile mfg. co.

After the police had sternly reprimanded James Williams for imitating a copyrighted burglar and given him as honourable a discharge as the department was capable of, Mrs. Williams re-arrested him and swept him into an angle of the station-house. James Williams regarded her with one eye. He always said that Donovan closed the other while somebody was holding his good right hand. Never before had he given her a word of reproach or of reproof.

"If you can explain," he began rather stiffly, "why you——"

"Dear," she interrupted, "listen. It was an hour's pain and trial to you. I did it for her—I mean the girl who spoke to me on the coach. I was so happy, Jim—so happy with you that I didn't dare to refuse that happiness to another. Jim, they were married only this morning—those two; and I wanted him to get away. While they were struggling with you I saw him slip from behind his tree and hurry across the park. That's all of it, dear—I had to do it."

Thus does one sister of the plain gold band know another who stands in the enchanted light that shines but once and briefly for each one. By rice and satin bows does mere man become aware of weddings. But bride knoweth bride at the glance of an eye. And between them swiftly passes comfort and meaning in a language that man and widows wot not of.

An Adjustment of Nature

IN AN art exhibition the other day I saw a painting that had been sold for $5,000. The painter was a young scrub out of the West named Kraft, who had a favourite food and a pet theory. His pabulum was an unquenchable belief in the Unerring Artistic Adjustment of Nature. His theory was fixed around corned-beef hash with poached egg. There was a story behind the picture, so I went home and let it drip out of a fountain-pen. The idea of Kraft—but that is not the beginning of the story.

Three years ago Kraft, Bill Judkins (a poet), and I took our meals at Cypher's, on Eighth Avenue. I say "took." When we had money, Cypher got it "off of" us, as he expressed it. We had no credit; we went in, called for food and ate it. We paid or we did not pay. We had confidence in Cypher's sullenness and smouldering ferocity. Deep down in his sunless soul he was either a prince, a fool or an artist. He sat at a worm-eaten desk, covered with files of waiters' checks so old that I was sure the bottommost one was for clams that Hendrik Hudson had eaten and paid for. Cypher had the power, in common with Napoleon III. and the goggle-eyed perch, of throwing a film over his eyes, rendering opaque the windows of his soul. Once when we left him unpaid, with egregious excuses, I looked back and saw him shaking with inaudible laughter behind his film. Now and then we paid up back scores.

But the chief thing at Cypher's was Milly. Milly was a waitress. She was a grand example of Kraft's theory of the artistic adjustment of nature. She belonged, largely, to waiting, as Minerva did to the art of scrapping, or Venus to the science of serious flirtation. Pedestalled and in bronze she might have stood with the noblest of her heroic sisters as "Liver-and-Bacon Enlivening the World." She belonged to Cypher's. You expected to see her colossal figure loom through that reeking blue cloud of smoke from frying fat just as you expect the Palisades to appear through a drifting Hudson River fog. There amid the steam of vegetables and the vapours of acres of "ham and," the crash of crockery, the clatter of steel, the screaming of "short orders," the cries of the hungering and all the horrid tumult of feeding man, surrounded by swarms of the buzzing winged beasts bequeathed us by Pharaoh, Milly steered her magnificent way like some great liner cleaving among the canoes of howling savages.

Our Goddess of Grub was built on lines so majestic that they could be followed only with awe. Her sleeves were always rolled above her elbows. She could have taken us three musketeers in her two hands and dropped us out of the window. She had seen fewer years than any of us, but she was of such superb Eve-hood and simplicity that she mothered us from the beginning. Cypher's store of eatables she poured out upon us with royal indifference to price and quantity, as from a cornucopia that knew no exhaustion. Her voice rang like a great silver bell; her smile was many-toothed and frequent; she seemed like a yellow sunrise on mountain tops. I never saw her but I thought of the Yosemite. And yet, somehow, I could never think of her as existing outside of Cypher's. There nature had placed her, and she had taken root and grown mightily. She seemed happy, and took her few poor dollars on Saturday nights with the flushed pleasure of a child that receives an unexpected donation.

It was Kraft who first voiced the fear that each of us must have held latently. It came up apropos, of course, of certain questions of art at which we were hammering. One of us compared the harmony existing between a Haydn symphony and pistache ice cream to the exquisite congruity between Milly and Cypher's.

"There is a certain fate hanging over Milly," said Kraft, "and if it overtakes her she is lost to Cypher's and to us."

"She will grow fat?" asked Judkins, fearsomely.

"She will go to night school and become refined?" I ventured anxiously.

"It is this," said Kraft, punctuating in a puddle of spilled coffee with a stiff forefinger. "Cæsar had his Brutus—the cotton has its bollworm, the chorus girl has her Pittsburger, the summer boarder has his poison ivy, the hero has his Carnegie medal, art has its Morgan, the rose has its——"

"Speak," I interrupted, much perturbed. "You do not think that Milly will begin to lace?"

"One day," concluded Kraft, solemnly, "there will come to

Cypher's for a plate of beans a millionaire lumberman from Wisconsin, and he will marry Milly."

"Never!" exclaimed Judkins and I, in horror.

"A lumberman," repeated Kraft, hoarsely.

"And a millionaire lumberman!" I sighed, despairingly.

"From Wisconsin!" groaned Judkins.

We agreed that the awful fate seemed to menace her. Few things were less improbable. Milly, like some vast virgin stretch of pine woods, was made to catch the lumberman's eye. And well we knew the habits of the Badgers, once fortune smiled upon them. Straight to New York they hie, and lay their goods at the feet of the girl who serves them beans in a beanery. Why, the alphabet itself connives. The Sunday newspaper's headliner's work is cut for him.

"Winsome Waitress Wins Wealthy Wisconsin Woodsman."

For a while we felt that Milly was on the verge of being lost to us.

It was our love of the Unerring Artistic Adjustment of Nature that inspired us. We could not give her over to a lumberman, doubly accursed by wealth and provincialism. We shuddered to think of Milly, with her voice modulated and her elbows covered, pouring tea in the marble teepee of a tree murderer. No! In Cypher's she belonged—in the bacon smoke, the cabbage perfume, the grand, Wagnerian chorus of hurled ironstone china and rattling casters.

Our fears must have been prophetic, for on that same evening the wildwood discharged upon us Milly's preordained confiscator—our fee to adjustment and order. But Alaska and not Wisconsin bore the burden of the visitation.

We were at our supper of beef stew and dried apples when he trotted in as if on the heels of a dog team, and made one of the mess at our table. With the freedom of the camps he assaulted our ears and claimed the fellowship of men lost in the wilds of a hash house. We embraced him as a specimen, and in three minutes we had all but died for one another as friends.

He was rugged and bearded and wind-dried. He had just come off the "trail," he said, at one of the North River ferries. I fancied I could see the snow dust of Chilcoot yet powdering his shoulders. And then he strewed the table with the nuggets, stuffed ptarmigans, bead work and seal pelts of the returned Klondiker, and began to prate to us of his millions.

"Bank drafts for two millions," was his summing up, "and a thousand a day piling up from my claims. And now I want some beef stew and canned peaches. I never got off the train since I mushed out of Seattle, and I'm hungry. The stuff the niggers feed you on Pullmans don't count. You gentlemen order what you want."

And then Milly loomed up with a thousand dishes on her bare arm—loomed up big and white and pink and awful as Mount Saint Elias—with a smile like day breaking in a gulch. And the Klondiker threw down his pelts and nuggets as dross, and let his jaw fall half-way, and stared at her. You could almost see the diamond tiaras on Milly's brow and the hand-embroidered silk Paris gowns that he meant to buy for her.

At last the bollworm had attacked the cotton—the poison ivy was reaching out its tendrils to entwine the summer boarder—the millionaire lumberman, thinly disguised as the Alaskan miner, was about to engulf our Milly and upset Nature's adjustment.

Kraft was the first to act. He leaped up and pounded the Klondiker's back. "Come out and drink," he shouted. "Drink first and eat afterward." Judkins seized one arm and I the other. Gaily, roaringly, irresistibly, in jolly-good-fellow style, we dragged him from the restaurant to a café, stuffing his pockets with his embalmed birds and indigestible nuggets.

There he rumbled a roughly good-humoured protest. "That's the girl for my money," he declared. "She can eat out of my skillet the rest of her life. Why, I never see such a fine girl. I'm going back there and ask her to marry me. I guess she won't want to sling hash any more when she sees the pile of dust I've got."

"You'll take another whiskey and milk now," Kraft persuaded, with Satan's smile. "I thought you up-country fellows were better sports."

Kraft spent his puny store of coin at the bar and then gave Judkins and me such an appealing look that we went down to the last dime we had in toasting our guest.

Then, when our ammunition was gone and the Klondiker, still somewhat sober, began to babble again of Milly, Kraft whispered into his ear such a polite, barbed insult relating to people who were miserly with their funds, that the miner crashed down handful after handful of silver and notes, calling for all the fluids in the world to drown the imputation.

Thus the work was accomplished. With his own guns we drove him from the field. And then we had him carted to a distant small hotel and put to bed with his nuggets and baby seal-skins stuffed around him.

"He will never find Cypher's again," said Kraft. "He will propose to the first white apron he sees in a dairy restaurant to-morrow. And Milly—I mean the Natural Adjustment—is saved!"

And back to Cypher's went we three, and, finding customers scarce, we joined hands and did an Indian dance with Milly in the centre.

This, I say, happened three years ago. And about that time a little luck descended upon us three, and we were enabled to buy costlier and less wholesome food than Cypher's. Our paths separated, and I saw Kraft no more and Judkins seldom.

But, as I said, I saw a painting the other day that was sold for $5,000. The title was "Boadicea," and the figure seemed to fill all out-of-doors. But of all the picture's admirers who stood before it, I believe I was the only one who longed for Boadicea to stalk from her frame, bringing me corned-beef hash with poached egg.

I hurried away to see Kraft. His satanic eyes were the same, his hair was worse tangled, but his clothes had been made by a tailor.

"I didn't know," I said to him.

"We've bought a cottage in the Bronx with the money," said he. "Any evening at 7."

"Then," said I, "when you led us against the lumberman—the—Klondiker—it wasn't altogether on account of the Unerring Artistic Adjustment of Nature?"

"Well, not altogether," said Kraft, with a grin.

A Midsummer Knight's Dream

"The knights are dead;
Their swords are rust.
Except a few who have to hust-
Le all the time
To raise the dust."

DEAR READER: It was summertime. The sun glared down upon the city with pitiless ferocity. It is difficult for the sun to be ferocious and exhibit compunction simultaneously. The heat was—oh, bother thermometers!—who cares for standard measures, anyhow? It was so hot that—

The roof gardens put on so many extra waiters that you could hope to get your gin fizz now—as soon as all the other people got theirs. The hospitals were putting in extra cots for bystanders. For when little woolly dogs loll their tongues out and say "woof, woof!" at the fleas that bite 'em, and nervous old black bombazine ladies screech "Mad dog!" and policemen begin to shoot, somebody is going to get hurt. The man from Pompton, N. J., who always wears an overcoat in July, had turned up in a Broadway hotel drinking hot Scotches and enjoying his annual ray from the calcium. Philanthropists were petitioning the Legislature to pass a bill requiring builders to make tenement fire-escapes more commodious, so that families might die all together of the heat instead of one or two at a time. So many men were telling you about the number of baths they took each day that you wondered how they got along after the real lessee of the apartment came back to town and thanked 'em for taking such good care of it. The young man who called loudly for cold beef and beer in the restaurant, protesting that roast pullet and Burgundy was really too heavy for such weather, blushed when he met your eye, for you had heard him all winter calling, in modest tones, for the same ascetic viands. Soup, pocketbooks, shirt waists, actors and baseball excuses grew thinner. Yes, it was summertime.

A man stood at Thirty-fourth street waiting for a downtown

car. A man of forty, gray-haired, pink-faced, keen, nervous, plainly dressed, with a harassed look around the eyes. He wiped his forehead and laughed loudly when a fat man with an outing look stopped and spoke with him.

"No, siree," he shouted with defiance and scorn. "None of your old mosquito-haunted swamps and skyscraper mountains without elevators for me. When I want to get away from hot weather I know how to do it. New York, sir, is the finest summer resort in the country. Keep in the shade and watch your diet, and don't get too far away from an electric fan. Talk about your Adirondacks and your Catskills! There's more solid comfort in the borough of Manhattan than in all the rest of the country together. No, siree! No tramping up perpendicular cliffs and being waked up at 4 in the morning by a million flies, and eating canned goods straight from the city for me. Little old New York will take a few select summer boarders; comforts and conveniences of homes—that's the ad. that I answer every time."

"You need a vacation," said the fat man, looking closely at the other. "You haven't been away from town in years. Better come with me for two weeks, anyhow. The trout in the Beaverkill are jumping at anything now that looks like a fly. Harding writes me that he landed a three-pound brown last week."

"Nonsense!" cried the other man. "Go ahead, if you like, and boggle around in rubber boots wearing yourself out trying to catch fish. When I want one I go to a cool restaurant and order it. I laugh at you fellows whenever I think of you hustling around in the heat in the country thinking you are having a good time. For me Father Knickerbocker's little improved farm with the big shady lane running through the middle of it."

The fat man sighed over his friend and went his way. The man who thought New York was the greatest summer resort in the country boarded a car and went buzzing down to his office. On the way he threw away his newspaper and looked up at a ragged patch of sky above the housetops.

"Three pounds!" he muttered, absently. "And Harding isn't a liar. I believe, if I could—but it's impossible—they've got to have another month—another month at least."

In his office the upholder of urban midsummer joys dived,

headforemost, into the swimming pool of business. Adkins, his clerk, came and added a spray of letters, memoranda and telegrams.

At 5 o'clock in the afternoon the busy man leaned back in his office chair, put his feet on the desk and mused aloud:

"I wonder what kind of bait Harding used."

She was all in white that day; and thereby Compton lost a bet to Gaines. Compton had wagered she would wear light blue, for he knew that was his favorite color, and Compton was a millionaire's son, and that almost laid him open to the charge of betting on a sure thing. But white was her choice, and Gaines held up his head with twenty-five's lordly air.

The little summer hotel in the mountains had a lively crowd that year. There were two or three young college men and a couple of artists and a young naval officer on one side. On the other there were enough beauties among the young ladies for the correspondent of a society paper to refer to them as a "bevy." But the moon among the stars was Mary Sewell. Each one of the young men greatly desired to arrange matters so that he could pay her millinery bills, and fix the furnace, and have her do away with the "Sewell" part of her name forever. Those who could stay only a week or two went away hinting at pistols and blighted hearts. But Compton stayed like the mountains themselves, for he could afford it. And Gaines stayed because he was a fighter and wasn't afraid of millionaire's sons, and—well, he adored the country.

"What do you think, Miss Mary?" he said once. "I knew a duffer in New York who claimed to like it in the summer time. Said you could keep cooler there than you could in the woods. Wasn't he an awful silly? I don't think I could breathe on Broadway after the 1st of June."

"Mamma was thinking of going back week after next," said Miss Mary with a lovely frown.

"But when you think of it," said Gaines, "there are lots of jolly places in town in the summer. The roof gardens, you know, and the—er—the roof gardens."

Deepest blue was the lake that day—the day when they had the mock tournament, and the men rode clumsy farm horses around in a glade in the woods and caught curtain rings on the end of a lance. Such fun!

Cool and dry as the finest wine came the breath of the shadowed forest. The valley below was a vision seen through an opal haze. A white mist from hidden falls blurred the green of a hand's breadth of tree tops half-way down the gorge. Youth made merry hand-in-hand with young summer. Nothing on Broadway like that.

The villagers gathered to see the city folks pursue their mad drollery. The woods rang with the laughter of pixies and naiads and sprites. Gaines caught most of the rings. His was the privilege to crown the queen of the tournament. He was the conquering knight—as far as the rings went. On his arm he wore a white scarf. Compton wore light blue. She had declared her preference for blue, but she wore white that day.

Gaines looked about for the queen to crown her. He heard her merry laugh, as if from the clouds. She had slipped away and climbed Chimney Rock, a little granite bluff, and stood there, a white fairy among the laurels, fifty feet above their heads.

Instantly he and Compton accepted the implied challenge. The bluff was easily mounted at the rear, but the front offered small hold to hand or foot. Each man quickly selected his route and began to climb. A crevice, a bush, a slight projection, a vine or tree branch—all of these were aids that counted in the race. It was all foolery—there was no stake; but there was youth in it, cross reader, and light hearts, and something else that Miss Clay writes so charmingly about.

Gaines gave a great tug at the root of a laurel and pulled himself to Miss Mary's feet. On his arm he carried the wreath of roses; and while the villagers and summer boarders screamed and applauded below he placed it on the queen's brow.

"You are a gallant knight," said Miss Mary.

"If I could be your true knight always," began Gaines, but Miss Mary laughed him dumb, for Compton scrambled over the edge of the rock one minute behind time.

What a twilight that was when they drove back to the hotel! The opal of the valley turned slowly to purple, the dark woods framed the lake as a mirror, the tonic air stirred the very soul in

one. The first pale stars came out over the mountain tops where
yet a faint glow of——

"I beg your pardon, Mr. Gaines," said Adkins.

The man who believed New York to be the finest summer
resort in the world opened his eyes and kicked over the muci-
lage bottle on his desk.

"I—I believe I was asleep," he said.

"It's the heat," said Adkins. "It's something awful in the city
these"——

"Nonsense!" said the other. "The city beats the country ten
to one in summer. Fools go out tramping in muddy brooks and
wear themselves out trying to catch little fish as long as your
finger. Stay in town and keep comfortable—that's my idea."

"Some letters just came," said Adkins. "I thought you might
like to glance at them before you go."

Let us look over his shoulder and read just a few lines of one
of them:

> My Dear, Dear Husband: Just received your letter ordering
> us to stay another month. . . . Rita's cough is almost gone. . . .
> Johnny has simply gone wild like a little Indian. . . . Will be the
> making of both children. . . . work so hard, and I know that your
> business can hardly afford to keep us here so long. . . . best man
> that ever . . . you always pretend that you like the city in sum-
> mer. . . . trout fishing that you used to be so fond of . . . and all
> to keep us well and happy . . . come to you if it were not doing
> the babies so much good. . . . I stood last evening on Chimney
> Rock in exactly the same spot where I was when you put the
> wreath of roses on my head. . . . through all the world . . . when
> you said you would be my true knight . . . fifteen years ago, dear,
> just think! . . . have always been that to me . . . ever and ever,
>
>   Mary.

The man who said he thought New York the finest summer
resort in the country dropped into a café on his way home and
had a glass of beer under an electric fan.

"Wonder what kind of a fly old Harding used," he said to
himself.

An Unfinished Story

W E NO longer groan and heap ashes upon our heads when the flames of Tophet are mentioned. For, even the preachers have begun to tell us that God is radium, or ether or some scientific compound, and that the worst we wicked ones may expect is a chemical reaction. This is a pleasing hypothesis; but there lingers yet some of the old, goodly terror of orthodoxy.

There are but two subjects upon which one may discourse with a free imagination, and without the possibility of being controverted. You may talk of your dreams; and you may tell what you heard a parrot say. Both Morpheus and the bird are incompetent witnesses; and your listener dare not attack your recital. The baseless fabric of a vision, then, shall furnish my theme—chosen with apologies and regrets instead of the more limited field of pretty Polly's small talk.

I had a dream that was so far removed from the higher criticism that it had to do with the ancient, respectable, and lamented bar-of-judgment theory.

Gabriel had played his trump; and those of us who could not follow suit were arraigned for examination. I noticed at one side a gathering of professional bondsmen in solemn black and collars that buttoned behind; but it seemed there was some trouble about their real estate titles; and they did not appear to be getting any of us out.

A fly cop—an angel policeman—flew over to me and took me by the left wing. Near at hand was a group of very prosperous-looking spirits arraigned for judgment.

"Do you belong with that bunch?" the policeman asked.

"Who are they?" was my answer.

"Why," said he, "they are——"

But this irrelevant stuff is taking up space that the story should occupy.

Dulcie worked in a department store. She sold Hamburg edging, or stuffed peppers, or automobiles, or other little trinkets such as they keep in department stores. Of what she earned, Dulcie received six dollars per week. The remainder was credited to her and debited to somebody else's account in the ledger kept by G—— Oh, primal energy, you say, Reverend Doctor—Well then, in the Ledger of Primal Energy.

During her first year in the store, Dulcie was paid five dollars per week. It would be instructive to know how she lived on that amount. Don't care? Very well; probably you are interested in larger amounts. Six dollars is a larger amount. I will tell you how she lived on six dollars per week.

One afternoon at six, when Dulcie was sticking her hat-pin within an eighth of an inch of her *medulla oblongata*, she said to her chum, Sadie—the girl that waits on you with her left side:

"Say, Sade, I made a date for dinner this evening with Piggy."

"You never did!" exclaimed Sadie admiringly. "Well, ain't you the lucky one? Piggy's an awful swell; and he always takes a girl to swell places. He took Blanche up to the Hoffman House one evening, where they have swell music, and you see a lot of swells. You'll have a swell time, Dulce."

Dulcie hurried homeward. Her eyes were shining, and her cheeks showed the delicate pink of life's—real life's—approaching dawn. It was Friday; and she had fifty cents left of her last week's wages.

The streets were filled with the rush-hour floods of people. The electric lights of Broadway were glowing—calling moths from miles, from leagues, from hundreds of leagues out of darkness around to come in and attend the singeing school. Men in accurate clothes, with faces like those carved on cherry stones by the old salts in sailors' homes, turned and stared at Dulcie as she sped, unheeding, past them. Manhattan, the night-blooming cereus, was beginning to unfold its dead-white, heavy-odoured petals.

Dulcie stopped in a store where goods were cheap and bought an imitation lace collar with her fifty cents. That money was to have been spent otherwise—fifteen cents for supper, ten cents for breakfast, ten cents for lunch. Another dime was to be added to her small store of savings; and five cents was to be squandered for licorice drops—the kind that made your cheek look like the toothache, and last as long. The licorice was an extravagance—almost a carouse—but what is life without pleasures?

Dulcie lived in a furnished room. There is this difference

between a furnished room and a boarding-house. In a furnished room, other people do not know it when you go hungry.

Dulcie went up to her room—the third floor back in a West Side brownstone-front. She lit the gas. Scientists tell us that the diamond is the hardest substance known. Their mistake. Landladies know of a compound beside which the diamond is as putty. They pack it in the tips of gas-burners; and one may stand on a chair and dig at it in vain until one's fingers are pink and bruised. A hairpin will not remove it; therefore let us call it immovable.

So Dulcie lit the gas. In its one-fourth-candle-power glow we will observe the room.

Couch-bed, dresser, table, washstand, chair—of this much the landlady was guilty. The rest was Dulcie's. On the dresser were her treasures—a gilt china vase presented to her by Sadie, a calendar issued by a pickle works, a book on the divination of dreams, some rice powder in a glass dish, and a cluster of artificial cherries tied with a pink ribbon.

Against the wrinkly mirror stood pictures of General Kitchener, William Muldoon, the Duchess of Marlborough, and Benvenuto Cellini. Against one wall was a plaster of Paris plaque of an O'Callahan in a Roman helmet. Near it was a violent oleograph of a lemon-coloured child assaulting an inflammatory butterfly. This was Dulcie's final judgment in art; but it had never been upset. Her rest had never been disturbed by whispers of stolen copes; no critic had elevated his eyebrows at her infantile entomologist.

Piggy was to call for her at seven. While she swiftly makes ready, let us discreetly face the other way and gossip.

For the room, Dulcie paid two dollars per week. On week-days her breakfast cost ten cents; she made coffee and cooked an egg over the gaslight while she was dressing. On Sunday mornings she feasted royally on veal chops and pineapple fritters at "Billy's" restaurant, at a cost of twenty-five cents—and tipped the waitress ten cents. New York presents so many temptations for one to run into extravagance. She had her lunches in the department-store restaurant at a cost of sixty cents for the week: dinners were $1.05. The evening papers—show me a New Yorker going without his daily paper!—came to six cents; and two Sunday papers—one for the personal column and the other to read—were ten cents. The total amounts to $4.76. Now, one has to buy clothes, and——

I give it up. I hear of wonderful bargains in fabrics, and of miracles performed with needle and thread; but I am in doubt. I hold my pen poised in vain when I would add to Dulcie's life some of those joys that belong to woman by virtue of all the unwritten, sacred, natural, inactive ordinances of the equity of heaven. Twice she had been to Coney Island and had ridden the hobby-horses. 'Tis a weary thing to count your pleasures by summers instead of by hours.

Piggy needs but a word. When the girls named him, an undeserving stigma was cast upon the noble family of swine. The words-of-three-letters lesson in the old blue spelling book begins with Piggy's biography. He was fat; he had the soul of a rat, the habits of a bat, and the magnanimity of a cat. . . . He wore expensive clothes; and was a connoisseur in starvation. He could look at a shop-girl and tell you to an hour how long it had been since she had eaten anything more nourishing than marshmallows and tea. He hung about the shopping districts, and prowled around in department stores with his invitations to dinner. Men who escort dogs upon the streets at the end of a string look down upon him. He is a type; I can dwell upon him no longer; my pen is not the kind intended for him; I am no carpenter.

At ten minutes to seven Dulcie was ready. She looked at herself in the wrinkly mirror. The reflection was satisfactory. The dark blue dress, fitting without a wrinkle, the hat with its jaunty black feather, the but-slightly-soiled gloves—all representing self-denial, even of food itself—were vastly becoming.

Dulcie forgot everything else for a moment except that she was beautiful, and that life was about to lift a corner of its mysterious veil for her to observe its wonders. No gentleman had ever asked her out before. Now she was going for a brief moment into the glitter and exalted show.

The girls said that Piggy was a "spender." There would be a grand dinner, and music, and splendidly dressed ladies to look at, and things to eat that strangely twisted the girls' jaws when they tried to tell about them. No doubt she would be asked out again.

There was a blue pongee suit in a window that she knew—by

saving twenty cents a week instead of ten, in—let's see—Oh, it would run into years! But there was a second-hand store in Seventh Avenue where——

Somebody knocked at the door. Dulcie opened it. The landlady stood there with a spurious smile, sniffing for cooking by stolen gas.

"A gentleman's downstairs to see you," she said. "Name is Mr. Wiggins."

By such epithet was Piggy known to unfortunate ones who had to take him seriously.

Dulcie turned to the dresser to get her handkerchief; and then she stopped still, and bit her underlip hard. While looking in her mirror she had seen fairyland and herself, a princess, just awakening from a long slumber. She had forgotten one that was watching her with sad, beautiful, stern eyes—the only one there was to approve or condemn what she did. Straight and slender and tall, with a look of sorrowful reproach on his handsome, melancholy face, General Kitchener fixed his wonderful eyes on her out of his gilt photograph frame on the dresser.

Dulcie turned like an automatic doll to the landlady.

"Tell him I can't go," she said dully. "Tell him I'm sick, or something. Tell him I'm not going out."

After the door was closed and locked, Dulcie fell upon her bed, crushing her black tip, and cried for ten minutes. General Kitchener was her only friend. He was Dulcie's ideal of a gallant knight. He looked as if he might have a secret sorrow, and his wonderful moustache was a dream, and she was a little afraid of that stern yet tender look in his eyes. She used to have little fancies that he would call at the house sometime, and ask for her, with his sword clanking against his high boots. Once, when a boy was rattling a piece of chain against a lamp-post she had opened the window and looked out. But there was no use. She knew that General Kitchener was away over in Japan, leading his army against the savage Turks; and he would never step out of his gilt frame for her. Yet one look from him had vanquished Piggy that night. Yes, for that night.

When her cry was over Dulcie got up and took off her best dress, and put on her old blue kimono. She wanted no dinner. She sang two verses of "Sammy." Then she became intensely interested in a little red speck on the side of her nose. And after that was attended to, she drew up a chair to the rickety table, and told her fortune with an old deck of cards.

"The horrid, impudent thing!" she said aloud. "And I never gave him a word or a look to make him think it!"

At nine o'clock Dulcie took a tin box of crackers and a little pot of raspberry jam out of her trunk, and had a feast. She offered General Kitchener some jam on a cracker; but he only looked at her as the sphinx would have looked at a butterfly—if there are butterflies in the desert.

"Don't eat it if you don't want to," said Dulcie. "And don't put on so many airs and scold so with your eyes. I wonder if you'd be so superior and snippy if you had to live on six dollars a week."

It was not a good sign for Dulcie to be rude to General Kitchener. And then she turned Benvenuto Cellini face downward with a severe gesture. But that was not inexcusable; for she had always thought he was Henry VIII., and she did not approve of him.

At half-past nine Dulcie took a last look at the pictures on the dresser, turned out the light, and skipped into bed. It's an awful thing to go to bed with a good-night look at General Kitchener, William Muldoon, the Duchess of Marlborough, and Benvenuto Cellini.

This story really doesn't get anywhere at all. The rest of it comes later—sometime when Piggy asks Dulcie again to dine with him, and she is feeling lonelier than usual, and General Kitchener happens to be looking the other way; and then——

As I said before, I dreamed that I was standing near a crowd of prosperous-looking angels, and a policeman took me by the wing and asked if I belonged with them.

"Who are they?" I asked.

"Why," said he, "they are the men who hired working-girls, and paid 'em five or six dollars a week to live on. Are you one of the bunch?"

"Not on your immortality," said I. "I'm only the fellow that set fire to an orphan asylum, and murdered a blind man for his pennies."

The City of Dreadful Night

"$\mathbf{D}$URING THE recent warmed-over spell," said my friend Carney, driver of express wagon No. 8,606, "a good many opportunities was had of observing human nature through peekaboo waists.

"The Park Commissioner and the Commissioner of Polis and the Forestry Commission gets together and agrees to let the people sleep in the parks until the Weather Bureau gets the thermometer down again to a living basis. So they draws up open-air resolutions and has them O. K.'d by the Secretary of Agriculture, Mr. Comstock and the Village Improvement Mosquito Exterminating Society of South Orange, N. J.

"When the proclamation was made opening up to the people by special grant the public parks that belong to 'em, there was a general exodus into Central Park by the communities existing along its borders. In ten minutes after sundown you'd have thought that there was an undress rehearsal of a potato famine in Ireland and a Kishineff massacre. They come by families, gangs, clambake societies, clans, clubs and tribes from all sides to enjoy a cool sleep on the grass. Them that didn't have oil stoves brought along plenty of blankets, so as not to be upset with the cold and discomforts of sleeping outdoors. By building fires of the shade trees and huddling together in the bridle paths, and burrowing under the grass where the ground was soft enough, the likes of 5,000 head of people successfully battled against the night air in Central Park alone.

"Ye know I live in the elegant furnished apartment house called the Beersheba Flats, over against the elevated portion of the New York Central Railroad.

"When the order come to the flats that all hands must turn out and sleep in the park, according to the instructions of the consulting committee of the City Club and the Murphy Draying, Returfing and Sodding Company, there was a look of a couple of fires and an eviction all over the place.

"The tenants began to pack up feather beds, rubber boots, strings of garlic, hot-water bags, portable canoes and scuttles of coal to take along for the sake of comfort. The sidewalk looked like a Russian camp in Oyama's line of march. There was wailing and lamenting up and down stairs from Danny Geoghegan's flat on the top floor to the apartments of Missis Goldsteinupski on the first.

"'For why,' says Danny, coming down and raging in his blue yarn socks to the janitor, 'should I be turned out of me comfortable apartmints to lay in the dirty grass like a rabbit? 'Tis like Jerome to stir up trouble wid small matters like this instead of——'

"'Whist!' says Officer Reagan on the sidewalk, rapping with his club. ''Tis not Jerome. 'Tis by order of the Polis Commissioner. Turn out every one of yez and hike yerselves to the park.'

"Now, 'twas a peaceful and happy home that all of us had in them same Beersheba Flats. The O'Dowds and the Steinowitzes and the Callahans and the Cohens and the Spizzinellis and the McManuses and the Spiegelmayers and the Joneses— all nations of us, we lived like one big family together. And when the hot nights come along we kept a line of childher reaching from the front door to Kelly's on the corner, passing along the cans of beer from one to another without the trouble of running after it. And with no more clothing on than is provided for in the statutes, sitting in all the windies, with a cool growler in every one, and your feet out in the air, and the Rosenstein girls singing on the fire-escape of the sixth floor, and Patsy Rourke's flute going in the eighth, and the ladies calling each other synonyms out the windies, and now and then a breeze sailing in over Mister Depew's Central—I tell you the Beersheba Flats was a summer resort that made the Catskills look like a hole in the ground. With his person full of beer and his feet out the windy and his old woman frying pork chops over a charcoal furnace and the childher dancing in cotton slips on the sidewalk around the organ-grinder and the rent paid for a week—what does a man want better on a hot night than that? And then comes this ruling of the polis driving people out o' their comfortable homes to sleep in parks—'twas for all the world like a ukase of them Russians—'twill be heard from again at next election time.

"Well, then, Officer Reagan drives the whole lot of us to the park and turns us in by the nearest gate. 'Tis dark under the trees, and all the childher sets up to howling that they want to go home.

"'Ye'll pass the night in this stretch of woods and scenery,' says Officer Reagan. ''Twill be fine and imprisonment for insoolting the Park Commissioner and the Chief of the Weather Bureau if ye refuse. I'm in charge of thirty acres between here and the Agyptian Monument, and I advise ye to give no trouble. 'Tis sleeping on the grass yez all have been condemned to by the authorities. Yez'll be permitted to leave in the morning, but ye must retoorn be night. Me orders was silent on the subject of bail, but I'll find out if 'tis required and there'll be bondsmen at the gate.'

"There being no lights except along the automobile drives, us 179 tenants of the Beersheba Flats prepared to spend the night as best we could in the raging forest. Them that brought blankets and kindling wood was best off. They got fires started and wrapped the blankets round their heads and laid down, cursing, in the grass. There was nothing to see, nothing to drink, nothing to do. In the dark we had no way of telling friend or foe except by feeling the noses of 'em. I brought along me last winter overcoat, me tooth-brush, some quinine pills and the red quilt off the bed in me flat. Three times during the night somebody rolled on me quilt and stuck his knees against the Adam's apple of me. And three times I judged his character by running me hand over his face, and three times I rose up and kicked the intruder down the hill to the gravelly walk below. And then some one with a flavor of Kelly's whisky snuggled up to me, and I found his nose turned up the right way, and I says: 'Is that you, then, Patsey?' and he says, 'It is, Carney. How long do you think it'll last?'

"'I'm no weather-prophet,' says I, 'but if they bring out a strong anti-Tammany ticket next fall it ought to get us home in time to sleep on a bed once or twice before they line us up at the polls.'

"'A-playing of my flute into the airshaft,' says Patsey Rourke, 'and a-perspiring in me own windy to the joyful noise of the passing trains and the smell of liver and onions and a-reading of the latest murder in the smoke of the cooking is well enough for me,' says he. 'What is this herding us in grass for, not to mention the crawling things with legs that walk up the trousers of us, and the Jersey snipes that peck at us, masquerading under the name and denomination of mosquitoes. What is it all for, Carney, and the rint going on just the same over at the flats?'

"''Tis the great annual Municipal Free Night Outing Lawn Party,' says I, 'given by the polis, Hetty Green and the Drug Trust. During the heated season they hold a week of it in the principal parks. 'Tis a scheme to reach that portion of the people that's not worth taking up to North Beach for a fish fry.'

"'I can't sleep on the ground,' says Patsey, 'wid any benefit. I have the hay fever and the rheumatism, and me ear is full of ants.'

"Well, the night goes on, and the ex-tenants of the Flats groans and stumbles around in the dark, trying to find rest and recreation in the forest. The childher is screaming with the coldness, and the janitor makes hot tea for 'em and keeps the fires going with the signboards that point to the Tavern and the Casino. The tenants try to lay down on the grass by families in the dark, but you're lucky if you can sleep next to a man from the same floor or believing in the same religion. Now and then a Murphy, accidental, rolls over on the grass of a Rosenstein, or a Cohen tries to crawl under the O'Grady bush, and then there's a feeling of noses and somebody is rolled down the hill to the driveway and stays there. There is some hair-pulling among the women folks, and everybody spanks the nearest howling kid to him by the sense of feeling only, regardless of its parentage and ownership. 'Tis hard to keep up the social distinctions in the dark that flourish by daylight in the Beersheba Flats. Mrs. Rafferty, that despises the asphalt that a Dago treads on, wakes up in the morning with her feet in the bosom of Antonio Spizzinelli. And Mike O'Dowd, that always threw peddlers downstairs as fast as he came upon 'em, has to unwind old Isaacstein's whiskers from around his neck, and wake up the whole gang at daylight. But here and there some few got acquainted and overlooked the discomforts of the elements. There was five engagements to be married announced at the flats the next morning.

"About midnight I gets up and wrings the dew out of my hair, and goes to the side of the driveway and sits down. At one side of the park I could see the lights in the streets and houses; and I was thinking how happy them folks was who could chase the duck and smoke their pipes at their windows, and keep cool and pleasant like nature intended for 'em to.

"Just then an automobile stops by me, and a fine-looking, well-dressed man steps out.

"'Me man,' says he, 'can you tell me why all these people are lying around on the grass in the park? I thought it was against the rules.'

"''Twas an ordinance,' says I, 'just passed by the Polis Department and ratified by the Turf Cutters' Association, providing that all persons not carrying a license number on their rear axles shall keep in the public parks until further notice. Fortunately, the orders comes this year during a spell of fine weather, and the mortality, except on the borders of the lake and along the automobile drives, will not be any greater than usual.'

"'Who are these people on the side of the hill?' asks the man.

"'Sure,' says I, 'none others than the tenants of the Beersheba Flats—a fine home for any man, especially on hot nights. May daylight come soon!'

"'They come here be night,' says he, 'and breathe in the pure air and the fragrance of the flowers and trees. They do that,' says he, 'coming every night from the burning heat of dwellings of brick and stone.'

"'And wood,' says I. 'And marble and plaster and iron.'

"'The matter will be attended to at once,' says the man, putting up his book.

"'Are ye the Park Commissioner?' I asks.

"'I own the Beersheba Flats,' says he. 'God bless the grass and the trees that give extra benefits to a man's tenants. The rents shall be raised fifteen per cent. to-morrow. Good-night,' says he."

The Skylight Room

FIRST MRS. Parker would show you the double parlours. You would not dare to interrupt her description of their advantages and of the merits of the gentleman who had occupied them for eight years. Then you would manage to stammer forth the confession that you were neither a doctor nor a dentist. Mrs. Parker's manner of receiving the admission was such that you could never afterward entertain the same feeling toward your parents, who had neglected to train you up in one of the professions that fitted Mrs. Parker's parlours.

Next you ascended one flight of stairs and looked at the second-floor-back at $8. Convinced by her second-floor manner that it was worth the $12 that Mr. Toosenberry always paid for it until he left to take charge of his brother's orange plantation in Florida near Palm Beach, where Mrs. McIntyre always spent the winters that had the double front room with private bath, you managed to babble that you wanted something still cheaper.

If you survived Mrs. Parker's scorn, you were taken to look at Mr. Skidder's large hall room on the third floor. Mr. Skidder's room was not vacant. He wrote plays and smoked cigarettes in it all day long. But every room-hunter was made to visit his room to admire the lambrequins. After each visit, Mr. Skidder, from the fright caused by possible eviction, would pay something on his rent.

Then—oh, then—if you still stood on one foot, with your hot hand clutching the three moist dollars in your pocket, and hoarsely proclaimed your hideous and culpable poverty, nevermore would Mrs. Parker be cicerone of yours. She would honk loudly the word "Clara," she would show you her back, and march downstairs. Then Clara, the coloured maid, would escort you up the carpeted ladder that served for the fourth flight, and show you the Skylight Room. It occupied 7 × 8 feet of floor space at the middle of the hall. On each side of it was a dark lumber closet or storeroom.

In it was an iron cot, a washstand and a chair. A shelf was the dresser. Its four bare walls seemed to close in upon you like the sides of a coffin. Your hand crept to your throat, you gasped, you looked up as from a well—and breathed once more. Through the glass of the little skylight you saw a square of blue infinity.

"Two dollars, suh," Clara would say in her half-contemptuous, half-Tuskegeenial tones.

One day Miss Leeson came hunting for a room. She carried a typewriter made to be lugged around by a much larger lady. She was a very little girl, with eyes and hair that had kept on growing after she had stopped and that always looked as if they were saying: "Goodness me! Why didn't you keep up with us?"

Mrs. Parker showed her the double parlours. "In this closet," she said, "one could keep a skeleton or anæsthetic or coal——"

"But I am neither a doctor nor a dentist," said Miss Leeson, with a shiver.

Mrs. Parker gave her the incredulous, pitying, sneering, icy stare that she kept for those who failed to qualify as doctors or dentists, and led the way to the second floor back.

"Eight dollars?" said Miss Leeson. "Dear me! I'm not Hetty if I do look green. I'm just a poor little working girl. Show me something higher and lower."

Mr. Skidder jumped and strewed the floor with cigarette stubs at the rap on his door.

"Excuse me, Mr. Skidder," said Mrs. Parker, with her demon's smile at his pale looks. "I didn't know you were in. I asked the lady to have a look at your lambrequins."

"They're too lovely for anything," said Miss Leeson, smiling in exactly the way the angels do.

After they had gone Mr. Skidder got very busy erasing the tall, black-haired heroine from his latest (unproduced) play and inserting a small, roguish one with heavy, bright hair and vivacious features.

"Anna Held'll jump at it," said Mr. Skidder to himself, putting his feet up against the lambrequins and disappearing in a cloud of smoke like an aërial cuttlefish.

Presently the tocsin call of "Clara!" sounded to the world the state of Miss Leeson's purse. A dark goblin seized her, mounted a Stygian stairway, thrust her into a vault with a glimmer of light in its top and muttered the menacing and cabalistic words "Two dollars!"

"I'll take it!" sighed Miss Leeson, sinking down upon the squeaky iron bed.

Every day Miss Leeson went out to work. At night she brought home papers with handwriting on them and made copies with her typewriter. Sometimes she had no work at night, and then she would sit on the steps of the high stoop with the other roomers. Miss Leeson was not intended for a skylight room when the plans were drawn for her creation. She was gay-hearted and full of tender, whimsical fancies. Once she let Mr. Skidder read to her three acts of his great (unpublished) comedy, "It's No Kid; or, The Heir of the Subway."

There was rejoicing among the gentlemen roomers whenever Miss Leeson had time to sit on the steps for an hour or two. But Miss Longnecker, the tall blonde who taught in a public school and said, "Well, really!" to everything you said, sat on the top step and sniffed. And Miss Dorn, who shot at the moving ducks at Coney every Sunday and worked in a department store, sat on the bottom step and sniffed. Miss Leeson sat on the middle step, and the men would quickly group around her.

Especially Mr. Skidder, who had cast her in his mind for the star part in a private, romantic (unspoken) drama in real life. And especially Mr. Hoover, who was forty-five, fat, flush and foolish. And especially very young Mr. Evans, who set up a hollow cough to induce her to ask him to leave off cigarettes. The men voted her "the funniest and jolliest ever," but the sniffs on the top step and the lower step were implacable.

I pray you let the drama halt while Chorus stalks to the footlights and drops an epicedian tear upon the fatness of Mr. Hoover. Tune the pipes to the tragedy of tallow, the bane of bulk, the calamity of corpulence. Tried out, Falstaff might have rendered more romance to the ton than would have Romeo's rickety ribs to the ounce. A lover may sigh, but he must not puff. To the train of Momus are the fat men remanded. In vain beats the faithfullest heart above a 52-inch belt. Avaunt, Hoover! Hoover, forty-five, flush and foolish, might carry off Helen herself; Hoover, forty-five, flush, foolish and fat is meat for perdition. There was never a chance for you, Hoover.

As Mrs. Parker's roomers sat thus one summer's evening,

Miss Leeson looked up into the firmament and cried with her little gay laugh:

"Why, there's Billy Jackson! I can see him from down here, too."

All looked up—some at the windows of skyscrapers, some casting about for an airship, Jackson-guided.

"It's that star," explained Miss Leeson, pointing with a tiny finger. "Not the big one that twinkles—the steady blue one near it. I can see it every night through my skylight. I named it Billy Jackson."

"Well, really!" said Miss Longnecker. "I didn't know you were an astronomer, Miss Leeson."

"Oh, yes," said the small star gazer, "I know as much as any of them about the style of sleeves they're going to wear next fall in Mars."

"Well, really!" said Miss Longnecker. "The star you refer to is Gamma, of the constellation Cassiopeia. It is nearly of the second magnitude, and its meridian passage is——"

"Oh," said the very young Mr. Evans, "I think Billy Jackson is a much better name for it."

"Same here," said Mr. Hoover, loudly breathing defiance to Miss Longnecker. "I think Miss Leeson has just as much right to name stars as any of those old astrologers had."

"Well, really!" said Miss Longnecker.

"I wonder whether it's a shooting star," remarked Miss Dorn. "I hit nine ducks and a rabbit out of ten in the gallery at Coney Sunday."

"He doesn't show up very well from down here," said Miss Leeson. "You ought to see him from my room. You know you can see stars even in the daytime from the bottom of a well. At night my room is like the shaft of a coal mine, and it makes Billy Jackson look like the big diamond pin that Night fastens her kimono with."

There came a time after that when Miss Leeson brought no formidable papers home to copy. And when she went out in the morning, instead of working, she went from office to office and let her heart melt away in the drip of cold refusals transmitted through insolent office boys. This went on.

There came an evening when she wearily climbed Mrs.

Parker's stoop at the hour when she always returned from her dinner at the restaurant. But she had had no dinner.

As she stepped into the hall Mr. Hoover met her and seized his chance. He asked her to marry him, and his fatness hovered above her like an avalanche. She dodged, and caught the balustrade. He tried for her hand, and she raised it and smote him weakly in the face. Step by step she went up, dragging herself by the railing. She passed Mr. Skidder's door as he was red-inking a stage direction for Myrtle Delorme (Miss Leeson) in his (unaccepted) comedy, to "pirouette across stage from L to the side of the Count." Up the carpeted ladder she crawled at last and opened the door of the skylight room.

She was too weak to light the lamp or to undress. She fell upon the iron cot, her fragile body scarcely hollowing the worn springs. And in that Erebus of a room she slowly raised her heavy eyelids, and smiled.

For Billy Jackson was shining down on her, calm and bright and constant through the skylight. There was no world about her. She was sunk in a pit of blackness, with but that small square of pallid light framing the star that she had so whimsically and oh, so ineffectually named. Miss Longnecker must be right; it was Gamma, of the constellation Cassiopeia, and not Billy Jackson. And yet she could not let it be Gamma.

As she lay on her back she tried twice to raise her arm. The third time she got two thin fingers to her lips and blew a kiss out of the black pit to Billy Jackson. Her arm fell back limply.

"Good-bye, Billy," she murmured faintly. "You're millions of miles away and you won't even twinkle once. But you kept where I could see you most of the time up there when there wasn't anything else but darkness to look at, didn't you? . . . Millions of miles. . . . Good-bye, Billy Jackson."

Clara, the coloured maid, found the door locked at 10 the next day, and they forced it open. Vinegar, and the slapping of wrists and burnt feathers proving of no avail, some one ran to 'phone for an ambulance.

In due time it backed up to the door with much gong-clanging, and the capable young medico, in his white linen coat, ready, active, confident, with his smooth face half debonair, half grim, danced up the steps.

"Ambulance call to 49," he said briefly. "What's the trouble?"

"Oh, yes, doctor," sniffed Mrs. Parker, as though her trouble that there should be trouble in the house was the greater. "I can't think what can be the matter with her. Nothing we could do would bring her to. It's a young woman, a Miss Elsie—yes, a Miss Elsie Leeson. Never before in my house——"

"What room?" cried the doctor in a terrible voice, to which Mrs. Parker was a stranger.

"The skylight room. It——"

Evidently the ambulance doctor was familiar with the location of skylight rooms. He was gone up the stairs, four at a time. Mrs. Parker followed slowly, as her dignity demanded.

On the first landing she met him coming back bearing the astronomer in his arms. He stopped and let loose the practised scalpel of his tongue, not loudly. Gradually Mrs. Parker crumpled as a stiff garment that slips down from a nail. Ever afterward there remained crumples in her mind and body. Sometimes her curious roomers would ask her what the doctor said to her.

"Let that be," she would answer. "If I can get forgiveness for having heard it I will be satisfied."

The ambulance physician strode with his burden through the pack of hounds that follow the curiosity chase, and even they fell back along the sidewalk abashed, for his face was that of one who bears his own dead.

They noticed that he did not lay down upon the bed prepared for it in the ambulance the form that he carried, and all that he said was: "Drive like h—l, Wilson," to the driver.

That is all. Is it a story? In the next morning's paper I saw a little news item, and the last sentence of it may help you (as it helped me) to weld the incidents together.

It recounted the reception into Bellevue Hospital of a young woman who had been removed from No. 49 East —— street, suffering from debility induced by starvation. It concluded with these words:

"Dr. William Jackson, the ambulance physician who attended the case, says the patient will recover."

The Poet and the Peasant

THE OTHER day a poet friend of mine, who has lived in close communion with nature all his life, wrote a poem and took it to an editor.

It was a living pastoral, full of the genuine breath of the fields, the song of birds, and the pleasant chatter of trickling streams.

When the poet called again to see about it, with hopes of a beefsteak dinner in his heart, it was handed back to him with the comment:

"Too artificial."

Several of us met over spaghetti and Dutchess County chianti, and swallowed indignation with the slippery forkfuls.

And there we dug a pit for the editor. With us was Conant, a well-arrived writer of fiction—a man who had trod on asphalt all his life, and who had never looked upon bucolic scenes except with sensations of disgust from the windows of express trains.

Conant wrote a poem and called it "The Doe and the Brook." It was a fine specimen of the kind of work you would expect from a poet who had strayed with Amaryllis only as far as the florist's windows, and whose sole ornithological discussion had been carried on with a waiter. Conant signed this poem, and we sent it to the same editor.

But this has very little to do with the story.

Just as the editor was reading the first line of the poem, on the next morning, a being stumbled off the West Shore ferryboat, and loped slowly up Forty-second Street.

The invader was a young man with light blue eyes, a hanging lip and hair the exact color of the little orphan's (afterward discovered to be the earl's daughter) in one of Mr. Blaney's plays. His trousers were corduroy, his coat short-sleeved, with buttons in the middle of his back. One bootleg was outside the corduroys. You looked expectantly, though in vain, at his straw hat for ear holes, its shape inaugurating the suspicion that it had been ravaged from a former equine possessor. In his hand was a valise—description of it is an impossible task; a

Boston man would not have carried his lunch and law books to his office in it. And above one ear, in his hair, was a wisp of hay—the rustic's letter of credit, his badge of innocence, the last clinging touch of the Garden of Eden lingering to shame the gold-brick men.

Knowingly, smilingly, the city crowds passed him by. They saw the raw stranger stand in the gutter and stretch his neck at the tall buildings. At this they ceased to smile, and even to look at him. It had been done so often. A few glanced at the antique valise to see what Coney "attraction" or brand of chewing gum he might be thus dinning into his memory. But for the most part he was ignored. Even the newsboys looked bored when he scampered like a circus clown out of the way of cabs and street cars.

At Eighth Avenue stood "Bunco Harry," with his dyed mustache and shiny, good-natured eyes. Harry was too good an artist not to be pained at the sight of an actor overdoing his part. He edged up to the countryman, who had stopped to open his mouth at a jewelry store window, and shook his head.

"Too thick, pal," he said, critically—"too thick by a couple of inches. I don't know what your lay is; but you've got the properties on too thick. That hay, now—why, they don't even allow that on Proctor's circuit any more."

"I don't understand you, mister," said the green one. "I'm not lookin' for any circus. I've just run down from Ulster County to look at the town, bein' that the hayin's over with. Gosh! but it's a whopper. I thought Poughkeepsie was some punkins; but this here town is five times as big."

"Oh, well," said "Bunco Harry," raising his eyebrows, "I didn't mean to butt in. You don't have to tell. I thought you ought to tone down a little, so I tried to put you wise. Wish you success at your graft, whatever it is. Come and have a drink, anyhow."

"I wouldn't mind having a glass of lager beer," acknowledged the other.

They went to a café frequented by men with smooth faces and shifty eyes, and sat at their drinks.

"I'm glad I come across you, mister," said Haylocks. "How'd you like to play a game or two of seven-up? I've got the keerds."

He fished them out of Noah's valise—a rare, inimitable deck, greasy with bacon suppers and grimy with the soil of cornfields.

"Bunco Harry" laughed loud and briefly.

"Not for me, sport," he said, firmly. "I don't go against that make-up of yours for a cent. But I still say you've overdone it. The Reubs haven't dressed like that since '79. I doubt if you could work Brooklyn for a key-winding watch with that layout."

"Oh, you needn't think I ain't got the money," boasted Haylocks. He drew forth a tightly rolled mass of bills as large as a teacup, and laid it on the table.

"Got that for my share of grandmother's farm," he announced. "There's $950 in that roll. Thought I'd come to the city and look around for a likely business to go into."

"Bunco Harry" took up the roll of money and looked at it with almost respect in his smiling eyes.

"I've seen worse," he said, critically. "But you'll never do it in them clothes. You want to get light tan shoes and a black suit and a straw hat with a colored band, and talk a good deal about Pittsburg and freight differentials, and drink sherry for breakfast in order to work off phony stuff like that."

"What's his line?" asked two or three shifty-eyed men of "Bunco Harry" after Haylocks had gathered up his impugned money and departed.

"The queer, I guess," said Harry. "Or else he's one of Jerome's men. Or some guy with a new graft. He's too much hayseed. Maybe that his—I wonder now—oh, no, it couldn't have been real money."

Haylocks wandered on. Thirst probably assailed him again, for he dived into a dark groggery on a side street and bought beer. Several sinister fellows hung upon one end of the bar. At first sight of him their eyes brightened; but when his insistent and exaggerated rusticity became apparent their expressions changed to wary suspicion.

Haylocks swung his valise across the bar.

"Keep that a while for me, mister," he said, chewing at the end of a virulent claybank cigar. "I'll be back after I knock around a spell. And keep your eye on it, for there's $950 inside of it, though maybe you wouldn't think so to look at me."

Somewhere outside a phonograph struck up a band piece,

and Haylocks was off for it, his coat-tail buttons flopping in the middle of his back.

"Divvy, Mike," said the men hanging upon the bar, winking openly at one another.

"Honest, now," said the bartender, kicking the valise to one side. "You don't think I'd fall to that, do you? Anybody can see he ain't no jay. One of McAdoo's come-on squad, I guess. He's a shine if he made himself up. There ain't no parts of the country now where they dress like that since they run rural free delivery to Providence, Rhode Island. If he's got nine-fifty in that valise it's a ninety-eight cent Waterbury that's stopped at ten minutes to ten."

When Haylocks had exhausted the resources of Mr. Edison to amuse he returned for his valise. And then down Broadway he gallivanted, culling the sights with his eager blue eyes. But still and evermore Broadway rejected him with curt glances and sardonic smiles. He was the oldest of the "gags" that the city must endure. He was so flagrantly impossible, so ultra rustic, so exaggerated beyond the most freakish products of the barn-yard, the hayfield and the vaudeville stage, that he excited only weariness and suspicion. And the wisp of hay in his hair was so genuine, so fresh and redolent of the meadows, so clamorously rural that even a shell-game man would have put up his peas and folded his table at the sight of it.

Haylocks seated himself upon a flight of stone steps and once more exhumed his roll of yellow-backs from the valise. The outer one, a twenty, he shucked off and beckoned to a newsboy.

"Son," said he, "run somewhere and get this changed for me. I'm mighty nigh out of chicken feed. I guess you'll get a nickel if you'll hurry up."

A hurt look appeared through the dirt on the newsy's face.

"Aw, watchert'ink! G'wan and get yer funny bill changed yerself. Dey ain't no farm clothes yer got on. G'wan wit yer stage money."

On a corner lounged a keen-eyed steerer for a gambling-house. He saw Haylocks, and his expression suddenly grew cold and virtuous.

"Mister," said the rural one. "I've heard of places in this here town where a fellow could have a good game of old sledge or peg a card at keno. I got $950 in this valise, and I come down from old Ulster to see the sights. Know where a fellow could get action on about $9 or $10? I'm goin' to have some sport, and then maybe I'll buy out a business of some kind."

The steerer looked pained, and investigated a white speck on his left forefinger nail.

"Cheese it, old man," he murmured, reproachfully. "The Central Office must be bughouse to send you out looking like such a gillie. You couldn't get within two blocks of a sidewalk crap game in them Tony Pastor props. The recent Mr. Scotty from Death Valley has got you beat a crosstown block in the way of Elizabethan scenery and mechanical accessories. Let it be skiddoo for yours. Nay, I know of no gilded halls where one may bet a patrol wagon on the ace."

Rebuffed again by the great city that is so swift to detect artificialities, Haylocks sat upon the curb and presented his thoughts to hold a conference.

"It's my clothes," said he; "durned if it ain't. They think I'm a hayseed and won't have nothin' to do with me. Nobody never made fun of this hat in Ulster County. I guess if you want folks to notice you in New York you must dress up like they do."

So Haylocks went shopping in the bazaars where men spake through their noses and rubbed their hands and ran the tape line ecstatically over the bulge in his inside pocket where reposed a red nubbin of corn with an even number of rows. And messengers bearing parcels and boxes streamed to his hotel on Broadway within the lights of Long Acre.

At 9 o'clock in the evening one descended to the sidewalk whom Ulster County would have foresworn. Bright tan were his shoes; his hat the latest block. His light gray trousers were deeply creased; a gay blue silk handkerchief flapped from the breast pocket of his elegant English walking coat. His collar might have graced a laundry window; his blond hair was trimmed close; the wisp of hay was gone.

For an instant he stood, resplendent, with the leisurely air of a boulevardier concocting in his mind the route for his evening pleasures. And then he turned down the gay, bright street with the easy and graceful tread of a millionaire.

But in the instant that he had paused the wisest and keenest eyes in the city had enveloped him in their field of vision. A stout man with gray eyes picked two of his friends with a lift of his eyebrows from the row of loungers in front of the hotel.

"The juiciest jay I've seen in six months," said the man with gray eyes. "Come along."

It was half-past eleven when a man galloped into the West Forty-seventh Street Police Station with the story of his wrongs.

"Nine hundred and fifty dollars," he gasped, "all my share of grandmother's farm."

The desk sergeant wrung from him the name Jabez Bull-tongue, of Locust Valley farm, Ulster County, and then began to take descriptions of the strong-arm gentlemen.

When Conant went to see the editor about the fate of his poem, he was received over the head of the office boy into the inner office that is decorated with the statuettes by Rodin and J. G. Brown.

"When I read the first line of 'The Doe and the Brook,'" said the editor, "I knew it to be the work of one whose life has been heart to heart with Nature. The finished art of the line did not blind me to that fact. To use a somewhat homely comparison, it was as if a wild, free child of the woods and fields were to don the garb of fashion and walk down Broadway. Beneath the apparel the man would show."

"Thanks," said Conant. "I suppose the check will be round on Thursday, as usual."

The morals of this story have somehow gotten mixed. You can take your choice of "Stay on the Farm" or "Don't Write Poetry."

The Plutonian Fire

THERE ARE a few editor men with whom I am privileged to come in contact. It has not been long since it was their habit to come in contact with me. There is a difference.

They tell me that with a large number of the manuscripts that are submitted to them come advices (in the way of a boost) from the author asseverating that the incidents in the story are true. The destination of such contributions depends wholly upon the question of the inclosure of stamps. Some are returned, the rest are thrown on the floor in a corner on top of a pair of gum shoes, an overturned statuette of the Winged Victory, and a pile of old magazines containing a picture of the editor in the act of reading the latest copy of *Le Petit Journal*, right side up—you can tell by the illustrations. It is only a legend that there are waste baskets in editors' offices.

Thus is truth held in disrepute. But in time truth and science and nature will adapt themselves to art. Things will happen logically, and the villain be discomfited instead of being elected to the board of directors. But in the meantime fiction must not only be divorced from fact, but must pay alimony and be awarded custody of the press despatches.

This preamble is to warn you off the grade crossing of a true story. Being that, it shall be told simply, with conjunctions substituted for adjectives wherever possible, and whatever evidences of style may appear in it shall be due to the lino-type man. It is a story of the literary life in a great city, and it should be of interest to every author within a 20-mile radius of Gosport, Ind., whose desk holds a MS. story beginning thus: "While the cheers following his nomination were still ringing through the old court-house, Harwood broke away from the congratulating handclasps of his henchmen and hurried to Judge Creswell's house to find Ida."

Pettit came up out of Alabama to write fiction. The Southern papers had printed eight of his stories under an editorial caption identifying the author as the son of "the gallant Major Pettingill Pettit, our former County Attorney and hero of the battle of Lookout Mountain."

594

Pettit was a rugged fellow, with a kind of shame-faced culture, and my good friend. His father kept a general store in a little town called Hosea. Pettit had been raised in the pine-woods and broom-sedge fields adjacent thereto. He had in his gripsack two manuscript novels of the adventures in Picardy of one Gaston Laboulaye, Vicompte de Montrepos, in the year 1329. That's nothing. We all do that. And some day when we make a hit with the little sketch about a newsy and his lame dog, the editor prints the other one for us—or "on us," as the saying is—and then—and then we have to get a big valise and peddle those patent air-draft gas burners. At $1.25 everybody should have 'em.

I took Pettit to the red-brick house which was to appear in an article entitled "Literary Landmarks of Old New York," some day when we got through with it. He engaged a room there, drawing on the general store for his expenses. I showed New York to him, and he did not mention how much narrower Broadway is than Lee Avenue in Hosea. This seemed a good sign, so I put the final test.

"Suppose you try your hand at a descriptive article," I suggested, "giving your impressions of New York as seen from the Brooklyn Bridge. The fresh point of view, the——"

"Don't be a fool," said Pettit. "Let's go have some beer. On the whole I rather like the city."

We discovered and enjoyed the only true Bohemia. Every day and night we repaired to one of those palaces of marble and glass and tilework, where goes on a tremendous and sounding epic of life. Valhalla itself could not be more glorious and sonorous. The classic marble on which we ate, the great, light-flooded, vitreous front, adorned with snow-white scrolls; the grand Wagnerian din of clanking cups and bowls, the flashing staccato of brandishing cutlery, the piercing recitative of the white-aproned grub-maidens at the morgue-like banquet tables; the recurrent lied-motif of the cash-register—it was a gigantic, triumphant welding of art and sound, a deafening, soul-uplifting pageant of heroic and emblematic life. And the beans were only ten cents. We wondered why our fellow-artists cared to dine at sad little tables in their so-called Bohemian restaurants; and we shuddered lest they should seek out our resorts and make them conspicuous with their presence.

Pettit wrote many stories, which the editors returned to him. He wrote love stories, a thing I have always kept free from, holding the belief that the well-known and popular sentiment is not properly a matter for publication, but something to be privately handled by the alienists and florists. But the editors had told him that they wanted love stories, because they said the women read them.

Now, the editors are wrong about that, of course. Women do not read the love stories in the magazines. They read the poker-game stories and the recipes for cucumber lotion. The love stories are read by fat cigar drummers and little ten-year-old girls. I am not criticising the judgment of editors. They are mostly very fine men, but a man can be but one man, with individual opinions and tastes. I knew two associate editors of a magazine who were wonderfully alike in almost everything. And yet one of them was very fond of Flaubert, while the other preferred gin.

Pettit brought me his returned manuscripts, and we looked them over together to find out why they were not accepted. They seemed to me pretty fair stories, written in a good style, and ended, as they should, at the bottom of the last page.

They were well constructed and the events were marshalled in orderly and logical sequence. But I thought I detected a lack of living substance—it was much as if I gazed at a symmetrical array of presentable clamshells from which the succulent and vital inhabitants had been removed. I intimated that the author might do well to get better acquainted with his theme.

"You sold a story last week," said Pettit, "about a gun fight in an Arizona mining town in which the hero drew his Colt's .45 and shot seven bandits as fast as they came in the door. Now, if a six-shooter could——"

"Oh, well," said I, "that's different. Arizona is a long way from New York. I could have a man stabbed with a lariat or chased by a pair of chaparreras if I wanted to, and it wouldn't be noticed until the usual error-sharp from around McAdams Junction isolates the erratum and writes in to the papers about it. But you are up against another proposition. This thing they call love is as common around New York as it is in Sheboygan during the young onion season. It may be mixed here with a little commercialism—they read Byron, but they look up

Bradstreet's, too, while they're among the B's, and Brigham also if they have time—but it's pretty much the same old internal disturbance everywhere. You can fool an editor with a fake picture of a cowboy mounting a pony with his left hand on the saddle horn, but you can't put him up a tree with a love story. So, you've got to fall in love and then write the real thing."

Pettit did. I never knew whether he was taking my advice or whether he fell an accidental victim.

There was a girl he had met at one of these studio contrivances—a glorious, impudent, lucid, open-minded girl with hair the color of Culmbacher, and a good-natured way of despising you. She was a New York girl.

Well (as the narrative style permits us to say infrequently), Pettit went to pieces. All those pains, those lover's doubts, those heart-burnings and tremors of which he had written so unconvincingly were his. Talk about Shylock's pound of flesh! Twenty-five pounds Cupid got from Pettit. Which is the usurer?

One night Pettit came to my room exalted. Pale and haggard but exalted. She had given him a jonquil.

"Old Hoss," said he, with a new smile flickering around his mouth, "I believe I could write that story to-night—the one, you know, that is to win out. I can feel it. I don't know whether it will come out or not, but I can feel it."

I pushed him out of my door. "Go to your room and write it," I ordered. "Else I can see your finish. I told you this must come first. Write it to-night and put it under my door when it is done. Put it under my door to-night when it is finished—don't keep it until to-morrow."

I was reading my bully old pal Montaigne at two o'clock when I heard the sheets rustle under my door. I gathered them up and read the story.

The hissing of geese, the languishing cooing of doves, the braying of donkeys, the chatter of irresponsible sparrows—these were in my mind's ear as I read. "Suffering Sappho!" I exclaimed to myself. "Is this the divine fire that is supposed to ignite genius and make it practicable and wage-earning?"

The story was sentimental drivel, full of whimpering soft-heartedness and gushing egoism. All the art that Pettit had acquired was gone. A perusal of its buttery phrases would have made a cynic of a sighing chambermaid.

In the morning Pettit came to my room. I read him his doom mercilessly. He laughed idiotically.

"All right, Old Hoss," he said, cheerily, "make cigar-lighters of it. What's the difference? I'm going to take her to lunch at Claremont to-day."

There was about a month of it. And then Pettit came to me bearing an invisible mitten, with the fortitude of a dish-rag. He talked of the grave and South America and prussic acid; and I lost an afternoon getting him straight. I took him out and saw that large and curative doses of whiskey were administered to him. I warned you this was a true story—'ware your white ribbons if you follow this tale. For two weeks I fed him whiskey and Omar, and read to him regularly every evening the column in the evening paper that reveals the secrets of female beauty. I recommend the treatment.

After Pettit was cured he wrote more stories. He recovered his old-time facility and did work just short of good enough. Then the curtain rose on the third act.

A little, dark-eyed, silent girl from New Hampshire, who was studying applied design, fell deeply in love with him. She was the intense sort, but externally *glacé*, such as New England sometimes fools us with. Pettit liked her mildly, and took her about a good deal. She worshipped him, and now and then bored him.

There came a climax when she tried to jump out of a window, and he had to save her by some perfunctory, unmeant wooing. Even I was shaken by the depths of the absorbing affection she showed. Home, friends, traditions, creeds went up like thistledown in the scale against her love. It was really discomposing.

One night again Pettit sauntered in, yawning. As he had told me before, he said he felt that he could do a great story, and as before I hunted him to his room and saw him open his inkstand. At one o'clock the sheets of paper slid under my door.

I read that story, and I jumped up, late as it was, with a whoop of joy. Old Pettit had done it. Just as though it lay there, red and bleeding, a woman's heart was written into the lines. You couldn't see the joining, but art, exquisite art, and pulsing nature had been combined into a love story that took you by the throat like the quinsy. I broke into Pettit's room and beat him on the back and called him names—names high up in the galaxy of the immortals that we admired. And Pettit yawned and begged to be allowed to sleep.

On the morrow, I dragged him to an editor. The great man read, and, rising, gave Pettit his hand. That was a decoration, a wreath of bay, and a guarantee of rent.

And then old Pettit smiled slowly. I call him Gentleman Pettit now to myself. It's a miserable name to give a man, but it sounds better than it looks in print.

"I see," said old Pettit, as he took up his story and began tearing it into small strips. "I see the game now. You can't write with ink, and you can't write with your own heart's blood, but you can write with the heart's blood of some one else. You have to be a cad before you can be an artist. Well, I am for old Alabam and the Major's store. Have you got a light, Old Hoss?"

I went with Pettit to the dépôt and died hard.

"Shakespeare's sonnets?" I blurted, making a last stand. "How about him?"

"A cad," said Pettit. "They give it to you, and you sell it—love, you know. I'd rather sell ploughs for father."

"But," I protested, "you are reversing the decision of the world's greatest——"

"Good-by, Old Hoss," said Pettit.

"Critics," I continued. "But—say—if the Major can use a fairly good salesman and bookkeeper down there in the store, let me know, will you?"

The Last Leaf

IN A little district west of Washington Square the streets have run crazy and broken themselves into small strips called "places." These "places" make strange angles and curves. (One street crosses itself a time or two. An artist once discovered a valuable possibility in this street. Suppose a collector with a bill for paints, paper and canvas should, in traversing this route, suddenly meet himself coming back, without a cent having been paid on account!)

So, to quaint old Greenwich Village the art people soon came prowling, hunting for north windows and eighteenth-century gables and Dutch attics and low rents. Then they imported some pewter mugs and a chafing dish or two from Sixth avenue, and became a "colony."

At the top of a squatty, three-story brick Sue and Johnsy had their studio. "Johnsy" was familiar for Joanna. One was from Maine; the other from California. They had met at the *table d'hôte* of an Eighth street "Delmonico's," and found their tastes in art, chicory salad and bishop sleeves so congenial that the joint studio resulted.

That was in May. In November a cold, unseen stranger, whom the doctors called Pneumonia, stalked about the colony, touching one here and there with his icy finger. Over on the east side this ravager strode boldly, smiting his victims by scores, but his feet trod slowly through the maze of the narrow and moss-grown "places."

Mr. Pneumonia was not what you would call a chivalric old gentleman. A mite of a little woman with blood thinned by California zephyrs was hardly fair game for the red-fisted, short-breathed old duffer. But Johnsy he smote; and she lay, scarcely moving, on her painted iron bedstead, looking through the small Dutch window-panes at the blank side of the next brick house.

One morning the busy doctor invited Sue into the hallway with a shaggy, gray eyebrow.

"She has one chance in—let us say, ten," he said; as he shook down the mercury in his clinical thermometer. "And that chance is for her to want to live. This way people have of lining-up on the side of the undertaker makes the entire pharmacopeia look silly. Your little lady has made up her mind that she's not going to get well. Has she anything on her mind?"

"She—she wanted to paint the Bay of Naples some day," said Sue.

"Paint?—bosh! Has she anything on her mind worth thinking about twice—a man, for instance?"

"A man?" said Sue, with a jews-harp twang in her voice. "Is a man worth—but, no, doctor; there is nothing of the kind."

"Well, it is the weakness, then," said the doctor. "I will do all that science, so far as it may filter through my efforts, can accomplish. But whenever my patient begins to count the carriages in her funeral procession I subtract 50 per cent. from the curative power of medicines. If you will get her to ask one question about the new winter styles in cloak sleeves I will promise you a one-in-five chance for her, instead of one in ten."

After the doctor had gone Sue went into the workroom and cried a Japanese napkin to a pulp. Then she swaggered into Johnsy's room with her drawing board, whistling ragtime.

Johnsy lay, scarcely making a ripple under the bedclothes, with her face toward the window. Sue stopped whistling, thinking she was asleep.

She arranged her board and began a pen-and-ink drawing to illustrate a magazine story. Young artists must pave their way to Art by drawing pictures for magazine stories that young authors write to pave their way to Literature.

As Sue was sketching a pair of elegant horse-show riding trousers and a monocle on the figure of the hero, an Idaho cowboy, she heard a low sound, several times repeated. She went quickly to the bedside.

Johnsy's eyes were open wide. She was looking out the window and counting—counting backward.

"Twelve," she said, and a little later "eleven"; and then "ten," and "nine"; and then "eight" and "seven," almost together.

Sue looked solicitously out the window. What was there to count? There was only a bare, dreary yard to be seen, and the blank side of the brick house twenty feet away. An old, old ivy vine, gnarled and decayed at the roots, climbed half way up the brick wall. The cold breath of autumn had stricken its leaves from the vine until its skeleton branches clung, almost bare, to the crumbling bricks.

"What is it, dear?" asked Sue.

"Six," said Johnsy, in almost a whisper. "They're falling faster now. Three days ago there were almost a hundred. It made my head ache to count them. But now it's easy. There goes another one. There are only five left now."

"Five what, dear. Tell your Sudie."

"Leaves. On the ivy vine. When the last one falls I must go, too. I've known that for three days. Didn't the doctor tell you?"

"Oh, I never heard of such nonsense," complained Sue, with magnificent scorn. "What have old ivy leaves to do with your getting well? And you used to love that vine so, you naughty girl. Don't be a goosey. Why, the doctor told me this morning that your chances for getting well real soon were—let's see exactly what he said—he said the chances were ten to one! Why, that's almost as good a chance as we have in New York when we ride on the street cars or walk past a new building. Try to take some broth now, and let Sudie go back to her drawing, so she can sell the editor man with it, and buy port wine for her sick child, and pork chops for her greedy self."

"You needn't get any more wine," said Johnsy, keeping her eyes fixed out the window. "There goes another. No, I don't want any broth. That leaves just four. I want to see the last one fall before it gets dark. Then I'll go, too."

"Johnsy, dear," said Sue, bending over her, "will you promise me to keep your eyes closed, and not look out the window until I am done working? I must hand those drawings in by to-morrow. I need the light, or I would draw the shade down."

"Couldn't you draw in the other room?" asked Johnsy, coldly.

"I'd rather be here by you," said Sue. "Besides, I don't want you to keep looking at those silly ivy leaves."

"Tell me as soon as you have finished," said Johnsy, closing her eyes, and lying white and still as a fallen statue, "because I want to see the last one fall. I'm tired of waiting. I'm tired of thinking. I want to turn loose my hold on everything, and go sailing down, down, just like one of those poor, tired leaves."

"Try to sleep," said Sue. "I must call Behrman up to be my model for the old hermit miner. I'll not be gone a minute. Don't try to move 'till I come back."

Old Behrman was a painter who lived on the ground floor beneath them. He was past sixty and had a Michael Angelo's Moses beard curling down from the head of a satyr along the body of an imp. Behrman was a failure in art. Forty years he had wielded the brush without getting near enough to touch the hem of his Mistress's robe. He had been always about to paint a masterpiece, but had never yet begun it. For several years he had painted nothing except now and then a daub in the line of commerce or advertising. He earned a little by serving as a model to those young artists in the colony who could not pay the price of a professional. He drank gin to excess, and still talked of his coming masterpiece. For the rest he was a fierce little old man, who scoffed terribly at softness in any one, and who regarded himself as especial mastiff-in-waiting to protect the two young artists in the studio above.

Sue found Behrman smelling strongly of juniper berries in his dimly lighted den below. In one corner was a blank canvas on an easel that had been waiting there for twenty-five years to receive the first line of the masterpiece. She told him of Johnsy's fancy, and how she feared she would, indeed, light and fragile as a leaf herself, float away when her slight hold upon the world grew weaker.

Old Behrman, with his red eyes plainly streaming, shouted his contempt and derision for such idiotic imaginings.

"Vass!" he cried. "Is dere people in de world mit der foolishness to die because leafs dey drop off from a confounded vine? I haf not heard of such a thing. No, I vill not bose as a model for your fool hermit-dunderhead. Vy do you allow dot silly pusiness to come in der prain of her? Ach, dot poor lettle Miss Johnsy."

"She is very ill and weak," said Sue, "and the fever has left her mind morbid and full of strange fancies. Very well, Mr. Behrman, if you do not care to pose for me, you needn't. But I think you are a horrid old—old flibbertigibbet."

"You are just like a woman!" yelled Behrman. "Who said I vill not bose? Go on. I come mit you. For half an hour I haf

peen trying to say dot I am ready to bose. Gott! dis is not any
blace in which one so goot as Miss Yohnsy shall lie sick. Some
day I vill baint a masterpiece, and ve shall all go avay. Gott! yes."

Johnsy was sleeping when they went upstairs. Sue pulled the
shade down to the window-sill, and motioned Behrman into
the other room. In there they peered out the window fearfully
at the ivy vine. Then they looked at each other for a moment
without speaking. A persistent, cold rain was falling, mingled
with snow. Behrman, in his old blue shirt, took his seat as the
hermit-miner on an upturned kettle for a rock.

When Sue awoke from an hour's sleep the next morning she
found Johnsy with dull, wide-open eyes staring at the drawn
green shade.

"Pull it up; I want to see," she ordered, in a whisper.

Wearily Sue obeyed.

But, lo! after the beating rain and fierce gusts of wind that
had endured through the livelong night, there yet stood out
against the brick wall one ivy leaf. It was the last on the vine.
Still dark green near its stem, but with its serrated edges tinted
with the yellow of dissolution and decay, it hung bravely from
a branch some twenty feet above the ground.

"It is the last one," said Johnsy. "I thought it would surely
fall during the night. I heard the wind. It will fall to-day, and I
shall die at the same time."

"Dear, dear!" said Sue, leaning her worn face down to the
pillow, "think of me, if you won't think of yourself. What would
I do?"

But Johnsy did not answer. The lonesomest thing in all the
world is a soul when it is making ready to go on its mysterious,
far journey. The fancy seemed to possess her more strongly as
one by one the ties that bound her to friendship and to earth
were loosed.

The day wore away, and even through the twilight they
could see the lone ivy leaf clinging to its stem against the wall.
And then, with the coming of the night, the north wind was
again loosed, while the rain still beat against the windows and
pattered down from the low Dutch eaves.

When it was light enough Johnsy, the merciless, commanded
that the shade be raised.

The ivy leaf was still there.

Johnsy lay for a long time looking at it. And then she called to Sue, who was stirring her chicken broth over the gas stove.

"I've been a bad girl, Sudie," said Johnsy. "Something has made that last leaf stay there to show me how wicked I was. It is a sin to want to die. You may bring me a little broth now, and some milk with a little port in it, and—no; bring me a hand-mirror first; and then pack some pillows about me, and I will sit up and watch you cook."

An hour later she said:

"Sudie, some day I hope to paint the Bay of Naples."

The doctor came in the afternoon, and Sue had an excuse to go into the hallway as he left.

"Even chances," said the doctor, taking Sue's thin, shaking hand in his. "With good nursing you'll win. And now I must see another case I have downstairs. Behrman, his name is—some kind of an artist, I believe. Pneumonia, too. He is an old, weak man, and the attack is acute. There is no hope for him; but he goes to the hospital to-day to be made more comfortable."

The next day the doctor said to Sue: "She's out of danger. You've won. Nutrition and care now—that's all."

And that afternoon Sue came to the bed where Johnsy lay, contentedly knitting a very blue and very useless woolen shoulder scarf, and put one arm around her, pillows and all.

"I have something to tell you, white mouse," she said. "Mr. Behrman died of pneumonia to-day in the hospital. He was ill only two days. The janitor found him on the morning of the first day in his room downstairs helpless with pain. His shoes and clothing were wet through and icy cold. They couldn't imagine where he had been on such a dreadful night. And then they found a lantern, still lighted, and a ladder that had been dragged from its place, and some scattered brushes, and a palette with green and yellow colors mixed on it, and—look out the window, dear, at the last ivy leaf on the wall. Didn't you wonder why it never fluttered or moved when the wind blew? Ah, darling, it's Behrman's masterpiece—he painted it there the night that the last leaf fell."

Elsie in New York

No, BUMPTIOUS reader, this story is not a continuation of the Elsie series. But if your Elsie had lived over here in our big city there might have been a chapter in her books not very different from this.

Especially for the vagrant feet of youth are the roads of Manhattan beset "with pitfall and with gin." But the civic guardians of the young have made themselves acquainted with the snares of the wicked, and most of the dangerous paths are patrolled by their agents, who seek to turn straying ones away from the peril that menaces them. And this will tell you how they guided my Elsie safely through all peril to the goal that she was seeking.

Elsie's father had been a cutter for Fox & Otter, cloaks and furs, on lower Broadway. He was an old man, with a slow and limping gait, so a pot-hunter of a newly licensed chauffeur ran him down one day when livelier game was scarce. They took the old man home, where he lay on his bed for a year and then died, leaving $2.50 in cash and a letter from Mr. Otter offering to do anything he could to help his faithful old employee. The old cutter regarded this letter as a valuable legacy to his daughter, and he put it into her hands with pride as the shears of the dread Cleaner and Repairer snipped off his thread of life.

That was the landlord's cue; and forth he came and did his part in the great eviction scene. There was no snowstorm ready for Elsie to steal out into, drawing her little red woollen shawl about her shoulders, but she went out, regardless of the unities. And as for the red shawl—back to Blaney with it! Elsie's fall tan coat was cheap, but it had the style and fit of the best at Fox & Otter's. And her lucky stars had given her good looks, and eyes as blue and innocent as the new shade of note paper, and she had $1 left of the $2.50. And the letter from Mr. Otter. Keep your eye on the letter from Mr. Otter. That is the clue. I desire that everything be made plain as we go. Detective stories are so plentiful now that they do not sell.

And so we find Elsie, thus equipped, starting out in the world to seek her fortune. One trouble about the letter from Mr. Otter was that it did not bear the new address of the firm, which had moved about a month before. But Elsie thought she could find it. She had heard that policemen, when politely addressed, or thumbscrewed by an investigation committee, will give up information and addresses. So she boarded a down-town car at One Hundred and Seventy-seventh street and rode south to Forty-second, which she thought must surely be the end of the island. There she stood against the wall undecided, for the city's roar and dash was new to her. Up where she had lived was rural New York, so far out that the milkmen awaken you in the morning by the squeaking of pumps instead of the rattling of cans.

A kind-faced, sunburned young man in a soft-brimmed hat went past Elsie into the Grand Central Depot. That was Hank Ross, of the Sunflower Ranch, in Idaho, on his way home from a visit to the East. Hank's heart was heavy, for the Sunflower Ranch was a lonesome place, lacking the presence of a woman. He had hoped to find one during his visit who would conge-nially share his prosperity and home, but the girls of Gotham had not pleased his fancy. But, as he passed in, he noted, with a jumping of his pulses, the sweet, ingenuous face of Elsie and her pose of doubt and loneliness. With true and honest West-ern impulse he said to himself that here was his mate. He could love her, he knew; and he would surround her with so much comfort, and cherish her so carefully that she would be happy, and make two sunflowers grow on the ranch where there grew but one before.

Hank turned and went back to her. Backed by his never before questioned honesty of purpose, he approached the girl and removed his soft-brimmed hat. Elsie had but time to sum up his handsome frank face with one shy look of modest ad-miration when a burly cop hurled himself upon the ranchman, seized him by the collar and backed him against the wall. Two blocks away a burglar was coming out of an apartment-house with a bag of silverware on his shoulder; but that is neither here nor there.

"Carry on yez mashin' tricks right before me eyes, will yez?" shouted the cop. "I'll teach yez to speak to ladies on me beat that ye're not acquainted with. Come along."

Elsie turned away with a sigh as the ranchman was dragged away. She had liked the effect of his light blue eyes against his tanned complexion. She walked southward, thinking herself already in the district where her father used to work, and hoping to find some one who could direct her to the firm of Fox & Otter.

But did she want to find Mr. Otter? She had inherited much of the old cutter's independence. How much better it would be if she could find work and support herself without calling on him for aid!

Elsie saw a sign "Employment Agency" and went in. Many girls were sitting against the wall in chairs. Several well-dressed ladies were looking them over. One white-haired, kind-faced old lady in rustling black silk hurried up to Elsie.

"My dear," she said in a sweet, gentle voice, "are you looking for a position? I like your face and appearance so much. I want a young woman who will be half maid and half companion to me. You will have a good home and I will pay you $30 a month."

Before Elsie could stammer forth her gratified acceptance, a young woman with gold glasses on her bony nose and her hands in her jacket pockets seized her arm and drew her aside.

"I am Miss Ticklebaum," said she, "of the Association for the Prevention of Jobs Being Put Up on Working Girls Looking for Jobs. We prevented forty-seven girls from securing positions last week. I am here to protect you. Beware of any one who offers you a job. How do you know that this woman does not want to make you work as a breaker-boy in a coal mine or murder you to get your teeth? If you accept work of any kind without permission of our association you will be arrested by one of our agents."

"But what am I to do?" asked Elsie. "I have no home or money. I must do something. Why am I not allowed to accept this kind lady's offer?"

"I do not know," said Miss Ticklebaum. "That is the affair of our Committee on the Abolishment of Employers. It is my duty simply to see that you do not get work. You will give me your name and address and report to our secretary every Thursday. We have 600 girls on the waiting list who will in time be allowed to accept positions as vacancies occur on our roll of Qualified Employers, which now comprises twenty-seven names. There is prayer, music and lemonade in our chapel the third Sunday of every month."

Elsie hurried away after thanking Miss Ticklebaum for her timely warning and advice. After all, it seemed that she must try to find Mr. Otter.

But after walking a few blocks she saw a sign, "Cashier wanted," in the window of a confectionery store. In she went and applied for the place, after casting a quick glance over her shoulder to assure herself that the job-preventer was not on her trail.

The proprietor of the confectionery was a benevolent old man with a peppermint flavor, who decided, after questioning Elsie pretty closely, that she was the very girl he wanted. Her services were needed at once, so Elsie, with a thankful heart, drew off her tan coat and prepared to mount the cashier's stool.

But before she could do so a gaunt lady wearing steel spectacles and black mittens stood before her, with a long finger pointing, and exclaimed: "Young woman, hesitate!"

Elsie hesitated.

"Do you know," said the black-and-steel lady, "that in accepting this position you may this day cause the loss of a hundred lives in agonizing physical torture and the sending as many souls to perdition?"

"Why, no," said Elsie, in frightened tones. "How could I do that?"

"Rum," said the lady—"the demon rum. Do you know why so many lives are lost when a theatre catches fire? Brandy balls. The demon rum lurking in brandy balls. Our society women while in theatres sit grossly intoxicated from eating these candies filled with brandy. When the fire fiend sweeps down upon them they are unable to escape. The candy stores are the devil's distilleries. If you assist in the distribution of these insidious confections you assist in the destruction of the bodies and souls of your fellow-beings, and in the filling of our jails, asylums and almshouses. Think, girl, ere you touch the money for which brandy balls are sold.

"Dear me," said Elsie, bewildered. "I didn't know there was rum in brandy balls. But I must live by some means. What shall I do?"

"Decline the position," said the lady, "and come with me. I will tell you what to do."

After Elsie had told the confectioner that she had changed her mind about the cashiership she put on her coat and followed the lady to the sidewalk, where awaited an elegant victoria.

"Seek some other work," said the black-and-steel lady, "and assist in crushing the hydra-headed demon rum." And she got into the victoria and drove away.

"I guess that puts it up to Mr. Otter again," said Elsie, ruefully, turning down the street. "And I'm sorry, too, for I'd much rather make my way without help."

Near Fourteenth street Elsie saw a placard tacked on the side of a doorway that read: "Fifty girls, neat sewers, wanted immediately on theatrical costumes. Good pay."

She was about to enter, when a solemn man, dressed all in black, laid his hand on her arm.

"My dear girl," he said, "I entreat you not to enter that dressing-room of the devil."

"Goodness me!" exclaimed Elsie, with some impatience. "The devil seems to have a cinch on all the business in New York. What's wrong about the place?"

"It is here," said the solemn man, "that the regalia of Satan—in other words, the costumes worn on the stage—are manufactured. The stage is the road to ruin and destruction. Would you imperil your soul by lending the work of your hands to its support? Do you know, my dear girl, what the theatre leads to? Do you know where actors and actresses go after the curtain of the playhouse has fallen upon them for the last time?"

"Sure," said Elsie. "Into vaudeville. But do you think it would be wicked for me to make a little money to live on by sewing? I must get something to do pretty soon."

"The flesh-pots of Egypt," exclaimed the reverend gentleman, uplifting his hands. "I beseech you, my child, to turn away from this place of sin and iniquity."

"But what will I do for a living?" asked Elsie. "I don't care to sew for this musical comedy, if it's as rank as you say it is; but I've got to have a job."

"The Lord will provide," said the solemn man. "There is a free Bible class every Sunday afternoon in the basement of the cigar store next to the church. Peace be with you. Amen. Farewell."

Elsie went on her way. She was soon in the downtown district where factories abound. On a large brick building was a gilt sign, "Posey & Trimmer, Artificial Flowers." Below it was hung a newly stretched canvas bearing the words, "Five hundred girls wanted to learn trade. Good wages from the start. Apply one flight up."

Elsie started toward the door, near which were gathered in groups some twenty or thirty girls. One big girl with a black straw hat tipped down over her eyes stepped in front of her.

"Say, you'se," said the girl, "are you'se goin' in there after a job?"

"Yes," said Elsie; "I must have work."

"Now, don't do it," said the girl. "I'm chairman of our Scab Committee. There's 400 of us girls locked out just because we demanded 50 cents a week raise in wages, and ice water, and for the foreman to shave off his mustache. You're too nice a looking girl to be a scab. Wouldn't you please help us along by trying to find a job somewhere else, or would you'se rather have your face pushed in?"

"I'll try somewhere else," said Elsie.

She walked aimlessly eastward on Broadway, and there her heart leaped to see the sign, "Fox & Otter," stretching entirely across the front of a tall building. It was as though an unseen guide had led her to it through the by-ways of her fruitless search for work.

She hurried into the store and sent in to Mr. Otter by a clerk her name and the letter he had written her father. She was shown directly into his private office.

Mr. Otter arose from his desk as Elsie entered and took both hands with a hearty smile of welcome. He was a slightly corpulent man of nearly middle age, a little bald, gold spectacled, polite, well dressed, radiating.

"Well, well, and so this is Beatty's little daughter! Your father was one of our most efficient and valued employees. He left nothing? Well, well. I hope we have not forgotten his faithful services. I am sure there is a vacancy now among our models. Oh, it is easy work—nothing easier."

Mr. Otter struck a bell. A long-nosed clerk thrust a portion of himself inside the door.

"Send Miss Hawkins in," said Mr. Otter. Miss Hawkins came.

"Miss Hawkins," said Mr. Otter, "bring for Miss Beatty to try on one of those Russian sable coats and—let's see—one of those latest model black tulle hats with white tips."

Elsie stood before the full-length mirror with pink cheeks and quick breath. Her eyes shone like faint stars. She was beautiful. Alas! she was beautiful.

I wish I could stop this story here. Confound it! I will. No; it's got to run it out. I didn't make it up. I'm just repeating it.

I'd like to throw bouquets at the wise cop, and the lady who rescues Girls from Jobs, and the prohibitionist who is trying to crush brandy balls, and the sky pilot who objects to costumes for stage people (there are others), and all the thousands of good people who are at work protecting young people from the pitfalls of a great city; and then wind up by pointing out how they were the means of Elsie reaching her father's benefactor and her kind friend and rescuer from poverty. This would make a fine Elsie story of the old sort. I'd like to do this; but there's just a word or two to follow.

While Elsie was admiring herself in the mirror, Mr. Otter went to the telephone booth and called up some number. Don't ask me what it was.

"Oscar," said he, "I want you to reserve the same table for me this evening. . . . What? Why, the one in the Moorish room to the left of the shrubbery. . . . Yes; two. . . . Yes, the usual brand; and the '85 Johannisburger with the roast. If it isn't the right temperature I'll break your neck. . . . No; not her . . . No, indeed . . . A new one—a peacherino, Oscar, a peacherino!"

Tired and tiresome reader, I will conclude, if you please, with a paraphrase of a few words that you will remember were written by him—by him of Gad's Hill, before whom, if you doff not your hat, you shall stand with a covered pumpkin—aye, sir, a pumpkin.

Lost, Your Excellency. Lost, Associations and Societies. Lost, Right Reverends and Wrong Reverends of every order. Lost, Reformers and Lawmakers, born with heavenly compassion in your hearts, but with the reverence of money in your souls. And lost thus around us every day.

The Purple Dress

W<small>E ARE</small> to consider the shade known as purple. It is a color justly in repute among the sons and daughters of man. Emperors claim it for their especial dye. Good fellows everywhere seek to bring their noses to the genial hue that follows the commingling of the red and blue. We say of princes that they are born to the purple; and no doubt they are, for the colic tinges their faces with the royal tint equally with the snub-nosed countenance of a woodchopper's brat. All women love it—when it is the fashion.

And now purple is being worn. You notice it on the streets. Of course other colors are quite stylish as well—in fact, I saw a lovely thing the other day in olive green albatross, with a triple-lapped flounce skirt trimmed with insert squares of silk, and a draped fichu of lace opening over a shirred vest and double puff sleeves with a lace band holding two gathered frills—but you see lots of purple too. Oh, yes, you do; just take a walk down Twenty-third street any afternoon.

Therefore Maida—the girl with the big brown eyes and cinnamon-colored hair in the Bee-Hive Store—said to Grace—the girl with the rhinestone brooch and pepperment-pepsin flavor to her speech—"I'm going to have a purple dress—a tailor-made purple dress—for Thanksgiving."

"Oh, are you," said Grace, putting away some 7½ gloves into the 6¾ box. "Well, it's red for me. You see more red on Fifth avenue. And the men all seem to like it."

"I like purple best," said Maida. "And old Schlegel has promised to make it for $8. It's going to be lovely. I'm going to have a plaited skirt and a blouse coat trimmed with a band of galloon under a white cloth collar with two rows of—"

"Sly boots!" said Grace with an educated wink.

"—soutache braid over a surpliced white vest; and a plaited basque and—"

"Sly boots—sly boots!" repeated Grace.

"—plaited gigot sleeves with a drawn velvet ribbon over an inside cuff. What do you mean by saying that?"

"You think Mr. Ramsay likes purple. I heard him say yesterday he thought some of the dark shades of red were stunning."

"I don't care," said Maida. "I prefer purple, and them that don't like it can just take the other side of the street."

Which suggests the thought that after all, the followers of purple may be subject to slight delusions. Danger is near when a maiden thinks she can wear purple regardless of complexions and opinions; and when Emperors think their purple robes will wear forever.

Maida had saved $18 after eight months of economy; and this had bought the goods for the purple dress and paid Schlegel $4 on the making of it. On the day before Thanksgiving she would have just enough to pay the remaining $4. And then for a holiday in a new dress—can earth offer anything more enchanting?

Old Bachman, the proprietor of the Bee-Hive Store, always gave a Thanksgiving dinner to his employees. On every one of the subsequent 364 days, excusing Sundays, he would remind them of the joys of the past banquet and the hopes of the coming ones, thus inciting them to increased enthusiasm in work. The dinner was given in the store on one of the long tables in the middle of the room. They tacked wrapping paper over the front windows; and the turkeys and other good things were brought in the back way from the restaurant on the corner. You will perceive that the Bee-Hive was not a fashionable department store, with escalators and pompadours. It was almost small enough to be called an emporium; and you could actually go in there and get waited on and walk out again. And always at the Thanksgiving dinners Mr. Ramsay—

Oh, bother! I should have mentioned Mr. Ramsay first of all. He is more important than purple or green, or even the red cranberry sauce.

Mr. Ramsay was the head clerk; and as far as I am concerned I am for him. He never pinched the girls' arms when he passed them in dark corners of the store; and when he told them stories when business was dull and the girls giggled and said: "Oh, pshaw!" it wasn't G. Bernard they meant at all. Besides being a gentleman, Mr. Ramsay was queer and original in other ways. He was a health crank, and believed that people should never eat anything that was good for them. He was violently opposed to anybody being comfortable, and coming in out of snow storms, or wearing overshoes, or taking medicine, or coddling themselves in any way. Every one of the ten girls in the store had little pork-chop-and-fried-onion dreams every night of becoming Mrs. Ramsay. For, next year old Bachman was going to take him in for a partner. And each one of them knew that if she should catch him she would knock those cranky health notions of his sky high before the wedding cake indigestion was over.

Mr. Ramsay was master of ceremonies at the dinners. Always they had two Italians in to play a violin and harp and had a little dance in the store.

And here were two dresses being conceived to charm Ramsay—one purple and the other red. Of course, the other eight girls were going to have dresses too, but they didn't count. Very likely they'd wear some shirt-waist-and-black-skirt-affairs—nothing as resplendent as purple or red.

Grace had saved her money, too. She was going to buy her dress ready-made. "Oh, what's the use of bothering with a tailor—when you've got a figger it's easy to get a fit—the ready-made are intended for a perfect figger—except I have to have 'em all taken in at the waist—the average figger is so large waisted."

The night before Thanksgiving came. Maida hurried home, keen and bright with the thoughts of the blessed morrow. Her thoughts were of purple, but they were white themselves—the joyous enthusiasm of the young for the pleasures that youth must have or wither. She knew purple would become her, and—for the thousandth time she tried to assure herself that it was purple Mr. Ramsay said he liked and not red. She was going home first to get the $4 wrapped in a piece of tissue paper in the bottom drawer of her dresser, and then she was going to pay Schlegel and take the dress home herself.

Grace lived in the same house. She occupied the hall room above Maida's.

At home Maida found clamor and confusion. The landlady's tongue clattering sourly in the halls like a churn dasher dabbling in buttermilk. And then Grace came down to her room crying with eyes as red as any dress.

"She says I've got to get out," said Grace. "The old beast.

Because I owe her $4. She's put my trunk in the hall and locked the door. I can't go anywhere else. I haven't got a cent of money."

"You had some yesterday," said Maida.

"I paid it on my dress," said Grace. "I thought she'd wait till next week for the rent."

Sniffle, sniffle, sob, sniffle.

Out came—out it had to come—Maida's $4.

"You blessed darling," cried Grace, now a rainbow instead of sunset. "I'll pay the mean old thing and then I'm going to try on my dress. I think it's heavenly. Come up and look at it. I'll pay the money back, a dollar a week—honest I will."

Thanksgiving.

The dinner was to be at noon. At a quarter to twelve Grace switched into Maida's room. Yes, she looked charming. Red was her color. Maida sat by the window in her old cheviot skirt and blue waist darning a st—. Oh, doing fancy work.

"Why, goodness me! ain't you dressed yet?" shrilled the red one. "How does it fit in the back? Don't you think these velvet tabs look awful swell? Why ain't you dressed, Maida?"

"My dress didn't get finished in time," said Maida. "I'm not going to the dinner."

"That's too bad. Why, I'm awful sorry Maida. Why don't you put on anything and come along—it's just the store folks, you know, and they won't mind."

"I was set on my purple," said Maida. "If I can't have it I won't go at all. Don't bother about me. Run along or you'll be late. You look awful nice in red."

At her window Maida sat through the long morning and past the time of the dinner at the store. In her mind she could hear the girls shrieking over a pull-bone, could hear old Bachman's roar over his own deeply-concealed jokes, could see the diamonds of fat Mrs. Bachman, who came to the store only on Thanksgiving days, could see Mr. Ramsay moving about alert, kindly, looking to the comfort of all.

At four in the afternoon, with an expressionless face and a lifeless air she slowly made her way to Schlegel's shop and told him she could not pay the $4 due on the dress.

"Gott!" cried Schlegel, angrily. "For what do you look so glum? Take him away. He is ready. Pay me some time. Haf I not seen you pass mine shop every day in two years? If I make clothes is it that I do not know how to read beoples because? You will pay me some time when you can. Take him away. He is made goot; and if you look bretty in him all right. So. Pay me when you can."

Maida breathed a millionth part of the thanks in her heart, and hurried away with her dress. As she left the shop a smart dash of rain struck upon her face. She smiled and did not feel it.

Ladies who shop in carriages, you do not understand. Girls whose wardrobes are charged to the old man's account, you cannot begin to comprehend—you could not understand why Maida did not feel the cold dash of the Thanksgiving rain.

At five o'clock she went out upon the street wearing her purple dress. The rain had increased, and it beat down upon her in a steady, wind-blown pour. People were scurrying home and to cars with close-held umbrellas and tight buttoned raincoats. Many of them turned their heads to marvel at this beautiful, serene, happy-eyed girl in the purple dress walking through the storm as though she were strolling in a garden under summer skies.

I say you do not understand it, ladies of the full purse and varied wardrobe. You do not know what it is to live with a perpetual longing for pretty things—to starve eight months in order to bring a purple dress and a holiday together. What difference if it rained, hailed, blew, snowed, cycloned?

Maida had no umbrella nor overshoes. She had her purple dress and she walked abroad. Let the elements do their worst. A starved heart must have one crumb during a year. The rain ran down and dripped from her fingers.

Some one turned a corner and blocked her way. She looked up into Mr. Ramsay's eyes, sparkling with admiration and interest.

"Why, Miss Maida," said he, "you look simply magnificent in your new dress. I was greatly disappointed not to see you at our dinner. And of all the girls I ever knew, you show the greatest sense and intelligence. There is nothing more healthful and invigorating than braving the weather as you are doing. May I walk with you?"

And Maida blushed and sneezed.

The Gift of the Magi

ONE DOLLAR and eighty-seven cents. That was all. And sixty cents of it was in pennies. Pennies saved one and two at a time by bulldozing the grocer and the vegetable man and the butcher until one's cheeks burned with the silent imputation of parsimony that such close dealing implied. Three times Della counted it. One dollar and eighty-seven cents. And the next day would be Christmas.

There was clearly nothing to do but flop down on the shabby little couch and howl. So Della did it. Which instigates the moral reflection that life is made up of sobs, sniffles, and smiles, with sniffles predominating.

While the mistress of the home is gradually subsiding from the first stage to the second, take a look at the home. A furnished flat at $8 per week. It did not exactly beggar description, but it certainly had that word on the lookout for the mendicancy squad.

In the vestibule below was a letter-box into which no letter would go, and an electric button from which no mortal finger could coax a ring. Also appertaining thereunto was a card bearing the name "Mr. James Dillingham Young."

The "Dillingham" had been flung to the breeze during a former period of prosperity when its possessor was being paid $30 per week. Now, when the income was shrunk to $20, the letters of "Dillingham" looked blurred, as though they were thinking seriously of contracting to a modest and unassuming D. But whenever Mr. James Dillingham Young came home and reached his flat above he was called "Jim" and greatly hugged by Mrs. James Dillingham Young, already introduced to you as Della. Which is all very good.

Della finished her cry and attended to her cheeks with the powder rag. She stood by the window and looked out dully at a grey cat walking a grey fence in a grey backyard. To-morrow would be Christmas Day, and she had only $1.87 with which to buy Jim a present. She had been saving every penny she could for months, with this result. Twenty dollars a week doesn't go far. Expenses had been greater than she had calculated. They always are. Only $1.87 to buy a present for Jim. Her Jim. Many a happy hour she had spent planning for something nice for him. Something fine and rare and sterling—something just a little bit near to being worthy of the honour of being owned by Jim.

There was a pier-glass between the windows of the room. Perhaps you have seen a pier-glass in an $8 flat. A very thin and very agile person may, by observing his reflection in a rapid sequence of longitudinal strips, obtain a fairly accurate conception of his looks. Della, being slender, had mastered the art.

Suddenly she whirled from the window and stood before the glass. Her eyes were shining brilliantly, but her face had lost its colour within twenty seconds. Rapidly she pulled down her hair and let it fall to its full length.

Now, there were two possessions of the James Dillingham Youngs in which they both took a mighty pride. One was Jim's gold watch that had been his father's and his grandfather's. The other was Della's hair. Had the Queen of Sheba lived in the flat across the airshaft, Della would have let her hair hang out the window some day to dry just to depreciate Her Majesty's jewels and gifts. Had King Solomon been the janitor, with all his treasures piled up in the basement, Jim would have pulled out his watch every time he passed, just to see him pluck at his beard from envy.

So now Della's beautiful hair fell about her, rippling and shining like a cascade of brown waters. It reached below her knee and made itself almost a garment for her. And then she did it up again nervously and quickly. Once she faltered for a minute and stood still while a tear or two splashed on the worn red carpet.

On went her old brown jacket; on went her old brown hat. With a whirl of skirts and with the brilliant sparkle still in her eyes, she fluttered out the door and down the stairs to the street.

Where she stopped the sign read: "Mme. Sofronie. Hair Goods of All Kinds." One flight up Della ran, and collected herself, panting. Madame, large, too white, chilly, hardly looked the "Sofronie."

"Will you buy my hair?" asked Della.

"I buy hair," said Madame. "Take yer hat off and let's have a sight at the looks of it."

Down rippled the brown cascade.

"Twenty dollars," said Madame, lifting the mass with a practised hand.

"Give it to me quick," said Della.

Oh, and the next two hours tripped by on rosy wings. Forget the hashed metaphor. She was ransacking the stores for Jim's present.

She found it at last. It surely had been made for Jim and no one else. There was no other like it in any of the stores, and she had turned all of them inside out. It was a platinum fob chain simple and chaste in design, properly proclaiming its value by substance alone and not by meretricious ornamentation—as all good things should do. It was even worthy of The Watch. As soon as she saw it she knew that it must be Jim's. It was like him. Quietness and value—the description applied to both. Twenty-one dollars they took from her for it, and she hurried home with the 87 cents. With that chain on his watch Jim might be properly anxious about the time in any company. Grand as the watch was, he sometimes looked at it on the sly on account of the old leather strap that he used in place of a chain.

When Della reached home her intoxication gave way a little to prudence and reason. She got out her curling irons and lighted the gas and went to work repairing the ravages made by generosity added to love. Which is always a tremendous task, dear friends—a mammoth task.

Within forty minutes her head was covered with tiny, close-lying curls that made her look wonderfully like a truant school-boy. She looked at her reflection in the mirror long, carefully, and critically.

"If Jim doesn't kill me," she said to herself, "before he takes a second look at me, he'll say I look like a Coney Island chorus girl. But what could I do—oh! what could I do with a dollar and eighty-seven cents?"

At 7 o'clock the coffee was made and the frying-pan was on the back of the stove hot and ready to cook the chops.

Jim was never late. Della doubled the fob chain in her hand and sat on the corner of the table near the door that he always entered. Then she heard his step on the stair away down on the first flight, and she turned white for just a moment. She had a habit of saying little silent prayers about the simplest everyday things, and now she whispered: "Please God, make him think I am still pretty."

The door opened and Jim stepped in and closed it. He looked thin and very serious. Poor fellow, he was only twenty-two—and to be burdened with a family! He needed a new overcoat and he was without gloves.

Jim stopped inside the door, as immovable as a setter at the scent of quail. His eyes were fixed upon Della, and there was an expression in them that she could not read, and it terrified her. It was not anger, nor surprise, nor disapproval, nor horror, nor any of the sentiments that she had been prepared for. He simply stared at her fixedly with that peculiar expression on his face.

Della wriggled off the table and went for him.

"Jim, darling," she cried, "don't look at me that way. I had my hair cut off and sold it because I couldn't have lived through Christmas without giving you a present. It'll grow out again—you won't mind, will you? I just had to do it. My hair grows awfully fast. Say 'Merry Christmas!' Jim, and let's be happy. You don't know what a nice—what a beautiful, nice gift I've got for you."

"You've cut off your hair?" asked Jim, laboriously, as if he had not arrived at that patent fact yet even after the hardest mental labour.

"Cut it off and sold it," said Della. "Don't you like me just as well, anyhow? I'm me without my hair, ain't I?"

Jim looked about the room curiously.

"You say your hair is gone?" he said, with an air almost of idiocy.

"You needn't look for it," said Della. "It's sold, I tell you—sold and gone, too. It's Christmas Eve, boy. Be good to me, for it went for you. Maybe the hairs of my head were numbered," she went on with a sudden serious sweetness, "but nobody could ever count my love for you. Shall I put the chops on, Jim?"

Out of his trance Jim seemed quickly to wake. He enfolded his Della. For ten seconds let us regard with discreet scrutiny some inconsequential object in the other direction. Eight dollars a week or a million a year—what is the difference? A mathematician or a wit would give you the wrong answer. The magi brought valuable gifts, but that was not among them. This dark assertion will be illuminated later on.

Jim drew a package from his overcoat pocket and threw it upon the table.

"Don't make any mistake, Dell," he said, "about me. I don't think there's anything in the way of a haircut or a shave or a shampoo that could make me like my girl any less. But if you'll unwrap that package you may see why you had me going a while at first."

White fingers and nimble tore at the string and paper. And then an ecstatic scream of joy; and then, alas! a quick feminine change to hysterical tears and wails, necessitating the immediate employment of all the comforting powers of the lord of the flat.

For there lay The Combs—the set of combs, side and back, that Della had worshipped for long in a Broadway window. Beautiful combs, pure tortoise shell, with jewelled rims—just the shade to wear in the beautiful vanished hair. They were expensive combs, she knew, and her heart had simply craved and yearned over them without the least hope of possession. And now, they were hers, but the tresses that should have adorned the coveted adornments were gone.

But she hugged them to her bosom, and at length she was able to look up with dim eyes and a smile and say: "My hair grows so fast, Jim!"

And then Della leaped up like a little singed cat and cried, "Oh, oh!"

Jim had not yet seen his beautiful present. She held it out to him eagerly upon her open palm. The dull precious metal seemed to flash with a reflection of her bright and ardent spirit.

"Isn't it a dandy, Jim? I hunted all over town to find it. You'll have to look at the time a hundred times a day now. Give me your watch. I want to see how it looks on it."

Instead of obeying, Jim tumbled down on the couch and put his hands under the back of his head and smiled.

"Dell," said he, "let's put our Christmas presents away and keep 'em a while. They're too nice to use just at present. I sold the watch to get the money to buy your combs. And now suppose you put the chops on."

The magi, as you know, were wise men—wonderfully wise men—who brought gifts to the Babe in the manger. They invented the art of giving Christmas presents. Being wise, their gifts were no doubt wise ones, possibly bearing the privilege of exchange in case of duplication. And here I have lamely related to you the uneventful chronicle of two foolish children in a flat who most unwisely sacrificed for each other the greatest treasures of their house. But in a last word to the wise of these days let it be said that of all who give gifts these two were the wisest. Of all who give and receive gifts, such as they are wisest. Everywhere they are wisest. They are the magi.

The Duel

T HE GODS, lying beside their nectar on 'Lympus and peeping over the edge of the cliff, perceive a difference in cities.
Although it would seem that to their vision towns must appear
as large or small ant-hills without special characteristics, yet it
is not so. Studying the habits of ants from so great a height
should be but a mild diversion when coupled with the soft
drink that mythology tells us is their only solace. But doubtless they have amused themselves by the comparison of villages and towns; and it will be no news to them (nor, perhaps,
to many mortals), that in one particularity New York stands
unique among the cities of the world. This shall be the theme
of a little story addressed to the man who sits smoking with
his Sabbath-slippered feet on another chair, and to the woman
who snatches the paper for a moment while boiling greens or
a narcotized baby leaves her free. With these I love to sit upon
the ground and tell sad stories of the death of Kings.

New York City is inhabited by 4,000,000 mysterious
strangers; thus beating Bird Centre by three millions and half
a dozen nine's. They came here in various ways and for many
reasons—Hendrik Hudson, the art schools, green goods, the
stork, the annual dressmakers' convention, the Pennsylvania
Railroad, love of money, the stage, cheap excursion rates, brains,
personal column ads., heavy walking shoes, ambition, freight
trains—all these have had a hand in making up the population.

But every man Jack when he first sets foot on the stones of
Manhattan has got to fight. He has got to fight at once until
either he or his adversary wins. There is no resting between
rounds, for there are no rounds. It is slugging from the first. It
is a fight to a finish.

Your opponent is the City. You must do battle with it from
the time the ferry-boat lands you on the island until either it is
yours or it has conquered you. It is the same whether you have
a million in your pocket or only the price of a week's lodging.

The battle is to decide whether you shall become a New
Yorker or turn the rankest outlander and Philistine. You must
be one or the other. You cannot remain neutral. You must be

for or against—lover or enemy—bosom friend or outcast. And, oh, the city is a general in the ring. Not only by blows does it seek to subdue you. It woos you to its heart with the subtlety of a siren. It is a combination of Delilah, green Chartreuse, Beethoven, chloral and John L. in his best days.

In other cities you may wander and abide as a stranger man as long as you please. You may live in Chicago until your hair whitens, and be a citizen and still prate of beans if Boston mothered you, and without rebuke. You may become a civic pillar in any other town but Knickerbocker's, and all the time publicly sneering at its buildings, comparing them with the architecture of Colonel Telfair's residence in Jackson, Miss., whence you hail, and you will not be set upon. But in New York you must be either a New Yorker or an invader of a modern Troy, concealed in the wooden horse of your conceited provincialism. And this dreary preamble is only to introduce to you the unimportant figures of William and Jack.

They came out of the West together, where they had been friends. They came to dig their fortunes out of the big city.

Father Knickerbocker met them at the ferry, giving one a right-hander on the nose and the other an uppercut with his left, just to let them know that the fight was on.

William was for business; Jack was for Art. Both were young and ambitious; so they countered and clinched. I think they were from Nebraska or possibly Missouri or Minnesota. Anyhow, they were out for success and scraps and scads, and they tackled the city like two Lochinvars with brass knucks and a pull at the City Hall.

Four years afterward William and Jack met at luncheon. The business man blew in like a March wind, hurled his silk hat at a waiter, dropped into the chair that was pushed under him, seized the bill of fare, and had ordered as far as cheese before the artist had time to do more than nod. After the nod a humorous smile came into his eyes.

"Billy," he said, "you're done for. The city has gobbled you up. It has taken you and cut you to its pattern and stamped you with its brand. You are so nearly like ten thousand men I have seen to-day that you couldn't be picked out from them if it weren't for your laundry marks."

"Camembert," finished William. "What's that? Oh, you've

still got your hammer out for New York, have you? Well, little
old Noisyville-on-the-Subway is good enough for me. It's giving me mine. And, say, I used to think the West was the whole
round world—only slightly flattened at the poles whenever
Bryan ran. I used to yell myself hoarse about the free expense,
and hang my hat on the horizon, and say cutting things in
the grocery to little soap drummers from the East. But I'd
never seen New York, then, Jack. Me for it from the rathskellers
up. Sixth Avenue is the West to me now. Have you heard this
fellow Crusoe sing? The desert isle for him, I say, but my wife
made me go. Give me May Irwin or E. S. Willard any time."

"Poor Billy," said the artist, delicately fingering a cigarette.
"You remember, when we were on our way to the East, how
we talked about this great, wonderful city, and how we meant
to conquer it and never let it get the best of us? We were going
to be just the same fellows we had always been, and never let it
master us. It has downed you, old man. You have changed from
a maverick into a butterick."

"Don't see exactly what you are driving at," said William. "I
don't wear an alpaca coat with blue trousers and a seersucker
vest on dress occasions, like I used to do at home. You talk
about being cut to a pattern—well, ain't the pattern all right?
When you're in Rome you've got to do as the Dagoes do. This
town seems to me to have other alleged metropolises skinned
to flag stations. According to the railroad schedule I've got in
my mind, Chicago and Saint Jo and Paris, France, are asterisk
stops—which means you wave a red flag and get on every other
Tuesday. I like this little suburb of Tarrytown-on-the-Hudson.
There's something or somebody doing all the time. I'm clearing $8,000 a year selling automatic pumps, and I'm living like
kings-up. Why, yesterday, I was introduced to John W. Gates. I
took an auto ride with a wine agent's sister. I saw two men run
over by a street car, and I seen Edna May play in the evening.
Talk about the West, why, the other night I woke everybody
up in the hotel hollering. I dreamed I was walking on a board
sidewalk in Oshkosh. What have you got against this town,
Jack? There's only one thing in it that I don't care for, and that's
a ferry-boat."

The artist gazed dreamily at the cartridge paper on the wall.
"This town," said he, "is a leech. It drains the blood of the

country. Whoever comes to it accepts a challenge to a duel. Abandoning the figure of the leech, it is a juggernaut, a Moloch, a monster to which the innocence, the genius, and the beauty of the land must pay tribute. Hand to hand every newcomer must struggle with the leviathan. You've lost, Billy. It shall never conquer me. I hate it as one hates sin or pestilence or—the color work in a ten-cent magazine. I despise its very vastness and power. It has the poorest millionaires, the littlest great men, the haughtiest beggars, the plainest beauties, the lowest skyscrapers, the dolefulest pleasures of any town I ever saw. It has caught you, old man, but I will never run beside its chariot wheels. It glosses itself as the Chinaman glosses his collars. Give me the domestic finish. I could stand a town ruled by wealth or one ruled by an aristocracy; but this is one controlled by its lowest ingredients. Claiming culture, it is the crudest; asseverating its pre-eminence, it is the basest; denying all outside values and virtue, it is the narrowest. Give me the pure air and the open heart of the West country. I would go back there to-morrow if I could."

"Don't you like this *filet mignon*?" said William. "Shucks, now, what's the use to knock the town! It's the greatest ever. I couldn't sell one automatic pump between Harrisburg and Tommy O'Keefe's saloon, in Sacramento, where I sell twenty here. And have you seen Sara Bernhardt in 'Andrew Mack' yet?"

"The town's got you, Billy," said Jack.

"All right," said William. "I'm going to buy a cottage on Lake Ronkonkoma next summer."

At midnight Jack raised his window and sat close to it. He caught his breath at what he saw, though he had seen and felt it a hundred times.

Far below and around lay the city like a ragged purple dream. The irregular houses were like the broken exteriors of cliffs lining deep gulches and winding streams. Some were mountainous; some lay in long, monotonous rows like the basalt precipices hanging over desert cañons. Such was the background of the wonderful, cruel, enchanting, bewildering, fatal, great city. But into this background were cut myriads of brilliant parallelograms and circles and squares through which glowed many colored lights. And out of the violet and purple depths ascended like the city's soul sounds and odors and thrills that make up the civic body. There arose the breath of gaiety unrestrained, of love, of hate, of all the passions that man can know. There below him lay all things, good or bad, that can be brought from the four corners of the earth to instruct, please, thrill, enrich, despoil, elevate, cast down, nurture or kill. Thus the flavor of it came up to him and went into his blood.

There was a knock on his door. A telegram had come for him. It came from the West, and these were its words:

"Come back home and the answer will be yes.

"Dolly."

He kept the boy waiting ten minutes, and then wrote the reply: "Impossible to leave here at present." Then he sat at the window again and let the city put its cup of mandragora to his lips again.

After all it isn't a story; but I wanted to know which one of the heroes won the battle against the city. So I went to a very learned friend and laid the case before him. What he said was: "Please don't bother me; I have Christmas presents to buy."

So there it rests; and you will have to decide for yourself.

The Rubaiyat of a Scotch Highball

THIS DOCUMENT is intended to strike somewhere between a temperance lecture and the "Bartender's Guide." Relative to the latter, drink shall swell the theme and be set forth in abundance. Agreeably to the former, not an elbow shall be crooked.

Bob Babbitt was "off the stuff." Which means—as you will discover by referring to the unabridged dictionary of Bohemia—that he had "cut out the booze"; that he was "on the water wagon." The reason for Bob's sudden attitude of hostility toward the "demon rum"—as the white ribboners miscall whiskey (see the "Bartender's Guide"), should be of interest to reformers and saloon-keepers.

There is always hope for a man who, when sober, will not concede or acknowledge that he was ever drunk. But when a man will say (in the apt words of the phrase-distiller), "I had a beautiful skate on last night," you will have to put stuff in his coffee as well as pray for him.

One evening on his way home Babbitt dropped in at the Broadway bar that he liked best. Always there were three or four fellows there from the downtown offices whom he knew. And then there would be highballs and stories, and he would hurry home to dinner a little late but feeling good, and a little sorry for the poor Standard Oil Company. On this evening as he entered he heard some one say: "Babbitt was in last night as full as a boiled owl."

Babbitt walked to the bar, and saw in the mirror that his face was as white as chalk. For the first time he had looked Truth in the eyes. Others had lied to him; he had dissembled with himself. He was a drunkard, and had not known it. What he had fondly imagined was a pleasant exhilaration had been maudlin intoxication. His fancied wit had been drivel; his gay humors nothing but the noisy vagaries of a sot. But, never again!

"A glass of seltzer," he said to the bartender.

A little silence fell upon the group of his cronies, who had been expecting him to join them.

"Going off the stuff, Bob?" one of them asked politely and with more formality than the highballs ever called forth.

"Yes," said Babbitt.

Some one of the group took up the unwashed thread of a story he had been telling; the bartender shoved over a dime and a nickel change from the quarter, ungarnished with his customary smile; and Babbitt walked out.

Now, Babbitt had a home and a wife—but that is another story. And I will tell you that story, which will show you a better habit and a worse story than you could find in the man who invented the phrase.

It began away up in Sullivan County, where so many rivers and so much trouble begins—or begin; how would you say that? It was July, and Jessie was a summer boarder at the Mountain Squint Hotel, and Bob, who was just out of college, saw her one day—and they were married in September. That's the tabloid novel—one swallow of water, and it's gone.

But those July days!

Let the exclamation point expound it, for I shall not. For particulars you might read up on "Romeo and Juliet," and Abraham Lincoln's thrilling sonnet about "You can fool some of the people," &c., and Darwin's works.

But one thing I must tell you about. Both of them were mad over Omar's Rubaiyat. They knew every verse of the old bluffer by heart—not consecutively, but picking 'em out here and there as you fork the mushrooms in a fifty-cent steak à la Bordelaise. Sullivan County is full of rocks and trees; and Jessie used to sit on them, and—please be good—used to sit on the rocks; and Bob had a way of standing behind her with his hands over her shoulders holding her hands, and his face close to hers, and they would repeat over and over their favorite verses of the old tent-maker. They saw only the poetry and philosophy of the lines then—indeed, they agreed that the Wine was only an image, and that what was meant to be celebrated was some divinity, or maybe Love or Life. However, at that time neither of them had tasted the stuff that goes with a sixty-cent *table d'hôte*.

Where was I? Oh, they married and came to New York. Bob showed his college diploma, and accepted a position filling inkstands in a lawyer's office at $15 a week. At the end of two years he had worked up to $50, and gotten his first taste of Bohemia—the kind that won't stand the borax and formaldehyde tests.

They had two furnished rooms and a little kitchen. To Jess, accustomed to the mild but beautiful savor of a country town, the dreggy Bohemia was sugar and spice. She hung fish seines on the walls of her rooms, and bought a rakish-looking sideboard, and learned to play the banjo. Twice or thrice a week they dined at French or Italian *tables d'hôte* in a cloud of smoke, and brag and unshorn hair. Jess learned to drink a cocktail in order to get the cherry. At home she smoked a cigarette after dinner. She learned to pronounce Chianti, and leave her olive stones for the waiter to pick up. Once she essayed to say la, la, la! in a crowd; but got only as far as the second one. They met one or two couples while dining out and became friendly with them. The sideboard was stocked with Scotch and rye and a liqueur. They had their new friends in to dinner and all were laughing at nothing by 1 A.M. Some plastering fell in the room below them, for which Bob had to pay $4.50. Thus they footed it merrily on the ragged frontiers of the country that has no boundary lines or government.

And soon Bob fell in with his cronies and learned to keep his foot on the little rail six inches above the floor for an hour or so every afternoon before he went home. Drink always rubbed him the right way, and he would reach his rooms as jolly as a sandboy. Jessie would meet him at the door, and generally they would dance some insane kind of a rigadoon about the floor by way of greeting. Once when Bob's feet became confused and he tumbled headlong over a footstool Jessie laughed so heartily and long that he had to throw all the couch pillows at her to make her hush.

In such wise life was speeding for them on the day when Bob Babbitt first felt the power that the giftie gi'ed him.

But let us get back to our lamb and mint sauce.

When Bob got home that evening he found Jessie in a long apron cutting up a lobster for the Newburg. Usually when Bob came in mellow from his hour at the bar his welcome was hilarious, though somewhat tinctured with Scotch smoke.

By screams and snatches of song and certain audible testimonials to domestic felicity was his advent proclaimed. When she heard his foot on the stairs the old maid in the hall room always stuffed cotton into her ears. At first Jessie had shrunk from the rudeness and flavor of these spiritual greetings, but as the fog of the false Bohemia gradually encompassed her she came to accept them as love's true and proper greeting.

Bob came in without a word, smiled, kissed her neatly but noiselessly, took up a paper and sat down. In the hall room the old maid held her two plugs of cotton poised, filled with anxiety.

Jessie dropped lobster and knife and ran to him with frightened eyes.

"What's the matter, Bob, are you ill?"

"Not at all, dear."

"Then what's the matter with you?"

"Nothing."

Hearken, brethren. When She-who-has-a-right-to-ask interrogates you concerning a change she finds in your mood answer her thus: Tell her that you, in a sudden rage, have murdered your grandmother; tell her that you have robbed orphans and that remorse has stricken you; tell her your fortune is swept away; that you are beset by enemies, by bunions, by any kind of malevolent fate; but do not, if peace and happiness are worth as much as a grain of mustard seed to you—do not answer her "Nothing."

Jessie went back to the lobster in silence. She cast looks of darkest suspicion at Bob. He had never acted that way before.

When dinner was on the table she set out the bottle of Scotch and the glasses. Bob declined.

"Tell you the truth, Jess," he said. "I've cut out the drink. Help yourself, of course. If you don't mind I'll try some of the seltzer straight."

"You've stopped drinking?" she said, looking at him steadily and unsmilingly. "What for?"

"It wasn't doing me any good," said Bob. "Don't you approve of the idea?"

Jessie raised her eyebrows and one shoulder slightly.

"Entirely," she said with a sculptured smile. "I could not conscientiously advise any one to drink or smoke, or whistle on Sunday."

The meal was finished almost in silence. Bob tried to make

talk, but his efforts lacked the stimulus of previous evenings. He felt miserable, and once or twice his eye wandered toward the bottle, but each time the scathing words of his bibulous friend sounded in his ear, and his mouth set with determination.

Jessie felt the change deeply. The essence of their lives seemed to have departed suddenly. The restless fever, the false gayety, the unnatural excitement of the shoddy Bohemia in which they had lived had dropped away in the space of the popping of a cork. She stole curious and forlorn glances at the dejected Bob, who bore the guilty look of at least a wife-beater or a family tyrant.

After dinner the colored maid who came in daily to perform such chores cleared away the things. Jessie, with an unreadable countenance, brought back the bottle of Scotch and the glasses and a bowl of cracked ice and set them on the table.

"May I ask," she said, with some of the ice in her tones, "whether I am to be included in your sudden spasm of good-ness? If not, I'll make one for myself. It's rather chilly this evening, for some reason."

"Oh, come now, Jess," said Bob good-naturedly, "don't be too rough on me. Help yourself, by all means. There's no danger of your overdoing it. But I thought there was with me; and that's why I quit. Have yours, and then let's get out the banjo and try over that new quickstep."

"I've heard," said Jessie in the tones of the oracle, "that drinking alone is a pernicious habit. No, I don't think I feel like playing this evening. If we are going to reform we may as well abandon the evil habit of banjo-playing, too."

She took up a book and sat in her little willow rocker on the other side of the table. Neither of them spoke for half an hour.

And then Bob laid down his paper and got up with a strange, absent look on his face and went behind her chair and reached over her shoulders, taking her hands in his, and laid his face close to hers.

In a moment to Jessie the walls of the seine-hung room van-ished, and she saw the Sullivan County hills and rills. Bob felt her hands quiver in his as he began the verse from old Omar:

> "Come, fill the Cup, and in the Fire of Spring
> The Winter Garment of Repentance fling:

The Bird of Time has but a little way
To fly—and Lo! the Bird is on the Wing!"

And then he walked to the table and poured a stiff drink of Scotch into a glass.

But in that moment a mountain breeze had somehow found its way in and blown away the mist of the false Bohemia.

Jessie leaped and with one fierce sweep of her hand sent the bottle and glasses crashing to the floor. The same motion of her arm carried it around Bob's neck, where it met its mate and fastened tight.

"Oh, my God, Bobbie—not that verse—I see now. I wasn't always such a fool, was I? The other one, boy—the one that says: 'Remould it to the Heart's Desire.' Say that one—'to the Heart's Desire.'"

"I know that one," said Bob. "It goes:

> "'Ah! Love, could you and I with Him conspire
> To grasp this sorry Scheme of Things entire
> Would not we—'"

"Let me finish it," said Jessie.

> "'Would not we shatter it to bits—and then
> Remould it nearer to the Heart's Desire!'"

"It's shattered all right," said Bob, crunching some glass under his heel.

In some dungeon below the accurate ear of Mrs. Pickens, the landlady, located the smash.

"It's that wild Mr. Babbitt coming home soused again," she said. "And he's got such a nice little wife, too!"

The Buyer from Cactus City

IT IS well that hay fever and colds do not obtain in the health-ful vicinity of Cactus City, Texas, for the dry goods empo-rium of Navarro & Platt, situated there, is not to be sneezed at.

Twenty thousand people in Cactus City scatter their silver coin with liberal hands for the things that their hearts desire. The bulk of this semiprecious metal goes to Navarro & Platt. Their huge brick building covers enough ground to graze a dozen head of sheep. You can buy of them a rattlesnake-skin necktie, an automobile or an eighty-five dollar, latest style, ladies' tan coat in twenty different shades. Navarro & Platt first introduced pennies west of the Colorado River. They had been ranchmen with business heads, who saw that the world did not necessarily have to cease its revolutions after free grass went out.

Every spring, Navarro, senior partner, fifty-five, half Spanish, cosmopolitan, able, polished, had "gone on" to New York to buy goods. This year he shied at taking up the long trail. He was undoubtedly growing older; and he looked at his watch several times a day before the hour came for his siesta.

"John," he said, to his junior partner, "you shall go on this year to buy the goods."

Platt looked tired.

"I'm told," said he, "that New York is a plumb dead town; but I'll go. I can take a whirl in San Antone for a few days on my way and have some fun."

Two weeks later a man in a Texas full dress suit—black frock coat, broad-brimmed soft white hat, and lay-down collar 3–4 inch high, with black, wrought iron necktie—entered the wholesale cloak and suit establishment of Zizzbaum & Son, on lower Broadway.

Old Zizzbaum had the eye of an osprey, the memory of an elephant and a mind that unfolded from him in three move-ments like the puzzle of the carpenter's rule. He rolled to the front like a brunette polar bear, and shook Platt's hand.

"And how is the good Mr. Navarro in Texas?" he said. "The

trip was too long for him this year, so? We welcome Mr. Platt instead."

"A bull's eye," said Platt, "and I'd give forty acres of unirrigated Pecos County land to know how you did it."

"I knew," grinned Zizzbaum, "just as I know that the rainfall in El Paso for the year was 28.5 inches, or an increase of 15 inches, and that therefore Navarro & Platt will buy a $15,000 stock of suits this spring instead of $10,000, as in a dry year. But that will be to-morrow. There is first a cigar in my private office that will remove from your mouth the taste of the ones you smuggle across the Rio Grande and like—because they are smuggled."

It was late in the afternoon and business for the day had ended. Zizzbaum left Platt with a half-smoked cigar, and came out of the private office to Son, who was arranging his diamond scarfpin before a mirror, ready to leave.

"Abey," he said, "you will have to take Mr. Platt around to-night and show him things. They are customers for ten years. Mr. Navarro and I we played chess every moment of spare time when he came. That is good, but Mr. Platt is a young man and this is his first visit to New York. He should amuse easily."

"All right," said Abey, screwing the guard tightly on his pin. "I'll take him on. After he's seen the Flatiron and the head waiter at the Hotel Astor and heard the phonograph play 'Under the Old Apple Tree' it'll be half past ten, and Mr. Texas will be ready to roll up in his blanket. I've got a supper engagement at 11.30, but he'll be all to the Mrs. Winslow before then."

The next morning at 10 Platt walked into the store ready to do business. He had a bunch of hyacinths pinned on his lapel. Zizzbaum himself waited on him. Navarro & Platt were good customers, and never failed to take their discount for cash.

"And what did you think of our little town?" asked Zizzbaum, with the fatuous smile of the Manhattanite.

"I shouldn't care to live in it," said the Texan. "Your son and I knocked around quite a little last night. You've got good water, but Cactus City is better lit up."

"We've got a few lights on Broadway, don't you think, Mr. Platt?"

"And a good many shadows," said Platt. "I think I like your horses best. I haven't seen a crowbait since I've been in town."

Zizzbaum led him upstairs to show the samples of suits.

"Ask Miss Asher to come," he said to a clerk.

Miss Asher came, and Platt, of Navarro & Platt, felt for the first time the wonderful bright light of romance and glory descend upon him. He stood still as a granite cliff above the cañon of the Colorado, with his wide-open eyes fixed upon her. She noticed his look and flushed a little, which was contrary to her custom.

Miss Asher was the crack model of Zizzbaum & Son. She was of the blond type known as "medium," and her measurements even went the required 38-25-42 standard a little better. She had been at Zizzbaum's two years, and knew her business. Her eye was bright, but cool; and had she chosen to match her gaze against the optic of the famed basilisk, that fabulous monster's gaze would have wavered and softened first. Incidentally, she knew buyers.

"Now, Mr. Platt," said Zizzbaum, "I want you to see these princess gowns in the light shades. They will be the thing in your climate. This first, if you please, Miss Asher."

Swiftly in and out of the dressing-room the prize model flew, each time wearing a new costume and looking more stunning with every change. She posed with absolute self-possession before the stricken buyer, who stood, tongue-tied and motionless, while Zizzbaum orated oilily of the styles. On the model's face was her faint, impersonal professional smile that seemed to cover something like weariness or contempt.

When the display was over Platt seemed to hesitate. Zizzbaum was a little anxious, thinking that his customer might be inclined to try elsewhere. But Platt was only looking over in his mind the best building sites in Cactus City, trying to select one on which to build a house for his wife-to-be—who was just then in the dressing-room taking off an evening gown of lavender and tulle.

"Take your time, Mr. Platt," said Zizzbaum. "Think it over to-night. You won't find anybody else meet our prices on goods like these. I'm afraid you're having a dull time in New York, Mr. Platt. A young man like you—of course, you miss the society of the ladies. Wouldn't you like a nice young lady to take out to dinner this evening? Miss Asher, now, is a very nice young lady; she will make it agreeable for you."

"Why, she doesn't know me," said Platt, wonderingly. "She doesn't know anything about me. Would she go? I'm not acquainted with her."

"Would she go?" repeated Zizzbaum, with uplifted eyebrows. "Sure, she would go. I will introduce you. Sure, she would go."

He called Miss Asher loudly.

She came, calm and slightly contemptuous, in her white shirt waist and plain black skirt.

"Mr. Platt would like the pleasure of your company to dinner this evening," said Zizzbaum, walking away.

"Sure," said Miss Asher, looking at the ceiling. "I'd be much pleased. Nine-eleven West Twentieth street. What time?"

"Say seven o'clock."

"All right, but please don't come ahead of time. I room with a school teacher, and she doesn't allow any gentlemen to call in the room. There isn't any parlor, so you'll have to wait in the hall. I'll be ready."

At half past seven Platt and Miss Asher sat at a table in a Broadway restaurant. She was dressed in a plain, filmy black. Platt didn't know that it was all a part of her day's work.

With the unobtrusive aid of a good waiter he managed to order a respectable dinner, minus the usual Broadway preliminaries.

Miss Asher flashed upon him a dazzling smile.

"Mayn't I have something to drink?" she asked.

"Why, certainly," said Platt. "Anything you want."

"A dry Martini," she said to the waiter.

When it was brought and set before her Platt reached over and took it away.

"What is this?" he asked.

"A cocktail, of course."

"I thought it was some kind of tea you ordered. This is liquor. You can't drink this. What is your first name?"

"To my intimate friends," said Miss Asher, freezingly, "it is 'Helen.'"

"Listen, Helen," said Platt, leaning over the table. "For many years every time the spring flowers blossomed out on the prairies I got to thinking of somebody that I'd never seen or heard of. I knew it was you the minute I saw you yesterday. I'm going back home to-morrow, and you're going with me. I know it, for I saw it in your eyes when you first looked at me. You needn't kick, for you've got to fall into line. Here's a little trick I picked out for you on my way over."

He flicked a two-carat diamond solitaire ring across the table. Miss Asher flipped it back to him with her fork.

"Don't get fresh," she said, severely.

"I'm worth a hundred thousand dollars," said Platt. "I'll build you the finest house in West Texas."

"You can't buy me, Mr. Buyer," said Miss Asher, "if you had a hundred million. I didn't think I'd have to call you down. You didn't look like the others to me at first, but I see you're all alike."

"All who?" asked Platt.

"All you buyers. You think because we girls have to go out to dinner with you or lose our jobs that you're privileged to say what you please. Well, forget it. I thought you were different from the others, but I see I was mistaken."

Platt struck his fingers on the table with a gesture of sudden, illuminating satisfaction.

"I've got it!" he exclaimed, almost hilariously—"the Nicholson place, over on the north side. There's a big grove of live oaks and a natural lake. The old house can be pulled down and the new one set further back."

"Put out your pipe," said Miss Asher. "I'm sorry to wake you up, but you fellows might as well get wise, once for all, to where you stand. I'm supposed to go to dinner with you and help jolly you along so you'll trade with old Zizzy, but don't expect to find me in any of the suits you buy."

"Do you mean to tell me," said Platt, "that you go out this way with customers, and they all—they all talk to you like I have?"

"They all make plays," said Miss Asher. "But I must say that you've got 'em beat in one respect. They generally talk diamonds, while you've actually dug one up."

"How long have you been working, Helen?"

"Got my name pat, haven't you? I've been supporting myself for eight years. I was a cash girl and a wrapper and then a shop girl until I was grown, and then I got to be a suit model. Mr. Texas Man, don't you think a little wine would make this dinner a little less dry?"

"You're not going to drink wine any more, dear. It's awful to think how—— I'll come to the store to-morrow and get you. I want you to pick out an automobile before we leave. That's all we need to buy here."

"Oh, cut that out. If you knew how sick I am of hearing such talk."

After the dinner they walked down Broadway and came upon Diana's little wooded park. The trees caught Platt's eye at once, and he must turn along under the winding walk beneath them. The lights shone upon two bright tears in the model's eyes.

"I don't like that," said Platt. "What's the matter?"

"Don't you mind," said Miss Asher. "Well, it's because—well, I didn't think you were that kind when I first saw you. But you are all alike. And now will you take me home, or will I have to call a cop?"

Platt took her to the door of her boarding-house. They stood for a minute in the vestibule. She looked at him with such scorn in her eyes that even his heart of oak began to waver. His arm was half way around her waist, when she struck him a stinging blow on the face with her open hand.

As he stepped back a ring fell from somewhere and bounded on the tiled floor. Platt groped for it and found it.

"Now, take your useless diamond and go, Mr. Buyer," she said.

"This was the other one—the wedding ring," said the Texan, holding the smooth gold band on the palm of his hand.

Miss Asher's eyes blazed upon him in the half darkness.

"Was that what you meant?—did you"—

Somebody opened the door from inside the house.

"Good-night," said Platt. "I'll see you at the store to-morrow."

Miss Asher ran up to her room and shook the school teacher until she sat up in bed ready to scream "Fire!"

"Where is it?" she cried.

"That's what I want to know," said the model. "You've studied geography, Emma, and you ought to know. Where is a town called Cac—Cac—Carac—Caracas City, I think they called it?"

"How dare you wake me up for that?" said the school teacher. "Caracas is in Venezuela, of course."

"What's it like?"

"Why, it's principally earthquakes and negroes and monkeys and malarial fever and volcanoes."

"I don't care," said Miss Asher, blithely; "I'm going there to-morrow."

The Harbinger

L ONG BEFORE the springtide is felt in the dull bosom of the yokel does the city man know that the grass-green goddess is upon her throne. He sits at his breakfast eggs and toast, begirt by stone walls, opens his morning paper and sees journalism leave vernalism at the post.

For, whereas, spring's couriers were once the evidence of our finer senses, now the Associated Press does the trick.

The warble of the first robin in Hackensack, the stirring of the maple sap in Bennington, the budding of the pussy willows along Main Street in Syracuse, the first chirp of the bluebird, the swan song of the Blue Point, the annual tornado in St. Louis, the plaint of the peach pessimist from Pompton, N. J., the regular visit of the tame wild goose with a broken leg to the pond near Bilgewater Junction, the base attempt of the Drug Trust to boost the price of quinine foiled in the House by Congressman Jinks, the first tall poplar struck by lightning and the usual stunned picknickers who had taken refuge, the first crack of the ice jam in the Allegheny River, the finding of a violet in its mossy bed by the correspondent at Round Corners—these are the advance signs of the burgeoning season that are wired into the wise city, while the farmer sees nothing but winter upon his dreary fields.

But these be mere externals. The true harbinger is the heart. When Strephon seeks his Chloe and Mike his Maggie, then only is spring arrived and the newspaper report of the five-foot rattler killed in Squire Pettigrew's pasture confirmed.

Ere the first violet blew, Mr. Peters, Mr. Ragsdale and Mr. Kidd sat together on a bench in Union Square and conspired. Mr. Peters was the D'Artagnan of the loafers three. He was the dingiest, the laziest, the sorriest brown blot against the green background of any bench in the park. But just then he was the most important of the trio.

Mr. Peters had a wife. This had not heretofore affected his standing with Ragsy and Kidd. But today it invested him with a peculiar interest. His friends, having escaped matrimony, had shown a disposition to deride Mr. Peters for his venture on that troubled sea. But at last they had been forced to acknowledge that either he had been gifted with a large foresight or that he was one of Fortune's lucky sons.

For, Mrs. Peters had a dollar. A whole dollar bill, good and receivable by the Government for customs, taxes and all public dues. How to get possession of that dollar was the question up for discussion by the three musty musketeers.

"How do you know it was a dollar?" asked Ragsy, the immensity of the sum inclining him to scepticism.

"The coalman seen her have it," said Mr. Peters. "She went out and done some washing yesterday. And look what she give me for breakfast—the heel of a loaf and a cup of coffee, and her with a dollar!"

"It's fierce," said Ragsy.

"Say, we go up and punch 'er and stick a towel in 'er mouth and cop the coin," suggested Kidd, viciously. "Y' ain't afraid of a woman, are you?"

"She might holler and have us pinched," demurred Ragsy. "I don't believe in slugging no woman in a houseful of people."

"Gent'men," said Mr. Peters, severely, through his russet stubble, "remember that you are speaking of my wife. A man who would lift his hand to a lady except in the way of——"

"Maguire," said Ragsy, pointedly, "has got his bock beer sign out. If we had a dollar we could——"

"Hush up!" said Mr. Peters, licking his lips. "We got to get that case note somehow, boys. Ain't what's a man's wife's his? Leave it to me. I'll go over to the house and get it. Wait here for me."

"I've seen 'em give up quick, and tell you where it's hid if you kick 'em in the ribs," said Kidd.

"No man would kick a woman," said Peters, virtuously. "A little choking—just a touch on the windpipe—that gets away with 'em—and no marks left. Wait for me. I'll bring back that dollar, boys."

High up in a tenement-house between Second Avenue and the river lived the Peterses in a back room so gloomy that the landlord blushed to take the rent for it. Mrs. Peters worked at sundry times, doing odd jobs of scrubbing and washing. Mr. Peters had a pure, unbroken record of five years without having earned a penny. And yet they clung together, sharing each other's hatred and misery, being creatures of habit. Of habit, the power that keeps the earth from flying to pieces; though there is some silly theory of gravitation.

Mrs. Peters reposed her 200 pounds on the safer of the two chairs and gazed stolidly out the one window at the brick wall opposite. Her eyes were red and damp. The furniture could have been carried away on a pushcart, but no pushcart man would have removed it as a gift.

The door opened to admit Mr. Peters. His fox-terrier eyes expressed a wish. His wife's diagnosis located correctly the seat of it, but misread it hunger instead of thirst.

"You'll get nothing more to eat till night," she said, looking out of the window again. "Take your hound-dog's face out of the room."

Mr. Peters's eye calculated the distance between them. By taking her by surprise it might be possible to spring upon her, overthrow her, and apply the throttling tactics of which he had boasted to his waiting comrades. True, it had been only a boast; never yet had he dared to lay violent hands upon her; but with the thoughts of the delicious, cool bock or Culmbacher bracing his nerves, he was near to upsetting his own theories of the treatment due by a gentleman to a lady. But, with his loafer's love for the more artistic and less strenuous way, he chose diplomacy first, the high card in the game—the assumed attitude of success already attained.

"You have a dollar," he said, loftily, but significantly in the tone that goes with the lighting of a cigar—when the properties are at hand.

"I have," said Mrs. Peters, producing the bill from her bosom and crackling it, teasingly.

"I am offered a position in a—in a tea store," said Mr. Peters. "I am to begin work to-morrow. But it will be necessary for me to buy a pair of——"

"You are a liar," said Mrs. Peters, reinterring the note. "No tea store, nor no A B C store, nor no junk shop would have you. I rubbed the skin off both me hands washin' jumpers and overalls to make that dollar. Do you think it come out of them suds to buy the kind you put into you? Skiddoo! Get your mind off of money."

Evidently the poses of Talleyrand were not worth one

hundred cents on that dollar. But diplomacy is dexterous. The artistic temperament of Mr. Peters lifted him by the straps of his congress gaiters and set him on new ground. He called up a look of desperate melancholy to his eyes.

"Clara," he said, hollowly, "to struggle further is useless. You have always misunderstood me. Heaven knows I have striven with all my might to keep my head above the waves of misfortune, but——"

"Cut out the rainbow of hope and that stuff about walkin' one by one through the narrow isles of Spain," said Mrs. Peters, with a sigh. "I've heard it so often. There's an ounce bottle of carbolic on the shelf behind the empty coffee can. Drink hearty."

Mr. Peters reflected. What next! The old expedients had failed. The two musty musketeers were awaiting him hard by the ruined château—that is to say, on a park bench with rickety cast-iron legs. His honor was at stake. He had engaged to storm the castle single-handed and bring back the treasure that was to furnish them wassail and solace. And all that stood between him and the coveted dollar was his wife, once a little girl whom he could—aha!—why not again? Once with soft words he could, as they say, twist her around his little finger. Why not again? Not for years had he tried it. Grim poverty and mutual hatred had killed all that. But Ragsy and Kidd were waiting for him to bring the dollar!

Mr. Peters took a surreptitiously keen look at his wife. Her formless bulk overflowed the chair. She kept her eyes fixed out the window in a strange kind of trance. Her eyes showed that she had been recently weeping.

"I wonder," said Mr. Peters to himself, "if there'd be anything in it."

The window was open upon its outlook of brick walls and drab, barren back yards. Except for the mildness of the air that entered it might have been midwinter yet in the city that turns such a frowning face to besieging spring. But spring doesn't come with the thunder of cannon. She is a sapper and a miner, and you must capitulate.

"I'll try it," said Mr. Peters to himself, making a wry face.

He went up to his wife and put his arm across her shoulders.

"Clara, darling," he said in tones that shouldn't have fooled a baby seal, "why should we have hard words? Ain't you my own tootsum wootsums?"

A black mark against you, Mr. Peters, in the sacred ledger of Cupid. Charges of attempted graft are filed against you, and of forgery and utterance of two of Love's holiest of appellations.

But the miracle of spring was wrought. Into the back room over the back alley between the black walls had crept the Harbinger. It was ridiculous, and yet—— Well, it is a rat trap, and you, madam and sir and all of us, are in it.

Red and fat and crying like Niobe or Niagara, Mrs. Peters threw her arms around her lord and dissolved upon him. Mr. Peters would have striven to extricate the dollar bill from its deposit vault, but his arms were bound to his sides.

"Do you love me, James?" asked Mrs. Peters.

"Madly," said James, "but——"

"You are ill!" exclaimed Mrs. Peters. "Why are you so pale and tired looking?"

"I feel weak," said Mr. Peters. "I——"

"Oh, wait; I know what it is. Wait, James. I'll be back in a minute."

With a parting hug that revived in Mr. Peters recollections of the Terrible Turk, his wife hurried out of the room and down the stairs.

Mr. Peters hitched his thumbs under his suspenders.

"All right," he confided to the ceiling. "I've got her going. I hadn't any idea the old girl was soft any more under the foolish rib. Well, sir; ain't I the Claude Melnotte of the lower East Side? What? It's a 100 to 1 shot that I get the dollar. I wonder what she went out for. I guess she's gone to tell Mrs. Muldoon on the second floor, that we're reconciled. I'll remember this. Soft soap! And Ragsy was talking about slugging her!"

Mrs. Peters came back with a bottle of sarsaparilla.

"I'm glad I happened to have that dollar," she said. "You're all run down, honey."

Mr. Peters had a tablespoonful of the stuff inserted into him. Then Mrs. Peters sat on his lap and murmured:

"Call me tootsum wootsums again, James."

He sat still, held there by his materialized goddess of spring. Spring had come.

On the bench in Union Square Mr. Ragsdale and Mr. Kidd squirmed, tongue-parched, awaiting D'Artagnan and his dollar.

"I wish I had choked her at first," said Mr. Peters to himself.

Brickdust Row

BLINKER WAS displeased. A man of less culture and poise and wealth would have sworn. But Blinker always remembered that he was a gentleman—a thing that no gentleman should do. So he merely looked bored and sardonic while he rode in a hansom to the center of disturbance, which was the Broadway office of Lawyer Oldport, who was agent for the Blinker estate.

"I don't see," said Blinker, "why I should be always signing confounded papers. I am packed, and was to have left for the North Woods this morning. Now I must wait until to-morrow morning. I hate night trains. My best razors are, of course, at the bottom of some unidentifiable trunk. It is a plot to drive me to bay rum and a monologueing, thumb-handed barber. Give me a pen that doesn't scratch. I hate pens that scratch."

"Sit down," said double-chinned, gray Lawyer Oldport. "The worst has not been told you. Oh, the hardships of the rich! The papers are not yet ready to sign. They will be laid before you to-morrow at eleven. You will miss another day. Twice shall the barber tweak the helpless nose of a Blinker. Be thankful that your sorrows do not embrace a hair-cut."

"If," said Blinker, rising, "the act did not involve more signing of papers I would take my business out of your hands at once. Give me a cigar, please."

"If," said Lawyer Oldport, "I had cared to see an old friend's son gulped down at one mouthful by sharks I would have ordered you to take it away long ago. Now, let's quit fooling, Alexander. Besides the grinding task of signing your name some thirty times to-morrow, I must impose upon you the consideration of a matter of business—of business, and I may say humanity or right. I spoke to you about this five years ago, but you would not listen—you were in a hurry for a coaching trip, I think. The subject has come up again. The property—"

"Oh, property!" interrupted Blinker. "Dear Mr. Oldport, I think you mentioned to-morrow. Let's have it all at one dose to-morrow—signatures and property and snappy rubber bands and that smelly sealing-wax and all. Have luncheon with me?

Well, I'll try to remember to drop in at eleven to-morrow. Morning."

The Blinker wealth was in lands, tenements and hereditaments, as the legal phrase goes. Lawyer Oldport had once taken Alexander in his little pulmonary gasoline runabout to see the many buildings and rows of buildings that he owned in the city. For Alexander was sole heir. They had amused Blinker very much. The houses looked so incapable of producing the big sums of money that Lawyer Oldport kept piling up in banks for him to spend.

In the evening Blinker went to one of his clubs, intending to dine. Nobody was there except some old fogies playing whist who spoke to him with grave politeness and glared at him with savage contempt. Everybody was out of town. But here he was kept in like a schoolboy to write his name over and over on pieces of paper. His wounds were deep.

Blinker turned his back on the fogies, and said to the club steward who had come forward with some nonsense about cold fresh salmon roe:

"Symons, I'm going to Coney Island." He said it as one might say: "All's off; I'm going to jump into the river."

The joke pleased Symons. He laughed within a sixteenth of a note of the audibility permitted by the laws governing employees.

"Certainly, sir," he tittered. "Of course, sir, I think I can see you at Coney, Mr. Blinker."

Blinker got a paper and looked up the movements of Sunday steamboats. Then he found a cab at the first corner and drove to a North River pier. He stood in line, as democratic as you or I, and bought a ticket, and was trampled upon and shoved forward until, at last, he found himself on the upper deck of the boat staring brazenly at a girl who sat alone upon a camp stool. But Blinker did not intend to be brazen; the girl was so wonderfully good looking that he forgot for one minute that he was the prince incog, and behaved just as he did in society.

She was looking at him, too, and not severely. A puff of wind threatened Blinker's straw hat. He caught it warily and settled it again. The movement gave the effect of a bow. The girl nodded and smiled, and in another instant he was seated at her side. She was dressed all in white, she was paler than Blinker imagined milkmaids and girls of humble stations to be, but she was as tidy as a cherry blossom, and her steady, supremely frank gray eyes looked out from the intrepid depths of an unshadowed and untroubled soul.

"How dare you raise your hat to me?" she asked, with a smile-redeemed severity.

"I didn't," Blinker said, but he quickly covered the mistake by extending it to "I didn't know how to keep from it after I saw you."

"I do not allow gentlemen to sit by me to whom I have not been introduced," she said, with a sudden haughtiness that deceived him. He rose reluctantly, but her clear, teasing laugh brought him down to his chair again.

"I guess you weren't going far," she declared, with beauty's magnificent self-confidence.

"Are you going to Coney Island?" asked Blinker.

"Me?" She turned upon him wide-open eyes full of bantering surprise. "Why, what a question! Can't you see that I'm riding a bicycle in the park?" Her drollery took the form of impertinence.

"And I am laying brick on a tall factory chimney," said Blinker. "Mayn't we see Coney together? I'm all alone and I've never been there before."

"It depends," said the girl, "on how nicely you behave. I'll consider your application until we get there."

Blinker took pains to provide against the rejection of his application. He strove to please. To adopt the metaphor of his nonsensical phrase, he laid brick upon brick on the tall chimney of his devoirs until, at length, the structure was stable and complete. The manners of the best society come around finally to simplicity; and as the girl's way was that naturally, they were on a mutual plane of communication from the beginning.

He learned that she was twenty, and her name was Florence; that she trimmed hats in a millinery shop; that she lived in a furnished room with her best chum Ella, who was cashier in a shoe store; and that a glass of milk from the bottle on the window-sill and an egg that boils itself while you twist up your hair makes a breakfast good enough for any one. Florence laughed when she heard "Blinker."

"Well," she said. "It certainly shows that you have imagination. It gives the 'Smiths' a chance for a little rest, anyhow."

They landed at Coney, and were dashed on the crest of a great human wave of mad pleasure-seekers into the walks and avenues of Fairyland gone into vaudeville.

With a curious eye, a critical mind and a fairly withheld judgment Blinker considered the temples, pagodas and kiosks of popularized delights. Hoi polloi trampled, hustled and crowded him. Basket parties bumped him; sticky children tumbled, howling, under his feet, candying his clothes. Insolent youths strolling among the booths with hard-won canes under one arm and easily won girls on the other, blew defiant smoke from cheap cigars into his face. The publicity gentlemen with megaphones, each before his own stupendous attraction, roared like Niagara in his ears. Music of all kinds that could be tortured from brass, reed, hide or string, fought in the air to gain space for its vibrations against its competitors. But what held Blinker in awful fascination was the mob, the multitude, the proletariat shrieking, struggling, hurrying, panting, hurling itself in incontinent frenzy, with unabashed abandon, into the ridiculous sham palaces of trumpery and tinsel pleasures. The vulgarity of it, its brutal overriding of all the tenets of repression and taste that were held by his caste, repelled him strongly.

In the midst of his disgust he turned and looked down at Florence by his side. She was ready with her quick smile and upturned, happy eyes, as bright and clear as the water in trout pools. The eyes were saying that they had the right to be shining and happy, for was their owner not with her (for the present) Man, her Gentleman Friend and holder of the keys to the enchanted city of fun?

Blinker did not read her look accurately, but by some miracle he suddenly saw Coney aright.

He no longer saw a mass of vulgarians seeking gross joys. He now looked clearly upon a hundred thousand true idealists. Their offenses were wiped out. Counterfeit and false though the garish joys of these spangled temples were, he perceived that deep under the gilt surface they offered saving and apposite balm and satisfaction to the restless human heart. Here, at least, was the husk of Romance, the empty but shining casque of Chivalry, the breath-catching though safe-guarded dip and flight of Adventure, the magic carpet that transports you to the realms of fairyland, though its journey be through but a few poor yards of space. He no longer saw a rabble, but his brothers seeking the ideal. There was no magic of poesy here or of art; but the glamour of their imagination turned yellow calico into cloth of gold and the megaphones into the silver trumpets of joy's heralds.

Almost humbled, Blinker rolled up the shirt sleeves of his mind and joined the idealists.

"You are the lady doctor," he said to Florence. "How shall we go about doing this jolly conglomeration of fairy tales, incorporated?"

"We will begin there," said the Princess, pointing to a fun pagoda on the edge of the sea, "and we will take them all in, one by one."

They caught the eight o'clock returning boat and sat, filled with pleasant fatigue against the rail in the bow, listening to the Italians' fiddle and harp. Blinker had thrown off all care. The North Woods seemed to him an uninhabitable wilderness. What a fuss he had made over signing his name—pooh! he could sign it a hundred times. And her name was as pretty as she was—"Florence," he said it to himself a great many times.

As the boat was nearing its pier in the North River a two-funnelled, drab, foreign-looking sea-going steamer was dropping down toward the bay. The boat turned its nose in toward its slip. The steamer veered as if to seek midstream, and then yawed, seemed to increase its speed and struck the Coney boat on the side near the stern, cutting into it with a terrifying shock and crash.

While the six hundred passengers on the boat were mostly tumbling about the decks in a shrieking panic the captain was shouting at the steamer that it should not back off and leave the rent exposed for the water to enter. But the steamer tore its way out like a savage sawfish and cleaved its heartless way, full speed ahead.

The boat began to sink at its stern, but moved slowly toward the slip. The passengers were a frantic mob, unpleasant to behold.

Blinker held Florence tightly until the boat had righted itself. She made no sound or sign of fear. He stood on a camp stool, ripped off the slats above his head and pulled down a number of the life preservers. He began to buckle one around Florence. The rotten canvas split and the fraudulent granulated cork came pouring out in a stream. Florence caught a handful of it and laughed gleefully.

"It looks like breakfast food," she said. "Take it off. They're no good."

She unbuckled it and threw it on the deck. She made Blinker sit down, and sat by his side and put her hand in his. "What'll you bet we don't reach the pier all right?" she said, and began to hum a song.

And now the captain moved among the passengers and compelled order. The boat would undoubtedly make her slip, he said, and ordered the women and children to the bow, where they could land first. The boat, very low in the water at the stern, tried gallantly to make his promise good.

"Florence," said Blinker, as she held him close by an arm and hand, "I love you."

"That's what they all say," she replied, lightly.

"I am not one of 'they all,'" he persisted. "I never knew any one I could love before. I could pass my life with you and be happy every day. I am rich. I can make things all right for you."

"That's what they all say," said the girl again, weaving the words into her little, reckless song.

"Don't say that again," said Blinker in a tone that made her look at him in frank surprise.

"Why shouldn't I say it?" she asked calmly. "They all do."

"Who are 'they'?" he asked, jealous for the first time in his existence.

"Why, the fellows I know."

"Do you know so many?"

"Oh, well, I'm not a wall flower," she answered with modest complacency.

"Where do you see these—these men? At your home?"

"Of course not. I meet them just as I did you. Sometimes on the boat, sometimes in the park, sometimes on the street. I'm a pretty good judge of a man. I can tell in a minute if a fellow is one who is likely to get fresh."

"What do you mean by 'fresh'?"

"Why, try to kiss you—me, I mean."

"Do any of them try that?" asked Blinker, clenching his teeth.

"Sure. All men do. You know that."

"Do you allow them?"

"Some. Not many. They won't take you out anywhere unless you do."

She turned her head and looked searchingly at Blinker. Her eyes were as innocent as a child's. There was a puzzled look in them, as though she did not understand him.

"What's wrong about my meeting fellows?" she asked, wonderingly.

"Everything," he answered, almost savagely. "Why don't you entertain your company in the house where you live? Is it necessary to pick up Tom, Dick and Harry on the streets?"

She kept her absolutely ingenuous eyes upon his.

"If you could see the place where I live you wouldn't ask that. I live in Brickdust Row. They call it that because there's red dust from the bricks crumbling over everything. I've lived there for more than four years. There's no place to receive company. You can't have anybody come to your room. What else is there to do? A girl has got to meet the men, hasn't she?"

"Yes," he said, hoarsely. "A girl has got to meet a—has got to meet the men."

"The first time one spoke to me on the street," she continued, "I ran home and cried all night. But you get used to it. I meet a good many nice fellows at church. I go on rainy days and stand in the vestibule until one comes up with an umbrella. I wish there was a parlor, so I could ask you to call, Mr. Blinker—are you really sure it isn't 'Smith,' now?"

The boat landed safely. Blinker had a confused impression of walking with the girl through quiet crosstown streets until she stopped at a corner and held out her hand.

"I live just one more block over," she said. "Thank you for a very pleasant afternoon."

Blinker muttered something and plunged northward till he found a cab. A big, gray church loomed slowly at his right. Blinker shook his fist at it through the window.

"I gave you a thousand dollars last week," he cried under

his breath, "and she meets them in your very doors. There is something wrong; there is something wrong."

At eleven the next day Blinker signed his name thirty times with a new pen provided by Lawyer Oldport.

"Now let me go to the woods," he said surlily.

"You are not looking well," said Lawyer Oldport. "The trip will do you good. But listen, if you will, to that little matter of business of which I spoke to you yesterday, and also five years ago. There are some buildings, fifteen in number, of which there are new five-year leases to be signed. Your father contemplated a change in the lease provisions, but never made it. He intended that the parlors of these houses should not be sub-let, but that the tenants should be allowed to use them for reception rooms. These houses are in the shopping district, and are mainly tenanted by young working girls. As it is they are forced to seek companionship outside. This row of red brick—"

Blinker interrupted him with a loud, discordant laugh.

"Brickdust Row for an even hundred," he cried. "And I own it. Have I guessed right?"

"The tenants have some such name for it," said Lawyer Oldport.

Blinker arose and jammed his hat down to his eyes.

"Do what you please with it," he said harshly. "Remodel it, burn it, raze it to the ground. But, man, it's too late I tell you. It's too late. It's too late. It's too late. It's too late."

"Girl"

I N GILT letters on the ground glass of the door of room No. 962 were the words: "Robbins & Hartley, Brokers." The clerks had gone. It was past five, and with the solid tramp of a drove of prize Percherons, scrubwomen were invading the cloud-capped twenty-story office building. A puff of red-hot air flavoured with lemon peelings, soft-coal smoke and train oil came in through the half-open windows.

Robbins, fifty, something of an overweight beau, and addicted to first nights and hotel palm-rooms, pretended to be envious of his partner's commuter's joys.

"Going to be something doing in the humidity line tonight," he said. "You out-of-town chaps will be the people, with your katydids and moonlight and long drinks and things out on the front porch."

Hartley, twenty-nine, serious, thin, good-looking, nervous, sighed and frowned a little.

"Yes," said he, "we always have cool nights in Floralhurst, especially in the winter."

A man with an air of mystery came in the door and went up to Hartley.

"I've found where she lives," he announced in the portentous half-whisper that makes the detective at work a marked being to his fellow men.

Hartley scowled him into a state of dramatic silence and quietude. But by that time Robbins had got his cane and set his tie pin to his liking, and with a debonair nod went out to his metropolitan amusements.

"Here is the address," said the detective in a natural tone, being deprived of an audience to foil.

Hartley took the leaf torn out of the sleuth's dingy memorandum book. On it were pencilled the words "Vivienne Arlington, No. 341 East —th Street, care of Mrs. McComus."

"Moved there a week ago," said the detective. "Now, if you want any shadowing done, Mr. Hartley, I can do you as fine a job in that line as anybody in the city. It will be only $7 a day and expenses. Can send in a daily typewritten report, covering——"

"You needn't go on," interrupted the broker. "It isn't a case of that kind. I merely wanted the address. How much shall I pay you?"

"One day's work," said the sleuth. "A tenner will cover it."

Hartley paid the man and dismissed him. Then he left the office and boarded a Broadway car. At the first large crosstown artery of travel he took an eastbound car that deposited him in a decaying avenue, whose ancient structures once sheltered the pride and glory of the town.

Walking a few squares, he came to the building that he sought. It was a new flathouse, bearing carved upon its cheap stone portal its sonorous name, "The Vallambrosa." Fire-escapes zigzagged down its front—these laden with household goods, drying clothes, and squalling children evicted by the midsummer heat. Here and there a pale rubber plant peeped from the miscellaneous mass, as if wondering to what kingdom it belonged—vegetable, animal or artificial.

Hartley pressed the "McComus" button. The door latch clicked spasmodically—now hospitably, now doubtfully, as though in anxiety whether it might be admitting friends or duns. Hartley entered and began to climb the stairs after the manner of those who seek their friends in city flat-houses—which is the manner of a boy who climbs an apple-tree, stopping when he comes upon what he wants.

On the fourth floor he saw Vivienne standing in an open door. She invited him inside, with a nod and a bright, genuine smile. She placed a chair for him near a window, and poised herself gracefully upon the edge of one of those Jekyll-and-Hyde pieces of furniture that are masked and mysteriously hooded, unguessable bulks by day and inquisitorial racks of torture by night.

Hartley cast a quick, critical, appreciative glance at her before speaking, and told himself that his taste in choosing had been flawless.

Vivienne was about twenty-one. She was of the purest Saxon type. Her hair was a ruddy golden, each filament of the neatly gathered mass shining with its own lustre and delicate graduation of colour. In perfect harmony were her ivory-clear complexion and deep sea-blue eyes that looked upon the world with the ingenuous calmness of a mermaid or the pixie of an undiscovered mountain stream. Her frame was strong and yet possessed the grace of absolute naturalness. And yet with all her Northern clearness and frankness of line and colouring, there seemed to be something of the tropics in her—something of languor in the droop of her pose, of love of ease in her ingenious complacency of satisfaction and comfort in the mere act of breathing—something that seemed to claim for her a right as a perfect work of nature to exist and be admired equally with a rare flower or some beautiful, milk-white dove among its sober-hued companions.

She was dressed in a white waist and dark skirt—that discreet masquerade of goose-girl and duchess.

"Vivienne," said Hartley, looking at her pleadingly, "you did not answer my last letter. It was only by nearly a week's search that I found where you had moved to. Why have you kept me in suspense when you knew how anxiously I was waiting to see you and hear from you?"

The girl looked out the window dreamily.

"Mr. Hartley," she said hesitatingly, "I hardly know what to say to you. I realize all the advantages of your offer, and sometimes I feel sure that I could be contented with you. But, again, I am doubtful. I was born a city girl, and I am afraid to bind myself to a quiet suburban life."

"My dear girl," said Hartley, ardently, "have I not told you that you shall have everything that your heart can desire that is in my power to give you? You shall come to the city for the theatres, for shopping and to visit your friends as often as you care to. You can trust me, can you not?"

"To the fullest," she said, turning her frank eyes upon him with a smile. "I know you are the kindest of men, and that the girl you get will be a lucky one. I learned all about you when I was at the Montgomerys'."

"Ah!" exclaimed Hartley, with a tender, reminiscent light in his eye; "I remember well the evening I first saw you at the Montgomerys'. Mrs. Montgomery was sounding your praises to me all the evening. And she hardly did you justice. I shall never forget that supper. Come, Vivienne, promise me. I want you. You'll never regret coming with me. No one else will ever give you as pleasant a home."

The girl sighed and looked down at her folded hands.

A sudden jealous suspicion seized Hartley.

"Tell me, Vivienne," he asked, regarding her keenly, "is there another—is there some one else?"

A rosy flush crept slowly over her fair cheeks and neck.

"You shouldn't ask that, Mr. Hartley," she said, in some confusion. "But I will tell you. There is one other—but he has no right—I have promised him nothing."

"His name?" demanded Hartley, sternly.

"Townsend."

"Rafford Townsend!" exclaimed Hartley, with a grim tightening of his jaw. "How did that man come to know you? After all I've done for him——"

"His auto has just stopped below," said Vivienne, bending over the window-sill. "He's coming for his answer. Oh, I don't know what to do!"

The bell in the flat kitchen whirred. Vivienne hurried to press the latch button.

"Stay here," said Hartley. "I will meet him in the hall."

Townsend, looking like a Spanish grandee in his light tweeds, Panama hat and curling black mustache, came up the stairs three at a time. He stopped at sight of Hartley and looked foolish.

"Go back," said Hartley, firmly, pointing downstairs with his forefinger.

"Hullo!" said Townsend, feigning surprise. "What's up? What are you doing here, old man?"

"Go back," repeated Hartley, inflexibly. "The Law of the Jungle. Do you want the Pack to tear you in pieces? The kill is mine."

"I came here to see a plumber about the bathroom connections," said Townsend, bravely.

"All right," said Hartley. "You shall have that lying plaster to stick upon your traitorous soul. But, go back."

Townsend went downstairs, leaving a bitter word to be wafted up the draught of the staircase. Hartley went back to his wooing.

"Vivienne," said he, masterfully. "I have got to have you. I will take no more refusals or dilly-dallying."

"When do you want me?" she asked.

"Now. As soon as you can get ready."

She stood calmly before him and looked him in the eye.

"Do you think for one moment," she said, "that I would enter your home while Héloise is there?"

Hartley cringed as if from an unexpected blow. He folded his arms and paced the carpet once or twice.

"She shall go," he declared grimly. Drops stood upon his brow. "Why should I let that woman make my life miserable? Never have I seen one day of freedom from trouble since I have known her. You are right, Vivienne. Héloise must be sent away before I can take you home. But she shall go. I have decided. I will turn her from my doors."

"When will you do this?" asked the girl.

Hartley clinched his teeth and bent his brows together.

"To-night," he said, resolutely. "I will send her away to-night."

"Then," said Vivienne, "my answer is 'yes.' Come for me when you will."

She looked into his eyes with a sweet, sincere light in her own. Hartley could scarcely believe that her surrender was true, it was so swift and complete.

"Promise me," he said feelingly, "on your word and honour."

"On my word and honour," repeated Vivienne, softly.

At the door he turned and gazed at her happily, but yet as one who scarcely trusts the foundations of his joy.

"To-morrow," he said, with a forefinger of reminder uplifted.

"To-morrow," she repeated with a smile of truth and candour.

In an hour and forty minutes Hartley stepped off the train at Floralhurst. A brisk walk of ten minutes brought him to the gate of a handsome two-story cottage set upon a wide and well-tended lawn. Halfway to the house he was met by a woman with jet-black braided hair and flowing white summer gown, who half strangled him without apparent cause.

When they stepped into the hall she said:

"Mamma's here. The auto is coming for her in half an hour. She came to dinner, but there's no dinner."

"I've something to tell you," said Hartley. "I thought to

break it to you gently, but since your mother is here we may as well out with it."

He stooped and whispered something at her ear.

His wife screamed. Her mother came running into the hall. The dark-haired woman screamed again—the joyful scream of a well-beloved and petted woman.

"Oh, mamma!" she cried ecstatically, "what do you think? Vivienne is coming to cook for us! She is the one that stayed with the Montgomerys a whole year. And now, Billy, dear," she concluded, "you must go right down into the kitchen and discharge Héloise. She has been drunk again the whole day long."

The Trimmed Lamp

O F COURSE there are two sides to the question. Let us look at the other. We often hear "shop-girls" spoken of. No such persons exist. There are girls who work in shops. They make their living that way. But why turn their occupation into an adjective? Let us be fair. We do not refer to the girls who live on Fifth Avenue as "marriage-girls."

Lou and Nancy were chums. They came to the big city to find work because there was not enough to eat at their homes to go around. Nancy was nineteen; Lou was twenty. Both were pretty, active, country girls who had no ambition to go on the stage.

The little cherub that sits up aloft guided them to a cheap and respectable boarding-house. Both found positions and became wage-earners. They remained chums. It is at the end of six months that I would beg you to step forward and be introduced to them. Meddlesome Reader: My Lady friends, Miss Nancy and Miss Lou. While you are shaking hands please take notice—cautiously—of their attire. Yes, cautiously; for they are as quick to resent a stare as a lady in a box at the horse show is.

Lou is a piece-work ironer in a hand laundry. She is clothed in a badly-fitting purple dress, and her hat plume is four inches too long; but her ermine muff and scarf cost $25, and its fellow beasts will be ticketed in the windows at $7.98 before the season is over. Her cheeks are pink, and her light blue eyes bright. Contentment radiates from her.

Nancy you would call a shop-girl—because you have the habit. There is no type; but a perverse generation is always seeking a type; so this is what the type should be. She has the high-ratted pompadour, and the exaggerated straight-front. Her skirt is shoddy, but has the correct flare. No furs protect her against the bitter spring air, but she wears her short broadcloth jacket as jauntily as though it were Persian lamb! On her face and in her eyes, remorseless type-seeker, is the typical shop-girl expression. It is a look of silent but contemptuous revolt against cheated womanhood; of sad prophecy of the vengeance to come. When she laughs her loudest the look is still there. The same look can be seen in the eyes of Russian peasants; and those of us left will see it some day on Gabriel's face when he comes to blow us up. It is a look that should wither and abash man; but he has been known to smirk at it and offer flowers—with a string tied to them.

Now lift your hat and come away, while you receive Lou's cheery "See you again," and the sardonic, sweet smile of Nancy that seems, somehow, to miss you and go fluttering like a white moth up over the housetops to the stars.

The two waited on the corner for Dan. Dan was Lou's steady company. Faithful? Well he was on hand when Mary would have had to hire a dozen subpoena servers to find her lamb.

"Ain't you cold, Nance?" said Lou. "Say, what a chump you are for working in that old store for $8. a week! I made $18.50 last week. Of course ironing ain't as swell work as selling lace behind a counter, but it pays. None of us ironers make less than $10. And I don't know that it's any less respectful work, either."

"You can have it," said Nancy, with uplifted nose. "I'll take my eight a week and hall bedroom. I like to be among nice things and swell people. And look what a chance I've got! Why, one of our glove girls married a Pittsburg—steel maker, or blacksmith or something—the other day worth a million dollars. I'll catch a swell myself some time. I ain't bragging on my looks or anything; but I'll take my chances where there's big prizes offered. What show would a girl have in a laundry?"

"Why, that's where I met Dan," said Lou, triumphantly. "He came in for his Sunday shirt and collars and saw me at the first board, ironing. We all try to get to work at the first board. Ella Maginnis was sick that day, and I had her place. He said he noticed my arms first, how round and white they was. I had my sleeves rolled up. Some nice fellows come into laundries. You can tell 'em by their bringing their clothes in suit cases, and turning in the door sharp and sudden."

"How can you wear a waist like that, Lou?" said Nancy gazing down at the offending article with sweet scorn in her heavy-lidded eyes. "It shows fierce taste."

"This waist?" cried Lou, with wide-eyed indignation. "Why, I paid $16. for this waist. It's worth twenty-five. A woman left it to be laundered, and never called for it. The boss sold it to me. It's got yards and yards of hand embroidery on it. Better talk about that ugly, plain thing you've got on."

"This ugly, plain thing," said Nancy, calmly, "was copied from one that Mrs. Van Alstyne Fisher was wearing. The girls say her bill in the store last year was $12,000. I made mine, myself. It cost me $1.50. Ten feet away you couldn't tell it from hers."

"Oh, well," said Lou, good-naturedly, "if you want to starve and put on airs, go ahead. But I'll take my job and good wages; and after hours give me something as fancy and attractive to wear as I am able to buy."

But just then Dan came—a serious young man with a ready-made necktie, who had escaped the city's brand of frivolity—an electrician earning $30. per week who looked upon Lou with the sad eyes of Romeo, and thought her embroidered waist a web in which any fly should delight to be caught.

"My friend, Mr. Owens—shake hands with Miss Danforth," said Lou.

"I'm mighty glad to know you, Miss Danforth," said Dan, with outstretched hand. "I've heard Lou speak of you so often."

"Thanks," said Nancy, touching his fingers with the tips of her cool ones, "I've heard her mention you—a few times."

Lou giggled.

"Did you get that handshake from Mrs. Van Alstyne Fisher, Nance?" she asked.

"If I did, you can feel safe in copying it," said Nancy.

"Oh, I couldn't use it at all. It's too stylish for me. It's intended to set off diamond rings, that high shake is. Wait till I get a few and then I'll try it."

"Learn it first," said Nancy wisely, "and you'll be more likely to get the rings."

"Now, to settle this argument," said Dan, with his ready, cheerful smile, "let me make a proposition. As I can't take both of you up to Tiffany's and do the right thing, what do you say to a little vaudeville? I've got the tickets. How about looking at stage diamonds since we can't shake hands with the real sparklers?"

The faithful squire took his place close to the curb; Lou next, a little peacocky in her bright and pretty clothes; Nancy on the inside, slender, and soberly clothed as the sparrow, but with the true Van Alstyne Fisher walk—thus they set out for their evening's moderate diversion.

I do not suppose that many look upon a great department store as an educational institution. But the one in which Nancy worked was something like that to her. She was surrounded by beautiful things that breathed of taste and refinement. If you live in an atmosphere of luxury, luxury is yours whether your money pays for it, or another's.

The people she served were mostly women whose dress, manners, and position in the social world were quoted as criterions. From them Nancy began to take toll—the best from each according to her view.

From one she would copy and practice a gesture, from another an eloquent lifting of an eyebrow, from others, a manner of walking, of carrying a purse, of smiling, of greeting a friend, of addressing "inferiors in station." From her best beloved model, Mrs. Van Alstyne Fisher, she made requisition for that excellent thing, a soft, low voice as clear as silver and as perfect in articulation as the notes of a thrush. Suffused in the aura of this high social refinement and good breeding, it was impossible for her to escape a deeper effect of it. As good habits are said to be better than good principles, so, perhaps, good manners are better than good habits. The teachings of your parents may not keep alive your New England conscience; but if you sit on a straight-back chair and repeat the words "prisms and pilgrims" forty times the devil will flee from you. And when Nancy spoke in the Van Alstyne Fisher tones she felt the thrill of *noblesse oblige* to her very bones.

There was another source of learning in the great departmental school. Whenever you see three or four shop-girls gather in a bunch and jingle their wire bracelets as an accompaniment to apparently frivolous conversation, do not think that they are there for the purpose of criticizing the way Ethel does her back hair. The meeting may lack the dignity of the deliberative bodies of man; but it has all the importance of the occasion on which Eve and her first daughter first put their heads together to make Adam understand his proper place in the household. It is Woman's Conference for Common Defense and Exchange of Strategical Theories of Attack and Repulse upon and against the World, which is a Stage, and Man, its Audience who Persists in

Throwing Bouquets Thereupon. Woman, the most helpless of the young of any animal—with the fawn's grace but without its fleetness; with the bird's beauty but without its power of flight; with the honey-bee's burden of sweetness but without its—Oh, let's drop that simile—some of us may have been stung.

During this council of war they pass weapons one to another, and exchange stratagems that each has devised and formulated out of the tactics of life.

"I says to 'im," says Sadie, "ain't you the fresh thing! Who do you suppose I am, to be addressing such a remark to me? And what do you think he says back to me?"

The heads, brown, black, flaxen, red, and yellow bob together; the answer is given; and the parry to the thrust is decided upon, to be used by each thereafter in passages-at-arms with the common enemy, man.

Thus Nancy learned the art of defense; and to women successful defense means victory.

The curriculum of a department store is a wide one. Perhaps no other college could have fitted her as well for her life's ambition—the drawing of a matrimonial prize.

Her station in the store was a favored one. The music room was near enough for her to hear and become familiar with the works of the best composers—at least to acquire the familiarity that passed for appreciation in the social world in which she was vaguely trying to set a tentative and aspiring foot. She absorbed the educating influence of art wares, of costly and dainty fabrics, of adornments that are almost culture to women.

The other girls soon became aware of Nancy's ambition. "Here comes your millionaire, Nance," they would call to her whenever any man who looked the rôle approached her counter. It got to be a habit of men, who were hanging about while their women folk were shopping, to stroll over to the handkerchief counter and dawdle over the cambric squares. Nancy's imitation high-bred air and genuine dainty beauty was what attracted. Many men thus came to display their graces before her. Some of them may have been millionaires; others were certainly no more than their sedulous apes. Nancy learned to discriminate. There was a window at the end of the handkerchief counter; and she could see the rows of vehicles waiting for the shoppers in the street below. She looked, and perceived that automobiles differ as well as do their owners.

Once a fascinating gentleman bought four dozen handkerchiefs, and wooed her across the counter with a King Cophetua air. When he had gone one of the girls said:

"What's wrong, Nance, that you didn't warm up to that fellow? He looks the swell article, all right, to me."

"Him?" said Nancy, with her coolest, sweetest, most impersonal, Van Alstyne Fisher smile; "not for mine. I saw him drive up outside. A 12 H.P. machine and an Irish chauffeur! And you saw what kind of handkerchiefs he bought—silk! And he's got dactylis on him. Give me the real thing or nothing, if you please."

Two of the most "refined" women in the store—a forelady and a cashier—had a few "swell gentlemen friends" with whom they now and then dined. Once they included Nancy in an invitation. The dinner took place in a spectacular café whose tables are engaged for New Year's eve a year in advance. There were two "gentlemen friends"—one without any hair on his head—high living ungrew it; and we can prove it—the other a young man whose worth and sophistication he impressed upon you in two convincing ways—he swore that all the wine was corked; and he wore diamond cuff buttons. This young man perceived irresistible excellencies in Nancy. His taste ran to shop-girls; and here was one that added the voice and manners of his high social world to the franker charms of her own caste. So, on the following day, he appeared in the store and made her a serious proposal of marriage over a box of hemstitched, grass-bleached Irish linens. Nancy declined. A brown pompadour ten feet away had been using her eyes and ears. When the rejected suitor had gone she heaped carboys of upbraidings and horror upon Nancy's head.

"What a terrible little fool you are! That fellow's a millionaire—he's a nephew of old Van Skittles himself. And he was talking on the level, too. Have you gone crazy, Nance?"

"Have I?" said Nancy. "I didn't take him, did I? He isn't a millionaire so hard that you could notice it, anyhow. His family only allows him $20,000 a year to spend. The bald-headed fellow was guying him about it the other night at supper."

The brown pompadour came nearer and narrowed her eyes.

"Say, what do you want?" she inquired, in a voice hoarse for lack of chewing-gum. "Ain't that enough for you? Do you want to be a Mormon, and marry Rockefeller and Gladstone Dowie and the King of Spain and the whole bunch? Ain't $20,000 a year good enough for you?"

Nancy flushed a little under the level gaze of the black, shallow eyes.

"It wasn't altogether the money, Carrie," she explained. "His friend caught him in a rank lie the other night at dinner. It was about some girl he said he hadn't been to the theater with. Well, I can't stand a liar. Put everything together—I don't like him; and that settles it. When I sell out it's not going to be on any bargain day. I've got to have something that sits up in a chair like a man, anyhow. Yes, I'm looking out for a catch; but it's got to be able to do something more than make a noise like a toy bank."

"The physiopathic ward for yours!" said the brown pompadour, walking away.

These high ideas, if not ideals—Nancy continued to cultivate on $8. per week. She bivouacked on the trail of the great unknown "catch," eating her dry bread and tightening her belt day by day. On her face was the faint, soldierly, sweet, grim smile of the preordained man-hunter. The store was her forest; and many times she raised her rifle at game that seemed broad-antlered and big; but always some deep unerring instinct—perhaps of the huntress, perhaps of the woman—made her hold her fire and take up the trail again.

Lou flourished in the laundry. Out of her $18.50 per week she paid $6. for her room and board. The rest went mainly for clothes. Her opportunities for bettering her taste and manners were few compared with Nancy's. In the steaming laundry there was nothing but work, work and her thoughts of the evening pleasures to come. Many costly and showy fabrics passed under her iron; and it may be that her growing fondness for dress was thus transmitted to her through the conducting metal.

When the day's work was over Dan awaited her outside, her faithful shadow in whatever light she stood.

Sometimes he cast an honest and troubled glance at Lou's clothes that increased in conspicuity rather than in style; but this was no disloyalty; he deprecated the attention they called to her in the streets.

And Lou was no less faithful to her chum. There was a law that Nancy should go with them on whatsoever outings they might take. Dan bore the extra burden heartily and in good cheer. It might be said that Lou furnished the color, Nancy the tone, and Dan the weight of the distraction-seeking trio. The escort, in his neat but obviously ready-made suit, his ready-made tie and unfailing, genial, ready-made wit never startled or clashed. He was of that good kind that you are likely to forget while they are present, but remember distinctly after they are gone.

To Nancy's superior taste the flavor of these ready-made pleasures was sometimes a little bitter: but she was young; and youth is a gourmand, when it cannot be a gourmet.

"Dan is always wanting me to marry him right away," Lou told her once. "But why should I. I'm independent. I can do as I please with the money I earn; and he never would agree for me to keep on working afterward. And say, Nance, what do you want to stick to that old store for, and half starve and half dress yourself? I could get you a place in the laundry right now if you'd come. It seems to me that you could afford to be a little less stuck-up if you could make a good deal more money."

"I don't think I'm stuck-up, Lou," said Nancy, "but I'd rather live on half rations and stay where I am. I suppose I've got the habit. It's the chance that I want. I don't expect to be always behind a counter. I'm learning something new every day. I'm right up against refined and rich people all the time—even if I do only wait on them; and I'm not missing any pointers that I see passing around."

"Caught your millionaire yet?" asked Lou with her teasing laugh.

"I haven't selected one yet," answered Nancy. "I've been looking them over."

"Goodness! the idea of picking over 'em! Don't you ever let one get by you Nance—even if he's a few dollars shy. But of course you're joking—millionaires don't think about working girls like us."

"It might be better for them if they did," said Nancy, with

cool wisdom. "Some of us could teach them how to take care of their money."

"If one was to speak to me," laughed Lou, "I know I'd have a duck-fit."

"That's because you don't know any. The only difference between swells and other people is you have to watch 'em closer. Don't you think that red silk lining is just a little bit too bright for that coat, Lou?"

Lou looked at the plain, dull olive jacket of her friend.

"Well, no I don't—but it may seem so beside that faded-looking thing you've got on."

"This jacket," said Nancy, complacently, "has exactly the cut and fit of one that Mrs. Van Alstyne Fisher was wearing the other day. The material cost me $3.98. I suppose hers cost about $100. more."

"Oh, well," said Lou lightly, "it don't strike me as millionaire bait. Shouldn't wonder if I catch one before you do, anyway."

Truly it would have taken a philosopher to decide upon the values of the theories held by the two friends. Lou, lacking that certain pride and fastidiousness that keeps stores and desks filled with girls working for the barest living, thumped away gaily with her iron in the noisy and stifling laundry. Her wages supported her even beyond the point of comfort; so that her dress profited until sometimes she cast a sidelong glance of impatience at the neat but inelegant apparel of Dan—Dan the constant, the immutable, the undeviating.

As for Nancy, her case was one of tens of thousands. Silk and jewels and laces and ornaments and the perfume and music of the fine world of good-breeding and taste—these were made for woman; they are her equitable portion. Let her keep near them if they are a part of life to her, and if she will. She is no traitor to herself, as Esau was; for she keeps her birthright and the pottage she earns is often very scant.

In this atmosphere Nancy belonged; and she throve in it and ate her frugal meals and schemed over her cheap dresses with a determined and contented mind. She already knew woman; and she was studying man, the animal, both as to his habits and eligibility. Some day she would bring down the game that she wanted; but she promised herself it would be what seemed to her the biggest and the best, and nothing smaller.

Thus she kept her lamp trimmed and burning to receive the bridegroom when he should come.

But, another lesson she learned, perhaps unconsciously. Her standard of values began to shift and change. Sometimes the dollar-mark grew blurred in her mind's eye, and shaped itself into letters that spelled such words as "truth" and "honor" and now and then just "kindness." Let us make a likeness of one who hunts the moose or elk in some mighty wood. He sees a little dell, mossy and embowered, where a rill trickles, babbling to him of rest and comfort. At these times the spear of Nimrod himself grows blunt.

So, Nancy wondered sometimes if Persian lamb was always quoted at its market value by the hearts that it covered.

One Thursday evening Nancy left the store and turned across Sixth Avenue westward to the laundry. She was expected to go with Lou and Dan to a musical comedy.

Dan was just coming out of the laundry when she arrived. There was a queer, strained look on his face.

"I thought I would drop around to see if they had heard from her," he said.

"Heard from who?" asked Nancy. "Isn't Lou there?"

"I thought you knew," said Dan. "She hasn't been here or at the house where she lived since Monday. She moved all her things from there. She told one of the girls in the laundry she might be going to Europe."

"Hasn't anybody seen her anywhere?" asked Nancy.

Dan looked at her with his jaws set grimly, and a steely gleam in his steady gray eyes.

"They told me in the laundry," he said, harshly, "that they saw her pass yesterday—in an automobile. With one of the millionaires, I suppose, that you and Lou were forever busying your brains about."

For the first time Nancy quailed before a man. She laid her hand that trembled slightly on Dan's sleeve.

"You've no right to say such a thing to me Dan—as if I had anything to do with it!"

"I didn't mean it that way," said Dan, softening. He fumbled in his vest pocket.

"I've got the tickets for the show to-night," he said, with a gallant show of lightness. "If you—"

Nancy admired pluck whenever she saw it.

"I'll go with you, Dan," she said.

Three months went by before Nancy saw Lou again.

At twilight one evening the shop-girl was hurrying home along the border of a little quiet park. She heard her name called, and wheeled about in time to catch Lou rushing into her arms.

After the first embrace they drew their heads back as serpents do, ready to attack or to charm, with a thousand questions trembling on their swift tongues. And then Nancy noticed that prosperity had descended upon Lou, manifesting itself in costly furs, flashing gems, and creations of the tailors' art.

"You little fool!" cried Lou, loudly and affectionately. "I see you are still working in that store, and as shabby as ever. And how about that big catch you were going to make—nothing doing yet, I suppose?"

And then Lou looked, and saw that something better than prosperity had descended upon Nancy—something that shone brighter than gems in her eyes and redder than a rose in her cheeks, and that danced like electricity anxious to be loosed from the tip of her tongue.

"Yes, I'm still in the store," said Nancy, "but I'm going to leave it next week. I've made my catch—the biggest catch in the world. You won't mind now Lou, will you?—I'm going to be married to Dan—to Dan!—he's my Dan now—why, Lou!"

Around the corner of the park strolled one of those new-crop, smooth-faced young policemen that are making the force more endurable—at least to the eye. He saw a woman with an expensive fur coat and diamond-ringed hands crouching down against the iron fence of the park sobbing turbulently, while a slender, plainly-dressed working girl leaned close, trying to console her. But the Gibsonian cop, being of the new order, passed on, pretending not to notice, for he was wise enough to know that these matters are beyond help, so far as the power he represents is concerned, though he rap the pavement with his nightstick till the sound goes up to the furthermost stars.

Proof of the Pudding

S PRING WINKED a vitreous optic at Editor Westbrook, of the
Minerva Magazine, and deflected him from his course. He
had lunched in his favorite corner of a Broadway hotel, and was
returning to his office when his feet became entangled in the
lure of the vernal coquette. Which is by way of saying that he
turned eastward in Twenty-sixth Street, safely forded the spring
freshet of vehicles in Fifth Avenue, and meandered along the
walks of budding Madison Square.

The lenient air and the settings of the little park almost
formed a pastoral; the color motif was green—the presiding
shade at the creation of man and vegetation.

The callow grass between the walks was the color of verdi-
gris, a poisonous green, reminiscent of the horde of derelict
humans that had breathed upon the soil during the summer
and autumn. The bursting tree buds looked strangely familiar
to those who had botanized among the garnishings of the fish
course of a forty-cent dinner. The sky above was of that pale
aquamarine tint that hallroom poets rhyme with "true" and
"Sue" and "coo." The one natural and frank color visible was
the ostensible green of the newly painted benches—a shade
between the color of a pickled cucumber and that of a last
year's fast-black cravenette raincoat. But, to the city-bred eye
of Editor Westbrook, the landscape appeared a masterpiece.

And now, whether you are of those who rush in, or of the
gentle concourse that fears to tread, you must follow in a brief
invasion of the editor's mind.

Editor Westbrook's spirit was contented and serene. The
April number of the *Minerva* had sold its entire edition before
the tenth day of the month—a newsdealer in Keokuk had written that he could have sold fifty copies more if he had had 'em.
The owners of the magazine had raised his (the editor's) salary;
he had just installed in his home a jewel of a recently imported
cook who was afraid of policemen; and the morning papers
had published in full a speech he had made at a publishers'
banquet. Also there were echoing in his mind the jubilant notes
of a splendid song that his charming young wife had sung to

him before he left his up-town apartment that morning. She was taking enthusiastic interest in her music of late, practising early and diligently. When he had complimented her on the improvement in her voice she had fairly hugged him for joy at his praise. He felt, too, the benign, tonic medicament of the trained nurse, Spring, tripping softly adown the wards of the convalescent city.

While Editor Westbrook was sauntering between the rows of park benches (already filling with vagrants and the guardians of lawless childhood) he felt his sleeve grasped and held. Suspecting that he was about to be panhandled, he turned a cold and unprofitable face, and saw that his captor was—Dawe—Shackleford Dawe, dingy, almost ragged, the genteel scarcely visible in him through the deeper lines of the shabby.

While the editor is pulling himself out of his surprise, a flashlight biography of Dawe is offered.

He was a fiction writer, and one of Westbrook's old acquaintances. At one time they might have called each other old friends. Dawe had some money in those days, and lived in a decent apartment house near Westbrook's. The two families often went to theatres and dinners together. Mrs. Dawe and Mrs. Westbrook became "dearest" friends. Then one day a little tentacle of the octopus, just to amuse itself, ingurgitated Dawe's capital, and he moved to the Gramercy Park neighborhood where one, for a few groats per week, may sit upon one's trunk under eight-branched chandeliers and opposite Carrara marble mantels and watch the mice play upon the floor. Dawe thought to live by writing fiction. Now and then he sold a story. He submitted many to Westbrook. The *Minerva* printed one or two of them; the rest were returned. Westbrook sent a careful and conscientious personal letter with each rejected manuscript, pointing out in detail his reasons for considering it unavailable. Editor Westbrook had his own clear conception of what constituted good fiction. So had Dawe. Mrs. Dawe was mainly concerned about the constituents of the scanty dishes of food that she managed to scrape together. One day Dawe had been spouting to her about the excellencies of certain French writers. At dinner they sat down to a dish that a hungry schoolboy could have encompassed at a gulp. Dawe commented.

"It's Maupassant hash," said Mrs. Dawe. "It may not be art, but I do wish you would do a five-course Marion Crawford serial with an Ella Wheeler Wilcox sonnet for dessert. I'm hungry."

As far as this from success was Shackleford Dawe when he plucked Editor Westbrook's sleeve in Madison Square. That was the first time the editor had seen Dawe in several months.

"Why, Shack, is this you?" said Westbrook, somewhat awkwardly, for the form of his phrase seemed to touch upon the other's changed appearance.

"Sit down for a minute," said Dawe, tugging at his sleeve. "This is my office. I can't come to yours, looking as I do. Oh, sit down—you won't be disgraced. Those half-plucked birds on the other benches will take you for a swell porch-climber. They won't know you are only an editor."

"Smoke, Shack?" said Editor Westbrook, sinking cautiously upon the virulent green bench. He always yielded gracefully when he did yield.

Dawe snapped at the cigar as a kingfisher darts at a sunperch, or a girl pecks at a chocolate cream.

"I have just——" began the editor.

"Oh, I know; don't finish," said Dawe. "Give me a match. You have just ten minutes to spare. How did you manage to get past my office-boy and invade my sanctum? There he goes now, throwing his club at a dog that couldn't read the 'Keep off the Grass' signs."

"How goes the writing?" asked the editor.

"Look at me," said Dawe, "for your answer. Now don't put on that embarrassed, friendly-but-honest look and ask me why I don't get a job as a wine agent or a cab driver. I'm in the fight to a finish. I know I can write good fiction and I'll force you fellows to admit it yet. I'll make you change the spelling of 'regrets' to 'c-h-e-q-u-e' before I'm done with you."

Editor Westbrook gazed through his nose-glasses with a sweetly sorrowful, omniscient, sympathetic, skeptical expression—the copyrighted expression of the editor beleaguered by the unavailable contributor.

"Have you read the last story I sent you—'The Alarum of the Soul'?" asked Dawe.

"Carefully. I hesitated over that story, Shack, really I did. It had some good points. I was writing you a letter to send with it when it goes back to you. I regret——"

"Never mind the regrets," said Dawe, grimly. "There's neither salve nor sting in 'em any more. What I want to know is *why*. Come, now; out with the good points first."

"The story," said Westbrook, deliberately, after a suppressed sigh, "is written around an almost original plot. Characterization—the best you have done. Construction—almost as good, except for a few weak joints which might be strengthened by a few changes and touches. It was a good story, except——"

"I can write English, can't I?" interrupted Dawe.

"I have always told you," said the editor, "that you had a style."

"Then the trouble is the——"

"Same old thing," said Editor Westbrook. "You work up to your climax like an artist. And then you turn yourself into a photographer. I don't know what form of obstinate madness possesses you, Shack, but that is what you do with everything that you write. No, I will retract the comparison with the photographer. Now and then photography, in spite of its impossible perspective, manages to record a fleeting glimpse of truth. But you spoil every dénouement by those flat, drab, obliterating strokes of your brush that I have so often complained of. If you would rise to the literary pinnacle of your dramatic scenes, and paint them in the high colors that art requires, the postman would leave fewer bulky, self-addressed envelopes at your door."

"Oh, fiddles and footlights!" cried Dawe, derisively. "You've got that old sawmill drama kink in your brain yet. When the man with the black mustache kidnaps golden-haired Bessie you are bound to have the mother kneel and raise her hands in the spotlight and say: 'May high heaven witness that I will rest neither night nor day till the heartless villain that has stolen me child feels the weight of a mother's vengeance!'"

Editor Westbrook conceded a smile of impervious complacency.

"I think," said he, "that in real life the woman would express herself in those words or in very similar ones."

"Not in a six hundred nights' run anywhere but on the stage," said Dawe hotly. "I'll tell you what she'd say in real life. She'd say: 'What! Bessie led away by a strange man? Good Lord! It's one trouble after another! Get my other hat, I must hurry around to the police-station. Why wasn't somebody looking after her, I'd like to know? For God's sake, get out of my way or I'll never get ready. Not that hat—the brown one with the velvet bows. Bessie must have been crazy; she's usually shy of strangers. Is that too much powder? Lordy! How I'm upset!'

"That's the way she'd talk," continued Dawe. "People in real life don't fly into heroics and blank verse at emotional crises. They simply can't do it. If they talk at all on such occasions they draw from the same vocabulary that they use every day, and muddle up their words and ideas a little more, that's all."

"Shack," said Editor Westbrook impressively, "did you ever pick up the mangled and lifeless form of a child from under the fender of a street car, and carry it in your arms and lay it down before the distracted mother? Did you ever do that and listen to the words of grief and despair as they flowed spontaneously from her lips?"

"I never did," said Dawe. "Did you?"

"Well, no," said Editor Westbrook, with a slight frown. "But I can well imagine what she would say."

"So can I," said Dawe.

And now the fitting time had come for Editor Westbrook to play the oracle and silence his opinionated contributor. It was not for an unarrived fictionist to dictate words to be uttered by the heroes and heroines of the *Minerva Magazine*, contrary to the theories of the editor thereof.

"My dear Shack," said he, "if I know anything of life I know that every sudden, deep and tragic emotion in the human heart calls forth an apposite, concordant, conformable and proportionate expression of feeling. How much of this inevitable accord between expression and feeling should be attributed to nature, and how much to the influence of art, it would be difficult to say. The sublimely terrible roar of the lioness that has been deprived of her cubs is dramatically as far above her customary whine and purr as the kingly and transcendent utterances of Lear are above the level of his senile vaporings. But it is also true that all men and women have what may be called a sub-conscious dramatic sense that is awakened by a sufficiently deep and powerful emotion—a sense unconsciously acquired from literature and the stage that prompts them to express those emotions in language befitting their importance and histrionic value."

"And in the name of the seven sacred saddle-blankets of Sagittarius, where did the stage and literature get the stunt?" asked Dawe.

"From life," answered the editor, triumphantly.

The story writer rose from the bench and gesticulated eloquently but dumbly. He was beggared for words with which to formulate adequately his dissent.

On a bench nearby a frowzy loafer opened his red eyes and perceived that his moral support was due a downtrodden brother.

"Punch him one, Jack," he called hoarsely to Dawe. "W'at's he come makin' a noise like a penny arcade for amongst gen'lemen that comes in the Square to set and think?"

Editor Westbrook looked at his watch with an affected show of leisure.

"Tell me," asked Dawe, with truculent anxiety, "what especial faults in 'The Alarum of the Soul' caused you to throw it down?"

"When Gabriel Murray," said Westbrook, "goes to his telephone and is told that his fiancée has been shot by a burglar, he says—I do not recall the exact words, but——"

"I do," said Dawe. "He says: 'Damn Central; she always cuts me off.' (And then to his friend) 'Say, Tommy, does a thirty-two bullet make a big hole? It's kind of hard luck, ain't it? Could you get me a drink from the sideboard, Tommy? No; straight; nothing on the side.'"

"And again," continued the editor, without pausing for argument, "when Berenice opens the letter from her husband informing her that he has fled with the manicure girl, her words are—let me see——"

"She says," interposed the author: "'Well, what do you think of that!'"

"Absurdly inappropriate words," said Westbrook, "presenting an anti-climax—plunging the story into hopeless bathos. Worse yet; they mirror life falsely. No human being ever uttered banal colloquialisms when confronted by sudden tragedy."

"Wrong," said Dawe, closing his unshaven jaws doggedly.

"I say no man or woman ever spouts 'highfalutin' talk when they go up against a real climax. They talk naturally and a little worse."

The editor rose from the bench with his air of indulgence and inside information.

"Say, Westbrook," said Dawe, pinning him by the lapel, "would you have accepted 'The Alarum of the Soul' if you had believed that the actions and words of the characters were true to life in the parts of the story that we discussed?"

"It is very likely that I would, if I believed that way," said the editor. "But I have explained to you that I do not."

"If I could prove to you that I am right?"

"I'm sorry, Shack, but I'm afraid I haven't time to argue any further just now."

"I don't want to argue," said Dawe. "I want to demonstrate to you from life itself that my view is the correct one."

"How could you do that?" asked Westbrook, in a surprised tone.

"Listen," said the writer, seriously. "I have thought of a way. It is important to me that my theory of true-to-life fiction be recognized as correct by the magazines. I've fought for it for three years, and I'm down to my last dollar, with two months' rent due."

"I have applied the opposite of your theory," said the editor, "in selecting the fiction for the *Minerva Magazine*. The circulation has gone up from ninety thousand to——"

"Four hundred thousand," said Dawe. "Whereas it should have been boosted to a million."

"You said something to me just now about demonstrating your pet theory."

"I will. If you 'll give me about half an hour of your time I'll prove to you that I am right. I'll prove it by Louise."

"Your wife!" exclaimed Westbrook. "How?"

"Well, not exactly by her, but *with* her," said Dawe. "Now, you know how devoted and loving Louise has always been. She thinks I'm the only genuine preparation on the market that bears the old doctor's signature. She's been fonder and more faithful than ever, since I've been cast for the neglected genius part."

"Indeed, she is a charming and admirable life companion,"

agreed the editor. "I remember what inseparable friends she and Mrs. Westbrook once were. We are both lucky chaps, Shack, to have such wives. You must bring Mrs. Dawe up some evening soon, and we'll have one of those informal chafing-dish suppers that we used to enjoy so much."

"Later," said Dawe. "When I get another shirt. And now I'll tell you my scheme. When I was about to leave home after breakfast—if you can call tea and oatmeal breakfast—Louise told me she was going to visit her aunt in Eighty-ninth Street. She said she would return home at three o'clock. She is always on time to a minute. It is now——"

Dawe glanced toward the editor's watch pocket.

"Twenty-seven minutes to three," said Westbrook, scanning his time-piece.

"We have just enough time," said Dawe. "We will go to my flat at once. I will write a note, address it to her and leave it on the table where she will see it as she enters the door. You and I will be in the dining-room concealed by the portières. In that note I'll say that I have fled from her forever with an affinity who understands the needs of my artistic soul as she never did. When she reads it we will observe her actions and hear her words. Then we will know which theory is the correct one—yours or mine."

"Oh, never!" exclaimed the editor, shaking his head. "That would be inexcusably cruel. I could not consent to have Mrs. Dawe's feelings played upon in such a manner."

"Brace up," said the writer. "I guess I think as much of her as you do. It's for her benefit as well as mine. I've got to get a market for my stories in some way. It won't hurt Louise. She's healthy and sound. Her heart goes as strong as a ninety-eight-cent watch. It'll last for only a minute, and then I'll step out and explain to her. You really owe it to me to give me the chance, Westbrook."

Editor Westbrook at length yielded, though but half willingly. And in the half of him that consented lurked the vivisectionist that is in all of us. Let him who has not used the scalpel rise and stand in his place. Pity 'tis that there are not enough rabbits and guinea-pigs to go around.

The two experimenters in Art left the Square and hurried

eastward and then to the south until they arrived in the Gramercy neighborhood. Within its high iron railings the little park had put on its smart coat of vernal green, and was admiring itself in its fountain mirror. Outside the railings the hollow square of crumbling houses, shells of a bygone gentry, leaned as if in ghostly gossip over the forgotten doings of the vanished quality. *Sic transit gloria urbis.*

A block or two north of the Park, Dawe steered the editor again eastward, then, after covering a short distance, into a lofty but narrow flathouse burdened with a floridly over-decorated façade. To the fifth story they toiled, and Dawe, panting, pushed his latch-key into the door of one of the front flats.

When the door opened Editor Westbrook saw, with feelings of pity, how meanly and meagerly the rooms were furnished.

"Get a chair, if you can find one," said Dawe, "while I hunt up pen and ink. Hello, what's this? Here's a note from Louise. She must have left it there when she went out this morning."

He picked up an envelope that lay on the centre-table and tore it open. He began to read the letter that he drew out of it; and once having begun it aloud he so read it through to the end. These are the words that Editor Westbrook heard:

"Dear Shackleford:

"By the time you get this I will be about a hundred miles away and still a-going. I've got a place in the chorus of the Occidental Opera Co., and we start on the road to-day at twelve o'clock. I didn't want to starve to death, and so I decided to make my own living. I'm not coming back. Mrs. Westbrook is going with me. She said she was tired of living with a combination phonograph, iceberg and dictionary, and she's not coming back, either. We've been practising the songs and dances for two months on the quiet. I hope you will be successful, and get along all right. Good-bye.   Louise."

Dawe dropped the letter, covered his face with his trembling hands, and cried out in a deep, vibrating voice:

"My God, why hast thou given me this cup to drink? Since she is false, then let Thy Heaven's fairest gifts, faith and love, become the jesting by-words of traitors and fiends!"

Editor Westbrook's glasses fell to the floor. The fingers of one hand fumbled with a button on his coat as he blurted between his pale lips:

"*Say, Shack, ain't that a hell of a note? Wouldn't that knock you off your perch, Shack? Ain't it hell, now, Shack—ain't it?*"

The Memento

Miss Lynnette D'Armande turned her back on Broadway. This was but tit for tat, because Broadway had often done the same thing to Miss D'Armande. Still, the "tats" seemed to have it, for the ex-leading lady of the "Reaping the Whirlwind" company had everything to ask of Broadway, while there was no vice-versâ.

So Miss Lynnette D'Armande turned the back of her chair to her window that overlooked Broadway, and sat down to stitch in time the lisle-thread heel of a black silk stocking. The tumult and glitter of the roaring Broadway beneath her window had no charm for her; what she greatly desired was the stifling air of a dressing-room on that fairyland street and the roar of an audience gathered in that capricious quarter. In the meantime, those stockings must not be neglected. Silk does wear out so, but—after all, isn't it just the only goods there is?

The Hotel Thalia looks on Broadway as Marathon looks on the sea. It stands like a gloomy cliff above the whirlpool where the tides of two great thoroughfares clash. Here the player-bands gather at the end of their wanderings, to loosen the buskin and dust the sock. Thick in the streets around it are booking-offices, theatres, agents, schools, and the lobster-palaces to which those thorny paths lead.

Wandering through the eccentric halls of the dim and fusty Thalia, you seem to have found yourself in some great ark or caravan about to sail, or fly, or roll away on wheels. About the house lingers a sense of unrest, of expectation, of transientness, even of anxiety and apprehension. The halls are a labyrinth. Without a guide, you wander like a lost soul in a Sam Loyd puzzle.

Turning any corner, a dressing-sack or a *cul-de-sac* may bring you up short. You meet alarming tragedians stalking in bath-robes in search of rumored bathrooms. From hundreds of rooms come the buzz of talk, scraps of new and old songs, and the ready laughter of the convened players.

Summer has come; their companies have disbanded, and they take their rest in their favorite caravansary, while they besiege the managers for engagements for the coming season.

At this hour of the afternoon the day's work of tramping the rounds of the agents' offices is over. Past you, as you ramble distractedly through the mossy halls, flit audible visions of houris, with veiled, starry eyes, flying tag-ends of things and a swish of silk, bequeathing to the dull hallways an odor of gaiety and a memory of *frangipanni*. Serious young comedians, with versatile Adam's apples, gather in doorways and talk of Booth. Far-reaching from somewhere comes the smell of ham and red cabbage, and the crash of dishes on the American plan.

The indeterminate hum of life in the Thalia is enlivened by the discreet popping—at reasonable and salubrious intervals—of beer-bottle corks. Thus punctuated, life in the genial hostel scans easily—the comma being the favorite mark, semicolons frowned upon, and periods barred.

Miss D'Armande's room was a small one. There was room for her rocker between the dresser and the washstand if it were placed longitudinally. On the dresser were its usual accoutrements, plus the ex-leading lady's collected souvenirs of road engagements and photographs of her dearest and best professional friends.

At one of these photographs she looked twice or thrice as she darned, and smiled friendlily.

"I'd like to know where Lee is just this minute," she said, half-aloud.

If you had been privileged to view the photograph thus flattered, you would have thought at the first glance that you saw the picture of a many-petalled white flower, blown through the air by a storm. But the floral kingdom was not responsible for that swirl of petalous whiteness.

You saw the filmy, brief skirt of Miss Rosalie Ray as she made a complete heels-over-head turn in her wistaria-entwined swing, far out from the stage, high above the heads of the audience. You saw the camera's inadequate representation of the graceful, strong kick, with which she, at this exciting moment, sent flying, high and far, the yellow silk garter that each evening spun from her agile limb and descended upon the delighted audience below.

You saw, too, amid the black-clothed, mainly masculine patrons of select vaudeville a hundred hands raised with the hope of staying the flight of the brilliant aërial token.

Forty weeks of the best circuits this act had brought Miss Rosalie Ray, for each of two years. She did other things during her twelve minutes—a song and dance, imitations of two or three actors who are but imitations of themselves, and a balancing feat with a step-ladder and feather-duster; but when the blossom-decked swing was let down from the flies, and Miss Rosalie sprang smiling into the seat, with the golden circlet conspicuous in the place whence it was soon to slide and become a soaring and coveted guerdon—then it was that the audience rose in its seat as a single man—or presumably so—and indorsed the specialty that made Miss Ray's name a favorite in the booking-offices.

At the end of the two years Miss Ray suddenly announced to her dear friend, Miss D'Armande, that she was going to spend the summer at an antediluvian village on the north shore of Long Island, and that the stage would see her no more.

Seventeen minutes after Miss Lynnette D'Armande had expressed her wish to know the whereabouts of her old chum, there were sharp raps at her door.

Doubt not that it was Rosalie Ray. At the shrill command to enter she did so, with something of a tired flutter, and dropped a heavy hand-bag on the floor. Upon my word, it was Rosalie, in a loose, travel-stained automobileless coat, closely tied brown veil with yard-long, flying ends, gray walking-suit and tan oxfords with lavender overgaiters.

When she threw off her veil and hat, you saw a pretty enough face, now flushed and disturbed by some unusual emotion, and restless, large eyes with discontent marring their brightness. A heavy pile of dull auburn hair, hastily put up, was escaping in crinkly, waving strands and curling, small locks from the confining combs and pins.

The meeting of the two was not marked by the effusion vocal, gymnastical, osculatory and catechetical that distinguishes the greetings of their unprofessional sisters in society. There was a brief clinch, two simultaneous labial dabs and they stood on the same footing of the old days. Very much like the short salutations of soldiers or of travellers in foreign wilds are the welcomes between the strollers at the corners of their criss-cross roads.

"I've got the hall-room two flights up above yours," said Rosalie, "but I came straight to see you before going up. I didn't know you were here till they told me."

"I've been in since the last of April," said Lynnette. "And I'm going on the road with a 'Fatal Inheritance' company. We open next week in Elizabeth. I thought you'd quit the stage, Lee. Tell me about yourself."

Rosalie settled herself with a skilful wriggle on the top of Miss D'Armande's wardrobe trunk, and leaned her head against the papered wall. From long habit, thus can peripatetic leading ladies and their sisters make themselves as comfortable as though the deepest armchairs embraced them.

"I'm going to tell you, Lynn," she said, with a strangely sardonic and yet carelessly resigned look on her youthful face. "And then to-morrow I'll strike the old Broadway trail again, and wear some more paint off the chairs in the agents' offices. If anybody had told me any time in the last three months up to four o'clock this afternoon that I'd ever listen to that 'Leave-your-name-and-address' rot of the booking bunch again, I'd have given 'em the real Mrs. Fiske laugh. Loan me a handkerchief, Lynn. Gee! but those Long Island trains are fierce. I've got enough soft-coal cinders on my face to go on and play *Topsy* without using the cork. And, speaking of corks—got anything to drink, Lynn?"

Miss D'Armande opened a door of the wash-stand and took out a bottle.

"There's nearly a pint of Manhattan. There's a cluster of carnations in the drinking glass, but——"

"Oh, pass the bottle. Save the glass for company. Thanks! That hits the spot. The same to you. My first drink in three months!

"Yes, Lynn, I quit the stage at the end of last season. I quit it because I was sick of the life. And especially because my heart and soul were sick of men—of the kind of men we stage people have to be up against. You know what the game is to us—it's a fight against 'em all the way down the line from the manager who wants us to try his new motor-car to the bill-posters who want to call us by our front names.

"And the men we have to meet after the show are the worst of all. The stage-door kind, and the manager's friends who take us to supper and show their diamonds and talk about seeing 'Dan' and 'Dave' and 'Charlie' for us. They're beasts, and I hate 'em.

"I tell you, Lynn, it's the girls like us on the stage that ought to be pitied. It's girls from good homes that are honestly ambitious and work hard to rise in the profession, but never do get there. You hear a lot of sympathy sloshed around on chorus girls and their fifteen dollars a week. Piffle! There ain't a sorrow in the chorus that a lobster cannot heal.

"If there's any tears to shed, let 'em fall for the actress that gets a salary of from thirty to forty-five dollars a week for taking a leading part in a bum show. She knows she'll never do any better; but she hangs on for years, hoping for the 'chance' that never comes.

"And the fool plays we have to work in! Having another girl roll you around the stage by the hind legs in a 'Wheelbarrow Chorus' in a musical comedy is dignified drama compared with the idiotic things I've had to do in the thirty-centers.

"But what I hated most was the men—the men leering and blathering at you across tables, trying to buy you with Würzburger or Extra Dry, according to their estimate of your price. And the men in the audiences, clapping, yelling, snarling, crowding, writhing, gloating—like a lot of wild beasts, with their eyes fixed on you, ready to eat you up if you come in reach of their claws. Oh, how I hate 'em!

"Well, I'm not telling you much about myself, am I, Lynn?

"I had two hundred dollars saved up, and I cut the stage the first of the summer. I went over on Long Island and found the sweetest little village that ever was, called Soundport, right on the water. I was going to spend the summer there, and study up on elocution, and try to get a class in the fall. There was an old widow lady with a cottage near the beach who sometimes rented a room or two just for company, and she took me in. She had another boarder, too—the Reverend Arthur Lyle.

"Yes, he was the head-liner. You're on, Lynn. I'll tell you all of it in a minute. It's only a one-act play.

"The first time he walked on, Lynn, I felt myself going; the first lines he spoke, he had me. He was different from the men in audiences. He was tall and slim, and you never heard him come in the room, but you *felt* him. He had a face like a picture of a knight—like one of that Round Table bunch—and a voice like a 'cello solo. And his manners!

"Lynn, if you'd take John Drew in his best drawing-room scene and compare the two, you'd have John arrested for disturbing the peace.

"I'll spare you the particulars; but in less than a month Arthur and I were engaged. He preached at a little one-night stand of a Methodist church. There was to be a parsonage the size of a lunch-wagon, and hens and honeysuckles when we were married. Arthur used to preach to me a good deal about Heaven, but he never could get my mind quite off those honeysuckles and hens.

"No; I didn't tell him I'd been on the stage. I hated the business and all that went with it; I'd cut it out forever, and I didn't see any use of stirring things up. I was a good girl, and I didn't have anything to confess, except being an elocutionist, and that was about all the strain my conscience would stand.

"Oh, I tell you, Lynn, I was happy. I sang in the choir and attended the sewing society, and recited that 'Annie Laurie' thing with the whistling stunt in it, 'in a manner bordering upon the professional,' as the weekly village paper reported it. And Arthur and I went rowing, and walking in the woods, and clamming, and that poky little village seemed to me the best place in the world. I'd have been happy to live there always, too, if——

"But one morning old Mrs. Gurley, the widow lady, got gossipy while I was helping her string beans on the back porch, and began to gush information, as folks who rent out their rooms usually do. Mr. Lyle was her idea of a saint on earth—as he was mine, too. She went over all his virtues and graces, and wound up by telling me that Arthur had had an extremely romantic love-affair, not long before, that had ended unhappily. She didn't seem to be on to the details, but she knew that he had been hit pretty hard. He was paler and thinner, she said, and he had some kind of a remembrance or keepsake of the lady in a little rosewood box that he kept locked in his desk drawer in his study.

"'Several times,' says she, 'I've seen him gloomerin' over that box of evenings, and he always locks it up right away if anybody comes into the room.'

"Well, you can imagine how long it was before I got Arthur by the wrist and led him down stage and hissed in his ear.

"That same afternoon we were lazying around in a boat among the water-lilies at the edge of the bay.

"'Arthur,' says I, 'you never told me you'd had another love-affair. But Mrs. Gurley did,' I went on, to let him know I knew. I hate to hear a man lie.

"'Before you came,' says he, looking me frankly in the eye, 'there was a previous affection—a strong one. Since you know of it, I will be perfectly candid with you.'

"'I am waiting,' says I.

"'My dear Ida,' says Arthur—of course I went by my real name, while I was in Soundport—'this former affection was a spiritual one, in fact. Although the lady aroused my deepest sentiments, and was, as I thought, my ideal woman, I never met her, and never spoke to her. It was an ideal love. My love for you, while no less ideal, is different. You wouldn't let that come between us.'

"'Was she pretty?' I asked.

"'She was very beautiful,' said Arthur.

"'Did you see her often?' I asked.

"'Something like a dozen times,' says he.

"'Always from a distance?' says I.

"'Always from quite a distance,' says he.

"'And you loved her?' I asked.

"'She seemed my ideal of beauty and grace—and soul,' says Arthur.

"'And this keepsake that you keep under lock and key, and moon over at times, is that a remembrance from her?'

"'A memento,' says Arthur, 'that I have treasured.'

"'Did she send it to you?'

"'It came to me from her,' says he.

"'In a roundabout way?' I asked.

"'Somewhat roundabout,' says he, 'and yet rather direct.'

"'Why didn't you ever meet her?' I asked. 'Were your positions in life so different?'

"'She was far above me,' says Arthur. 'Now, Ida,' he goes on, 'this is all of the past. You're not going to be jealous, are you?'

"'Jealous!' says I. 'Why, man, what are you talking about? It makes me think ten times as much of you as I did before I knew about it.'

"And it did, Lynn—if you can understand it. That ideal love was a new one on me, but it struck me as being the most beautiful and glorious thing I'd ever heard of. Think of a man loving a woman he'd never even spoken to, and being faithful just to what his mind and heart pictured her! Oh, it sounded great to me. The men I'd always known come at you with either diamonds, knock-out-drops or a raise of salary,—and their ideals!—well, we'll say no more.

"Yes, it made me think more of Arthur than I did before. I couldn't be jealous of that far-away divinity that he used to worship, for I was going to have him myself. And I began to look upon him as a saint on earth, just as old lady Gurley did.

"About four o'clock this afternoon a man came to the house for Arthur to go and see somebody that was sick among his church bunch. Old lady Gurley was taking her afternoon snore on a couch, so that left me pretty much alone.

"In passing by Arthur's study I looked in, and saw his bunch of keys hanging in the drawer of his desk, where he'd forgotten 'em. Well, I guess we're all to the Mrs. Bluebeard now and then, ain't we, Lynn? I made up my mind I'd have a look at that memento he kept so secret. Not that I cared what it was—it was just curiosity.

"While I was opening the drawer I imagined one or two things it might be. I thought it might be a dried rosebud she'd dropped down to him from a balcony, or maybe a picture of her he'd cut out of a magazine, she being so high up in the world.

"I opened the drawer, and there was the rosewood casket about the size of a gent's collar-box. I found the little key in the bunch that fitted it, and unlocked it and raised the lid.

"I took one look at that memento, and then I went to my room and packed my trunk. I threw a few things into my grip, gave my hair a flirt or two with a side-comb, put on my hat, and went in and gave the old lady's foot a kick. I'd tried awfully hard to use proper and correct language while I was there for Arthur's sake, and I had the habit down pat, but it left me then.

"'Stop sawing gourds,' says I, 'and sit up and take notice.

The ghost's about to walk. I'm going away from here, and I owe you eight dollars. The expressman will call for my trunk.'

"I handed her the money.

"'Dear me, Miss Crosby!' says she. 'Is anything wrong? I thought you were pleased here. Dear me, young women are so hard to understand, and so different from what you expect 'em to be.'

"'You're damn right,' says I. 'Some of 'em are. But you can't say that about men. *When you know one man you know 'em all!* That settles the human-race question.'

"And then I caught the four-thirty-eight, soft-coal unlimited; and here I am."

"You didn't tell me what was in the box, Lee," said Miss D'Armande, anxiously.

"One of those yellow silk garters that I used to kick off my leg into the audience during that old vaudeville swing act of mine. Is there any of the cocktail left, Lynn?"

A Night in New Arabia

THE GREAT city of Bagdad-on-the-Subway is caliph-ridden. Its palaces, bazaars, khans, and byways are thronged with Al Rashids in divers disguises, seeking diversion and victims for their unbridled generosity. You can scarcely find a poor beggar whom they are willing to let enjoy his spoils unsuccored, nor a wrecked unfortunate upon whom they will not reshower the means of fresh misfortune. You will hardly find anywhere a hungry one who has not had the opportunity to tighten his belt in gift libraries, nor a poor pundit who has not blushed at the holiday basket of celery-crowned turkey forced resoundingly through his door by the eleemosynary press.

So then, fearfully through the Harun-haunted streets creep the one-eyed calenders, the Little Hunchback and the Barber's Sixth Brother, hoping to escape the ministrations of the roving horde of caliphoid sultans.

Entertainment for many Arabian nights might be had from the histories of those who have escaped the largesse of the army of Commanders of the Faithful. Until dawn you might sit on the enchanted rug and listen to such stories as are told of the powerful genie Roc-Ef-El-Er who sent the Forty Thieves to soak up the oil plant of Ali Baba; of the good Caliph Kar-Neg-Ghe, who gave away palaces; of the Seven Voyages of Sailbad, the Sinner, who frequented wooden excursion steamers among the islands; of the Fisherman and the Bottle; of the Barmecides' Boarding house; of Aladdin's rise to wealth by means of his Wonderful Gas-meter.

But now, there being ten sultans to one Sheherazade, she is held too valuable to be in fear of the bowstring. In consequence the art of narrative languishes. And, as the lesser caliphs are hunting the happy poor and the resigned unfortunate from cover to cover in order to heap upon them strange mercies and mysterious benefits, too often comes the report from Arabian headquarters that the captive refused "to talk."

This reticence, then, in the actors who perform the sad comedies of their philanthropy-scourged world, must, in a degree, account for the shortcomings of this painfully gleaned tale, which shall be called

THE STORY OF THE CALIPH WHO ALLEVIATED HIS CONSCIENCE

Old Jacob Spraggins mixed for himself some Scotch and lithia water at his $1,200 oak sideboard. Inspiration must have resulted from its imbibition, for immediately afterward he struck the quartered oak soundly with his fist and shouted to the empty dining room:

"By the coke ovens of hell, it must be that ten thousand dollars! If I can get that squared, it'll do the trick."

Thus, by the commonest artifice of the trade, having gained your interest, the action of the story will now be suspended, leaving you grumpily to consider a sort of dull biography beginning fifteen years before.

When old Jacob was young Jacob he was a breaker boy in a Pennsylvania coal mine. I don't know what a breaker boy is; but his occupation seems to be standing by a coal dump with a wan look and a dinner-pail to have his picture taken for magazine articles. Anyhow, Jacob was one. But, instead of dying of overwork at nine, and leaving his helpless parents and brothers at the mercy of the union strikers' reserve fund, he hitched up his galluses, put a dollar or two in a side proposition now and then, and at forty-five was worth $20,000,000.

There now! it's over. Hardly had time to yawn, did you? I've seen biographies that—but let us dissemble.

I want you to consider Jacob Spraggins, Esq., after he had arrived at the seventh stage of his career. The stages meant are, first, humble origin; second, deserved promotion; third, stockholder; fourth, capitalist; fifth, trust magnate; sixth, rich malefactor; seventh, caliph; eighth, χ. The eighth stage shall be left to the higher mathematics.

At fifty-five Jacob retired from active business. The income of a czar was still rolling in on him from coal, iron, real estate, oil, railroads, manufactories, and corporations, but none of it touched Jacob's hands in a raw state. It was a sterilized increment, carefully cleaned and dusted and fumigated until it arrived at its ultimate stage of untainted, spotless checks in the white fingers of his private secretary. Jacob built a three-million-dollar palace on a corner lot fronting on Nabob Avenue, city of New Bagdad, and began to feel the mantle of the late H. A. Rashid descending upon him. Eventually Jacob slipped the mantle under his collar, tied it in a neat four-in-hand, and became a licensed harrier of our Mesopotamian proletariat.

When a man's income becomes so large that the butcher actually sends him the kind of steak he orders, he begins to think about his soul's salvation. Now, the various stages or classes of rich men must not be forgotten. The capitalist can tell you to a dollar the amount of his wealth. The trust magnate "estimates" it. The rich malefactor hands you a cigar and denies that he has bought the P. D. & Q. The caliph merely smiles and talks about Hammerstein and the musical lasses. There is a record of tremendous altercation at breakfast in a "Where-to-Dine-Well" tavern between a magnate and his wife, the rift within the loot being that the wife calculated their fortune at a figure $3,000,000 higher than did her future *divorcé*. Oh, well, I, myself, heard a similar quarrel between a man and his wife because he found fifty cents less in his pockets than he thought he had. After all, we are all human—Count Tolstoi, R. Fitzsimmons, Peter Pan, and the rest of us.

Don't lose heart because the story seems to be degenerating into a sort of moral essay for intellectual readers.

There will be dialogue and stage business pretty soon.

When Jacob first began to compare the eyes of needles with the camels in the Zoo he decided upon organized charity. He had his secretary send a check for one million to the Universal Benevolent Association of the Globe. You may have looked down through a grating in front of a decayed warehouse for a nickel that you had dropped through. But that is neither here nor there. The Association acknowledged receipt of his favor of the 24th ult. with enclosure as stated. Separated by a double line, but still mighty close to the matter under the caption of "Oddities of the Day's News" in an evening paper, Jacob Spraggins read that one "Jasper Spargyous" had "donated $100,000 to the U. B. A. of G." A camel may have a stomach for each day in the week; but I dare not venture to accord him whiskers, for fear of the Great Displeasure at Washington; but if he have whiskers, surely not one of them will seem to have been inserted in the eye of a needle by that effort of that rich man to enter the K. of H. The right is reserved to reject any and all bids; signed, S. Peter, secretary and gatekeeper.

Next, Jacob selected the best endowed college he could scare up and presented it with a $200,000 laboratory. The college did not maintain a scientific course, but it accepted the money and built an elaborate lavatory instead, which was no diversion of funds so far as Jacob ever discovered.

The faculty met and invited Jacob to come over and take his A B C degree. Before sending the invitation they smiled, cut out the C, added the proper punctuation marks, and all was well.

While walking on the campus before being capped and gowned, Jacob saw two professors strolling nearby. Their voices, long adapted to indoor acoustics, undesignedly reached his ear.

"There goes the latest *chevalier d'industrie*," said one of them, "to buy a sleeping powder from us. He gets his degree to-morrow."

"*In foro conscientiæ*," said the other. "Let's 'eave 'arf a brick at 'im."

Jacob ignored the Latin, but the brick pleasantry was not too hard for him. There was no mandragora in the honorary draught of learning that he had bought. That was before the passage of the Pure Food and Drugs Act.

Jacob wearied of philanthropy on a large scale.

"If I could see folks made happier," he said to himself—"if I could see 'em myself and hear 'em express their gratitude for what I done for 'em it would make me feel better. This donatin' funds to institutions and societies is about as satisfactory as dropping money into a broken slot machine."

So Jacob followed his nose, which led him through unswept streets to the homes of the poorest.

"The very thing!" said Jacob. "I will charter two river steamboats, pack them full of these unfortunate children and—say ten thousand dolls and drums and a thousand freezers of ice cream, and give them a delightful outing up the Sound. The sea breezes on that trip ought to blow the taint off some of this money that keeps coming in faster than I can work it off my mind."

Jacob must have leaked some of his benevolent intentions, for an immense person with a bald face and a mouth that looked as if it ought to have a "Drop Letters Here" sign over it hooked a finger around him and set him in a space between a barber's pole and a stack of ash cans. Words came out of the post-office slit—smooth, husky words with gloves on 'em, but sounding as if they might turn to bare knuckles any moment.

"Say, Sport, do you know where you are at? Well, dis is Mike O'Grady's district you're buttin' into—see? Mike's got de stomach-ache privilege for every kid in dis neighborhood—see? And if dere's any picnics or red balloons to be dealt out here, Mike's money pays for 'em—see? Don't you butt in, or something'll be handed to you. Youse d—— settlers and reformers with your social ologies and your millionaire detectives have got dis district in a hell of a fix, anyhow. With your college students and professors rough-housing de soda-water stands and dem rubber-neck coaches fillin' de streets, de folks down here are 'fraid to go out of de houses. Now, you leave 'em to Mike. Dey belongs to him, and he knows how to handle 'em. Keep on your own side of de town. Are you some wiser now, uncle, or do you want to scrap wit' Mike O'Grady for de Santa Claus belt in dis district?"

Clearly, that spot in the moral vineyard was preëmpted. So Caliph Spraggins menaced no more the people in the bazaars of the East Side. To keep down his growing surplus he doubled his donations to organized charity, presented the Y. M. C. A. of his native town with a $10,000 collection of butterflies, and sent a check to the famine sufferers in China big enough to buy new emerald eyes and diamond-filled teeth for all their gods. But none of these charitable acts seemed to bring peace to the caliph's heart. He tried to get a personal note into his benefactions by tipping bell-boys and waiters $10 and $20 bills. He got well snickered at and derided for that by the minions who accept with respect gratuities commensurate to the service performed. He sought out an ambitious and talented but poor young woman, and bought for her the star part in a new comedy. He might have gotten rid of $50,000 more of his cumbersome money in this philanthropy if he had not neglected to write letters to her. But she lost the suit for lack of evidence, while his capital still kept piling up, and his *optikos needleorum camelibus*—or rich man's disease—was unrelieved.

In Caliph Spraggins's $3,000,000 home lived his sister Henrietta, who used to cook for the coal miners in a twenty-five-cent eating house in Coketown, Pa., and who now would have offered John Mitchell only two fingers of her hand to shake. And his daughter Celia, nineteen, back from boarding-school and from being polished off by private instructors in the restaurant languages and those études and things.

Celia is the heroine. Lest the artist's delineation of her charms on this very page humbug your fancy, take from me her authorized description. She was a nice-looking, awkward, loud, rather bashful, brown-haired girl, with a sallow complexion, bright eyes, and a perpetual smile. She had a wholesome, Spraggins-inherited love for plain food, loose clothing, and the society of the lower classes. She had too much health and youth to feel the burden of wealth. She had a wide mouth that kept the peppermint-pepsin tablets rattling like hail from the slot-machine wherever she went, and she could whistle hornpipes. Keep this picture in mind; and let the artist do his worst.

Celia looked out of her window one day and gave her heart to the grocer's young man. The receiver thereof was at that moment engaged in conceding immortality to his horse and calling down upon him the ultimate fate of the wicked; so he did not notice the transfer. A horse should stand still when you are lifting a crate of strictly new-laid eggs out of the wagon.

Young lady reader, you would have liked that grocer's young man yourself. But you wouldn't have given him your heart, because you are saving it for a riding-master, or a shoe-manufacturer with a torpid liver, or something quiet but rich in gray tweeds at Palm Beach. Oh, I know about it. So I am glad the grocer's young man was for Celia, and not for you.

The grocer's young man was slim and straight and as confident and easy in his movements as the man in the back of the magazines who wears the new frictionless roller suspenders. He wore a gray bicycle cap on the back of his head, and his hair was straw-colored and curly, and his sunburned face looked like one that smiled a good deal when he was not preaching the doctrine of everlasting punishment to delivery-wagon horses. He slung imported A1 fancy groceries about as though they were only the stuff he delivered at boarding-houses; and when he picked up his whip, your mind instantly recalled Mr. Tackett and his air with the buttonless foils.

Tradesmen delivered their goods at a side gate at the rear of the house. The grocer's wagon came about ten in the morning. For three days Celia watched the driver when he came, finding something new each time to admire in the lofty and almost contemptuous way he had of tossing around the choicest gifts of Pomona, Ceres, and the canning factories. Then she consulted Annette.

To be explicit, Annette McCorkle, the second housemaid, who deserves a paragraph herself. Annette Fletcherized large numbers of romantic novels which she obtained at a free public library branch (donated by one of the biggest caliphs in the business). She was Celia's sidekicker and chum, though Aunt Henrietta didn't know it, you may hazard a bean or two.

"Oh, canary-bird seed!" exclaimed Annette. "Ain't it a corkin' situation? You a heiress, and fallin' in love with him on sight! He's a sweet boy, too, and above his business. But he ain't suspectible like the common run of grocer's assistants. He never pays no attention to me."

"He will to me," said Celia.

"Riches——" began Annette, unsheathing the not unjustifiable feminine sting.

"Oh, you're not so beautiful," said Celia, with her wide, disarming smile. "Neither am I; but he sha'n't know that there's any money mixed up with my looks, such as they are. That's fair. Now, I want you to lend me one of your caps and an apron, Annette."

"Oh, marshmallows!" cried Annette. "I see. Ain't it lovely? It's just like 'Lurline, the Left-Handed; or, A Buttonhole Maker's Wrongs.' I'll bet he'll turn out to be a count."

There was a long hallway (or "passageway," as they call it in the land of the Colonels) with one side latticed, running along the rear of the house. The grocer's young man went through this to deliver his goods. One morning he passed a girl in there with shining eyes, sallow complexion, and wide, smiling mouth, wearing a maid's cap and apron. But as he was cumbered with a basket of Early Drumhead lettuce and Trophy tomatoes and three bunches of asparagus and six bottles of the most expensive Queen olives, he saw no more than that she was one of the maids.

But on his way out he came up behind her, and she was whistling "Fisher's Hornpipe" so loudly and clearly that all the piccolos in the world should have disjointed themselves and crept into their cases for shame.

The grocer's young man stopped and pushed back his cap until it hung on his collar button behind.

"That's out o' sight, Kid," said he.

"My name is Celia, if you please," said the whistler, dazzling him with a three-inch smile.

"That's all right. I'm Thomas McLeod. What part of the house do you work in?"

"I'm the—the second parlor maid."

"Do you know the 'Falling Waters'?"

"No," said Celia, "we don't know anybody. We got rich too quick—that is, Mr. Spraggins did."

"I'll make you acquainted," said Thomas McLeod. "It's a strathspey—a first cousin to a hornpipe."

If Celia's whistling put the piccolos out of commission, Thomas McLeod's surely made the biggest flutes hunt their holes. He could actually whistle *bass*.

When he stopped Celia was ready to jump into his delivery wagon and ride with him clear to the end of the pier and on to the ferry-boat of the Charon line.

"I'll be around to-morrow at 10:15," said Thomas, "with some spinach and a case of carbonic."

"I'll practice that what-you-may-call-it," said Celia. "I can whistle a fine second."

The processes of courtship are personal, and do not belong to general literature. They should be chronicled in detail only in advertisements of iron tonics and in the secret by-laws of the Woman's Auxiliary of the Ancient Order of the Rat Trap. But genteel writing may contain a description of certain stages of its progress without intruding upon the province of the X-ray or of park policemen.

A day came when Thomas McLeod and Celia lingered at the end of the latticed "passage."

"Sixteen a week isn't much," said Thomas, letting his cap rest on his shoulder blades.

Celia looked through the lattice-work and whistled a dead march. Shopping with Aunt Henrietta the day before, she had paid that much for a dozen handkerchiefs.

"Maybe I'll get a raise next month," said Thomas. "I'll be around to-morrow at the same time with a bag of flour and the laundry soap."

"All right," said Celia. "Annette's married cousin pays only $20 a month for a flat in the Bronx."

Never for a moment did she count on the Spraggins money. She knew Aunt Henrietta's invincible pride of caste and pa's mightiness as a Colossus of cash, and she understood that if she chose Thomas she and her grocer's young man might go whistle for their living.

Another day came, Thomas violating the dignity of Nabob Avenue with "The Devil's Dream," whistled keenly between his teeth.

"Raised to eighteen a week yesterday," he said. "Been pricing flats around Morningside. You want to start untying those apron strings and unpinning that cap, old girl."

"Oh, Tommy!" said Celia, with her broadest smile. "Won't that be enough? I got Betty to show me how to make a cottage pudding. I guess we could call it a flat pudding if we wanted to."

"And tell no lie," said Thomas.

"And I can sweep and polish and dust—of course, a parlor maid learns that. And we could whistle duets of evenings."

"The old man said he'd raise me to twenty at Christmas if Bryan couldn't think of any harder name to call a Republican than a 'postponer,'" said the grocer's young man.

"I can sew," said Celia; "and I know that you must make the gas company's man show his badge when he comes to look at the meter; and I know how to put up quince jam and window curtains."

"Bully! you're all right, Cele. Yes, I believe we can pull it off on eighteen."

As he was jumping into the wagon the second parlor maid braved discovery by running swiftly to the gate.

"And, oh, Tommy, I forgot," she called, softly. "I believe I could make your neckties."

"Forget it," said Thomas decisively.

"And another thing," she continued. "Sliced cucumbers at night will drive away cockroaches."

"And sleep, too, you bet," said Mr. McLeod. "Yes, I believe if I have a delivery to make on the West Side this afternoon I'll look in at a furniture store I know over there."

It was just as the wagon dashed away that old Jacob Spraggins struck the sideboard with his fist and made the mysterious remark about ten thousand dollars that you perhaps remember. Which justifies the reflection that some stories, as well as life, and puppies thrown into wells, move around in circles. Painfully but briefly we must shed light on Jacob's words.

The foundation of his fortune was made when he was twenty. A poor coal-digger (ever hear of a rich one?) had saved a dollar or two and bought a small tract of land on a hillside on which he tried to raise corn. Not a nubbin. Jacob, whose nose was a divining-rod, told him there was a vein of coal beneath. He bought the land from the miner for $125 and sold it a month afterward for $10,000. Luckily the miner had enough left of his sale money to drink himself into a black coat opening in the back, as soon as he heard the news.

And so, forty years afterward, we find Jacob illuminated with the sudden thought that if he could make restitution of this sum of money to the heirs or assigns of the unlucky miner, respite and Nepenthe might be his.

And now must come swift action, for we have here some four thousand words and not a tear shed and never a pistol, joke, safe, nor bottle cracked.

Old Jacob hired a dozen private detectives to find the heirs, if any existed, of the old miner, Hugh McLeod.

Get the point? Of course I know as well as you do that Thomas is going to be the heir. I might have concealed the name; but why always hold back your mystery till the end? I say, let it come near the middle so people can stop reading there if they want to.

After the detectives had trailed false clues about three thousand dollars—I mean miles—they cornered Thomas at the grocery and got his confession that Hugh McLeod had been his grandfather, and that there were no other heirs. They arranged a meeting for him and old Jacob one morning in one of their offices.

Jacob liked the young man very much. He liked the way he looked straight at him when he talked, and the way he threw his bicycle cap over the top of a rose-colored vase on the centre-table.

There was a slight flaw in Jacob's system of restitution. He did not consider that the act, to be perfect, should include confession. So he represented himself to be the agent of the purchaser of the land who had sent him to refund the sale price for the ease of his conscience.

"Well, sir," said Thomas, "this sounds to me like an illustrated post-card from South Boston with 'We're having a good time here' written on it. I don't know the game. Is this ten thousand dollars money, or do I have to save so many coupons to get it?"

Old Jacob counted out to him twenty five-hundred-dollar bills.

That was better, he thought, than a check. Thomas put them thoughtfully into his pocket.

"Grandfather's best thanks," he said, "to the party who sends it."

Jacob talked on, asking him about his work, how he spent his leisure time, and what his ambitions were. The more he saw and heard of Thomas, the better he liked him. He had not met many young men in Bagdad so frank and wholesome.

"I would like to have you visit my house," he said. "I might help you in investing or laying out your money. I am a very wealthy man. I have a daughter about grown, and I would like for you to know her. There are not many young men I would care to have call on her."

"I'm obliged," said Thomas. "I'm not much at making calls. It's generally the side entrance for mine. And, besides, I'm engaged to a girl that has the Delaware peach crop killed in the blossom. She's a parlor maid in a house where I deliver goods. She won't be working there much longer, though. Say, don't forget to give your friend my grandfather's best regards. You'll excuse me now; my wagon's outside with a lot of green stuff that's got to be delivered. See you again, sir."

At eleven Thomas delivered some bunches of parsley and lettuce at the Spraggins mansion. Thomas was only twenty-two; so, as he came back, he took out the handful of five-hundred-dollar bills and waved them carelessly. Annette took a pair of eyes as big as creamed onions to the cook.

"I told you he was a count," she said, after relating. "He never would carry on with me."

"But you say he showed money," said the cook.

"Hundreds of thousands," said Annette. "Carried around loose in his pockets. And he never would look at me."

"It was paid to me to-day," Thomas was explaining to Celia outside. "It came from my grandfather's estate. Say, Cele, what's the use of waiting now? I'm going to quit the job to-night. Why can't we get married next week?"

"Tommy," said Celia, "I'm no parlor maid. I've been fooling you. I'm Miss Spraggins—Celia Spraggins. The newspapers say I'll be worth forty million dollars some day."

Thomas pulled his cap down straight on his head for the first time since we have known him.

"I suppose then," said he, "I suppose then you'll not be marrying me next week. But you *can* whistle."

"No," said Celia, "I'll not be marrying you next week. My father would never let me marry a grocer's clerk. But I'll marry you to-night, Tommy, if you say so."

Old Jacob Spraggins came home at 9:30 P.M., in his motor car. The make of it you will have to surmise sorrowfully; I am giving you unsubsidized fiction; had it been a street car I could have told you its voltage and the number of flat wheels it had. Jacob called for his daughter; he had bought a ruby necklace for her, and wanted to hear her say what a kind, thoughtful, dear old dad he was.

There was a brief search in the house for her, and then came Annette, glowing with the pure flame of truth and loyalty well mixed with envy and histrionics.

"Oh, sir," said she, wondering if she should kneel, "Miss Celia's just this minute running away out of the side gate with a young man to be married. I couldn't stop her, sir. They went in a cab."

"What young man?" roared old Jacob.

"A millionaire, if you please, sir—a rich nobleman in disguise.

He carries his money with him, and the red peppers and the onions was only to blind us, sir. He never did seem to take to me."

Jacob rushed out in time to catch his car. The chauffeur had been delayed by trying to light a cigarette in the wind.

"Here, Gaston, or Mike, or whatever you call yourself, scoot around the corner quicker than blazes and see if you can see a cab. If you do, run it down."

There was a cab in sight a block away. Gaston, or Mike, with his eyes half shut and his mind on his cigarette, picked up the trail, neatly crowded the cab to the curb and pocketed it.

"What t'ell you doin'?" yelled the cabman.

"Pa!" shrieked Celia.

"Grandfather's remorseful friend's agent!" said Thomas. "Wonder what's on his conscience now."

"A thousand thunders!" said Gaston, or Mike. "I have no other match."

"Young man," said old Jacob, severely, "how about that parlor maid you were engaged to?"

A couple of years afterward old Jacob went into the office of his private secretary.

"The Amalgamated Missionary Society solicits a contribution of $30,000 toward the conversion of the Koreans," said the secretary.

"Pass 'em up," said Jacob.

"The University of Plumville writes that its yearly endowment fund of $50,000 that you bestowed upon it is past due."

"Tell 'em it's been cut out."

"The Scientific Society of Clam Cove, Long Island, asks for $10,000 to buy alcohol to preserve specimens."

"Waste basket."

"The Society for Providing Healthful Recreation for Working Girls wants $20,000 from you to lay out a golf course."

"Tell 'em to see an undertaker."

"Cut 'em all out," went on Jacob. "I've quit being a good thing. I need every dollar I can scrape or save. I want you to write to the directors of every company that I'm interested in and recommend a 10 per cent. cut in salaries. And say—I noticed half a cake of soap lying in a corner of the hall as I came in. I want you to speak to the scrubwoman about waste. I've got no money to throw away. And say—we've got vinegar pretty well in hand, haven't we?"

"The Globe Spice & Seasons Company," said the secretary, "controls the market at present."

"Raise vinegar two cents a gallon. Notify all our branches."

Suddenly Jacob Spraggins's plump red face relaxed into a pulpy grin. He walked over to the secretary's desk and showed a small red mark on his thick forefinger.

"Bit it," he said, "darned if he didn't, and he ain't had the tooth three weeks—Jaky McLeod, my Celia's kid. He'll be worth a hundred millions by the time he's twenty-one if I can pile it up for him."

As he was leaving, old Jacob turned at the door, and said:

"Better make that vinegar raise three cents instead of two. I'll be back in an hour and sign the letters."

The true history of the Caliph Harun Al Rashid relates that toward the end of his reign he wearied of philanthropy, and caused to be beheaded all his former favorites and companions of his "Arabian Nights" rambles. Happy are we in these days of enlightenment, when the only death warrant the caliphs can serve on us is in the form of a tradesman's bill.

Strictly Business

I SUPPOSE you know all about the stage and stage people. You've been touched with and by actors, and you read the newspaper criticisms and the jokes in the weeklies about the Rialto and the chorus girls and the long-haired tragedians. And I suppose that a condensed list of your ideas about the mysterious stageland would boil down to something like this:

Leading ladies have five husbands, paste diamonds, and figures no better than your own (madam) if they weren't padded. Chorus girls are inseparable from peroxide, Panhards and Pittsburg. All shows walk back to New York on tan oxford and railroad ties. Irreproachable actresses reserve the comic-landlady part for their mothers on Broadway and their step-aunts on the road. Kyrle Bellew's real name is Boyle O'Kelley. The ravings of John McCullough in the phonograph were stolen from the first sale of the Ellen Terry memoirs. Joe Weber is funnier than E. H. Sothern; but Henry Miller is getting older than he was.

All theatrical people on leaving the theatre at night drink champagne and eat lobsters until noon the next day. After all, the moving pictures have got the whole bunch pounded to a pulp.

Now, few of us know the real life of the stage people. If we did, the profession might be more overcrowded than it is. We look askance at the players with an eye full of patronizing superiority—and we go home and practise all sorts of elocution and gestures in front of our looking glasses.

Latterly there has been much talk of the actor people in a new light. It seems to have been divulged that instead of being motoring bacchanalians and diamond-hungry *loreleis* they are businesslike folk, students and ascetics with childer and homes and libraries, owning real estate, and conducting their private affairs in as orderly and unsensational a manner as any of us good citizens who are bound to the chariot wheels of the gas, rent, coal, ice, and wardmen.

Whether the old or the new report of the sock-and-buskiners be the true one is a surmise that has no place here. I offer you merely this little story of two strollers; and for proof of its truth

I can show you only the dark patch above the cast-iron handle of the stage-entrance door of Keetor's old vaudeville theatre made there by the petulant push of gloved hands too impatient to finger the clumsy thumb-latch—and where I last saw Cherry whisking through like a swallow into her nest, on time to the minute, as usual, to dress for her act.

The vaudeville team of Hart & Cherry was an inspiration. Bob Hart had been roaming through the Eastern and Western circuits for four years with a mixed-up act comprising a monologue, three lightning changes with songs, a couple of imitations of celebrated imitators, and a buck-and-wing dance that had drawn a glance of approval from the bass-viol player in more than one house—than which no performer ever received more satisfactory evidence of good work.

The greatest treat an actor can have is to witness the pitiful performance with which all other actors desecrate the stage. In order to give himself this pleasure he will often forsake the sunniest Broadway corner between Thirty-fourth and Forty-fourth to attend a matinée offering by his less gifted brothers. Once during the lifetime of a minstrel joke one comes to scoff and remains to go through with that most difficult exercise of Thespian muscles—the audible contact of the palm of one hand against the palm of the other.

One afternoon Bob Hart presented his solvent, serious, well-known vaudevillian face at the box-office window of a rival attraction and got his d. h. coupon for an orchestra seat.

A, B, C, and D glowed successively on the announcement spaces and passed into oblivion, each plunging Mr. Hart deeper into gloom. Others of the audience shrieked, squirmed, whistled and applauded; but Bob Hart, "All the Mustard and a Whole Show in Himself," sat with his face as long and his hands as far apart as a boy holding a hank of yarn for his grandmother to wind into a ball.

But when H came on, "The Mustard" suddenly sat up straight. H was the happy alphabetical prognosticator of Winona Cherry, in Character Songs and Impersonations. There were scarcely more than two bites to Cherry; but she delivered the merchandise tied with a pink cord and charged to the old man's account. She first showed you a deliciously dewy and ginghamy country girl with a basket of property daisies who informed you ingenuously that there were other things to be learned at the old log school-house besides cipherin' and nouns, especially "When the Teach-er Kept Me in." Vanishing, with a quick flirt of gingham apron-strings, she reappeared in considerably less than a "trice" as a fluffy "Parisienne"—so near does Art bring the old red mill to the Moulin Rouge. And then——

But you know the rest. And so did Bob Hart; but he saw somebody else. He thought he saw that Cherry was the only professional on the short order stage that he had seen who seemed exactly to fit the part of "Helen Grimes" in the sketch he had written and kept tucked away in the tray of his trunk. Of course Bob Hart, as well as every other normal actor, grocer, newspaper man, professor, curb broker, and farmer, has a play tucked away somewhere. They tuck 'em in trays of trunks, trunks of trees, desks, haymows, pigeonholes, inside pockets, safe-deposit vaults, handboxes, and coal cellars, waiting for Mr. Frohman to call. They belong among the fifty-seven different kinds.

But Bob Hart's sketch was not destined to end in a pickle jar. He called it "Mice Will Play." He had kept it quiet and hidden away ever since he wrote it, waiting to find a partner who fitted his conception of "Helen Grimes." And here was "Helen" herself, with all the innocent abandon, the youth, the sprightliness, and the flawless stage art that his critical taste demanded.

After the act was over Hart found the manager in the box office, and got Cherry's address. At five the next afternoon he called at the musty old house in the West Forties and sent up his professional card.

By daylight, in a secular shirtwaist and plain *voile* skirt, with her hair curbed and her Sister of Charity eyes, Winona Cherry might have been playing the part of Prudence Wise, the deacon's daughter, in the great (unwritten) New England drama not yet entitled anything.

"I know your act, Mr. Hart," she said after she had looked over his card carefully. "What did you wish to see me about?"

"I saw you work last night," said Hart. "I've written a sketch that I've been saving up. It's for two; and I think you can do the other part. I thought I'd see you about it."

"Come in the parlor," said Miss Cherry. "I've been wishing for something of the sort. I think I'd like to act instead of doing turns."

Bob Hart drew his cherished "Mice Will Play" from his pocket, and read it to her.

"Read it again, please," said Miss Cherry.

And then she pointed out to him clearly how it could be improved by introducing a messenger instead of a telephone call, and cutting the dialogue just before the climax while they were struggling for the pistol, and by completely changing the lines and business of Helen Grimes at the point where her jealousy overcomes her. Hart yielded to all her strictures without argument. She had at once put her finger on the sketch's weaker points. That was her woman's intuition that he had lacked. At the end of their talk Hart was willing to stake the judgment, experience, and savings of his four years of vaudeville that "Mice Will Play" would blossom into a perennial flower in the garden of the circuits. Miss Cherry was slower to decide. After many puckerings of her smooth young brow and tappings on her small, white teeth with the end of a lead pencil she gave out her dictum.

"Mr. Hart," said she, "I believe your sketch is going to win out. That Grimes part fits me like a shrinkable flannel after its first trip to a handless hand laundry. I can make it stand out like the colonel of the Forty-fourth Regiment at a Little Mothers' Bazaar. And I've seen you work. I know what you can do with the other part. But business is business. How much do you get a week for the stunt you do now?"

"Two hundred," answered Hart.

"I get one hundred for mine," said Cherry. "That's about the natural discount for a woman. But I live on it and put a few simoleons every week under the loose brick in the old kitchen hearth. The stage is all right. I love it; but there's something else I love better—that's a little country home, some day, with Plymouth Rock chickens and six ducks wandering around the yard.

"Now, let me tell you, Mr. Hart, I am STRICTLY BUSINESS. If you want me to play the opposite part in your sketch, I'll do it. And I believe we can make it go. And there's something else I want to say: There's no nonsense in my make-up; I'm *on the level*, and I'm on the stage for what it pays me, just as other girls work in stores and offices. I'm going to save my money to keep me when I'm past doing my stunts. No Old Ladies' Home or Retreat for Imprudent Actresses for me.

"If you want to make this a business partnership, Mr. Hart, with all nonsense cut out of it, I'm in on it. I know something about vaudeville teams in general; but this would have to be one in particular. I want you to know that I'm on the stage for what I can cart away from it every pay-day in a little manila envelope with nicotine stains on it, where the cashier has licked the flap. It's kind of a hobby of mine to want to cravenette myself for plenty of rainy days in the future. I want you to know just how I am. I don't know what an all-night restaurant looks like; I drink only weak tea; I never spoke to a man at a stage entrance in my life, and I've got money in five savings banks."

"Miss Cherry," said Bob Hart in his smooth, serious tones, "you're in on your own terms. I've got 'strictly business' pasted in my hat and stenciled on my make-up box. When I dream of nights I always see a five-room bungalow on the north shore of Long Island, with a Jap cooking clam broth and duckling in the kitchen, and me with the title deeds to the place in my pongee coat pocket, swinging in a hammock on the side porch, reading Stanley's 'Explorations into Africa.' And nobody else around. You never was interested in Africa, was you, Miss Cherry?"

"Not any," said Cherry. "What I'm going to do with my money is to bank it. You can get four per cent. on deposits. Even at the salary I've been earning, I've figured out that in ten years I'd have an income of about $50 a month just from the interest alone. Well, I might invest some of the principal in a little business—say, trimming hats or a beauty parlor, and make more."

"Well," said Hart, "you've got the proper idea all right, all right, anyhow. There are mighty few actors that amount to anything at all who couldn't fix themselves for the wet days to come if they'd save their money instead of blowing it. I'm glad you've got the correct business idea of it, Miss Cherry. I think the same way; and I believe this sketch will more than double what both of us earn now when we get it shaped up."

The subsequent history of "Mice Will Play" is the history of all successful writings for the stage. Hart & Cherry cut it, pieced it, remodeled it, performed surgical operations on the dialogue and business, changed the lines, restored 'em, added more, cut 'em out, renamed it, gave it back the old name, rewrote it, substituted a dagger for the pistol, restored the pistol—put the sketch through all the known processes of condensation and improvement.

They rehearsed it by the old-fashioned boarding-house clock in the rarely used parlor until its warning click at five minutes to the hour would occur every time exactly half a second before the click of the unloaded revolver that Helen Grimes used in rehearsing the thrilling climax of the sketch.

Yes, that was a thriller and a piece of excellent work. In the act a real 32-caliber revolver was used loaded with a real cartridge. Helen Grimes, who is a Western girl of decidedly Buffalo Billish skill and daring, is tempestuously in love with Frank Desmond, the private secretary and confidential prospective son-in-law of her father, "Arapahoe" Grimes, quarter-million-dollar cattle king, owning a ranch that, judging by the scenery, is in either the Bad Lands or Amagansett, L. I. Desmond (in private life Mr. Bob Hart) wears puttees and Meadow Brook Hunt riding trousers, and gives his address as New York, leaving you to wonder why he comes to the Bad Lands or Amagansett (as the case may be) and at the same time to conjecture mildly why a cattleman should want puttees about his ranch with a secretary in 'em.

Well, anyhow, you know as well as I do that we all like that kind of play, whether we admit it or not—something along in between "Bluebeard, Jr.," and "Cymbeline" played in the Russian.

There were only two parts and a half in "Mice Will Play." Hart and Cherry were the two, of course; and the half was a minor part always played by a stage hand, who merely came in once in a Tuxedo coat and a panic to announce that the house was surrounded by Indians, and to turn down the gas fire in the grate by the manager's orders.

There was another girl in the sketch—a Fifth Avenue society swelless—who was visiting the ranch and who had sirened Jack Valentine when he was a wealthy clubman on lower Third Avenue before he lost his money. This girl appeared on the stage only in the photographic state—Jack had her Sarony stuck up on the mantel of the Amagan—of the Bad Lands droring room. Helen was jealous, of course.

And now for the thriller. Old "Arapahoe" Grimes dies of angina pectoris one night—so Helen informs us in a stage-ferryboat whisper over the footlights—while only his secretary was present. And that same day he was known to have had $647,000 in cash in his (ranch) library just received for the sale of a drove of beeves in the East (that accounts for the prices we pay for steak!). The cash disappears at the same time. Jack Valentine was the only person with the ranchman when he made his (alleged) croak.

"Gawd knows I love him; but if he has done this deed——" you sabe, don't you? And then there are some mean things said about the Fifth Avenue Girl—who doesn't come on the stage—and can we blame her, with the vaudeville trust holding down prices until one actually must be buttoned in the back by a call boy, maids cost so much?

But, wait. Here's the climax. Helen Grimes, chaparralish as she can be, is goaded beyond imprudence. She convinces herself that Jack Valentine is not only a falsetto, but a financier. To lose at one fell swoop $647,000 and a lover in riding trousers with angles in the sides like the variations on the chart of a typhoid-fever patient is enough to make any perfect lady mad. So, then!

They stand in the (ranch) library, which is furnished with mounted elk heads (didn't the Elks have a fish fry in Amagansett once?), and the dénouement begins. I know of no more interesting time in the run of a play unless it be when the prologue ends.

Helen thinks Jack has taken the money. Who else was there to take it? The box-office manager was at the front on his job; the orchestra hadn't left their seats; and no man could get past "Old Jimmy," the stage doorman, unless he could show a Skye terrier or an automobile as a guarantee of eligibility.

Goaded beyond imprudence (as before said), Helen says to Jack Valentine: "Robber and thief—and worse yet, stealer of trusting hearts, this should be your fate!"

With that out she whips, of course, the trusty 32-caliber.

"But I will be merciful," goes on Helen. "You shall live—that will be your punishment. I will show you how easily I could have sent you to the death that you deserve. There is *her* picture on the mantel. I will send through her more beautiful face the bullet that should have pierced your craven heart."

And she does it. And there's no fake blank cartridges or assistants pulling strings. Helen fires. The bullet—the actual bullet—goes through the face of the photograph—and then strikes the hidden spring of the sliding panel in the wall—and lo! the panel slides, and there is the missing $647,000 in convincing stacks of currency and bags of gold. It's great. You know how it is. Cherry practised for two months at a target on the roof of her boarding house. It took good shooting. In the sketch she had to hit a brass disk only three inches in diameter, covered by wall paper in the panel; and she had to stand in exactly the same spot every night, and the photo had to be in exactly the same spot, and she had to shoot steady and true every time.

Of course old "Arapahoe" had tucked the funds away there in the secret place; and, of course, Jack hadn't taken anything except his salary (which really might have come under the head of "obtaining money under"; but that is neither here nor there); and, of course, the New York girl was really engaged to a concrete house contractor in the Bronx; and, necessarily, Jack and Helen ended in a half-Nelson—and there you are.

After Hart and Cherry had gotten "Mice Will Play" flawless, they had a try-out at a vaudeville house that accommodates. The sketch was a house wrecker. It was one of those rare strokes of talent that inundates a theatre from the roof down. The gallery wept; and the orchestra seats, being dressed for it, swam in tears.

After the show the booking agents signed blank checks and pressed fountain pens upon Hart and Cherry. Five hundred dollars a week was what it panned out.

That night at 11.30 Bob Hart took off his hat and bade Cherry good night at her boarding-house door.

"Mr. Hart," said she thoughtfully, "come inside just a few minutes. We've got our chance now to make good and to make money. What we want to do is to cut expenses every cent we can, and save all we can."

"Right," said Bob. "It's business with me. You've got your scheme for banking yours; and I dream every night of that bungalow with the Jap cook and nobody around to raise trouble. Anything to enlarge the net receipts will engage my attention."

"Come inside just a few minutes," repeated Cherry, deeply thoughtful. "I've got a proposition to make to you that will reduce our expenses a lot and help you work out your own future and help me work out mine—and all on business principles."

"Mice Will Play" had a tremendously successful run in New York for ten weeks—rather neat for a vaudeville sketch—and then it started on the circuits. Without following it, it may be said that it was a solid drawing card for two years without a sign of abated popularity.

Sam Packard, manager of one of Keetor's New York houses, said of Hart & Cherry:

"As square and high-toned a little team as ever came over the circuit. It's a pleasure to read their names on the booking list. Quiet, hard workers, no Johnny and Mabel nonsense, on the job to the minute, straight home after their act, and each of 'em as gentlemanlike as a lady. I don't expect to handle any attractions that give me less trouble or more respect for the profession."

And now, after so much cracking of a nutshell, here is the kernel of the story:

At the end of its second season "Mice Will Play" came back to New York for another run at the roof gardens and summer theatres. There was never any trouble in booking it at the top-notch price. Bob Hart had his bungalow nearly paid for, and Cherry had so many savings-deposit bank books that she had begun to buy sectional bookcases on the instalment plan to hold them.

I tell you these things to assure you, even if you can't believe it, that many, very many of the stage people are workers with abiding ambitions—just the same as the man who wants to be president, or the grocery clerk who wants a home in Flatbush, or a lady who is anxious to flop out of the Count-pan into the Prince-fire. And I hope I may be allowed to say, without chipping into the contribution basket, that they often move in a mysterious way their wonders to perform.

But, listen.

At the first performance of "Mice Will Play" in New York at the new Westphalia (no hams alluded to) Theatre, Winona Cherry was nervous. When she fired at the photograph of the Eastern beauty on the mantel, the bullet, instead of penetrating the photo and then striking the disk, went into the lower left side of Bob Hart's neck. Not expecting to get it there, Hart collapsed neatly, while Cherry fainted in a most artistic manner.

The audience, surmising that they viewed a comedy instead of a tragedy in which the principals were married or reconciled, applauded with great enjoyment. The Cool Head, who always graces such occasions, rang the curtain down, and two platoons of scene shifters respectively and more or less respectfully removed Hart & Cherry from the stage. The next turn went on, and all went as merry as an alimony bell.

The stage hands found a young doctor at the stage entrance who was waiting for a patient with a decoction of Am. B'ty roses. The doctor examined Hart carefully and laughed heartily.

"No headlines for you, Old Sport," was his diagnosis. "If it had been two inches to the left it would have undermined the carotid artery as far as the Red Front Drug Store in Flatbush and Back Again. As it is, you just get the property man to bind it up with a flounce torn from any one of the girls' Valenciennes and go home and get it dressed by the parlor-floor practitioner on your block, and you'll be all right. Excuse me; I've got a serious case outside to look after."

After that Bob Hart looked up and felt better. And then to where he lay came Vincente, the Tramp Juggler, great in his line. Vincente, a solemn man from Brattleboro, Vt., named Sam Griggs at home, sent toys and maple sugar home to two small daughters from every town he played. Vincente had moved on the same circuits with Hart & Cherry, and was their peripatetic friend.

"Bob," said Vincente in his serious way, "I'm glad it's no worse. The little lady is wild about you."

"Who?" asked Hart.

"Cherry," said the juggler. "We didn't know how bad you were hurt; and we kept her away. It's taking the manager and three girls to hold her."

"It was an accident, of course," said Hart. "Cherry's all right. She wasn't feeling in good trim or she couldn't have done it.

There's no hard feelings. She's strictly business. The doctor says I'll be on the job again in three days. Don't let her worry."

"Man," said Sam Griggs severely, puckering his old, smooth, lined face, "are you a chess automaton or a human pincushion? Cherry's crying her heart out for you—calling 'Bob, Bob,' every second, with them holding her hands and keeping her from coming to you."

"What's the matter with her?" asked Hart, with wide-open eyes. "The sketch'll go on again in three days. I'm not hurt bad, the doctor says. She won't lose out half a week's salary. I know it was an accident. What's the matter with her?"

"You seem to be blind, or a sort of a fool," said Vincente. "The girl loves you and is almost mad about your hurt. What's the matter with *you*? Is she nothing to you? I wish you could hear her call you."

"Loves me?" asked Bob Hart, rising from the stack of scenery on which he lay. "Cherry loves me? Why, it's impossible."

"I wish you could see her and hear her," said Griggs.

"But, man," said Bob Hart, sitting up, "it's impossible. It's impossible, I tell you. I never dreamed of such a thing."

"No human being," said the Tramp Juggler, "could mistake it. She's wild for love of you. How have you been so blind?"

"But, my God," said Bob Hart, rising to his feet, "*it's too late*. It's too late, I tell you, Sam; *it's too late*. It can't be. You must be wrong. It's *impossible*. There's some mistake."

"She's crying for you," said the Tramp Juggler. "For love of you she's fighting three, and calling your name so loud they don't dare to raise the curtain. Wake up, man."

"For love of me?" said Bob Hart with staring eyes. "Don't I tell you it's too late? It's too late, man. Why, *Cherry and I have been married two years!*"

The Third Ingredient

THE (SO-CALLED) Vallambrosa Apartment-House is not an apartment-house. It is composed of two old-fashioned, brownstone-front residences welded into one. The parlor floor of one side is gay with the wraps and headgear of a modiste; the other is lugubrious with the sophistical promises and grisly display of a painless dentist. You may have a room there for two dollars a week or you may have one for twenty dollars. Among the Vallambrosa's roomers are stenographers, musicians, brokers, shop-girls, space-rate writers, art students, wire-tappers, and other people who lean far over the banister-rail when the door-bell rings.

This treatise shall have to do with but two of the Vallambrosians—though meaning no disrespect to the others.

At six o'clock one afternoon Hetty Pepper came back to her third-floor rear $3.50 room in the Vallambrosa with her nose and chin more sharply pointed than usual. To be discharged from the department store where you have been working four years, and with only fifteen cents in your purse, does have a tendency to make your features appear more finely chiseled.

And now for Hetty's thumb-nail biography while she climbs the two flights of stairs.

She walked into the Biggest Store one morning four years before with seventy-five other girls, applying for a job behind the waist department counter. The phalanx of wage-earners formed a bewildering scene of beauty, carrying a total mass of blond hair sufficient to have justified the horseback gallops of a hundred Lady Godivas.

The capable, cool-eyed, impersonal, young, bald-headed man whose task it was to engage six of the contestants, was aware of a feeling of suffocation as if he were drowning in a sea of frangipanni, while white clouds, hand-embroidered, floated about him. And then a sail hove in sight. Hetty Pepper, homely of countenance, with small, contemptuous, green eyes and chocolate-colored hair, dressed in a suit of plain burlap and a common-sense hat, stood before him with every one of her twenty-nine years of life unmistakably in sight.

"You're on!" shouted the bald-headed young man, and was saved. And that is how Hetty came to be employed in the Biggest Store. The story of her rise to an eight-dollar-a-week salary is the combined stories of Hercules, Joan of Arc, Una, Job, and Little-Red-Riding-Hood. You shall not learn from me the salary that was paid her as a beginner. There is a sentiment growing about such things, and I want no millionaire store-proprietors climbing the fire-escape of my tenement-house to throw dynamite bombs into my skylight boudoir.

The story of Hetty's discharge from the Biggest Store is so nearly a repetition of her engagement as to be monotonous.

In each department of the store there is an omniscient, omnipresent, and omnivorous person carrying always a mile-age book and a red necktie, and referred to as a "buyer." The destinies of the girls in his department who live on (see Bureau of Victual Statistics)—so much per week are in his hands.

This particular buyer was a capable, cool-eyed, impersonal, young, bald-headed man. As he walked along the aisles of his department he seemed to be sailing on a sea of frangipanni, while white clouds, machine-embroidered, floated around him. Too many sweets bring surfeit. He looked upon Hetty Pepper's homely countenance, emerald eyes, and chocolate-colored hair as a welcome oasis of green in a desert of cloying beauty. In a quiet angle of a counter he pinched her arm kindly, three inches above the elbow. She slapped him three feet away with one good blow of her muscular and not especially lily-white right. So, now you know why Hetty Pepper came to leave the Biggest Store at thirty minutes' notice, with one dime and a nickel in her purse.

This morning's quotations list the price of rib beef at six cents per (butcher's) pound. But on the day that Hetty was "released" by the B. S. the price was seven and one-half cents. That fact is what makes this story possible. Otherwise, the extra four cents would have—

But the plot of nearly all the good stories in the world is concerned with shorts who were unable to cover; so you can find no fault with this one.

Hetty mounted with her rib beef to her $3.50 third-floor back. One hot, savory beef-stew for supper, a night's good sleep, and

she would be fit in the morning to apply again for the tasks of
Hercules, Joan of Arc, Una, Job, and Little-Red-Riding-Hood.

In her room she got the granite-ware stew-pan out of the
2×4-foot china—er—I mean earthenware closet, and began
to dig down in a rats'-nest of paper bags for the potatoes and
onions. She came out with her nose and chin just a little sharper
pointed.

There was neither a potato nor an onion. Now, what kind
of a beef-stew can you make out of simply beef? You can
make oyster-soup without oysters, turtle-soup without turtles,
coffee-cake without coffee, but you can't make beef-stew without potatoes and onions.

But rib beef alone, in an emergency, can make an ordinary
pine door look like a wrought-iron gambling-house portal to
the wolf. With salt and pepper and a tablespoonful of flour
(first well stirred in a little cold water) 'twill serve—'tis not so
deep as a lobster à la Newburg nor so wide as a church festival
doughnut; but 'twill serve.

Hetty took her stew-pan to the rear of the third-floor hall.
According to the advertisements of the Vallambrosa there was
running water to be found there. Between you and me and the
water-meter, it only ambled or walked through the faucets; but
technicalities have no place here. There was also a sink where
housekeeping roomers often met to dump their coffee grounds
and glare at one another's kimonos.

At this sink Hetty found a girl with heavy, gold-brown, artistic hair and plaintive eyes, washing two large "Irish" potatoes.
Hetty knew the Vallambrosa as well as any one not owning
"double hextra-magnifying eyes" could compass its mysteries.
The kimonos were her encyclopædia, her "Who's What?" her
clearinghouse of news, of goers and comers. From a rose-pink
kimono edged with Nile green she had learned that the girl
with the potatoes was a miniature-painter living in a kind of
attic—or "studio," as they prefer to call it—on the top floor.
Hetty was not certain in her mind what a miniature was; but it
certainly wasn't a house; because house-painters, although they
wear splashy overalls and poke ladders in your face on the street,
are known to indulge in a riotous profusion of food at home.

The potato girl was quite slim and small, and handled her

potatoes as an old bachelor uncle handles a baby who is cutting teeth. She had a dull shoemaker's knife in her right hand, and she had begun to peel one of the potatoes with it.

Hetty addressed her in the punctiliously formal tone of one who intends to be cheerfully familiar with you in the second round.

"Beg pardon," she said, "for butting into what's not my business, but if you peel them potatoes you lose out. They're new Bermudas. You want to scrape 'em. Lemme show you."

She took a potato and the knife, and began to demonstrate.

"Oh, thank you," breathed the artist. "I didn't know. And I *did* hate to see the thick peeling go; it seemed such a waste. But I thought they always had to be peeled. When you've got only potatoes to eat, the peelings count, you know."

"Say, kid," said Hetty, staying her knife, "you ain't up against it, too, are you?"

The miniature artist smiled starvedly.

"I suppose I am. Art—or, at least, the way I interpret it—doesn't seem to be much in demand. I have only these potatoes for my dinner. But they aren't so bad boiled and hot, with a little butter and salt."

"Child," said Hetty, letting a brief smile soften her rigid features, "Fate has sent me and you together. I've had it handed to me in the neck, too; but I've got a chunk of meat in my room as big as a lap-dog. And I've done everything to get potatoes except pray for 'em. Let's me and you bunch our commissary departments and make a stew of 'em. We'll cook it in my room. If we only had an onion to go in it! Say, kid, you haven't got a couple of pennies that 've slipped down into the lining of your last winter's sealskin, have you? I could step down to the corner and get one at old Giuseppe's stand. A stew without an onion is worse'n a matinée without candy."

"You may call me Cecilia," said the artist. "No; I spent my last penny three days ago."

"Then we'll have to cut the onion out instead of slicing it in," said Hetty. "I'd ask the janitress for one, but I don't want 'em hep just yet to the fact that I'm pounding the asphalt for another job. But I wish we did have an onion."

In the shop-girl's room the two began to prepare their supper. Cecilia's part was to sit on the couch helplessly and beg to be allowed to do something, in the voice of a cooing ring-dove. Hetty prepared the rib beef, putting it in cold salted water in the stew-pan and setting it on the one-burner gas-stove.

"I wish we had an onion," said Hetty, as she scraped the two potatoes.

On the wall opposite the couch was pinned a flaming, gorgeous advertising picture of one of the new ferry-boats of the P. U. F. F. Railroad that had been built to cut down the time between Los Angeles and New York City one-eighth of a minute.

Hetty, turning her head during her continuous monologue, saw tears running from her guest's eyes as she gazed on the idealized presentment of the speeding, foam-girdled transport.

"Why, say, Cecilia, kid," said Hetty, poising her knife, "is it as bad art as that? I ain't a critic; but I thought it kind of brightened up the room. Of course, a manicure-painter could tell it was a bum picture in a minute. I'll take it down if you say so. I wish to the holy Saint Potluck we had an onion."

But the miniature miniature-painter had tumbled down, sobbing, with her nose indenting the hard-woven drapery of the couch. Something was here deeper than the artistic temperament offended at crude lithography.

Hetty knew. She had accepted her rôle long ago. How scant the words with which we try to describe a single quality of a human being! When we reach the abstract we are lost. The nearer to Nature that the babbling of our lips comes, the better do we understand. Figuratively (let us say), some people are Bosoms, some are Hands, some are Heads, some are Muscles, some are Feet, some are Backs for burdens.

Hetty was a Shoulder. Hers was a sharp, sinewy shoulder; but all her life people had laid their heads upon it, metaphorically or actually, and had left there all or half their troubles. Looking at Life anatomically, which is as good a way as any, she was preordained to be a Shoulder. There were few truer collar-bones anywhere than hers.

Hetty was only thirty-three, and she had not yet outlived the little pang that visited her whenever the head of youth and beauty leaned upon her for consolation. But one glance in her mirror always served as an instantaneous pain-killer. So she gave one pale look into the crinkly old looking-glass on the wall above the gas-stove, turned down the flame a little lower from the bubbling beef and potatoes, went over to the couch, and lifted Cecilia's head to its confessional.

"Go on and tell me, honey," she said. "I know now that it ain't art that's worrying you. You met him on a ferry-boat, didn't you? Go on, Cecilia, kid, and tell your—your Aunt Hetty about it."

But youth and melancholy must first spend the surplus of sighs and tears that waft and float the barque of romance to its harbor in the delectable isles. Presently, through the stringy tendons that formed the bars of the confessional, the penitent—or was it the glorified communicant of the sacred flame?—told her story without art or illumination.

"It was only three days ago. I was coming back on the ferry from Jersey City. Old Mr. Schrum, an art dealer, told me of a rich man in Newark who wanted a miniature of his daughter painted. I went to see him and showed him some of my work. When I told him the price would be fifty dollars he laughed at me like a hyena. He said an enlarged crayon twenty times the size would cost him only eight dollars.

"I had just enough money to buy my ferry ticket back to New York. I felt as if I didn't want to live another day. I must have looked as I felt, for I saw *him* on the row of seats opposite me, looking at me as if he understood. He was nice-looking, but oh, above everything else, he looked kind. When one is tired or unhappy or hopeless, kindness counts more than anything else.

"When I got so miserable that I couldn't fight against it any longer, I got up and walked slowly out the rear door of the ferry-boat cabin. No one was there, and I slipped quickly over the rail and dropped into the water. Oh, friend Hetty, it was cold, cold!

"For just one moment I wished I was back in the old Vallambrosa, starving and hoping. And then I got numb, and didn't care. And then I felt that somebody else was in the water close by me, holding me up. *He* had followed me, and jumped in to save me.

"Somebody threw a thing like a big, white doughnut at us, and he made me put my arms through the hole. Then the ferry-boat backed, and they pulled us on board. Oh, Hetty, I was so ashamed of my wickedness in trying to drown myself;

and, besides, my hair had all tumbled down and was sopping wet, and I was such a sight.

"And then some men in blue clothes came around; and *he* gave them his card, and I heard him tell them he had seen me drop my purse on the edge of the boat outside the rail, and in leaning over to get it I had fallen overboard. And then I remembered having read in the papers that people who try to kill themselves are locked up in cells with people who try to kill other people, and I was afraid.

"But some ladies on the boat took me downstairs to the furnace-room and got me nearly dry and did up my hair. When the boat landed, *he* came and put me in a cab. He was all dripping himself, but laughed as if he thought it was all a joke. He begged me, but I wouldn't tell him my name nor where I lived, I was so ashamed."

"You were a fool, child," said Hetty, kindly. "Wait till I turn the light up a bit. I wish to Heaven we had an onion."

"Then he raised his hat," went on Cecilia, "and said: 'Very well. But I'll find you, anyhow. I'm going to claim my rights of salvage.' Then he gave money to the cab-driver and told him to take me where I wanted to go, and walked away. What is 'salvage,' Hetty?"

"The edge of a piece of goods that ain't hemmed," said the shop-girl. "You must have looked pretty well frazzled out to the little hero boy."

"It's been three days," moaned the miniature-painter, "and he hasn't found me yet."

"Extend the time," said Hetty. "This is a big town. Think of how many girls he might have to see soaked in water with their hair down before he would recognize you. The stew's getting on fine—but oh, for an onion! I'd even use a piece of garlic if I had it."

The beef and potatoes bubbled merrily, exhaling a mouth-watering savor that yet lacked something, leaving a hunger on the palate, a haunting, wistful desire for some lost and needful ingredient.

"I came near drowning in that awful river," said Cecilia, shuddering.

"It ought to have more water in it," said Hetty; "the stew, I mean. I'll go get some at the sink."

"It smells good," said the artist.

"That nasty old North River?" objected Hetty. "It smells to me like soap factories and wet setter-dogs—oh, you mean the stew. Well, I wish we had an onion for it. Did he look like he had money?"

"First, he looked kind," said Cecilia. "I'm sure he was rich; but that matters so little. When he drew out his bill-folder to pay the cabman you couldn't help seeing hundreds and thousands of dollars in it. And I looked over the cab doors and saw him leave the ferry station in a motor-car; and the chauffeur gave him his bearskin to put on, for he was sopping wet. And it was only three days ago."

"What a fool!" said Hetty, shortly.

"Oh, the chauffeur wasn't wet," breathed Cecilia. "And he drove the car away very nicely."

"I mean *you*," said Hetty. "For not giving him your address."

"I never give my address to chauffeurs," said Cecilia, haughtily.

"I wish we had one," said Hetty, disconsolately.

"What for?"

"For the stew, of course—oh, I mean an onion."

Hetty took a pitcher and started to the sink at the end of the hall.

A young man came down the stairs from above just as she was opposite the lower step. He was decently dressed, but pale and haggard. His eyes were dull with the stress of some burden of physical or mental woe. In his hand he bore an onion—a pink, smooth, solid, shining onion as large around as a ninety-eight-cent alarm-clock.

Hetty stopped. So did the young man. There was something Joan of Arc-ish, Herculean, and Una-ish in the look and pose of the shop-lady—she had cast off the rôles of Job and Little-Red-Riding-Hood. The young man stopped at the foot of the stairs and coughed distractedly. He felt marooned, held up, attacked, assailed, levied upon, sacked, assessed, panhandled, browbeaten, though he knew not why. It was the look in Hetty's eyes that did it. In them he saw the Jolly Roger fly to the masthead and an able seaman with a dirk between his teeth scurry up the ratlines and nail it there. But as yet he did not know that the cargo he carried was the thing that had caused him to be so nearly blown out of the water without even a parley.

"*Beg* your pardon," said Hetty, as sweetly as her dilute acetic acid tones permitted, "but did you find that onion on the stairs? There was a hole in the paper bag; and I've just come out to look for it."

The young man coughed for half a minute. The interval may have given him the courage to defend his own property. Also, he clutched his pungent prize greedily, and, with a show of spirit, faced his grim waylayer.

"No," he said huskily, "I didn't find it on the stairs. It was given to me by Jack Bevens, on the top floor. If you don't believe it, ask him. I'll wait until you do."

"I know about Bevens," said Hetty, sourly. "He writes books and things up there for the paper-and-rags man. We can hear the postman guy him all over the house when he brings them thick envelopes back. Say—do you live in the Vallambrosa?"

"I do not," said the young man. "I come to see Bevens sometimes. He's my friend. I live two blocks west."

"What are you going to do with the onion?—*begging* your pardon," said Hetty.

"I'm going to eat it."

"Raw?"

"Yes: as soon as I get home."

"Haven't you got anything else to eat with it?"

The young man considered briefly.

"No," he confessed; "there's not another scrap of anything in my diggings to eat. I think old Jack is pretty hard up for grub in his shack, too. He hated to give up the onion, but I worried him into parting with it."

"Man," said Hetty, fixing him with her world-sapient eyes, and laying a bony but impressive finger on his sleeve, "you've known trouble, too, haven't you?"

"Lots," said the onion owner, promptly. "But this onion is my own property, honestly come by. If you will excuse me, I must be going."

"Listen," said Hetty, paling a little with anxiety. "Raw onion is a mighty poor diet. And so is a beef-stew without one. Now, if you're Jack Bevens' friend, I guess you're nearly right. There's a little lady—a friend of mine—in my room there at the end of the hall. Both of us are out of luck; and we had just potatoes and meat between us. They're stewing now. But it ain't got any soul. There's something lacking to it. There's certain things in life that are naturally intended to fit and belong together. One is pink cheese-cloth and green roses, and one is ham and eggs, and one is Irish and trouble. And the other one is beef and potatoes *with* onions. And still another one is people who are up against it and other people in the same fix."

The young man went into a protracted paroxysm of coughing. With one hand he hugged his onion to his bosom.

"No doubt; no doubt," said he, at length. "But, as I said, I must be going, because—"

Hetty clutched his sleeve firmly.

"Don't be a Dago, Little Brother. Don't eat raw onions. Chip it in toward the dinner and line yourself inside with the best stew you ever licked a spoon over. Must two ladies knock a young gentleman down and drag him inside for the honor of dining with 'em? No harm shall befall you, Little Brother. Loosen up and fall into line."

The young man's pale face relaxed into a grin.

"Believe I'll go with you," he said, brightening. "If my onion is good as a credential, I'll accept the invitation gladly."

"It's good as that, but better as seasoning," said Hetty. "You come and stand outside the door till I ask my lady friend if she has any objections. And don't run away with that letter of recommendation before I come out."

Hetty went into her room and closed the door. The young man waited outside.

"Cecilia, kid," said the shop-girl, oiling the sharp saw of her voice as well as she could, "there's an onion outside. With a young man attached. I've asked him in to dinner. You ain't going to kick, are you?"

"Oh, dear!" said Cecilia, sitting up and patting her artistic hair. She cast a mournful glance at the ferry-boat poster on the wall.

"Nit," said Hetty. "It ain't him. You're up against real life now. I believe you said your hero friend had money and automobiles. This is a poor skeezicks that's got nothing to eat but an onion. But he's easy-spoken and not a freshy. I imagine he's been a gentleman, he's so low down now. And we need the onion. Shall I bring him in? I'll guarantee his behavior."

"Hetty, dear," sighed Cecilia, "I'm so hungry. What difference does it make whether he's a prince or a burglar? I don't care. Bring him in if he's got anything to eat with him."

Hetty went back into the hall. The onion man was gone. Her heart missed a beat, and a gray look settled over her face except on her nose and cheek-bones. And then the tides of life flowed in again, for she saw him leaning out of the front window at the other end of the hall. She hurried there. He was shouting to some one below. The noise of the street overpowered the sound of her footsteps. She looked down over his shoulder, saw whom he was speaking to, and heard his words. He pulled himself in from the window-sill and saw her standing over him.

Hetty's eyes bored into him like two steel gimlets.

"Don't lie to me," she said, calmly. "What were you going to do with that onion?"

The young man suppressed a cough and faced her resolutely. His manner was that of one who had been bearded sufficiently.

"I was going to eat it," said he, with emphatic slowness; "just as I told you before."

"And you have nothing else to eat at home?"

"Not a thing."

"What kind of work do you do?"

"I am not working at anything just now."

"Then why," said Hetty, with her voice set on its sharpest edge, "do you lean out of windows and give orders to chauffeurs in green automobiles in the street below?"

The young man flushed, and his dull eyes began to sparkle.

"Because, madam," said he, in *accelerando* tones, "I pay the chauffeur's wages and I own the automobile—and also this onion—this onion, madam."

He flourished the onion within an inch of Hetty's nose. The shop-lady did not retreat a hair's-breadth.

"Then why do you eat onions," she said, with biting contempt, "and nothing else?"

"I never said I did," retorted the young man, heatedly. "I said I had nothing else to eat where I live. I am not a delicatessen storekeeper."

"Then why," pursued Hetty, inflexibly, "were you going to eat a raw onion?"

"My mother," said the young man, "always made me eat one for a cold. Pardon my referring to a physical infirmity; but you may have noticed that I have a very, very severe cold. I was going to eat the onion and go to bed. I wonder why I am standing here and apologizing to you for it."

"How did you catch this cold?" went on Hetty, suspiciously.

The young man seemed to have arrived at some extreme height of feeling. There were two modes of descent open to him—a burst of rage or a surrender to the ridiculous. He chose wisely; and the empty hall echoed his hoarse laughter.

"You're a dandy," said he. "And I don't blame you for being careful. I don't mind telling you. I got wet. I was on a North River ferry a few days ago when a girl jumped overboard. Of course, I—"

Hetty extended her hand, interrupting his story.

"Give me the onion," she said.

The young man set his jaw a trifle harder.

"Give me the onion," she repeated.

He grinned, and laid it in her hand.

Then Hetty's infrequent, grim, melancholy smile showed itself. She took the young man's arm and pointed with her other hand to the door of her room.

"Little Brother," she said, "go in there. The little fool you fished out of the river is there waiting for you. Go on in. I'll give you three minutes before I come. Potatoes is in there, waiting. Go on in, Onions."

After he had tapped at the door and entered, Hetty began to peel and wash the onion at the sink. She gave a gray look at the gray roofs outside, and the smile on her face vanished by little jerks and twitches.

"But it's us," she said, grimly, to herself, "it's *us* that furnishes the beef."

The Higher Pragmatism

HERE TO go for wisdom has become a question of serious import. The ancients are discredited; Plato is boiler-plate; Aristotle is tottering; Marcus Aurelius is reeling; Æsop has been copyrighted by Indiana; Solomon is too solemn; you couldn't get anything out of Epictetus with a pick.

The ant, which for many years served as a model of intelligence and industry in the school-readers, has been proven to be a doddering idiot and a waster of time and effort. The owl to-day is hooted at. Chautauqua conventions have abandoned culture and adopted diabolo. Graybeards give glowing testimonials to the venders of patent hair-restorers. There are typographical errors in the almanacs published by the daily newspapers. College professors have become—

But there shall be no personalities.

To sit in classes, to delve into the encyclopedia or the past-performances page, will not make us wise. As the poet says, "Knowledge comes, but wisdom lingers." Wisdom is dew, which, while we know it not, soaks into us, refreshes us, and makes us grow. Knowledge is a strong stream of water turned on us through a hose. It disturbs our roots.

Then, let us rather gather wisdom. But how to do so requires knowledge. If we know a thing, we know it; but very often we are not wise to it that we are wise, and—

But let's go on with the story.

II

Once upon a time I found a ten-cent magazine lying on a bench in a little city park. Anyhow, that was the amount he asked me for when I sat on the bench next to him. He was a musty, dingy, and tattered magazine, with some queer stories bound in him, I was sure. He turned out to be a scrap-book.

"I am a newspaper reporter," I said to him, to try him. "I have been detailed to write up some of the experiences of the unfortunate ones who spend their evenings in this park. May I ask you to what you attribute your downfall in—"

I was interrupted by a laugh from my purchase—a laugh so rusty and unpractised that I was sure it had been his first for many a day.

"Oh, no, no," said he. "You ain't a reporter. Reporters don't talk that way. They pretend to be one of us, and say they've just got in on the blind baggage from St. Louis. I can tell a reporter on sight. Us park bums get to be fine judges of human nature. We sit here all day and watch the people go by. I can size up anybody who walks past my bench in a way that would surprise you."

"Well," I said, "go on and tell me. How do you size me up?"

"I should say," said the student of human nature with unpardonable hesitation, "that you was, say, in the contracting business—or maybe worked in a store—or was a sign-painter. You stopped in the park to finish your cigar, and thought you'd get a little free monologue out of me. Still, you might be a plasterer or a lawyer—it's getting kind of dark, you see. And your wife won't let you smoke at home."

I frowned gloomily.

"But, judging again," went on the reader of men, "I'd say you ain't got a wife."

"No," said I, rising restlessly. "No, no, no, I ain't. But I *will* have, by the arrows of Cupid! That is, if—"

My voice must have trailed away and muffled itself in uncertainty and despair.

"I see you have a story yourself," said the dusty vagrant—impudently, it seemed to me. "Suppose you take your dime back and spin your yarn for me. I'm interested myself in the ups and downs of unfortunate ones who spend their evenings in the park."

Somehow, that amused me. I looked at the frowsy derelict with more interest. I did have a story. Why not tell it to him? I had told none of my friends. I had always been a reserved and bottled-up man. It was psychical timidity or sensitiveness—perhaps both. And I smiled to myself in wonder when I felt an impulse to confide in this stranger and vagabond.

"Jack," said I.

"Mack," said he.

"Mack," said I, "I'll tell you."

"Do you want the dime back in advance?" said he.

I handed him a dollar.

"The dime," said I, "was the price of listening to *your* story."

"Right on the point of the jaw," said he. "Go on."

And then, incredible as it may seem to the lovers in the world who confide their sorrows only to the night wind and the gibbous moon, I laid bare my secret to that wreck of all things that you would have supposed to be in sympathy with love.

I told him of the days and weeks and months that I had spent in adoring Mildred Telfair. I spoke of my despair, my grievous days and wakeful nights, my dwindling hopes and distress of mind. I even pictured to this night-prowler her beauty and dignity, the great sway she had in society, and the magnificence of her life as the elder daughter of an ancient race whose pride overbalanced the dollars of the city's millionaires.

"Why don't you cop the lady out?" asked Mack, bringing me down to earth and dialect again.

I explained to him that my worth was so small, my income so minute, and my fears so large that I hadn't the courage to speak to her of my worship. I told him that in her presence I could only blush and stammer, and that she looked upon me with a wonderful, maddening smile of amusement.

"She kind of moves in the professional class, don't she?" asked Mack.

"The Telfair family—" I began, haughtily.

"I mean professional beauty," said my hearer.

"She is greatly and widely admired," I answered, cautiously.

"Any sisters?"

"One."

"You know any more girls?"

"Why, several," I answered. "And a few others."

"Say," said Mack, "tell me one thing—can you hand out the dope to other girls? Can you chin 'em and make matinée eyes at 'em and squeeze 'em? You know what I mean. You're just shy when it comes to this particular dame—the professional beauty—ain't that right?"

"In a way you have outlined the situation with approximate truth," I admitted.

"I thought so," said Mack, grimly. "Now, that reminds me of my own case. I'll tell you about it."

I was indignant, but concealed it. What was this loafer's case or anybody's case compared with mine? Besides, I had given him a dollar and ten cents.

"Feel my muscle," said my companion, suddenly, flexing his biceps. I did so mechanically. The fellows in gyms are always asking you to do that. His arm was as hard as cast-iron.

"Four years ago," said Mack, "I could lick any man in New York outside of the professional ring. Your case and mine is just the same. I come from the West Side—between Thirtieth and Fourteenth—I won't give the number on the door. I was a scrapper when I was ten, and when I was twenty no amateur in the city could stand up four rounds with me. 'S a fact. You know Bill McCarty? No? He managed the smokers for some of them swell clubs. Well, I knocked out everything Bill brought up before me. I was a middle-weight, but could train down to a welter when necessary. I boxed all over the West Side at bouts and benefits and private entertainments, and was never put out once.

"But, say, the first time I put my foot in the ring with a professional I was no more than a canned lobster. I dunno how it was—I seemed to lose heart. I guess I got too much imagination. There was a formality and publicness about it that kind of weakened my nerve. I never won a fight in the ring. Light-weights and all kinds of scrubs used to sign up with my manager and then walk up and tap me on the wrist and see me fall. The minute I seen the crowd and a lot of gents in evening clothes down in front, and seen a professional come inside the ropes, I got as weak as ginger-ale.

"Of course, it wasn't long till I couldn't get no backers, and I didn't have any more chances to fight a professional—or many amateurs, either. But lemme tell you—I was as good as most men inside the ring or out. It was just that dumb, dead feeling I had when I was up against a regular that always done me up.

"Well, sir, after I had got out of the business, I got a mighty grouch on. I used to go round town licking private citizens and all kinds of unprofessionals just to please myself. I'd lick cops in dark streets and car-conductors and cab-drivers and draymen whenever I could start a row with 'em. It didn't make any difference how big they were, or how much science they had, I got away with 'em. If I'd only just have had the confidence in the ring that I had beating up the best men outside of it, I'd be wearing black pearls and heliotrope silk socks to-day.

"One evening I was walking along near the Bowery, thinking about things, when along comes a slumming-party. About six or seven they was, all in swallowtails, and these silk hats that don't shine. One of the gang kind of shoves me off the sidewalk. I hadn't had a scrap in three days, and I just says, 'De-light-ed!' and hits him back of the ear.

"Well, we had it. That Johnnie put up as decent a little fight as you'd want to see in the moving pictures. It was on a side street, and no cops around. The other guy had a lot of science, but it only took me about six minutes to lay him out.

"Some of the swallowtails dragged him up against some steps and began to fan him. Another one of 'em comes over to me and says:

"'Young man, do you know what you've done?'

"'Oh, beat it,' says I. 'I've done nothing but a little punching-bag work. Take Freddy back to Yale and tell him to quit studying sociology on the wrong side of the sidewalk.'

"'My good fellow,' says he, 'I don't know who you are, but I'd like to. You've knocked out Reddy Burns, the champion middle-weight of the world! He came to New York yesterday, to try to get a match on with Jim Jeffries. If you—'

"But when I come out of my faint I was laying on the floor in a drug-store saturated with aromatic spirits of ammonia. If I'd known that was Reddy Burns, I'd have got down in the gutter and crawled past him instead of handing him one like I did. Why, if I'd ever been in a ring and seen him climbing over the ropes, I'd have been all to the sal volatile.

"So that's what imagination does," concluded Mack. "And, as I said, your case and mine is simultaneous. You'll never win out. You can't go up against the professionals. I tell you, it's a park bench for yours in this romance business."

Mack, the pessimist, laughed harshly.

"I'm afraid I don't see the parallel," I said, coldly. "I have only a very slight acquaintance with the prize-ring."

The derelict touched my sleeve with his forefinger, for emphasis, as he explained his parable.

"Every man," said he, with some dignity, "has got his lamps on something that looks good to him. With you, it's this dame that you're afraid to say your say to. With me, it was to win out in the ring. Well, you'll lose just like I did."

"Why do you think I shall lose?" I asked warmly.

"'Cause," said he, "you're afraid to go in the ring. You dassen't stand up before a professional. Your case and mine is just the same. You're a amateur; and that means that you'd better keep outside of the ropes."

"Well, I must be going," I said, rising and looking with elaborate care at my watch.

When I was twenty feet away the park-bencher called to me.

"Much obliged for the dollar," he said. "And for the dime. But you'll never get 'er. You're in the amateur class."

"Serves you right," I said to myself, "for hobnobbing with a tramp. His impudence!"

But, as I walked, his words seemed to repeat themselves over and over again in my brain. I think I even grew angry at the man.

"I'll show him!" I finally said, aloud. "I'll show him that I can fight Reddy Burns, too—even knowing who he is."

I hurried to a telephone-booth and rang up the Telfair residence.

A soft, sweet voice answered. Didn't I know that voice? My hand holding the receiver shook.

"Is that *you*?" said I, employing the foolish words that form the vocabulary of every talker through the telephone.

"Yes, this is I," came back the answer in the low, clear-cut tones that are an inheritance of the Telfairs. "Who is it, please?"

"It's me," said I, less ungrammatically than egotistically. "It's me, and I've got a few things that I want to say to you right now and immediately and straight to the point."

"*Dear* me," said the voice. "Oh, it's you, Mr. Arden!"

I wondered if any accent on the first word was intended; Mildred was fine at saying things that you had to study out afterward.

"Yes," said I. "I hope so. And now to come down to brass tacks." I thought that rather a vernacularism, if there is such a word, as soon as I had said it; but I didn't stop to apologize. "You know, of course, that I love you, and that I have been in that idiotic state for a long time. I don't want any more foolishness about it—that is, I mean I want an answer from you right now. Will you marry me or not? Hold the wire, please. Keep out, Central. Hello, hello! Will you, or will you *not*?"

That was just the uppercut for Reddy Burns' chin. The answer came back:

"Why, Phil, dear, of course I will! I didn't know that you— that is, you never said—oh, come up to the house, please—I can't say what I want to over the 'phone. You are so importunate. But please come up to the house, won't you?"

Would I?

I rang the bell of the Telfair house violently. Some sort of a human came to the door and shooed me into the drawing-room.

"Oh, well," said I to myself, looking at the ceiling, "any one can learn from any one. That was a pretty good philosophy of Mack's, anyhow. He didn't take advantage of his experience, but I get the benefit of it. If you want to get into the professional class, you've got to—"

I stopped thinking then. Some one was coming down the stairs. My knees began to shake. I knew then how Mack had felt when a professional began to climb over the ropes. I looked around foolishly for a door or a window by which I might escape. If it had been any other girl approaching, I mightn't have—

But just then the door opened, and Bess, Mildred's younger sister, came in. I'd never seen her look so much like a glorified angel. She walked straight up to me, and—and—

I'd never noticed before what perfectly wonderful eyes and hair Elizabeth Telfair had.

"Phil," she said, in the Telfair, sweet, thrilling tones, "why didn't you tell me about it before? I thought it was sister you wanted all the time, until you telephoned to me a few minutes ago!"

I suppose Mack and I always will be hopeless amateurs. But, as the thing has turned out in my case, I'm mighty glad of it.

No Story

To avoid having this book hurled into a corner of the room by the suspicious reader, I will assert in time that this is not a newspaper story. You will encounter no shirt-sleeved, omniscient city editor, no prodigy "cub" reporter just off the farm, no scoop, no story—no anything.

But if you will concede me the setting of the first scene in the reporters' room of the *Morning Beacon*, I will repay the favor by keeping strictly my promises set forth above.

I was doing space-work on the *Beacon*, hoping to be put on a salary. Some one had cleared with a rake or a shovel a small space for me at the end of a long table piled high with exchanges, *Congressional Records*, and old files. There I did my work. I wrote whatever the city whispered or roared or chuckled to me on my diligent wanderings about its streets. My income was not regular.

One day Tripp came in and leaned on my table. Tripp was something in the mechanical department—I think he had something to do with the pictures, for he smelled of photographers' supplies, and his hands were always stained and cut up with acids. He was about twenty-five and looked forty. Half of his face was covered with short, curly red whiskers that looked like a door-mat with the "welcome" left off. He was pale and unhealthy and miserable and fawning, and an assiduous borrower of sums ranging from twenty-five cents to a dollar. One dollar was his limit. He knew the extent of his credit as well as the Chemical National Bank knows the amount of H_2O that collateral will show on analysis. When he sat on my table he held one hand with the other to keep both from shaking. Whiskey. He had a spurious air of lightness and bravado about him that deceived no one, but was useful in his borrowing because it was so pitifully and perceptibly assumed.

This day I had coaxed from the cashier five shining silver dollars as a grumbling advance on a story that the Sunday editor had reluctantly accepted. So if I was not feeling at peace with the world, at least an armistice had been declared; and I was beginning with ardor to write a description of the Brooklyn Bridge by moonlight.

"Well, Tripp," said I, looking up at him rather impatiently, "how goes it?" He was looking to-day more miserable, more cringing and haggard and downtrodden than I had ever seen him. He was at that stage of misery where he drew your pity so fully that you longed to kick him.

"Have you got a dollar?" asked Tripp, with his most fawning look and his dog-like eyes that blinked in the narrow space between his high-growing matted beard and his low-growing matted hair.

"I have," said I; and again I said, "I have," more loudly and inhospitably, "and four besides. And I had hard work cork-screwing them out of old Atkinson, I can tell you. And I drew them," I continued, "to meet a want—a hiatus—a demand—a need—an exigency—a requirement of exactly five dollars."

I was driven to emphasis by the premonition that I was to lose one of the dollars on the spot.

"I don't want to borrow any," said Tripp, and I breathed again. "I thought you'd like to get put onto a good story," he went on. "I've got a rattling fine one for you. You ought to make it run a column at least. It 'll make a dandy if you work it up right. It 'll probably cost you a dollar or two to get the stuff. I don't want anything out of it myself."

I became placated. The proposition showed that Tripp appreciated past favors, although he did not return them. If he had been wise enough to strike me for a quarter then he would have got it.

"What is the story?" I asked, poising my pencil with a finely calculated editorial air.

"I'll tell you," said Tripp. "It's a girl. A beauty. One of the howlingest Amsden's Junes you ever saw. Rosebuds covered with dew—violets in their mossy bed—and truck like that. She's lived on Long Island twenty years and never saw New York City before. I ran against her on Thirty-fourth Street. She'd just got in on the East River ferry. I tell you, she's a beauty that would take the hydrogen out of all the peroxides in the world. She stopped me on the street and asked me where she could find George Brown. Asked me where she could find *George Brown in New York City*! What do you think of that?

"I talked to her, and found that she was going to marry a young farmer named Dodd—Hiram Dodd—next week. But it seems that George Brown still holds the championship in her youthful fancy. George had greased his cowhide boots some years ago, and came to the city to make his fortune. But he forgot to remember to show up again at Greenburg, and Hiram got in as second-best choice. But when it comes to the scratch Ada—her name's Ada Lowery—saddles a nag and rides eight miles to the railroad station and catches the 6.45 A.M. train for the city. Looking for George, you know—you understand about women—George wasn't there, so she wanted him.

"Well, you know, I couldn't leave her loose in Wolf-town-on-the-Hudson. I suppose she thought the first person she inquired of would say: 'George Brown?—why, yes—lemme see—he's a short man with light-blue eyes, ain't he? Oh yes—you'll find George on One Hundred and Twenty-fifth Street, right next to the grocery. He's bill-clerk in a saddle-and-harness store.' That's about how innocent and beautiful she is. You know those little Long Island water-front villages like Greenburg—a couple of duck-farms for sport, and clams and about nine summer visitors for industries. That's the kind of a place she comes from. But, say—you ought to see her!

"What could I do? I don't know what money looks like in the morning. And she'd paid her last cent of pocket-money for her railroad ticket except a quarter, which she had squandered on gum-drops. She was eating them out of a paper bag. I took her to a boarding-house on Thirty-second Street where I used to live, and hocked her. She's in soak for a dollar. That's old Mother McGinnis' price per day. I'll show you the house."

"What words are these, Tripp?" said I. "I thought you said you had a story. Every ferryboat that crosses the East River brings or takes away girls from Long Island."

The premature lines on Tripp's face grew deeper. He frowned seriously from his tangle of hair. He separated his hands and emphasized his answer with one shaking forefinger.

"Can't you see," he said, "what a rattling fine story it would make? You could do it fine. All about the romance, you know, and describe the girl, and put a lot of stuff in it about true love, and sling in a few stickfuls of funny business—joshing the Long Islanders about being green, and, well—you know how to do it. You ought to get fifteen dollars out of it, anyhow. And it 'll cost you only about four dollars. You'll make a clear profit of eleven."

"How will it cost me four dollars?" I asked, suspiciously.

"One dollar to Mrs. McGinnis," Tripp answered, promptly, "and two dollars to pay the girl's fare back home."

"And the fourth dimension?" I inquired, making a rapid mental calculation.

"One dollar to me," said Tripp. "For whiskey. Are you on?"

I smiled enigmatically and spread my elbows as if to begin writing again. But this grim, abject, specious, subservient, burr-like wreck of a man would not be shaken off. His forehead suddenly became shiningly moist.

"Don't you see," he said, with a sort of desperate calmness, "that this girl has got to be sent home to-day—not to-night nor to-morrow, but to-day? I can't do anything for her. You know, I'm the janitor and corresponding secretary of the Down-and-Out Club. I thought you could make a newspaper story out of it and win out a piece of money on general results. But, anyhow, don't you see that she's got to get back home before night?"

And then I began to feel that dull, leaden, soul-depressing sensation known as the sense of duty. Why should that sense fall upon one as a weight and a burden? I knew that I was doomed that day to give up the bulk of my store of hard-wrung coin to the relief of this Ada Lowery. But I swore to myself that Tripp's whiskey dollar would not be forthcoming. He might play knight-errant at my expense, but he would indulge in no wassail afterward, commemorating my weakness and gullibility. In a kind of chilly anger I put on my coat and hat.

Tripp, submissive, cringing, vainly endeavoring to please, conducted me *via* the street-cars to the human pawn-shop of Mother McGinnis. I paid the fares. It seemed that the collodion-scented Don Quixote and the smallest minted coin were strangers.

Tripp pulled the bell at the door of the mouldy red-brick boarding-house. At its faint tinkle he paled, and crouched as a rabbit makes ready to spring away at the sound of a hunting-dog. I guessed what a life he had led, terror-haunted by the coming footsteps of landladies.

"Give me one of the dollars—quick!" he said.

The door opened six inches. Mother McGinnis stood there with white eyes—they were white, I say—and a yellow face, holding together at her throat with one hand a dingy pink flannel dressing-sack. Tripp thrust the dollar through the space without a word, and it bought us entry.

"She's in the parlor," said the McGinnis, turning the back of her sack upon us.

In the dim parlor a girl sat at the cracked marble centre-table weeping comfortably and eating gum-drops. She was a flawless beauty. Crying had only made her brilliant eyes brighter. When she crunched a gum-drop you thought only of the poetry of motion and envied the senseless confection. Eve at the age of five minutes must have been a ringer for Miss Ada Lowery at nineteen or twenty. I was introduced, and a gum-drop suffered neglect while she conveyed to me a naïve interest, such as a puppy dog (a prize winner) might bestow upon a crawling beetle or a frog.

Tripp took his stand by the table, with the fingers of one hand spread upon it, as an attorney or a master of ceremonies might have stood. But he looked the master of nothing. His faded coat was buttoned high, as if it sought to be charitable to deficiencies of tie and linen. I thought of a Scotch terrier at the sight of his shifty eyes in the glade between his tangled hair and beard. For one ignoble moment I felt ashamed of having been introduced as his friend in the presence of so much beauty in distress. But evidently Tripp meant to conduct the ceremonies, whatever they might be. I thought I detected in his actions and pose an intention of foisting the situation upon me as material for a newspaper story, in a lingering hope of extracting from me his whiskey dollar.

"My friend" (I shuddered), "Mr. Chalmers," said Tripp, "will tell you, Miss Lowery, the same that I did. He's a reporter, and he can hand out the talk better than I can. That's why I brought him with me." (O Tripp, wasn't it the *silver*-tongued orator you wanted?) "He's wise to a lot of things, and he'll tell you now what's best to do."

I stood on one foot, as it were, as I sat in my rickety chair.

"Why—er—Miss Lowery," I began, secretly enraged at Tripp's awkward opening, "I am at your service, of course, but—er—as I haven't been apprized of the circumstances of the case, I—er—"

"Oh," said Miss Lowery, beaming for a moment, "it ain't as bad as that—there ain't any circumstances. It's the first time I've ever been in New York except once when I was five years old, and I had no idea it was such a big town. And I met Mr.—Mr. Snip on the street and asked him about a friend of mine, and he brought me here and asked me to wait."

"I advise you, Miss Lowery," said Tripp, "to tell Mr. Chalmers all. He's a friend of mine" (I was getting used to it by this time), "and he'll give you the right tip."

"Why, certainly," said Miss Ada, chewing a gum-drop toward me. "There ain't anything to tell except that—well, everything's fixed for me to marry Hiram Dodd next Thursday evening. Hi has got two hundred acres of land with a lot of shore-front, and one of the best truck-farms on the Island. But this morning I had my horse saddled up—he's a white horse named Dancer— and I rode over to the station. I told 'em at home I was going to spend the day with Susie Adams. It was a story, I guess, but I don't care. And I came to New York on the train, and I met Mr.—Mr. Flip on the street and asked him if he knew where I could find G—G—"

"Now, Miss Lowery," broke in Tripp, loudly, and with much bad taste, I thought, as she hesitated with her word, "you like this young man, Hiram Dodd, don't you? He's all right, and good to you, ain't he?"

"Of course I like him," said Miss Lowery, emphatically. "Hi's all right. And of course he's good to me. So is everybody."

I could have sworn it myself. Throughout Miss Ada Lowery's life all men would be good to her. They would strive, contrive, struggle, and compete to hold umbrellas over her hat, check her trunk, pick up her handkerchief, and buy for her soda at the fountain.

"But," went on Miss Lowery, "last night I got to thinking about G—George, and I—"

Down went the bright gold head upon her dimpled, clasped hands on the table. Such a beautiful April storm! Unrestrainedly she sobbed. I wished I could have comforted her. But I was not George. And I was glad I was not Hiram—and yet I was sorry, too.

By-and-by the shower passed. She straightened up, brave and half-way smiling. She would have made a splendid wife, for crying only made her eyes more bright and tender. She took a gum-drop and began her story.

"I guess I'm a terrible hayseed," she said, between her little gulps and sighs, "but I can't help it. G—George Brown and I were sweethearts since he was eight and I was five. When he was nineteen—that was four years ago—he left Greenburg and went to the city. He said he was going to be a policeman or a railroad president or something. And then he was coming back for me. But I never heard from him any more. And I—I—liked him."

Another flow of tears seemed imminent, but Tripp hurled himself into the crevasse and dammed it. Confound him, I could see his game. He was trying to make a story of it for his sordid ends and profit.

"Go on, Mr. Chalmers," said he, "and tell the lady what's the proper caper. That's what I told her—you'd hand it to her straight. Spiel up."

I coughed, and tried to feel less wrathful toward Tripp. I saw my duty. Cunningly I had been inveigled, but I was securely trapped. Tripp's first dictum to me had been just and correct. The young lady must be sent back to Greenburg that day. She must be argued with, convinced, assured, instructed, ticketed, and returned without delay. I hated Hiram and despised George; but duty must be done. *Noblesse oblige* and only five silver dollars are not strictly romantic compatibles, but sometimes they can be made to jibe. It was mine to be Sir Oracle, and then pay the freight. So I assumed an air that mingled Solomon's with that of the general passenger agent of the Long Island Railroad.

"Miss Lowery," said I, as impressively as I could, "life is rather a queer proposition, after all." There was a familiar sound to these words after I had spoken them, and I hoped Miss Lowery had never heard Mr. Cohan's song. "Those whom we first love we seldom wed. Our earlier romances, tinged with the magic radiance of youth, often fail to materialize." The last three words sounded somewhat trite when they struck the air. "But those fondly cherished dreams," I went on, "may cast a pleasant afterglow on our future lives, however impracticable and vague they may have been. But life is full of realities as well as visions and dreams. One cannot live on memories. May I ask, Miss Lowery, if you think you could pass a happy—that is, a contented and harmonious life with Mr.—er—Dodd—if in other ways than romantic recollections he seems to—er—fill the bill, as I might say?"

"Oh, Hi's all right," answered Miss Lowery. "Yes, I could get along with him fine. He's promised me an automobile and a motor-boat. But somehow, when it got so close to the time I was to marry him, I couldn't help wishing—well, just thinking about George. Something must have happened to him or he'd have written. On the day he left, he and me got a hammer and a chisel and cut a dime into two pieces. I took one piece and he took the other, and we promised to be true to each other and always keep the pieces till we saw each other again. I've got mine at home now in a ring-box in the top drawer of my dresser. I guess I was silly to come up here looking for him. I never realized what a big place it is."

And then Tripp joined in with a little grating laugh that he had, still trying to drag in a little story or drama to earn the miserable dollar that he craved.

"Oh, the boys from the country forget a lot when they come to the city and learn something. I guess George, maybe, is on the bum, or got roped in by some other girl, or maybe gone to the dogs on account of whiskey or the races. You listen to Mr. Chalmers and go back home, and you'll be all right."

But now the time was come for action, for the hands of the clock were moving close to noon. Frowning upon Tripp, I argued gently and philosophically with Miss Lowery, delicately convincing her of the importance of returning home at once. And I impressed upon her the truth that it would not be absolutely necessary to her future happiness that she mention to Hi the wonders or the fact of her visit to the city that had swallowed up the unlucky George.

She said she had left her horse (unfortunate Rosinante) tied to a tree near the railroad station. Tripp and I gave her instructions to mount the patient steed as soon as she arrived and ride home as fast as possible. There she was to recount the exciting adventure of a day spent with Susie Adams. She could "fix" Susie—I was sure of that—and all would be well.

And then, being susceptible to the barbed arrows of beauty, I warmed to the adventure. The three of us hurried to the ferry, and there I found the price of a ticket to Greenburg to be but a dollar and eighty cents. I bought one, and a red, red rose with the twenty cents for Miss Lowery. We saw her aboard her ferryboat, and stood watching her wave her handkerchief at us until it was the tiniest white patch imaginable. And then Tripp and I faced each other, brought back to earth, left dry and desolate in the shade of the sombre verities of life.

The spell wrought by beauty and romance was dwindling. I looked at Tripp and almost sneered. He looked more care-worn, contemptible, and disreputable than ever. I fingered the two silver dollars remaining in my pocket and looked at him with the half-closed eyelids of contempt. He mustered up an imitation of resistance.

"Can't you get a story out of it?" he asked, huskily. "Some sort of a story, even if you have to fake part of it?"

"Not a line," said I. "I can fancy the look on Grimes' face if I should try to put over any slush like this. But we've helped the little lady out, and that 'll have to be our only reward."

"I'm sorry," said Tripp, almost inaudibly. "I'm sorry you're out your money. Now, it seemed to me like a find of a big story, you know—that is, a sort of thing that would write up pretty well."

"Let's try to forget it," said I, with a praiseworthy attempt at gayety, "and take the next car 'cross town."

I steeled myself against his unexpressed but palpable desire. He should not coax, cajole, or wring from me the dollar he craved. I had had enough of that wild-goose chase.

Tripp feebly unbuttoned his coat of the faded pattern and glossy seams to reach for something that had once been a hand-kerchief deep down in some obscure and cavernous pocket. As he did so I caught the shine of a cheap silver-plated watch-chain across his vest, and something dangling from it caused me to stretch forth my hand and seize it curiously. It was the half of a silver dime that had been cut in halves with a chisel.

"What!" I said, looking at him keenly.

"Oh yes," he responded, dully. "George Brown, *alias* Tripp. What's the use?"

Barring the W. C. T. U., I'd like to know if anybody disapproves of my having produced promptly from my pocket Tripp's whiskey dollar and unhesitatingly laying it in his hand.

FINAL STORIES

Let Me Feel Your Pulse

S o I went to a doctor.

"How long has it been since you took any alcohol into your system?" he asked.

Turning my head sidewise, I answered, "Oh, quite awhile."

He was a young doctor, somewhere between twenty and forty. He wore heliotrope socks, but he looked like Napoleon. I liked him immensely.

"Now," said he, "I am going to show you the effect of alcohol upon your circulation." I think it was "circulation" he said; though it may have been "advertising."

He bared my left arm to the elbow, brought out a bottle of whiskey, and gave me a drink. He began to look more like Napoleon. I began to like him better.

Then he put a tight compress on my upper arm, stopped my pulse with his fingers, and squeezed a rubber bulb connected with an apparatus on a stand that looked like a thermometer. The mercury jumped up and down without seeming to stop anywhere; but the doctor said it registered two hundred and thirty-seven or one hundred and sixty-five or some such number.

"Now," said he, "you see what alcohol does to the blood-pressure."

"It's marvellous," said I, "but do you think it a sufficient test? Have one on me, and let's try the other arm." But, no!

Then he grasped my hand. I thought I was doomed and he was saying good-bye. But all he wanted to do was to jab a needle into the end of a finger and compare the red drop with a lot of fifty-cent poker chips that he had fastened to a card.

"It's the hæmoglobin test," he explained. "The colour of your blood is wrong."

"Well," said I, "I know it should be blue; but this is a country of mix-ups. Some of my ancestors were cavaliers; but they got thick with some people on Nantucket Island, so——"

"I mean," said the doctor, "that the shade of red is too light."

"Oh," said I, "it's a case of matching instead of matches."

The doctor then pounded me severely in the region of the

chest. When he did that I don't know whether he reminded me most of Napoleon or Battling or Lord Nelson. Then he looked grave and mentioned a string of grievances that the flesh is heir to—mostly ending in "itis." I immediately paid him fifteen dollars on account.

"Is or are it or some or any of them necessarily fatal?" I asked. I thought my connection with the matter justified my manifesting a certain amount of interest.

"All of them," he answered cheerfully. "But their progress may be arrested. With care and proper continuous treatment you may live to be eighty-five or ninety."

I began to think of the doctor's bill. "Eighty-five would be sufficient, I am sure," was my comment. I paid him ten dollars more on account.

"The first thing to do," he said, with renewed animation, "is to find a sanitarium where you will get a complete rest for a while, and allow your nerves to get into a better condition. I myself will go with you and select a suitable one."

So he took me to a mad-house in the Catskills. It was on a bare mountain frequented only by infrequent frequenters. You could see nothing but stones and boulders, some patches of snow, and scattered pine trees. The young physician in charge was most agreeable. He gave me a stimulant without applying a compress to the arm. It was luncheon time, and we were invited to partake. There were about twenty inmates at little tables in the dining room. The young physician in charge came to our table and said: "It is a custom with our guests not to regard themselves as patients, but merely as tired ladies and gentlemen taking a rest. Whatever slight maladies they may have are never alluded to in conversation."

My doctor called loudly to a waitress to bring some phosphoglycerate of lime hash, dog-bread, bromo-seltzer pancakes, and nux vomica tea for my repast. Then a sound arose like a sudden wind storm among pine trees. It was produced by every guest in the room whispering loudly, "Neurasthenia!"—except one man with a nose, whom I distinctly heard say, "Chronic alcoholism." I hope to meet him again. The physician in charge turned and walked away.

An hour or so after luncheon he conducted us to the

workshop—say fifty yards from the house. Thither the guests had been conducted by the physician in charge's understudy and sponge-holder—a man with feet and a blue sweater. He was so tall that I was not sure he had a face; but the Armour Packing Company would have been delighted with his hands.

"Here," said the physician in charge, "our guests find relaxation from past mental worries by devoting themselves to physical labour—recreation, in reality."

There were turning-lathes, carpenters' outfits, clay-modelling tools, spinning-wheels, weaving-frames, treadmills, bass drums, enlarged-crayon-portrait apparatuses, blacksmith forges, and everything, seemingly, that could interest the paying lunatic guests of a first-rate sanitarium.

"The lady making mud pies in the corner," whispered the physician in charge, "is no other than—Lula Lulington, the authoress of the novel entitled 'Why Love Loves.' What she is doing now is simply to rest her mind after performing that piece of work."

I had seen the book. "Why doesn't she do it by writing another one instead?" I asked.

As you see, I wasn't as far gone as they thought I was.

"The gentleman pouring water through the funnel," continued the physician in charge, "is a Wall Street broker broken down from overwork."

I buttoned my coat.

Others he pointed out were architects playing with Noah's arks, ministers reading Darwin's "Theory of Evolution," lawyers sawing wood, tired-out society ladies talking Ibsen to the blue-sweatered sponge-holder, a neurotic millionaire lying asleep on the floor, and a prominent artist drawing a little red wagon around the room.

"You look pretty strong," said the physician in charge to me. "I think the best mental relaxation for you would be throwing small boulders over the mountainside and then bringing them up again."

I was a hundred yards away before my doctor overtook me.

"What's the matter?" he asked.

"The matter is," said I, "that there are no aeroplanes handy. So I am going to merrily and hastily jog the foot-pathway to yon station and catch the first unlimited-soft-coal express back to town."

"Well," said the doctor, "perhaps you are right. This seems hardly the suitable place for you. But what you need is rest—absolute rest and exercise."

That night I went to a hotel in the city, and said to the clerk: "What I need is absolute rest and exercise. Can you give me a room with one of those tall folding beds in it, and a relay of bellboys to work it up and down while I rest?"

The clerk rubbed a speck off one of his finger nails and glanced sidewise at a tall man in a white hat sitting in the lobby. That man came over and asked me politely if I had seen the shrubbery at the west entrance. I had not, so he showed it to me and then looked me over.

"I thought you had 'em," he said, not unkindly, "but I guess you're all right. You'd better go see a doctor, old man."

A week afterward my doctor tested my blood pressure again without the preliminary stimulant. He looked to me a little less like Napoleon. And his socks were of a shade of tan that did not appeal to me.

"What you need," he decided, "is sea air and companionship."

"Would a mermaid—" I began; but he slipped on his professional manner.

"I myself," he said, "will take you to the Hotel Bonair off the coast of Long Island and see that you get in good shape. It is a quiet, comfortable resort where you will soon recuperate."

The Hotel Bonair proved to be a nine-hundred-room fashionable hostelry on an island off the main shore. Everybody who did not dress for dinner was shoved into a side dining-room and given only a terrapin and champagne table d'hôte. The bay was a great stamping ground for wealthy yachtsmen. The *Corsair* anchored there the day we arrived. I saw Mr. Morgan standing on deck eating a cheese sandwich and gazing longingly at the hotel. Still, it was a very inexpensive place. Nobody could afford to pay their prices. When you went away you simply left your baggage, stole a skiff, and beat it for the mainland in the night.

When I had been there one day I got a pad of monogrammed telegraph blanks at the clerk's desk and began to wire to all my friends for get-away money. My doctor and I played one game of croquet on the golf links and went to sleep on the lawn.

When we got back to town a thought seemed to occur to him suddenly. "By the way," he asked, "how do you feel?"

"Relieved of very much," I replied.

Now a consulting physician is different. He isn't exactly sure whether he is to be paid or not, and this uncertainty insures you either the most careful or the most careless attention. My doctor took me to see a consulting physician. He made a poor guess and gave me careful attention. I liked him immensely. He put me through some coördination exercises.

"Have you a pain in the back of your head?" he asked. I told him I had not.

"Shut your eyes," he ordered, "put your feet close together, and jump backward as far as you can."

I always was a good backward jumper with my eyes shut, so I obeyed. My head struck the edge of the bathroom door, which had been left open and was only three feet away. The doctor was very sorry. He had overlooked the fact that the door was open. He closed it.

"Now touch your nose with your right forefinger," he said.

"Where is it?" I asked.

"On your face," said he.

"I mean my right forefinger," I explained.

"Oh, excuse me," said he. He reopened the bathroom door, and I took my finger out of the crack of it. After I had performed the marvellous digito-nasal feat I said:

"I do not wish to deceive you as to symptoms, Doctor; I really have something like a pain in the back of my head." He ignored the symptom and examined my heart carefully with a latest-popular-air-penny-in-the-slot ear-trumpet. I felt like a ballad.

"Now," he said, "gallop like a horse for about five minutes around the room."

I gave the best imitation I could of a disqualified Percheron being led out of Madison Square Garden. Then, without dropping in a penny, he listened to my chest again.

"No glanders in our family, Doc," I said.

The consulting physician held up his forefinger within three inches of my nose. "Look at my finger," he commanded.

"Did you ever try Pears'——" I began; but he went on with his test rapidly.

"Now look across the bay. At my finger. Across the bay. At my finger. At my finger. Across the bay. Across the bay. At my finger. Across the bay." This for about three minutes.

He explained that this was a test of the action of the brain. It seemed easy to me. I never once mistook his finger for the bay. I'll bet that if he had used the phrases: "Gaze, as it were, unpreoccupied, outward—or rather laterally—in the direction of the horizon, underlaid, so to speak, with the adjacent fluid inlet," and "Now, returning—or rather, in a manner, withdrawing your attention, bestow it upon my upraised digit"—I'll bet, I say, that Henry James himself could have passed the examination.

After asking me if I had ever had a grand uncle with curvature of the spine or a cousin with swelled ankles, the two doctors retired to the bathroom and sat on the edge of the bath tub for their consultation. I ate an apple, and gazed first at my finger and then across the bay.

The doctors came out looking grave. More: they looked tombstones and Tennessee-papers-please-copy. They wrote out a diet list to which I was to be restricted. It had everything that I had ever heard of to eat on it, except snails. And I never eat a snail unless it overtakes me and bites me first.

"You must follow this diet strictly," said the doctors.

"I'd follow it a mile if I could get one-tenth of what's on it," I answered.

"Of next importance," they went on, "is outdoor air and exercise. And here is a prescription that will be of great benefit to you."

Then all of us took something. They took their hats, and I took my departure.

I went to a druggist and showed him the prescription.

"It will be $2.87 for an ounce bottle," he said.

"Will you give me a piece of your wrapping cord?" said I.

I made a hole in the prescription, ran the cord through it, tied it around my neck, and tucked it inside. All of us have a little superstition, and mine runs to a confidence in amulets.

Of course there was nothing the matter with me, but I was very ill. I couldn't work, sleep, eat, or bowl. The only way I could get any sympathy was to go without shaving for four days. Even then somebody would say: "Old man, you look as hardy as a pine knot. Been up for a jaunt in the Maine woods, eh?"

Then, suddenly, I remembered that I must have outdoor air and exercise. So I went down South to John's. John is an approximate relative by verdict of a preacher standing with a little book in his hands in a bower of chrysanthemums while a hundred thousand people looked on. John has a country house seven miles from Pineville. It is at an altitude and on the Blue Ridge Mountains in a state too dignified to be dragged into this controversy. John is mica, which is more valuable and clearer than gold.

He met me at Pineville, and we took the trolley car to his home. It is a big, neighbourless cottage on a hill surrounded by a hundred mountains. We got off at his little private station, where John's family and Amaryllis met and greeted us. Amaryllis looked at me a trifle anxiously.

A rabbit came bounding across the hill between us and the house. I threw down my suit-case and pursued it hotfoot. After I had run twenty yards and seen it disappear, I sat down on the grass and wept disconsolately.

"I can't catch a rabbit any more," I sobbed. "I'm of no further use in the world. I may as well be dead."

"Oh, what is it—what is it, Brother John?" I heard Amaryllis say.

"Nerves a little unstrung," said John, in his calm way. "Don't worry. Get up, you rabbit-chaser, and come on to the house before the biscuits get cold." It was about twilight, and the mountains came up nobly to Miss Murfree's descriptions of them.

Soon after dinner I announced that I believed I could sleep for a year or two, including legal holidays. So I was shown to a room as big and cool as a flower garden, where there was a bed as broad as a lawn. Soon afterward the remainder of the household retired, and then there fell upon the land a silence.

I had not heard a silence before in years. It was absolute. I raised myself on my elbow and listened to it. Sleep! I thought that if I only could hear a star twinkle or a blade of grass sharpen itself I could compose myself to rest. I thought once that I heard a sound like the sail of a catboat flapping as it veered about in a breeze, but I decided that it was probably only a tack in the carpet. Still I listened.

Suddenly some belated little bird alighted upon the window-sill, and, in what he no doubt considered sleepy tones, enunciated the noise generally translated as "cheep!"

I leaped into the air.

"Hey! what's the matter down there?" called John from his room above mine.

"Oh, nothing," I answered, "except that I accidentally bumped my head against the ceiling."

The next morning I went out on the porch and looked at the mountains. There were forty-seven of them in sight. I shuddered, went into the big hall sitting room of the house, selected "Pancoast's Family Practice of Medicine" from a bookcase, and began to read. John came in, took the book away from me, and led me outside. He has a farm of three hundred acres furnished with the usual complement of barns, mules, peasantry, and harrows with three front teeth broken off. I had seen such things in my childhood, and my heart began to sink.

Then John spoke of alfalfa, and I brightened at once. "Oh, yes," said I, "wasn't she in the chorus of—let's see——"

"Green, you know," said John, "and tender, and you plow it under after the first season."

"I know," said I, "and the grass grows over her."

"Right," said John. "You know something about farming, after all."

"I know something of some farmers," said I, "and a sure scythe will mow them down some day."

On the way back to the house a beautiful and inexplicable creature walked across our path. I stopped irresistibly fascinated, gazing at it. John waited patiently, smoking his cigarette. He is a modern farmer. After ten minutes he said: "Are you going to stand there looking at that chicken all day? Breakfast is nearly ready."

"A chicken?" said I.

"A White Orpington hen, if you want to particularize."

"A White Orpington hen?" I repeated, with intense interest. The fowl walked slowly away with graceful dignity, and I followed like a child after the Pied Piper. Five minutes more were allowed me by John, and then he took me by the sleeve and conducted me to breakfast.

After I had been there a week I began to grow alarmed. I was sleeping and eating well and actually beginning to enjoy life. For a man in my desperate condition that would never do. So I sneaked down to the trolley-car station, took the car for Pineville, and went to see one of the best physicians in town. By this time I knew exactly what to do when I needed medical treatment. I hung my hat on the back of a chair, and said rapidly:

"Doctor, I have cirrhosis of the heart, indurated arteries, neurasthenia, neuritis, acute indigestion, and convalescence. I am going to live on a strict diet. I shall also take a tepid bath at night and a cold one in the morning. I shall endeavour to be cheerful, and fix my mind on pleasant subjects. In the way of drugs I intend to take a phosphorous pill three times a day, preferably after meals, and a tonic composed of the tinctures of gentian, cinchona, calisaya, and cardamom compound. Into each teaspoonful of this I shall mix tincture of nux vomica, beginning with one drop and increasing it a drop each day until the maximum dose is reached. I shall drop this with a medicine-dropper, which can be procured at a trifling cost at any pharmacy. Good morning."

I took my hat and walked out. After I had closed the door I remembered something that I had forgotten to say. I opened it again. The doctor had not moved from where he had been sitting, but he gave a slightly nervous start when he saw me again.

"I forgot to mention," said I, "that I shall also take absolute rest and exercise."

After this consultation I felt much better. The reëstablishing in my mind of the fact that I was hopelessly ill gave me so much satisfaction that I almost became gloomy again. There is nothing more alarming to a neurasthenic than to feel himself growing well and cheerful.

John looked after me carefully. After I had evinced so much interest in his White Orpington chicken he tried his best to divert my mind, and was particular to lock his hen house of nights. Gradually the tonic mountain air, the wholesome food, and the daily walks among the hills so alleviated my malady that I became utterly wretched and despondent. I heard of a country doctor who lived in the mountains nearby. I went to see him and told him the whole story. He was a gray-bearded man with clear, blue, wrinkled eyes, in a home-made suit of gray jeans.

In order to save time I diagnosed my case, touched my nose with my right forefinger, struck myself below the knee to make my foot kick, sounded my chest, stuck out my tongue, and asked him the price of cemetery lots in Pineville.

lie lit his pipe and looked at me for about three minutes. "Brother," he said, after a while, "you are in a mighty bad way. There's a chance for you to pull through, but it's a mighty slim one."

"What can it be?" I asked eagerly. "I have taken arsenic and gold, phosphorus, exercise, nux vomica, hydrotherapeutic baths, rest, excitement, codein, and aromatic spirits of ammonia. Is there anything left in the pharmacopœia?"

"Somewhere in these mountains," said the doctor, "there's a plant growing—a flowering plant that'll cure you, and it's about the only thing that will. It's of a kind that's as old as the world; but of late it's powerful scarce and hard to find. You and I will have to hunt it up. I'm not engaged in active practice now: I'm getting along in years; but I'll take your case. You'll have to come every day in the afternoon and help me hunt for this plant till we find it. The city doctors may know a lot about new scientific things, but they don't know much about the cures that nature carries around in her saddle-bags."

So every day the old doctor and I hunted the cure-all plant among the mountains and valleys of the Blue Ridge. Together we toiled up steep heights so slippery with fallen autumn leaves that we had to catch every sapling and branch within our reach to save us from falling. We waded through gorges and chasms, breast-deep with laurel and ferns; we followed the banks of mountain streams for miles; we wound our way like Indians through brakes of pine—road side, hill side, river side, mountain side we explored in our search for the miraculous plant.

As the old doctor said, it must have grown scarce and hard to find. But we followed our quest. Day by day we plumbed the valleys, scaled the heights, and tramped the plateaus in search of the miraculous plant. Mountain-bred, he never seemed to tire. I often reached home too fatigued to do anything except fall into bed and sleep until morning. This we kept up for a month.

One evening after I had returned from a six-mile tramp with the old doctor, Amaryllis and I took a little walk under the trees near the road. We looked at the mountains drawing their royal-purple robes around them for their night's repose.

"I'm glad you're well again," she said. "When you first came you frightened me. I thought you were really ill."

"Well again!" I almost shrieked. "Do you know that I have only one chance in a thousand to live?"

Amaryllis looked at me in surprise. "Why," said she, "you are as strong as one of the plough-mules, you sleep ten or twelve hours every night, and you are eating us out of house and home. What more do you want?"

"I tell you," said I, "that unless we find the magic—that is, the plant we are looking for—in time, nothing can save me. The doctor tells me so."

"What doctor?"

"Doctor Tatum—the old doctor who lives halfway up Black Oak Mountain. Do you know him?"

"I have known him since I was able to talk. And is that where you go every day—is it he who takes you on these long walks and climbs that have brought back your health and strength? God bless the old doctor."

Just then the old doctor himself drove slowly down the road in his rickety old buggy. I waved my hand at him and shouted that I would be on hand the next day at the usual time. He stopped his horse and called to Amaryllis to come out to him. They talked for five minutes while I waited. Then the old doctor drove on.

When we got to the house Amaryllis lugged out an encyclopædia and sought a word in it. "The doctor said," she told me, "that you needn't call any more as a patient, but he'd be glad to see you any time as a friend. And then he told me to look up my name in the encyclopædia and tell you what it means. It seems to be the name of a genus of flowering plants, and also the name of a country girl in Theocritus and Virgil. What do you suppose the doctor meant by that?"

"I know what he meant," said I. "I know now."

A word to a brother who may have come under the spell of the unquiet Lady Neurasthenia.

The formula was true. Even though gropingly at times, the physicians of the walled cities had put their fingers upon the specific medicament.

And so for the exercise one is referred to good Doctor Tatum on Black Oak Mountain—take the road to your right at the Methodist meeting house in the pine-grove.

Absolute rest and exercise!

What rest more remedial than to sit with Amaryllis in the shade, and, with a sixth sense, read the wordless Theocritan idyl of the gold-bannered blue mountains marching orderly into the dormitories of the night?

The Snow Man

HOUSED AND windowpaned from it, the greatest wonder to little children is the snow. To men, it is something like a crucible in which their world melts into a white star ten million miles away. The man who can stand the test is a Snow Man; and this is his reading by Fahrenheit, Réaumur, or Moses's carven tables of stone.

Night had fluttered a sable pinion above the cañon of Big Lost River, and I urged my horse toward the Bay Horse Ranch because the snow was deepening. The flakes were as large as an hour's circular tatting by Miss Wilkin's ablest spinster, betokening a heavy snowfall and less entertainment and more adventure than the completion of the tatting could promise. I knew Ross Curtis of the Bay Horse, and that I would be welcome as a snow-bound pilgrim, both for hospitality's sake and because Ross had few chances to confide in living creatures who did not neigh, bellow, bleat, yelp, or howl, during his discourse.

The ranch house was just within the jaws of the cañon where its builder may have fatuously fancied that the timbered and rocky walls on both sides would have protected it from the wintry Colorado winds; but I feared the drift. Even now through the endless, bottomless rift in the hills—the speaking tube of the four winds—came roaring the voice of the proprietor to the little room on the top floor.

At my "hello," a ranch hand came from an outer building and received my thankful horse. In another minute, Ross and I sat by a stove in the dining-room of the four-room ranch house, while the big, simple welcome of the household lay at my disposal. Fanned by the whizzing norther, the fine, dry snow was sifted and bolted through the cracks and knot holes of the logs. The cook room, without a separating door, appended.

In there I could see a short, sturdy, leisurely and weather-beaten man moving with professional sureness about his red-hot stove. His face was solid and unreadable—something like that of a great thinker, or of one who had no thoughts to conceal. I thought his eye seemed unwarrantably superior to the elements and to the man, but quickly attributed that to the characteristic self-importance of a petty chef. "Camp cook" was the niche that I gave him in the Hall of Types; and he fitted it as an apple fits a dumpling.

Cold it was, in spite of the glowing stove; and Ross and I sat and talked, shuddering frequently, half from nerves and half from the freezing draughts. So he brought the bottle, and the cook brought boiling water, and we made prodigious hot toddies against the attacks of Boreas. We clinked glasses often. They sounded like icicles dropping from the eaves, or like the tinkle of a thousand prisms on a Louis XIV chandelier that I once heard at a boarder's dance in the parlor of a ten-a-week boarding-house in Gramercy Square. *Sic transit.*

Silence in the terrible beauty of the snow and of the Sphinx and of the stars; but they who believe that all things, from a without-wine table d'hôte to the crucifixion, may be interpreted through music, might have found a nocturne or a symphony to express the isolation of that blotted-out world. The clink of glass and bottle, the aeolian chorus of the wind in the house crannies, its deeper trombone through the cañon below, and the Wagnerian crash of the cook's pots and pans, united in a fit, discordant melody, I thought. No less welcome an accompaniment was the sizzling of broiling ham and venison cutlets, indorsed by the solvent fumes of true Java, bringing rich promises of comfort to our yearning souls.

The cook brought the smoking supper to the table. He nodded to me democratically as he cast the heavy plates around as though he were pitching quoits or hurling the discus. I looked at him with some appraisement and curiosity, and much conciliation. There was no prophet to tell us when that drifting evil outside might cease to fall; and it is well, when snow-bound, to stand somewhere within the radius of the cook's favorable consideration. But I could read neither favor nor disapproval in the face and manner of our pot-wrestler.

He was about five feet, nine inches, and two hundred pounds of commonplace, bull-necked, pink-faced, callous calm. He wore brown duck trousers too tight and too short, and a blue flannel shirt with sleeves rolled above his elbows. There was a sort of grim, steady scowl on his features that looked to me as though he had fixed it there purposely as a protection against the weakness of an inherent amiability that, he fancied, were better concealed. And then I let supper usurp his brief occupancy of my thoughts.

"Draw up, George," said Ross. "Let's all eat while the grub's hot."

"You fellows go on and chew," answered the cook. "I ate mine in the kitchen before sundown."

"Think it'll be a big snow, George?" asked the ranchman.

George had turned to reënter the cook room. He moved slowly around, and, looking at his face, it seemed to me that he was turning over the wisdom and knowledge of centuries in his head.

"It might," was his delayed reply.

At the door of the kitchen he stopped and looked back at us. Both Ross and I held our knives and forks poised and gave him our regard. Some men have the power of drawing the attention of others without speaking a word. Their attitude is more effective than a shout.

"And again it mightn't," said George, and went back to his stove.

After we had eaten, he came in and gathered the emptied dishes. He stood for a moment, with his spurious frown deepened.

"It might stop any minute," he said, "or it might keep it up for days."

At the farther end of the cook room I saw George pour hot water into his dishpan, light his pipe, and put the tableware through its required lavation. He then carefully unwrapped from a piece of old saddle blanket a paper-back book, and settled himself to read by his dim oil lamp.

And then the ranchman threw tobacco on the cleared table and set forth again the bottles and glasses; and I saw that I stood in a deep channel through which the long dammed flood of his discourse would soon be booming. But I was half content, comparing my fate with that of the late Thomas Tucker, who had to sing for his supper, thus doubling the burdens of both himself and his host.

"Snow is a hell of a thing," said Ross, by way of a foreword. "It ain't, somehow, it seems to me, salubrious. I can stand water and mud and two inches below zero and a hundred and ten in the shade and medium-sized cyclones, but this here fuzzy white stuff naturally gets me all locoed. I reckon the reason it rattles you is because it changes the look of things so much. It's like you had a wife and left her in the morning with the same old blue cotton wrapper on, and rides in of a night and runs across her all outfitted in a white silk evening frock, waving an ostrich-feather fan, and monkeying with a posy of lily flowers. Wouldn't it make you look for your pocket compass? You'd be liable to kiss her before you collected your presence of mind."

By and by, the flood of Ross's talk was drawn up into the clouds (so it pleased me to fancy) and there condensed into the finer snowflakes of thought; and we sat silent about the stove, as good friends and bitter enemies will do. I thought of Ross's preamble about the mysterious influence upon man exerted by that ermine-lined monster that now covered our little world, and knew he was right.

Of all the curious knickknacks, mysteries, puzzles, Indian gifts, rat-trap, and well-disguised blessings that the gods chuck down to us from the Olympian peaks, the most disquieting and evil-bringing is the snow. By scientific analysis it is absolute beauty and purity—so, at the beginning we look doubtfully at chemistry.

It falls upon the world, and lo! we live in another. It hides in a night the old scars and familiar places with which we have grown heartsick or enamored. So, as quietly as we can, we hustle on our embroidered robes and hie us on Prince Camaralzaman's horse or in the reindeer sleigh into the white country where the seven colors converge. This is when our fancy can overcome the bane of it.

But in certain spots of the earth comes the snow-madness, made known by people turned wild and distracted by the bewildering veil that has obscured the only world they know. In the cities, the white fairy who sets the brains of her dupes whirling by a wave of her wand is cast for the comedy rôle. Her diamond shoe buckles glitter like frost; with a pirouette she invites the spotless carnival.

But in the waste places the snow is sardonic. Sponging out the world of the outliers, it gives no foothold on another sphere in return. It makes of the earth a firmament under foot;

it leaves us clawing and stumbling in space in an inimical fifth element whose evil outdoes its strangeness and beauty. There Nature, low comedienne, plays her tricks on man. Though she has put him forth as her highest product, it appears that she has fashioned him with what seems almost incredible carelessness and indexterity. One-sided and without balance, with his two halves unequally fashioned and joined, must he ever jog his eccentric way. The snow falls, the darkness caps it, and the ridiculous man-biped strays in accurate circles until he succumbs in the ruins of his defective architecture.

In the throat of the thirsty the snow is vitriol. In appearance as plausible as the breakfast food of the angels, it is as hot in the mouth as ginger, increasing the pangs of the water-famished. It is a derivative from water, air, and some cold, uncanny fire from which the caloric has been extracted. Good has been said of it; even the poets, crazed by its spell and shivering in their attics under its touch, have indited permanent melodies commemorative of its beauty.

Still, to the saddest overcoated optimist it is a plague—a corroding plague that Pharaoh successfully sidestepped. It beneficently covers the wheat fields, swelling the crop—and the Flour Trust gets us by the throat like a sudden quinsy. It spreads the tail of its white kirtle over the red seams of the rugged north—and the Alaskan short story is born. Etiolated perfidy, it shelters the mountain traveler burrowing from the icy air—and, melting to-morrow, drowns his brother in the valley below.

At its worst it is lock and key and crucible, and the wand of Circe. When it corrals man in lonely ranches, mountain cabins, and forest huts, the snow makes apes and tigers of the hardiest. It turns the bosoms of weaker ones to glass, their tongues to infants' rattles, their hearts to lawlessness and spleen. It is not all from the isolation; the snow is not merely a blockader; it is a Chemical Test. It is a good man who can show a reaction that is not chiefly composed of a drachm or two of potash and magnesia, with traces of Adam, Ananias, Nebuchadnezzar, and the fretful porcupine.

This is no story, you say; well, let it begin.

There was a knock at the door (is the opening not full of context and reminiscence, oh best buyers of best sellers?).

We drew the latch, and in stumbled Étienne Girod (as he afterwards named himself). But just then he was no more than a worm struggling for life, enveloped in a killing white chrysalis.

We dug down through snow, overcoats, mufflers, and waterproofs, and dragged forth a living thing with a Van Dyck beard and marvelous diamond rings. We put it through the approved curriculum of snow-rubbing, hot milk, and teaspoonful doses of whisky, working him up to a graduating class entitled to a diploma of three fingers of rye in half a glassful of hot water. One of the ranch boys had already come from the quarters at Ross's bugle-like yell and kicked the stranger's staggering pony to some sheltered corral where beasts were entertained.

Let a paragraphic biography of Girod intervene.

Étienne was an opera singer originally, we gathered; but adversity and the snow had made him *non compos vocis*. The adversity consisted of the stranded San Salvador Opera Company, a period of hotel second-story work, and then a career as a professional palmist, jumping from town to town. For, like other professional palmists, every time he worked the Heart Line too strongly he immediately moved along the Line of Least Resistance. Though Étienne did not confide this to us, we surmised he had moved out into the dusk about twenty minutes ahead of a constable, and had thus encountered the snow. In his most sacred blue language he dilated upon the subject of snow; for Étienne was Paris-born and loved the snow with the same passion that an orchid does.

"Mee-ser-rhable!" commented Étienne, and took another three fingers.

"Complete, cast-iron, pussy-footed, blank . . . blank!" said Ross, and followed suit.

"Rotten," said I.

The cook said nothing. He stood in the door, weighing our outburst; and insistently from behind that frozen visage I got two messages (*via* the M.A.M. wireless). One was that George considered our vituperation against the snow childish; the other was that George did not love Dagoes. Inasmuch as Étienne was a Frenchman, I concluded I had the message wrong. So I queried the other: "Bright eyes, you don't really mean Dagoes, do you?" and over the wireless came three deathly, psychic taps: "Yes." Then I reflected that to George all foreigners were probably "Dagoes." I had once known another camp cook who had thought Mons., Sig. and Millie (Trans-Mississippi for Mlle.) were Italian given names; this cook used to marvel therefore at the paucity of Neo-Roman precognomens, and therefore why not——

I have said that snow is a test of men. For one day, two days, Étienne stood at the window, Fletcherizing his finger nails and shrieking and moaning at the monotony. To me, Étienne was just about as unbearable as the snow; and so, seeking relief, I went out on the second day to look at my horse, slipped on a stone, broke my collar-bone, and thereafter underwent not the snow test, but the test of flat-on-the-back. A test that comes once too often for any man to stand.

However, I bore up cheerfully. I was now merely a spectator, and from my couch in the big room I could lie and watch the human interplay with that detached, impassive, impersonal feeling which French writers tell us is so valuable to the litterateur, and American writers to the faro-dealer.

"I shall go crazy in this abominable, mee-ser-rhable place!" was Étienne's constant prediction.

"Never knew Mark Twain to bore me before," said Ross, over and over. He sat by the other window, hour after hour, a box of Pittsburg stogies of the length, strength, and odor of a Pittsburg graft scandal deposited on one side of him, and "Roughing It," "The Jumping Frog," and "Life on the Mississippi" on the other. For every chapter he lit a new stogie, puffing furiously. This, in time, gave him a recurrent premonition of cramps, gastritis, smoker's colic, or whatever it is they have in Pittsburg after a too deep indulgence in graft scandals. To fend off the colic, Ross resorted time and again to old Doctor Still's Amber-Colored U. S. A. Colic Cure. Result, after forty-eight hours—nerves.

"Positive fact, I never knew Mark Twain to make me tired before. Positive fact." Ross slammed "Roughing It" on the floor. "When you're snow-bound this away you want tragedy, I guess. Humor just seems to bring out all your cussedness. You read a man's poor, pitiful attempts to be funny and it makes you so nervous you want to tear the book up, get out your bandana, and have a good, long cry."

At the other end of the room, the Frenchman took his finger

nails out of his mouth long enough to exclaim: "Humor! Humor at such a time as thees! My God, I shall go crazy in thees abominable——"

"Supper," announced George.

These meals were not the meals of Rabelais who said, "the great God makes the planets and we make the platters neat." By that time, the ranch-house meals were not affairs of gusto; they were mental distraction, not bodily provender. What they were to be later shall never be forgotten by Ross or me or Étienne.

After supper, the stogies and finger nails began again. My shoulder ached wretchedly, and with half-closed eyes I tried to forget it by watching the deft movements of the stolid cook.

Suddenly I saw him cock his ear, like a dog. Then, with a swift step, he moved to the door, threw it open, and stood there.

The rest of us had heard nothing.

"What is it, George?" asked Ross.

The cook reached out his hand into the darkness alongside the jamb. With careful precision he prodded something. Then he made one careful step into the snow. His back muscles bulged a little under the arms as he stooped and lightly lifted a burden. Another step inside the door, which he shut methodically behind him, and he dumped the burden at a safe distance from the fire.

He stood up and fixed us with a solemn eye. None of us moved under that Orphic suspense until,

"A woman," remarked George.

Miss Willie Adams was her name. Vocation, school-teacher. Present avocation, getting lost in the snow. Age, yum-yum (the Persian for twenty). Take to the woods if you would describe Miss Adams. A willow for grace; a hickory for fiber; a birch for the clear whiteness of her skin; for eyes, the blue sky seen through tree-tops; the silk in cocoons for her hair; her voice, the murmur of the evening June wind in the leaves; her mouth, the berries of the wintergreen; fingers as light as ferns; her toe as small as a deer track. General impression upon the dazed beholder—you could not see the forest for the trees.

Psychology, with a capital P and the foot of a lynx, at this juncture stalks into the ranch house. Three men, a cook, a pretty young woman—all snow-bound. Count me out of it, as I did not count, anyway. I never did, with women. Count the cook out, if you like. But note the effect upon Ross and Étienne Girod.

Ross dumped Mark Twain in a trunk and locked the trunk. Also, he discarded the Pittsburg scandals. Also, he shaved off a three days' beard.

Étienne, being French, began on the beard first. He pomaded it, from a little tube of grease *Hongroise* in his vest pocket. He combed it with a little aluminum comb from the same vest pocket. He trimmed it with manicure scissors from the same vest pocket. His light and Gallic spirits underwent a sudden, miraculous change. He hummed a blithe San Salvador Opera Company tune; he grinned, smirked, bowed, pirouetted, twiddled, twaddled, twisted, and tooralooed. Gayly, the notorious troubadour, could not have equaled Étienne.

Ross's method of advance was brusque, domineering. "Little woman," he said, "you're welcome here!"—and with what he thought subtle double meaning—"welcome to stay here as long as you like, snow or no snow."

Miss Adams thanked him a little wildly, some of the wintergreen berries creeping into the birch bark. She looked around hurriedly, as if seeking escape. But there was none, save the kitchen and the room allotted her. She made an excuse and disappeared into her own room.

Later I, feigning sleep, heard the following:

"Mees Adams, I was almos' to perish—die—of monotony w'en your fair and beautiful face appear in thees mee-ser-rhable house." I opened my starboard eye. The beard was being curled furiously around a finger, the Svengali eye was rolling, the chair was being hunched closer to the school-teacher's. "I am French—you see—temperamental—nervous! I cannot endure thees dull hours in thees ranch house; *but*—a woman comes! Ah!" The shoulders gave nine 'rahs and a tiger. "What a difference! All is light and gay; ever'ting smile w'en you smile. You have 'eart, beauty, grace. My 'eart comes back to me w'en I feel your 'eart. So!" He laid his hand upon his vest pocket. From this vantage point he suddenly snatched at the school-teacher's own hand. "Ah! Mees Adams, if I could only tell you how I ad——"

"Dinner—" remarked George. He was standing just behind the Frenchman's ear. His eyes looked straight into the schoolteacher's eyes. After thirty seconds of survey, his lips moved, deep in the flinty frozen maelstrom of his face: "Dinner," he concluded, "will be ready in two minutes."

Miss Adams jumped to her feet, relieved. "I must get ready for dinner," she said brightly, and went into her room.

Ross came in fifteen minutes late. After the dishes had been cleaned away, I waited until a propitious time when the room was temporarily ours alone, and told him what had happened.

He became so excited that he lit a stogy without thinking. "Yeller-hided, unwashed, palm-readin' skunk," he said under his breath. "I'll shoot him full o' holes if he don't watch out— talkin' that way to my wife!"

I gave a jump that set my collarbone back another week. "Your wife!" I gasped.

"Well, I mean to make her that," he announced.

The air in the ranch house the rest of that day was tense with pent-up emotions, oh best buyers of best sellers.

Ross watched Miss Adams as a hawk does a hen; he watched Étienne as a hawk does a scarecrow. Étienne watched Miss Adams as a weasel does a henhouse. He paid no attention to Ross.

The condition of Miss Adams, in the rôle of sought-after, was feverish. Lately escaped from the agony and long torture of the white cold, where for hours Nature had kept the little school-teacher's vision locked in and turned upon herself, nobody knows through what profound, feminine introspections she had gone. Now, suddenly cast among men, instead of finding relief and security, she beheld herself plunged anew into other discomforts. Even in her own room she could hear the loud voices of her imposed suitors. "I'll blow you full o' holes!" shouted Ross. "Witnesses," shrieked Étienne, waving his hand at the cook and me. She could not have known the previous harassed condition of the men, fretting under indoor conditions. All she knew was, that where she had expected the frank freemasonry of the West, she found the subtle tangle of two men's minds, bent upon exacting whatever romance there might be in her situation.

She tried to dodge Ross and the Frenchman by spells of

nursing me. They also came over to help nurse. This combination aroused such a natural state of invalid cussedness on my part that they all were forced to retire. Once she did manage to whisper: "I am so worried here. I don't know what to do."

To which I replied, gently, hitching up my shoulder, that I was a hunch-savant and that the Eighth House under this sign, the Moon being in Virgo, showed that everything would turn out all right.

But twenty minutes later I saw Étienne reading her palm and felt that perhaps I might have to recast her horoscope, and try for a dark man coming with a bundle.

Toward sunset, Étienne left the house for a few moments and Ross, who had been sitting taciturn and morose, having unlocked Mark Twain, made another dash. It was typical Ross talk.

He stood in front of her and looked down majestically at that cool and perfect spot where Miss Adams' forehead met the neat part in her fragrant hair. First, however, he cast a desperate glance at me. I was in a profound slumber.

"Little woman," he began, "it's certainly tough for a man like me to see you bothered this way. You"—gulp—"you have been alone in this world too long. You need a protector. I might say that at a time like this you need a protector the worst kind—a protector who would take a three-ring delight in smashing the saffron-colored kisser off of any yeller-skinned skunk that made himself obnoxious to you. Hem. Hem. I am a lonely man, Miss Adams. I have so far had to carry on my life without the"—gulp—"sweet radiance"—gulp—"of a woman around the house. I feel especially doggoned lonely at a time like this, when I am pretty near locoed from havin' to stall indoors, and hence it was with delight I welcomed your first appearance in this here shack. Since then I have been packed jam full of more different kinds of feelings, ornery, mean, dizzy, and superb, than has fallen my way in years." Miss Adams made a useless movement toward escape. The Ross chin stuck firm. "I don't want to annoy you, Miss Adams, but, by heck, if it comes to that you'll have to be annoyed. And I'll have to have my say. This palm-ticklin' slob of a Frenchman ought to be kicked off the place and if you'll say the word, off he goes. But I don't want to do the wrong thing. You've got to show a preference.

I'm gettin' around to the point, Miss—Miss Willie, in my own brick fashion. I've stood about all I can stand these last two days and somethin's got to happen. The suspense hereabouts is enough to hang a sheepherder. Miss Willie"—he lassoed her hand by main force—"just say the word. You need somebody to take your part all your life long. Will you mar——"

"Supper," remarked George, tersely, from the kitchen door.

Miss Adams hurried away.

Ross turned angrily. "You——"

"I have been revolving it in my head," said George.

He brought the coffeepot forward heavily. Then gravely the big platter of pork and beans. Then somberly the potatoes. Then profoundly the biscuits. "I been revolving it in my mind. There ain't no use waitin' any longer for Swengalley. Might as well eat now."

From my excellent vantage-point on the couch I watched the progress of that meal. Ross muddled, glowering, disappointed; Étienne, eternally blandishing, attentive, ogling; Miss Adams nervous, picking at her food, hesitant about answering questions, almost hysterical; now and then the solid, flitting shadow of the cook, passing behind their backs like a Dreadnought in a fog.

I used to own a clock which gurgled in its throat three minutes before it struck the hour. I know, therefore, the slow freight of Anticipation. For I have awakened at three in the morning, heard the clock gurgle and waited those three minutes for the three strokes I knew were to come. *Alors.* In Ross's ranch house that night the slow freight of Climax whistled in the distance.

Étienne began it after supper. Miss Adams had suddenly displayed a lively interest in the kitchen layout and I could see her in there, chatting brightly at George—not with him—the while he ducked his head and rattled his pans.

"My fren," said Étienne, exhaling a large cloud from his cigarette and patting Ross lightly on the shoulder with a be-diamonded hand which hung limp from a yard or more of bony arm, "I see I mus' be frank with you. Firs', because we are rivals; second, because you take these matters so serious. I—I am Franchman. I love the women"—he threw back his curls, bared his yellow teeth, and blew an unsavory kiss toward the kitchen. "It is, I suppose, a trait of my nation. All Franchmen love the women—pretty women. Now, look: Here I am!" He spread out his arms. "Cold outside! I detes' the col-l-l'! Snow! I abominate the mees-ser-rhable snow! Two men! This"—pointing to me—"an' this!" Pointing to Ross. "I am distracted! For two whole days I stan' at the window an' tear my 'air! I am nervous, upset, pr-r-ro-foun'ly distress inside my 'ead! An' suddenly—be'old! A woman—a nice, pretty, charming innocen' young woman! I, naturally, rejoice. I become myself again—gay, light-'earted, 'appy. I address myself to mademoiselle; it passes the time. That, m'sieu', is wot the women are for—pass the time! Entertainment—like the music, like the wine!

"They appeal to the mood, the caprice, the temperamen'. To play with thees woman, follow her through her humor, pursue her—ah! that is the mos' delightful way to sen' the hours about their business."

Ross banged the table. "Shut up, you miserable yeller pup!" he roared. "I object to your pursuin' anything or anybody in my house. Now, you listen to me, you—" He picked up the box of stogies and used it on the table as an emphasizer. The noise of it awoke the attention of the girl in the kitchen. Unheeded, she crept into the room. "I don't know anything about your French ways of lovemakin', an' I don't care. In my section of the country, it's the best man wins. And I'm the best man here, and don't you forget it! This girl's goin' to be mine. There ain't going to be any playing, or philandering, or palm reading about it. I've made up my mind I'll have this girl, and that settles it. My word is law in this neck o' the woods. She's mine and as soon as she says she's mine, you pull out." The box made one final, tremendous punctuation point.

Étienne's bravado was unruffled. "Ah! that is no way to win a woman," he smiled, easily. "I make prophecy you will never win 'er that way. No. Not thees woman. She mus' be played along an' then keessed, this charming, delicious little creature. One keess! An' then you 'ave her." Again he displayed his unpleasant teeth. "I make you a bet I will keess her——"

As a cheerful chronicler of deeds done well, it joys me to relate that the hand which fell upon Étienne's amorous lips was not his own. There was one sudden sound, as of a mule kicking a lath fence, and then—through the swinging doors of oblivion for Étienne.

I had seen this blow delivered. It was an aloof, unstudied, almost absent-minded affair. I had thought the cook was rehearsing the proper method of turning a flapjack.

Silently, lost in thought, he stood there scratching his head. Then he began rolling down his sleeves.

"You'd better get your things on, Miss, and we'll get out of here," he decided. "Wrap up warm."

I heard her heave a little sigh of relief as she went to get her cloak, sweater, and hat.

Ross jumped to his feet, and said: "George, what are you goin' to do?"

George, who had been headed in my direction, slowly swiveled around and faced his employer. "Bein' a camp cook, I ain't overburdened with hosses," George enlightened us. "Therefore, I am going to try to borrow this feller's here."

For the first time in four days my soul gave a genuine cheer. "If it's for Lochinvar purposes, go as far as you like," I said grandly.

The cook studied me a moment, as if trying to find an insult in my words. "No," he replied. "It's for mine and the young lady's purposes, and we'll go only three miles—to Hicksville. Now let me tell you somethin', Ross." Suddenly I was confronted with the cook's chunky back and I heard a low, curt, carrying voice shoot through the room at my host. George had wheeled just as Ross started to speak. "You're nutty. That's what's the matter with you. You can't stand the snow. You're gettin' nervouser and nuttier every day. That and this Dago"—he jerked a thumb at the half-dead Frenchman in the corner—"has got you to the point where I thought I better horn in. I got to revolvin' it around in my mind and I seen if somethin' wasn't done, and done soon, there'd be murder around here and maybe"—his head gave an imperceptible list toward the girl's room—"worse."

He stopped, but he held up a stubby finger to keep any one else from speaking. Then he plowed slowly through the drift of his ideas. "About this here woman. I know you, Ross, and I know what you reely think about women. If she hadn't happened in here durin' this here snow, you'd never have given two thoughts to the whole woman question. Likewise, when the storm clears, and you and the boys go hustlin' out, this here whole business'll clear out of your head and you won't think of a skirt again until Kingdom Come. Just because o' this snow here, don't forget you're livin' in the selfsame world you was in four days ago. And you're the same man, too. Now, what's the use o' gettin' all snarled up over four days of stickin' in the house? That there's what I been revolvin' in my mind and this here's the decision I've come to."

He plodded to the door and shouted to one of the ranch heads to saddle my horse.

Ross lit a stogy and stood thoughtful in the middle of the room. Then he began: "I've a durn good notion, George, to knock your confounded head off and throw you into that snowbank; if——"

"You're wrong, mister. That ain't a durned good notion you've got. It's durned bad. Look here!" He pointed steadily out of doors until we were both forced to follow his finger. "You're in here for more'n a week yet." After allowing this fact to sink in, he barked out at Ross: "Can *you* cook?" Then at me: "Can *you* cook?" Then he looked at the wreck of Étienne and sniffed.

There was an embarrassing silence as Ross and I thought solemnly of a foodless week.

"If you just use hoss sense," concluded George, "and don't go for to hurt my feelin's, all I want to do is to take this young gal down to Hicksville; and then I'll head back here and cook fer you."

The horse and Miss Adams arrived simultaneously, both of them very serious and quiet. The horse because he knew what he had before him in that weather; the girl because of what she had left behind.

Then all at once I awoke to a realization of what the cook was doing. "My God, man!" I cried, "aren't you afraid to go out in that snow?"

Behind my back I heard Ross mutter, "Not him."

George lifted the girl daintily up behind the saddle, drew on his gloves, put his foot in the stirrup and turned to inspect me leisurely.

As I passed slowly in his review, I saw in my mind's eye the algebraic equation of Snow, the equals sign, and the answer in the man before me.

"Snow is my last name," said George. He swung into the saddle and they started cautiously out into the darkening swirl of fresh new currency just issuing from the Snowdrop Mint. The girl, to keep her place, clung happily to the sturdy figure of the camp cook.

I brought three things away from Ross Curtis's ranch house—yea, four. One was the appreciation of snow, which I have so humbly tried here to render; (2) was a collarbone, of which I am extra careful; (3) was a memory of what it is to eat very, extremely, terribly bad food for a week; and (4) was the cause of (3)—a little note delivered at the end of the week and hand-painted in blue pencil on a sheet of meat paper.

"I cannot come back there to that there job. Mrs. Snow say no, George. I been revolvin' it in my mind; considerin' circumstances she's right."

The Dream

MURRAY DREAMED a dream.

Both psychology and science grope when they would explain to us the strange adventures of our immaterial selves when wandering in the realm of "Death's twin brother, Sleep." This story will not attempt to be illuminative; it is no more than a record of Murray's dream. One of the most puzzling phases of that strange waking sleep is that dreams which seem to cover months or even years may take place within a few seconds or minutes.

Murray was waiting in his cell in the ward of the condemned. An electric arc light in the ceiling of the corridor shone brightly upon his table. On a sheet of white paper an ant crawled wildly here and there as Murray blocked his way with an envelope. The electrocution was set for eight o'clock in the evening. Murray smiled at the antics of the wisest of insects.

There were seven other condemned men in the chamber. Since he had been there Murray had seen three taken out to their fate: one gone mad and fighting like a wolf caught in a trap; one, no less mad, offering up a sanctimonious lip-service to Heaven; the third, a weakling, collapsed and strapped to a board. He wondered with what credit to himself his own heart, foot, and face would meet his punishment; for this was his evening. He thought it must be nearly eight o'clock.

Opposite his own in the two rows of cells was the cage of Bonifacio, the Sicilian slayer of his betrothed and of two officers who came to arrest him. With him Murray had played checkers many a long hour, each calling his move to his unseen opponent across the corridor.

Bonifacio's great booming voice with its indestructible singing quality called out,

"Eh, Meestro Murray; how you feel—all-a right—yes?"

"All right, Bonifacio," said Murray steadily, as he allowed the ant to crawl upon the envelope and then dumped it gently on the stone floor.

"Dat's good-a, Meestro Murray. Men like us, we must-a die like-a men. My time come nex'-a week. All-a right. Remember,

777

Meestro Murray, I beat-a you dat las' game of da check. Maybe we play again some-a time. I don'-a know. Maybe we have to call-a de move damn-a loud to play de check where dey goin' send us."

Bonifacio's hardened philosophy, followed closely by his deafening, musical peal of laughter, warmed rather than chilled Murray's numbed heart. Yet, Bonifacio had until next week to live.

The cell-dwellers heard the familiar, loud click of the steel bolts as the door at the end of the corridor was opened. Three men came to Murray's cell and unlocked it. Two were prison guards; the other was "Len"—no; that was in the old days; now the Reverend Leonard Winston, a friend and neighbor from their barefoot days.

"I got them to let me take the prison chaplain's place," he said, as he gave Murray's hand one short, strong grip. In his left hand he held a small Bible, with his forefinger marking a page.

Murray smiled slightly and arranged two or three books and some penholders orderly on his small table. He would have spoken, but no appropriate words seemed to present themselves to his mind.

The prisoners had christened this cell-house, eighty feet long, twenty-eight feet wide, Limbo Lane. The regular guard of Limbo Lane, an immense, rough, kindly man, drew a pint bottle of whiskey from his pocket and offered it to Murray, saying:

"It's the regular thing, you know. All has it who feel like they need a bracer. No danger of it becoming a habit with 'em, you see."

Murray drank deep into the bottle.

"That's the boy!" said the guard. "Just a little nerve tonic, and everything goes smooth as silk."

They stepped into the corridor, and each one of the doomed seven knew. Limbo Lane is a world on the outside of the world; but it has learned, when deprived of one or more of the five senses, to make another sense supply the deficiency. Each one knew that it was nearly eight, and that Murray was to go to the chair at eight. There is also in the many Limbo Lanes an aristocracy of crime. The man who kills in the open, who beats his enemy or pursuer down, flushed by the primitive emotions and the ardor of combat, holds in contempt the human rat, the spider, and the snake.

So, of the seven condemned only three called their farewells to Murray as he marched down the corridor between the two guards—Bonifacio, Marvin, who had killed a guard while trying to escape from the prison, and Bassett, the train-robber, who was driven to it because the express-messenger wouldn't raise his hands when ordered to do so. The remaining four smoldered, silent, in their cells, no doubt feeling their social ostracism in Limbo Lane society more keenly than they did the memory of their less picturesque offenses against the law.

Murray wondered at his own calmness and nearly indifference. In the execution room were about twenty men, a congregation made up of prison officers, newspaper reporters and lookers on who had succeeded

Here, in the very middle of a sentence, the hand of Death interrupted the telling of O. Henry's last story. He had planned to make this story different from his others—the beginning of a new series in a style he had not previously attempted. "I want to show the public," he said, "that I can write something new— new for me, I mean—a story without slang, a straightforward dramatic plot treated in a way that will come nearer my idea of real story-writing." Before starting to write the present story, he outlined briefly how he intended to develop it: Murray, the criminal accused and convicted of the brutal murder of his sweetheart—a murder prompted by jealous rage—at first faces the death penalty, calm and, to all outward appearances, indifferent to his fate. As he nears the electric chair he is overcome by a revulsion of feeling. He is left dazed, stupefied, stunned. The entire scene in the death-chamber—the witnesses, the spectators, the preparations for execution—become unreal to him. The thought flashes through his brain that a terrible mistake is being made. Why is *he* being strapped to the chair? What has *he* done? What crime has *he* committed? In the few moments while the straps are being adjusted a vision comes to him. He dreams a dream. He sees a little country cottage, bright, sun-lit, nestling in a bower of flowers. A woman is there, and a little child. He speaks with them and finds that they are his wife, his child—and the cottage their home. So, after all, it is a mistake. Some one has frightfully, irretrievably blundered. The accusation, the trial, the conviction, the sentence to death in the electric chair—all a dream. He takes his wife in his arms and kisses the child. Yes, here is happiness. It *was* a dream. Then—at a sign from the prison warden the fatal current is turned on.

MURRAY HAD DREAMED THE WRONG DREAM.

CHRONOLOGY

NOTE ON THE TEXTS

NOTES

Chronology

1862 Born William Sidney Porter on September 11 in Greensboro, North Carolina, the second of three sons of Alger-
non Sidney Porter and Mary Jane Virginia Swaim. Father,
born August 22, 1825, in Guilford County, North Carolina, attended Jefferson Medical College in Pennsylvania
in 1845–46, although he never graduated, and during
the Civil War treats Confederate soldiers at a hospital set
up at the Edgeworth Female Seminary in Greensboro.
Known as a heavy drinker and a distracted parent, he is
preoccupied with the notion of inventing a perpetual
motion machine modeled on a waterwheel. Mother, born
February 12, 1833, in Greensboro, is the daughter of the
editor of the Greensboro *Patriot*. Parents married April 15,
1858. Brother Shirley Worth, called Shell, born in August
1860; he will spend much of his working life as a laborer in
Carolina lumber camps.

1865 Brother David born March 26. Mother dies of tuberculosis, September 26. Porter, father, and brothers move to
the home of paternal grandmother, Ruth Porter, who runs
a boardinghouse there. Infant David dies of tuberculosis
soon afterward.

1867–76 Enrolls in the small private school operated by a maternal
aunt, Evalina Swaim, known as "Miss Lina"; he will be a
student there for the next nine years. Becomes known for
his shyness, his occasional practical jokes, and his skill at
drawing cartoons and likenesses. His love of reading is
encouraged by Miss Swain; favorites include the works
of Charles Dickens and Sir Walter Scott, Sir Richard
Burton's *The Anatomy of Melancholy*, Edward FitzGerald's
translation of *Rubáiyát of Omar Khayyám*, and Edward
William Lane's translation of *The Arabian Nights*. He later
writes, "I did more reading between my thirteenth and
nineteenth years than I have done in all the years since."

1877 His formal schooling at an end, begins to work in the
drugstore of his father's brother, Clark Porter.

1881   Becomes a member of the North Carolina Pharmaceutical Association, and thus a registered pharmacist. Becomes known for his sketches—in both pictures and words—of customers.

1882–83   Suffers from a bad cough. Thinking that a pharmacy is a poor environment, a local doctor, James K. Hall, invites Porter to travel with him and his family in March on a trip to Texas, where the Halls' four sons live. Stays at the sheep ranch of one of the sons, Richard, in La Salle County, and spends two years there, sleeping outdoors for the most part. Makes frequent visits to another Hall son, Lee, a former Texas Ranger turned rancher. Does a minimal amount of ranch work; occasionally serves as ranch cook. In a letter home, describes his changed appearance: "long hair, part of a new sombrero, Mexican spurs," and "wild, untamed aspect." Teaches himself Spanish. Produces forty illustrations for a book, never published, to be called *Carbondale Days*.

1884–85   In March, moves to Austin, the capital of Texas and the fourth largest city in the state. Initially stays at the home of another family from Greensboro with four sons, the Harrells. About three months after his arrival in town, gets a job as a drug clerk at Morley Brothers' Drug Store but quits in less than three months and is unemployed for the better part of a year. Starts submitting skits and verses to magazines, with no acceptances. Wins a place in a singing group, the Hill City Quartet, which performs frequently around town. Courts Lollie Cave, and, in a private joke with her, calls himself "O. Henry," his first use of the name. She turns down his marriage proposal (she later reports). Begins courting Athol Estes, an Austin high school girl originally from Tennessee.

1886   In the fall, is hired as a bookkeeper in an Austin real estate firm, for a salary of $100 a month.

1887   Takes a job as a draftsman in the Texas Land Office, where he will work for four years. Becomes engaged to Athol in June, just before her high school graduation. On July 1, they meet by chance in Austin and—without informing Athol's mother or stepfather—are married at the residence of the Reverend R. K. Smoot, pastor of the Southern Presbyterian Church. Starts publishing humorous verse, sketches, and jokes in the Detroit *Free Press* and a New

York publication called *Truth* (which paid him $6 for two pieces).

1888   Athol becomes pregnant. The couple rents a house on the 500 block of East Fourth Street in Austin. A son is born on May 6 but lives only a few hours.

1889   Produces twenty-six illustrations for a book by J. W. Wilbarger, *Indian Depredations in Texas.* Moves to a cottage at 505 East Eleventh Street. On September 30, Athol gives birth to a daughter, Margaret Worth. Athol recovers slowly from the birth and shows symptoms of tuberculosis, from which her father had died. For the rest of her life, she suffers effects from the illness.

1891   Loses job in the Land Office because his political patron is forced out of his own position. Hired as a teller at the First National Bank.

1894   Buys a printing press and with a friend, James P. Crane, starts a weekly humorous publication they will eventually call *The Rolling Stone.* It never reaches a circulation more than 1,500. Most of the content of the eight-page paper is produced by Porter himself, writing in his spare time from his work at the First National Bank. In December, discrepancies are found in his books at the bank, and he resigns.

1895   In April, *The Rolling Stone* suspends publication. At a U.S. grand jury hearing in July, bank examiner F. B. Gray provides evidence that on fifty occasions Porter embezzled bank funds, for a total of $5,654.20; bank employees testify, to the contrary, that the discrepancies were a result of an unfortunate series of errors. He is not indicted. In October, accepts a job as a writer at *The Houston Post* at a salary of $15 a week (later raised to $25) and moves to Houston, later joined by Athol and Margaret. Contributes cartoons and writes a daily column, "Some Postscripts," for which he adopts the pen name "The Post Man."

1896   In February, as a result of F. B. Gray's efforts, Porter's case is resubmitted to the grand jury and he is indicted. He is arrested in Houston and taken to Austin, where he is released on bond after two days in jail and returns to Houston. Begins to write longer sketches for the *Post* that anticipate the themes and technique of his later work. Leaves Houston by train in July, ostensibly to return to

Austin to stand trial. In fact, he travels to New Orleans, where he takes temporary newspaper jobs. After several weeks, travels by boat to Honduras, the only Central American country that has no extradition laws with the United States.

1897 In January, because of Athol's poor health, returns to Austin, again traveling through New Orleans, to turn himself in. Spends most of his time over the next several months nursing his wife. Athol Estes Porter dies July 25, at the age of twenty-nine. Sells his first proper short story, "The Miracle of Lava Canyon," a western tale, to the McClure Syndicate, which publishes it under the byline W. S. Porter.

1898 Embezzlement trial begins in February. Asks family and friends to stay away from courtroom; does not speak in his own defense during the three-day trial. Witnesses, backed up by documents, testify that in 1894, two separate deposits, totaling about $850, were made at the First National Bank, that Porter received the cash, and that he did not record the transactions. Deliberating less than a day, the jury reaches a guilty verdict. Continues to submit short stories, now as "Sydney Porter." In March, sentenced to five years in the Ohio State Penitentiary, the lightest sentence allowed by law. Enters the penitentiary on April 25. Shortly after his arrival, assigned to be night druggist in the prison hospital and given his own apartment in the hospital wing. Adopts the habit of working on short stories after midnight. Over the course of three years in prison, produces fourteen stories, several submitted under the name "O. Henry"; three of them are published while he is in the penitentiary. His mother-in-law and Margaret travel to Tennessee, and later to Pittsburgh, where Athol's stepfather, P. G. Roach, takes possession of a hotel. Margaret is told that her father is a traveling salesman.

1900 Given the job of secretary to the steward of the prison, which he considers, he writes to his mother-in-law, "the best position connected with this place. . . . I . . . am absolutely without supervision of any kind."

1901 Released from prison on July 24, his sentence reduced by two years for good behavior. Travels to Pittsburgh where he is reunited with Margaret, now almost twelve. Spends roughly nine months there, during which nine stories are published in national magazines. The majority carry the byline O. Henry.

1902   Gilman Hall, the editor of *Ainslee's,* to which Porter has contributed several stories and poems, advances $200 to make it possible for Porter to travel to New York. Arrives in early April; Margaret remains in Pittsburgh with her grandparents. Takes up residence in a hotel on West 24th Street in Manhattan. Consumes alcohol heavily, averaging, according to a friend, two bottles of whiskey a day. Publishes seventeen stories over the course of the year. Conceals his time in prison from his friends and associates; will continue to do so for the rest of his life.

1903   In December, contracts with the *Sunday World* newspaper to contribute a short story every week, for $100 a story. The arrangement lasts more than two years and produces 113 stories, including "The Furnished Room," "That Last Leaf," and "The Gift of the Magi." From this point on, all his work is signed "O. Henry."

1904   An article in *The Critic* identifies O. Henry as "Sydney Porter, a gentleman from Texas." Moves to a house on East 24th Street, near Madison Square, and shortly thereafter to nearby Irving Place. In November, McClure, Phillips & Co. publishes *Cabbages and Kings,* a book of interconnected stories set in a fictional Central American country. McClure will publish all of his books for the next four years. Reviews are generally good, with the *Bookman* calling it "a book of very unusual interest and cleverness."

1905   Signs a five-year, first-reading contract with *Munsey's* magazine; he will be paid ten cents a word for accepted stories. Corresponds with a boyhood sweetheart, Sara Lindsay Coleman, who is still living in North Carolina.

1906   In April, publishes *The Four Million,* a collection of stories set in New York and almost entirely taken from his contributions to the *World.* Title is a reference to both the approximate population of New York and "The 400," a list of socially prominent residents of the city published in the *New York Times* in 1892. Receives mainly positive reviews.

1907   His output, prodigious for the previous five years, begins to slacken; publishes only eleven stories over the course of the year. Publishes two collections of his past work, *The Trimmed Lamp: And Other Stories of the Four Million* in April and *Heart of the West* in October. The latter contains western-set stories, to a large extent from early in

his writing career, and receives unfavorable reviews, the
Nation's reviewer calling it "cheaply clever." Moves from
Irving Place and settles in the Caledonia Hotel on West
26th Street. Sara Coleman travels to New York, and on
September 11 (his birthday) they meet for the first time
since childhood. He proposes marriage but cautions her
not to respond till she has returned home and received
a letter from him. The letter describes his conviction and
imprisonment—apparently the first time he has told the
full story since his release. She accepts; they are married
November 27 in Asheville, North Carolina. Gilman Hall
is the best man. The couple honeymoon in Hot Springs,
North Carolina. On return to New York, they take an
apartment at the Chelsea Hotel, on West 23rd Street;
Porter works at the Caledonia. The marriage is unhappy
from the start.

1908   Aware of the need for money to support his wife and
daughter (who now lives with the household) and maintain rooms in two hotels, plus a summer cottage at Good
Ground, Long Island, increases his production, publishing
twenty-nine stories over the year. In the fall, moves to
an apartment on Washington Place. *The Voice of the City:
Further Stories of the Four Million*, his third collection of
New York stories, is published in May and receives good
reviews. An essay in the *North American Review* says O.
Henry "has breathed new life into the short story." Writes
eleven new stories about a con man named "Jeff Peters";
along with three previously published ones, they make up
a book called *The Gentle Grafter*, published by McClure,
in October. Doubleday, Page & Company becomes his
publisher and, for the first time, he earns royalties on his
books. The company advances Porter $1,500 to write a
novel, but he apparently never begins work on it.

1909   Complains to friends and associates of poor health.
Publishes only eight stories and two collections of past
work, *Roads of Destiny* in April and *Options* in October.
Continues discussions with Doubleday about his proposed
novel, which he intends to call *The Rat Trap* and which,
he writes to an editor, will take its "hero . . . through
all the main phases of life—wild adventure, city, society,
something of the 'under world.'" In April, interviewed for
the first and last time, by *The New York Times*. Sits for a
photographic portrait by W. M. Van der Wyde. Spends the

bulk of his working time collaborating with Franklin P. Adams on a musical comedy, *Lo!*, based on Porter's story "To Him Who Waits." *Lo!* opens in Aurora, Illinois, on August 25; plays in midwestern cities for fourteen weeks before folding in December. Accepts $500 from a theatrical producer, George Tyler, for the rights to his story "A Retrieved Reformation." In the autumn, joins Sara in North Carolina, in hopes of improving his health. Appears to give up drinking.

1910   The adaptation of "A Retrieved Reformation," written by Paul Armstrong and titled *Alias Jimmy Valentine,* opens in Chicago and ultimately becomes a worldwide success. Returns to New York (Sara remains in North Carolina), ostensibly to work on another play for Tyler, an adaptation of his story "The World and the Door." Health steadily deteriorates. Another collection of New York stories, *Strictly Business: More Stories of the Four Million,* is published in March. Begins a story for *Hampton's* called "The Snow Man" and one for *Cosmopolitan,* "The Dream." Rarely leaves his room at the Caledonia. On June 3, telephones a friend, Anne Partlan, for help. She arrives to find him semiconscious and a doctor has him admitted to Polyclinic Hospital on East 34th Street. Diagnosed with cirrhosis of the liver, diabetes, and a dilated heart. Dies on the morning of June 5, some three months before his forty-eighth birthday. His last words are "Send for Mr. Hall." The New York *Herald* reports the cause of death as cirrhosis of the liver. A staff writer for *Hampton's*, Harris Merton Lyons, completes "The Snow Man"; "The Dream" is left unfinished. After a funeral at the Little Church Around the Corner, his body is taken to Asheville by train, and buried there in Riverside Cemetery.

Note on the Texts

This volume contains 101 sketches and short stories by O. Henry written over the course of his career and published from 1894 to 1911.

O. Henry (born William Sidney Porter) was a prolific writer, especially given the fact that he produced all of his mature work in the thirteen-year span from 1898 to his death in 1910, and more than half of it from 1903 through 1906. In 1958, a staff member at his publisher, Doubleday, produced an internal memorandum itemizing all of O. Henry's published short stories. (The memo is now in the collection of the University of Virginia Library.) It listed 264 titles, including 244 published in magazines and newspapers and collected in books, and twenty stories included in *Cabbages and Kings* (1904) and *The Gentle Grafter* (1908) but never previously published. In addition, from 1894 to 1896, O. Henry published several hundred pieces, first in an Austin, Texas–based humor magazine he edited, *The Rolling Stone*, and then in *The Houston Post*, where he was a staff writer. These works—many of which were subsequently collected posthumously in *Rolling Stones* (1912), *Postscripts* (1923), and *O. Henry Encore* (1939)—range from comical paragraphs to satiric sketches to longer pieces that anticipate his mature short stories. Finally, there are three stories—"The Ghost That Came to Old Angles," "Pursuing Ideals," and "Return of the Songster"—that the writer apparently submitted to magazines in 1898 but were rejected and never published (manuscripts of these stories are in the University of Virginia library). "The Miracle of Lava Canyon," written about the same time, was syndicated nationally by McClure's Syndicate in 1898 under the name "W. S. Porter." His first story to appear in a magazine was "Whistling Dick's Christmas Stocking," published in *McClure's* in 1899 under the name "O. Henry." Over the next few years his works appeared under a variety of bylines, including Sydney Porter (he had changed the spelling of his middle name in his Texas days), Olivier Henry, and S. H. Peters. From the fall of 1903 until his death, he exclusively used O. Henry.

The collections of O. Henry's stories published in his lifetime, besides those mentioned above, were *The Four Million* (1906), *The Trimmed Lamp* (1907), *Heart of the West* (1907), *The Voice of the City* (1908), *Roads of Destiny* (1909), *Options* (1909), and *Strictly Business* (1910). The other posthumous collections were *Whirligigs* (1910), *Sixes and Sevens* (1911), *Waifs and Strays* (1917), and *O. Henryana* (1920). Only in a handful of cases was there any duplication in these books. The author's involvement in the development of the collections was limited; he played a part in choosing the titles for the collections and in several instances changed the title of an individual story: "Raggles" became "The Making of a New Yorker," and, notably, "Gifts of the Magi" became "The Gift of the Magi." Most of the first half dozen collections were thematically organized: *The Four Million* and *The Voice of the City* gathered New York stories, *Heart of the West* Western stories, *Cabbages and Kings* the Central America–set linked stories, and *The Gentle Grafter* the Jeff Peters stories. The contents of subsequent collections were selected by his publisher based on what uncollected material was at hand. The texts of the stories were generally not altered between their periodical and book publications. There were no British editions during the author's lifetime. Doubleday republished O. Henry's short story collections in several editions of uniform volumes from 1912 to 1929 and also gathered his collected writings in editions ranging from one to three volumes, the first in 1926 and the most recent in 1953. In 1945, the Modern Library published a collection of thirty-eight stories that has continuously been in print since. (The book could not be described as representative, as only two stories are set in the West and it does not include anything from *The Gentle Grafter*.) In 1998, all of O. Henry's works entered the public domain, and since then there have been numerous anthologies, recently including e-books.

The stories selected for this volume represent the editor's judgment of O. Henry's best stories, with an attempt to reflect, as well, the principal strains in his work; the geographical section headings loosely follow the course of O. Henry's life. For those stories collected during O. Henry's lifetime, the source of the text in this volume is the first American edition. This volume also includes texts from three collections that were published in the months following O. Henry's death in June 1910, as work on the collections would have finished months in advance: *Whirligigs*, published by Doubleday, Page & Company in September 1910; *The Two Women*, published in Boston by Small, Maynard and Company in December 1910; and *Sixes and Sevens*, published by Doubleday, Page & Company in October 1911.

O. Henry was not directly involved in the publication of *The Two Women*, which collects the stories "A Fog in Santone" and "A Medley of Moods" (an alternate version of the story "Blind Man's Holiday"). However, Witter Bynner, in whose name *The Two Women* was copyrighted, wrote in a letter to O. Henry bibliographer Paul S. Clarkson that "in return for a few favors, [O. Henry] handed me the manuscripts of two stories which he said were not much good but might, if ever he grew famous, prove to be a recompense. Later, when I was with Small, Maynard and Company I mentioned the fact and the firm asked if they might not publish the two in a volume. I wrote

Mrs. Porter [O. Henry's widow, the former Sara Lindsay Coleman] about the case and received her assent to the project."

For stories not collected during O. Henry's lifetime or immediately thereafter, the first periodical publication is the source of the text in this volume, except in the following cases, in which the original periodical publication is not known to be extant:

"Bexar Scrip No. 2692" was originally published in Porter's humorous weekly *The Rolling Stone* (March 5, 1894). It was collected posthumously in *Rolling Stones* (New York: Doubleday, Page & Company, 1912), pp. 217–30. The text from *Rolling Stones* is the source of the text in this volume.

"Three Paragraphs" was originally published in *The Rolling Stone* (September 22, 1894). It was collected posthumously in *O. Henryana* (New York: Doubleday, Page & Company, 1920), pp. 8–12. The text from *O. Henryana* is the source of the text in this volume.

In addition, three stories in this volume have never been previously published. The texts of these stories, "The Ghost That Came to Old Angles," "Pursuing Ideals," and "Return of the Songster," are taken from O. Henry's manuscripts, which are in the Papers of O. Henry (William Sydney Porter), Box 1, Folders 2–4, Accession #6333-i, Special Collections, University of Virginia Library, Charlottesville, Virginia.

The following is a list of the stories included in this volume, in the order of their appearance, giving the first periodical appearance of each text as well as the source of the text in this volume. The most common sources are indicated by title alone:

Cabbages and Kings (New York: McClure, Phillips & Co., 1904).

The Four Million (New York: McClure, Phillips & Co., 1906).

The Trimmed Lamp (New York: McClure, Phillips & Co., 1907).

Heart of the West (New York: The McClure Company, 1907).

The Voice of the City (New York: The McClure Company, 1908).

The Gentle Grafter (New York: The McClure Company, 1908).

Roads of Destiny (New York: Doubleday, Page & Company, 1909).

Options (New York: Harper & Brothers, 1909).

Strictly Business (New York: Doubleday, Page & Company, 1910).

Whirligigs (New York: Doubleday, Page & Company, 1910).

The Two Women (Boston: Small, Maynard and Company, 1910).

Sixes and Sevens (Garden City, New York: Doubleday, Page & Company, 1911).

Rolling Stones (Garden City, New York: Doubleday, Page & Company, 1912).

Waifs and Strays (Garden City, New York: Doubleday, Page & Company, 1917).

O. Henryana (Garden City, New York: Doubleday, Page & Company, 1920).

Postscripts (Garden City, New York: Doubleday, Page & Company, 1923).

O. Henry Encore (Garden City, New York: Doubleday, Page & Company, 1936).

EARLY SKETCHES, STORIES, AND REPORTAGE

"Bexar Scrip No. 2692," *The Rolling Stone* (March 5, 1894); this issue appears to no longer be extant. *Rolling Stones*, pp. 217–30.

"Three Paragraphs," *The Rolling Stone* (September 22, 1894); this issue appears to no longer be extant. *O. Henryana*, pp. 8–12.

"A Personal Insult," *The Houston Post* (December 12, 1895), p. 4; posthumously collected in *Postscripts*.

"When the Train Comes In: Outline Sketches at the Grand Central Depot," *The Houston Post* (December 16, 1895), p. 4; posthumously collected in *O. Henry Encore*.

"Why He Hesitated," *The Houston Post* (December 18, 1895), p. 6; posthumously collected in *Postscripts*.

"Something for Baby," *The Houston Post* (December 21, 1895), p. 4; posthumously collected in *Postscripts*.

"Too Wise," *The Houston Post* (December 24, 1895), p. 6; posthumously collected in *Postscripts*.

"The Return of the Songster," c. 1895. Papers of O. Henry, University of Virginia Library, Charlottesville, Va.

"Book Reviews," *The Houston Post* (February 23, 1896), p. 6; posthumously collected in *Postscripts*.

"Guessed Everything Else," *The Houston Post* (March 21, 1896), p. 4; posthumously collected in *Postscripts*.

"In Mezzotint," *The Houston Post* (April 26, 1896), p. 18; posthumously collected in *O. Henry Encore*.

"The Barber Talks," *The Houston Post* (May 31, 1896), p. 9; posthumously collected in *O. Henry Encore*.

"The Ghost That Came to Old Angles," c. 1897. Papers of O. Henry, University of Virginia Library, Charlottesville, Va.

"Pursuing Ideals," c. 1897. Papers of O. Henry, University of Virginia Library, Charlottesville, Va.

"The Miracle of Lava Canyon," McClure's Syndicate (*The Omaha Daily Bee*) (September 17, 1898), p. 9.

COUNTRY

"Whistling Dick's Christmas Stocking," *McClure's* (December 1899); *Roads of Destiny*, pp. 311–34.

"A Retrieved Reformation," *Cosmopolitan* (April 1903) under the title "A Retrieved Reform"; *Roads of Destiny*, pp. 161–72.

"Confessions of a Humorist," *Ainslee's*, Vol. 12, No. 3 (October 1903), pp. 62–66; posthumously collected in *Waifs and Strays*.

"A Ramble in Aphasia," *Metropolitan* (February 1905); *Strictly Business*, pp. 129–46.

"Blind Man's Holiday," *Ainslee's* (December 1905); *Whirligigs*, pp. 259–87. It was also collected in *The Two Women* with the title "A Medley of Moods."

"The Ransom of Red Chief," *The Saturday Evening Post* (July 6, 1907); *Whirligigs*, pp. 100–115.

"A Municipal Report," *Hampton's* (November 1909); *Strictly Business*, pp. 147–71.

WEST

"A Fog in Santone: A Meteorological Sketch," c. 1901. *The Two Women*, pp. 9–28; it subsequently appeared in *Cosmopolitan* (October 1912).

"Friends in San Rosario," *Ainslee's* (April 1902); *Roads of Destiny*, pp. 186–205.

"Round the Circle," *Everybody's Magazine*, Vol. 7, No. 4 (October 1902), pp. 388–90; posthumously collected in *Waifs and Strays*.

"Hearts and Hands," *Everybody's Magazine*, Vol. 7, No. 6 (December 1902), pp. 581–82; posthumously collected in *Waifs and Strays*.

"The Lonesome Road," *Ainslee's* (September 1903); *Roads of Destiny*, pp. 364–76.

"The Pimienta Pancakes," *McClure's* (December 1903); *Heart of the West*, pp. 62–77.

"Holding Up a Train," *McClure's* (April 1904); *Sixes and Sevens*, pp. 46–63.

"The Ransom of Mack," *McClure's* (December 1904); *Heart of the West*, pp. 22–31.

"Christmas by Injunction," *New York Sunday World* (December 11, 1904); *Heart of the West*, pp. 288–305.

"The Handbook of Hymen," *Munsey's* (July 1906); *Heart of the West*, pp. 44–61.

"The Caballero's Way," *Everybody's Magazine* (July 1907); *Heart of the West*, pp. 200–218.

"The Moment of Victory," *Munsey's* (June 1908); *Options*, pp. 186–208.

"Buried Treasure," *Ainsley's* (July 1908); *Options*, pp. 128–46.

"The Last of the Troubadours," *Everybody's Magazine* (July 1908); *Sixes and Sevens*, pp. 3–20.

"The Hiding of Black Bill," *Everybody's Magazine* (October 1908); *Options*, pp. 45–66.

"A Technical Error," *Munsey's* (February 1910); *Whirligigs*, pp. 125–34.
"The Friendly Call," *Associated Sunday Magazine* (syndicated, *The Washington Post*) (July 10, 1910), pp. 7, 22–23.

TROPICS

"Shoes," originally part of a longer story titled "The Lotus and the Cockleburrs," published in *Everybody's Magazine* (October 1903); *Cabbages and Kings*, pp. 225–41.
"Ships," originally part of a longer story titled "The Lotus and the Cockleburrs," published in *Everybody's Magazine* (October 1903); *Cabbages and Kings*, pp. 242–56.
"A Ruler of Men," *Everybody's Magazine*, Vol. 15, No. 2 (August 1906), pp. 157–67.
"Next to Reading Matter," *Everybody's Magazine* (December 1907); *Roads of Destiny*, pp. 68–87.

THE GENTLE GRAFTER

"The Atavism of John Tom Little Bear," *Everybody's Magazine*, Vol. 9, No. 1 (July 1903), pp. 57–64; posthumously collected in *Rolling Stones*.
"Conscience in Art," McClure's Syndicate (Summer 1908); *The Gentle Grafter*, pp. 126–36.
"The Man Higher Up," McClure's Syndicate (Summer 1908); *The Gentle Grafter*, pp. 137–59.

NEW YORK

"The Social Triangle," *New York Sunday World* (December 13, 1903); *The Trimmed Lamp*, pp. 121–29.
"A Little Local Colour," *New York Sunday World* (January 10, 1904); *Whirligigs*, pp. 231–39.
"A Newspaper Story," *New York Sunday World* (January 17, 1904); *Whirligigs*, pp. 209–14.
"After Twenty Years," *New York Sunday World* (February 14, 1904); *The Four Million*, pp. 214–20.
"Lost on Dress Parade," *New York Sunday World* (February 28, 1904); *The Four Million*, pp. 221–31.
"The Complete Life of John Hopkins," *New York Sunday World* (April 17, 1904); *The Voice of the City*, pp. 11–20.
"The Rubber Plant's Story," *New York Sunday World* (May 15, 1904), p. 8; posthumously collected in *Waifs and Strays*.

"A Dinner at ———— *: The Adventures of an Author with His Own Hero," *The Critic*, Vol. 44, No. 6 (June 1904), pp. 530–34; posthumously collected in *Rolling Stones*.

"A Comedy in Rubber," *New York Sunday World* (June 19, 1904); *The Voice of the City*, pp. 67–74.

"The Pride of the Cities," *New York Sunday World* (July 3, 1904); *Sixes and Sevens*, pp. 38–45.

"The Foreign Policy of Company 99," *New York Sunday World* (July 31, 1904); *The Trimmed Lamp*, pp. 139–49.

"The Furnished Room," *New York Sunday World* (August 14, 1904); *The Four Million*, pp. 239–50.

"The Love-Philtre of Ikey Schoenstein," *New York Sunday World* (October 2, 1904); *The Four Million*, pp. 118–26.

"The Rathskeller and the Rose," *New York Sunday World* (October 9, 1904); *The Voice of the City*, pp. 178–86.

"A Sacrifice Hit," *New York Sunday World* (October 16, 1904); *Whirligigs*, pp. 152–58.

"The Coming-Out of Maggie," *New York Sunday World* (November 20, 1904); *The Four Million*, pp. 68–80.

"The Cop and the Anthem," *New York Sunday World* (December 4, 1904); *The Four Million*, pp. 89–99.

"The Green Door," *New York Sunday World* (December 18, 1904); *The Four Million*, pp. 150–63.

"The Badge of Policeman O'Roon," *New York Sunday World* (December 25, 1904); *The Trimmed Lamp*, pp. 81–88.

"The Making of a New Yorker," *New York Sunday World* (January 1, 1905), under the title "Raggles; or the Making of a New Yorker"; *The Trimmed Lamp*, pp. 102–10.

"Psyche and the Pskyscraper," *New York Sunday World* (January 15, 1905); *Strictly Business*, pp. 172–81.

"Man About Town," *New York Sunday World* (March 5, 1905); *The Four Million*, pp. 81–88.

"Springtime à la Carte," *New York Sunday World* (April 2, 1905); *The Four Million*, pp. 139–49.

"Extradited from Bohemia," *New York Sunday World* (April 23, 1905); *The Voice of the City*, pp. 199–208.

"Tommy's Burglar," *New York Sunday World* (May 14, 1905); *Whirligigs*, pp. 215–22.

"The Girl and the Graft," *New. York Sunday World* (May 28, 1905); *Strictly Business*, pp. 89–98.

"Sisters of the Golden Circle," *New York Sunday World* (July 2, 1905); *The Four Million*, pp. 196–206.

"An Adjustment of Nature," *New York Sunday World* (July 16, 1905); *The Four Million*, pp. 100–108.

"A Midsummer Knight's Dream," *New York Sunday World* (July 23, 1905); *The Trimmed Lamp*, pp. 189–97.

"An Unfinished Story," *McClure's* (August 1905); *The Four Million*, pp. 173–84.

"The City of Dreadful Night," *New York Sunday World* (August 13, 1905); *The Voice of the City*, pp. 141–48.

"The Skylight Room," *New York Sunday World* (August 20, 1905); *The Four Million*, pp. 47–57.

"The Poet and the Peasant," *New York Sunday World* (September 10, 1905); *Strictly Business*, pp. 72–81.

"The Plutonian Fire," *New York Sunday World* (September 24, 1905), originally published with the subtitle "Being the Curious Love Affair of the Man from Alabama"; *The Voice of the City*, pp. 105–14.

"The Last Leaf," *New York Sunday World* (October 15, 1905); *The Trimmed Lamp*, pp. 198–208.

"Elsie in New York," *New York Sunday World* (October 22, 1905); *The Trimmed Lamp*, pp. 249–60.

"The Purple Dress," *New York Sunday World* (November 5, 1905); *The Trimmed Lamp*, pp. 130–38.

"The Gift of the Magi," *New York Sunday World* (December 10, 1905), under the title "Gifts of the Magi"; *The Four Million*, pp. 16–25.

"The Duel," *New York Sunday World* (January 7, 1906); *Strictly Business*, pp. 294–301.

"The Rubaiyat of a Scotch Highball," *New York Sunday World* (February 25, 1906); *The Trimmed Lamp*, pp. 32–41.

"The Buyer from Cactus City," *New York Sunday World* (March 4, 1906); *The Trimmed Lamp*, pp. 70–80.

"The Harbinger," *New York Sunday World* (March 18, 1906); *The Voice of the City*, pp. 49–57.

"Brickdust Row," *New York Sunday World* (July 1, 1906); *The Trimmed Lamp*, pp. 89–101.

"Girl," *New York Sunday World* (July 15, 1906); *Whirligigs*, pp. 81–88.

"The Trimmed Lamp," *McClure's* (August 1906); *The Trimmed Lamp*, pp. 3–21.

"Proof of the Pudding," *Broadway Magazine* (May 1907); *Strictly Business*, pp. 240–54.

"The Memento," *Ainslee's* (February 1908); *The Voice of the City*, pp. 229–43.

"A Night in New Arabia," *Everybody's Magazine* (March 1908); *Strictly Business*, pp. 209–30.

"Strictly Business," *Hampton's* (August 1908); *Strictly Business*, pp. 3–20.

"The Third Ingredient," *Everybody's Magazine* (December 1908); *Options*, pp. 22–44.

"The Higher Pragmatism," *Munsey's* (March 1909); *Options*, pp. 250–63.

"No Story," first published as "The Point of the Story" in *Red Book Magazine* (November 1903), this revised version was published in *Cosmopolitan* (June 1909); *Options*, pp. 232–49.

FINAL STORIES

"Let Me Feel Your Pulse," *Cosmopolitan* (July 1910), under the title "Adventures in Neurasthenia: Some Experiences of a Nerve-Sick Man Seeking Health"; *Sixes and Sevens*, pp. 154–73.

"The Snow Man," *Hampton's Magazine*, Vol. 25, No. 2 (August 1910), pp. 231–38; left unfinished at Porter's death, it was finished by H. M. Lyons and posthumously collected in *Waifs and Strays*.

"The Dream," *Cosmopolitan*, Vol. 49, No. 4 (September 1910), pp. 444–47; posthumously collected in *Rolling Stones*.

This volume presents the texts of the original printings chosen for inclusion here, but it does not attempt to reproduce features of their typographic design. The texts are presented without change, except for the correction of typographical errors. Spelling, punctuation, and capitalization are often expressive features, and they are not altered, even when inconsistent or irregular. The following is a list of typographical errors corrected, cited by page and line number: 14.13, mother!; 20.4, tootache; 34.28, Whisky; 40.21, as artist; 41.37, ghost.; 42.6, "Isn't it—?; 43.10, it—"; 49.39, embodiement; 53.13, Canon; 53.15, wildness; 54.26, Arizona. Dan; 63.25, mangificent; 74.6, all',; 95.24, Corurac; 104.9, suit case; 162.17, began morphine; 167.4, teller, was; 189.7, I, says; 189.14, lady, You; 189.39, shouts 'you; 192.4, 'I 'll; 192.29, Perry; 192.33, We; 204.36, snoozer.'; 219.5, neary; 234.11, a elegant; 280.13, *sunt* Namely::; 313.14, spashed; 314.11, George; 314.13, Chihauhau; 327.1, Let; 343.16, Liberators."; 389.27, pawn—"; 396.27, 'Most; 405.14, á; 407.25, dinning; 428.3, your prefer."; 437.4, avenue; 437.6, d'hote; 440.4, little.; 440.9, dish."; 468.27, woman; 473.4, Blue-Light; 476.1, ¶hours; 478.13, heydey; 503.34, *d'hote*; 509.29, opprobious; 511.21, Spain.; 518.36, hear; 552.16, [new ¶ at "'Friend,']; 565.25, grin."; 569.6, breath; 601.9, jewsharp; 605.9, said.; 613.25, me for red; 613.35, [no ¶ before "—plaited]; 615.19, ready-made. Oh; 615.23, waisted.; 615.30, Ramsey; 616.1, "She's; 616.34, Ramsey; 617.31, Ramsey's; 627.24, Bernardt; 630.37, *d'hote.*; 633.3, scatching; 633.13, with as; 636.14, ended,; 653.1, Forence; 667.23, bottons; 726.21, go you,"; 739.32, themouldly; 771.25, plam; 773.19, cook?.

Notes

In the notes below, the reference numbers denote page and line of this volume (the line count includes chapter headings). No note is made for material included in the eleventh edition of *Merriam Webster's Collegiate Dictionary*. Biblical references are keyed to the King James Version; references to Shakespeare to *The Riverside Shakespeare*, ed. G. Blakemore Evans (Boston: Houghton Mifflin, 1974). For further biographical background, references to other studies, and more detailed notes, see C. Alphonso Smith, *O. Henry Biography* (New York: Doubleday, Page, 1916); Gerald Langford, *Alias O. Henry: A Biography of William Sidney Porter* (New York: Macmillan, 1957); and Paul S. Clarkson, *A Bibliography of William Sidney Porter* (Caldwell, OH: Caxton Publishers, 1938).

EARLY SKETCHES, STORIES, AND REPORTAGE

3.3   General Land Office] Constructed in 1856–57, the former Texas General Land Office is now a visitor center. William Sidney Porter worked there as a draftsman from 1887 to 1891.

3.7   "castled crag of Drachenfels"] "The castled crag of Drachenfels / Frowns o'er the wide and winding Rhine," Canto III, section LV from "Childe Harold's Pilgrimage" (1812–18) by George Gordon, Lord Byron (1788–1824). The Drachenfels (German for "Dragon's Rock") is a hill in western Germany.

15.9   "The Ancient Mariner"] Cf. "The Rime of the Ancient Mariner," poem (1798) by Samuel Taylor Coleridge (1772–1834). O. Henry misquotes the opening line: "It is an ancient Mariner."

15.19   daisy cutters] Baseball slang for ground balls.

18.19–20   North American Review . . . Puck and Judge] The *North American Review* was a serious literary magazine, while the other two titles were weekly magazines of humor and satire.

28.1–2   Strange we do not prize . . . has flown:] The first two lines of "If We Knew" (1867) by May Riley Smith (1843–1927). It was frequently anthologized and provided the text of the hymn "Scatter Seeds of Kindness." The rest of the verse in the story is O. Henry's invention.

29.2   UNABRIDGED DICTIONARY by Noah Webster] *Webster's International Dictionary of the English Language* (1890). Noah Webster (1758–1843) published several editions of an English dictionary, beginning in 1828. After his death, the rights to the Webster name were sold to George and Charles Merriam.

29.14   Houston City Directory, by Morrison & Fourmy] *Morrison & Fourmy's General Directory of the City of Houston*, published biannually from 1882 to 1894.

34.2   THE POST man] A persona Porter frequently adopted in his pieces for the *Houston Post*.

40.12–15   'Would die, . . . sweet to live"] Stanza XVIII of "Maud" (1854) by Alfred, Lord Tennyson (1809–1892).

52.2   Siskiwah county, Ari.] There is no such county in Arizona.

53.8   Lava canyon] Lava Canyon of the Colorado River is upstream from the Grand Canyon in Grand Canyon National Park. In the story, it is an invented town.

55.5   the eyes of Melpomene] In Greek mythology, the muse of tragedy.

55.5–6   the heart of the ancient British queen whose name she bore] Boadicea, also known as Boudica, British Celtic queen who led an uprising against occupying Roman forces in the first century C.E.

55.33   Gila monsters] Venomous lizards found in the southwestern U.S.

COUNTRY

97.8   Young Hyson] Variety of green tea that comes from the Anhui province of China.

99.8–9   tartar emetic and Rochelle salt Ant. et Pot. Tart. and Sod. et Pot. Tart.] Two medicines familiar to contemporary pharmacists: tartar emetic (formal name Antimony Potassium Tartrate), which is toxic in high doses, and Rochelle salt (Potassium-Sodium Tartrate).

99.26   magnesia carbonate or the pulverized glycerrhiza radix?] Magnesia carbonate is an antacid as well as an anticaking agent. *Glycerrhizae radix* or licorice root, a mainstay of traditional Chinese medicine, has been used to treat a variety of conditions.

108.16   *trois-quartz*] French: *trois-quarts*, or three-quarters.

123.24–25   Ciaran of Clonmacnoise, Cormac McCullenan and Cuan O'Lochain] Saint Ciaran of Clonmacnoise (c. 516–c. 549 C.E.), Irish abbot known for his asceticism. Cormac mac Cuilennáin (836–908 C.E.), Irish bishop, king of Cashel (902–8 C.E.), and author of *Sanas Cormaic*, an encyclopedic glossary of more than 1,400 Irish words. Cuon O'Lothchain, the chief ollam, or bard, of Ireland until his death in 1024 C.E.

131.18–19   niggerhead rock] Regional slang for a dark-colored rock or boulder.

131.26   "King Herod,"] Herod the Great, Roman client-king of Judea (c. 72–c. 4 B.C.E.) under Rome, who according to biblical accounts ordered the massacre of all male children two years old and younger near Bethlehem.

WEST

157.19   Ozone] In the 1890s it was widely thought that ozone gas could be used to treat tuberculosis.

157.24   Litmus paper tests] When exposed to ozone, paper coated with potassium iodide and cornstarch will turn purple.

158.5   muriate] Chlorine gas, used as a method of suicide.

159.6   "Twenty-four."] The normal respiration rate for adults is twelve to twenty breaths per minute.

159.32   Kentucky Belle] Brand of whiskey made by R. S. Strader & Son, Lexington, Kentucky.

159.37   Uncle Mark Hanna] Mark Hanna (1837–1904), jocularly known as "Uncle Mark," Ohio industrialist and Republican political operative.

160.8–11   "*En las tardes . . . mas infeliz.*"] Spanish: In the afternoons umbrellas of winter / In the meadow of Morar I recline / And I curse my amazing destiny— / A most unhappy life. The verse is likely O. Henry's creation.

161.22   Phthisis] Tuberculosis.

171.9   Shiloh and Fort Pillow] Civil War battles that took place in 1862 and 1864, respectively.

179.13   Nueces and the Frio] Rivers that converge south of San Antonio, Texas.

184.3   B. & M. express] The Burlington and Missouri River Railroad, a rail company headquartered in Omaha, Nebraska.

187.20   Aransas Pass] A Texas city on the Gulf of Mexico.

200.33   Epicurus] Greek philosopher (341–270 B.C.E.) whose beliefs centered on the importance of friendship and simple pleasures and the acceptance of death's inevitability.

206.2   The man who told me these things] Alphonso J. "Al" Jennings (1863–1961), Virginia-born train robber and later film actor, politician, and author, who met and befriended Porter in Honduras. They renewed their acquaintance at the Ohio State Penitentiary when both men were serving there.

207.27   The Santa Fé flyer] The Atchison, Topeka & Santa Fe Railway, chartered in 1859. A flyer is a fast train.

210.5-7   high silk hat . . . Prince Albert] Prince Albert of Great Britain

(1819–1861) created a fashion trend for top hats when he began wearing them frequently in the 1850s.

210.9   French harp] Harmonica.

210.19–20   Prettiest little gal . . . told me so.] "Prettiest Little Girl in the County-O," traditional song.

213.23   Cimarron] A branch of the Santa Fe Trail.

213.27   Washington City] Washington, D.C.

215.5   Daltons] The Dalton Gang, an outlaw group active 1890–92.

215.9–10   M. K. & T. flyer] Missouri-Kansas-Texas Railway.

215.15   Katy] Slang for Missouri-Kansas-Texas Railway, from its "KT" stock symbol.

216.7   his "sider,"] Possibly sidekick.

217.12   buck at faro?] The card game Faro was sometimes referred to as "Bucking the Tiger."

217.16   Buckle's History of Civilisation] *History of Civilization in England,* a proposed fourteen-volume work by Henry Thomas Buckle (1821–1862), only one volume of which was published, in 1857.

217.19–20   Sep Winner's Self-Instructor for the Banjo] Septimus "Sep" Winner (1827–1902), American songwriter, publisher, and author of *Winner's New Primer for the Banjo* (1892).

217.33   "Old Zip Coon"] Minstrel song, sung to the tune of "Turkey in the Straw."

218.9   Alfred] City in Maine.

218.40   "Buffalo Gals, Can't You Come Out To-night,"] "Buffalo Gals" (1844), traditional song.

219.9   Lick Observatory] Astronomical observatory opened in 1888 and operated by the University of California.

219.27–28   Mary-Jane infirmity] Possibly a reference to Buster Brown's sweetheart, Mary Jane, in the "Buster Brown" comic strip (1902–21) by Richard F. Outcault (1863–1928).

219.37   the snow scene from the "Two Orphans."] *The Two Orphans,* theatrical melodrama by French dramatists Adolphe d'Ennery and Eugène Cormon, which premiered in 1874. An English version was produced the same year and was widely performed. A pivotal scene takes place in the snow outside a church.

223.2   Yellowhammer] No such town exists. A yellowhammer is a bird common in the American South.

223.11   from the Gila country . . . the Pecos] The Gila River, a tributary of the Colorado River flowing through New Mexico and Arizona. The Salt River, a tributary of the Gila, in Arizona. The Pecos River originates in north-central New Mexico and flows into Texas.

223.29   the Mariposas] *Mariposa* is the Spanish word for "butterfly." The reference in the story is obscure.

224.31   seen the elephant and the owl] "To see the elephant," common nineteenth-century expression meaning to endure an unusually trying experience. Sometimes rendered as "I've seen the elephant and heard the owl."

224.32   seidlitz powder] Generic name for a common laxative.

225.7   Chuck-a-luck] A dice game.

225.9   "Come and Kiss Me, Ma Honey,"] Possibly a reference to the popular song "Little Sweetheart Come Kiss Me" (1873).

226.11   William Cullen Longfellow] Combination of the American poets William Cullen Bryant (1794–1878) and Henry Wadsworth Longfellow (1807–1882).

228.8   Swiss Family Robinsons] *The Swiss Family Robinson* (1812), novel by Johann David Wyss (1743–1818) about a family shipwrecked in the East Indies who survive on a tropical island.

230.30   'Pussy Wants a Corner'] Also called Puss in the Corner, a game in which players occupy spots in a room and at a signal try to exchange places before an additional player can reach one of the vacant spots.

230.30   'King William.'] Children's kissing game in which the party sings a song beginning, "King William Was King James's Son."

234.12   Bitter Root Mountains] Bitterroot Mountains, range spanning parts of western Montana and eastern Idaho.

236.1   seven-up] Card game, also known as All Four.

236.9–10   "Herkimer's Handbook of Indispensable Information."] Likely a satirical reference to *The Indispensable Handbook of Useful and Practical Information: Pertaining to the Household, the Trades and the Professions* by George Lowell Austin (1878).

238.28–29   *pro re nata*] Latin: under present circumstances.

240.29   Ruby Ott] *Rubáiyát of Omar Khayyám*, title given by English poet Edward FitzGerald (1809–1883) to his 1859 translation of verses attributed to the Persian poet Omar Khayyam (1048–1131).

243.34   Jalap and Jerusalem oakseed] Substances commonly prescribed as purgatives.

245.1   *The Caballero's Way*] While it literally means "horseman," *caballero* also connotes qualities of a gentleman.

245.21   *jacal*] Spanish: adobe-style housing structure.

247.29   *gitanas*] Spanish: the Romani people of Spain.

248.3   *chivo*] Spanish: goat.

249.26–27   Don't you monkey . . . what I'll do—] Opening of "Bang Bang Lulu," traditional American song.

250.27   *vaquero*] Spanish: cowboy.

250.28   *tienda*] Spanish: store.

251.16   '*El Chivato*,'] Spanish: the Villain.

253.15   *canciones de amor*] Spanish: love songs.

255.34   *tule*] Bulrush.

257.2   war veteran aged twenty-nine] "The Moment of Victory" was published in 1908. The Spanish-American War took place in 1898.

257.6   the Don] Slang for Spaniard.

257.7   Greater Antilles] Island group in the Caribbean Ocean, including Cuba.

257.12   Mindanao] The second largest island in the Philippines.

258.5   San Augustine] City in East Texas.

258.17   fools and angels] "Fools rush in where angels dare to tread," proverb originating in "An Essay on Criticism" (1711), poem by Alexander Pope (1688–1744).

258.24   germans] Sausages.

258.28   *Two Orphans*] See note 219.37.

259.31   fly] Fashionable.

260.5   the battleship *Maine* was blown up] U.S. Navy ship that sank in Havana Harbor in February 1898, contributing to start of the Spanish-American War.

260.6   Joe Bailey] Joseph Bailey (1862–1929), member of the U.S. House of Representatives from Texas, 1891–1901, and U.S. senator, 1901–13.

260.6–7   Ben Tillman] Benjamin Tillman (1847–1918), U.S. senator from South Carolina, 1895–1918.

260.8   Mason & Hamlin's line] Mason & Hamlin was a Massachusetts piano manufacturer. The Mason-Dixon line was considered the boundary between slave and free states before the Civil War.

260.11–12   'We're coming, Father William. . . and then some,'] The Civil War poem "We Are Coming, Father Abra'am" by Joseph S. Gibbons begins, "We are coming Father Abraham—300,000 more." "William" here is William McKinley (1843–1901), U.S. president from 1897 to 1901.

261.24   *caballard*] Spanish: band of horses.

261.34   'Upton's Tactics,'] Emory Upton (1839–1881), a general in the Union Army during the Civil War, wrote a number of books on military tactics that were influential in the U.S. Army.

262.9   Lord Chesterfield ring rules] Probably a reference to the Marquess of Queensberry Rules, a boxing code published in 1867.

263.9   Lady of Shalott] "The Lady of Shalott," 1833 poem by Alfred, Lord Tennyson (1809–1892).

263.11   Cisalpine Alps in Germany] Nonsensical. "Cisalpine" means the southern side of the Alps, and Germany is north of the Alps.

264.10–11   Queen Sophia Christina] Possibly Charlotte Sophia of Mecklenburg-Strelitz (1744–1818), queen consort of George III of England.

264.11   Charlie Culberson] Charles Culberson (1855–1925), U.S. senator from Texas, 1899–1923.

265.10   Good Templar's] The Independent Order of Good Templars, a fraternal organization advocating Temperance founded in 1850.

266.12   Bury St. Edmunds] Town in southeast England.

266.15   Roosevelt-Democrat] Member of the Democratic Party who supported Theodore Roosevelt (1858–1919), a Republican, who was president from 1901 to 1909.

266.34   James Whitcomb Ryan] Cf. James Whitcomb Riley (1849–1916), American poet.

269.6   bucket-shops] Unauthorized establishments in which patrons gambled on financial markets.

269.33   *racibus humanus*] I.e., human race. "Racibus" is not a word in Latin.

270.32   *Orgetorix, Rex Helvetii*] Orgetorix, the leader of the Helvetian people in the first century B.C.E.

271.31   *charco*] Spanish: water hole.

273.15–16   King Philip of Spain] King Philip II (1526–1598) granted land to colonists in Texas and New Mexico.

273.24   varas] Vara, a Texas unit of measurement equal to 33.33 inches.

275.26   Anacreon] Greek lyric poet (c. 582–c. 485 B.C.E.).

279.5   saleratus] Leavening agent commonly used in baking bread.

279.21   Bravo del Norte] Designation of Rio Grande in Mexico.

280.13   *omnæ personæ in tres partes divisæ sunt*] Latin: all people are divided into three parts. Cf. Julius Caesar's *Commentaries on the Gallic War*: "Omnia Gallia in tres partes divisa est."

280.19   Dante Alighieri face] Italian poet (1265–1321) who was described by poet Giovanni Boccaccio (1313–1375) as "his face was long, his nose aquiline."

280.29   Beatrice] Dante's beloved.

281.8–9   Bulwer-Lytton . . . Warwick] A central figure in the historical novel *The Last of the Barons* (1843), by the English writer and politician Edward Bulwer-Lytton (1803–1873), is Richard Neville, the 16th Earl of Warwick (1428–1471).

282.21   Tommy Tucker] The English nursery rhyme "Little Tommy Tucker" begins, "Little Tommy Tucker / Sings for his supper."

283.3   *vaqueros*] Spanish: cowboys.

284.1   *paisano* bird] Spanish: the greater roadrunner.

284.6   *vaciero*] Spanish: supply agent for sheep or goat camps.

285.8   *vita simplex*] Latin: simple life.

285.38   Frio City] Also known as Frio Town, town on the Frio River in Frio County, Texas, now a ghost town.

286.8   Spanish Fandango] Guitar instrumental arranged by American artist and musician Henry Worrall (1825–1902).

288.27–30   Athos . . . D'Artagnan] Athos, Aramis, Porthos, and d'Artagnan (a native of Gascony), characters in *The Three Musketeers* (1844) by Alexandre Dumas (1802–1870).

290.2   Wellington beak] Arthur Wellesley, 1st Duke of Wellington (1769–1852) and British prime minister, 1828–30 and 1834, was known for his large nose.

292.4   Zollicoffer] Felix Zollicoffer (1812–1862), Confederate general killed in action during the Civil War.

292.11   Crusoe's goat] In *Robinson Crusoe* (1719) by Daniel Defoe (c. 1660–1731), Crusoe forgets about his tamed goat for a week and it nearly starves.

293.12   Joe Weber] American vaudeville comedian (1867–1942), part of the team Weber and Fields.

293.14   'Curfew Shall Not Ring To-night,'] "Curfew Must Not Ring Tonight" (1867), popular narrative poem by American poet Rose Hartwick Thorpe (1850–1939).

293.19   M. K. & T.] See note 215.9–10.

294.31   seven-up] See note 236.1.

295.27   Buffalo Bill] William Frederick Cody (1846–1917), who began his touring Wild West show in 1874.

297.8–10   'Imperial Cæsar . . . wind away'] *Hamlet*, V.i.199–200.

298.4 Katy] See note 215.15.

298.10 baa-a-rum] Bay rum, popular aftershave application.

299.3 State of South Dakota] South Dakota became a state in 1889.

299.6 P. R. R.] The Pennsylvania Railroad.

299.21 mines of Gondola] Golconda Diamonds, mined in southern India.

299.30–31 Philip Steins] In the biblical book of Judges, the Philistines bribed Delilah to find the source of Samson's strength.

300.40 saleratus] See note 279.5.

302.13 Creek Nation] The American Indian Muskogee Creek Confederacy, originally from the southeastern United States but forcibly removed in the 1830s to modern Oklahoma.

302.15–16 bitten the grass . . . Nebuchadnezzars] Cf. Daniel 4, especially verses 31–33.

303.2–3 Muscogee] Later more commonly spelled Muskogee, city in eastern Indian Territory, later Oklahoma. See also note 302.13.

304.27 "The Gipsy's Curse."] Lengthy speech made by a gypsy in *Guy Mannering* (1815), novel by Sir Walter Scott (1771–1832).

304.30–31 Belasco's] David Belasco (1853–1931), American theatrical impresario.

304.39–305.1 "The Cowboy's Lament"] Traditional song, also known as "The Streets of Laredo."

305.39 the "Unabridged."] See note 29.2.

307.15 Chandler] City in central Indian Territory, later Oklahoma, opened by a land run in September 1891.

308.3 Saltillo] No such town currently exists.

312.26 Piute] American Indian tribe.

TROPICS

321.13 *mozo*] Spanish: male servant.

325.34 Spitzbergen] An island in northern Norway, which has an Arctic climate.

330.31 dolcy far nienty] *Dolce far niente*, Italian expression meaning "sweet idleness."

331.34–35 Satan sowing tares . . . Paul planting] Cf. Matthew 13 and 1 Corinthians 3:6.

332.16   *Qué picadores diablos!*] Spanish: What devilish stickers!

333.5   *Juez de la Paz*] Spanish: Justice of the Peace.

333.6   twenty stone] Two hundred and eighty pounds.

333.7   *pulperia*] Spanish: bar or tavern.

339.3–4   became Elijahs . . . played the raven] In 1 Kings 17:2, the prophet Elijah is fed by ravens.

340.5–6   The annual parade . . . ex-snakes of Ireland?] The St. Patrick's Day Parade in New York City.

340.16–17   "Ridpath's History of the World . . . the Equator."] *History of the World* (1894), an eight-volume work by John C. Ridpath (1840–1900).

341.3   Anthony Hope] English novelist (1863–1933), author of *The Prisoner of Zenda* (1894).

343.20   yellow-back] Cheap novel bound in bright-colored fabric or paper.

343.29–30   rockaways and old-style barouches] Types of horse-drawn carriages.

345.23   Botica Española] General store.

345.31   Spanish Fandango] See note 286.8.

346.1–2   sextet in a 'Florodora' road company] *Florodora*, musical comedy that opened in the London West End in 1899 and on Broadway in 1900, famous for its sextet of chorines, who became known as "The Florodora Girls."

351.8   straight front] A type of corset.

352.39   Mrs. Humphry Ward] Mary Augusta Ward (1851–1920), British novelist.

354.38   Richmond Hobson Davis] The writer Richard Harding Davis (1864–1916).

355.15   afrites] Or ifrits. In Arabian and Muslim mythology, demons.

355.16   fisherman's vase] In one of the stories in *One Thousand and One Nights*, a fisherman finds a genie in a vase.

356.27   alcalde] Municipal magistrate.

356.29   *chuchula*] Apparently an invention of O. Henry's.

356.40   *perissodactyle ungulates*] Perissodactyl, or odd-toed, ungulates, a taxonomic order including horses and tapirs.

357.1   Cordilleras] Chain of mountains, a term commonly used in reference to the Andes.

357.34   Loeb] William Loeb (1866–1937), secretary to President Theodore Roosevelt.

357.35   Duma] Russian legislative body, which had little legislative power during the reign, 1894–1917, of the autocratic Nicholas II (1868–1918).

358.14–15   Herr Mees] Hermes.

358.35   when T. R. is at Oyster Bay] Theodore Roosevelt's summer home was in Oyster Bay, New York.

359.5–6   Nebuchadnezzars; they bit the grass] See note 302.15–16.

359.22   Little Big High Low Jacks-in-the-game] Reference to the card game Pitch, or High Low Jack.

359.35   Faust's wooing of Marguerite] In *Faust*, a play by Johann von Goethe (1749–1832), Faust is in love with Gretchen, sometimes called Marguerite.

365.22   'A Life on the Ocean Wave'] Popular song (1838) by Epes Sargent, set to music by Henry Russell.

THE GENTLE GRAFTER

371.4   Hadji] In Islam, title given to one who has made the pilgrimage to Mecca.

371.32   teetotum] A kind of gambling spinning top.

372.38–39   'When Knighthood Was in Flower'] Popular novel (1898) by American writer Charles Major (1856–1913), published under the pen name Edwin Caskoden.

373.18   Manitou] To the Algonquin tribes, the great spirit or spiritual life force.

374.10   Boy Avenger] Name taken by the character Bromley Chitterlings in the novel *Drift from Two Shores* (1878) by American author Bret Harte (1836–1902).

374.29   Tammany cartoon] Editorial cartoons critiquing the Tammany Hall New York political machine sometimes depicted its leaders as American Indians.

374.31   Howells] William Dean Howells (1837–1920), American author of realistic novels.

375.35   feendenuman shape] I.e., fiend in human shape.

377.35   fakir] A Hindu wonder worker; also a swindler.

382.5   Buffalo Bill matinée] See note 295.27.

384.25   nature fakers] Term used by Theodore Roosevelt in a September 1907 article decrying some literary naturalists.

388.21   Connecticut wrappers] Tobacco grown in the Connecticut River Valley and used to wrap cigars.

388.33   Rameses II.] King of Egypt from 1279 to 1213 B.C.E.

388.34   Queen Isis] Isis, major Egyptian goddess.

389.16–17   B. & O. westbound] Baltimore and Ohio Railroad.

390.31   John D. Napoleons] I.e., John D. Rockefeller and Napoleon Bonaparte.

391.36   A., T. & S. F.] Atcheson, Topeka and Santa Fe Railroad.

392.6–7   Phœbe Snow's job] Fictional character created in 1902 to advertise the cleanliness of the Delaware, Lackawanna and Western Railroad.

392.35   Raffles] A. J. Raffles, the "gentleman thief" in a series of stories by English author E. W. Hornung (1866–1921).

393.28   Luther Burbank] American botanist (1849–1926).

394.5–6   General Raven's . . . Elijah] In Greek mythology, ravens were associated with Apollo, the god of prophecy. See also note 339.3–4 for Elijah and the ravens.

395.23–24   English pokes] Poke collar, a kind of collar with projecting ends.

398.7   tinkers' chorus] "The Tinkers' Song," from the comic opera *Robin Hood* (1890) by Reginald De Koven, Harry B. Smith, and Clement Scott.

398.31–32   Industrial Christian Science . . . Mrs. Eddy] Mary Baker Eddy (1821–1910) founded Christian Science, a religion that holds that sickness can be cured by prayer.

398.33   gold-dust twins] Fictional characters used to advertise Gold Dust Washing Powder.

400.17–18   cold proposition . . . Robert E. Peary and Charlie Fairbanks] Peary, American explorer of the Arctic (1856–1920). Charles W. Fairbanks (1852–1918), vice president of the United States, 1905–9. As U.S. senator from Indiana, 1897–1905, he helped settle the Alaska boundary dispute.

400.31–32   Pasteur institute] A medical research foundation named after Louis Pasteur (1822–1895).

401.23   Autolycan] Autolycus, a thief in Greek mythology.

NEW YORK

405.27–28   McMahan . . . Upon him the Tiger purred] Possibly a reference to Timothy "Big Tim" Sullivan (1862–1913), leader of the Tammany Hall political machine on the Lower East Side. Tammany Hall was customarily represented as a tiger.

406.36–37   Hester . . . Chrystie . . . Delancey] Streets on the Lower East Side of New York, home in the early twentieth century to most of New York's immigrant Jewish population.

411.34 wind-jammers] Talkative persons, windbags.

411.37–412.1 Marx and Hyndman and Kautsky] Karl Marx (1818–1883), German philosopher and author of *The Communist Manifesto*. Henry Hyndman (1842–1921), British Marxist. Karl Kautsky (1854–1938), Czech-German Marxist philosopher.

412.1 shines!] Fools.

412.4 takes the rag off the bush] Takes the cake.

412.5 skookum house] Prison.

412.11 Bowery] Street and section in lower Manhattan then known for crime and other lowlife activity.

412.16 "Shinny on your own side!"] Mind your business.

412.19 mazuma] Money.

412.22 spifflicated] Overcome, defeated.

412.24 Cobden] Richard Cobden (1804–1865), British manufacturer and politician known for his defense of free trade.

412.25 biff] Hit, strike.

414.18 cull] Friend, mate.

415.5–6 Marco Polo and Mungo Park] Polo, Italian explorer (1254–1324). Park, Scottish explorer (1771–1806).

417.9 *vade mecum*] A pocket handbook.

418.19 spider-wheel] A metal wheel with wire spokes.

419.1 whisht!] Hush.

419.17 braid] Fabric in the form of a band, used as trim.

419.26 jagerfonteins] Jagersfontein, town in South Africa famous for its diamond mine.

425.1 Dress Parade] A display of clothes, or fashion show.

425.19 Flatiron Building] Triangular New York office building completed in 1902.

426.5–6 cheviot and worsted] Kinds of wool.

428.34 Fuss and Feathers] Excessive bustle and display.

428.34 Bacillus] Rod-shaped bacterium, used figuratively for disease.

429.3 Larchmont] Wealthy New York suburb on Long Island Sound.

429.40–430.1   that avenue . . . highway of Mammon] Fifth Avenue.

432.4   Kootenai Falls] Waterfall near Libby, Montana.

432.20   "The Storm"] Painting (1880) by French artist Pierre August Cot (1837–1883).

433.21   colorado-maduro] A kind of cigar wrapper.

435.18   grouch] Complaint.

437.7   Bourke Cockran] William Bourke Cockran (1854–1923), New York Democratic politician.

437.20   lares and penates] A person's or household's possessions, from Lares and Penates, Roman gods who were guardians of the household.

437.30   pony ballet] Kick-line routine developed in the 1890s by British choreographer John Tiller, featuring chorus girls dressed as ponies. The term was later generally applied to synchronized dance performances.

437.35   angel] The financial backer of a theatrical production.

441.13   b. and s.] Brandy and soda.

441.36   See advertising column] Restaurants and other businesses sometimes paid newspapers for favorable mentions in articles.

442.25   the way the story runs] See also "The Badge of Policeman O'Roon," pp. 509–13.

442.26–27   "Rugged Riders,"] Cf. the Rough Riders, the popular name for the first U.S. Volunteer Cavalry regiment in the Spanish-American War (1898), who were commanded by Theodore Roosevelt (1858–1919).

450.3   upas tree] A tree in the mulberry and fig family whose latex is poisonous.

450.5   Cerberus and Argus] In Greek mythology, Cerberus was a multi-headed dog who guarded the gates of Hades, and Argus was a hundred-eyed monster.

450.6   Rubberer] Variant of "rubbernecker," overly inquisitive or gawping person.

450.7   Caoutchouc] Tree-derived substance from which rubber is manufactured.

450.10   Martians] In H. G. Wells's *War of the Worlds* (1897), the narrator describes the invading Martians as having "a pair of very large, dark-coloured eyes" that dominate their noseless faces and as moving around the landscape by piloting large machines.

450.18   Senator Depew] Chauncey Depew (1834–1928), U.S. senator from New York from 1899 until 1911.

450.19 Chuck Connors] George Washington "Chuck" Connors (c. 1852–1913), Tammany Hall boss known as "the Mayor of Chinatown."

451.13 Duke of Roxburgh married] In November 1903, Henry John Innes-Ker, the 8th Duke of Roxburghe, married Mary Goelet, daughter of the wealthy New York real estate businessman Ogden Goelet.

452.6 ex-Mayor Low] Seth Low (1850–1916), mayor of New York City from 1902 to 1903.

452.16 Bricklets] Ice-cream product formed into a rectangular shape.

453.13 The Big Church in the Middle of the Block] Perhaps a reference to the Church of the Transfiguration, popularly known as the Little Church Around the Corner, on East 29th Street in Manhattan.

453.28 Laura Jean Libbey] Popular New York–based writer (1862–1924) known as the "working-girl" novelist for her many stories with such characters.

455.2 Kipling] From the dedication of English author Rudyard Kipling's poetry collection *The Seven Seas* (1896).

455.8 roof-garden] Hammerstein's Roof Garden, which opened in 1899, began a trend of summertime outdoor rooftop cafés and vaudeville theaters in New York.

456.6 Doctor Wiley] Harvey Wiley (1844–1930), American chemist and a leader in the passage of the Pure Food and Drug Act of 1906.

456.31 Flatiron Building] See note 425.19.

457.34 Langley flying machine] Langley Aerodrome, unsuccessful flying machine designed in the 1890s by Samuel Langley (1834–1906).

458.20 Depew and Ford] For Depew, see note 450.18. Simeon Ford (1855–1933), owner of the Grand Union Hotel and well-known raconteur.

459.16 Sousa's band] John Philip Sousa (1854–1932), American composer and bandleader.

459.16 the repeating candidate] William Jennings Bryan (1860–1925), Democratic candidate for president in 1896, 1900, and 1908.

460.4 war map] The Russo-Japanese War was fought from 1904 to 1905.

460.16 Yalu] The Battle of the Yalu River (1904) was a victory for Japan.

460.35 Jeffries's] James "Jim" Jeffries (1875–1953), world heavyweight champion, 1899–1905.

461.18–19 denarii—scudi—kopecks—pfennigs—pilasters] The first four are the currencies, respectively, of ancient Rome, various Italian states up to the nineteenth century, Russia, and Germany. A pilaster is a column that protrudes from a wall.

462.24   seidlitz powder] See note 224.32.

465.34   Kuropatkin] Alexsey Kuropatkin (1848–1925), Russian minister of war from 1898 to 1904.

466.7–8   *lares et penates*] See note 437.20.

468.16   The Huguenot Lovers] "A Huguenot" (1852), painting by John Everett Millais (1829–1896).

468.17   The First Quarrel] "Their First Quarrel," drawing by Charles Dana Gibson (1867–1944).

468.17   The Wedding Breakfast] Painting (1862) by George Elgar Hicks (1824–1914).

468.17–18   Psyche at the Fountain] "Psyche at a Fountain" (1900), painting by Guillaume Seignac (1870–1924).

473.3–4   where the distance between the two streets is the shortest] That would place the store on Houston Street in lower Manhattan.

476.26   Lochinvar] Knight who is the hero of the ballad "Marmion" (1808) by Sir Walter Scott (1771–1832).

478.8   "broiler,"] Chorus girl.

478.23   dub] Oaf.

478.30   John Drew or Jim Corbett] Drew, American stage actor (1853–1927). James "Gentleman Jim" Corbett (1866–1933), American heavyweight who worked as an actor after his retirement from boxing in 1903.

479.5   Thespis] Greek poet of the sixth century B.C.E. said to be the first person to speak, rather than chant or sing, as an actor in a drama.

483.18   ticket-chopper] Employee who shredded New York subway customers' tickets.

484.1–2   "The Rise and Fall of Silas Latham"] Novel (1885) by William Dean Howells (1837–1920).

484.3   "The Boss"] *The Boss, and How He Came to Rule New York*, novel (1903) by Alfred Henry Lewis (1857–1914).

484.3–4   "In the Bishop's Carriage"] Novel (1904) by Miriam Michelson (1870–1942).

484.5   "The Deliverance"] Novel (1904) by Ellen Glasgow (1873–1945).

484.7–8   "The Queen's Quair"] Historical novel (1904) by Maurice Hewlett (1861–1923).

486.12–13   Big Church in the Middle of the Block] See note 453.13.

487.12   Mazuma] See note 412.19.

489.23   Cop] Look at, notice.

489.24   push] Crowd, set.

489.38   Beau Brummel] George Bryan "Beau" Brummell (1778–1840), English dandy.

490.13   Pipe] Look at.

490.13   floor-walker] Employee who supervises a section of a store or shop.

491.3   "Big Mike" O'Sullivan] See note 405.27–28.

491.19   perfectos] Cigars.

493.4   Lizzie-boy] Effeminate man, homosexual.

495.20   the Island] Blackwell's Island (now called Roosevelt Island), a narrow island in New York's East River, site of a municipal prison from the early nineteenth century until 1935.

495.22   Boreas] Greek god of the north wind.

499.9   Hartford College] Comedic mangling of Harvard College, Yale's traditional football foe.

502.27   Palisades] Steep cliffs along the west side of the Hudson River opposite Manhattan, once frequently used as a site for duels.

502.30   tierce] Fencing maneuver.

502.31   crow to pick] Disagreement, bone to pick.

503.10   Sidereal System] A system of astrology that uses different dates than the more commonly used tropical system to divide the year among the twelve zodiac signs.

503.19   Rudolf Steiner] Also the name of an Austrian-born spiritualist (1861–1925).

503.39   "Junie's Love Test,"] Novel (1886) by Laura Jean Libbey, for whom see note 453.28.

506.20   "Himmel!"] Good heavens!

506.30   election bets] Contemporary fad of betting on elections with odd stakes, such as rolling a peanut for a specified number of blocks.

507.12   "fines"] Wage deductions for minor offenses.

509.10   Gentle Riders] See note 442.26–27.

509.24   up-hill charge] The Battle of San Juan Hill, Cuba, a decisive U.S. victory in the Spanish-American War.

509.25   Democrats] In the 1904 campaign, Democrats unsuccessfully used Roosevelt's Rough Riders experience as evidence that Roosevelt was too "impulsive" and "sensational" to be president.

510.2   bobbies] Police officers.

514.30   Mrs. Partington] Comical character known for her malapropisms created by American author Benjamin Penhallow Shillaber (1814–1890).

515.2–3   Dockstader's minstrels] Vaudeville troupe led by Lew Dockstader, stage name of George Alfred Clapp (1856–1924).

521.14   D. P. W.] Department of Public Works.

521.21–22   the nation that keeps us . . . fugues and fruit] Italy.

522.31   Hoosac Tunnel] A 4.75-mile-long railroad tunnel in western Massachusetts.

523.37   Beloochistan] Belochistan, a province in Pakistan.

524.35   sidereal system] See note 503.10.

524.35   Epictetus] Greek stoic philosopher (c. 55–c. 135 C.E.).

525.25   "Arcturus——"] The brightest star in the northern constellation Boötes.

527.32   'rounder'] Wealthy, fashionable man; playboy.

527.33   Mrs. Fish's receptions] Marion "Mamie" Fish (1853–1915), New York socialite.

527.34   Lotos Club] Gentlemen's club in New York.

528.3–4   hydrogen derivatives] Probably a reference to women who dye their hair blonde with hydrogen peroxide.

528.9   heimgangers] Stay-at-homes.

528.38   fly] Fashionable.

528.39   push] See note 489.24.

528.39–529.1   bump to the rail] A horse-racing maneuver in which a jockey crowds his opponent to the outside.

529.1   between the Flatirons] A part of Broadway, known for its theaters and nightclubs, stretching from the Flatiron Building at 23rd Street to the *New York Times* headquarters at 42nd Street.

529.30   roof garden] See note 455.8.

530.3–4   'Let's All Go Up to Maud's'] Popular song (1904) by Joseph C. Farrell and Kerry Mills.

530.19   Rubber] See note 450.6.

531.2   Santos-Dumont] Alberto Santos-Dumont (1873–1932), Brazilian aviation pioneer.

532.15 Hackett matinee] James K. Hackett (1869–1926), American actor.

532.17–18 gentleman who announced . . . open] Pistol, in Shakespeare's *The Merry Wives of Windsor*, II.ii.2–3, who says, "the world's mine oyster, Which I with sword will open."

532.35 throw the five . . . coloured gentleman's head] African Dodger, carnival game in which an African American man would stick his head through a curtain and attempt to dodge objects, such as eggs or baseballs, thrown at him.

533.26 "In the Good Old Summertime"] "In the Good Old Summer Time," popular song (1903) by George Evans and Ren Shields.

535.7–8 *diminuendo con amore*] Italian: quietly, with love.

536.24 Mukden] City in Manchuria, site of decisive battle (1905) in the Russo-Japanese War in which Russian forces retreated.

536.25–26 "The Cloister and the Hearth,"] Historical novel (1861) by Charles Reade (1814–1884). The main character is Gerard Eliassoen, a young Dutch scribe; Denys is his companion.

538.16–17 Bastien Le Page and Gérôme?] French painters Jules Bastien-Lepage (1848–1884) and Jean-Léon Gérôme (1824–1904).

538.37 Rosa Bonheur] French painter and sculptor (1822–1899).

539.24 Comstockized] Anthony Comstock (1844–1915), moralistic crusader against "obscenity." The adjective presumably suggests that Medora's shirtwaist is demure.

540.11 Würzburger] Beer brewed in Würzburg, Germany.

541.12 White Lane] Broadway, also known as the Great White Way.

541.13 pad] Leave, walk away.

541.21 maul-stick] Sometimes mahlstick, used by painters as a rest for the hand while painting.

541.23 Jerome or Gérôme] William Travers Jerome (1859–1934), New York district attorney, 1902–9. For Gérôme, see note 538.16–17.

541.29 Prax Italys!] Praxiteles (fl. 370–330 B.C.E.), Greek sculptor.

541.30 Venus Anno Dominis] Reference to "Venus Annodomini," short story (1886) by Rudyard Kipling (1865–1936).

542.25–26 Camille, Lola Montez, Royal Mary, Zaza] Camille, tragic heroine of the novel *La Dame aux Camélias* (1848) by Alexandre Dumas *fils*, as well as the opera *La traviata* (1853) by Giuseppe Verdi. Lola Montez (1821–61), Irish singer and actress who became the mistress of King Ludwig I of Bavaria and died of syphilis. Mary, Queen of Scots (1542–1587), who was executed for treason. Zaza, the title character, a prostitute, of a play (1898) by Pierre Berton and Charles Simon.

542.29   King of Belgium] Leopold II (1835–1909), known for his many mistresses.

543.2   Carter] Mrs. Leslie Carter (c. 1857–1937) played the title role in the American production of *Zaza* (1899).

544.7   St. George Rathbone's] St. George Rathborne (1854–1938), American author known for his adventure stories and dime novels.

544.29   Metropolitan] Metropolitan Opera.

544.29   De Reszke] Jean de Reszke (1850–1925), Polish tenor who retired from performing in 1902.

544.32   Caruso] Enrico Caruso (1873–1921), Italian tenor who made his American debut at the Metropolitan Opera in 1903 and who was considered to be de Reszke's successor.

546.14   Tony Pastor] American vaudeville impresario (1837–1908).

546.16   'Parsifal'] Opera (1882) by Richard Wagner (1813–1883).

546.19   B. Cory Kilvert] Benjamin Sayre Cory Kilvert, Canadian-born illustrator (1879–1946), known for his depictions of children.

547.17   the unities] The theory, derived from Aristotle, that a play should have a single action occurring in a single place and within the course of a single day.

547.23   S. P. C. C.] Society for the Prevention of Cruelty to Children, founded in New York in 1874.

548.21–22   Château de Beychsvelle] Château Beychevelle, wine from the Bordeaux region of France.

549.21   "The Banks of the Wabash"] "On the Banks of the Wabash, Far Away," song (1897) by Paul Dresser (1857–1906).

549.34   Chaldean] Chaldea, country located in southeastern Mesopotamia, which existed roughly from the tenth century until the sixth century B.C.E.

550.18–19   the kangaroo walk] Fad that involved walking with a "hoppy, springy stride and a swinging relaxation of the arms."

550.22   pneumatic] Relating to a woman with a well-rounded figure.

551.18   frangipangi] Probably frangipane, a sweet, almond-flavored filling used in baking.

551.22   'Elsie's School Days'] Martha Finley (1828–1909) wrote *Elsie Dinsmore*, a series of children's novels with a moralistic, Christian slant, published from 1867 to 1905. *Elsie's School Days* was not one of them.

551.36   Carnegie] Andrew Carnegie (1835–1919), Scottish-American industrialist known for his philanthropy, especially funding public libraries.

552.2   Red Leary] John "Red" Leary (died 1888), bank robber.

555.2   RUBBERNECK] See note 450.6.

556.1   Golden Way] Presumably Fifth Avenue.

556.8   Vanderbilts] Descendants of Cornelius Vanderbilt (1794–1877), American business magnate.

556.8–9   Grand Central depot] Vanderbilt built the Grand Central Depot in 1869–71 to unite three separate railroads that ran to 42nd Street into a single station.

556.15   Chuck Connors] See note 450.19.

556.16   Parkhurst] Charles Henry Parkhurst (1842–1933), Presbyterian clergyman and anti-Tammany crusader.

556.17   "Bishop" Potter] Henry C. Potter (1834–1908), Episcopal bishop of New York, 1888–1908.

557.28   cardiaphone] Cardiophone, electrical stethoscope for listening to the heart.

557.34   Bluebeard's chamber] "Bluebeard," French folktale in which a wealthy man murders his wives and deposits their corpses in an underground chamber that his new wife is not allowed to enter.

561.19   Hendrik Hudson] Henry (in Dutch, Hendrik) Hudson (c. 1565–1611), English navigator who explored the area around present-day New York in 1609.

561.21   Napoleon III.] Also called Louis-Napoléon (1808–1873), the last emperor of France, 1852–70.

561.34   Palisades] See note 502.27.

562.35–36   Carnegie medal] In 1904, the industrialist Andrew Carnegie (see also note 551.36) established a fund that annually awarded medals and cash grants to people who risked their lives helping others.

562.36   Morgan] John Pierpont Morgan (1837–1913), American financier known for his art collection.

563.37   North River] Hudson River.

563.38   Chilcoot] Chilkoot Pass, high mountain pass in Alaska and British Columbia.

564.10–11   Mount Saint Elias] Mountain on the border of Alaska and the Yukon Territory of Canada.

565.21 "Boadicea,"] See note 55.5–6.

566.12 roof gardens] See note 455.8.

566.21 ray from the calcium] Sunshine.

567.21 Beaverkill] River in upstate New York.

567.29 Father Knickerbocker's] Mythical symbol of New York, based on early Dutch settlers.

569.27–28 Miss Clay] Bertha M. Clay, American pen name of Charlotte M. Brame (1836–1884), English author of romantic short stories and novels. After her death, works by other writers continued to be issued under the "Bertha Clay" name.

571.11 Morpheus] In Greek mythology, a god associated with sleep and dreams.

571.16–17 higher criticism] School that examines the historical context in which a text, especially the Bible, was written.

571.19 Gabriel] Angel traditionally said to play a trumpet blast to herald Jesus's return to earth.

571.33–34 Hamburg edging] A kind of embroidered work used for trimming.

572.15 Hoffman House] Restaurant and hotel at Broadway and 25th Street in Manhattan.

573.19–20 General Kitchener] Herbert Kitchener (1850–1916), British army officer.

573.20 William Muldoon] Wrestling champion (1852–1933) and proponent of the physical culture movement.

573.20 Duchess of Marlborough] Sarah Churchill (1660–1744), influential English courtier.

573.21 Benvenuto Cellini] Italian sculptor (1500–1571).

575.39 "Sammy."] Song (1902) by Edward Hutchison and James O'Dea.

577.5 peekaboo waists] Shirtwaists made with embroidery or sheer fabric such that the flesh behind them could be seen.

577.18 Kishineff massacre] Anti-Jewish pogroms that took place in Kishinev, Russia, in 1903 and 1905.

577.32 the City Club] Nongovernmental organization advocating for civic improvement in New York.

578.1 Oyama's] Ōyama Iwao (1842–1916), Japanese field marshal and leader in several victorious land battles in the Russo-Japanese War (1904–5).

578.8   Jerome] See note 541.23.

578.28   Mister Depew's] For Chauncey Depew, see note 450.18. In 1905, he was chairman of the board of the New York Central Railroad.

578.37   ukase] Edict of the Russian government.

580.5   Hetty Green] Henrietta Green (1834–1916), businesswoman and financier.

580.8   North Beach] Popular beach at the Bowery and Flushing Bays in Queens.

580.16–17   the Tavern and the Casino] Restaurants located in Central Park: Black Horse Tavern, located near Fifth Avenue and 102nd Street, and the Casino, near Fifth Avenue and 72nd Street.

583.6   Tuskegeenial] I.e., the Tuskegee Institute, African American educational institution in Alabama founded by Booker T. Washington (1856–1915).

583.19–20   I'm not Hetty if I do look green] For Hetty Green, see note 580.5.

583.33   Anna Held'll] Broadway performer (c. 1872–1918) known for her appearances in Florenz Ziegfeld productions.

584.33   Momus] The god of mockery in Greek mythology.

588.21   Amaryllis] Nymph in the bucolic idylls of Theocritus, Greek poet of the third century B.C.E.

588.31–32   Mr. Blaney's plays] Charles E. Blaney (1866–1944), American playwright known for his melodramas.

590.25   The queer] Counterfeit money.

590.25–26   Jerome's] See note 541.23.

591.7   jay] Rustic, simpleton.

591.7   McAdoo's] WIlliam McAdoo (1853–1930), New York City police commissioner, 1904–5.

591.8   shine] Fool.

591.11   Waterbury] Clock from the Waterbury Clock Company, Waterbury, Connecticut.

591.26   yellow-backs] Gold certificates.

591.39   old sledge] Card game.

592.7   Central Office] Headquarters for a vaudeville touring company.

592.8   gillie] Yokel or simpleton.

592.9   Tony Pastor] See note 546.14.

592.9–10   Mr. Scotty from Death Valley] Walter Edward Perry Scott (1872–1954), also known as Death Valley Scotty, a prospector and con man known for his fraudulent gold mine schemes.

592.12   skiddoo] Bad luck, exit.

592.26   Long Acre] Longacre Square in midtown Manhattan, renamed Times Square in 1904.

593.15   J. G. Brown] John George Brown (1831–1913), British-born American artist known for his paintings of street urchins.

594.11–12   Winged Victory] The Winged Victory of Samothrace, Greek statue of the second century B.C.E., which has been displayed at the Louvre since 1883.

594.13   *Le Petit Journal*] French newspaper with international circulation.

596.34   chaparreras] Chaps, leather riding pants without a seat.

597.1   Bradstreet's] Weekly business publication.

597.1   Brigham] Perhaps Albert Perry Brigham (1855–1932), American geologist and author of *Geographic Influences in American History* (1903).

597.11   Culmbacher] A dark lager beer, usually spelled Kulmbacher.

598.5   Claremont] The Claremont Inn, restaurant on the banks of the Hudson River at 124th Street in New York.

598.13   Omar] See note 240.29.

600.18   "Delmonico's,"] Famous restaurant near Wall Street in lower Manhattan. Eighth Street is a principal street in Greenwich Village.

600.19   bishop sleeves] Style of clothing in which a full, loose sleeve is gathered into a cuff.

606.3   the Elsie series] See note 551.22.

606.7   "with pitfall and with gin."] "Oh Thou, who didst with pitfall and with gin," opening line of Quatrain 38 of *The Rubáiyát of Omar Khayyám* (see note 240.29)

606.26   the unities] See note 547.17.

612.33   Gad's Hill] Summer house of English novelist Charles Dickens (1812–1870).

612.36   Lost, Your Excellency] Cf. Dickens, *Bleak House* (1852–53): "Dead, your Majesty. Dead, my lords and gentlemen. Dead, Right Reverends and Wrong Reverends of every order. Dead, men and women, born with Heavenly compassion in your hearts. And dying thus around us every day."

614.37   G. Bernard] George Bernard Shaw (1856–1950), Irish playwright.

624.16–17   sit upon the ground . . . death of Kings] *Richard II,* III.ii.155–56.

624.19   Bird Centre] Fictional small town created by cartoonist John T. McCutcheon (1870–1949).

624.21   Hendrik Hudson] See note 561.19.

625.5   chloral] Chemical used to make chloral hydrate, a sedative.

625.5   John L.] John L. Sullivan (1858–1918), American heavyweight boxer.

625.10   Knickerbocker's] See note 567.29.

625.27   Lochinvars] See note 476.26.

626.5   Bryan] See note 459.16.

626.10   Crusoe] See note 292.11.

626.11   May Irwin or E. S. Willard] Irwin, comedian and vaudeville performer (1862–1938). Edward Smith Willard, English actor (1853–1915).

626.18   butterick] E. Butterick & Co., firm that publishes sewing patterns.

626.31–32   John W. Gates] American industrial magnate (1855–1911).

626.33   Edna May] Edna May Pettie (1878–1948), American actress.

627.24   Sara Bernhardt in 'Andrew Mack'] Sarah Bernhardt (1844–1923), French-born actress. Andrew Mack (1863–1931), Irish American actor, singer, and comedian. There was no such play with that title.

629.3   "Bartenders Guide."] Book by bartender Jeremiah "Jerry" P. Thomas (1830–1885) first published in 1862 and reissued under several different titles.

629.11   white ribboners] The symbol of the Woman's Christian Temperance Movement.

629.17   skate] Alcoholic bender.

629.26   full] Drunk.

629.26   boiled owl] A drunk person.

630.24   Omar's Rubaiyat] See note 240.29.

631.2–3   borax and formaldehyde tests] Tests for detecting the presence of alcohol.

631.33   giftie gi'ed] Cf. "To a Louse" by Robert Burns (1759–1796): "O wad some Power the giftie gie us [Oh would some power the gift give us] / To see oursels as ithers see us!"

633.38–634.2   "Come, fill the Cup, . . . on the Wing!"] Cf. Quatrain 21 of *The Rubáiyát of Omar Khayyám*.

634.16–21   "'Ah! Love, could you . . . Heart's Desire!'"] Quatrain 99 of *The Rubáiyát of Omar Khayyám*.

636.23   Flatiron] See note 425.19.

636.24–25 'Under the Old Apple Tree'] "In the Shade of the Old Apple Tree," popular song (1905) written by Harry Williams and Egbert Van Alstyne.

636.27 Mrs. Winslow] Mrs. Winslow's Soothing Syrup, patent medicine for calming teething children, which contained generous levels of alcohol and morphine sulfate.

636.40 crowbait] Worn-out, emaciated horse.

639.39 cash girl] Messenger in a store who takes money from a customer to a cashier and returns with change.

640.11 Diana's] *Diana*, sculpture by Augustus Saint-Gaudens (1848–1907), which was installed at the top of the second Madison Square Garden building (demolished 1925).

642.12 Blue Point] Small oyster, typically from the South Shore of Long Island.

642.25 Strephon seeks his Chloe] A married couple in the poem "Strephon and Chloe" by Jonathan Swift (1667–1745).

642.30 D'Artagnan] See note 288.27–30.

644.20 Culmbacher] See note 597.11.

644.35 A B C store] Dry goods store.

644.38 Skiddoo!] Get out, leave.

645.3 congress gaiters] Ankle boots with elasticated sides.

645.12 carbolic] Carbolic acid, substance used as a disinfectant that is toxic in large doses.

646.22 Terrible Turk] Stage name of Turkish professional wrestler Yusuf İsmail (c. 1857–1898).

646.27 Claude Melnotte] Romantic character in the play *The Lady of Lyons* (1838) by Edward Bulwer-Lytton (1803–1873).

649.29 North River] Hudson River.

667.4 King Cophetua] African king who, in the sixteenth-century ballad "The King and the Beggar-Maid," falls instantly in love with a beggar.

668.4 Gladstone Dowie] A son (1877–1945) of Scottish-Australian evangelist John Alexander Dowie (1847–1907).

668.18 physiopathic] Having to do with disorders attributed to neural dysfunction.

670.4 duck-fit] Bout of hysterics.

670.32 Esau . . . keeps her birthright] Old Testament figure who sold his birthright for a bowl of stew; cf. Genesis 25.

671.10   Nimrod] Biblical figure called "a mighty hunter before the LORD."

672.32   Gibsonian cop] Term coined by New York police commissioner Theodore A. Bingham (1858–1934) to refer to young, good-looking police officers.

675.2   Marion Crawford] Francis Marion Crawford (1854–1909), prolific American novelist.

675.3   Ella Wheeler Wilcox] American poet (1850–1919).

681.7   *Sic transit gloria urbis*] *Latin:* Thus passes the glory of the city.

683.17   Marathon] Coastal town in southern Greece.

683.29–30   Sam Loyd puzzle] Samuel Loyd (1841–1911), American chess player and puzzle creator.

684.9   *frangipanni*] See note 551.18.

684.10   Booth] Edwin Booth (1833–1893), American actor.

686.25   play *Topsy* without using the cork] African American character in *Uncle Tom's Cabin* (1852) by Harriet Beecher Stowe (1811–1896). The novel was frequently dramatized, with Topsy played by a white actor in blackface.

686.29   Manhattan] Cocktail made with rye whiskey and sweet vermouth.

687.23   Würzburger] See note 540.11.

687.23   Extra Dry] Champagne.

688.5   John Drew] John Drew, Jr., American stage actor (1853–1927).

688.21   'Annie Laurie'] Scottish song dating from the early eighteenth century.

690.22   Mrs. Bluebeard] For Bluebeard, see note 557.34. *Mr. Bluebeard* was a 1903 Broadway production starring Eddie Foy.

692.4   Al Rashids] Hārūn al-Rashīd, Muslim caliph, or ruler, in the eighth and ninth centuries C.E.

692.13   Harun-haunted] See previous note.

692.14–15   one-eyed calendars . . . the Barber's Sixth Brother.] Characters in *The Arabian Nights*. Calendars were an order of dervishes who dedicated themselves to fasting and prayer.

692.25   Barmecides'] Barmecide, character in *The Arabian Nights*.

693.6   lithia water] Mineral water containing lithium salts.

694.16   Hammerstein] Willie Hammerstein (1875–1914), New York theater manager and impresario and father of the lyricist Oscar Hammerstein II.

694.23–24   R. Fitzsimmons] Robert "Bob" Fitzsimmons (1863–1917), British boxer.

694.28–29   eyes of needles with the camels] Cf. Matthew 19:24.

695.27   Pure Food and Drugs Act] Pure Food and Drug Act, U.S. law passed in 1906.

697.2–3   *optikos needleorum camelibus*] Nonsense phrase referring to Matthew 19:24.

697.7   John Mitchell] Mitchell (1870–1919) was president of the United Mine Workers.

698.11   Pomona] City in California known for its production of oranges.

698.14   Fletcherized] Chewed thoroughly, based on the principles of Horace Fletcher (1849–1919).

699.6   "Fisher's Hornpipe"] Traditional Celtic tune.

699.17   'Falling Waters'] Song (1874) by J. L. Truax.

699.21   strathspey] Slow Scottish dance.

699.29   carbonic] Carbonic acid, used in indigestion remedies.

700.17   "The Devil's Dream,"] Traditional fiddle tune.

700.20   Morningside] Morningside Avenue, street in upper Manhattan.

700.30–31   Bryan couldn't think . . . 'postponer,'] For Bryan, see note 459.16. In 1907, Bryan called William Howard Taft "The Great Postponer."

701.27   Nepenthe] In Greek literature and mythology, a drug that causes forgetfulness.

706.10   Panhards] French automobile.

706.14   Kyrle Bellew's real name] Harold Kyrle Bellew, English actor (1850–1911).

706.14–15   The ravings of John McCullough] Irish-born American actor (1832–1885). A popular phonograph record titled "The Ravings of John McCullough" supposedly depicted McCullough late in life, when he suffered from general paresis, or paralytic dementia.

706.16   Ellen Terry] English actress (1847–1928).

706.16–17   Joe Weber . . . E. H. Sothern . . . Henry Miller] Weber, American vaudeville comedian (1867–1942); Edward Hugh Sothern, American actor (1859–1933); Miller, English-born American actor (1859–1926).

708.17–18   Mr. Frohman] Charles Frohman (1856–1915), theatrical manager and producer.

708.18–19   fifty-seven different kinds] "57 Pickle Varieties," slogan of the H.J. Heinz Company.

710.23   Stanley's 'Explorations into Africa.'] The Welsh American explorer and journalist Henry Morton Stanley (1841–1904) wrote several books about his travels, though none with this title.

711.19   L. I.] Long Island.

711.20   Meadow Brook Hunt] Meadowbrook Hunt Club, Westbury, New York.

711.28   "Bluebeard, Jr.,"] Musical production conceived by and starring Eddie Foy (1856–1928).

717.32   frangipanni] See note 551.18.

718.4   Una] Lady of the Redcrosse Knight in *The Faerie Queene* (1590) by Edmund Spenser (c. 1552–1599).

719.30   "Who's What?"] "Who's What and Why in America," a series of comic biographies by humorist John Kendrick Bangs (1862–1922).

729.11   Chautauqua conventions] Movement that brought speakers, concerts, and educational instruction to communities around the country.

729.12   diabolo] Game in which a two-headed top is balanced on a string suspended between two sticks.

729.19   "Knowledge comes, but wisdom lingers."] From "Locksley Hall" (1835) by Alfred, Lord Tennyson (1809–1892).

731.16   cop the lady out] Woo, win over.

731.33   chin 'em] Talk with.

732.35   grouch] Complaint.

733.23   Jim Jeffries] See note 460.35.

737.32   Amsden's Junes] Variety of peach.

737.37   hydrogen out of all the peroxides] See note 528.3–4.

739.37   collodion] Solution used in developing photographs.

742.35–36   "life is rather a queer . . . Mr. Cohan's song] "Life's a Funny Proposition After All," song (1904) by George M. Cohan (1878–1942).

743.38   Rosinante] Broken-down horse, from Don Quixote's horse in Miguel de Cervantes's novel (1605, 1615).

745.3   W. C. T. U.] Woman's Christian Temperance Union

FINAL STORIES.

750.2   Battling or Lord Nelson] Oscar "Battling Nelson" (1882–1954), Danish American boxer who was world lightweight champion, 1905–6 and 1908–10. Horatio Nelson (1758–1805), vice admiral in the British navy.

750.32–33   lime hash . . . nux vomica tea] Lime hash, given to children by dentists to build up the lime salts in their teeth. Dog bread, a simple type of cornbread. Nux vomica, derived from seeds of the strychnine tree and used to treat a variety of ailments in traditional medicine.

751.4–5   Armour Packing Company] Armour & Company, Chicago meat-packing firm founded in 1867.

761.6   Réaumur] René Antoine Ferchault de Réaumur (1683–1757), French scientist for whom a temperature scale was named.

763.36   Thomas Tucker] See note 282.21.

764.26–27   Prince Camaralzaman's] Character in *The Arabian Nights.*

765.35–36   potash and magnesia] Ingredients in carbonate, a remedy for indigestion.

765.36   Ananias] A member of the early Christian community who was struck dead for lying to God in Acts 5.

765.36   Nebuchadnezzar] See note 302.15–16.

766.15   *non compos vocis*] Latin: of unsound voice.

767.7   Fletcherizing] See note 698.14.

767.25–26   "Roughing . . . Mississippi."] Works by Mark Twain, pen name of American author Samuel Clemens (1835–1910): *Roughing It* (1872), "The Celebrated Jumping Frog of Calaveras County" (1865), and *Life on the Mississippi* (1883).

768.5–6   Rabelais who said . . . platters neat."] In *Gargantua and Pantagruel* (1532–64), the French author François Rabelais (c. 1494–1553) wrote, "The great God made the planets, and we make the platters neat."

769.9   *Hongroise*] A brand of pomade, used on beards and mustaches.

772.21   Dreadnought] A type of battleship.

774.19   Lochinvar] See note 476.26.

777.5   "Death's twin brother, Sleep."] From *The Rubáiyát of Omar Khayyám.* See note 240.29.

This book is set in 10 point ITC Galliard, a face designed
for digital composition by Matthew Carter and based
on the sixteenth-century face Granjon. The paper is acid-free
lightweight opaque that will not turn yellow or brittle with age.
The binding is sewn, which allows the book to open easily and lie flat.
The binding board is covered in Brillianta, a woven rayon cloth
made by Van Heek–Scholco Textielfabrieken, Holland.
Composition by Gopa & Ted2, Inc.
Printing by Sheridan Grand Rapids, Grand Rapids MI.
Binding by Dekker Bookbinding, Wyoming MI.
Designed by Bruce Campbell.

THE LIBRARY OF AMERICA SERIES

Library of America fosters appreciation of America's literary heritage by publishing, and keeping permanently in print, authoritative editions of America's best and most significant writing. An independent nonprofit organization, it was founded in 1979 with seed funding from the National Endowment for the Humanities and the Ford Foundation.

5